TOO YOUNG TO DIE

TOO YOUNG TO DIE

PIVOT LAB CHRONICLES™ BOOK ONE

MICHAEL ANDERLE

LMBPN Publishing
PMB 196, 2540 South Maryland Pkwy
Las Vegas, NV 89109

First US Edition, June, 2020
eBook ISBN: 978-1-64202-962-8
Print ISBN: 978-1-64202-963-5

THE TOO YOUNG TO DIE TEAM

Thanks to the Beta Readers
John Ashmore, Theresa Holmes, Nicole Emens, Larry Omans, Allen Collins

Thanks to the JIT Readers

Allen Collins
Angel LaVey
Billie Leigh Kellar
Dave Hicks
Deb Mader
Diane L. Smith
Jeff Eaton
Jeff Goode
Kerry Mortimer

If I've missed anyone, please let me know!

Editor
The Skyhunter Editing Team

PART I

PROLOGUE

Jacob's favorite part of MMORPGs by far was that you could be another you. Not someone else entirely because you could never be that, but you could find out who you were if you were dropped into the middle of, say, a fantasy world with a rusty sword and nothing else.

He liked to think he was the same in either world. A straight talker, he liked to give people the benefit of the doubt until they blew it and once they did, he immediately leapt to conclusions about their character.

It was why he wasn't part of the public relations part of the PIVOT team, generally speaking. As Amber liked to say, no part of that cycle was helpful in PR.

She, meanwhile, took her opportunity in the game world to be a—mostly—more "woohoo" version of herself. In real life, she was five feet two inches of terrifying muscle, with a head of curls that could put Medusa to shame. She had studied engineering with Jacob and Nick at MIT, and she managed to meld creativity and an intuitive grasp of design with one of the most coldly analytical minds Jacob had ever seen.

Which made her druids both fascinating and pants-pissingly

frightening. You never knew if she would preach about the harmony of the natural world, slit someone's throat…or both.

Nick, meanwhile, was such a dialed-up version of himself that he was insane. He wanted everyone to love him and poured time into learning the backstory of every NPC. When monsters attacked the group, he felt personally betrayed.

His two friends had learned a very simple way to deal with this. They let him get as far as he could in terms of winning people over and killed those he had no success with. While they had agreed never to tell him about this strategy, both of them had to admit it was likely he would notice someday. He might be a pathological people-pleaser but he was also quite intelligent.

They'd deal with that when they came to it.

Right now, Jacob listened to Amber and Nick argue about the best way forward.

"No," she stated, "because the villager said there were dozens of orcs in the hills, and if we stop to talk to all of them, it'll take us *a thousand years* to reach the next settlement. And it's midnight, man. I'm tired."

"I won't talk to *all* the orcs," he argued. "I merely thought I'd try to find the leader and talk to him about the attacks on the village."

"Okay, but…" Jacob could practically see her rubbing her forehead. "Here's the thing. It's late, the orcs will *not listen to you*, and it would be so much easier to take the side road, log out at the inn, and come back and kill them all tomorrow."

"Kill them?" Nick sounded aghast.

"I'm only jumping ahead," Amber said grumpily. "It's where we'll end up. Jacob, back me up on this one."

"Nuh-uh." He laughed. "I won't get in the middle of this one." He typed out a PM to Amber: *Remember the rule?*

Yeah, it works, her answer agreed, *but it takes so long.*

To be fair, you once said that about a McDonald's order.

They had fries already made!

Jacob laughed but forgot to mute himself, and Nick took this as a condemnation of his strategy.

"It's always worth talking to people," he said grumpily. "Plus, if I resolve five more disputes, I'll get Diplomat Level Twenty-three."

"There it is," Amber said and sounded grimly amused. "Nick's a people-pleaser and this game turned it up to eleven because now, he gets little gold stars when he does it."

Nick muttered on his end of the voice chat, and Jacob decided to wrangle the two of them. "Let's go up the mountain path. If it looks like an ambush, we turn and go back to the village behind us. If they immediately want to parlay, we save and come back tomorrow. If it's smooth sailing, we log out at the next village."

The two of them muttered but as he'd expected, they began to walk with him. They even joked about the next day's lunches. For years, the three of them had lived together and Jacob had only recently moved out. He felt a little pang and could imagine the way the kitchen had smelled while they were cooking.

It wasn't something he wanted to spend his time thinking about, though. He liked his new place, and it wasn't like the three of them didn't see each other every day at work. They were on the cusp of making their startup's principal technology workable, and once they had that, investors would pour in to help them fund the rest.

"The rest" was a game. PIVOT might be founded on virtual reality and reading brain waves, but all that scanning technology wouldn't do jack if they didn't create themselves a world. All three of them had worked on PIVOT, in fact, in order to make their dreams of truly *living* in a game world come true.

The problem was, while a crack team of three MIT-trained engineers could absolutely build a prototype of an immersive VR experience given several years and some funding, it turned out that a team of three could *not* make a sprawling, immersive MMORPG. There was simply too much to do.

This game, for instance, had made incredible waves when it came out—its AI and voice recognition software were top-notch, and the sheer depth of each of the quests was breathtaking. Instead of being stuck on one questline or having to choose between a few dialogue options, you could approach problems in your own way—it was why

Nick could try to talk it out with the orcs or Amber could simply go in with fireballs.

The PIVOT team needed to make a game that could rival some of the best games out there, and they needed to *not* do what Forever Echo had done and piss off a number of big industry players. The second one, as far as Jacob could tell, wouldn't be a problem because they had no way to accomplish the first.

They needed to find solutions for that one.

He kept his character moving and took the time to appreciate how twilight looked in this zone. After a magical explosion of some kind, the area was bathed in drifting fallout—gorgeous, like embers on the wind, but also dangerous if you were touched by too many. The village behind them had tall walls and, even in the middle-ages aesthetic, an abundance of pseudo-greenhouses kept vegetables safe.

When Jacob moved around the bend in the road, however, he stopped in confusion.

"Guys."

The conversation on the voice chat stopped and the other two took the corner at a sprint.

"Orcs?" Amber had her staff out.

"No, look at the sign." Jacob started his character forward again and the three of them crowded around the sign and clicked it.

DEAR PLAYER-

THANK YOU FOR YOUR TIME IN OUR WORLD. UNFORTU-NATELY, WE CAN NO LONGER AFFORD TO KEEP MAKING THIS GAME. WE ARE GLAD TO HAVE SHARED THIS MUCH OF OUR WORLD WITH YOU AND HOPE YOU HAVE ENJOYED YOUR TIME. PLEASE FEEL FREE TO ENJOY EXISTING COPIES OF THE GAME, BUT OUR MULTIPLAYER SERVERS WILL SHUT DOWN ON JANUARY 31.

SINCERELY, THE FOREVER ECHO TEAM

"Wait." Amber sounded lost. "The game's shutting down?"

"The game can't shut down," Nick said. "So many people love it."

"Oh, for fuck's sake, Nick, not everyone is motivated only by that. It says they can't afford to keep going." She sighed regretfully. "I knew their subscription numbers weren't good but *damn*—I'm gonna miss this one, guys. This sucks. It sucks so hard."

Jacob turned to look over the valley behind them. The game was one of the most amazing he'd played in a long while. It had an immersive feel to it, real enough to hook you in but unreal enough to be an entirely new world.

Then, something occurred to him. "Wait." His brain had shifted into overdrive. "Wait. Wait, wait, wait."

"Wait, wait, wait?" Amber said.

"Wait, wait, wait, wait, wait…" Nick chanted now. "Wait! Wait!" He laughed when Amber joined in.

"I'm trying to think and you're not making it easy!" Jacob called over the sound of their chanting. He pushed his headset off his ears and lowered his head into his hands. Yes. This could be workable—it could be very workable.

He put his earphones on and grimaced when he heard the other two still chanting.

"Hey, listen here, kiddos." He flicked the microphone a few times. "I have an idea. It means we don't have to stop playing this game."

"We hide their servers so they can't shut them off," Amber said. "Excellent. I like it."

"Or," Jacob said, drawing the word out, "we *buy* them."

"In case you haven't noticed, *kiddo*, we're broker than broke right now. We can't simply buy games for—ohhhh." Amber caught up. "Oh, that could work."

"Look, I haven't slept in a while," Nick interjected, "so I want to make sure I'm parsing this correctly. You two want to buy this game… and start some kind of paid, worldwide Thunderdome thing, right?"

Jacob guffawed. "I'm not crazy, right? We could do this. Adapting an existing game to VR has to be easier than building an entire game. They have all the assets in place, the story…we could do this."

"We could do this," his friends confirmed in unison.

"Okay, it's past midnight. Let's all go to bed and if it still sounds like a good idea in the morning, we'll buy it."

A growl behind them interrupted their plans.

"Goddammit, Jacob," Amber said, "this is why you don't have long conversations in orc-infested territory. All right, everyone. Let's murder some orcs."

"No!" Nick pounded on his desk. "We talk to them—"

A fireball streaked toward them.

"I think talking time is over, buddy," Jacob told him. "For the forest! For the villagers! For glory!"

CHAPTER ONE

Nick's smoothie, which had seemed like a good idea when he ordered the box of mixes delivered to his house, had now begun to separate into two distinct and equally unappealing sections at the bottom of his Nalgene bottle. For some reason, he couldn't stop watching it.

With a sigh, Amber picked it up and lobbed it at the sink. It missed and bounced off the floor on the other side of the counter. After she'd stared at it for a moment, she shrugged as if to say, "Good enough", and looked at him.

"Can we focus now?" she asked.

"I don't know." He slouched in his chair. "Will you keep saying depressing things?"

"If by 'depressing things' you mean the numbers in our financial reports, then *yes*." She gave him a smile that showed her teeth. "Let me put it this way, Mr. Ryan. Neither of us will leave this office until we have a plan in place."

"That's not fair," Nick complained. "Jacob doesn't have to be here. Why do I?" He picked at his sleeve. "Lucky bastard, having his grandmother in the ICU."

Amber's kick, when it came, was direct and to a particularly sensitive part of his shin. She jabbed a finger at him. "You *never* say things like that," she told him severely.

He nodded, chastened. Put her in front of a problem and she would do whatever it took to solve it. It was one of the things that made her an incredible engineer—and one of the reasons he hoped she would never decide to take up politics. Or a military career.

Nick shuddered. The thought of Amber in charge of high-grade explosives was *terrifying*.

But as utilitarian and cold-eyed as she could be about problem-solving, she had no tolerance for black humor. Make a joke she thought was tempting fate or mocking someone's pain, and she'd let you know about it immediately.

You knew you'd *really* messed up when she devolved into Spanish. Once, he and Jacob had secretly recorded one of her rants and translated it later—a lengthy process due to the fact that popular translation dictionaries didn't have quite as varied a vocabulary as their friend. The results had convinced them both to never get on her bad side.

Now, Nick cleared his throat, leaned forward on the table, and paused briefly when the rusted metal legs creaked. They'd retired to the kitchenette part of the offices for a working lunch, which hadn't exactly worked out. Amber had forgotten to order food and his food…

Well, whatever that was, you couldn't call it food. His stomach rumbled and he grimaced.

"It's not *so* bad," he said after he'd stared at the numbers for a few more minutes. "I mean…it's not much worse than last quarter."

Her sigh was less angry than despairing. "But it *is* worse," she said. She sat with her head tipped back and stared at the ceiling. "We made a thing that…" Her voice trailed off and she sighed again.

Nick cleared his throat awkwardly. The numbers hadn't been great for a while now, but he hadn't realized she was this worried about it. He'd watched things work out for them, over and over, from the early technological hurdles to the Hail Mary presentations they'd given time and again to investors.

Something always came through. This was Silicon Valley. Money was nothing and there was always someone willing to pay for the latest cool thing.

Now, he tried to reassure her. "Amber." He leaned back and waited until she opened her eyes and looked at him. "Things come through. They always come through. We'll think of something."

"I don't want to think of *something*," she said, her tone crisp. "I don't want to patch this until it's two months from now and we're looking at another quarterly loss, and we're deeper in the red."

"By then, we'll have plenty of interest." He saw her face harden and held a hand up. "No, no, I don't think you're giving this enough credit. Let me get the—"

"*Nick—*"

"The articles!" he called over his shoulder. His mother had printed them and sent them to him, although he'd rolled his eyes at them when he opened the envelope. Now, however, they would make a good case to show Amber.

He dodged around the glass-walled laboratory. One of the pods was open and looked rather like a cross between an iPod, a spa bed, and a tanning booth, and another two hummed faintly as they processed information. Their operating systems were updating with the latest story components for the MMORPG, and the LED panels around the side flashed orange as they did so.

Nearby, a sterilized compartment held the headset hookups and a veritable wealth of heart rate monitors, blood pressure cuffs, and thermometers were piled in a basket in the corner.

"Nick," Amber said again, as he returned to the room. She had rolled the sleeves of her Henley up and pulled her hair into a ponytail. "The problem isn't—"

"'PIVOT unveils the first look at its groundbreaking virtual reality pods,'" he quoted with a flourish. He propped one foot on his folding chair and leaned forward, really hamming it up. "Listen to this. 'One of the most popular booths by far at E3 this year was PIVOT, who gave live demos of what they simply call pods. These come preprogrammed with a surprisingly gripping MMORPG called Alt IRL, which—'"

She stretched impatiently and twitched the printout out of his hand. Without breaking eye contact, she flipped to the second page of the review, paused for a moment to find the section she was looking for, and read aloud. "'While the Kickstarter campaign raised four hundred and thirty-eight percent of its goal, early prototypes of the pod, priced at seven thousand dollars apiece, have not found a significant market.'" She tossed the sheet of paper onto the table and fixed him with a steady look. "The problem isn't the interest. Nick, people can't *afford* it."

"So we rent them," he said.

"Jesus Christ, we've gone over every freaking scenario and there is not *one* that is viable." Amber waved her hands as if she tried not to swipe the whole set of papers off the table. "For. The. Last. Time. The numbers don't work."

"They will work," Nick assured her. "They'll work until the price point comes down."

"But it *doesn't* come down." Her face was pale. She pulled a piece of paper out of the pile and didn't even have to look to check which one it was. That alone showed him how many times she'd been through this. "It's like…it's like making a bigger LED TV, *si?* The expensive part is making it, not the materials. And in our case, we gotta maintain them too. They need updates. They need regular checks to make sure they don't turn someone's brainstem into a Krispy Kreme—"

"There's an image I'm never gonna be able to get out of my head," he muttered.

"Nick, we need every one of these machines running at fifty dollars an hour, ten hours a day, three hundred and sixty-five simply to break even." Her eyes had shadows under them, and he wondered when last she had slept. "And that's the machines. That's not renting the space to use them. It's not the advertising or the tech support or the sales or the shipping or…" She sighed and said bitterly, "It's an expensive toy."

Nick's eyebrows raised. He'd never heard her say something like *this* before and he was a little thrown. He scratched his ear and considered. "Uh...Amber."

"What?" She didn't look at him.

"Are you okay?" He folded his arms awkwardly over his chest. "You seem a little down."

"What gave it away?" She looked at him with a flash of her trademark humor.

That made him feel a little better. His friend was still in there somewhere. He and Amber had met at MIT eight years before when she was dating Jacob, and although that relationship had broken up within a couple of weeks, the three of them had been inseparable since. They'd all gotten their first apartment together, helped each other through a string of job rejections, heartbreaks, and family disappointment, and—

Oh.

"Your parents called," he said. "Didn't they?"

Amber gave him a hollow-eyed look and blew out a breath.

Nick fiddled with one of the pieces of paper on the table. He didn't like to say too much when it came to her parents because if he did, he'd end up saying things she didn't like and she'd tell him he was only mad at his parents.

Which was true. His parents and hers were very much alike. Of the three of them, only Jacob had a family that supported his life choices. Nick and Amber, on the other hand, got regular calls about how they should go to grad school, or get married, or move back home.

She folded her arms to mirror his stance. "They said they put up with everything because I told them I would change the world," she said bitterly. "And now, I'm making toys for rich kids."

"Toys for...what does that even mean?" He rolled his eyes. "And what do they mean, put up with *everything*? What's everything?"

"*This.*" She made a dismissive gesture at herself. At his frown, she sighed. "Oh, come on, like you haven't noticed my mom always asking me if I have a man?"

"I thought that was merely what parents did," he joked.

Amber tried to smile, but her heart wasn't in it. "They don't get me. God, I sound like I'm thirteen and writing bad poetry. But I thought…Nick, I thought they'd figure it out someday, you know? I wanted to go dirt bike racing for my Quinceañera. I never liked wearing skirts. I've told them since I was a kid that I didn't want to have babies. I only…I always thought they would believe me someday." She crossed one booted foot over her knee. "And now, the stupid thing is, they understand me enough to make it all hurt."

"What d'you mean?" Nick leaned forward.

"I wanted to help people!" Her eyes were suspiciously bright. "I intended to write the programs that…I don't know. I planned to work for people curing diseases. *I* was gonna cure diseases. And I thought maybe this would all get off the ground and I could go do that, you know?"

"You don't want to do this?" He looked over his shoulder at the pods. "I thought you liked building this."

"I did—I do! It's not that!" She hunched her shoulders. "But it's falling apart and now, I've spent four years doing something that'll go down the tubes and I haven't done any of the stuff I wanted to do and what can I even say to them? That—" She sighed.

"You know…" Nick cleared his throat. "My sister said to me not too long ago that making Mom and Dad happy wasn't the price I had to pay to be happy myself." He raised his eyebrows at her. "Maybe that's worth—oh, hey, is that Jacob?"

A door had opened and closed at the front of the building.

"He said he'd be back when he could." Amber straightened and her anxiety seemed to melt away into gladness.

This was one of the things Nick wished her parents could see about her. She was one of the kindest people he knew, so happy about her friends' well-being that their good news could make her forget even total misery on her part.

But when Jacob walked into the room, it was clear that what he had to report wasn't good news at all. He didn't look like he'd slept in days and he had the air of someone walking through a nightmare.

"Jacob?" Nick tried to catch his friend's eyes. "Uh…"

"Is everything okay?" Amber's voice was a thread of sound.

Jacob looked at them and his eyes were bloodshot. From the momentary confusion on his face, he didn't seem to remember how he'd wound up at the office. Nick pushed a chair toward him and went to start a pot of coffee. What the man *really* needed was sleep, but he wasn't sure how soon that would happen.

"What's wrong?" she asked gently. Over their friend's head, her gaze locked with Nick's. A week before, Jacob's grandmother had suffered a stroke and there had been numerous close calls since then.

"They're going to…" Jacob's voice trailed off. "They have to…take her off life support." His face crumpled as he said it and he bent forward over his legs, his arms wrapped tightly around his chest.

"I thought she was getting better," Nick said quietly. "I thought the doctors said—"

"They did." Jacob hadn't moved. "But we don't have time."

Neither Amber nor Nick could make anything of this.

He straightened finally and his face was stricken. "The doctor says it could be weeks," he managed to say. He saw the looks on their faces. "We can't—it's—" He took a piece of paper out of his pocket and handed it to Amber.

Nick watched her eyebrows raise.

"Jesus Christ." She shook her head. "This can't be right. Five thousand dollars a *day*?"

Jacob remained silent.

"A *day*?" she mouthed again in Nick's direction.

He came to look over her shoulder as he opened the coffee bag, and his jaw dropped. She wasn't kidding. Between all the various services and scans and monitoring thus far, it was costing that much or more to keep Jacob's grandmother in the hospital. He leaned closer.

"It kind of puts our price tag into perspective, doesn't it?"

From the way she went still, he thought he'd fucked up enough to have another angry tirade in Spanish. But when she turned her head, there was something new in her eyes.

Hope.

"Yes," she said. "Yes, it does, doesn't it?"

Nick stared at her for a moment before he straightened abruptly. "Oh, you can't be serious."

Amber had turned to look at the pods. "It's climate-controlled," she said carefully. "The oxygen levels can be adjusted. It's made to allow easy monitoring of brain waves, heart rate, blood pressure... And what's the one thing people have tried to figure out how to do for coma patients? Re-engage them. Wake them up. A game, an interactive game that breaks through all their outer perceptions—"

"You can't be serious," he said again and couldn't seem to think at all. His mind whirled.

But Jacob had looked up with the first real human emotion they'd seen from him in days. "She could come *here*," he said. "She could—she could come here. Guys, you'd do that for me?"

Amber began to laugh. "For you, for...anyone. Jacob, don't you get it? If your family can't afford this, how many other people can't afford it?" She looked at Nick. "I'm not crazy, right? We found our target market."

"And..." He slung an arm around her shoulders. "I don't want to be too on the nose here, but it looks like you may have found a way to help people and cure diseases."

"Holy shit." Her eyes widened. "Okay, Mr. Hopeful Selling Person. You gotta get ready. We need to make a *lot* of calls, and you are the most personable one of us."

Even Jacob laughed. "She's right. She's—hang on, my mom's calling." He stood and headed into the offices as he took the call. "What's up, Mom? You won't believe what we thought of."

"We could do this." Amber leaned on her chair and a smile broke through on her face. "We could actually *do* this!" She smacked the table. "Investors, ha. Who needs 'em?" Then, she leaned sideways slightly. "Jacob?"

He stood in the doorway. "She, uh...she passed." He slid his phone into his pocket. "She's gone."

"Jacob." Nick stepped to his side and Amber joined them. "I'm so sorry, buddy. Why don't we get you home? We'll get a meal in you, see if your family needs help with anything—"

"No." Jacob stood a little straighter. "They have it under control and we have work to do."

"The quarterly statements can wait a while," Amber said.

"No," Jacob said. "Not that." He looked at them. "There are so many people in ICUs all over the country right now. That means numerous families trying to find a way to pay for it. The sooner we get this thing up and running, the better." He looked at Nick. "Start making calls."

CHAPTER TWO

"It's a Valkyrie," Tina said.

"Huh?" Justin looked at her in confusion.

"My tattoo?" She looked at her arm, where something peeked out from under her t-shirt. "I thought you were looking at my arm."

In point of fact, he had stared into the middle of nowhere and wished he was literally anywhere else.

He hadn't wanted to come on this date. His past experiences with dating hadn't exactly inspired confidence, and there was something hopelessly awkward to him about striking up a conversation with someone he didn't even know as if there were a simple, easy way to get from Point A to Point B.

Point B, of course, being marriage, babies, and a house with beige carpets.

Unfortunately, after several weeks of browbeating from his mother and dark comments from his father about how someone who couldn't even afford his own apartment shouldn't ignore simple requests from his parents, Justin was there and he did have to find something to say.

The amusing part of this was that however his parents had pictured Tina Castro, he was fairly sure it wasn't anywhere *close* to reality. There was no way they would have gone from almost constantly getting on his case about his job, his prospects, and graduate school to setting him up with a woman who had worn ripped jeans and a sweatshirt out on a first date. They would expect…

Pearls, probably. And a nice sweater.

He could not imagine Tina in pearls and a sweater. He could imagine it even less when she waved her hand in front of his face. "Hellooooo?"

"Sorry." Justin took a sip of his beer—which he'd forgotten was beer—choked, and pounded his fist on his chest a few times. "God, this sucks. I'm sorry you're out with me."

She gave him a curious look and took a sip of her beer. She spun the bottle in her hands as she looked at him. "You're not what I expected," she told him.

"I know," he said with feeling. "Trust me, I know."

"My mother made such a big deal of you on the phone," she said and rolled her eyes. "'Senator *Williams's* son, Tina.'" She adopted a mocking falsetto. "Honestly? I pictured khakis and a polo with the collar flipped up."

"Yeah, well." He found a shred of humor. "So were my parents."

Tina almost spat out her mouthful of beer. "So, it's like that, is it? Interesting."

Justin shrugged and hunched his shoulders. "I guess. Why'd you come out with me if you thought I was gonna be a tool?"

"I hadn't planned to." She looked around. "Then you suggested an arcade for our first date and I thought, 'Huh. I wonder what's up with this dude?' So here I am." She wiggled her fingers. "Of course, I kind of expected that if you intended to disappoint your parents, you'd really go for it." One eyebrow arched.

He opened his mouth, realized he had nothing to say, and closed it.

"Oh, come on." Tina shifted in her chair. "I should have—" She leaned back as the waiter set plastic baskets of jalapeno poppers and fries on the table. "Thanks," she told him. When he was gone, she picked up a jalapeno popper and contemplated it before she took a bite. "I should have known our parents would only set us up if they were having trouble with both of us," she said around the mouthful of food, "but I don't get why you're a problem."

"Do you see khakis?" he asked, not entirely sure what was going on. He had no idea what she meant by going for it.

"No, but…where's your mohawk? Where are your tattoos?" She squinted at him. "Did you knock up a gold-digging girlfriend or something?"

Justin snorted.

"So, not that." Tina tapped her chin and made a show of looking skyward as she thought. "Ohhhh, you got high and crashed their car—nice, shiny Porsche SUV, right?"

"Lexus, actually." He raised an eyebrow. "But no. I haven't done either of those two things."

"You haven't gotten high? Jesus Christ. Okay, are they disappointed because you're so boring?"

"Hey!" He had been having fun but he was now genuinely annoyed. "I'm not boring, okay? I do stuff. It's simply that they don't care about my stuff. I stream games. I'm damned good at it, too. And—" He saw the look on her face. "Yeah. Yeah, I'm a huge nerd, okay? So, why don't you leave and think of something to tell our parents. Don't worry, mine will be all too willing to believe I screwed it up."

"Dude." Tina set her beer down and looked at him. "I won't walk away because you're a nerd, okay?" She cleared her throat. "Look, I was…uh, making a joke. It didn't work. My bad." She held her pinky finger out. "No more bad jokes, pinky swear."

Justin ignored her finger and took a sip of his beer. He merely wanted to be home. "Look, I'm not a drug-snorting, failing-out-of-school, bankrupt disappointment. I'm simply boring, okay? I never liked playing football and I didn't bring home girlfriends with the hair and the nails and the purses and whatever. Honestly? My parents would probably be happier if I'd knocked up some chick." He swirled his beer in the bottle.

His parents wouldn't be happy, of course. They'd be furious. He'd get a huge lecture on how he was letting his father down and endangering the family's livelihood. How a senator couldn't afford to have that kind of thing going on in their family.

But at least they'd understand it. This—the streaming online, the video games—they didn't get that at all.

"I know how it is," Tina said after a moment. "I think…well, that my parents wish I was a little more boring. No drugs. No tattoos. No piercings."

"You don't have any piercings," he said distractedly.

"Not that you can see." When he looked up, she had a very smug look on her face.

Justin hoped it was dark enough that she couldn't see his expression.

"My parents *freaked* when they saw my first tattoo," she said, apparently taking pity on him. "And it was so basic, too." She held one hand up to show a tiny infinity symbol on the inside of her wrist. "I thought I was sooooo deep." She paused. "I was sixteen. I probably don't have to tell you that."

Despite himself, he laughed.

"So, what about you?" She gave him a look. "Why haven't you done any of that stuff?"

"What do you mean?"

"I meant what I said before. You're a huge disappointment, apparently—so why not lean into it? Do all the shit you want to do that they wouldn't approve of." She raised an eyebrow.

Justin shrugged. "Like what, though?"

"*I* don't know." She frowned at him. "I mean…what's the thing you'd do if there were no consequences?"

"Uh…" Justin tried to think of something and came up blank. "Buy a nice gaming setup? Oh, there was a chair I looked at a while back. It looked so damned comfortable. For real, this thing was amazing, all leather—"

"Oh, my God," Tina said. She looked into the middle distance for a moment and seemed to come to a decision. "Okay, finish your beer."

"What?"

"Right now. One drink. Finish it." She folded her arms.

He was about to scoff at her but looked at his beer. It occurred to him that he'd never gone to any of the big parties at his prep school—those everyone snuck off-campus to. He'd heard stories, though, and always kind of wondered what was so fun about them.

Maybe this was his chance to find out. He tipped his head back and drank the beer in one gulp, wiped a stray drop from the corner of his mouth, and looked at her. "Okay, now what?"

"Now finish mine." Tina pushed hers across the table. She gave a delighted laugh when she saw his face. "It's gonna be good, I promise. Finish it—go on."

It was easier to do the second time around. Justin drained the glass and put it on the table so hard it tipped.

"Okay," she said and leaned closer. "Now you gotta choose."

Justin looked around at the games. "Sega Rally Championship."

"Maybe on the second date," Tina said. "You know, depending on how this one goes."

He flushed and hoped she wouldn't notice. "So, what do I have to choose?"

"You'll decide which beach we go to." Tina pulled a twenty out of her pocket and put it on the table before she beckoned to him. "Come on."

"I downed two beers and you want me to drive—"

"I'll drive, come on." She took his hand and towed him away. He hadn't realized before how short she was. "So, which beach?"

"Why are we going to the beach?"

Tina stopped so suddenly that he collided with her. She stood on her tiptoes to whisper in his ear. "We're going skinny dipping."

"*What?*" Justin straightened abruptly.

"Yup." She gave him a grin and yanked him out into the spring night.

"I can't—wait—" He stopped. "Are we doing this?"

"What are you worried about?" she asked him, her arms folded.

"Uh—I don't know. Getting arrested?"

"That's what makes it fun," Tina retorted. She caught his hand again and towed him to a car in the corner of the lot—a beat-up turquoise vehicle that might very well have been made before either one of them was born. "Get in."

Justin was about to protest until he thought it through. Really thought it through.

Skinny dipping.

Both of them.

He got in the car.

"Ha," Tina turned the car on and backed out. "I knew you had a wild streak somewhere."

"We'll see about that." He grasped the handle above his seat as she pulled out onto the empty street at high speed and the tires squealed. "Hang on a second. I still need to put on my seatbelt—"

She grinned, turned the radio up, and danced in her seat as she drove. "So, which beach?" she called over the sound of the music.

"I don't know." The beer was beginning to hit. Justin leaned his head back against the seat. "You choose."

"Okay." She made a sharp turn, so close to oncoming traffic that they left a series of angry horns in their wake. "God, people are so stuffy," she commented and laughed.

"Holy shit," Justin muttered.

"Oh, come on. You didn't get hurt, did you?" Tina grinned at him and stretched her hand to take his. "Just you wait, preppy boy. You're gonna find out how awesome it is to get a little wild, and our parents will regret *ever* setting us up."

She turned the wheel and the car skidded around a corner. The tires squealed again. She cast a glance at him and laughed. "Now you're getting into it. Choose some music."

"Right." He leaned forward and pressed the radio. "Uh, rock?"

"Whatever you want." She drummed her hands on the steering wheel. "Wait, *shit*—"

His head jerked and his gaze immediately focused on the puppy. A ball of fluff that couldn't be more than a couple of months old stood scared and frozen in the middle of the street.

Only for a moment, though, because Tina had jerked the wheel to the side in a desperate effort to avoid it. Justin's head had begun to turn to make sure it wouldn't run the wrong way—not that he could do anything about it, of course—before a massive bang shattered conscious thought and something hit him hard all across his body.

In the street, the puppy cowered, stared at the smoking pile of metal, and whimpered. It could hear its name but didn't know where to go. The world was too big and full of fast things and loud noises. When at last footsteps stepped close behind it, the animal looked at its owner and knew something was very wrong.

"Oh, no," she said. She scooped it up and cradled it against her chest, but her hand was over her mouth. "Oh, no. Sam—*Sam!* Call 911!"

CHAPTER THREE

"All *right*." Nick laid out two spiral-bound folios of information in front of Amber and Jacob. "Who's ready for the sales pitch?"

"Did you say you needed a day and a half because you wanted to get it all put together nicely?" Jacob asked. He looked at the cover and binding. "I suppose it looks nice, but you don't need to impress us. We're all in, buddy."

"It's my job to make things look nice," he replied serenely.

The truth, of course, was that he had claimed it would take a day and a half because it meant Jacob could go home and sleep. In reality, he could have whipped up most of this presentation in a couple of hours, but his friend looked like warmed-over oatmeal and frankly, they all needed sleep and food as well.

And, as it turned out, it was lucky he'd asked for the extra time.

"Should we get started?" he asked.

"Sounds good." Amber lifted the remote and turned down the volume on the TV in the corner, which displayed a market report on the tech sector. "Okay, Mr. Salesman. Dazzle us."

Nick grinned. "So, as you both know, the cost of a night in an ICU is prohibitive. On page two, you can see the range of values nationwide. It varies wildly between hospitals, even in the same cities, but the one unifying factor? It's insanely expensive.

"Now, you might think it's all markups. And it is true, there are many markups. We can show that definitively by examining the operating costs of hospitals in other first-world nations and controlling for energy costs, et cetera. That's on page three."

Amber, who had yet to meet a spreadsheet she didn't like, drank this in happily. Jacob, who had seen all this firsthand recently, seemed a little more despondent about it.

"However," Nick said, "it's not all markups. Running the equipment genuinely is expensive, and part of that is because it's several distinct systems, each of which needs to talk to the others, receive updates, et cetera, et cetera, et cetera." He waved a hand expansively. "Which brings us to the numbers you've all waited for. Flip to page four, if you would."

Both his companions turned the page and looks of extreme surprise settled on their faces.

"Whoa," Amber said quietly. "Okay, I knew…I knew. But it's crazy to *see* it."

Jacob stared quietly at the numbers. On the table, one of his hands was in constant motion. The fingers danced over and around each other the way he did when he was deep in thought or stressed. It had become an inside joke in their class at MIT that he could have powered a small plant with his hand motions during exams.

The diagram on the page showed expected costs over time for a patient in the ICU in two scenarios. The first was in the current technological setup and the second in one of the PIVOT pods. A thick line ran horizontally along the page, and Nick didn't smile as he pointed to it.

"This? It's the median savings of an American family. Look how quickly it gets eaten away by a regular ICU stay."

Amber shook her head quietly. Beside her, Jacob looked like he wanted to burn the world down.

"Over a two-week stay, which is the median, the costs of running our pod doesn't even touch that line," Nick said. "And I'm pleased to report that the modifications to the already-manufactured pods cost almost nothing and would come out even when producing new ones."

"You're kidding." Amber flipped a page ahead and began to read, her brows drawn together in concentration. "Holy shit, you're right."

"I haven't even reached the best part yet." He grinned.

"You haven't?" She looked up.

"Nope." He put his folder on the table and leaned on his hands to fix them both with a smug look. "We have a whole set of research showing that things like our game could help bring people out of comas faster and recover more of their brain function."

Amber frowned now. She and Jacob exchanged a look.

"I knew it was a theory," Jacob said, "but I didn't think it had been studied."

"There was a huge study on it." Nick couldn't stop smiling. This alone had been worth the extra time. "Dr. Dubois at American University. He went through an insanely rigorous process with neurosurgeons, psychiatrists, neuroscientists—the whole nine yards. They even did a set of very, very successful tests on mice."

"Not…humans?" She raised an eyebrow. "Nick, I gotta say, I don't think the mouse ICU market is all that big."

"You're not thinking of how many mice we could fit in one of those at a time," Jacob objected.

"Oh, you make a good point."

"Guys." Nick laughed. "Focus. The results were all good. They were *really* good."

"So why isn't there already a product on the market?" Amber shrugged. "There must be something you didn't see—"

"Well, you see, IterNext Corp was seeking approval at the same time for a different method of treating patients in comas." He raised an eyebrow. "Somehow, out of nowhere…the FDA approval didn't come through for Dubois."

"Wait." Jacob frowned at him. "Who blocked it?"

"Well, I don't have any idea *officially*, but the head of the FDA accepted a real cushy post on the board of IterNext when he retired." Nick shook his head.

"Fuck that." His friend was furious. "They don't get to do things like that! These are people's lives they're playing with. If we make this public—"

"Nothing will happen," Amber said quietly.

Both men looked at her in surprise.

"Look." She shrugged. "They *can* get away with things like that. It's how it works in Washington. Money buys influence. That's how it's been forever."

"And you'll seriously simply give up because a few lobbyists—" Jacob's voice was rising.

"I'm not giving up. I'm saying everyone who gets into congress winds up doing things like this!" She waved her hands to encompass the room to emphasize the idea of everyone. "Every election cycle, there's a new set of people who will shake things up, and has the system changed at all? No. So before we go all-in on this, I want us to understand that we're probably…tilting at a windmill."

A long pause followed while the two men digested her statement.

"Where did you get windmills from?" Nick asked finally.

"It's a reference," Amber said wearily.

"To what?"

"I don't know. My dad says it all the time." She shrugged. "It means you're doing something futile."

"This isn't futile, though." Jacob stabbed a finger onto the sheet of paper. "This got blocked, okay? Sure. But that was before we had the resources we have now. Before people could do things like write a song about an airline destroying their guitar and have it go viral on Twitter and before people could dredge up videos and photos from decades ago and destroy someone's whole career."

"Your eyes are looking a little crazy," Amber told him.

"Maybe we can't change how politics works from inside the system," Jacob said dangerously, "but we can sure as hell make a ton of people mad that there's a cheap way to make people better and the FDA didn't approve testing. It's not like no one's talking about this lately. We have our moment."

"We don't have any allies," she pointed out wearily. "We can't simply take this up ourselves. Who will we go to? This kind of thing needs someone to sponsor a bill. It needs someone to make calls. Most of all, it needs someone in the senate, and in case you haven't noticed, we don't have much spare cash lying around."

Jacob leaned back in his chair for a moment, his jaw set. He shook his head angrily. "No. This isn't the end of it. We don't have a product, a problem, a solution, and research that backs it, all for nothing. Nick, can you get in touch with this Dubois guy?"

Amber shook her head in exasperation, but Nick wasn't entirely sure what would happen if he told Jacob no right now. She was right. The man had a crazy look in his eye.

"What harm could it do to call him?" he asked her.

"Well, no harm yet, but…." She sighed. "Okay, have it your way. I'll make more coffee. If we all get offed by big pharma lobbyists, I will haunt you two."

"We'll also be dead," Nick pointed out as he dialed.

"I'll find a way." The look on her face was remarkably convincing.

He spun in his office chair as the phone rang. When he began to think Dr. Dubois had no answering machine, a brusque voice said, "Yes?"

"Uh. Hi." He cleared his throat. "Is this Dr. Dubois?"

"Yes. Is this important? I was heading out."

"Uh, I'll be quick. Yes, it's important." Nick looked at the others and mouthed, "The doctor is in." "I'm calling about your study on using low-level electric currents to stimulate brain activity."

There was a long pause. "Are you a journalist?" Dubois asked finally.

"No. I'm an engineer." Nick hesitated, then took the plunge. "My friends and I made a device that, it turns out, is very close to what you had envisaged. We recently found your research and we wanted to meet. We're in the bay area, and—"

"Huh." The doctor cut him off. "Send me your resume, kid, with schematics. I'll get back to you." He hung up without a goodbye.

Nick put the phone down carefully. "Well, he's interesting. A little like Professor Elling at high speed."

Amber raised her eyebrows.

"Guys?" Jacob turned the TV up. "Look at that for a second."

Amber craned her neck to see better. The TV displayed a broadcast of footage taken from a chopper. Ambulances were crowded around a crumpled piece of metal that looked like it might once have been a car before it met a tree at high speed. Two pictures flashed on the screen. One was of a young woman with dark hair and a mischievous smile, captured in a candid photo. The other portrayed an uncomfortable-looking young man in a sport coat and tie, probably a senior class photo.

"Car accident?" she said. "None of us live near there, man."

"Look who he is, though." Jacob pointed to the text that scrolled across the bottom. ***THE PASSENGER, JUSTIN WILLIAMS, IS THE SON OF JUNIOR SENATOR TAD WILLIAMS. WILLIAMS, WHO WAS ELECTED IN 2018...***

"Oh," she said softly.

"Oh," Jacob echoed. He gave her a determined look. "It seems we might have found our pull in the senate, doesn't it?"

CHAPTER FOUR

Tad Williams had grown accustomed to thinking of his son as an overgrown child. At six feet two inches, with his father's broad-shouldered build and a good education, Justin had all the makings of a good looking, successful man. He shouldn't be living at home at the age of twenty-four, playing video games all day long with no earthly ambition.

The fact was that lately, he hadn't even been able to look at his son without feeling annoyed.

It was amazing how quickly things changed. He looked at him now, lying still under the blankets of the hospital bed, and all he could think about was when he was still small enough to pick up. When he'd carried him to bed, his blond head pillowed on his shoulder, tiny arms around his neck, and eyes drooping.

He even *looked* small right now. His chest barely moved and his face was horrifying.

The doctors said they kept the lights dim so that if he woke, it wouldn't be hard for him to open his eyes, but he suspected it was so that he and his wife couldn't see how bad the bruising was. Half of Justin's face looked almost purple, and another bruise was visible at the neck of his hospital gown—the seatbelt had probably made that one.

The doctor said his collarbone had been knocked out of place.

Why that was enough to make his heart squeeze, he didn't know, but he fumbled blindly for Mary's hand. When her fingers tightened around his, he looked at her and their eyes met.

Justin didn't know it, but he wasn't the only one with a lazy streak. At eighteen, all Tad had wanted to do with his life was work on cars and maybe get a job in the factory in town. He hadn't cared much about college or a career.

That was until her father sat him down. He had thought he knew where the conversation was going, and he'd never been more wrong in his life.

"I think you like my Mary," Harry had told him. "And she likes you. I like you too."

Tad had smiled.

"We like you," Harry had added, "because we know the man you could be. I think Mary would give anything to make you that man, Tad." When he'd blinked, suddenly aware that this conversation was going sideways, Harry leaned forward and looked him right in the eyes. "I like you, Tad," he'd said again. "And I like to think that if you woke up at forty-five and realized you'd made my daughter miserable because you never lived up to what she knew you could be, you'd hate that."

Tad had braced for The Talk, the one all the boys his age expected —you hurt my little girl, and—

But all Harry had said was, "The thing is, Tad, Mary can't ever make you that man. Only you can do that." He'd clapped Tad on the shoulder and offered him a beer.

It was a story he had waited to tell Justin since he'd first learned he was having a son. He'd had ideas about him coming to him with girl problems, about throwing a football, about glowing reports from teachers and the young man's ambitions—would he be a doctor? An entrepreneur? A lawyer?

But nothing had turned out like he wanted. The man he'd worked so hard to be had made his wife proud, but it hadn't been enough of an example for his son.

Mary's blue eyes were sad. She hadn't cried yet and had held herself together, on the brink, until now. "You're blaming yourself," she said. She could always see what was happening inside his head.

Tad found he couldn't say anything to that. His voice would break if he did.

"It's not your fault," she told him. "It's hers." Her voice had changed now. She looked at the bed with the angriest expression he'd ever seen on his wife's face. Tears rolled down her cheeks at last, but her expression wasn't one of grief.

It was one of rage.

"Ninety," she said. Her face twisted at the number. "Ninety miles per hour and—"

He reached out but she didn't lean into his arms.

"And she's *fine*!" She slammed her hand on the arm of the chair. At last, she collapsed, her face in one hand, and rocked slowly. "She's fine —she's sleeping, just *sleeping*, and he's—"

Tad leaned forward to wrap his arms around her. His eyes were tightly closed and all he could think was that he couldn't cry because she needed him right now.

"It isn't fair," Mary whispered, her words barely coherent around the sobs. "And it's my fault. I set him up on the date and he never would have met her if I hadn't."

He cupped the side of her face and leaned his forehead against hers. "None of this was your fault," he told her. "Imagine what Father LeMarc would think if he heard you say that."

She pressed her lips together and took a shuddering breath.

A knock at the door made them draw apart and they both looked at the entrance as it opened to admit a doctor. She was quiet and watchful, her black hair streaked with grey, brown eyes deep-set, and a distinct arch to her nose.

"Mr. and Mrs. Williams." Her voice was quiet. "I'm Dr. Goli, the attending physician. May I come in?"

"Yes." Mary wiped her face. "Yes, of course. I'm sorry."

"There is no need to apologize." The doctor crossed the room to them. "I was here when your son came in, and I am happy to say that he stabilized quickly and has remained stable since then. There were two dislocations but no breaks, and there are no signs of internal bleeding."

They both nodded.

When the doctor hesitated, however, Tad braced himself.

"Unfortunately, your son suffered extensive trauma to the head," Dr. Goli said. "At this point, his prognosis is not clear."

Mary grasped his hand harder than he knew she could. "When will you know?" Her voice was level.

The doctor folded her hands around the clipboard. "I wish I could say, Mrs. Williams. Unfortunately, there's very little we can do for traumatic brain injuries at this stage. The brain sometimes heals itself, but there's no way to know if it will or how long it will take. It's entirely possible that your son could wake up tomorrow and be completely fine."

Mary paused and took a deep breath. "And it's possible he'll never wake up," she said. "Isn't it?"

Dr. Goli hesitated before she nodded. "That is a possibility, yes. In all likelihood, his recovery to full health would take some time."

"I see."

Tad's phone vibrated in his pocket and he looked at the number of the insurance company.

"I need to take this," he told his wife.

She nodded as frustration flitted across her face but it was gone in an instant.

He didn't want her to think he was stepping away for no reason but he also didn't want her to worry, the way he did, that this call might be the insurance company denying their claim. He left the room wordlessly and answered the call in the hallway. "This is Tad Williams."

"Mr. Williams." The voice was warm but brisk. "This is Matthew Heigl with Unity Insurance, calling about your claim."

"Yes?" He closed his eyes briefly.

"I'm pleased to say that it has been approved," the agent said. "Your son is covered for up to five hundred thousand dollars and—"

"Oh, thank God." Tad sank onto a bench that didn't exist and looked around to see if anyone had noticed. Thankfully, the hallway was empty. He leaned against the wall, shaking. Relief made him light-headed. Five hundred thousand dollars would be more than enough.

"Now, we haven't yet received the bill for the life flight and the initial surgeries," the agent continued.

"How much does a life flight normally cost?" Tad asked.

"I can't give any specific numbers, sir."

"Ballpark it for me, Heigl." He looked heavenward and prayed for patience. "What's the average?"

"Roughly forty-five thousand dollars." The agent's voice was subdued.

Tad gripped the phone. "Could you say that again?"

"The average for a life flight is about forty-five thousand dollars," the agent repeated. "That, of course, does not include the original emergency services response or any of the surgeries. Or the hospital stay."

"I'm…" Tad looked at the door. Inside that room, a doctor was telling his wife that Justin might be under for an indeterminate amount of time.

"You'll also want to account for physical therapy after he's released," the agent added.

"How long?" he asked.

"It would vary based on what type of physical therapy he needs."

"No. How long will he be covered in the hospital?" He thought he felt the phone creak in his grip.

"Um." The agent seemed to guess from his tone—correctly—that a noncommittal answer would be the wrong choice. "About three months, sir. Without accounting for physical therapy."

"Thank you." Tad hung up and stared at the blank wall in front of him.

Three months. Three months without counting the rehabilitation. Three months after which…

What was he supposed to do then? He was a junior senator and didn't have the reserves the older senators did. He didn't have the connections, either.

Alone in the hallway, Tad squeezed his hands until his nails began to break the skin on his palms.

What the hell was he going to do?

CHAPTER FIVE

Today's work at the office had been done hastily, with aides running in and out of Tad's sun-drenched office, bringing briefs and chattering message reports and watering the plants until he had to usher them all out of the room simply for a moment of quiet.

He had promised himself he would make coffee when he was done with this call. Unfortunately, after three days of sleeping in hospital chairs, he had begun to fantasize about a nice, big mug of coffee with foam at the edges. It would taste so good. The heat would feel so good.

This was a bad sign and he shook himself to clear the thought. Normally, he didn't even like coffee.

There was a beep. "Mr. Williams?" The voice on the other end of the line was chipper and pleasant. It was the kind of voice that came from a twenty-two-year-old with no responsibilities and the ability to bounce back from a night without sleep.

"Yes?"

"Mr. Metcalfe is on the line."

"Senator Williams." Dru Metcalfe's voice was easy and affable. "Thank you for calling me back so quickly."

"Yes, sir." Tad took a deep breath and tried to keep his eyes from drifting closed. "You wanted to speak to me?"

"Yes. I'm calling on behalf of Raymond White, the CEO at Iter-Next. He saw a report in the news about your son."

He tried to make sense of this in his head. "Yes?" he said finally when nothing gelled.

"Now, you may not realize it, but Mr. White has a close relationship with the administrative board at Bay Health Hospital, and he knows that in this kind of situation, costs can be…surprising."

Tad straightened a little. "They were something of a shock," he admitted. He tried to keep his voice neutral but his heart beat faster. This couldn't be the type of break he was hoping for, could it?

"Simply put, Mr. White would like to take care of the issue for you," Metcalfe went on. "Some of the bills can be negotiated—they can always be negotiated, can't they?" He gave a charming laugh. "But that can still leave a great deal. Mr. White doesn't want that to add to your family's burden right now."

"That's very generous, sir." There was a moment where Tad felt like he could breathe again for the first time since the police had called him. The house he and Mary had fixed up together was safe. Their nest egg would survive this.

But then he remembered who he was talking to.

He didn't want to say something to ruin his mental image, but he needed to. The mirage needed to disappear before he grew too attached to it. He had the vague idea that if he merely thanked the man and hung up the phone before he could tell him the quid pro quo, he might be too embarrassed to call back…but he knew that wouldn't work.

"And what does Mr. White want in return?" he asked evenly.

If he hoped to embarrass Metcalfe, he was disappointed.

"As you know, Senator, the regulatory market in Washington can be fickle. Reasonable business interests often take a back seat."

"Yes." Tad did know that.

Unfortunately, he was fairly sure he and Metcalfe did not agree on the definition of the term "reasonable business interests."

"IterNext works hard to make sure their products and services provide groundbreaking medical care," the man told him. He seemed to have settled into the presentation now. "They give America the next generation of advances, and they want to help as many people as possible live long, healthy lives."

He wouldn't be able to get out of this without the full spiel, would he? Tad darted a sad look at the coffee machine. He really should have started it before the call. Lesson learned.

"Mr. Metcalfe, it's been a very busy morning—"

"Of course, Senator. To be very direct with you, Mr. White has no idea of the next time one of IterNext's lifesaving products will be unfairly blocked in the senate."

It took a long moment for him to realize what the lobbyist was saying. He'd expected a sales pitch and had hoped against hope that it would be something he could support in good conscience, and this was anything but.

"He wants a blank check." His voice had begun to harden and he told himself not to get angry. Dru Metcalfe had something to offer, and it was something he desperately needed. Without the man's help, where would he find another offer like this?

But was the price tag one he could pay in good conscience? Especially when he couldn't know what it would entail until it happened.

"Mr. White merely needs to know that he has someone he can count on to make common-sense decisions," Metcalfe said soothingly. "Too many senators end up choosing their stance before they even know the facts of a case. Knowing there's someone who can listen to reason will be a weight off his mind."

Go to hell. Or…what was it he'd overheard Justin say on his headset the other day? *Get in the sea?* He wanted to say it so badly. This was the type of thing he'd planned to say since the day he decided to run for the senate. That was why he'd gone into politics, dammit. Too many people were bought, captive to interests that weren't only neutral to voters but actively went entirely against the voters' interests.

Tad picked up a picture from his desk—Justin, aged five and in a life vest, grinned from the deck of his uncle's boat.

He needs you right now. And he especially needs you to not be a hothead. There's a line you can walk.

With the terrible sense that this was how it all began for too many people, he finally said, "I'll think about it, Mr. Metcalfe. If you're ever in the area, do stop by my office."

"Of course, Senator Williams. And again, we're all praying for Justin."

"Thank you." He placed the phone down.

He needed…he didn't know what he needed. For a brief moment, he had the mental image of sitting at Justin's bedside and asking him what he should do. But his son couldn't answer right now and even if he could, it had been years since they'd spoken with no animosity. Justin thought—

It hurt to acknowledge that he didn't know what he thought. He had seen the rolled eyes when he practiced campaign speeches and had heard Mary plead with him to come to one event, to dress up and support his father. He'd left before he could hear him say something he didn't want to remember.

Tad didn't realize he'd dialed the number until Mary said, "Hello?"

"Hello." He heard the tiredness in her voice. "How are you holding up over there?"

"I'm doing fine." He could tell she was smiling. "Take as long as you need. I know other people need you right now."

His gut twisted.

"Tad?" Her voice was concerned. "Are *you* all right?"

"I'm fine," he managed. "I could use a little more sleep. Or much more coffee."

Mary clucked her tongue. "And a year ago, you didn't even drink it. What's happening to you there in big politics?"

She was joking, but he squeezed his eyes shut and rested his forehead in his hand.

"Tad. Something is wrong, isn't it?" Her voice had no humor in it now. "What is it?"

"I had an offer," Tad said. "A blank check for a CEO in return for—a bribe. They offered me a bribe." Maybe if he said it out loud it would make it seem real or less ridiculous.

"You knew that would happen," she said evenly. "I'm surprised it took them this long, frankly." She paused and when he said nothing, she added, "Don't be upset, my love. You knew they would try. What they need is for someone to tell them no. Once other senators see it's possible, there'll be real change."

"What if…I didn't say no?" His voice broke a little.

Mary said nothing.

"They offered to pay Justin's medical bills." The words came out in a rush.

"Tad, we have insurance."

"He's covered up to five hundred thousand dollars." He hadn't wanted to tell her this but now, he couldn't seem to stop talking. "That's all. And I thought it would be enough, but he's already up over a hundred and it's thousands a day, Mary. Not only that, but he'll also need physical therapy when he gets out and we don't know how long it'll even take for him to wake up…" His voice trailed off and he clenched his free hand.

"I wish Justin could hear you," she said finally.

"What?"

"He thinks you're too idealistic." Her voice was distant. Tad could practically see her staring at the hospital bed where Justin lay amidst the monitors and wires. "He thinks you can't see how complicated life is. He said when push came to shove, you'd choose your principles over doing the expedient or self-serving thing."

He laughed bleakly. "I hope you're going somewhere good with this."

Mary laughed as well, although he could tell she was on the edge of tears. "I think it would do him good to know you want to do this for him," she said. "You campaigned on one thing, Tad, and you're ready to throw it all away."

"Do you think I should?" It seemed as if the ground shifted beneath him. He didn't know where he stood anymore. While he was desperate for her to say yes, he was terrified she would. "Mary, I can't do this alone."

"You don't have to." It was like she was there with him, holding his hand. The pressure in his chest eased. "I'm here, Tad. I'm always here."

She took a deep breath. "And, no. I don't think you should take the deal."

Her voice didn't even waver.

"You don't?" he almost whispered. God, what he wouldn't give to be able to gripe at Justin right now. What he wouldn't give to walk past his room and see him playing video games, or sleeping in, or slouching to the dinner table in sweatpants and an old t-shirt.

"No." Her voice was firm. "I don't know what the answer is, Tad, but I know it's not this—and you don't think it is, either. If you thought this was something you needed to do, you'd simply have done it. You wouldn't have called me."

Tad squeezed his eyes shut. "But what if—what if nothing else comes up?"

"Then we'll figure it out," his wife told him. "Don't compromise everything you are for this. I don't know if…if Justin will wake up." Her voice shook. "But if he does, he needs you—not the person you'd be if you did this."

They said their goodbyes and he hung up. He rested his face in his hands for a long moment before he pushed to his feet. He hadn't gotten there, he told himself, by cracking at the first sign of a problem. He would have coffee, he would get paperwork done, and he would find a way to make this work without Dru Metcalfe and his offer. This afternoon, before he returned to the hospital, he would call him and tell him as much.

He wasn't sure if it was adrenaline or purpose that sustained him, but he managed to make his way to the coffee machine and began to measure beans out. He had barely finished grinding them when one of his aides entered.

"Excuse me, Senator? Two men are here to speak to you about a medical device."

How quickly the blank check was getting called in. Tad gave a bleak smile. It looked like he'd tell Mr. Metcalfe off sooner rather than later.

"Send them in," he said over his shoulder. He heard their footsteps as he shook the grounds into the filter and said, "I'll be with you in a minute."

"Thank you for having us here, Senator." The line sounded rehearsed. "We have something truly groundbreaking to discuss with you today, something we believe will transform your life."

"Are you lobbyists or are you missionaries?" He poured the water into the machine, put the lid down, and pressed the *brew* button. "Because your presentation—" He turned and stopped in surprise.

The two men who stood there weren't lobbyists or if they were, they were the worst he'd ever seen. Instead of tailored suits, they wore dark-colored jeans bunched around the ankles rather than hemmed appropriately. One of them wore a button-down shirt and tie with a modicum of grace, but it looked like the shirt had been pulled hastily out of the back of his closet without being pressed. The other wore an unseasonable sweater, probably to hide a t-shirt.

Interestingly, both of them looked as exhausted as he was.

Tad considered them for a moment. "Aren't you two a little young to be piranhas for the DC elite?"

The one in the sweater looked at the one in the tie before he answered. "We're not piranhas, sir. We're engineers."

"Sometimes considered a close cousin," the other one joked with a flash of real humor, "but you're probably thinking of the team over in legal. We hate those stuck up bastards." He waited to see how the joke would land and when Tad didn't respond, he cleared his throat. "Senator, we think we can help your son."

"Really." Tad told himself there was no way this was good news. He decided to sit before he swayed too obviously on his feet and pulled his office chair out before he gestured to the two other chairs in front of his desk. "Sit. Right upfront, you tell me what you want in return."

"Uh…" The two men looked at each other.

"It's a piece of ICU equipment," the one with the tie said.

"It helps patients in comas," the other one added.

They wouldn't be straightforward either, would they? He resisted the urge to tell them to go away.

"Okay, first, who are you? You in the sweater, what's your name?"

"Jacob Zachary, sir."

"And you?" Tad nodded to the one in the tie.

"Nick Ryan, sir."

"Well." He leaned forward on his elbows. "Mr. Zachary. Mr. Ryan. Let me tell you a little about myself. I'm not a fan of long presentations. I'm also not a fan of quid pro quo deals. So if that's what you have for me today, you should do us both a favor and walk out that door, are we clear?"

Jacob looked like he wanted to do exactly that, but Nick leaned forward.

"Senator Williams, please hear us out. We've made a device that does all the normal functions of ICU equipment. It's called a pod." He pushed a piece of paper across the table at him. "It can monitor blood pressure and heart rate, provide a specific amount of oxygen, all of the normal stuff. It merely has something normal ICU equipment doesn't have—a way to engage a patient in a coma. A way to stimulate brain waves and jumpstart the brain's process of healing. We think it could work for your son."

Tad looked at the two of them. There wasn't anything practiced in these words, and he liked to think that what he saw on their faces was sincerity.

"Sir, my grandmother just died in the ICU," said Jacob. "She'd had a stroke, she wasn't waking up, and—"

"What does it cost?" he asked them.

He was talking favors and votes, but when they answered, it was clear they hadn't even thought of that. Nick swallowed twice before answering.

"It's about…well, five hundred dollars a day." He held up his hands. "But hear us out—"

"Five…hundred?" He did some quick math in his head, then pulled a calculator out of his desk drawer to check the numbers. He couldn't possibly have been right, could he?

But he had been. This machine would give Justin three more years to recover.

The two young men looked at him like they were afraid they'd blown it, but all he could do was smile.

"Tell me more," he said quietly.

"I don't want to promise anything," Nick said quietly.

Jacob looked angry. "My grandmother might have lived if she'd had something like this," he told his friend. He looked at Tad. "A doctor named DuBois conducted research several years ago about a device that would basically do the same thing ours does. He hadn't built one—he was trying to find out if it would be a good idea. His research showed it would but it was blocked."

"Blocked how?"

"Healthcare lobbyists." Jacob's hands clenched. "Sir, this research is *solid*. It could help people. But healthcare companies don't want people to get better. That's not how they get paid. They blocked DuBois's research and we need someone to help get ours through."

Tad hardly heard him. *Three years. More than enough time.* Justin would surely have woken up and they'd still have money for his physical therapy.

"Sir, I don't want to raise your hopes," Jacob said again. He shook his head at Nick. "You said you wanted straight talk, didn't you? It *is* experimental. No one's done this with a game before. That's what we would do. We'd give him a game that's like real life. For you or me, it would be like dreaming or using a VR set. We don't know what it would do to someone in a coma. If he dies in the game...we don't know how his brain would interpret that."

Tad, for whom the word "game" conjured mental images of Candy Land, realized they probably meant something like Justin had played. Call of Warfare. World of Legends. One of those.

"I have to talk to my wife about this," he said.

"Of course," Nick said.

"Sir," Jacob began, "if you're worried about the device—"

"Your friend's right, Mr. Zachary." He smiled. "I do like straight talk. You're not lying to me, and I like that. Let me talk to my wife and I'll get back to you. Does my aide have your information?"

"Yes." Jacob nodded. He and Nick exchanged a look, completely transparent in its hope.

"Good." He stood. "I'll be in touch. Yes, Annie, what is it?"

His aide had come around the door and she gave him a cautious smile. "A Mr. Metcalfe is here to see you," she said.

Tad had a vivid memory of himself saying, "Do stop by." He had thought it was a rote pleasantry when he said it but apparently, Metcalfe had taken him at his word. He sighed.

"Send him in, Annie. Gentlemen, I'll talk to you later."

CHAPTER SIX

Amber hunched over the compartment of the pod and tried to think of something other than the swirl of negative thoughts in her head. She didn't take any particular joy in being a pessimist. She'd much rather be an optimist, and if the whole world were like her lab, she would be one.

The whole world wasn't like her lab, though. Unfortunately, it wasn't even close. Instead of carefully-drawn schematics, there was absolute chaos. Instead of careful trial and error, in which every problem you encountered was simply your fault—and thus fixable— the world was full of situations that were not only chaotic but sometimes tailored toward failure.

She stole a glance at the corner of the room, where Dr. DuBois was sitting—or lying, in actual fact. Apparently, he had decided to take a nap.

He didn't look at all like she'd pictured him, which threw her off. She'd expected someone short and businesslike, either with his head entirely in the clouds like Nick or bleakly depressed in the wake of his defeat at the hands of lobbyists. Instead, he didn't seem to have any particular thoughts on whether the pod would work or not. He'd asked to see the game, played it for a couple of hours, and disappeared around the time Nick and Jacob left to see the senator.

When he'd returned, there had been popcorn in his beard and now, he was asleep on the couch.

And he still hadn't given any feedback on the pods.

Amber straightened and looked wearily at him. He was a perfect example of why she was worried right now. DuBois had done good research, she had to admit that. He'd tied together disparate groups in his field, resolved hanging questions, and written a rigorous study to which there was not yet any rebuttal.

It wasn't the quality of his work or ideas that had sunk him. Rather, it was someone who didn't want their profits to suffer and who could pay to make sure that wouldn't happen. If DuBois, with a full slate of researchers and the backing of American University, hadn't managed to get past them, what hope did PIVOT have?

The door banged open and she heard Jacob and Nick talking excitedly to one another as they came down the hall. A quick glance showed that DuBois had not even stirred, and Amber shrugged before she headed to the kitchenette to see what was going on.

"So?" She was surprised to see the happy looks on their faces.

"He wants to do it," Jacob reported.

"He's talking to his wife," Nick tempered.

Jacob rolled his eyes. "This guy? He's not all salesman, turns out. He tried *un*-selling the thing once we'd already made the sale."

Amber's eyebrows raised and her mouth twitched when Nick gave a soft moan and put his head in his hands. She'd seen many arguments between these two over the years, during which they went round and round with increasingly implausible suggestions of each other's parentage and what the other one could consider doing with a cactus, and the theater of it never got old. Now, she pulled a chair out and leaned back to watch.

"You didn't meet this guy," Nick told Amber. "He eats lobbyists for breakfast. He doesn't want to be oversold, and we've never had a coma patient in one of these. I gave him the facts, *which*"—he held a threatening finger up to stave off Jacob's protest—"ended up getting us the contract. He *liked* that we weren't selling him some pie in the sky dream."

Jacob rolled his eyes. "It will work," he said to no one in particular. "I don't know why everyone is so worried. It will work, and the sooner we get it on the market, the better." He shook his head and wandered into the lab, muttering something about upgrades.

His companions exchanged a glance.

"I didn't expect to be the voice of reason," Nick admitted. He lowered his voice slightly. "Buuuut let's say Jacob oversold a little."

Amber tilted her head to look and make sure their friend was out of earshot. "Are you surprised?" she asked Nick.

"Well…yeah." He waved his hands. "The dude's not a salesman."

"No," she said patiently, "but he *is* someone who just lost his grandmother and has an awful lot invested in this working." She rolled her eyes at the slow-dawning comprehension on Nick's face. "Yeah. This isn't coming out of nowhere, and we'll need to be real careful when we hit snags."

"If," he said warningly. "Don't tempt fate."

"Nick, you've been an engineer how long? *When.* There's a reason it's taken us four years to get here on this project. Jacob likes to talk about brains being computers, but they're so far beyond the computers we have that it's a miracle the two can even talk."

"I don't see why," a new voice said.

Amber and Nick both jumped and turned to where Dr. DuBois wandered sleepily into the kitchenette. He rummaged around in the cupboards, opened each one in turn to see what was inside, and turned to look at the two of them. "A laptop could understand a calculator," he said, as if that solved the whole problem, then wandered into the laboratory and left several boxes of tea and coffee on the counter and the cupboards open.

"What does he mean?" Nick mouthed at Amber.

She shrugged as she began to put the tea away, frowned, and went to lean in the doorway. "You're saying the problem isn't the human brain understanding computers, it's computers understanding what the brain says in response. Right?"

DuBois didn't bother to give a yes or a no. "The brain will fill in as much as it needs to. The computer says 'sky,' the brain builds a picture. But what happens when the brain says something that's beyond the computer's knowledge?"

"Nothing," Jacob said. "If you tell a computer to do something it can't interpret, it does nothing."

"If you're lucky," Nick argued. He came to stand in the doorway beside Amber. "If you're unlucky, you used language it knows and it tries to do something it can't." He swallowed. "And it crashes."

Jacob's face darkened and he marched to one of the pods to begin working on it. He kept his back to the two of them.

Dr. DuBois looked puzzled. "Why is he angry?" he asked Amber and Nick as he pointed at the man.

"They're talking about ways this could go wrong," Jacob said without looking around.

"I thought we were talking about computers," DuBois said vaguely. He shrugged after a moment. "So it goes wrong. What then?"

Jacob finally straightened. "Then we have a medical emergency," he said slowly. "And a dead person."

"That doesn't necessarily follow." The scientist raised an eyebrow. "You're falling prey to a classic logical fallacy, young man."

Amber thought their friend might have an aneurysm.

"What's the fallacy?" he asked far too nicely.

"You put too much moral weight on doing something different," DuBois told him. "You think if you put someone in this machine and they die, it will be your fault."

"It *will* be our fault," Amber said.

"People in comas die all the time," the man countered. "Do they do that because they're on a ventilator? Because they have surgery to stop internal bleeding? No. They die because they're in bad condition. You say you have a good piece of equipment." He waved his hand at the pods. "I agree. So if you have a good piece of equipment that can save people and you don't use it… Well, that's a choice, too, isn't it?" He gave them all a somewhat challenging look. "I'm going to go get more popcorn," he added before he disappeared.

A moment of absolute silence followed.

"I cannot figure that dude out," Amber said finally.

"He has a good point," Jacob replied. He looked at them. "There might be problems but there are problems with the way things are done now, too. We have to remember to not make it our fault if something goes wrong outside of our control."

She was a little more worried about what the legal system would think of things.

CHAPTER SEVEN

In person, Dru Metcalfe was tall with brown skin and close-cropped, curly black hair. He shook Tad's hand but his eyes were worried.

"Senator Williams, I hope you don't think I was eavesdropping, but I caught the tail end of that discussion." He folded his lanky form into one of the chairs and pressed his fingertips together. "I'm sorry they offered you something like that."

The senator leaned back in his chair and resisted the urge to narrow his eyes. "Why so?" he asked as neutrally as he could. He'd poured them both cups of coffee when the man entered the room and sipped his slowly. It was almost strong enough to raise someone from the dead, which was what he needed right now.

"The technology is untested," Metcalfe told him. "Who knows what problems might lurk down the road? This country has stringent testing protocols for a reason, Senator."

He took another sip of his coffee. "I thought you recently told me the protocols were too stringent," he said and he couldn't keep the amusement from creeping into his voice.

"Senator Williams." His visitor did not smile. "Politics aside, testing is important. Putting your son's life in the hands of those…" He paused as he tried to choose the correct word.

"Engineers," Tad supplied.

"Yes. They're not doctors, you know."

"They're working with one. Mr. Metcalfe—"

"You can't possibly be *considering* their offer." The man seemed horrified. "Senator, you do not need to take desperate measures right now. Mr. White is happy to fund as much care as your son needs."

"In return for my cooperation on the senate floor," he said flatly.

Metcalfe smiled gently. "Senator, believe it or not, I do understand your worries." He paused and deliberately let the moment hang. "We understand your fears that this might conflict with your morals. Trust me when I say this is as far from those concerns as it could be."

Tad couldn't help himself and raised an eyebrow. "Why don't you walk me through that one," he suggested. "Because my guess is that favor won't get called in until you need support for something I won't give it to. So why don't you tell me how there's no conflict?"

"Senator, which treatments go to the FDA for testing and which are blocked is not a matter of lives being saved," the man explained as if he were not at all fazed by this question. "It is a matter of politics. IterNext has strong competitors, each of them with their own lobbyists. Suppose all of them pursue the same avenue on…oh, heart disease." He gestured to show that this was only an example. "This is not a matter of whether or not people are cured. It is a matter of who gets the rights to cure them."

He leaned forward. "And that is not a game I want to play," he said simply.

Metcalfe stared at him, a little nonplussed.

"If there's truly no difference," he continued, "then why should I care if the other guy wins? Why shouldn't I simply let all of you duke it out and spend my time on other matters?"

"Because none of the rest of them have called to help you and your son." The lobbyist was not offended. In fact, he was all too calm. "Senator, I assure you, I understand. You don't want to be bought. This isn't being bought—it's finding complementary interests."

Tad said nothing. He tried to think of what Mary would say and could not.

"There is a reason quid pro quo has always existed," Metcalfe said easily. "Before it got a dirty name in the media, it was merely two people helping each other out. That's what we do, isn't it? It's why you got into politics—to help people out. Mr. White appreciates that, as do I. We even appreciate your candor about your worries." His smile did not falter at the disbelieving look he earned. "But quid pro quo is older than Washington, Senator—it's even older than the empire that named it. It isn't going anywhere, and if you refuse to take part, the only one you harm is yourself." He did not add "and your son" but the words were almost audible.

Tad looked out the window. When he had campaigned for this job, it had been so clear to him how the chain of corruption began—a small ask, a favor, a gift in return. Nothing you could object to. Nothing that even seemed wrong.

But it opened the door and every time, it got easier to say yes.

His path forward was clear. Justin's prognosis was uncertain, even in the ICU, and whether he stayed there or they transferred him to PIVOT's labs, he and Mary had decided that they would do this without Dru Metcalfe and his bribes.

"I'm not interested," he said simply.

Metcalfe nodded slightly. He opened his briefcase and withdrew two full-page, glossy photos and a written statement. When he pushed them across the desk, Tad's jaw dropped. The photos were of him standing with a woman in a sundress and heels, far too close for them simply to be having a friendly conversation. Behind them was the entrance to a hotel. The statement was from the woman and contained details of an affair and his offer of a payoff if she would remain silent.

The only slight problem with the allegation was that he had never had an affair. He was a good-looking man and he'd had offers, but Mary was the love of his life. She still made his heart race the way she had when they were sixteen.

That said, the absolute, blatant threat of the photos made him flush hot and cold. He pushed them across the desk so hard that they fluttered to the floor.

"This never happened," he said tightly.

The man smiled at him, almost pitying. "And we both know that doesn't matter," he said simply.

"*What?*"

"Senator Williams…" Metcalfe picked the papers up and put them in his briefcase. "Let us be honest with one another. What do voters like more than anything?"

"To see their interests represented," Tad snapped.

"Scandal," the man corrected him simply. He shook his head. "What do you think will happen if we put those photos out?"

"I'll make a statement to the press explaining what's going on," he told him. Mary wouldn't believe it. Surely she wouldn't believe it—

"You might even prove it," his visitor agreed.

Tad hesitated.

"But by the time you do that," the lobbyist told him, "your career will already be over. Have you ever seen a town hall meeting with voters who hate their representative? Yelling, throwing things? Can you imagine it, Senator? Can you imagine the speeches your opponents will give? It's too perfect, isn't it? The senator who couldn't be bought paying off his mistress."

- He saw red. "Why even pretend to play nice?" He almost growled the words. "Why the phone calls and why the fake concern for Justin?" The fact that Metcalfe had opened the door by pretending to care made him want to punch the man in the face.

"I am concerned for Justin," the lobbyist said. "As is Mr. White. We're not monsters, Senator Williams." He shook his head. "And as for why we began with a pleasant phone call—I much prefer it when things are pleasant. Don't you?"

Tad could hardly see straight he was so angry. The doubletalk was beyond infuriating. "If you like things to be pleasant, why did you have those photos in your briefcase?"

Metcalfe stood and buttoned his suit jacket. Now he *did* look pitying, and Tad hated him for that. "You're not the first senator to promise they wouldn't take bribes," he said. "Didn't you ever wonder why the others all left their morals behind in the end?" He went to the door and looked back. "Think about it, Senator," he said, and in the next moment, he was gone.

He stood and began to pace. All the urges he had right now—to drag Metcalfe into the back alley and teach him a lesson, to hold a press conference, to flip his desk over—were the opposite of productive. If he intended to do this, if he wanted to stay the course, he needed to be as cold and calculating as they were.

It was imperative that he be as *smart* as they were. Because, like an idiot, he'd expected that not taking bribes would be as simple as saying no to them. He hadn't expected blackmail, much less blackmail over something he'd never done.

Before all this began, he would have said that to cave now would be senseless. If he caved, it would be to betray everything he stood for.

But when he'd promised that, Justin's life and his career hadn't hung in the balance. If Metcalfe made good on his threats—and he had no doubt that he would—he could lose everything and his blackmailer would never suffer any consequences. Too late, he realized he should have held onto the forged images and perhaps approached law enforcement. Unfortunately, he'd been too surprised and perhaps naïve to think of that.

There had to be an answer. But what in the name of God *was* it?

CHAPTER EIGHT

Dru Metcalfe made sure to keep moving as he hurried out into the sunlight and got into his car. For one thing, he had a busy schedule. Senator Williams might be the only US senator in the city right now, but there were dozens more California senators taking vacations and visiting their home districts nearby. It was going to be a busy day.

That wasn't why he kept moving, though. He'd learned long ago that after a meeting like this, after turning the screws that would bring someone around to his side, he preferred to not think about it.

Dwelling on it all usually meant he didn't like the tone of his thoughts. He remembered things like his law school days and the pro bono clinics he served in before he graduated. It brought back the times when he'd held out for his first job, shared a studio apartment, and waited tables to make ends meet.

He also remembered the dinner where he'd told his friends about his new job—the one with the big salary and the annual bonus. A vivid recollection always surfaced of how he'd told them that he would take them all out for dinner at Christmas, how they would take the big corporations down from the outside and he would help them from the inside.

Inevitably, he remembered the first case he hadn't helped on.

A couple of years later, he'd moved away from New York. It was easy to not move in the same circles when one group watched for sales on toilet paper and the other drank a thousand-dollar bottle of champagne. Still, he hadn't liked the possibility of running into them all again.

It had been ten years since then, and he'd learned very well how to quiet the little voice in his head that told him this wasn't what he'd wanted to do with his life.

The thing was that it didn't matter. None of it mattered. Dru had told himself he would change the world, but that wasn't something anyone could do. The world was too big. You could make a ripple but the ripple died away soon after. Even if you thrashed around with all your strength, you would still go under and leave no trace. People like Raymond White and IterNext always won in the end.

So why not get some of the profits for himself?

He didn't even blame them. People went stupid when money was involved. Ethics went out of the window. It was simply human nature. There was no point in trying to rise above it when so many people didn't care. In the end, someone's personal interest would always trump a vague idea of doing the right thing.

No, the people he blamed—the ones he hated—were the ones like Tad Williams who told him to go to hell. Dru hated them for yelling at him as if he didn't know what went through their heads. He hated them for being stupid and not seeing the world as it really was, hated them when they refused his offers, and hated them even more when they broke.

But at least once they broke he never had to see them again.

He didn't think about Tad Williams any more while he drove. There was no point, after all. Dru had been the one to bring the news of Justin Williams's car crash to Raymond White. He'd known what that meant and he hadn't lied when he told Tad that it didn't matter which company he backed.

Nothing mattered, not in the end. What mattered was getting what you could while you were here.

Amber and Nick had gone out to get dinner. Well, get dinner and find DuBois, who wandered around outside like a lunatic.

And they'd whisper about him. Jacob knew that. He knew they thought he was too caught up in this and was disregarding the risks. That was the problem with being reasonably intelligent—you knew what other people thought and you knew they were right.

You merely couldn't stop yourself.

His grandmother had looked peaceful in the ICU. She hadn't been in pain and he knew that was a blessing. He shouldn't be angry about it.

But she looked like she was asleep—like she was already dead, and she shouldn't be. She should be alive and at home while they all tried to make her apple pie and she scolded them for adding too much cinnamon and stealing morsels of the dough. She'd slipped away because there was nothing to call her back and no way to get through to her.

Jacob whirled away from the pod. He wanted to punch something and it couldn't be this. This was the pod Amber had spent all day tinkering with. It didn't matter that she doubted it would work or that she was afraid they would be offed by Big Pharma. She was doing this because it was important to all of them that their work meant something—and because it was important to him.

In the same way, Nick had given Tad Williams the real facts rather than the inflated ones. They would do this so that PIVOT could succeed and Jacob could see a family get someone back.

He went to his desk, hesitated, and typed **JUSTIN WILLIAMS TAD WILLIAMS** into the search bar. It wasn't long before he'd found a trail through social media. The Facebook page had been locked down and scrubbed carefully—Tad Williams had clearly found a PR firm while running for congress—a LinkedIn page looked like someone else had set it up for him, but a YouTube channel might provide insight.

Jacob hesitated before he opened the page. The autoplay had a run-through of a game he hadn't seen in ages and before he knew it, he leaned back in his chair, laughed at some of the jokes, and even groaned in mock-horror when the character ran afoul of a cleverly-placed trap.

Movement behind him drew his attention and someone placed an open container of lo mein in his hand. Chopsticks already protruded from it. Amber and Nick drew stools up behind him, watched, and laughed with him. They ate as they watched princesses get saved, Master Chief dodge a particularly worrisome section of the final level in Halo 3, and some of the funnier bloopers from Portal.

When the food was gone and the videos were finished, Jacob leaned back in his chair and smiled at his friends.

"It's good to unwind," Nick told him. "None of us have done that enough lately."

"Honestly, if it had to be something, I thought we'd have found you watching Starcraft tournaments." Amber popped the last piece of chicken into her mouth and handed her takeout container to Nick, who was collecting them to throw away. "What made you decide to watch vintage game play-throughs?"

"First of all," Jacob told her, "if Halo 3 is vintage, we're ancient."

She laughed and smoothed the hair along the side of her head. "See these grays, friend? We're ancient. Next?"

"Don't remind me," he grumbled. "Second..." He looked at the screen. Justin's face was frozen in an exaggerated expression and inclined to point to where the subscribe button was. "Do you know who that is?"

"No." Nick shook his head and peered at the screen. "Ah, yes, MorePylons3000. I'd know that name anywhere."

Jacob lobbed a wadded-up napkin at him. "This is Justin Williams."

His friends stopped dead.

He looked at the screen again. While he had listened to the jokes and the awkward attempts at gaining subscribers, flashes of something had continually nagged at his consciousness.

Flashes of Tad Williams, he realized. Justin could be just as direct and to the point when he had a focus.

"This is why we're doing what we're doing," he said quietly.

No one argued with him this time. Amber squeezed his shoulder. "Nick told me what you said to the senator," she said. "I think you helped him see this was more than a sales pitch. I think you helped him see that his son would be in good hands with you—because you care. You freaking care. And that's more than those fuckers in the lobbyist firms can say."

Mary listened to the story of Dru Metcalfe and the forged papers in silence before she stretched her hand out to wrap her fingers around Tad's. When he looked at her, there was nothing in her face but concern.

"Well?" He laughed but it didn't quite sound like a laugh.

"Well, what?" She tilted her head to the side. It was the same gesture Justin used sometimes, and his heart constricted.

"Well..." He closed his eyes and exhaled slowly. "What do I do?"

"The same thing you planned to do," she said without missing a beat. Behind her, Justin's heart rate monitor beeped regularly. The bruises on his face had turned all different colors now. He wished he could joke with his son about that.

"How can I fight this?" he asked hopelessly. "How can I fight someone who can turn anything I do—anything I don't even do—into a scandal?"

Mary laughed then. It was a sound he hadn't heard since the night they came to the hospital. "If you can't win, why worry about losing?"

Tad stared at her.

"If you'd been born a woman," she told him, "you'd have known much earlier in life that there's no winning some fights. It doesn't matter what you do sometimes, you'll still somehow lose. Either you're loose, or you're a prude, or you're a bitch..." She squeezed his hand and shrugged. "When there's no winning, it hurts. It isn't fair. But it's freedom, too. It means you can do whatever you want to do. Look at it this way, Tad—one way, you give up everything that makes you respect yourself but the other way, someone lobs a scandal at you."

"I won't get to do anything I wanted to do in Congress if I am tossed out after one term," he murmured.

"You won't get to if you're a bought and paid-for puppet, either," Mary said sharply. "Anything else?"

"*Justin*," Tad whispered. "Justin needs us."

"Exactly." She leaned closer, her gaze locked on his. "Justin needs us. If we can't win, then we do what keeps Justin safest—and you know what I think? I think that means keeping him away from the people who are trying to blackmail you."

Tad leaned his head against hers for a moment. "What did I ever do to deserve you?"

Mary tilted her face up for a kiss. "Like I've never leaned on you?"

He smiled and kissed her again. Calm now, he held her close for a moment before he pulled his phone out. "Okay. I'll make the call."

CHAPTER NINE

Mary stood to the side and clutched Tad's hand while the nursing team worked.

Dr. Goli had been called in and had appeared with dark circles under her eyes but the same air of quiet competence. She was in constant, calm motion and stopped occasionally to touch a nurse on the shoulder and murmur a quiet suggestion before she moved on to the next.

Dr. DuBois, the doctor the PIVOT team had brought, couldn't be more different. His lab coat, although clean, looked as if it had been shoved in the bottom of his suitcase without being folded. He rocked rhythmically from his heels to the balls of his feet as he read Justin's file. Periodically, he would look vaguely at all the monitors before he refocused on the records again.

He didn't look nervous at all.

Mary couldn't decide which she preferred—nervousness or a lack of it. Dr. Goli and her team were clearly worried about this transfer. They took extra care as they replaced each monitor with one of those the PIVOT team had brought and made sure the power sources for each was sufficient. They ran a series of final checks that seemed interminable.

Part of her wondered if they took so long to give her and Tad time to call it all off.

After a final flurry of activity, Dr. Goli stepped back and took Dr. DuBois' arm to draw him gently out of the way. He complied without looking up from the charts as if he were used to people moving him around this way.

He murmured questions to his counterpart as the nursing team swung the hospital bed into motion. Dr. Goli had flatly refused to transfer Justin from one bed to another, which had necessitated a few tense calls while Tad had attempted to find a private ambulance service that would allow a full-sized hospital bed inside it.

Mary squeezed his hand as they began to walk behind the bed. While she knew how heavily this had weighed on him, she also knew how much he had borne alone for her sake. She could still remember him as he'd been at eighteen—as brilliant and handsome as he was now but with a wild streak, still more concerned with day to day happiness than with the long term or anyone else.

While she still wasn't sure what had changed in him that year, he had truly become the man she had only seen glimpses of up until then. It was why she didn't worry about Justin. Each person needed their purpose. Tad had found his in leadership and she had found hers in teaching. Both had found new depths of themselves in parenthood.

Justin simply needed to find what in him could change the world.

Which meant he had to survive this. Mary knew that Tad had leaned on her as much as she had leaned on him during this time, but the truth was that her confidence was built on nothing more than necessity. Justin *had* to survive. The alternative was unthinkable. The applicable rules and theories of science and medicine didn't matter.

He had to survive. If he didn't…she didn't want to think of what would happen so she didn't think of it.

They traveled down the hallways in silence. The team was always careful to take corners extremely slowly to make sure that no lateral pressure shifted Justin's head. They had added foam blocks to stabilize him but from their extreme care, it was clear how fragile his condition still was.

As if that wasn't enough, the lights in the hallway showed all too clearly how bad the crash had been. There was little of him that wasn't bruised at this point, from brilliant reds and purples to a sickly yellow-green at the edges. His lips were dry and a small split was visible, no longer bleeding, thank goodness.

Mary thought of the girl who'd driven him and who was already home with her parents and the anger rose again until she thought she would choke on it. She set it aside but did not forget it. She couldn't.

The private ambulance waiting outside was so nondescript that she might have taken it for an armored car if she didn't know better. The team of privately contracted paramedics inside exited and changed places with the hospital nursing staff. They worked efficiently as well but she saw their eyes linger on Justin and knew from their subdued demeanor that they rarely saw anything this bad.

When the bed was loaded—with more jerks and bangs than she had hoped for—she realized that the hospital team was gone. She looked around and shivered in the night air as she and Tad grasped each other's hands so hard that they ached.

"Mrs. Williams." Dr. DuBois looked at her now. "I assure you, Jordan is in good hands with me."

"Justin." The name came out of her mouth with a trace of horror. What was she doing with these people?

"Yes, of course." The doctor looked only vaguely discomfited. "Justin." He climbed into the ambulance.

"Mrs. Williams." A young man stood next to her. "Senator, good to see you again. Would you like to come in the ambulance?"

"Yes," Mary and Tad said together. They couldn't leave Justin. Not now.

"Right this way, then." The young man helped her up and moved to the front seat. The doors swung closed and the ambulance lurched into motion.

———

There were no sirens or lights. The ambulance, painted a deep red and black, slid through the city almost silently, which meant that Jacob was acutely aware of the way his heart pounded.

He tried not to look at Justin's parents, but the ambulance was set up with a series of mirrors to allow the driver to see into the rear and so it was easy for Jacob, in the passenger seat, to make use of them. They did not interfere with the paramedics or Dr. DuBois, nor did they touch their son—the doctors at the hospital must have told them how fragile his condition was right now.

They murmured to each other, he thought before he saw that their lips moved at the same time. They were praying, their gazes fixed on their son, and he thought it was more a way to give one another comfort than to comfort themselves. For a moment, he could only envy them. When he had been in the hospital the previous week, he had been alone.

To give them privacy, he looked away and watched the shops slide past. It was after midnight and only a few were open—a couple of bars and a café or two. There weren't many cars on the road, either.

Which was why the one behind them caught his attention before too long. He craned his neck to look in the side mirror and frowned. It was a nondescript vehicle and he couldn't see much about it.

The senator must have noticed his interest because he looked out the back windows. They were one-way so nothing on the inside of the ambulance would be visible, and that allowed Tad Williams to stand and put his face close to the glass.

There was a flash, which Jacob thought might have been the car behind them going over a tiny bump, but the senator drew back from the window sharply.

"That was a camera," he said.

"Do you want me to get away from them?" the driver asked. He looked at the hospital bed.

Jacob didn't want to make this decision. He knew what could go wrong and he wasn't ready to have that on his conscience. Rather than respond, he turned to wait for Justin's parents, who shared a single look.

"Step on it," the senator said. He sat hastily and swallowed hard.

The young engineer leaned back in his seat as the ambulance accelerated and the lights and sirens activated. Ahead of them, the few cars on the road pulled over sharply but the pursuing car didn't waver. It seemed to speed up as well. His heart pounded. Amber's throwaway threat about being offed by Big Pharma had been funny when she'd said it. They all knew she'd meant their careers might be stopped dead in the water and their company might be sunk.

But right now, with a car following an ambulance and people taking pictures of a boy in a coma, that idea had begun to seem far more literal.

"Get away from them," Jacob said in an undertone. "I don't like this."

"I don't like it, either." The driver increased his speed. "Come on, come on—"

The light he muttered to turned green at the last second and the ambulance rocketed through the intersection and made a slight turn at the end to merge onto a highway on-ramp. The car, which had increased speed, couldn't turn in time and went past with a screech of tires.

On the highway, the driver turned the lights and sirens off, took the immediate exit, and traversed the four-leaf clover in a tight, controlled turn that made Jacob clutch his armrest.

Behind them, an explosion of beeping erupted and paramedics began to call to one another. Jacob unbuckled his seatbelt and scrambled around, holding onto the seats to balance himself.

"What's going on?"

"The equipment's gone haywire," one of them said distractedly. She shoved past Jacob. "*Move.*"

The young engineer stood aside, his gaze fixed on Justin's parents. Their faces had gone gray.

"Don't worry," DuBois said and swung into action. He snatched a pair of scissors from one of the paramedics and made a single, practiced cut down the front of Justin's gown. The monitors were wildly erratic with respiration and heart rate off the charts, and Jacob clutched the back of the seats in consternation.

If Justin was truly deteriorating in condition, it brought all kinds of ramifications.

"Aha," the doctor said with satisfaction. He yanked a patch off Justin's chest and replaced it, wiggled one of the wires at its connection point, and held a button on one of the machines down. "You, turn that off." He gestured at a large set of machines but the paramedic seemed to know exactly what he meant.

A moment later, the set of beeps and whistles settled into their former, familiar rhythm. DuBois sat again, perfectly contented as if there hadn't been a crisis at all, although after a moment, he did lean forward to pull Justin's hospital robe closed again.

"Stop up there," he told the driver.

"Why?" The man risked a look back over his shoulder.

"I want to run into the drug store," the doctor said, "and get some popcorn."

In the silence that followed, the others stared at him open-mouthed.

"Does anyone else want anything?" DuBois asked as if this might be the reason for their looks.

Mary Williams drew in a breath, no doubt getting ready to rip him an entire series of new assholes, and Jacob intervened before the situation could degenerate.

"Our first priority is to get him hooked up," he told the man and put as much authority as he could into the words.

DuBois looked disappointed but subsided, and so did Mary.

Jacob took a deep breath and tried to calm his racing heart. That had been a close call in more ways than one.

The ambulance driver had done his job well and the car didn't catch up with them again. When they pulled into the lot at PIVOT's rented offices, there was no one else around at all and Tad breathed a sigh of relief. Jacob and the driver swung the doors open, and Tad and Mary were ushered professionally to one side as the paramedics began unloading Justin with far more speed than they'd used at the hospital.

Everyone, it seemed, had been unnerved by being followed.

Still, he was glad to see they were as professional as they had been before. They maneuvered the hospital bed out of the vehicle and toward the double doors that led into the interior.

This was the moment he had dreaded. When Dr. Goli had refused to oversee a transfer from a hospital bed to a more usual gurney, he had quietly promised himself he'd do anything he needed to do to keep Justin safe. If she wouldn't oversee it, they'd do it there, at the labs.

Now, he was rethinking that decision—especially when he saw the lobby of the building. He told himself that it was rented and the other tenants might be why the trash overflowed the bin and the stairs looked grimy.

But it wasn't exactly inspiring.

The transfer took all the paramedics, including those waiting inside with the gurney, and he had to expend his entire measure of self-control not to wince as they did so. At his side, Jacob Zachary stood rigidly with his hands locked behind his back. He suspected that the engineer tried to keep himself from looking worried.

That wasn't inspiring either.

The elevators took them up one floor before the paramedics wheeled the gurney down a long hallway. One of the fluorescent lights was out and another flickered like something from a horror movie.

At the end of the hallway, Jacob held the door open for them to wheel Justin through a kitchenette—with a rusted table and chairs pushed to one side to provide a clear path—and into a dimly-lit space that was half-lab and half-offices.

Mary's mouth opened in shock and she grasped Tad's hand tightly.

"This?" she whispered. Her voice quavered. "This is where they'll have him?"

Her whisper was barely audible to him, and none of the others heard it at all. In the corner of the lab section, two other PIVOT employees waited—Nick Ryan, who Tad had met earlier that day, and a woman with dark hair and long-lashed black eyes, dressed in black jeans under her lab coat.

The second transfer began immediately. Wires were switched while the machines shrieked and sank into their calm rhythm by turns, and the woman lifted Justin's arm with surprising care to slide one blood pressure cuff off and another on. Her fingers were gentle as she placed electronic pads on his ribs, but even she stood back to let DuBois take over when it came time to place the brain wave sensors.

"I can't watch," Mary whispered. "I can't." She hid her face in Tad's jacket. "The bruising, it's—"

"Mrs. Williams." Jacob stepped forward to hold his hand out and stood considerately between her and the activity in the lab. "May I get you some tea? I can explain all the steps that are taking place if you'd like, but you won't have to see it."

It was a kind offer and one Tad appreciated more than he could say. He squeezed Mary's hand as she left with the young man and drifted closer to the bed. She couldn't watch but he couldn't look away.

Gloves were fitted to Justin's hands, each containing a dozen or more white pads attached to wires. Output had begun to feed onto a machine he remembered was an EEG, and a monitor showed a static scan that must have come from an earlier MRI. He averted his eyes from that one. While he might not know which colors meant blood inside the brain, looking at his son's internal injuries was too much for him.

"Why haven't you transferred him into the pod yet?" he asked. His voice seemed too loud in the stillness.

The woman answered him as she pushed a syringe of something into Justin's IV hookup. "It's important to make sure the sensors are reading," she said. Her gaze flicked from his hand to the output on the machines and she stood aside to let DuBois adjust one of the pads. "If the sensors are able to integrate his scan data and begin tracking, it will make sense to move him. If not, the risk will not be worth it."

Tad swallowed hard.

DuBois, however, did not seem even slightly worried. "He's stable," he said and studied the output on the monitors. "It looks stronger than it was in the base scans, which is good. We should transfer him."

"Doctor." The woman immediately looked nervous. "We haven't given the drug time to—"

"There's no benefit to waiting," the doctor said briskly. "You two, begin the transfer. One of you, get the headset prepped."

"What drug?" Tad asked as the paramedics began to move his son's still body. He thought he would be sick. They hadn't said anything about drugs.

"It's a prototype I developed in my work," DuBois said. "The comatose brain can't process stimuli in the same way as a conscious brain. This prepares a patient for the audiovisual feeds. Of course, I didn't have a game quite like this one. Also, I added a paralytic agent. I don't want your son to attempt to move and possibly injure himself." Far from being worried, he seemed only intrigued. "You, careful with his legs. Simply because they're not broken doesn't mean you can drop them like that. Yes, very good. Now, get that IV hooked up."

"What's in the IV?" Tad asked. He couldn't stop himself.

"This is only saline," Nick told him soothingly. "The same as he had at the hospital. Since he's not eating or drinking, we want to make sure he's hydrated." He pointed to the feeding tube, which had been inserted before Justin left the hospital. "We've been thoroughly briefed on the exact mixture he should get and how often." He came to stand beside him and offered the same, comforting presence Jacob had shown for Mary. "You see how the machines are reading even while the lid is open? We'll be able to open it to move him, change him, bathe him, all of that. He'll receive the same care he had in the ICU, sir, I promise you."

Tad nodded, a single jerk of his head.

The woman and Dr. DuBois lowered a headset over Justin's forehead. It had been modified at the last minute with two long pieces of metal that would hold it up at the sides of his head so it would apply no pressure to his bruises. They threaded the wires for his patches through holes in the device and plugged them in, and the feed on the monitors flickered before it resumed.

"That's Amber Garcia," Nick told him in an undertone. "She was the one who made most of our breakthroughs on this headset. She knows more than anyone about how it interacts with the brain's feeds. Between her and Dr. DuBois, you have the best minds in the country in this room."

Tad did not reply. He watched Amber's face as she looked at the doctor. At his nod, she squared her shoulders and walked to one of the monitors. She closed her eyes briefly before she pressed one of the buttons.

Justin's body shivered. It was a tiny movement, but Tad saw it and he took a step forward without even being aware of it.

"What was that?"

"A mild shock," Amber said, her voice level. "It jump-starts the process. Your son's heart has not suffered any damage and we were cleared by Dr. Goli to apply up to four times as much electricity if we needed to."

"We don't need to," DuBois added unnecessarily. He folded his arms.

With a sudden wail, the machines burst into a frantic storm of beeping.

"What is it? What's going on?" Tad's voice was rising. "Turn it off! Turn it all off!"

"This is expected," the doctor called in response. "Normal," he corrected himself. "Wait a moment."

Nick's hand was around Tad's arm to hold him back, and before he could shake himself free, the machines subsided into their usual pattern of beeps. A new monitor booted up above the pod and words were displayed.

PLAYER_009

Across the room, Amber edged closer to Dr. DuBois.

"Player 9?" she said under her breath.

The man looked vaguely guilty. He gestured toward the senator, who looked like he wanted to break the pod apart with his bare hands. "We don't want him to think we haven't done this before."

"We *haven't* done this before," she all but hissed in reply.

"*He* doesn't need to know that," DuBois whispered. He looked at the series of monitors one by one and smiled with satisfaction. "Well, we're into the boot sequence. It'll be a while before we know how things are going."

"Very comforting," she told him. She resisted the urge to bury her head in her hands.

"So what now?" the senator asked.

"Now," the doctor said, "I'm going to get popcorn."

CHAPTER TEN

Instead of black, the sudden wash of blues and greens and a series of boot-up chimes were vaguely familiar enough that Justin found them immensely soothing.

WELCOME TO PIVOT, words on the screen announced.

He blinked, tried to adjust his body, and realized he must have been seated in one place too long—everything hurt. Perhaps he fell asleep while waiting for a VR game to load, he thought and had the sudden worry that one of his parents might have walked past his room and peeked in.

They didn't know how much more he made than the rent he paid, and they *definitely* wouldn't approve of him spending it like this. That was why he hadn't told them he bought a VR headset.

As he was about to remove the headset, an image of him flashed up on the screen.

Justin's jaw dropped. It was pixelated but it was definitely him. The character had the same lean height, the same incongruously broad shoulders, and the same arch in his nose. In fact, it was a little more pronounced than he remembered it being. What kind of photos did they use to build this model?

Also, he could not for the life of him remember buying this game. Had someone offered him a demo?

"Character creation activated," a pleasant voice told him. It sounded somewhat mischievous, not at all like the usual flat, computerized AI voices he was used to. It sounded almost like he imagined a pixie. *"You may choose your starting class."*

Three icons appeared on the side of the screen, each highlighted in shimmering metallics. The top one was the outline of a sword, the second was two crossed daggers, and the third was the quintessential druid staff, the knobbly wood curled into a spiral at the top.

Well, that was an easy choice. Justin tapped the image of the sword icon. The game didn't respond quite how it should but after a few attempts, he managed to make it work.

"Time to smash things," he said. Or, at least, he thought he said it. His voice didn't sound like it normally did.

Oh, hell, he wasn't on a stream, was he?

He hoped not.

His character spun, the view tipped crazily, and he whirled through a computer-generated starfield. He gave a low whistle. This kind of thing was pretty on a monitor but it was on a whole different level when you wore a VR headset. It was beautiful, but he had to fight the urge to give in to motion sickness.

"In ages past," a sad voice whispered, *"the universe was in harmony—"*

"Ugh," Justin said succinctly. He noticed a dull, chrome-colored button in the corner of the screen that read **SKIP** and pressed it. It was easier this time, although he still had some difficulty getting the set to respond to his hand motions. He'd have to remember to note that in his review.

Now, he was suspended in the star field and text appeared to scroll like the beginning of a Star Wars film.

WELCOME TO ALT REAL. YOU ARE ONE OF THE FIRST TO EXPERIENCE THIS UNIQUE, FULL-BODY VIRTUAL REALITY EXPERIENCE.

"That explains the bugs," he said and rolled his eyes.

That hurt more than it should have. Maybe he should take some ibuprofen.

Eh, in a minute. He pressed the **SKIP** button at the bottom.

Your story begins as a humble—

"Skip." Justin groaned. "Jesus. Enough with the freaking narrative. Gimme some gameplay."

The game obliged. The screen went black and when a new visual appeared, he stood in a field of tall grass. Birds called somewhere, he could see mountains in the distance, and there was a stand of trees over to his right. He looked around and raised his hands—one of which, he now saw, held the most battered, rusty sword he had ever seen in his life.

"Oh, come *on*," he griped. "Really? Where the hell did I get this thing?"

"Fatigue penalty," the AI announced. A red minus 1 floated through his field of vision.

"Fatigue penalty?" Justin asked, annoyed. "Are you *kidding* me with this? For this freaking sword?" He punctuated the words with several shakes of the disappointing weapon.

His reward was a flurry of minus ones.

He sighed.

"You'll notice you're not very good at this yet," the AI said, and he could swear it sounded smug. *"Do be careful to not put your eye out with that, adventurer. And would you like me to direct you to the nearest doctor for a tetanus shot?"*

"No. Thank you." He rolled his eyes. A snarky AI. He might like that a little more if his head didn't hurt so much.

Amber hunched over the screen, watching with Nick and Jacob, when DuBois entered with his party-size bag of popcorn. He popped a piece of caramel corn in his mouth and chewed before he licked his fingers.

"How is it going?" he asked.

"Not great," she said. "He skipped all the narrative. This does not bode well."

"Everyone skips that stuff," Nick objected.

"He's not exactly in any condition to skip it," she pointed out.

DuBois had frowned at the monitors and he now went to the table behind the pod. He readied a syringe, approached the IV drip, and seemed surprised when he noticed everyone in the room watching him.

"He's 'awake' now," the doctor explained and made finger quotes. "So he's aware that he's in pain."

Mary Williams made a strangled noise.

"This will help," the doctor told her confidently. "It's not narcotics or opioids, merely good, old-fashioned naproxen." He returned, stripped off the latex gloves, and picked up his bag of popcorn. "Now, let's see what you do next, kiddo."

<hr>

"Would you like a tutorial?" the AI asked. Justin might be imagining it but it sounded like it was enjoying itself.

"No," he told it. "I've played enough games, thank you."

"Are you sure?" it pressed. *"You haven't done so well thus far."*

"Are you finished?"

"Maybe." The sense of amusement rippled in its voice.

"Tutorials are for noobs," he insisted. "Plus, good game design should be intuitive. Aren't I supposed to review the game design here?"

The AI might as well have shrugged. *"It's your funeral,"* the voice said and disappeared.

On-screen, words appeared in shimmering bronze. **Quest 1: Scavenge Food**.

Justin looked around. There was grass, of course, but nothing that looked particularly edible. He didn't see any bushes or anything that glittered with the usual quest-item sparkles, so he set off toward the trees. As he walked, he could hear the faint sound of a stream somewhere reasonably close.

He hadn't gone far when the grass rustled nearby. Although he scanned the area cautiously, he didn't see anything noteworthy and so kept walking. After another few steps, a rabbit darted across his path.

Rabbits. Apparently, the food was rabbits. Hopefully, this complete disappointment of a sword had some kind of edge to it. He crept forward as carefully as he could and, at the water's edge, saw his quarry drinking from the stream. Carefully, Justin raised the sword and brought it down.

The animal disappeared and was replaced by two vaguely realistic drumstick icons, which floated into the middle of the screen, flashed, and vanished. On the left side of the screen, a bag icon flashed as well.

"Tutorials," he muttered. "Who needs 'em?"

SCAVENGE FOOD: 2/5, the screen read.

"*Congratulations,*" the AI announced, "*you have achieved Bunny-Slayer, Level One.*" The words also appeared on the screen in gold.

Justin had played games like this before. Whatever you did, you got better at it. If you fought with daggers, you leveled up daggers. If you chose persuasive dialogue options, you learned to convince people of your point of view.

Apparently, by the end of this, he would be a bunny slayer extraordinaire. He went in search of more rabbits and muttered, "Be vewwy, vewwy quiet…"

The next two only dropped one drumstick apiece, a process that reminded him a little too much of wandering around a different computerized forest, killing boars for their livers—and finding, in the process, dozens of inexplicably liver-less .

The real question, he decided, was how the rabbits had gotten the drumsticks. Maybe they had killed birds for them. Perhaps they had an advanced society that trapped, murdered, and cooked turkeys, #.

He snickered quietly but it cut short when he heard a growl from behind him. Turning swiftly as the hair on the back of his neck prickled, Justin came face to face with a wolf.

The thing about wolves was that you didn't realize quite how big they were until you saw one up close. This one was easily three and a half feet tall at the shoulder, and its eyes glowed a demonic-looking yellow. It growled again and lowered its head.

Panicked, he stumbled back and he must have tripped over something because in the next moment, he sprawled awkwardly. He hadn't fallen in real life, he could tell—there was no burst of pain—but his character's view tilted crazily.

As he scrambled upright, the AI said, *"Congratulations. You have achieved Clumsy, Level One."*

"Are you *serious* with this?" Justin called at the sky.

There was no answer, but unfortunately, there *was* still a wolf to deal with.

Amber frowned at the screen as bits of data flashed up in sequence.

"I don't understand," the senator said quietly in the background. "If he's playing a game, why can't we see it on the screen? We can hear him."

They could, and the dialogue hadn't exactly been reassuring until now—although they had all laughed at his "Be vewwy, vewwy quiet…"

"His brain is filling in the textures," Amber explained.

The senator looked bewildered and Nick hastened to explain. "We don't have an asset of a star, for instance," he said. "I mean—like, a 3D object in the game. We didn't model a yellow, five-pointed star and give it depth and make it all shiny. The game says 'star,' and Justin's brain interprets that. It puts in whatever he thinks of when he thinks of a star. Or a field. Or mountains."

"The game looks different for everyone," Amber concluded. "Some things, like the AI, are pre-recorded, but for other things, we use the brain. For instance, he's not really moving but he thinks he is and the game interprets that input." She raised her eyebrows at a certain line of code. "He's in the game and he's leveling things up. It *is* working. I —what's he doing now?"

"Being an idiot," DuBois said succinctly. "Oh, come on, kid, don't

—" He sighed and shook his head as he put a piece of popcorn in his mouth. "He's gonna get himself killed."

"Wait." Jacob looked at the others, all of whom wore identical expressions. "Killed how? You mean in the game, right?"

The doctor looked at them. "I told you this before, didn't I?"

"Told us what?" Amber asked him.

The doctor shrugged. "The brain is essentially a complex computer. Isn't that what you said the other day? Well—dying means he goes through a 'reboot.' In this condition, I don't know how he'll take it."

A tense pause followed. Jacob looked at the others.

"What is he saying to us?" he asked. His smile was forced.

"He's saying…" Amber looked like she wanted to stop talking, but the senator showed every intention to start kicking asses if no one answered him. "He's saying if Justin dies in the game…we don't know if it will kill him for real."

The words horrified her and even more so when they heard the sound of the bathroom door closing and Mary walked into the room. From the way her gaze flicked over the group, it was clear she knew something had happened.

"What's going on?" she asked.

"He's playing the game," DuBois said. He put a large palmful of popcorn in his mouth. "It's *fascinating*," he added, around his mouthful. "It's truly fascinating."

***

Before the wolf could lunge at him, Justin flailed at it with the sword. He saw the fatigue dialogue take one point from his health but he didn't have time to pay attention to it before he needed to fling himself sideways. He ended up in the stream, which was on par with his luck. At least pixelated clothes didn't get completely wet, although the game was somehow realistic enough to make his legs feel cold.

How did it do that?

The wolf thrust forward at him and he decided to work the rest out later. He swung the sword again and felt a jolt in his hands, if not his arms, and a negative four drifted from the wolf's body.

"Ha!" he yelled. "Take that, fucker."

Without warning, the wolf jumped. Its paws struck Justin's chest with an impact he didn't feel in his body so much as in his mind. The sky cartwheeled and he landed hard with an audible thud and a clatter of his sword. The wolf's head lowered and its snarl drowned out his involuntary yell before it ripped his arm with its teeth.

He almost felt the pain, the same way he'd almost felt the cold.

"You have been poisoned," the AI announced. *"Negative three health per second."*

"Yeah?" Justin sat and watched his attacker slink away. "So what do I do now?"

The answer, it turned out, was simple. He watched his health tick away—seven points, then four, then one—

"You have died," the AI said cheerfully as the screen went black.

CHAPTER ELEVEN

In the extended pause that followed, Amber and DuBois held their breath. She was fairly sure they were the only two who knew what the few lines of code on the screen meant. Everyone had heard that Justin had been poisoned, but only she and DuBois knew that his character had died.

Maybe, she thought hopefully, no one else would find out.

C'mon, c'mon, c'mon...

It wasn't her day. The heart rate monitor flat-lined, the EEG spiked crazily before it followed suit, and they could hear the sound as the blood pressure cuff inflated.

"Amber," Jacob said quietly. "Did he die in the game?"

Amber said nothing and was frozen with horror. She couldn't be watching this happen, could she?

Before her friend could repeat his question, the EEG scrambled again and reactivated. She exhaled a breath, which sounded too much like a sob for comfort. "Yes," she said. "He died in the game."

"*Fuck*," Justin's voice said emphatically.

"Stop swearing!" Mary looked horrified. She glanced at the others and then at the monitor. "And stop dying!"

Nick hid a snort of laughter with a sudden coughing fit.

"If there was ever a time for you to be good at a game, Justin," the senator said quietly, "it's now."

"Fascinating," DuBois said again. "Did you see that? The way the brain responds to the simple power of suggestion. It is truly extraordinary."

"Maybe too extraordinary," Tad muttered. He jerked his head and Amber, Nick, and Jacob followed him as he wandered a short distance away from the group. "Look, I don't know much about..." He waved his hand. "All this stuff. But isn't there something you can do? Some way to keep him from dying again? Can't you...." His voice trailed off.

Jacob looked at the screen as he considered the unfinished question and its implications. "I suppose we could put a block on the health bar," he said thoughtfully.

"Or simply nerf all the animals," Nick interjected.

"Or both," Amber summed up.

"That won't work," said DuBois.

All four of them turned to look at him. Apparently, his hearing was better than they thought—that, and he had no sense of shame about eavesdropping. He wandered closer to them, still licking caramel coating off his fingers.

"We can't reboot the entire game while he's inside it," Amber said, "but we can change the characteristics of the monsters that spawn live and we can segment his zone and reboot everything else."

"That's not what I mean." The doctor waved a hand. "No, I mean this will only work if there's the possibility of failure." He looked at all of them meaningfully as if they should understand exactly why that was true.

"Uh," Nick said finally. "Why, though?"

"Young man," he said severely, "I thought you read my research."

"I did!" He looked mortified and glanced at the senator. "I did," he assured him.

"I did, too," Amber said to DuBois, "and I don't know what you're talking about either."

The doctor looked at Jacob for backup and, as a last resort, to the senator. Amber raised her eyebrow. The politician didn't seem stupid but he also didn't seem like the type of person who read neuroscience papers between senate votes.

The doctor sighed. "We're preparing him for real life again," he said finally. "I thought you must have understood that because your game lined up so well with the conclusions in my paper. Real-life includes the chance of death at all moments. It is imperative that the patient begins normal function between their sympathetic and parasympathetic nervous system again."

"What's he talking about?" Nick muttered.

"He's talking about fight or flight," Amber explained. "Self-preservation instincts. He's saying that without those, the game won't make Justin better. Right?" She looked at DuBois.

"I just said that," he said plaintively. "But, yes. The point is to restore normal brain function. Something that is obviously a simulation and has no consequences for failure will not serve the purpose."

"Okay, so..." Senator Williams looked as if he struggled to keep calm. "You're telling me that I have to put my son in mortal danger in order to have a chance at him recovering?"

"Mr. Williams," the doctor said with surprising gentleness, "you're not putting him in mortal danger. Recovery from a traumatic brain injury on this scale is...rare. It's dangerous."

Amber could have hit him for saying that. She thought she saw the light in the senator's eyes die a little.

"The reason I did my research," DuBois said, "is because the human brain has a remarkable capacity to heal itself—if it can be reached socially. Locked away in your own head is a terrible way for most people to be. You're not putting your son in danger by doing this, you're giving him the chance to get out of it. What happened moments ago could have happened at any time in the ICU. The only difference is that now, it serves a purpose. It's reminding his brain how to work."

Amber stared at him. She hadn't expected that monologue to turn out inspiring but somehow, it had. She snuck a glance at the senator and saw that even he looked more hopeful now.

"I see," he said. "Is there anything more we can do tonight?"

"No," the doctor told them. "We've hired nursing staff, so between us and the nurses, there will always be someone taking care of your son. You two should rest."

"Thank you," Williams said. He looked at each of them. "Thank you to all of you. Your work is giving my son the chance to come back to us."

Then, as if exhausted by his show of charming, senatorial thanks, he seemed to collapse in on himself slightly and hunched his shoulders as he went to take his wife's hand.

"Thank you all," she told them as well, and her smile was warm.

<hr>

Justin woke in the same field with the same damned rusty sword—and a health bar that was very low.

"AI?" he asked.

"*Yes, Player underscore 009?*" The voice was infuriatingly bland and noncommittal.

"My name is Justin," he told it. If it wanted to be smug, goddammit, it would be smug while it used his correct name.

"*Noted, Player underscore 009.*"

He sighed and considered his options. "AI, please restart the tutorial for me."

"*I'm sorry, Player underscore 009, that is not an option at this time.*"

"Why not?" he asked and anger stirred. He reached up to take the VR headset off but his fingers didn't connect with anything. In fact, he wasn't sure he could feel them connecting with the headset.

Now that he thought of it, what could he feel? He wasn't quite sure.

"*May I suggest replenishing your health?*" the AI asked. Its smugness had returned in full force.

"Yeah, how *exactly* am I supposed to—oh, the weird rabbit legs." Justin jabbed with a finger until one of the packs opened and then stabbed at the rabbit legs, almost deleted them by accident, and finally managed to consume one of them. After the usual sound of video game chewing, his health bar climbed into the green and finally, to full.

"Good," he said. "Now what am I supposed to do?"

There was no answer, but the marker for his food scavenging quest flashed.

He did *not* like this AI.

With a sigh, he set off toward the stand of trees and the stream again. When the first rabbit dashed across his path, he raised the sword and waited for the next. With two more weird rabbit drumsticks, his quest was completed.

LEVEL 2 flashed across the screen with a triumphant burst of music.

"You have achieved Level Two," the AI told him.

"Yes, despite your best efforts," he retorted. "Now where's that fucking wolf? I want to avenge—well, myself." He set off through the grass and his feet crunched on the ground. This time, when he heard the growl, he was ready. He turned with a lunge and a slash and the wolf yipped in pain. It danced away sideways to crouch and bare its teeth.

"Yeah, what's up?" Justin asked. "I came back and I'm Level Two now, bitch. That's right, a hundred percent better. What are you gonna do with—no bitey!" He threw himself sideways as the beast snarled and charged, and his wild strike missed.

Fair enough. Physics was physics, after all, and apparently, this game had more realistic physics than usual.

"Clumsy, Level Two," the AI announced.

"Oh, you have *got* to be kidding me!" he yelled in response. "I don't have Bunny Slayer Level Two yet, but I have Clumsy Level Two? That is bitchy."

The AI made no response. Justin supposed that having won the argument by virtue of running the game world, it didn't have to say anything.

Anyway, he had a wolf to kill. He took two running steps, feinted right, and switched his sword to his left hand and slashed. This strike connected, the wolf yelped again, and a big chunk came off its health bar.

More satisfying, several achievements flashed up on the screen.

MOVIE-STYLE SWORDFIGHTING, LEVEL 1

AMBIDEXTROUS, LEVEL 1

CHUTZPAH, LEVEL 1

"What the heck is chutzpah?" Justin asked the AI. It didn't answer, and he devoted his attention to the animal again. It had become desperate and crouched like it intended to spring and bite him again.

He knew he couldn't let that happen. Before it could act, he charged it with a battle cry and dropped onto his stomach as the wolf launched itself into the air. It wasn't a total success, given that the creature's back feet caught him in the head, but he avoided the bite.

He also got Clumsy, Level Three.

"That one was on *purpose*," he told the AI. "You take that level back."

It did not.

His adversary might have thought it was snarling quietly as it snuck up on him, but Justin heard it. He turned and swung the blade forcefully and although he lost two points to fatigue—fair, he supposed—the wolf fell. It disappeared and left three copper coins and a scrap of fur, all of which disappeared into his inventory almost instantly.

"Excellent," Justin said. "Hey, AI? I don't suppose you have any more quests."

"There are no more quests at this time," the AI said.

"So…what am I supposed to do next?" he asked it.

Not unexpectedly, no answer was forthcoming.

"Great," he muttered. He looked around and thought he spied movement in the distance. A windmill, maybe? Something that looked like civilization, anyway. Keeping a careful lookout for more wolves, he made his way through the grass until he found a road—another good sign—and headed alongside the river and toward the town.

CHAPTER TWELVE

The village wasn't exactly close, and unlike most video games, Justin's character didn't automatically run everywhere. On the road, however, there were no more wolves, so he found he was happy to walk and use the time to study the scenery.

He couldn't quite get a handle on it. That was one of the things he noticed first. Sometimes, the textures didn't seem to load and then they loaded all at once. At other times, he could swear the shape of things changed. He noticed groups of trees that he was sure shouldn't go together, but when he looked back, they were suddenly all the correct types.

In all honesty, he didn't know what to make of that.

One thing that was like other video games was that time seemed to go faster in the game world than in the real world. The sun had barely begun to set as Justin reached the signpost at the edge of the village that read *RIVERBEND*.

"New zone discovered," the AI told him. *"Riverbend is a small village on the western edge of the Golian Plains."*

"Thank you," he replied.

"You're welcome," it told him promptly.

He stopped and squinted into the air, trying to sense whether there was some kind of trick in the AI's politeness, but there didn't seem to be.

The village, as it turned out, was amazing. It was realistic with broken cobblestones and dirt between them and houses of plaster and thatch, and it was also incredibly beautiful. The whole picture was as if someone had told him to imagine the most beautiful, cozy, picture-perfect English village he could. Some things were unfamiliar—instead of crosses, for instance, he saw elaborate windchimes hanging from the corners of the buildings.

All of it was soothing, however. Flowers climbed the walls of the cottages and roses bloomed in the hedgerows. He could hear chickens, cows, and dogs and once, he saw a cat streak across his path. Swallows darted through the air as night fell.

And the people were nothing like those in any game he'd ever seen. Some poured slops, weeded gardens, and lit lanterns. A few nodded as he went past and others looked at his sword, which resulted in an awkward few moments during which he tried to determine how to sheathe it. They called greetings to one another and the banter between them was comfortable and familiar as if the community was close-knit. He'd never seen a game so detailed.

Justin was content to wander and look around and finally saw the tavern. A wooden sign creaked faintly, a large flagon of beer emblazoned on it in black paint. He smiled as he wove through the crowd. Taverns were where the good stuff happened. He'd buy a drink, chat to other NPCs, and learn this game's rest mechanic.

It occurred to him that he was incredibly hungry. As soon as he was done in the tavern, he would shut the game down and order food. He'd probably missed dinner already, he realized. His parents wouldn't be happy with him.

With a sigh, he moved into the shadowed interior.

He paused in a corridor lined with sputtering lamps. The din of the tavern spilled into the small space, the walls papered with jobs on offer. He saw requests for rabbit slayers—*Aww, yeah, I can get that sweet, sweet, Bunny Slayer Level 5*—and someone to deal with the wolves on the plains—"Oh, *hell* no"—as well as requests for five bunches of a herb or ten rockworms.

He didn't want to know about the last one.

Some were so mundane that he laughed out loud.

ONE YOUNG PERSONE TO SCYTHE MY YARDE

SALE ON FLOUR AT THE FLOUR MILLE

How had he not heard about this game before? Despite his initial response, he was having an awesome time. He strolled the corridor and read each of the posters in turn. At the end, pinned to the door frame of the tavern itself, was a piece of paper that looked as if it had been taken down and put up several times, the top of it ripped and full of nail holes. Unlike the others, it wasn't written in an all-capital scrawl but instead, in a neat, practiced script.

WANTED: one adventurer to rescue a kidnapped maiden. Will be generously compensated. Speak to Mayor Hausen for details.

"Find Mayor Hausen," Justin said to himself. "Got it."

Inside the tavern, rough wooden tables were surrounded by men in the patched, worn clothes of day laborers. They drank from foaming mugs of ale and laughed with one another, and a few of them looked at Justin and gave him a nod.

It occurred to him that he wore stupid, Level One gear and a rusty sword and probably looked like a lunatic. Thankfully, NPCs didn't care about things like that. He threaded through the maze of tables, ducked under one or two low-hanging lanterns, and strode past the huge hearth to the bar.

The woman there was dressed in the most traditional tavern-wench costume he had ever seen. A white shirt peeked out from behind a close-fitting vest and her brown skirt was embroidered with flowers and leaves. She curtsied.

"What can I get for you, sir?"

"One ale." He leaned on the counter and smiled at her.

Sometimes, the game showed it was truly a game and the ale appeared on the bar in front of him without the tavern girl so much as moving from where she wiped a mug with a towel. After a few near misses, he managed to grasp the mug and lift it in her direction before he took a sip. The liquid didn't tip when he "drank," but it was lower when he set the mug down.

"That'll be a copper," the woman said to him.

An idea occurred to him.

"Only a copper?" Justin asked. He leaned forward to grin at her. "Surely I should pay for that smile too."

FLIRT, LEVEL 1 popped up on the screen.

He took another sip. The woman had smiled and looked away, clearly embarrassed, and he was curious—not only to see how extensive this game was in its programming but also to see what he could come up with. It wasn't like he'd ever be cheesy enough to do this in real life, after all. "They make a beauty like you handle the money?"

"Sir, I'm a betrothed woman." She looked flustered.

"Ah, who is the lucky man?" Justin looked at the room. None of the NPCs gave him a death glare, so that was good.

"Yannick Hausen," the woman said proudly. She raised her chin. "The mayor says Yannick can do better'n an innkeep's daughter, but Mayor Hausen's in here often enough. Or…he was." She had a sad expression now. "Before Zaara, of course."

"Of course," he said. "And tell me about your Yannick."

SILVER TONGUE, LEVEL 1 flashed across the screen, and the AI spoke over the woman's monologue.

"Good work, Player Underscore 009. A silver tongue will get you farther than a heart of gold."

"If you had a heart of gold, you'd be dead," Justin said succinctly.

The girl paused in mid-monologue. "I beg your pardon, sir?"

He weighed the idea of telling her that he was speaking to a familiar but discarded that plan. It didn't seem wise when he wasn't quite sure how the people there thought of demonic magic. "My apologies. Do go on."

She continued to speak while her character repeatedly picked up the same mug, wiped it dry with her towel, and put it down again. When she had run out of rapturous words about her fiancé—with the appropriate responses of "Mmm," and "Oh, really?" from Justin—she smiled at him.

"Can I get you anything else, sir?"

"I don't suppose you have pizza," he joked.

"I don't think so, sir." Well, there was the limit of the AI.

IMPOSSIBLE REQUESTS, LEVEL 1

"Oh, come on," he muttered and shrugged. "How about some stew?"

"Of course, sir." The meal appeared on the counter in front of him. "That'll be a copper, sir."

"You still won't tell me what it costs to see that beautiful smile of yours?"

A man appeared in the doorway to the kitchens. He was broad-shouldered and with a ruddy complexion. His shirt sleeves were rolled to show massive forearms with a tattoo of several interlocking circles on one, and he wore a stained apron made of canvas. He strode toward Justin.

"'Ey." His tone wasn't friendly. "My daughter asked ye for payment."

Normally, he would simply pay and be done with it. Well, *normally*, he wouldn't be in this situation at all. But it was funny how being in a game world made you want to try things you wouldn't ordinarily try.

"Now, now," he argued. "There are so many kinds of payment. I'm a new adventurer in town and you don't even want to tell me how I might help all of you?"

"She did," the bartender said. "The coin, *adventurer*."

"You know, I don't think so." He wanted to see what would happen. "That stew tasted a little pixel-y to me."

Behind him, he realized the bar had gone very quiet. When Justin turned with the mug still in his hand, he saw most of the men there were standing now. Many seemed to wear a band of blue cloth on one arm.

"Are you all in a club?" he joked.

"We're the town guard," one of them said. He smiled. "Let's chat, shall we?"

He was still trying to work out how to set the mug down and draw his sword again when the screen went black. Sounds of punches and kicks ensued and a flurry of red numbers floated on the screen. When the numbers stopped, his health bar flashed red and indicated that he had one point left.

The sounds of the blows made him wince and he could almost feel the pain each time a blow landed, but he was also laughing. This was amazing. You could smooth-talk bartenders there. Or you could flirt and walk out on your bill. The game gave you the option to step out of line.

Justin waited for the screen to clear and when it did, he wasn't disappointed. Stone walls and chains on his feet announced that he was in the town jail.

CHAPTER THIRTEEN

"Hey," a voice announced. "Look who's finally awake."

Justin sat and was rewarded by flashes of actual pain. He paused warily for a moment. That pain couldn't be real, could it? Of course it couldn't. It wasn't real. He'd probably merely sat for too long while he played the game.

His character looked sideways and noticed a dwarf watching him. He hadn't realized this game had multiple races, given that he hadn't been allowed to choose one on the character creation screen. That didn't seem very fair. He would put that in his review.

"Hi," he said.

"You were out for the better part of an hour," the dwarf informed him. "They dragged ye in looking like death warmed over. Course, even without those bruises, looks like ye'd be about as attractive as a bison's hairy arse." He laughed at his wit.

"Do you say things like that to everyone who comes in here?" The joke made him smile. Of course an NPC would say that to any character.

"Everyone who's as ugly as you," the dwarf said cheerfully, almost as if he were giving a compliment. "I'm Lyle Stout. And you are?"

"Justin," he said.

"Player underscore 009, huh?"

Oh, come on, that was uncalled for.

Did the AI make a rude noise or did he simply imagine it?

He examined Lyle. The dwarf's beard and hair were a ginger-red and decorated with small braids and metal beads. He wore carefully assembled leather armor with a giant tree embossed on the chest plate. When he saw Justin's scrutiny, Lyle jabbed a thumb at himself. "I'm one o' the king's finest—hic—operatives, I'll have ye know."

"Sure, sure." Justin was enjoying the hell out of this. He leaned against the wall and folded his arms. "So, how'd you end up in here?"

"Bah." Lyle waved a hand. "That bartender has it out for me. I told him I'd pay up."

"You skipped out on your drink, too?"

"Didn't pay for my ale?" Now the dwarf sounded outraged. "As if I would ever disrespect craftsmanship like that. That inkeep's a bloody genius when it comes to brewing. Best ale in the damned plains. And I should know. Hic!"

Justin could bet the dwarf knew about every tavern in this region.

"No, I'd never skip out on my bar tab." Lyle gave him a suspicious look as if he wondered if he might be one of that type of no-good bastard. "Innkeep's only angry I broke a bench." He waved a hand jovially. "I said to him, 'I'll pay, won't I? I always pay.'"

"How'd you break a bench?" he asked. He was curious despite himself. The furniture in the tavern had looked incredibly sturdy.

"With another bench," the dwarf said as if that explained everything.

"Sure."

A guard appeared in the hallway and squinted at the two of them. "The adventurer's awake now," he called down the hallway and disappeared as suddenly as he had come.

"So, will they let me out?" Justin asked. He shook his hands and was rewarded by the clank of chains.

"Can't rightly say," the dwarf told him. "Normally, Mayor Hausen brings the innkeep and we settle it, and soon as I do, I get let out. This time, though, it's been three days. Chafes my balls."

Justin stared at him.

"So, who are you?" Lyle asked. He hadn't missed a beat. "Haven't seen you around here before."

"I'm an adventurer," he told him. "Actually, I'm surprised you haven't heard of me. I've been saving villages from—*bunnies*—vicious animals for—*an hour*—the better part of a month now."

"Is that so?" The dwarf leaned close. "Well, I reckon I know why they're coming to get ye, then."

"Why?"

"Yer the type who can get into the damned tower," he announced.

"What tower?"

"You'll see." Lyle looked like he was enjoying this. "Do you like wizards, adventurer?"

Justin made a noncommittal noise.

"I'll be more specific, then." The dwarf leaned forward with a grin. "Do you like *killing* wizards, adventurer?"

"You're sending me to kill a wizard," he said blankly.

"Not me," his cellmate pointed out but didn't deign to explain any further. "Nope, definitely not me. Lucky for you, though. You'll get out of here—and, if you don't die, that'll be that!"

"If I don't die?" This game was so realistic sometimes that it was hard to remember he wouldn't die if his character did. That, and honestly, the last time he'd died in-game, it hadn't felt good. It almost felt like his heart was skipping beats.

"I'll tell you what you should do," Lyle said.

"Yes, please." Justin shook his head at himself. He was acting like the normal, boring version of himself right now, not the adventurer who smooth-talked tavern wenches and walked out on bills.

Not that he was very good at that.

"You should tell the mayor to let me out," his companion said.

He waited but apparently, that was the end of the statement. "Your…advice is to get the mayor to let you out? Then what?"

"What d'you mean, then what? Then I'll be out, won't I?" Lyle raised his eyebrows at him and sighed. "Oh, you're one of *those* adventurers. Always wanting to be paid, aren't ye? Well, you talk Mayor Hausen into letting me out and there'll be something in it for ye. As long as the wizard doesn't get ye." He laughed as if this were an uproariously funny joke.

Justin didn't think he agreed on that front. He sighed as the guards reappeared and the chains vanished off his wrists with a clanking sound effect.

"Mayor Hausen wants to see you," a guard announced. "Come with us, adventurer."

At least they weren't calling him Player Underscore 009. He shook his head and stood to follow them out of the cell.

"Remember!" Lyle Stout called after him. "Tell him to let me out! I'll buy you a drink before you go off to your doom."

He was still cackling like a madman when the door to the jail swung closed.

To Justin's surprise, it was still dark out. The guards led him across the town square and up a gentle hill. To his right, he could see the giant arms of the windmill turning and hear the sounds of it creaking. Dogs barked distantly and sometimes, he heard a squeak or the lowing of a cow.

It was only now that he noticed the ambient music in the game. It was subtle, so atmospheric that he hadn't realized that he was listening to it. A few notes played on a flute—like the kind of sound that might carry on the night air—were accompanied by the distant sound of a woman's voice as if singing a lullaby to her child. It was almost peaceful.

Almost.

There was a sense of foreboding about this place. You couldn't miss it. Everything was too picture-perfect and the guards were on edge. What kind of tiny village had this many guards, anyway?

He shivered in happy anticipation that he would be slaying

monsters in no time. Of course, he was currently dressed in the most noob clothes he'd ever worn and the game didn't seem to have mechanics he could use, but maybe the wizard would drop some good gear for him.

Or would this game be super-realistic and make him fight someone in leather armor if that was what he wanted to get instead of fighting a wizard in long, flowing robes? Justin scowled. That would piss him off, even if it would be hilarious to go around waving a sword while in blue, spangly robes. No one would see it coming.

He would also die. You never played a clothie if you could help it.

The mayor's mansion was like many other game houses Justin had been inside. The first floor contained very little and was merely one open room with a hearth and a rug and no kitchen. Bookshelves lined the walls, filled with books that were identical on each shelf.

Still, the way the mayor was seated in a chair by the fire, his face in shadow, was cool.

"Hello," Justin said cheerfully.

"Adventurer. I'm glad you could come." The mayor stood. "Am I correct that I am speaking to Player Underscore 009?"

This was becoming annoying. He rolled his eyes. "Yes, that's me. PU009. My friends call me, uh…" Yeah, it was not a catchy name.

"I'm glad it's you," the mayor said, and Justin's mouth twitched. Never mind. He was enjoying this glitch now. "You see, adventurer, I have a problem. My daughter has been kidnapped."

"Oh, really?" he asked. "You don't say. Would you be the one with the posters up in the tavern?"

"I have posted many rewards," the mayor said, "but the wizard, Sephith, is a master of dark magic and illusion. No one has been able to save Zaara."

"Cool," he responded. "So, what's the reward?"

"The reward is ten gold pieces," the mayor said. "This should tell you how dangerous the quest is, adventurer."

"No risk, no reward," he said. "I'll take it."

"Good." The mayor handed him a scroll that he had not held a moment before. These things were far more noticeable when playing an MMORPG in virtual reality, Justin thought. "This should tell you all that you need to know about Sephith."

A pop-up covered the screen now, made to look like parchment with old-school script that detailed Sephith's history and powers. He skipped through it as quickly as he could, and it was only when it disappeared that he felt a flash of misgiving. Skipping the tutorial hadn't been a great idea, after all.

On the other hand, he'd made it out of the starting zone with only one death. He was doing fine. He didn't need to know about Sephith.

"This will be a dangerous quest," the mayor told him. "If you have any questions about Sephith, you may ask me. I have learned much about him since he took Zaara."

Of all the things Justin was interested in right now, a long backstory was not one of them. "No, thanks. I know what I need to know."

"Will you take any companions with you?" the mayor asked. "I suggest you do. The other heroes went alone and their fate…was not what they hoped."

An idea occurred to him suddenly and he felt his face split into a wide grin. Oh, this would be good. This would be so, so good.

"I do have someone in mind," he said casually, "but I'll need your help."

"I will do anything I can to help, of course. My daughter's life is at stake."

Excellent. "I want Lyle Stout to help me," Justin said.

"Lyle Stout is the town drunk," the mayor said.

"Oh, sure," Justin replied, "but he's also very good at causing chaos, isn't he? I think that would be useful when we get to Sephith's tower. Why, I hear that only three days ago, he broke a bench with another bench. That's the kind of strength this quest could use. I don't suppose I could persuade you to let him out of jail for this? It would be a good way for him to work off his debt to the town, after all."

The mayor responded promptly: "Of course. Anything you need, adventurer. If you wish to be accompanied by Lyle Stout, I will arrange for his release from jail."

"Excellent." He felt the beginning of a laugh. He knew Lyle was an

NPC but Justin would have so much fun telling him exactly how he'd gotten him out of jail. The dwarf wanted to laugh about him ending up as another dead adventurer? Well, he could make a choice, couldn't he? Help on the quest or stay in that grimy old jail.

CHAPTER FOURTEEN

uBois watched the progress on the screen with a critical eye.
Justin's mind moved at unpredictable speeds. One moment, it would race along without any interruptions and the next, it would fall into a period of rest for up to an hour. What was interesting was that he did not seem to be aware of it. He would pick up with conversations exactly where he had left off.

DuBois appreciated that the characters in the game seemed inclined to wait as well. Everything hinged on interaction. If Justin did not interact, everyone else—what had Jacob called them? Some acronym—simply stood there. One of these days, the doctor would ask to see the inside of the game alongside their patient.

Not yet, however. The young man could still go critical at any minute and watching his brain in motion was fascinating.

The sound of voices behind him intruded and Nick came to stand at his shoulder and cleared his throat awkwardly.

He had learned over the years that when people did that, they usually wanted to say something. While he had never quite worked out why they didn't simply say whatever it was to start with, at least he understood the strange mannerism now. He looked at the engineer and waited patiently.

"The senator is here to see you, sir," Nick said.

"Hello," Tad Williams added as he strode across the floor.

DuBois thought about mentioning to the two of them that they could have skipped both the introduction and the throat-clearing but decided not to. People seemed to cling to these strange rituals, no matter how often he pointed out that they simply wasted time. He nodded a hello to the senator and chose a piece of cheese popcorn out of his bag. The trash can below his desk now overflowed with empty packets.

He didn't know it, but the three PIVOT employees had a bet going about the maximum number of bags he could finish in a day. Amber was currently winning.

"Dr. DuBois." The senator looked as if he had slept but not well. He was dressed in jeans and a sweatshirt, clothes in which he looked manifestly uncomfortable. "Since there hadn't been an update, I decided to come by to see how Justin is doing."

He put considerable stress on the first words, and the doctor looked vaguely at the calendar. It occurred to him that he probably should have updated them. How long had it been? He looked at his notes. Ah, three days.

Well, the senator surely couldn't be expecting miracles.

"Recovery from brain trauma can take a long time," he explained. "Justin is doing as well as can be expected. His brain function still shows the ability to understand and produce language."

"Were we worried about that?" Williams asked.

DuBois looked at Jacob, Nick, and Amber. She waved one hand, the palm out, in front of her face. Jacob drew one finger repeatedly across his neck. Nick shook his head and made scissor motions with two fingers. He had no idea what they were going for.

"There's no telling what might have been affected," he explained to the senator. "He might end up with aphasia—that's a difficulty with language."

"I thought you said he had no difficulty with language."

"I said he could understand and produce it," he said patiently. Didn't people ever listen? "Whether he will be able to speak it, write it, read it, or understand it aurally is another matter. Any one of the functions of language can be interrupted as well as other things. Partial paralysis is common, for instance. Or loss of function in the frontal lobe. He does seem to be making…strange decisions."

The senator looked stricken at this, and Amber swooped in.

"His decisions make very good sense to another gamer," she told the senator. "Justin appears to believe that he is reviewing this game on a video streaming platform. He sometimes notes glitches, for instance. I believe he is trying to find the limits of how the game operates."

The senator and DuBois exchanged a look. Neither of them knew what this meant.

"My point is," she said, "Justin has picked up very quickly that he can solve problems in multiple ways and he is doing that. This shows creativity, the ability to make choices…all kinds of higher brain function. He's interacting very well with the game."

"Then why can't he…" The senator took a deep breath. "My apologies, all of you. This is not my area of expertise."

"I understand entirely, sir," Amber said. "You can feel free to ask, however."

"If he can interact with the game and speak to people in the game, why can't he wake up?" Williams asked. His tone was admirably even, but DuBois saw from the flared nostrils and the clenched hands that the senator was upset. He moved as if to straighten a tie he was not wearing and shoved his hands in the pocket of his sweatshirt, which read *PHILLIPS EXETER* across the front.

"The mechanics of that aren't exactly certain," the doctor answered. He could see Amber trying to choose her words, and he had a hunch that she would spend more time doing that than talking. He took a moment to check the screen and make sure Justin was okay—he was—and returned his attention to Tad. "The human brain is enormously complex. What Justin is doing now—and what people do inside this game—is more similar to dreaming than to consciously processing information. As of now, dreaming is believed to be a cleaning mechanism for the brain. It processes information it already knows, takes limited inputs—for instance, how a person can wake up if they hear a loud noise—and in Justin's case, waits for the blood to drain away and the brain to heal."

"So he doesn't know…that he's asleep." The senator walked closer to the pod and extended his fingers as if he wanted to open it.

"Would you like to see him, sir?" Amber asked.

DuBois refrained from sighing. They would never get anywhere in this conversation, would they?

Williams nodded, and she checked several feeds before she opened the lid of the pod. Inside, Justin looked the same as he had before. His hair might be greasier. He had less muscle tone. Still, the doctor didn't see the point. The senator knew what his son looked like, surely.

"We should keep the lid closed," Amber said. "It keeps his environment as secure as possible and minimizes the chance that he'll wake up suddenly."

She waited until Tad nodded, which was a good thirty seconds. The man stared at his son, and even if DuBois didn't understand what was going on, he could see the pain in his face. Maybe, he thought, this was like when he would keep checking the monitors, even when he could hear that everything was fine. Sometimes, you wanted to see it for yourself. After all, the senator didn't know what all the readouts on the monitors meant.

Yes, that made sense now.

When Tad turned toward him, the doctor saw that the senator's eyes were suspiciously bright.

"Can we talk to him?" Williams asked.

"Of course." DuBois tilted his head. "He might not hear you, but you certainly can."

The senator looked briefly skyward. "So he can possibly hear," he said finally and carefully. "Can we…also be in the game?"

DuBois, Amber, Nick, and Jacob all looked at one another. A flurry of tiny gestures followed—raised eyebrows, shrugs, and finger wiggles. Then, when Tad wasn't looking, Nick and Amber gave a shrug and a hopeful-looking nod at DuBois.

"There might be," the doctor said. "We need to test it first, of course. Come back tomorrow."

"It would do Mary so much good," Tad said. "Both of us, to be honest. Knowing he's awake in there and alone—it's hard. I don't want him to be scared." He cleared his throat as if embarrassed. "I'll call tomorrow to arrange a time," he said and left abruptly.

When the door had closed, Jacob looked at DuBois. "We could definitely work on your bedside manner," he said and sounded exasperated. "Do you think it was necessary to list all the worst-case scenarios?"

"He *asked*," the man responded, puzzled.

Amber sank her head into her hands with a sigh. "Okay. Come on, we have so much to do. No, leave it, Jacob." She shook her head slightly. "This isn't a worthwhile discussion right now."

DuBois took a moment to ponder this, then shrugged. If they wouldn't talk to him about it, he could hardly force them to. He tipped the last of the popcorn into his mouth. "Is there another bag anywhere?"

"Of course," Nick said smoothly. "That's eight, right?" He smiled. "You keep eating." In an undertone, he added to Amber and Jacob, "I'll win this, you see if I don't."

CHAPTER FIFTEEN

The mayor accompanied the guards to the jail and left Justin in the house. He wandered around, twiddled his thumbs, and wished he had a video to watch. This game was certainly leaning into the story before it let him fight any more monsters.

When the mayor returned with Lyle, the dwarf was still tipsy. Squiggly lines practically came off him to show how much he smelled of booze, and he couldn't seem to walk straight. He gave Justin a look.

"What's this about a wizard?"

"I asked Mayor Hausen if he would release you from jail," Justin asked serenely. *Just like you asked, remember?* "Because I need you to help me fight the wizard."

"Oh, no." The dwarf shook his head. "No, no. I don't fight freaks of nature. Give me a good, honest brawl any day of the week, but I won't fight spells. You can't punch a spell."

"Yes, but you *can* punch a wizard," he pointed out. He sighed. "I understand if you don't want to join me, of course."

"Hmph. Yes. It's a ridiculous quest." Lyle swayed on his feet. "So, I'll be going now."

"Yes, back to the jail for you," he said smoothly. "Good luck with the innkeep whenever he decides to speak to you."

The dwarf stopped. The guards had stepped forward to take his arms. "Now, wait a minute," he said. "Yer sayin' I have to go back to jail?"

"Yes," Justin confirmed. He assumed that was the word the conversation branch would cue off of. It was masterfully done. "I asked the mayor if you could be let out to help me fight the wizard. If you don't come along—"

"That's ridiculous," Lyle said. "You can't throw me back in jail simply because I'm not stupid enough to go get myself killed!"

"You'd be a legend," he said. "And imagine the treasure inside a wizard's tower."

"Those instruments are evil," the mayor said at once. "The whole place should be burned."

"Now yer talkin' crazy, mayor." The dwarf considered the offer. "So he has an evil thing. You melt it down, get a good ingot out of it, and now you got something normal to sell, y'see?"

The mayor did not seem to like this, but Justin knew he would agree. After all, the game had made this quest a possibility, right?

"Very well," he said. "Take what you wish from the wizard's tower, but all potions are to be destroyed and all instruments are to be melted down. Books, you shall burn. Am I clear?"

Book burning? That's not a good look, bro. He shook his head. "Yes," he lied. He hoped his inventory could store a large number of books— clearly, they were worth something, and he wanted a spell to make his sword less lame. Maybe he could get it to light on fire in combat. He wondered how learning spells worked in this game.

"Very well," the mayor said again. "Now, I will be unable to outfit you, of course—budget cuts, I'm afraid. You understand."

The game writers, Justin thought, had worked in government somewhere. Hell, even his father would have enjoyed that joke.

And it wasn't like they needed the mayor's help, anyway. Lyle had spoken about a reward. Justin would cash it in early, buy himself new armor, and head off to kill the wizard—with a great distraction in tow.

The mayor waved them out of his house and the two of them left.

Lyle's player icon and health bar had appeared under Justin's in the top right corner of the screen. Apparently, he was a party member and like a party member, he followed him around.

He made sure to walk away from the guards before he asked, "So, where's the treasure?"

"What treasure?" the dwarf asked. "Hic," he added.

"The reward," he said. "You promised me a reward if I got you out, and it seems to me that I did that. So where is it?"

"Oh." Lyle looked around and hiccupped again. He seemed to appreciate the night air and the sounds of the owls. Contemplatively, he said, "I don't remember."

"You don't…remember?" This game would be the death of him.

"Well, I remember I put it behind a midden heap." The drunk nodded. "Good place to hide it. Everyone goes past the midden heap every day, see, but no one wants to stop there, ye ken?"

"Yes, I…I get that." He wasn't sure what a midden heap was but he was fairly sure he could get the idea. Something like a dump, perhaps. "So where's the midden heap?"

"There are many midden heaps."

"Oh, good." It seemed he would have to spend his night digging through pixelated garbage. At least he didn't have to smell it. "Well, let's go looking, then. Because one way or another, you'll pay for new armor for me."

<hr>

Lights still flickered in the windows as Justin looked through the town. He'd been enchanted by the settlement when he first saw it, but that hadn't been when he had to search around every house and back alley. Now, he began to dislike the fact that there was so much detail in this game. Couldn't this be a normal MMORPG village with five houses and three NPCs?

The first midden heap yielded nothing. He sighed, especially at the far too realistic game assets and squelching noises. At least his character didn't sink into the pile of garbage. He didn't think he could have dealt with that particular amount of realism.

"Not here," Lyle announced finally.

"Uh-huh." His entire body shuddered as a fly buzzed past him. Maybe the game designers should have spent their money making the liquid slosh in the beer mugs rather than adding realistic midden heaps.

That would go in the review, too.

They had reached the next midden heap when he heard footsteps and turned to see two men and another dwarf. They all had armor and weapons, and he suspected they would not be friendly NPCs. Were they a patrol group of mobs that showed up randomly in the towns at night?

"Well, well, well," one of them said. "If it isn't Lyle Stout."

Apparently not. Justin was annoyed that Lyle had gotten him in trouble but he remembered that they were searching midden heaps instead of fighting enemies. This was a good development.

Of course, he still didn't have any proper armor.

"Fellas." The dwarf waved. "I was looking for your money."

"*Their* money?" Justin asked, even more annoyed. That money was *his* for getting Lyle out of jail. He was beginning to understand, however, exactly why his new party member had been thrown into the jail so often.

His suspicions were only heightened when Lyle said, "Now, fellas…fellas. All of you will get what you were promised."

"That's the worst attempt I've ever seen to reassure someone," Justin told him.

The conversation didn't go anywhere, although that was because one of the bandits attacked. The man drew a dagger and smiled. "Well, maybe we remind you where you hid it, then—and get rid of some competition at the same time."

They meant him, he realized. He drew his sword and scowled when the bandits laughed.

"You plan to fight with that?" one of them asked him.

"Yeah, well, have you ever had tetanus?" He swung his sword as hard as he could at one of the men. A little fatigue point floated across the screen, which he knew to ignore by now. Besides, he had struck the bandit, who grunted in pain. "Yeah, that's right," he told him. "I'm not gonna get Silver Tongue Level Two out of this fight. I'm gonna get Bandit Slayer Level One."

No one appreciated his line, though, because his teammate barreled past him at full speed with a war cry. The dwarf launched into a flurry of punches and the two other bandits settled into fighting stances, their daggers out. Lyle had no weapons, but he didn't seem worried about that fact—and when Justin saw the bandit dwarf become airborne and career into the wall of the alleyway, he understood why.

He needed to focus on his attacker, though. His first slash with the sword again encountered only thin air and he circled away. When his attacker darted close with a dagger, Justin, trained on other video games, stepped into the charge and swung his weapon. He thought he felt a punch of pain across his ribs and he responded with a yell. This game was playing with his head. It had to be. It wasn't like a VR headset could hook into your brain, after all, right?

AVOIDABLE INJURIES, LEVEL 1 displayed across the screen.

"Yeah, yeah," he told the AI. "Very funny."

He thought he heard it snicker at him. At least his blow had connected as well, though, and the bandit looked like he was at half-health. The man lunged into the same attack again and this time, Justin stepped out of the way, took the haft of his sword in both hands, and stabbed it sideways as his opponent barreled past him. The bandit uttered a gurgling groan and fell heavily, and his body disappeared.

THAT'S A SWORD, NOT A PIKE, LEVEL 1.

Justin rolled his eyes as he went to help Lyle with his battle. The dwarf seemed to have taken some damage, but he yelled a series of insults at his attackers, apparently not at all cowed by his injuries. Fortunately, he was enough of a distraction that Justin was able to sneak up behind both attackers one by one and kill them.

He looted the bodies and darted a look at Lyle. "You should heal yourself. Have some ham or something."

"Hic." The dwarf stared at him. "What does ham do?"

"You know. Eat some food, recover some health."

His teammate gave him a look like he was insane. "A bandage is better for bleeding than a ham," he said as if he thought he might be a raving lunatic.

Justin couldn't help it and laughed aloud. This game had a good sense of humor, he'd give it that. He got serious again.

"All right. Time to find that treasure."

CHAPTER SIXTEEN

Midden heap number two went well until they encountered the bugs. It was considerably less squelchy, for one thing. There seemed to be a considerable number of boards and pieces of metal and so on and fewer flies. Justin liked that.

In the next moment, he realized exactly why there weren't scraps of vegetables and dozens of flies. The awareness was triggered by a sound he had never heard before, halfway between clicking and a squelch with maybe a hint of a rustle.

You didn't have to have heard the noise before to know what it was, though. He grasped his sword, turned, and prayed for it to be a glitch in the game.

The cockroach, however, was the size of a small dog.

It spread its wings, hissed, and leapt straight at him.

Jacob was carrying a box of takeout into the corridor when he heard Amber scream. He had never heard her scream before. They'd been mugged once in Boston, and it had been the muggers who wound up screaming.

He burst into a sprint and raced through the kitchen. In his head, dozens of mental images clamored, none of them good. Maybe the people following them the first night had snuck in while he was gone. Or maybe she had electrocuted herself on one of the new additions to the pods. Maybe something was catastrophically wrong with Justin.

He didn't expect to see Amber and Nick doubled over with silent laughter while they watched the monitors. Even DuBois was smiling, although in a bemused way.

Amber looked up. "Justin doesn't like bugs," she managed to say before she descended into giggles.

"What?" Jacob looked around, his heart pounding. "Wait—*what*? I heard you scream."

"Not me." She leaned on Nick's shoulder, practically sobbing with laughter.

"Well, you're the only girl here," he said. "So—" He stopped and looked at the screen. A laugh suddenly bubbled in his chest. "You're telling me…that was Justin?"

The others descended into gales of laughter and even DuBois chuckled.

"They're doing the quest where they search for the dwarf's treasure," Nick explained as he wiped his eyes. "Remember that one?"

"Ohhhh." He set the takeout bags on the floor and came to look, even though he couldn't quite read all the output on the screen. "Yeah, the one with the midden heaps. Those were nasty. And those bugs were big."

"And we didn't even do it in VR," Amber pointed out.

"Oh, God," Jacob said. He gave a full-body shudder. "That would be terrifying."

"Justin thinks so, too," Nick said. He stretched to take a handful of popcorn from DuBois's bag.

"That's cheating," Amber warned him. She settled in a chair. The audio that issued from Justin's wires was now a constant stream of profanities as well as heartfelt pleas to God and some of the saints. "You know, we're glad the parents weren't here when that happened. But, *damn*, that was funny."

Justin settled on a strategy he had decided to call, "Swing the sword every which way until eventually, all the giant cockroaches die." It wasn't a particularly catchy title, but it was about all he had the brainpower for at this particular moment.

"Fuck, fuck, fuck, fuck." Fatigue points flurried every which way and he should probably worry more about that, but these were giant cockroaches. Nature was not supposed to produce horrors like this. "Hail Mary, full of grace—"

Lyle, meanwhile, uttered little whoops every time one of his punches connected. He drove a fist down on a cockroach's head. "That'll teach you to bite me, you little bastard!"

"They bite?" Justin yelled, panicked. He drove his sword down and saw sparks when it connected with the cobblestones. These bugs were damned fast and he was not a fan of it. "Jesus Christ, how do I abandon a quest? Or—who's the patron saint of giant-ass bugs? Does this fall under Francis or what?"

The cockroaches swarmed around him, their pincers clicking, and Jason gave another scream he wasn't particularly proud of. He'd been happier when he knew they didn't bite. In desperation, he whipped his sword around his head like a helicopter rotor and was pleased to see fewer cockroaches when he was finished. All he could hope was that some of them were dead.

Lyle knocked one out of the air with a punch and a guffaw. "Now, *this*—this is the kind of brawl I like."

"Psychopath," he muttered.

The bugs didn't hit him, but his HP bar was over half gone from fatigue by the time the fight was over. His last kill—by plunging the sword straight down into a carapace—came with a sound he hoped never to hear again in his life. A moment of silence followed, punctuated only by the sounds of cows and owls.

"Well," Justin said. He cleared his throat and tried to recover some of his dignity. "I, uh…I got the first ten levels of Wild Flailing. So that's something." He looked around. "Lyle?" He could only hope that the dwarf hadn't been dragged off into a bug nest or something.

If he had, he would compose a nice eulogy and go home. There were limits to friendship.

Instead, his teammate popped up from behind the midden heap with a smile and a jingle of coins. "I found it!" he said triumphantly and held a pouch up. "Let's get a drink to celebrate, shall we?"

<hr>

Lyle accompanied him to the blacksmith's shop. His vociferous complaints about the money's best use didn't override his dynamics as one of the party, especially when Justin snatched the coin purse out of his hand and marched off.

The farther they got from that particular midden heap, the better.

The sun had finally begun to come up, which was a good sign. The dwarf still complained about beer and food, and Justin's stomach rumbled as well. Come to think of it, he *had* felt full after the stew he slurped at the inn, but that food was gone by now.

Also, it wasn't real. He had to remind himself of that. This game was damned good at convincing him that it was actually life or death. He'd even begun to imagine he could smell things in the game, which was ridiculous.

One more quest, he told himself, and he'd go to sleep. How long had he been up, anyway?

They found the blacksmith at the edge of town, working bellows at the fire in the back of his workshop. A young man stood in the front, dressed in a soot-stained apron and the same brown, nondescript clothing as everyone else in the village.

"Would you like to buy anything, sir?" he asked.

"Yes," Justin said, speaking over the dwarf's refusal. "Show me what you have for armor."

"Of course, sir." The shop's inventory appeared on the screen.

He scrolled through quickly. Everything was an upgrade, which was good, but he didn't have much money. So much for the dwarf's "reward." He rolled his eyes at the amount he had. Two silver and two copper. He'd be able to buy much better gear after defeating the wizard but he needed the gear to defeat the wizard.

Maybe he could wander around outside town and slay bunnies for a while. Nah. What was the worst that could happen if he gave this quest a try? He'd have multiple attempts at the quest. Probably.

Justin was beginning to wish he'd run the tutorial.

Finally, he chose a set of leather armor that had some of the best stats he could find and equipped it. A window popped up to display what it looked like and he was pleased to see it was even nicer than Lyle's, with a red wash on the edges of the leather panels and lacquered tiles around the ribs. It reminded him of some of the photos he'd seen of samurai armor.

He couldn't afford it, though. With a sigh, he equipped a different set—the very lowest tier the blacksmith offered. He could see black studs in the leather and a very suspicious set of scorch marks.

While he wasn't sure he wanted to know where this armor had come from, he would try to find out if there were dragons in the area. If his brain intended to treat this game like reality, he would make sure he didn't get turned into Justin the Crispy.

With another heartfelt sigh, he made the trade. He still had sixty-two copper, which meant he might be able to afford something on the weapons as well.

"Do you have any swords?" he asked. When he saw the prices, he heaved a third sigh. He had become good at sighing but apparently, that wasn't one of the things you got levels in. "Okay, can you do anything for my existing sword? Sharpen it, or—"

"Of course, sir. We'll remove some of the rust and sharpen it for you. Twenty copper."

"Done." Justin handed it over. He wasn't sure how it would work to remove the rust, given that the sword seemed to be largely composed of the stuff, but this was a game and game worlds were better than the real world in most ways.

For instance, the boy handed the sword directly to him and he didn't have to wait at all. The blade didn't look like it would ever be on a list of famous fantasy swords, but it was recognizably made of metal now and it did look sharper. He equipped it and saw that his damage had increased by almost fifty percent.

Excellent.

Did his armor...smell? It kind of smelled—like smoke and bacon or, at least, he hoped it was bacon. He thought of the scorch marks and felt a little queasy.

"Have a nice day, sir," the shop boy told him.

"You, too," he said automatically. He turned and ducked into the sunlight, only to see a man waiting for him. It was an NPC with a blue band of cloth around his arm and he held a small package.

The man's hand extended quickly and proffered the package.

"O...kay?" Justin took it, at which point the NPC simply stood where he was and blinked stupidly in the sunlight. After a moment of staring at him, Justin took a cautious step around him and walked away. At the end of the street, he looked back.

The NPC was still there and still stared at the side of the blacksmith's shop.

"We could have made that a little smoother," Jacob said to Nick.

"Hey," the other man protested. "I'm not a game designer. He delivered the package."

"So what will he do now?"

"I don't know." Nick stared at him. "I didn't tell him to do anything other than that."

Jacob sighed. Not for the first time, he reflected, it was damned good they'd bought the game rather than trying to make it themselves.

With no money left for a proper meal or an inn room, the two teammates headed out of town to make camp. It turned out there was a command for that, at which point the dwarf produced a campfire out of thin air—complete with a ring of stones—and Justin spent a few moments learning how to get the rabbit legs in his inventory to cook.

They smelled good—or, at least, he must be hungry enough that he imagined they smelled good. He sat on the ground and heaved a sigh. He'd never played anything quite this engrossing, glitches and all, but he was tired. He was suddenly so tired. His whole body seemed to ache.

Then, he remembered the package. He opened his inventory and found it, and the inventory screen disappeared to leave him with a strange bracelet in one hand. For a moment, he frowned, tried to decide what to do, and decided he'd play along. If this was a trick from the evil wizard, he'd at least have a good laugh about it. He slipped it onto his wrist.

He didn't turn into a frog but an image did pop up in front of him, superimposed over the now-frozen fire. Even Lyle was stilled in mid-motion.

The man in the picture had grey hair and a bushy beard and he wore a white lab coat.

"Hello, Justin," he said. "I'm Dr. DuBois."

CHAPTER SEVENTEEN

"You're who?" Justin asked blankly.

The image kept talking, however. Apparently, unlike the rest of the game, it wasn't something he could interact with.

"I am your doctor," the man explained. "You are in a coma, Justin. Everything you see around you is a game being fed into your nervous system through the use of a virtual reality scenario. Everything you need is supplied in the real world, although we have set up the feeding tube to be responsive to what you do in the game. If you ever get hungry, eat something and it will trigger the feeding tube to provide more nutrients to your body."

He sat in stunned silence. How could he be in a coma? He couldn't be in a coma.

But it explained why he'd never simply raised his hands and removed the VR headset. It explained why his hunger kept going away and all the body aches. He merely didn't know how he had gotten there.

"You were in a car accident," Dr. DuBois explained as if he could read his mind. He saw him look down at something and realized he was reading off a piece of paper that someone had given him. "You were on a blind date at an arcade and after you left, you were in a car crash. Your date was driving."

He shook his head. He still had no memory of this. No. It didn't make any sense. It didn't make any sense at all.

"Your mother and father want you to know that they love you," the doctor said. He looked off-screen at someone and whispered something. Justin could barely hear someone whisper words in response and DuBois shook his head slightly before he looked at the camera. "They are working around the clock to save you. In the meantime, this game is giving you the best chance of recovering. It is helping you relearn neural pathways you need to have and overall, heal your brain.

"However, you must be careful to not die in the game if you can avoid it. The brain is immensely open to the power of suggestion, and a player who dies in the game will often experience mild arrhythmia as the body briefly perceives itself to be dead. In your current condition, this is very dangerous for you."

Justin lowered his head into his hands. This wasn't happening. It absolutely wasn't. But he had begun to remember the arcade. He had started to see why he couldn't remember ever buying this game and why neither of his parents had come to interrupt him for dinner.

No, no, no...

"This bracelet should let us communicate," Dr. DuBois said. Again, he looked at the paper. "If you lose it, return to the N...P...C...who gave it to you and he can provide another one. Because we have never tried this form of communication before, it may have bugs and it may also have delays. If you ever want to send a message, press the blue jewel on the medallion and speak into it.

"One more thing." The doctor leaned slightly closer to the camera. "We can hear the vocalizations you make in the game, and it's my suggestion that you stop swearing so much. Your mother doesn't seem to like it. Oh—and we'll try to make sure to warn you when there will be more bugs." He leaned back and smiled. "You're doing very well, Jason."

"Justin," someone said from off-screen.

"Justin. Right. You're doing very well," DuBois said. "You're interacting well with the game and beginning to pick up more of the neural suggestions. Keep working through the game and it should give you the time and stimulus you need to heal. I will send another message when I can."

The image disappeared and the game world leapt into dizzying motion.

Once it settled, he looked around to try to ground himself. This was a nightmare. He didn't want to believe it but he knew on some level that it was real. If only he could remember the accident. He'd been at the arcade. To help him focus, he squinted and images flashed through his mind. The bottom of Tina's tattoo peeking out from her t-shirt. Her sliding her beer to him across the table. Her telling him that getting caught was half the fun—

Parts of him reacted to that particular memory, and he had a sudden, terrified fear that his body was visible and his parents were there. He cast about for a distraction, thought of the giant cockroaches, and shuddered in response. At least it did the trick.

He sighed with relief and buried his head in his hands. What had happened after that, though? He remembered darkness, Tina drumming her hands on the steering wheel, and the pleasant buzz of the beer in his bloodstream.

The dog. He recalled the dog running into the road.

And the way his whole body had lurched forward. He *remembered* the sickening moment of pain. His mouth opened in a silent scream.

The pace of the beeps had been wildly erratic while Justin listened to the message and now, it began to climb steadily.

"What's going on?" Mary asked worriedly. She had come on her own today and told them that Tad was in the office and she needed to see Justin. Even when they closed the pod lid again, she stayed, pulled a chair close to the pod, and rested her forehead on it.

"He's remembering," DuBois said. He looked like he was making a calculation in his head. "It was a risk whether to tell him or not. I decided it would be less stress on his nervous system if he expected to remember rather than having the memory come up at an unexpected time."

Amber nodded, but Mary couldn't make any sense of this. What did he mean?

The other woman saw her confusion and came to sit next to her. "Have you ever remembered something frightening?" she asked. "It can be scary. You start to sweat or your heart begins to race. Things like that. Justin is having that right now while he remembers the accident."

"Is he safe?" she whispered. The pace on the machines wasn't climbing anymore, but her heart was still in her throat.

"As safe as he can be," the other woman said. "Mrs. Williams, Justin *is* getting better. It may seem like a slow process but think of it like a broken arm, or—well, after having a baby. Stress on the body takes a long time to heal. Right now, much of that stress is in Justin's brain. We need to give it time."

Mary clutched her hand gratefully. "Thank you," she managed to say, "for everything you're doing." She looked around the lab. "Thank you to all of you. It seems almost scarier to see a window into Justin's mind right now." She extended a hand to touch the pod with trembling fingers. "It hurts to have him so close and know he's...almost awake but not be able to talk to him."

***

Justin paced around the campfire as night fell. Lyle had eaten big chunks of the meat and Justin's food had, exactly as DuBois told him, made him feel full.

He wanted to say something to his parents but he didn't know what.

Before he could change his mind, he held his wrist up, pressed the blue medallion, and began to speak.

"Mom, Dad—I got your message. This isn't easy to understand and I'm...scared." He didn't want to say that in front of his dad but it was out there now and he didn't think this had an erase message button. "I want you to know I wasn't trying to do anything stupid that night. Tina was driving because I had been drinking. I tried to—to get out of my shell a little, I guess. I love you a lot. I'll be more careful in the game now that I know." He pressed the button again to stop the recording. *Please don't let me die.* He wanted to say it out loud but he knew they were doing everything they could.

He sat and wrapped his arms around himself.

It scared him that he didn't know what to do next.

───

It was early evening when the senator arrived. He had changed again into his sweatshirt and jeans and he didn't smell wonderful. When he saw Jacob's face, he shrugged.

"I took a cab," he explained. "I'm trying to stay off their radar."

"Who are they?" he asked. Williams looked at him as if he were trying to make up his mind and Jacob shook his head. "They came after all of us in that ambulance. Who are they?"

"IterNext, I assume." DuBois had appeared in the kitchen without either of them noticing. He didn't seem particularly bothered by the knowledge. He took a carton of milk out of the fridge and poured himself a large glass. "They've watched me for years."

"It is IterNext," the senator confirmed. "But it's me they're after. They...offered to pay all Justin's medical bills if—" He sighed. "Well, it was a bribe. A blank check for them to call in a favor during a senate vote in the future."

"They do that?" Jacob was shocked. He didn't like to think of himself as naïve but bribery was something that was whispered about on news shows like a huge scandal. The idea of it happening like this was oddly jarring, not to mention the other facts. "And they followed your son's *ambulance*? What was that, a threat?" He looked down the corridor. "We don't have security here."

"I don't think you have to worry," the senator said dryly. "They'll hardly burst in with commandos. They'll merely ruin my career."

"And possibly mine!" Jacob said and waved his hands.

Amber stuck her head into the kitchenette. "We knew that was a possibility," she said. "Remember? I said we would get smashed through the floor by Big Pharma and *you* said something about how we were helping people, blah, blah, damn the torpedoes, full speed ahead." She waved her hand. "Well, here we are, buddy. Don't get cold feet now."

"What, now you're threatening me, too?" He looked at her, his expression one of a man betrayed.

She only rolled her eyes and disappeared.

Senator Williams smiled at him and headed into the other room to where his wife waited. They embraced the way they always did—as if the rest of the world ceased to exist for a moment. She laid her head on his shoulder and he smoothed her hair. She must have said something about the smell on his clothes because when she picked her head up, her nose was wrinkled and he was laughing.

"I have something for you two," DuBois told them. Jacob leaned in the doorway as the man set the speakers up to play Justin's message. Then, with uncommon tact, the doctor ushered the others out of the room and shut the door of the kitchenette.

They waited and caught snatches of Justin's voice on the monitor. All of them had heard it when he recorded it, and Nick had been suspiciously sniffly.

It wasn't long before Tad came to push the door open and beckon them inside. Mary had clearly been crying, and she still tried to repair her makeup.

"How is he doing?" the senator asked. "Mary told me that remembering the accident was difficult for him."

"It was," DuBois said. "The good news is that his reaction to that was much more in line with what a healthy person would experience than his reaction when he died in the game. It would appear that he is getting better."

"I want to talk to him," Tad said.

The doctor hesitated. "We can send another voice packet fairly easily," he said, "but we don't want to do this too often. Justin needs to focus on the game, which he can interact with, rather than having his focus on the outside world."

"I understand." Amber winced when Tad swallowed. "But I want him to hear our voices."

Wordlessly, the doctor pointed to the microphone and, with a few clicks on the computer, set it up to record before he ushered the others out again.

In the kitchenette, Amber narrowed her eyes at the doctor. "What are you worried about?"

"It's a balance," DuBois said without preamble. "We wanted him to believe the game was real. He knew it was a game, which helped to keep him from dying when his character died, but he needs a certain amount of immersion. If he doesn't get that, his brain won't have an incentive to heal. And if he does…"

Amber frowned. "What then?"

"So many people in comas never wake up," DuBois said. "They're locked off from the world forever. That could still be him."

CHAPTER EIGHTEEN

Justin wasn't sure if he slept or not and was even afraid of sleeping now. He was very aware of the fact that his body lay in a perpetual sleep and something about that made this version of consciousness all the more vital. If he went to sleep there, would he ever wake up?

Still, time slid away from him for a while and when the sun came up, he felt rested. Did his mind feel more acute or was that merely his imagination?

"Lyle," he said. "Wake up. We're going back to the inn."

The dwarf sat. "You have more money for beer?"

"We're not going to get beer," he said. "We're going to get quests so that we can level up—I mean, get better gear—before facing Sephith."

"Good," his teammate replied.

"What do you mean, good?" He looked at him suspiciously as Lyle made the campfire vanish. "I thought you wouldn't like this plan."

"The longer we wait before we face him, the better the chance you don't decide to do it at all," Lyle explained.

"You could theoretically run off," Justin pointed out.

"Oh, don't you say that, boy." The dwarf pointed a finger at him.

"That's a deathly insult where I come from. Yer lucky I'm not my father or ye'd be dead for that."

"What do you mean? I didn't insult you." He began to walk toward the town.

"You said I could run off and leave my obligations," Lyle told him. "I asked ye to get me out of jail and the price of that was to help ye with the wizard. I'm not turning my back on that. That'd be to betray my honor."

"Oh." Justin hadn't considered that. He wondered what Lyle would think about flaking on group plans to go out to Chili's or see a game, both of which he'd done recently.

Probably the same thing.

The town was bustling, and Justin was simply glad that none of the NPCs were inclined to arrest them for coming back before they defeated the wizard. He didn't want to try to explain to an NPC that time was meaningless when it came to even the most important quests.

At least, he hoped it was.

And if it wasn't, Zaara was made of pixels. If he had to, he would let her get offed in order to save himself. *Nothing personal, Zaara. I'm sure you're great. You're merely not real.*

He browsed the job postings again and selected a few that looked interesting—more rabbits to be killed, a few wolves, and a couple of bounties. Lyle suggested skinning the wolves and selling the pelts at the next town, and although that made him a little queasy, he decided the game probably wouldn't make it too graphic.

Anyway, they needed the coin.

It was only when they headed out of town again that he realized how angry he was. When he'd recorded the message to his parents, he'd been shaken and grateful to be alive. Now, he had begun to feel the next wave of emotions and they weren't anywhere near so positive.

They were the ones who had badgered him to go out on that date and who'd said his video games were holding him back. Had they apologized? No, of course not. *He'd* apologized because they were always on his case about messing up and they probably thought he was the one at fault.

Now, he was in a coma after a date he hadn't even wanted to go on and what did they use to keep him alive? Video games. He hadn't expected them to apologize but right now, he had begun to think they should.

And was Tina even alive? They hadn't bothered to mention that to the doctor.

Which probably meant she was dead. They'd gotten her killed, too. Justin knew that wasn't fair. Tina's driving had been way too fast. If they'd been going thirty, they could have swerved around the dog. If it had been forty, they'd still have crashed but not nearly so hard.

He'd seen the speedometer right before everything went dark.

Still, he would blame his parents for this one. Tina had tried to cheer him up after his parents basically told him he was a loser. She was right that if they'd played the night safe, his parents wouldn't have thought any better of him. They'd simply keep thinking he was a loser.

He was so lost in his thoughts that he hardly noticed the orc stepping onto the path in front of them.

"Ho, ho, ho," it said with a gravelly laugh. "Looks like meat's on the menu toni—"

Its head thudded onto the path and Justin stared at it, his chest heaving. "I'm having a moment here," he told it. Still, he had to admit, swinging a sword was a very satisfying way to deal with anger. When the other orcs attacked him from the forest, he grinned as he settled into a ready stance.

It occurred to him that he should be terrified. After all, if he messed this up, he might die—*really* die.

But he found he was laughing as he danced in and around the orcs' heavy fists. When he was angry, he wasn't afraid. He wasn't all up in his head about game mechanics. Plus, now he knew how to piss his parents off.

In the lab, Amber's mouth hung open as she listened to the audio from the game. What she heard had to be the most sacrilegious thing anyone had ever said. Its creativity was marred only by its exceedingly repetitive use of the word fuck.

"He wants to do *what* with the shroud of Turin?" Jacob asked through a mouthful of lo mein.

"I think he might have gone in the other direction with your suggestion about not swearing," Nick said to DuBois.

"Yes," the doctor said after a moment. "You know, I think that's true. He seemed so sorry in his voice message."

"He's not anymore," Jacob said with feeling. "I'd say our friend Justin, here, might be a little angry about life in general right now."

"He's angry," Amber said, "at his parents." She looked at them all. "I wish we knew why. And I wish he'd keep his heart rate in a good range." She shrugged. "But if we're wishing for things, we might as well wish that no one was in a coma and we had no market because I guess that's the only way we could avoid this kind of stress."

"Your mind makes the strangest leaps," DuBois said. "Chaos is a part of life, young lady. Now, is there any more popcorn or am I all out? I'm studying game design and it's a hungry business."

CHAPTER NINETEEN

The road to Sephith's keep wound through a series of surprisingly pretty marshes on a mountain plateau. The sharp peak of the mountain to the west was lit by the sun and the streams that ran down it shined so brightly that Justin sometimes had to look away.

Whatever had happened there, the ice-cold water collected on a large plateau before it tumbled slowly over the edge to continue its journey down the mountain. Patches of grass sprang up from the marsh at regular intervals, along with brilliant flowers and some kind of alien lily pad.

It was there that he learned to be wary of rabbits. When he'd taken the posting for mountain rabbit hides down, he'd pictured easy XP and a few more levels on his Bunny Slayer skill.

It turned out that mountain rabbits were not the same as the bunnies he'd killed on the plains. These, in a nod to urban legend, had antelope horns. They also had incredibly sharp teeth, which he first found out when Lyle uttered a bellow of surprise from behind him. Justin swung in time to see the dwarf swat something furry and fast-moving out of the air. Having seen fur, floppy ears, and horns, his brain was still trying to parse what it was when he heard a hiss from the marsh nearby and turned to see another crouched in a patch of grass.

The game had helpfully added a glowing star above its head to mark that it was a quest objective.

"Well, *that's* terrifying," Justin muttered before the rabbit attacked. He swung his pack up on instinct and shrieked when it latched on and glared at him through red-tinted eyes. Its teeth were embedded in the pack and if looks could kill, the creature was guilty of murder a hundred times over.

His reaction was purely reflexive. He made a few hopping turns and swung his bag in an exaggerated way until the animal lost its hold and sailed into the water. A yelp and a splash were immensely satisfying.

THINK OUTSIDE THE BOX, LEVEL 1 announced the game.

Well, it *had* worked. Justin looked at Lyle for a moment, saw the dwarf scanning the marshes worriedly, and drew his sword. If there were two of these animals, there were probably more and they'd *really* pissed the little bastards off now.

"Lyle," he said conversationally. He settled into a warrior's crouch, the sword held at an angle.

"Yeah?"

"Did you know this was what mountain rabbits were?" He liked playing with the AI to see how far the conversation options went, and —as usual—he wasn't disappointed.

"No," the dwarf said and sounded surly. "I always heard to not go into the mountains, but no one said why."

"It was the rabbits." He nodded to confirm his assumption. That seemed like his level of luck. He'd taken what he thought would be the easiest quests and this was what the game gave him. Maybe the AI was messing with him.

He remembered the doctor telling him he had to immerse himself in the game and that it was training his survival instincts. Were they trying to keep him out of his depth all the time?

Justin had never beaten anyone up, but he had a few people in mind for when he came out of this damned coma. He would level up his Beating Up Smug Assholes skill and, boy howdy, there would be hell to pay.

A rustle in a nearby patch of grass alerted him and he swung his sword as the rabbit hurtled out at full speed. "Hi-yah!"

"When ye're asked for pelts, it's a good idea to not cut the beast in half," Lyle called. After a flurry of punching sounds and a few hastily muttered oaths, a dead rabbit landed at Justin's feet. It didn't disappear, presumably because they were supposed to skin it. "There. Like that, ye ken?"

He had a sudden and intense urge to throw up. This game was too realistic sometimes. The next rustle made him wince and this time, he aimed carefully for the neck when he swung. In his quest to be careful, he missed the rabbit entirely but when it landed, he was ready. He stabbed the sword directly down on its head and made a gurgling, horrified noise as the sound effect.

Way too realistic, he decided.

When they had five rabbits, he poked Lyle in the arm. "Let's get out of here. Get these…uh, skinned."

"Right." The dwarf gathered three of the rabbits and exited the marsh at a dead run, leaving Justin to follow. He scooped up the remaining two, prayed that the game blood wouldn't stick around—he was beginning to smell things now—and left before he heard any tell-tale hissing.

Skinning the rabbits was, thankfully, something Lyle said he'd handle. The dwarf made a makeshift drying rack, which was to say he walked to a bush, made some thwacking motions as if he had an ax, produced a neatly-stacked pile of branches out of nowhere, and mysteriously produced a long pole like the ones peasants used to carry full water jugs. He hung the rabbits from it and headed back toward Riverbend with Justin, who made it a point to look anywhere but at his companion and the animals.

Just outside the town, Lyle set the drying rack down and began to skin the rabbits. He tossed the finished carcasses in Justin's direction, where they thankfully disappeared into little drumstick icons. The dwarf stowed the antlers in his pack, careful to leave enough of a nub of bone on each pelt that it was clear they'd slain actual mountain rabbits.

The two wandered until he found a shop with a stretched animal skin on the sign. Inside, the leatherworker was hanging a skin up to dry. The place had such a smell that he paused on the threshold. He half-expected **PANSY, LEVEL 1** to pop up on the screen, and he was fairly sure he'd rather be a pansy than smell this ever again.

"What can I do for you, sirs?" The leatherworker came over to them with a smile. His apron was stained with what was clearly blood.

"I have the five mountain rabbit pelts you posted for," Justin said. He gestured to the pile of pelts Lyle was carrying.

"Is that Lyle Stout?" the tanner asked and raised an eyebrow. "Well, by the Three, there's a thing I never imagined I'd see. I thought you only made your living with your fists, Stout."

"Ye can punch rabbits," the dwarf grunted.

"True enough." The tanner nodded to Justin. "Player Underscore 009, was it? Let me get your reward."

"Just a moment." He held a hand up. "Ten copper for five mountain rabbits isn't a worthwhile reward."

"You accepted the job, did you not?" The tanner laughed. "Those are the terms."

"If they were good terms, you wouldn't post for adventurers to fulfill them, would you?" Justin pointed to the hides. "A silver for the lot."

"A silver? You want me to go to ten times the price I offered." The tanner folded his arms now and stared obdurately at him.

"Yes. Or we'll take them on with us to East Newbrook." He had seen the signs pointing that way. The village was close to Sephith's keep, so they would need to travel toward it in the end anyway.

"Fifty copper," the tanner said after a pause.

"A silver," he said again, "but we'll throw in the antlers."

The tanner didn't smile but he nodded. "Done." He fished a silver coin out of the pouch at his belt and pointed to a table. "Let me see the pelts before I hand the money over."

Lyle spread them out and the tanner walked around the table several times. Finally, he handed the coin to Justin.

"Your work is as good as your bargaining," he said grudgingly. "Good luck on your travels, adventurer. I'll pay the same rate for any more pelts you bring—and twice that for the Rabbit Queen."

"Of course. My thanks." Justin bowed and headed out into the sunlight. He had no intention of ever hunting another mountain rabbit, and whatever the Rabbit Queen was, he made his mind up to stay as far away as possible.

This time, after their walk to the marshes, the two companions crossed that section of the path quickly. Whether it was fear or lost numbers, no more rabbits attacked them and they were able to reach Peak Crossing near midday.

Justin, to his amusement, discovered he was weary. His body was lying in a coma but his mind truly believed he was walking through rough terrain. He listened to the crunch of his "footsteps" on the rough path and looked over the valley as he walked closer.

This was a strange place. The sky almost twinkled there, something he chalked up to a glitch until he saw an actual spark tumble through the air. It drifted like a piece of flaming paper, light as air, and it carried a faint, rosy glow. He looked around in time to see another, this time bluish-green. He stretched toward it but was surprised by a rough shove from Lyle.

"Don't touch those," the dwarf said. "Keep moving."

"Why shouldn't I touch them?"

"Ye want magic sickness?" his companion asked rhetorically as he passed him. "Ye want yer blood to turn black an' yer insides to come alive an' yer eyes to turn to cursed jewels? That's what ye want?" Justin had learned that the more worried the dwarf became, the more his native accent came out.

"Excuse me, what?" He hurried after him.

"This is where it happened," Lyle called, not looking back. "Between Sephith and Kural."

"Okay, but where *what* happened?" He looked around. The valley didn't seem very welcoming. There was something about the trees and the grass that was slightly…wrong. The colors were off, as were the proportions. On the hillside in the distance, he could see a pine tree that had split into two and one piece grew off with a twisted lean. The music, still faint, had taken on a foreboding sound.

The dwarf turned. "Ye truly don't know?"

"I truly don't. I—oh, shit! Did I touch that one?"

Lyle shrugged. "We'll know soon enough, won't we? Well, why d'you think everyone's afraid of Sephith, eh? This valley was ruled by Kural. Not bad for a wizard." He started down the mountain again.

"Are wizards generally bad?" Justin asked. He was careful to avoid a few drifting embers as he followed.

"No worse'n anyone else," the dwarf said with a shrug. "But once ye have magic, why listen to anyone else? Why be a good lord? Kural was better'n people had any right to expect, so they put up with him just fine. Then Sephith killed him. Dunno why—some wizard dispute. The magic he used is still in the air. It burns what it touches. Some, it turns into his thralls. Some go mad. Sephith doesn't care."

Justin shuddered. In a world of technology, the fear was nuclear fallout. Here, the denizens of the valley lived through some kind of magical Chernobyl.

"There." Lyle pointed. "That's Sephith's tower, see?"

He did see. The tower was smaller than he expected, not exactly an Eye of Sauron. Indeed, it couldn't be more than five stories tall and it stood at the far end of the valley. He suspected it would be one of the only places there that got sunlight for most of the day. The rest of the valley lived in semi-darkness and tried to shield themselves from the fallout of his fight.

"Keep yer cloak up," Lyle called and he set off down the mountain to another, smaller plain with a stream running through it. "We need water."

"Is the water safe to drink?" Justin asked. One part of him said it was ridiculous for him to be afraid but the doctor had told him not to get himself killed. Drinking irradiated water in a very realistic game seemed like a bad choice to make.

"Of course it is." Lyle shook his head. "Ye don't know anything, do ye? Water is pure. It's the one thing as never gets touched by magic. Now, come on. Bring the canteens."

At least this wasn't a nightmare with glowing green puddles. He filed the knowledge away and followed him to the stream. They knelt to refill the canteens, and he marveled at the feel of the cold water on his hands. The more time he spent here, the more the game convinced him it was real.

Or maybe he was regaining brain function.

It was strange to think of himself as being in a coma when he was awake there. Justin shook his head in confusion. He was so lost in his thoughts that he didn't notice the floating ember until it was right near his face. He yelled in alarm, ducked away, and tumbled into the stream.

The water was a shock to the system. He felt the muscles in his ribs contract sharply and his heart gave a sideways leap. In panic, he reached for the air and found ground instead. He didn't know which way was up anymore.

His head emerged from the water and he gave one gasped breath before his sodden cloak pulled him under again.

He had to get out of there. The water had begun to chill him to the bone and the plateau wasn't large. If he reached the edge and went over the cliff, he was a goner. He wasted one useless moment trying to be Neo in the Matrix and reminded himself that this virtual reality wasn't real at all—but he'd spent too long there to believe it. It didn't matter that he knew it wasn't real. He could feel the cold and he could feel the water pressing against his mouth.

In that moment, all he knew was that if he breathed the water in or went over that cliff, he would believe on some level that he was dying.

Justin snatched at something—anything. His lungs screamed for air as his fingers slipped across the surface of one rock and found purchase on another. He pushed his feet onto the streambed as hard as he could and launched himself out of the water to sprawl on the bank of the stream. Only a few feet away, the edge of the plateau cut off sharply and he could hear the waterfall roar down the mountainside. He dragged in a full breath of air and lay there with his heart pounding.

"*Fuck.*"

SWIMMING, LEVELS 1 & 2, the screen announced. **JUST DON'T DROWN IN THE BATH!** He shut his eyes on the words and groaned. He was in no mood for humor right now.

"Ye all right?" Lyle's face swam into view. "I grabbed for ye, but the water moves fast. Good thing ye caught yourself." He sounded almost worried, although Justin knew he was imagining it.

He was alone there. The truth was that he was alone and he was dying in the real world. Maybe.

The dwarf suggested they make camp in a stand of trees where the branches would catch most of the drifting embers, and Justin was too tired to do anything but agree. He was glad that the game was set up for party members to make suggestions because right now, his brain had too much going on for him to think about anything else.

Lyle hummed to himself as he made a fire and after a while, Justin said, "If you could do anything you wanted in the game, what would it be?" He took a contemplative bite of his roasted rabbit. His brain, thankfully, made it taste like rotisserie chicken. He could deal with that.

"What game?" his companion asked.

Oh. Right. Justin swallowed his non-existent bite reflexively before answering. "I mean…in the world. What's your big aspiration in life? It can't be to spend your days in a village jail."

The dwarf pondered this. He didn't seem to be offended.

Well, of course he wasn't. He was an NPC and wasn't alive at all. Justin shook his head at his own stupidity. The longer he spent there, the more Lyle seemed like a friend. His brain was apparently desperate to not be alone.

"I want to find," Lyle said finally, "the strongest brew in the world…an' drink it." He took a bite of his rabbit. He seemed very pleased with his goal. "What about you, then?"

"I…don't know, actually." He knew he could simply speak the truth, but he found himself translating his words into the game's language. "I used to think I wanted to…well, to be a gladiator. Kind of. To play games for others to watch. Or tell stories. Like a…well, a bard?"

"Huh." The dwarf snorted and took another bite.

"My father didn't want that for me," he explained. "He wanted me to be a barrister." That was the word, right? "Or a…town councilman like him. Maybe a doctor."

"Sounds boring," Lyle said, which left Justin wondering if he was always programmed to say that or if the game's creators had a poor opinion of doctors, lawyers, and politicians. He couldn't exactly blame them, if so.

"I thought so, too," he said. "But now, I'm not so sure. Telling people about stories of defeating wizards isn't quite so fun…once you've done it."

"Piece of advice, kid." His companion finished his rabbit leg and threw the bone into the trees. "Once you live something like this, you take everything you can get as a reward. If Sephith doesn't turn you into a pile of ash, you might as well take the acclaim."

He nodded, but he wasn't sure he could agree. Not yet. Not now.

His hand vibrated and he looked at the medallion, which glowed. He should answer, he supposed, but he didn't want to anymore. After a slight hesitation, he took a deep breath before he pressed on the blue jewel.

The face that popped up was his father's.

Justin didn't even think. He closed the message and deleted it, then lay back as the game world lurched into motion around him. His father's last words to him hadn't been kind and he didn't want his brand of tough love now.

This was hard enough to deal with on his own. He didn't need to make it harder.

CHAPTER TWENTY

The next day dawned rainy and miserable, a fact which made Justin groan when he awoke to water dripping on his face. He was only more annoyed when Lyle uttered a satisfied "Ha!" at the weather.

"What's there to be so cheery about?" he muttered.

"The rain keeps the embers out of the air," the dwarf said succinctly. "This valley's the only place in the world where everyone goes out on rainy days. Ye can get more done. Come on, we've no time to lose."

"I'm not sure we have enough experience to defeat Sephith yet." Justin considered his words as they packed up the camp and revised them. "I mean, we should…get better armor. Learn more…punches."

"How many punches are there?" his teammate asked rhetorically. "And how are ye going to get stronger, lugging that tiny little sword around? Ye should get a battle ax. Of course, ye'd need to have grown up with one. Dwarven babies use them fer teethin'."

Justin rolled his eyes and started down the path with a chuckle.

They were about halfway down the slope when he noticed a dark-cloaked figure waiting for them in the road. He stopped abruptly and fought the urge to scream and run in the opposite direction.

"Lyle…the village down there. It's not called Silent Hill, by chance?"

"No," the dwarf said. After a moment, he added, "Silent Hill's off west. Why d'you ask?"

"No reason. Also, let's never go west."

"Fine by me," Lyle said. "Hey, who's that?"

"Yes, I wondered the same thing." A hysterical laugh bubbled in his chest. With his luck, this would be Sephith and he would die. He had gotten into a coma because of his parents' meddling, but it would be a video game that finished him off. It was the kind of thing that would be funny in a little while.

You know, when he was dead.

"Greetings, travelers." The figure shook his hood back to reveal an older man. His close-cropped hair was going gray and he was clean-shaven, a fact Lyle took in with a derisive snort. "I've been waiting for the travelers whose fire I saw last night. I'd guess you are them?"

Justin made a mental note to not build fires anymore. "Maybe. Who are you?"

"Merely an old mercenary." The man smiled. "And, like any old mercenary, I'm willing to offer coin to some young men if they'll go into danger on my behalf."

"He talks like a mercenary," Lyle said, after a moment.

"If he were a mercenary, wouldn't he want to go into danger?" he pointed out.

"How d'you think a mercenary gets old?" the dwarf asked him. "By doin' things like this. If he's smart, he also took their coin purses when they fell in battle."

The mercenary smiled and jingled a pouch at his belt. It sounded quite heavy.

"See?" Lyle asked. He folded his arms. "What's the job?"

"There's a house nearby," the man said. "And a book inside. I'll pay handsomely for it." He turned to point down the hill, where a crumbling cottage could be seen.

"So…what's in there is so terrifying," Justin said, "that you won't take two steps inside the door to get it. I don't think I'm interested."

"Hey, look at that." Lyle patted his shoulder. "You might get old, too."

"The house holds many secrets," the mercenary told them. "You'll find it perhaps doesn't look on the inside as it does on the outside. And if it holds any other riches, you may keep them. I only want the book."

"So what's in there to stop you from getting it?" Justin asked. He was beginning to get annoyed.

"Do you know what happened to Kural?" the man asked.

His skin prickled. He swallowed when he looked at the house. "No."

"No one does." The mercenary shrugged. "But his servants? Sephith took their bodies. He said that was all he needed. The spirits…well, he left them here."

Justin didn't think his eyes could get any wider. He'd never found haunted houses all that scary but he had a feeling this one would be different. This one actually *could* kill him.

"The choice is yours," the man said. "But if you go in, you should know the spirits can't be fought—not with your weapons or mine, anyway. They're of the spirit world and they're hungry for life. They'll fight you for your flesh if they catch you."

"I can see why you didn't lead with that," he muttered. He stared at the house.

A long pause followed.

"Oh, hell," Lyle said.

"What?" Justin looked at him.

"You're going to do it, aren't you?" the dwarf said. "You're actually considering it."

"It's a chance to learn more about Sephith," he pointed out. "And his capabilities."

"It's very simple," Lyle told him. "Sephith? Bad. Capabilities? Very dangerous. He can kill you."

"And apparently, he practices necromancy," he said. "That's new. I didn't know that before."

"Now you do! What more do you need inside that house o' horrors?"

Justin began to laugh. He wasn't quite sure why and he also wasn't sure he could stop. He clapped Lyle on the shoulder. "You know, I'm not sure." He started down the hill. "But I'll be damned if I spend the rest of my life jumping at shadows."

"He's going to die," Lyle said to the other man as he strode past.

The mercenary wisely said nothing.

———

From the outside, the cottage looked like it was barely big enough to hold a hearth and a bed, but the stones looked virtually untouched by time or weather. The only thing that had rotted was the thatch. It still held together, but Justin couldn't see how—it was blackened and seemed to be composed mostly of slime.

He decided not to try breathing through his nose.

"Think of Zaara," Lyle told him a little desperately.

"Huh?" Justin hesitated in confusion.

"The mayor's daughter!" The dwarf looked at him like he was crazy. "The girl ye're trying to save? Remember her? If ye die in there…well, Sephith's gonna keep her."

"Ah." He considered this. "Counter-point. If we can't defeat these ghosts, we probably can't defeat Sephith. So, instead of walking all the way across the valley simply to die there, we might as well die here…right?"

His companion covered his face with his hands. "Don't go above ground, me da said. They're all crazy, he said. Well, he was right."

"Probably," Justin replied cheerfully. "But you stayed, which means you're a little crazy too."

He realized that when all of this was over, he would *miss* Lyle—and this life too. Sure, he was stuck in this game, but he was surviving based on wits and he got to choose how to do that. Instead of living in a little cave of a room, certain that the next day would bring more of the same monotony, he was in a world where his choices mattered.

And honestly, he liked that.

The cottage had no windows so there was no way to know what was inside. He took a deep breath, blew it out, and opened the door as gently as he could. When it slid open silently rather than creaking, he couldn't tell if he was relieved or worried. The dwelling didn't look like Sephith's magic had forgotten it.

What he saw took his breath away.

"Holy Godspawn," Lyle muttered from behind him.

Justin took a disbelieving step into the cottage and had to stop himself from laughing. The interior was massive. Vaulted ceilings stretched so high above that they should be shrouded in shadow—but the stained-glass windows cast jewel-toned patterns over the walls and illuminated everything. Wherever this mansion existed, it was somewhere the sun was shining.

The marble floor, too, was a work of art. The sigil of circling flames, which was picked out in red and orange glass on the windows, was echoed in the stone. It shone as if it had just been polished. Barely a single mote of dust floated in the shafts of light from the windows.

He took one step and then another before he stopped to look at the room as a whole. This was the kind of ballroom Disney princesses waltzed in. Not one, not two, but three staircases lay at the opposite end, the center one wide enough for one person in elaborate robes and the other two sweeping out in two symmetrical arcs.

Kural apparently liked to make an entrance when he entertained.

Even Lyle was shocked into silence until one of them took too many steps into the hall. With a chime like the sound of a dozen bells at once, braziers sprang into existence along the walls. A carpet unrolled itself from the top of the center stairway and flicked across the floor so quickly that they barely made it out of the way.

"Welcome," a voice said, "to the Hall of Kural."

"We should go," the dwarf said decisively. "We should go *right now*."

Justin waved a hand for him to be quiet. He could hear something.

"Come on!" He caught Lyle's sleeve and began to run across the floor. It was a good thing his brain had gotten the hang of these game mechanics because he didn't have time to dither. With the room this big and this empty, there weren't many places to hide. Instead, there were two—under the right staircase or the left one.

The noise grew louder as he ran, and he had the sickening realization that he was running directly toward it. He might, in fact, be going to the worst place of all.

Well, it was too late to do anything about it. He raced into the space under the right set of stairs and yanked the dwarf into the shadows beside him.

Above them, two doors slammed open and he jumped enough to hit his head on the underside of the stairs. Mouthing silent curses, he leaned into the darkness and snuck a peek at the opposite set of stairs.

Just as he had suspected, spirits made their way down the staircases. They drifted eerily in procession. He couldn't tell what they had once been. Serving girls in flowing dresses? Guards with spears and swords? Kural clearly liked to make an impression, but was he the type who wanted to flaunt that he had a good life full of beautiful women or one who wanted to show off a massive army?

Not that it mattered now, he supposed.

The procession continued down the stairs and he peeked out far enough to see the ghosts form a line along the carpet.

"Welcome." The whisper was hair-raising. "Welcome, petitioner, to the hall of Kural."

Definitely serving girls in flowing dresses, Justin decided. Kural clearly liked to flaunt the good life in everyone else's faces.

"D'you think we could get halls like this when we defeat Sephith?" he whispered to Lyle.

"Shhh!" His companion waved his hands dramatically.

He merely shrugged in response.

"Did you have a plan?" the dwarf asked in a furious whisper.

"Well, there was nowhere else to hide but here."

"Or we could have left," Lyle pointed out.

"Oh, right." He nodded. "Yeah, that's a good point."

The dwarf slapped his hands over his eyes.

Justin considered his options but he noticed something strange—faint lines in the wall under the center staircase. It looked like it was made of solid stone to contrast with the unsupported, sweeping side staircases, but in actuality, there was a door there. He poked his teammate and pointed to the wall. How did they open it?

Lyle, surprisingly, seemed to know exactly where to look. He crouched to examine the door's outline and nodded. He crept closer, took a deep breath before he went into the potential sightline of the ghosts, and pushed on the outer edge of one of the doors. It slid open as silently as the main door to the cottage and he beckoned Justin inside before he followed him in and pushed it hastily behind them, leaving only a crack for light.

"How did you know how to do that?" Justin asked quietly.

"The door's dwarven-made," Lyle explained. "Kural had good taste. Now." He looked around. The light from the door fell evenly across the patch of floor where they stood but was jagged at the end. "I'd say this stairwell leads down to the kitchens...and up to his lordship's tower."

"Well, I think one of those is a better place to find a book," Justin suggested. "Come on." He started into the darkness.

SNEAK, LEVEL 1 the game told him. **FINISH THIS QUEST TO EARN SNEAK LEVEL 10.**

Now that was a good bonus but also a very bad sign of how difficult this quest would be.

The staircase went straight up, a mirror to the stairway above, until they reached what must have been the back wall. At that point, the floor leveled out and magical orbs illuminated.

"These would have been useful earlier," Lyle said.

"Shhh!" Justin waved a hand. The last time lights had come on, ghosts had followed. He noticed a spiral staircase ahead and jerked his head. "Come on, before anyone comes from the kitchens to steal our souls."

They reached the staircase as Justin heard the telltale hissing. Without speaking, they ran up the staircase as lightly as they could but luckily, the sound seemed to halt a short distance away. Perhaps the ghostly kitchen staff were pretending to lay out an imaginary meal. He shuddered at the thought.

The staircase seemed to ascend much farther than it should, and when he finally hit his head—something his nervous system did not like, all things considered—he realized he'd missed another dwarven door set in the curved wall. Again, Lyle found the hidden catch and the door opened as if its hinges had been oiled only the day before.

The two crept into a room that looked like the quintessential wizard's tower.

Or, rather, the quintessential wizard's tower after a tornado made of fire. The drapes had once been a rich purple but they now hung in tatters that held both charred pieces and glowing embers.

Justin had the strange, hair-raising idea that time had stopped entirely inside this castle and that if he were to go outside, he would find the mercenary frozen in the same place they'd left him. He looked at the books and saw one or two that should be falling from the shelves. They were frozen in mid-air instead. A few specks of ash didn't swirl in the sunlight but simply hung in the air.

Kural had apparently not been one for potions. There were no bubbling braziers and no glowing green or purple liquids. Small mercies, he thought. He glanced at Lyle. "Do you see anything you want?"

The dwarf shook his head. "This place is cursed. That mercenary will pay for anything he keeps from it, you mark my words."

Justin didn't think so. He began to think that what had happened there wasn't only Sephith's magic but also Kural's. This hall should have been looted by now. Surely Sephith wanted the books on the walls. Surely a human soul was worth more than a soulless body.

No, this looked like defenses that had been used too late and weren't quite sufficient to save everyone. What if Sephith hadn't made the husks but simply found the empty bodies?

Because Kural had tried to save his servants.

It was a theory he couldn't prove and he wasn't sure he'd ever know the full story, but he liked the idea. He looked at the walls. "Which book do you think the mercenary…" His gaze fell on one that glittered faintly golden but only when he looked at it out of the corner of his eye. "Never mind. Found it."

He strode to the shelf, ignored Lyle's warning, and pulled it down. His muscles—although faintly—told him that it was heavy. He hesitated and flipped it open.

"What are you *doing?*" the dwarf asked, horrified.

"Seeing what's so valuable," he said. "After all, it's more advantageous to seize the means of production than be adjacent to it."

"What?"

"It's from a book. One my father doesn't like." Justin gave a small, private smile. "This, however, looks like spells. Yeah. Definitely spells. 'Draw upon your magic to...' Huh. This must be an intermediate book. I wonder where you learn where the magic *is.* Maybe there's a glossary." He flipped to the last page of the book.

MAGIC UNLOCKED, the game announced.

"Oh, hey, look at that." He looked to where a mana bar had appeared alongside his health bar. "There was a glossary. Kind of."

"I suggest you read that fireball spell again," the AI said sweetly.

"Huh?" Justin looked up.

"I didn't say anything," the dwarf said. "Although...do you hear something?"

He heaved a sigh. "More ghosts. Look—uh, bluff as long as you can."

"Bluff?" Lyle asked.

"Pretend," he said and gestured to the door, "that these ghosts want you to pay them for their ale and you don't have any money. Because it's exactly like that, see. They want a spare body and yours isn't a spare. So start making excuses. I'm going to learn some spells."

"Why can't we simply punch them?" the dwarf demanded. "Or run!"

"The mercenary said we couldn't punch them, remember? They were made by magic so it stands to reason"—he flipped through the pages as quickly as he could— "that they can only be destroyed by magic. Ah, here we go. Fireball." He read quickly as ghosts began to stream through the doors. "Any moment now, Lyle."

"Greetings, esteemed servants of Kural," Lyle said pleasantly.

The ghosts surrounded them and stopped.

"We have journeyed far to bring you news of your master," the dwarf continued. "Kural was defeated on this earthly plane but left all of you here to make ready for his return."

"That's good," Justin muttered.

"Shut it," his companion said in an undertone. To the ghosts, he said, "Your master has sent us to bring him the last thing he needs for his return—this book. On the third new moon after the solstice, the rituals in this book will help him return to the mortal plane. He will appear and reward you well for guarding the keep in his absence."

A long pause followed.

"Liar." The ghosts spoke in one voice. "*Thieves.*"

"Fireballs!" Lyle yelled. "Now!"

"Aaaaaaaaah…" Justin blew his breath out and raised his hands. "You should probably duck."

The dwarf, thankfully, didn't question him and flung himself down. The ghosts surged forward at that, and Justin let loose with a fireball from one palm. It went straight through the first spirit but a moment later, the being shrieked and dissipated.

The others screamed.

He pointed at each distinct shape he could make out and fireballs erupted from his hands to tear long, ragged holes through the mass of ghosts. It was very much like smoke rings, he thought prosaically.

"Behind you!" his companion yelled.

Justin turned hastily enough that he tripped but thankfully, fireballs still worked when one was falling. Even the burst of pain along his side didn't stop the next one from streaking into his adversaries. As one rose into the air with a shriek and turned to arrow down, he shoved both hands out and—as he'd hoped—a larger fireball was launched.

The one he killed must have been the leader because the rest gave a final shriek and vanished through the walls.

PYROMANIAC, LEVELS 1-3, the game announced.

"I'll be damned," the AI said, "you did it."

He rolled his eyes and stood. "There we go. Let's get out of here with this thing."

"None too soon," the dwarf agreed. He banged through the main doors and went down the stairs faster than Justin would have thought possible. Lyle was apparently in no mood to stick around there. Nothing—not the dwarven stonework or the golden baubles—was enough of an incentive to keep him there.

Justin decided that was probably for the best. His mana bar was low, and he couldn't continue to shoot fireballs forever. He followed hurriedly as he tucked the book into his satchel. And, he reminded himself, he intended to get payment before he handed it over.

That, and maybe ask the mercenary to join their group. He had a good feeling about the man.

They made it to the door without any more spirits targeting them and Lyle practically wrenched it off its hinges to exit. It was still raining, which Justin acknowledged with a shiver and a flick of his hood over his head.

The mercenary waited exactly where they'd left him. He almost did look frozen in time, but when they approached, he raised his hooded head to look at them.

"You found it." Justin couldn't tell what the man thought of that.

"Yes." He folded his arms. "So, why did you want it?"

With only a smile, the mercenary vanished into thin air.

He stared at the place where he'd been and leaned sideways slightly, then leaned the other way. Although he narrowed his eyes in focus, he couldn't see the character at all.

"Do...do you still see him?" he asked Lyle in an undertone. This wouldn't be the first time a quest giver had glitched out of thin air in an MMORPG.

He'd better get the XP for this quest, though.

"No," the dwarf said. "He's gone. Didn't ye say that book taught ye magic?"

"Yes. I mean, a spell. Well, and the magic. And there are other spells." He brought up his inventory to make sure the book was still there. It was. "He'd have been able to become a wizard if he took it."

"Kid, sometimes you're real dumb," Lyle stated gruffly. He started down the road.

Justin hurried after him. "What does that mean?"

"A man vanishes into thin air and you say he could become a wizard? Wake up. He was one already."

He looked over his shoulder. "But why—"

"You want my advice, kid?" His companion shook his head. "What am I saying? Of course you don't want it. You opened a magic book and started reading. You went into a wizard's abandoned hideout. But if you *did* want my advice, I'd say this." He stopped and gave him a look. "Don't expect wizards to make sense. They're a nasty lot who've forgotten what it's like to be alive."

"Well, sure," Justin agreed. "But they also have castles full of beautiful serving girls."

The dwarf snorted. "I've seen what you humans think is beautiful and let me tell you, it's a miracle you ever have babies. Your women are all…" He gestured. "Spindly."

"Spindly?"

"And they have no beards!"

He spluttered with laughter. "Beards?"

"Only your men ever have beards," the dwarf said and grimaced with something close to distaste. "I call that unnatural."

Justin rolled his eyes and followed as he silently endured a monologue about beards and broad shoulders and whether or not a proper woman should be able to swing a battle-ax. His mind, however, was occupied with other things.

Was the man who had waited for them in the rain a wizard or was he more of an echo? He had seen him, heard his words, and retrieved the book. But if he was right about Kural, the wizard might have left something of himself behind to defeat Sephith.

Thoughtfully, he patted the book. However it had come about, he was glad it had—and for the first time, he looked forward to the next adventure.

CHAPTER TWENTY-ONE

Nick shifted to a more comfortable position in his chair and looked at the pod.

It had been one month since Justin had arrived. Although he hadn't woken up, his physical condition hadn't grown any worse and even Dr. Goli, who had come at the senator's request, grudgingly admitted that nothing was going wrong.

When PIVOT acquired Forever Echo, they'd been excited to be able to keep playing their favorite game. The AI had responded to the three of them, changed quests, opened different paths, and even learned one's language. It wasn't actually AI, of course, although the game developers had given it a deeply sarcastic way of responding to people.

Now, Nick thought they should probably write to the Forever Echo team and tell them what the game had become. It was saving lives.

"Helloooo." Amber snapped her fingers under his nose.

"Oh, sorry." He had rocked onto the back legs of his chair but now came down with a thump. "D'you want some champagne?"

"Maybe once we're turning a profit," she replied.

"Good call." He took a sip and made a face. "We'll be able to afford better champagne then."

Jacob snickered into his glass.

"No jokes," she said and pointed severely at them. "No celebrations. We've managed to keep the lights on and the pod running, but that's it. The three of us are living on bulk dehydrated noodles and we haven't been able to pay DuBois at all." She lowered her voice at the last statement but swept a hand in the direction of the doctor.

"Relax," Jacob told her. "I don't think he's noticed." He grinned. "I also don't think he sleeps." He cleared his throat. "And I know he doesn't shower enough." He waved a hand. "The point is, it's going fine. We'll be able to roll this out soon."

"Will we?" Amber leaned on the table to look at him. "The Williams have paid enough to run all this, but that was for us to break even—and, lest we forget, Justin *isn't improving*."

"He's interacting more fully with the game," Jacob pointed out. "He seems to be taking in more sensory input. He's learning various skills." Between the patient's long periods of unconsciousness, he had indeed shown an increased responsiveness to the game.

"He isn't waking up," she stated. "What's this worth if he doesn't wake up?"

"A ton of them don't wake up," he argued. "Some people lie in comas for years, Amber. Some of them…well, some of them die. We can't base this off one person and honestly? Even if he doesn't wake up, they've been able to get a message to him. He was able to send one back. We know now for a fact that people in comas can respond to a scenario that conscious brains can interpret. That's huge!"

"Right," she replied. There was panic in her eyes now. "Yes, of course it's wonderful! All we did was hook a comatose patient up to an experimental machine with no real proof of concept and no FDA approval! We won't go to jail at all."

"I think you have to be a doctor to get charged with medical malpractice," Nick said. Both his teammates glared at him and he shrugged. "I'm just saying. Justin's next of kin approved this, we have research that hasn't ever been overturned saying this was based on sound foundations…and he's still alive. I mean, that's a fair amount weighing in our favor."

Amber tipped her head back and covered her eyes with her hands.

"Amber." Jacob leaned forward on the table. "This was the right thing to do, right? We had a technology that could help someone, so we used it to help them. No matter what the law says, we did the right thing."

She pulled a chair out and sat, her shoulders hunched. "I don't doubt that we did the right thing. It's only… I used to think you could grow up, do the right thing, and people would *see* that you'd done the right thing and it would work out, right? But that isn't how it works. Look at DuBois."

The outside door opened and closed, and footsteps came down the hall toward them. When Senator Williams came into the kitchenette, he looked like he hadn't slept. His hair was disheveled and his eyes had bags under them. He gave a vague nod and moved to the coffee like a drone. When he couldn't find a cup, Nick could swear the man considered drinking out of the pot. He stood and put a mug in the senator's hand before he resumed his seat.

Tad drained the entire beverage. "Thank you," he muttered hoarsely. He rummaged in the cabinets and busied himself brewing a new pot.

"Is something wrong?" Amber asked tentatively.

"With Justin?" He looked up sharply. "He's all right, isn't he?"

"Justin is fine," she said patiently. "How are *you*?"

Williams sighed and leaned against the counter. "It's a…vote. Coming up."

The three PIVOT team members considered their response and made their decision together. When you'd been best friends for ten years, you tended to do that. They scooched their chairs together and Jacob went to get a fourth for the senator to sit.

Tad dropped into the chair with a nod. He was close to dead on his feet. "There's a measure coming before congress next week. On paper, it's boring. It merely reclassifies some types of emergency services."

"And yet," Jacob said with a theatrical flair, "I sense there's a dark side."

The senator gave him a look that suggested this was no joking matter, and from Jacob's wince, Amber had stomped on his foot under the table. She gestured for Williams to continue.

"The emergency procedures the paramedics used to keep Justin alive on the way to the hospital, things like that—they'd double in cost overnight as a result of their reclassification." The senator shook his head and chewed his lip. From the way it was cracking, he'd done that too much lately. "People already can't afford these things. We have a *good* insurance policy and it covers him for five hundred thousand dollars, but it wouldn't have lasted three months in the hospital after those procedures, and it would last so much less time after this bill. And that's not even including physical therapy or rehabilitation."

"So, it's a bad bill." Nick was confused. "Did they tack something onto it that you want or something?"

"No." The senator took a deep breath. "You see, they're trying to blackmail me."

Jacob had a very interested facial expression, which dissolved into a grimace when Amber kicked him again. "The plot thickens," he mouthed to Nick.

"Right after you came to talk to me the first time, the lobbyists came to ask me for a blank check. I told you that. What I didn't tell you was that they photoshopped some lovely photos of me and a woman at a hotel. Ultimately, I can have them analyzed and prove they are fraudulent, but that will take months and the damage will have already been done." The senator gave a dry laugh. "I tell you, what I wouldn't give to be out on dates instead of sifting through endless paperwork. With Mary, of course, but still." He lowered his head into one hand on the table, looked at the coffee machine to check its progress, and sighed. "And they have leverage—more leverage now."

"Oh?" Amber asked. She looked embarrassed by the silence but equally as embarrassed to have spoken.

"Insurance won't cover Justin's treatment," Tad told them. "They say it's experimental. Which means we have to pay out of pocket now." He looked at each one in turn. "We will," he assured them.

"That's not what we're worried about," she said, although Nick could see the worry in the set of her face. She would never let Justin's parents know how she felt about this, but Nick could see her panic rising.

"You should be," the senator said. He shook his head. "Because if I don't give the lobbyists what they want, my career in Washington is as good as over, and then where's the money to pay for anything?" He downed the last of the coffee in his cup and stared into space. "My constituents elected me to stop this kind of thing." They could tell he was speaking as much to himself as to any of them. "If I vote no, I lose my salary, I lose my reputation, I lose…" He looked into the other room and his face changed when he saw the pod. "And if I vote yes, they'll never re-elect me. And they shouldn't. I'll be another sellout. I'll be someone who backed the interests of the lobbyists over the people. So what am I supposed to do? What do I do with any of that, huh?"

Nick realized his hands were clenched and he wrapped them carefully around his mug. The three of them had spent the first four years of their adult life at MIT, believing that they were immersed in the toughest problems humanity had to solve. After that, it was the pressure cooker of Silicon Valley, where the money was endless and the next big idea was all anyone cared about. Both places had burned people out and had eaten them alive. He could name ten people off the top of his head who lived on the edge now and felt like failures for not establishing billion-dollar companies.

He hadn't thought politics was that bad. Honestly, he must have been naïve.

"We'll think of something," Jacob assured the senator. He nodded to his companions. "We'll find a way to get this covered and have the money taken care of, and…well, we aren't politicians, but we'll keep thinking about this, too. You shouldn't have to choose between your conscience and your son, sir."

The senator responded with a bitter smile. "I used to think the people who sold out were such greedy bastards," he said. "I wondered how they could go home at night and look their spouse in the eye, play with their kids, and feel like good people. Now I know what really went on."

"We'll find solutions," Jacob assured him again. "Come on, come see Justin. I'll tell you some of the progress he's made and Nick will bring you coffee as soon as it's ready."

They went into the other room to see the monitors DuBois was watching over, and Amber sighed.

"I sure hope we can live up to his promises," she said. "Now, if we can't do our jobs right, Justin dies *and* millions more people go into bankruptcy."

"We'll think of something," Nick told her. "I'm scared, too. When you were little, you thought you could do the right thing and it'd work out. Well, when I was little, I thought everything would work *itself* out. So clearly, I'm not the brightest bulb in the shed but also, Jacob is right. We both got here and we were able to help Justin." He nodded at her. "Right now, you're walking around looking like an aneurysm on legs and I'm downing a whole bottle of TUMS every night before bed, but we'll find the answers we need. I promise. We will."

CHAPTER TWENTY-TWO

The village of East Newbrook was deceptively far away from the mountain, and it took Justin and Lyle almost an hour to reach it. The lights glimmering through the rain seemed like an impossible promise until they finally stood at the swinging sign that announced the town limits.

If Riverbend had been a picture-perfect fantasy village, East Newbrook looked like it had been through the wringer. The houses were run-down, the walls crumbled, and the thatch had been haphazardly covered with mud, slate, and canvas. The only things that looked well-tended were strange little greenhouses outside almost every house.

Justin stopped to look at one. "What is that?"

"It's to protect the vegetables," Lyle explained. "What with those embers drifting down all the time, you can't eat anything you pick up. Around here, barns have four doors so you can have a safe way to open them, no matter how the wind is blowing, and all the vegetables are grown in those structures."

"They must be expensive," he said.

"The big explosion that caused the embers happened toward the start of the war between Sephith and Kural," his companion told him.

"Kural made sure everyone had these. Good thing, too. Sephith never would, that's for sure."

"Hey!" The shout came from an old man who hobbled to the fence to stare at them. "What're you looking at?"

"I'm new here," Justin explained in an attempt to placate him, "and my friend was explaining about the covering on your vegetable garden."

"It's not for sale," the man said and radiated unfriendliness.

"I'm not trying to buy, sir, merely looking around East Newbrook." He began to back away.

"Well, don't," the man told him. "I suggest you head back the way you came. You don't want to be here and we don't want you here."

Justin backed into the rain without answering and continued along the road. "These are not friendly people," he said to Lyle.

"Yer an outsider," the dwarf said with a casual shrug. "People don't usually like outsiders 'til there's coin involved."

"Good point." He looked around him. "Let's find the tavern."

"That's the first good idea you've had in days." His companion increased his pace. "This way."

He followed without protest. "How do you know where it is?"

"Always in the town square." The rain had begun to slow, and Lyle's voice floated through the patter. "Everyone wants a pint, don't they? Plus, with the rain gone, we might as well be inside."

The dwarf wasn't wrong. The tavern stood on the far edge of the town square. At the center were a fountain that didn't seem to have run for years and cobblestones that had not only grass growing between them but giant spikes of it and strange, nettle-like plants. Justin gave them a wide berth.

"Now, remember," he told his companion and slung an arm around his shoulders as they approached it, "we are not going to get in any fights with these people."

"I thought you said we were going to the tavern." Lyle sounded confused. "Didn't you say that?"

"Yes. But only to sell our goods, buy new supplies, and maybe have *one* pint," he cautioned. "No bar fights, Lyle. No breaking benches and especially not with other benches. We don't know the innkeeper here and I don't want to have to bargain you out of another jail."

The dwarf muttered a grumpy and inaudible response.

Inside, it was dark with smoke and Lyle disappeared almost immediately. With a sigh and a mental preparation for breaking up a bar fight later, Justin went to find the innkeeper or a merchant.

The man behind the counter was both, and he accepted the assortment of animal fur scraps, pieces of foraged plants, and giant cockroach carapaces with good humor. Justin, seeing the opportunity to ask a question he'd always wanted to ask, seized the moment.

"So, what do you do with all the things adventurers sell you?" he asked. He'd always imagined NPC merchants with piles of bone chips and beetle legs.

The game had anticipated this, though, and it was ready with its sarcasm. "We put them in the stew," the innkeeper explained. "I'd try today's, sir. We have plenty of jellyfish umbras. We had a visitor from the west, you see."

He swallowed painfully and tried not to throw up all over the bar. That was the most disgusting thing he'd ever heard.

Also, he now knew that the west of this settlement included a town called Silent Hill and stew made of jellyfish parts. He had begun to think it was the birthplace of all evil.

"Maybe later," he said. "Could I see what you have for armor?"

"Of course, sir." The innkeeper popped up a new menu, this one showing several pieces of leather armor. "I'm sure you'll find one to your liking in here."

"Thank you." He paged through until he found one that provided stats for both strength and mana regeneration. What he needed, he thought, was a one-handed sword—but he was getting ahead of himself. He didn't have all that much money right now.

With his new breastplate on—this one had less suspicious scorch marks on it—Justin ordered a piece of bread and cheese. He really wanted stew, but as the game now gave him tastes and smells, he was too nervous to try the concoction at this particular tavern.

"Ale?" the innkeeper asked.

"While you still have some, yes." After all, Lyle would probably drink them dry in an hour. They'd been on the road for two nights with not a single stop at a tavern. For all he knew, the dwarf had already purchased an entire barrel and was drinking out of the spigot.

One of the tavern wenches walked past with a tray of beers and Justin turned to stare. Video games had been doing fan service characters for years, of course, but it was rare that they were your size. Up close, the proportions looked a little more improbable, but he was willing to go with it.

When in Rome...

When she retraced her steps, he was ready with a smile. She stopped and curtsied. "Can I get you another ale, sir?"

"No need," he said and leaned on the bar. "The pleasure of speaking to you is enough."

She blushed and he felt a wave of both humor and annoyance. This was so easy in a game world—why wasn't it easy in real life? It seemed like when he spoke to women, he either managed to get completely tongue-tied or they simply walked away from him.

Which made buying groceries difficult, among other things.

"Why are you in town, sir?" She looked curiously at him.

"I'm here to kill the wizard," Justin said loudly. He smiled and lifted his ale to the waiting crowd. Hell, in the real world, he would never be the one who came back to a hero's welcome. He might as well get everything out of this game that he could.

To his surprise, the people at the tables began to mutter and cast him dark looks.

"I should go." The tavern wench tried to leave. ·

"Now, wait a minute." He leaned out to catch her hand. When she stopped, he felt a thrill. He was never brave enough to do things like this in real life. "Sephith has terrorized your people for years. Surely you should be happy to have someone kill him?" *Happy and maybe grateful.* If he was lucky.

The maid hesitated before she moved closer to speak in a whisper. "You don't understand, sir. Sephith can hear every word that is spoken in this valley. He is all-knowing and all-seeing. If we do not obey him—"

"What?" He leaned toward her. "If you do not obey him, what happens?"

"He takes those who do not obey to his tower." The maid looked terrified. "Them, and sometimes others, too. He demands that we give up our fellow villagers to him. We tried to resist at first, but it is better to choose rather than endure his revenge." She pulled away and said clearly and loudly, "I could never wish you luck in such an ill-advised venture, sir. It is an insult to all of us for you to threaten the wizard." She curtsied and left.

It was her way to protect herself, obviously. Justin reminded himself to see what she said when he returned after he'd killed the wizard. He would prove himself and they would see that they should have helped him. A little disgruntled, he took a bite of his bread and cheese and admitted to himself that he did not feel very charitable toward these villagers. Wasn't the playing character of a video game supposed to be the hero?

He had turned to the bar in a black mood when he felt a tap on his shoulder. He twisted to see a figure in a dark cloak.

"If you want to kill the wizard…" The voice was husky. "You can get in line. He's mine."

"The hell he is," Justin said. He stood and turned to face the stranger. "Why don't you look me in the eyes and tell me that, you coward."

The figure pushed back its hood to reveal a woman's face. She had dark hair and sharp features, as well as an all-black outfit that he couldn't see much of behind the cloak. She folded her arms over her chest.

"Who are you?"

"Who are *you*?" he countered.

"I asked first." She smiled and showed a great deal of teeth. "And before you start a bar fight, you might want to remember that I'm not the one who came in here and caused trouble."

He looked around and found the unfriendly gazes still fixed on him. He shrugged. "I'm Justin. What's it to you, whoever-you-are?"

"I'm Anna," the woman told him, "and if it's all the same to you, I'd rather not see another set of would-be heroes run up to that tower, only to come out as lich. It'll be hard enough to fight my way in there as it is. I don't need to fight your corpse too."

"You won't have to," he told her. "Because I'll kill him tonight. That ten gold is *mine.*"

She gave a derisive snort. "You can have your ten gold if that's what matters to you. I'll make sure to send it along when I get it. Of course, I can't do that if you're dead."

"Tell you what," Justin said. "Why don't we see who's better suited to this task? You and me, outside." No woman would beat him in combat. He had a sword and he had fireballs—he'd win decisively and he could continue with the quest. Maybe you got XP for dueling in this game.

A commotion ensued outside and someone shoved into the tavern. "Sephith is here!"

Screams followed this pronouncement. A few people tried to flee into the back of the inn, only for the innkeeper to march them toward the door. Everyone seemed terrified but resigned to the fact that they would have to face the wizard. He really had trained them to do his bidding.

Justin curled his lip. These people were pathetic and he intended to show them exactly how wrong they were to bow down to a wizard.

"Get out of my way," he said to the woman. He drew his blade. "I intend to kill the wizard."

"You'll end up like all the others," she all but spat at him. "Every single one of them was so determined to run out with their weapons drawn. You're a fool."

"And you're a coward like all the rest of them," he told her. "All talk and no action. I should have known." He looked around the bar. "Lyle!"

With a clatter from under one of the tables, Lyle rolled out and stumbled to his feet. "Hic—here! 'S there a fight?"

"The wizard's here," Justin called.

"Oh. Right." The dwarf ducked under the table again.

"No." Justin crossed toward him and caught him by the collar. "We'll fight him now."

"Shouldn't we learn more about him first?" his teammate argued.

"You really should," Anna said. She still had her arms folded.

"I didn't ask for any of your sage advice," he told her. "Now, why don't you stay in here while I take care of the wizard for you?"

Dragging Lyle behind him, he marched out into the town square.

CHAPTER TWENTY-THREE

When Mary arrived at the lab, she saw no other cars in the parking lot. She frowned as she exited the vehicle and carried her bags into the shadowy interior of the building. No more cars had followed them since the first night. As if realizing that the tactic hadn't worked, the lobbyists had returned to more effective strategies.

Threatening Justin's life indirectly.

Mary had no doubt that they were behind the insurance company denying coverage for Justin, even though they cited the reason as being experimental treatment. With his doctor weighing in and the relatively low costs, there had seemed to be hope that they would agree, but that was now well and truly dashed.

She marched down the hallway and her heart pounded in her chest. For some reason, she couldn't seem to get that to stop these days. She was always angry—at the lobbyists, at the girl who had crashed with Justin in her car, at the doctors for not being able to fix him, and even at Tad and herself, although she didn't know why. That was the problem with anger. The more you let it into your heart, the more it ate you from the inside out.

During all of this, she had avoided going to confession. Father

LeMarc was very kind. He had a way to straighten things in your mind. She knew that if she called at any time of day or night, he would be willing to meet and pray with her.

The problem was that she didn't need him to sort out what was in her head. She knew what lay below the anger and the emotion was the only thing holding her up in the crisis. As soon as the anger left, she would have only a terrible fear of all the possibilities and unknowns.

She pushed into the lab, prepared to see it empty and to be angry at the scientists, too. Instead, she saw the strange doctor hunched over the monitors as usual while he chewed a handful of popcorn. As she watched, he set his bag of popcorn down and began to type furiously, regularly consulting a set of notes.

Mary came closer. "How is he?"

Dr. DuBois looked at her. "Oh. It's you. Nothing is wrong." He looked at the screens, then at her. Consciously, he stopped typing. "What did you bring?"

"Oh." She began to take things out of the bags. "Some things from home. I know it's...silly. But I think it would do Justin good to have these things around him—it's only some toys, pictures of us, and old stuffed animals." She had managed not to cry while taking them out of storage, but it had been a close call. "Where can I set these?"

"Anywhere," he said confidently.

"Are you sure?" She had expected him to be more territorial about his lab. "I wouldn't think stuffed animals would be allowed."

"Every lab has stuffed animals," DuBois said vaguely as he typed a few more things. He took another mouthful of popcorn, saw her expression, and realized she needed more explanation. "You see, scientific equipment can be very finicky. Every lab has their rituals to keep them happy. Some use little figurines. Others use stuffed animals." He cleared his throat. "I assure you, we do not think this works. It's more of a...tradition."

"I find it charming." Mary set the toys out, smiling as she did so. She tended to think of scientists as people like Dr. DuBois with strange, inconsistent priorities and no grounding in the real world. The idea of them doing something as human as decorating their labs or trying to make machines work was endearing. She fought with her printer, and they fought with intricate scientific equipment.

She hoped they weren't fighting with the pod Justin was in. If they had as much trouble with it as she had with her printer, that would be a bad situation.

Her task complete, she looked at Dr. DuBois, who inspected one of the toys she had brought, a purple dragon with a figurine that rode it. He picked it up and seemed to take joy in the detail on its scales.

"Justin painted that," she told him. "He begged for the figurine and the paints for his birthday. He promised he would make something beautiful with it. We were surprised at how pretty it was. I guess he learned how to do all of this online from videos."

"He likes dragons?" the doctor asked her.

"Yes." It was pleasant to talk to someone who didn't judge this quite as harshly as her husband did. When she asked Justin about his video games, Tad always rolled his eyes and sighed. But sometimes, her son would light up when describing a particular game. "He always loved dragons. Some of his favorite children's books had them. We got him signed copies and stuffed animals. His favorite game was coming out with a new part this year and there would be dragons for players to ride. He was excited about it." She looked down and blinked her tears away. "I hope he gets to play it someday—wait, what are you doing?"

DuBois typed furiously on the keyboard.

"Well," he explained, "the game is quite adaptable. I should be able to add a dragon if there's an asset for it. Even if it's a rough asset, his brain fills the details in. Of course, I don't know if flying has been added as a mechanic yet. This will be a beta test, but we might be able to get in there." He added as if to himself, "That's if the wizard doesn't kill him. He should have taken that ally. I don't know where I went wrong there."

"If the wizard doesn't *what?*" Mary came to stare at the screen. She couldn't read any of the output, but this was where everything was happening. "Did you say the wizard might *kill* him? Couldn't that be deadly?"

"Oh. Ah." Dr. DuBois looked uncomfortable. "Um, well. Technically, yes." His eyes strayed to the monitor again.

"Don't look at the screen," she said. "Tell me what's going on!"

"What's going on is on the screen," he reminded her.

She had to admit he had a point.

The doctor sighed. "Let me start at the beginning. You see, the game—no, farther back. The AI—no. Well, the wizard—no."

Mary prayed for patience.

"You remember that the brain is most engaged when it believes the game is reality," DuBois said. "And the AI will respond to however you play, which increases that perception. Well, Justin is making some very interesting choices. For instance, he seems to have decided that fortune favors the bold."

She could not believe that. He had always loved stories with dragon riders and heroes but he had never been the kind of child who did bold things. She had waited for a rebellious teenager phase during which he would do things like take the family's car or stay out at parties, but that had never come.

Sometimes, she thought her husband would have been happier if Justin *had* done those things. If there had been actual fights, if he had challenged his authority, Tad would have recognized that. Instead, he sat silently while his father yelled at him. Justin didn't go out with girls Tad didn't approve of—in fact, he didn't go out with anyone at all. He didn't trash the house with parties. Instead, he simply played his games.

"Justin has never been…very bold," Mary told DuBois. She was sure the doctor must be mistaken about what he saw in the game. "Now that he knows a misstep in the game can cost him his life, he'll be careful with it."

He didn't look at her. She didn't know it, but he thought furiously about what she had said. He had been torn about communicating with Justin at all. Telling him outright that the game wasn't real could have had disastrous impacts on his ability to get into it, after all. But Amber had pointed out that he already believed it was a game and that telling him about the potentially deadly effects would draw him in.

DuBois had to admit that she'd been right. Still, it was interesting to see Justin being so bold and so reckless, given what Mary had told him.

"What is he doing now?" she asked.

"Right now, he's sleeping." He pointed to some of the output on the screen. "Only a few days of game time have elapsed, and that's only a few hours to him. He's still healing, which means he needs to sleep a lot, and since the game responds to his active input if he falls asleep, it merely waits for him to wake up."

Mary nodded. She didn't understand games but she assumed this was like falling asleep while reading a book.

The doctor heaved a sigh. "As I said, the game is responsive to the player's choices and Justin is behaving as if he's much stronger than he is." He tapped a few keys and another screen opened, filled with numbers that were equally incomprehensible to her. "This is the enemy Justin will face soon. When he behaves more boldly, the game adjusts the wizard to be stronger."

"Well…" She shook her head. "The game must be misunderstanding."

"It isn't," DuBois told her. "These are his choices. He is seeking the limits of the game, and by seeking them, he is pushing them. The game is becoming more difficult. That appears to be what he needs right now."

She stared at him, a little nonplussed. Given what she knew of him, she hadn't expected philosophical insight. "Are you suggesting that…children need limits and consequences?"

He looked at her as if she were crazy. "I'm saying that Justin's recovery depends on him activating his survival instincts," he said, "and the game will make itself as difficult as it needs to be to convince him he's in mortal danger."

Ah. So it had been science, after all, and not philosophy. That made more sense.

Mary's brain caught up with her and she realized what he had said.

"Wait—you're telling me that…Justin is pushing this until he *believes* he will die?"

"It would appear so." DuBois looked around. "Where did I put my popcorn?"

"Forget the popcorn! I know my son, and he's not one to walk into danger for no good reason."

"Oh, people never do things for no reason," the doctor told her. He found the bag of popcorn and began to select a careful ratio of caramel, cheese, and plain popcorn. "Even when the reason makes no sense to you, it does make sense to them. Trust me, I know. People always do strange things like lying and handicapping themselves."

For a split-second, she thought she could see the world as DuBois saw it. She thought of the little white lies that were part of everyday life and the way people refused to ask for what they wanted or tell the truth.

But no matter how the world looked, one thing was true. "I don't want him in danger," she said.

"He is in danger," DuBois said. "And it's necessary that he understand that. Humans can believe all manner of lies. He has to understand the danger he's in and believe it—then he can begin to wake up." He shrugged. "Or so my research suggests."

"So it *suggests?*" Mary wanted to tear her hair out. "Look, this is dangerous and I don't like an AI to make decisions. Can't you help him?"

"I tried," the doctor said. "I really did. I gave him a new party member, you see, someone who could help him fight the wizard."

"And?" She folded her arms and glared at him.

He seemed impervious to glares and merely shrugged. "They didn't hit it off. I don't think he likes her, which is weird because he seemed to like many of the tavern wenches. So I thought maybe he'd like a woman as a party member." He shook his head, baffled. "I even made her very much like him. It did *not* work."

Mary turned in a circle. She was fairly sure she would scream.

"Oh, he's waking up." DuBois sounded pleased.

"He's—well, *do* something!"

"I am going to do something," he said. He held out the bag of popcorn to her. "I'm going to watch. Popcorn?"

CHAPTER TWENTY-FOUR

The entire village was outside, incongruously dressed in cloaks now that the rain had stopped. Embers drifted on the wind again—beautiful, if you didn't know what they were. The people crowded close to the fountain in the middle of the square. Half seemed to have decided it was safer to look down, while others looked up unwillingly at the man above them.

Sephith's age was difficult to determine. His hair was still a glossy brown, tied back from the sides of his head in ornate braids. He would have looked like one of the elves from Lord of the Rings if it weren't for his clothing. It was black, ornate enough to show his wealth and faintly ragged enough to suggest decay and violence. Knives were thrust into his belt together with a rusty flail, both of which had old blood on them.

The wizard looked around with an expression of utter contempt. He saw the villagers before him and he hated them intensely. It was abundantly clear to Justin that he did not simply use them as toys—he *wanted* them to suffer.

"Certain thoughts and words have reached my ears," Sephith announced. His voice was amplified to boom around the town square. "Some of you are plotting to kill me. You believe that your pathetic lives have worth and that your feeble attempts to kill me will come to fruition. You wish to rally your people to attack me together."

There was a murmur of dissent. No one wanted to speak out too openly but people shook their heads as if they tried to assure the wizard that nothing was afoot that he should be angry about.

"Do not deny it," Sephith snapped at them. "You know what you must do. When someone speaks against me, you are to mete out justice in this very square. You are to keep the peace rather than let rebellion foment and spread. But have you done so?"

A tense silence followed his challenge.

"Or have you decided to protect the heretics among you?" he asked. "I think you have."

Justin was done with this speech. He began to push toward the front of the group. Someone caught his hand but he shook their grasp away. He intended to do this and he wouldn't let anyone stop him.

"I am a kind master," Sephith said. "Far kinder than you deserve. In the west, whole villages have their minds enslaved. They live only to serve wizards and are killed on a whim. Do I do such things? No. I kill only when my experiments require it and to keep the peace."

A little impatiently, Justin shoved people out of his way. They didn't seem to want to move but he wouldn't let them continue to be cowards. This man was a bully and a game boss, and he was determined to get the XP and the ten gold for defeating him, stat.

"And because you continue to force my hand," Sephith said, "I must keep the peace now. I require three lives to atone for this rebellion. Three, and my anger shall be sated. You may choose which three to give me."

The village erupted into cries for mercy. People shoved Justin out of the way as they crowded close to the fountain. They fell to their knees and stretched imploring hands to the wizard as they begged piteously for mercy in a community appeal.

"There shall be no mercy," Sephith thundered. "I gave you mercy when I let you live your pathetic lives without slave crowns on your heads and this is the thanks I get for that mercy. No, mercy only causes rebellion. If it is justice you require, it is justice I will give you."

Someone pulled Justin back sharply and a figure in all black pushed past him. Anna had her gaze fixed on the wizard and she muttered something under her breath. One hand hovered near the hilt of a dagger at her belt.

"Oh, no you don't." He clutched her cloak and yanked. She stumbled back with a yelp and the two of them struggled. They were close to evenly matched and for a few furious seconds, the sound of the crowd faded and all he could hear was the rasp of their breath and the regular dings as his Grappling skill updated itself.

"He's *mine*," she whispered in a tone close to a hiss. "You know nothing about him. You'll get yourself killed!"

"If you intended to kill him, you would have done it already," he retorted sharply. "You're all talk."

"And you only care about the glory!" Anna ducked under his arm and pushed to the front of the crowd. When he grasped her arm to haul her back, she twisted expertly out of his hold. "These people deserve more than to have you save them so you can kiss the tavern wenches!"

"You're merely angry no one wants to kiss *you*. And they don't want to kiss you because you're insufferable!"

She grinned at him. "I could say the same of you, couldn't I?"

That retort stung. Justin jerked away. "Screw you." He shoved her into the crowd, only for her to shove him in return.

The force of their physical exchange was enough to thrust the two of them onto a patch of open ground in front of the wizard.

Justin didn't wait. He was done with waiting and with pussy-footing around. Determined, he drew his sword and turned to face the villagers.

"Don't you hear his lies? He's the one with his foot on your neck and every time he lifts it a little, he tells you he's the one who saved your life. It isn't *mercy* to not enslave you. It isn't *justice* to take people when someone speaks out against him." He lifted his sword into the air. "Today, you'll see how a wizard *should* be dealt with."

He turned and lunged at the wizard. It was clear a moment into the jump that he wouldn't successfully stab Sephith in the heart, but there were other targets he could reach. He angled his sword toward the groin, decided at the last moment that he wasn't ready to do that to another man, and pointed slightly down to catch the wizard in the thigh.

The strike never connected. In fact, he didn't seem to have moved any closer to the wizard at all. Sephith held one hand out, the palm facing Justin, who remained suspended in midair.

"What a display of strength and justice," Sephith drawled. "As if you would recognize either, adventurer."

Something roared past Justin and he would have jumped if he'd been able to move at all. As it was, his heart apparently tried to leap sideways out of his chest and was, fortunately, stopped by his ribcage.

Anna's spell exploded around Sephith, and for an instant, the outlines of a magical shield were visible and gleamed in facets like a dragon's scales. She gave a triumphant yell and Justin was about to shout that she hadn't done any good at all when he saw what she'd intended.

At the center of her spell, surrounded by the explosion that had weakened Sephith's shields, had been a blade made of magic. It appeared that magic, like everything else, was vulnerable to a direct strike in a very small area. Propelled forward by the strength of the blast, her magical blade had burst through the shields. It hadn't gone far but it had drawn blood.

There was a moment of pure, terrified silence. The wizard raised his other hand to touch the blood on his cheek and looked at her with the coldest expression Justin had ever seen.

"That," he said quietly, "was a mis—"

Anna threw another spell without warning. The air around her target exploded once more and this time, he tumbled back. He snarled as he righted himself and rather than float, he stood instead on the rough cobblestones. The villagers pushed and shoved each other to get away.

She advanced as she hurled her next spell, followed closely by another. When she finally drew her daggers and surged at Sephith, the wizard was so distracted that his free hand faltered and Justin immediately plummeted.

"Ow," he protested from where he sprawled in a hard landing. He looked up as Sephith made a wrenching movement with one hand and Anna's knife was ripped from her fingers to hover in the air between them. It began to glow, first a dull orange and then cherry-red, before it turned white-hot and the metal splattered onto the stones. She jumped away with a cry of pain.

"This is what your defiance has earned you!" Sephith yelled. He advanced and held a roiling cloud of darkness between his two hands.

"For Stouthooooooooold!" yelled a gruff, familiar voice. The crowd scattered as Lyle burst out of cover and ran toward the wizard, his fists up and ready.

Sephith jerked aside. The black cloud in his hands disappeared as the dwarf plowed sideways into him and Justin gave a reflexive snort of laughter at the look of surprise on the wizard's face. He toppled sideways, only for his attacker to jump into the fray with his fists swinging.

"Ye can't punch a spell," Lyle yelled, "but ye can punch a wizard! Who's with me?"

For a moment, Justin thought the people around him might join the fight. If the dwarf had continued to win, he was sure they would have. They had feared the wizard for a very long time and he had killed God only knew how many of their friends and family. With Lyle inflicting real damage, they were ready for revenge.

Unfortunately, Sephith was as powerful a wizard as the stories claimed. An explosion ripped through the town square like a thunderclap and the dwarf catapulted away. He struck the side of the tavern with a deep thud and slid down to lie still.

"Lyle!" Justin yelled. Fury filled him and he pushed to his feet to attack.

"Look out!" a female voice yelled, and Anna tackled him sideways.

"Let me up!" He shoved her away. "God, you can't let *anyone* else—"

Then he saw what she'd pushed him away from. Sephith floated once more and the air around him was wreathed in green and black flames that were so hot, they melted the cobblestones. The heat wasn't as bad as it should be only a few feet away, but he still winced and the people cowered with cries of pain and fear.

"You have one day," the wizard boomed. "Be grateful I only ask for three lives in recompense for this rebellion. True justice would be far harder on all of you. If you do not send three sacrifices to my tower within a day, I shall take one from every family in the village."

He disappeared with a thunderclap, and the flames vanished with him. Justin edged forward slightly, saw that the cobblestones truly were melted, and wanted to throw up. He had almost been in the path of those flames. Without a doubt, he had very nearly been melted the same way the stone had.

Who was he kidding? He wouldn't even have melted and would simply have gone up in flames. His skin prickled.

The villagers were crying. Young children buried their faces in their parents' shoulders while townspeople argued between themselves, hissing names and accusations at one another. Anna walked quietly to where the remains of her dagger had cooled and become an inextricable part of the cobbles. Only the hilt of the weapon was recognizable.

Justin stared at the tower in the distance. His hatred was so intense that he forgot anything else for a while. Then, reality clicked in.

"*Lyle!*" With a curse, he ran to find his friend.

CHAPTER TWENTY-FIVE

"Interesting," DuBois said. "*Very* interesting."

"What's interesting?" Mary was sure she would lose her mind. She couldn't read the little lines of code that continually appeared on the screen, and the doctor kept forgetting to interpret them. Sometimes, she thought he was not telling her on purpose so that she wouldn't get worried about Justin, but that only made her paranoid when he genuinely forgot to translate.

"He survived his first encounter with the wizard," he said and stretched a little to pat her hand. "That's good."

"His...first encounter? He didn't beat the wizard?" She was fairly sure the character was supposed to be dead at the end of this, although that seemed bloodthirsty on her part.

"No," DuBois said. "I didn't expect that he would. What's interesting is that he and the two group °members are functioning as a team. They don't like each other but it is going fairly well." He swallowed more popcorn before he continued. "Also, he's beginning to get more deeply invested in the game world. I don't see any of his joke dialogue." He saw her confusion. "He used to say things that showed he knew it was a game but he hasn't said those as much."

"That's good, right?"

"That's very good," he assured her. "In fact—uh-oh."

***-

Lyle lay inert outside the tavern. Justin shoved villagers out of his way as he ran to his side and lowered his head to listen for breath. He couldn't see his teammate's sides moving.

Then, with a groan, the dwarf rolled onto his back and uttered a snore. Justin jerked back. His heart pounded with relief but the snore sounded like a water buffalo breathing through oatmeal. He had begun to wonder how he had managed to get a single moment of sleep since getting there.

"Lyle?" He shook the dwarf's shoulder and craned to check if there was any blood in his hair. He didn't see any. Maybe dwarves were built more sturdily than humans. "Lyle, wake up."

It occurred to him how weird it was to try to wake an injured person in the game while he lay comatose in a bed somewhere.

That was strange. For the duration of the fight, he had forgotten entirely that this was a game at all. When Sephith had held him suspended and melted the rocks, he had been furious, terrified, and ready for action—and there hadn't been any room in his mind for disbelief.

He shook his head. Now wasn't the time for that. Right now, Lyle needed help.

"Is he all right?" Anna asked. She had come to stand at his side.

"Yes," he said shortly. *No thanks to you.* "Help me get him up."

She came to loop Lyle's other arm around her shoulders and the two of them levered him upright. The dwarf's head flopped onto her shoulder before it lolled forward so his chin rested on his chest. He seemed half awake and stumbled as they walked him into the tavern. Sometimes, his feet found purchase on the ground but at other times, he seemed to sink into unconsciousness again.

Both Justin and Anna were panting by the time they got inside. Dwarves were heavy. Frankly, he was surprised the wall of the tavern didn't have a Lyle-shaped hole in it.

"I need to see a healer," he called. "The dwarf was injured fighting Sephith."

The innkeeper had come inside after the wizard disappeared and he gave them a dark look. "You troublemakers can get out of here. It was your meddling that made Sephith come in the first place."

"Now wait a minute," Anna said heatedly. "*He's* the one who ran his mouth. I showed up weeks ago and haven't caused any problems for anyone."

"Until now, you mean?" The man shook his head.

"Well, what's your long-term plan, then?" Anna snapped. "You'll simply wait while he picks the whole village off by twos and threes? Someone needs to deal with him!"

"I was *trying*," Justin said.

"Oh, shut up," she told him. "You made a big speech, gave him time to get ready, and ran straight at him with the worst sword I've ever seen."

He couldn't come up with a good retort to this and was thankfully saved by the tavern wench, who came to clear a table. She gestured for them to lay Lyle on it. Without seeming to care about the innkeeper's glare, she checked for a pulse and pulled his eyelids up.

"I thought so," she said finally. She wiped her hands on her apron. "Your friend's not hurt. He'll be fine."

"Then…why won't he wake up?" Justin asked. That seemed to be the million-dollar question these days.

"He's drunk," the wench said. She looked at Lyle and sighed. "I had my suspicions after how much he drank before the wizard got here."

"That was only ten minutes."

"And ten minutes is enough for a dwarf to put away half a barrel." She shrugged. "He'll be fine. I'm not saying he won't feel that hit on his head tomorrow, but he'll feel the drink worse."

Justin smiled and strolled toward her, but her expression turned stony.

"And my father's right. You should all leave."

He looked at Anna, who smirked. "Not a word," he told her.

"I'll be damned," she said. "That tavern wench isn't as easy a mark as I thought."

The sound of the crowd grew louder, and before he had a chance to respond, people streamed into the tavern. They shouted as one when they saw Lyle, Anna, and Justin.

"There they are!" someone yelled.

The crowd roared approval.

"I don't think I like this," Justin remarked.

"You really pissed them off," Anna told him.

"*I* pissed them off?"

"Yes, *you*. If you hadn't—" She stopped as the crowd pressed closer and looked at them, tight-lipped. "Yes?"

"Sephith wants three people," one of the men said. He pointed at them. "And we have three people right here, don't we?"

Uh-oh. Justin held his hands up. "Let's be reasonable. The three of us right here are the ones who can save you from the wizard."

"You didn't, did you?" the man asked. He turned to look at the crowd. "These three came here, started speaking against Sephith, and angered him! He came to take vengeance because of them. Why should any of us suffer for that?"

"Um…" He was forced to admit that this was a good point, but he wasn't stupid enough to say so out loud. He looked at his teammate. "Lyle!" Nothing was forthcoming, not even a snore. Regretting the necessity, he looked at Anna. "Any ideas?"

She cleared her throat nervously. "The wizard gave you a day," she told them. "There's time to discuss this. And, by *this*, I don't mean who to send as sacrifices but who to send as an attacking force."

Justin nodded. "As the lady asked, is your plan to live in constant fear and be picked off one by one when Sephith wants his fun?"

People looked at one another and muttered.

"We drove him away from here," Anna said and had warmed to the theme. "Other adventurers went into his tower alone and all of them failed, but the three of us managed to hurt him. If he could have killed us, he would have done it, wouldn't he? But he ran away. The more people we have, the better our chances."

"So, you did need us," he said in an undertone. "All that stuff about him being yours to kill?"

"You're not helping," Anna snapped in an undertone. "And that's a fair amount of big talk for someone who spent most of the fight stuck in midair until I distracted him enough to drop you!"

"That tower is full of his thralls," the leader told them. "Traps. Spells. You won't beat him and neither will we."

"So we lure him out!" Justin called. "Listen to me. *Listen* to me. I can help you."

The crowd hesitated, then began to advance on them.

"Fuck," he muttered. He threw a look at Anna. "This is all your fault."

"You know what, you're right." She gave him a venomous smile. "If it weren't for me, you'd be dead in a pile of ash right now and you wouldn't be dealing with this problem."

"You're insufferable," he told her.

"Well, look on the bright side," she told him. "At least you're taking me down with you."

***

Tad went to the lab straight from his last meeting of the day. He knew Mary had intended to go past the PIVOT offices and he wanted to make sure all was well. It made him a little anxious that he hadn't heard from her at all.

As he moved down the hallway, he could hear her in an intense discussion with Dr. DuBois, and he began to hurry. If something was wrong—

He couldn't bear to think of that.

When he burst into the room, Dr. DuBois was stabbing at the screen as he tried to explain something to Mary. She argued with him, although there was doubt in her voice. Neither of them had noticed him. He tilted his head to the side and narrowed his eyes as he moved quietly closer.

"But if they're sacrifices, they'll arrive at the tower with a significant disadvantage," she said.

Tad grimaced. He had not expected to hear his wife say that sentence.

"It gets them there as a group," DuBois countered, "which is good for Justin and Anna to bond."

"Bond how?" she asked suspiciously. "Please tell me he won't fall in love with a…video game…fake…made-up woman."

That sounded more like his wife. He adjusted his tie and waited.

"Bond as a comrade in arms," the doctor explained patiently. "I still don't quite understand the problem with that. He's ascribing very negative motivations to her. Of course, she's doing the same to him. Then again, she does have some basis for it. Maybe…he feels differently about female warriors than he feels about tavern wenches."

"That seems likely," Tad interjected.

Both looked at him.

"Tad!" Mary came to give him a hug and a kiss.

"Are you debating aspects of the game?" he asked. He slid an arm around her. "I never thought I'd see the day."

"It's complicated." She pointed to a pad of paper where she'd written notes about the game. He could see phrases such as *xp loss for dead villagers* and *debuff = handicap*. "The game isn't only one thing. It responds to what Justin does. That means the way he solves problems and the way he behaves can affect things down the line. It's not only about having a big sword. He needs allies, too."

"Ah." Tad sat with a sigh of relief. He was exhausted and he still had no idea what to do about the lobbyists. Right now, he simply tried not to think about it.

"Your son's imagination is remarkable," DuBois told him. "He sees layers behind the story and they begin to exist because he *creates* them. The game he is playing is richer because *he* is the one playing it."

He frowned. "The game isn't all…programmed?"

"It adapts," the doctor replied. "Its algorithms are truly incredible. Justin's interest and hunches have shaped a whole piece of the narrative in a way that may give him significant advantages. He isn't… entirely behaving like a hero. Yet. But he has a sense of purpose. He doesn't like simply standing around while people get away with things. He could technically have done anything on this quest—tried to bargain with the wizard, tried to take the village over and make the people his slaves instead of Sephith's. He's trying to save them, and he's invested in his friends surviving as well."

Mary noticed Tad's expression. "What's wrong?"

"He's…building all of this." He tried to clear his throat but there was a lump in it. "You remember when we'd go down to the river sometimes and—no, not *that*. And just read? You'd get books from the library sales for five cents and we'd climb into that tree and sit all afternoon."

"I'd forgotten that." She smiled at him. "We read some awful books."

"And some really good ones," Tad said. "I loved books like this—whole different worlds. I could never make something like that up. Justin can, though."

"Yes." Mary was still smiling at the memory when she turned to look at the pod. "He knows it's a game but he isn't simply going through the motions. He's building it. But he always did that kind of thing. Do you remember the stories he would make up for his friends in the one with the dice and the figurines?"

"No," Tad said.

"Oh, notebooks and *notebooks* full of stories. There are some at home."

"How could I never have seen that?" He moved to the pod. "How did I…just…not notice at all?"

Mary said nothing. She came to take his hand and he squeezed hers as he looked over the top of her head at DuBois.

"I want to send another message to him," Tad said.

"Justin knows you love him," she said.

"We haven't heard anything after the last one." He shook his head. "What if he didn't get it? I need to speak to him. I need to tell him—so many things."

Wordlessly, DuBois handed him the keyboard and he sat and began to type.

CHAPTER TWENTY-SIX

The cart jostled over the roads. It seemed as though a new pothole appeared every few seconds, each one bigger than the last and able to send the cart in a new direction. It would appear that Sephith didn't spend very much on the infrastructure in the valley.

Justin supposed it was the kind of thing that happened when you were able to fly everywhere you went. He flexed his fingers and scowled.

"For the last time," Anna said, "stop doing that." She and Justin were bound back to back with their hands and arms tied together. The situation was not one either of them was pleased about.

"I'm not trying to grope you!" he retorted. "I'm trying to maintain blood flow to my fingers. They're going numb. I swear if I wake up and I lost a hand—"

"You're already awake, genius."

"Whatever." He fought the urge to wrench at the bindings with every ounce of his strength. All it would accomplish would be to pull Anna over, and if she went, so would he—at which point, there was no way he could see that they'd manage to get upright again.

In the corner of the wagon, trussed to the side like a turkey, Lyle snored. Whatever he was dreaming about made him smile.

"I still say you wouldn't ever have gotten into that tower on your own," Justin said finally.

"Who says that was my plan?"

"You, when you marched up to me in the inn and told me Sephith was yours."

Anna didn't say anything to this.

"You go on about stupid choices, but if you'd come to me and asked to help, we wouldn't be in this situation," he pointed out.

"Yeah, well, we wouldn't be in this situation if you had asked around to see if anyone else was planning to kill Sephith either. You knew you weren't the only one who had been sent."

"If you were the last one the mayor of Riverbend sent, I can see why he sent me, too," he responded acerbically. After a moment's silence, he abruptly felt bad. "Look. I'm...I'm sorry. You're good with magic. You're probably good with daggers, too."

"When they don't melt." Anna sounded like she was trying not to cry, but she carried the joke off well enough. "And I suppose you should know—the mayor didn't send me. Also, my name isn't Anna. It's Zaara."

It took Justin a moment to place the name. "*Zaara?*" He tried to scramble and twist and almost made them tip over. "Fuck, ow. Wait. You're the mayor's daughter?" He craned to look at her with new respect. "You escaped the wizard...and you're going back to kill him? That's...kinda cool, actually."

Zaara gave an unwilling chuckle. "I wish. If I'd escaped, I would know what was in that tower. No, I...ran away." When she caught sight of his frown, she explained, "To kill the wizard."

"Then why does your father think you were kidnapped?"

"He doesn't but he's embarrassed because I ran off." She shrugged, a motion that yanked the rope on Justin's arms and made him hiss with pain. "If he says I went to fight Sephith, people will ask why he didn't send anyone with me. But if he says I ran away, they'll ask why. So he's trying to get adventurers to help without telling them what's going on." She blew out an annoyed breath. "Let me tell you that you don't know how little you should trust some men until you hear them discussing how a woman should repay them for being rescued. They had no idea I was listening when they said it."

"What did they say when you told them?" He was interested but could feel his cheeks burning with the knowledge that he might have said something similar.

"I didn't," Zaara said. "I was going to ask their help and tell them what I knew of Sephith, but when I heard that, I didn't. And the next day, they went off to the tower and got themselves killed. I feel kind of bad about that one."

"Well...they did go into the tower," he pointed out.

"Yes, but I could have helped and I didn't."

"They didn't ask." He shrugged, then paused. "I would have gotten killed, wouldn't I?"

"Cheer up," Zaara told him. "You still might."

That surprised a laugh out of him. The more she spoke, the more he was curious about her. "Why did you do it? Run away, I mean."

The three members of the PIVOT team were hard at work when DuBois chuckled quietly. Nick looked up from his financial spread-sheets as the doctor leaned closer to the screen with another low laugh.

"Here we go," the man said. He stretched his hand sideways without looking, picked up a new bag of popcorn, and opened it with his gaze fixed on the monitor. As he watched the readouts on the screen, he began to eat.

Jacob watched him for a moment, put another tick on the popcorn consumption chart, and went back to his schematics.

Justin listened as Zaara explained her history. Her father had wanted her to marry well—perhaps go to the city and marry a lord—so he had paid for every type of tutor he could think of. She knew how to play a lyre and a harpsichord, could speak three languages, had been taught to keep household accounts, could recite several entire epic poems by heart, and knew every court dance.

These things, however, had bored her. Although she enjoyed dancing, she had convinced the instructor to teach her tumbling as well. When her mathematics tutor ran out of accounting to teach her, she had asked the woman to teach her cryptography.

On her own, she had studied magic, thinking she might someday find a way to rid the nearby valley of the drifting embers. Although she had never gotten far enough to do that, she was able to do several spells, as Justin had seen. She had even bribed the blacksmith to give her an old, battered knife so that she could study how to wield daggers from one of the books in her father's library.

As the daughter of the town's mayor, Zaara had the freedom to do almost anything she wanted, but when her father found out about the lessons, he put a stop to them. Although Yannick, her elder brother, was allowed to continue his studies, she was expected to confine herself to ladylike pursuits.

When news of Sephith's triumph had come to Riverbend, she was only twelve. Wizard duels were few and far between but usually, a wizard did not try to take over additional territories, so no one worried very much. There were scattered reports of Sephith's cruelty, but it had only been earlier that year when word reached Riverbend of the abductions.

Yannick and Zaara had both begged their father to send someone to help East Newbrook. Unlike the villagers there, he could send word to one of the cities. He refused to help, however. Finally, he grudgingly posted a sign for an adventurer, but none of those sent ever returned.

"It needed a big expedition," she said. "But he wouldn't organize one, no matter how much we told him to. I didn't even think of going until he told me not to bother thinking about it because it wasn't my place. Then…I lost my temper."

Justin laughed. "You did it because he told you to stay out of it?"

"Not only because of that!" Zaara protested. "I knew how to wield daggers and cast some spells. I thought I would go to East Newbrook and wait for all the other adventurers to arrive. I would convince them to wait until we had enough numbers, and *then* we'd go. Plus, I assumed if I went, my father might send more people." She sighed. "I guess he still thinks one person can fix this. Either that or he doesn't care if I come back."

"I know how that goes," he said quietly.

She looked over her shoulder at him. "Did you run away, too?"

"Not...exactly." He tried to think about how he could explain his circumstances. "I'm far from home right now, and I'm not sure if my parents want me to come back." He swallowed. "I wasn't the son they wanted. I would play games with my friends. In the tavern, I would talk to people from all over the world. I heard amazing stories. I learned to trust people with my life, and each of them taught me something. My parents wanted me to have a trade, though."

"It's hard," Zaara said, "when your parents want one specific thing for you. They block your chance to do anything else and then what are you supposed to do? I don't want to marry a lord. I like East Newbrook and don't want to wear uncomfortable dresses and embroider all day."

"I don't want to argue cases in court," Justin agreed and sighed. He couldn't say he'd gotten very far with his choices, though. "Would you change anything? Now that you know how it ends?"

"It's not over yet, adventurer." Her voice was gentle. She considered his question. "But...yes. I think I would change one thing. I never said goodbye to my father. I wish I had." She looked down, silent as the carriage jounced down the road.

He was trying to think of something comforting to say when his wrist vibrated.

"What's that?" Zaara asked.

"It's my magical apple watch," he told her. "Uh—never mind. Look, can you feel the medallion on my wrist?"

"I think...yes. The circular one?"

"Yes." He stretched his wrist as far to the side as he could.

"Ow—ow! My shoulder doesn't bend like that."

"It's only for a moment," he promised her. He tilted his wrist so he would be able to see the message, then asked her, "Could you press the jewel in the center?"

"Does this get us out of our ropes?" Zaara asked in a hopeful whisper.

"If it did, we wouldn't still be tied together. No, it's…I'll explain later. Just press it."

She did, and the rest of the world froze as a blank white screen came up. He stared as script popped up. It wasn't the handwritten script he had grown accustomed to in this world but instead, the very regular typeface of a computer.

Justin, the note read. *I don't know how much time has passed in the game. Dr. DuBois says it's not very much. We miss you, though.*

I want to apologize to you. I don't think I ever told you what Mary's father said to me when I was eighteen. He said I would kick myself forever if I realized I hadn't been the man I could be. I hadn't had any focus in life before that. I only cared about shooting pool and drinking beers with my friends, but that comment made me shape up.

Justin sighed. While he hadn't heard that particular story, he'd heard versions of it. He didn't expect much from the rest of this letter.

It has been difficult to watch you sitting around, playing games. I wanted you to succeed and live up to your potential. It has taken this experience to make me see that you always were. I have listened to Dr. DuBois speaking about how these games work, how you can be a hero by creating a team around you and learning new skills. I think of how I heard you laughing when you played the games or of how you used to tell your mother about the stories you came up with for your games with friends.

Your video games aren't like me playing pool. I always thought I wanted you to grow up and achieve your potential, but what I was looking for was for you to have a life like mine. You weren't born to be a politician—although Dr. DuBois tells me that you're not too bad at enlisting help if you put your mind to it. When you wake up, I have a problem I could use your take on.

He blinked his eyes rapidly when he felt tears welling in them. Of all the things he had thought his father might say, he'd never imagined this. He'd never thought this was even within the realm of possibility.

All of us have things that are important to us, and one of those things for you is video games. I look forward to learning more about the games you play. I see now that loving you means loving all of who you are, not only the parts I understand.

One thing I always admired about you was your problem-solving ability. When you were little, there was nowhere we could hide the cookies that you wouldn't find them and get to them. We always bought your presents on Christmas Eve because you could find them otherwise. Whatever puzzles or trials you face in this game, you can overcome them the same way. Good luck and know that we are fighting for you as hard out here as you are fighting in there.

Also, your mother says not to fall in love with any tavern wenches.

Love, Dad

Justin laughed and exited the message. The world around him unfroze and the jostling resumed.

"Did anything happen?" Zaara asked. "I pressed it. Should I press it again?"

"No. Not yet." He chewed his lip. "Give me a minute. I'm thinking."

"I don't think we're all that far from the tower," she told him, "so think quickly."

He should have left the message up. Lesson learned. Justin considered the insights that had come from it.

His father had often told him about how he was aimless and had no ambition in his teenage years, but he had never listened. In large part, his refusal to listen was because he knew the man would follow up that story with an admonition for him to be strong, play touch football on the weekends, and get a wife and kids immediately.

Justin had never paused to think that maybe his father wanted him to start doing all those things because his life had gotten better when he had listened to the advice he wanted to impart to his son. To him, his father was the annoying man who looked good in a suit, crossed all the Ts and dotted all the Is, and did well in life because he'd been born with the good looks and charisma to make business deals.

He had never thought of him as someone who struggled—or had to work at all.

It was possible, he reflected now, that he'd been an idiot. He could remember nights when his father came home and sat at the dinner table with an exhausted expression. Memories surfaced of his parents speaking in low voices while he played with his trucks in the other room.

It gave him a fair amount to think about.

Unfortunately, he couldn't think about that right now, though. What he needed to focus on at this particular moment was how to kill Sephith and how to get the Christmas presents out of the video game. He snickered and could remember piling different chairs and boxes together to get onto the counters and look in all the cupboards. His parents had tried decoy presents one year, but he'd found the real ones too—they'd been at his grandparents' house.

"Any ideas?" Zaara whispered over her shoulder.

"One," Justin said cautiously. "But it might hurt."

She heaved a sigh and thought about it. "More or less than getting killed by a wizard?"

"Less."

"Then let's do it."

CHAPTER TWENTY-SEVEN

Justin wished he'd managed to study more of the spell book. He wasn't sure he could get it out of his inventory right now, and he ran the risk of it falling off the cart or being stolen by the cart driver.

Which left him with the one spell he knew. He curled his hand as far as he could and breathed in deeply before he closed his eyes and tried to picture flames. Sternly, he told his brain he didn't want a fireball. All he wanted was a little flame, enough to singe the rope.

"Ow!"

Too much fire, he realized. He cut the spell off hastily and pressed his bound hands into his back to smother the flames.

"Sorry, sorry. Let me try again."

"Again?" Zaara asked plaintively. "Really?" She sighed and twisted her hands in an effort to look at them. "Fine, fine. But only because you seem to be getting somewhere and I don't have a better idea."

"I can't tell you how much your support means to me," he said dryly.

It took three more attempts to get one of their hands untied and then the two of them scrabbled with their free hands to undo the other knots. From there, it was a massively undignified process of trying to work upward as one person slid down while the other slid up to free their arms from the ropes.

"Promise me something." She paused and panted halfway through the process.

"What?"

"We never speak of this."

"Agreed." Justin got his arms free, gave a sigh of relief, and promptly fell flat on his face when the cart went over another pothole. He rolled onto his back with a groan, pushed up to untie his feet, and snickered when Zaara sprawled a moment later.

"How do we wake the dwarf up?" she asked.

"I had an idea for that, too," he said.

"I hope for his sake it doesn't involve fire."

"Oh, it doesn't." He began to work on the ropes that held Lyle in place. When his teammate was finally down and free on the floor of the cart, he leaned close to hear what he muttered in his sleep. He made out the words "lovely beard," grinned, and set about preparing for his plan. With a silent apology to Lyle, he brought his hand up and slapped the dwarf as hard as he could.

He had no response.

"Huh," Zaara said. "Try again."

Justin slapped the other cheek this time, which seemed to do the trick. Lyle opened one eye, saw the blue sky, and tried to go back to sleep. It took three more slaps to wake him fully, only the final one of which he seemed to notice at all.

"Here, now. Why are you slapping me? And why does my arm hurt? And—"

He put his hand over the dwarf's mouth, motioned for quiet, and indicated for him to turn around and look at the wizard's tower. This close, it blotted the sky out entirely. He hadn't noticed from the other side of the valley, but it rose from the center of a large building.

Lyle gave him a confused look. "What?" he mouthed. He looked around the wagon, noted the untied ropes, and darted a suspicious look at the front of the conveyance.

"Later," Justin mouthed emphatically. He gestured to the three of them, made walking motions with his fingers, and pointed into the woods the road wound through. The dwarf, for whom this was not an appreciably strange situation, shrugged and proceeded to leap out of the cart without a backward glance. He threw his hands up and followed, and Zaara scrambled down behind him. The three of them pelted into the woods and didn't look back as the cart continued on its journey.

The woods extended as far as the walls of the palace, so they had excellent cover in which to circle toward it from the side. Lyle led the way and whistled a tune at one point before Zaara lobbed a branch at his head. Every once in a while, one of them would creep closer to see if they could see anyone on the walls, but there was no evidence that they were manned.

By mutual agreement, they had decided not to attempt entry through the front gate, and they were almost at the back of the building before they located a wooden gate. It was made of slats set widely apart and opened onto a small corridor of green grass. Storerooms could be seen, as well as gardens beyond.

Justin considered this and then pointed his palms at the gate. He closed his eyes, pictured a fireball, and let loose. With a little *woof* of noise, the fireball struck the metal lock, backfired, and bounced off his face. He flinched and cursed before there was a hiss behind him and the sound of water pattered onto leaves.

"You can't use a fireball," Zaara whispered. She shook her hand free of the water she'd summoned, took his place at the gate, and conjured a tiny vortex of air that swirled into the lock. With a series of clicks, the tumblers rotated into place and the gate swung open.

"You have to teach me that," he told her.

"We have to survive this plan of yours first," she whispered in response. She poked her head into the grounds, began to creep inside, and whispered, "Run! Follow me!"

Justin and Lyle raced after her as she sprinted down the avenue of green to hide behind a storehouse. The little square storehouses were made of stone and covered in slate. Nothing looked patched or worn

—Sephith could afford the best. Zaara motioned for them to be quiet and they remained motionless as a patrol of guards passed.

The guards didn't seem to pay particular attention to anything, and when they had moved on, Lyle said quietly, "Those'll be some of the villagers. Poor bastards."

"Maybe we could get them on our side," Justin pointed out. His companions both frowned at him. "What?"

"He means…" Zaara wrinkled her nose. "Those were the villagers' *bodies.*"

"Oh, God." His stomach heaved. "Oh, that's so bad."

"Where do you come from that only has one god?" she asked him. She waved a hand when he opened his mouth. "It's not important right now. We need to get to the tower, and I think I can tell you one of the problems we'll have to deal with."

"You hear it, too," Lyle said grumpily.

"Hear what?" Justin asked.

"Come with us," she told him. She beckoned for him to follow her and took a cautious step into the alleyway. "This way."

They crept forward and followed the path of the patrol, careful to always have one person peek around corners first. When they reached the edge of the outbuildings, his eyebrows raised. This place was bigger than he'd thought, and he began to think Kural had done the same tricks there that he did in the cottage. There was no way the grounds of the tower looked this big from outside.

The outer wall enclosed a large, open space with multiple distinct areas. Where they had entered, there were storehouses and the distant sound of a forge. Across the way, they could see horses being trained for some of the guards—live ones, Justin assumed. Between the stables and the trade area was a garden they stood on the edge of now.

The gardens had the same too-perfect look of fake plants, in his opinion. The greens were a little too bright, the hedges were a little too regular, and nothing seemed to move. However, the hedges would provide some cover as they sneaked toward the next wall, which enclosed the tower.

This place was huge. Also, it didn't look like Sephith used any of it. What a waste, he thought. If this were his castle…

Well, if it were his, he would probably be holed up in the top of the tower playing video games, so he couldn't judge the wizard on that score. He'd stick to judging him for the rampant serial murdering.

Patrols of guards went around the edge of the garden, but it was easy enough to avoid them if the group ran at a crouch and hid behind the hedges. Justin caught the smell of roses and, at one point, various herbs. He wondered vaguely if any of them were useful in magic but he probably wouldn't have time to learn any other spells or potions right now. They needed to move fast.

When they came to the edge of the garden, though, he saw what Lyle and Zaara had been complaining about. He'd heard rushing water but thought it must be a fountain in the middle of the garden.

Unfortunately, it wasn't. It was a moat.

Justin rested his chin in one hand. "Huh."

"Huh, indeed." Zaara looked at where the tower wall rose directly out of the water. "Any ideas for this one?"

He leaned out from behind one of the bushes to look at the front gate, where a drawbridge was evident, and noticed a smaller door on their side of the tower that looked like it would come straight down to form a bridge. Unfortunately, it looked as if it could only be opened from the inside.

Regretfully, he supposed it had been too much to hope for that Sephith would be stupid.

There was one thing they could use, however. Water poured out of a wide pipe at the base of the wall. It didn't look like the water went all the way to the top of it, which meant that someone might be able to swim up it. He pointed.

"That could work," Zaara said. "Although I don't swim."

Justin looked at Lyle.

"I can drink like a fish," the dwarf said, "but I can't swim like one. Although, come to think of it, I never have seen a fish drink ale."

He rolled his eyes and stripped his cloak and boots off. "I'll do it," he said. "I swam in that mountain stream, remember?" Plus, his gear had a buff to keep him from fatiguing as quickly. He didn't know how to say that in game language, so he merely grinned. "I'll get that drawbridge down for you soon." He waited for the next guard patrol to disappear behind the hedges before he slipped into the water and began to swim toward the pipe.

The water was cold, which he didn't like, and he began to worry that maybe there were sharks or eels in there. It provided a nice incentive to swim as fast as he could. He tried to minimize his splashing and eventually reached the pipe. It was an awkward maneuver to pull himself up and into it, but he managed it without too much flailing or splashing.

Once inside, he half-swam, half crawled into the darkness. Every once in a while, he touched the wall of the pipe cautiously to make sure it wasn't branching off. He could see a distant light ahead that grew brighter as he approached. Given how tired he felt by this point, all he could hope was that it wasn't some kind of heavenly door.

When he drew closer, he realized he was staring at a pool of water that bubbled from somewhere and came into this pipe as well as many others. Justin was close to the pool itself when he saw a bucket plunge and he froze. He remained still and tried not to move forward or backward while the bucket was reeled up. Voices called to one another and receded.

He didn't know when he would get another chance. Quickly, he swam out into the pool itself, found cracks in the wall, and climbed up. He was in the tower now, he thought. Windows high up let tiny shafts of sunlight in and the walls were hung with hams, onions, bandages, and barrels of ale.

With a grin, he told himself he should *not* tell Lyle this was there until they were done with their mission.

Justin made his way to the wall and left a sopping wet trail behind him. He tried one of the doors that led back in the direction of the pipe. It opened onto a garden that was filled with herbs and lined with hedges, as well as being patrolled by far too many guards for his liking.

But there was one thing he saw on the side of the outer wall—the door that could turn into a drawbridge. Justin eased out of the door, closed it as quietly as he could, and took shelter behind one of the nearby hedges.

He heard footsteps come closer and then recede and had the sickening realization that there had been several sets of footsteps but no conversation and no breathing. Lyle had been right. These must be the villagers and the servants Sephith had turned into lifeless husks.

Justin wondered briefly what the wizard did with all the souls but decided he didn't want to know.

As soon as he had the opportunity, he darted through the garden and tapped his fingers with impatience on his legs each time he was forced to stop and wait. He had to remind himself that patience was a critical part of sneaking and puzzle games. The guards moved in three sets and each circled their section of the garden in a different way, which meant he could only move when the three circles were aligned correctly. There was no point in trying to be quicker about it if he would immediately be killed.

It took him a while to reach the wall, but when he was almost there, shouts at the front gate made him hesitate. The cart must have arrived. Justin waited as several of the guards peeled away to make sure this wasn't an invasion.

He wouldn't have a better chance than this. Seizing his moment while all the guards were facing away from him, he pushed the narrow drawbridge sharply and held onto the chain to slow its descent once it opened.

On the far bank, Zaara and Lyle raced to meet it and bounded onto it in a moment.

"You did it!" she told him. She carried his boots and cloak.

"Quick," he said. "I'm not sure we can do this without—"

"Hey!" They froze at the call.

"Being caught," he finished. "Aw, man, I couldn't even get my boots on first?"

CHAPTER TWENTY-EIGHT

Tad finished sorting the piles of documents on his desk into piles by session and began to slide them into folders. He had eventually bowed to the necessity that he could not read every relevant document for every session, so he had devised a system whereby his aides provided a one-paragraph overview of each document and recommended the most important two. In addition, they gave him a one-page briefing of numbers. He prepared his questions himself.

His constituents hadn't sent him there to be a figurehead in a suit, after all.

He needed to be on point today. Several spending bills were coming up, and he had begun to wonder how both parties had produced such wildly ineffective strategies. They were so ridiculous that he couldn't even try to find a middle road. As a junior senator, he did not yet have much pull but he had prepared his questions carefully, nonetheless.

A knock sounded on his door and one of his aides looked in. "Senator? Mr. Metcalfe is here to see you." The young man caught the flicker on his face. "I informed him that several votes were coming up in a few minutes."

He smiled. "Thank you, Jeff. I do have to leave in a few minutes but I'll see what Mr. Metcalfe wants. Show him in."

"Yes, sir." The aide opened the door and stepped aside to allow Dru Metcalfe in.

Tad decided to take a page out of his wife's playbook. His blue-blooded grandmother hadn't been a fan of her grandson's country girlfriend, and Mary had displayed a remarkable knack for setting the older woman off her guard. He looked up neutrally as Metcalfe sat opposite him.

"Coffee, Mr. Metcalfe?"

"Oh, no, I won't trouble you."

"It's no trouble." He went to pour the coffee himself. "Sugar? Cream?" Looking at the severe tailoring on the other man's suit, he was quite sure that Metcalfe never had either.

"Sugar," his visitor said after a moment. He accepted the cup and murmured his thanks, took a sip, and blinked as if trying to remember why he'd come.

Tad hid a smile as he sat. "What can I do for you?"

Metcalfe set the coffee on the desk. There was a hint of mistrust in his eyes. "I came to see if you had given any more thought to our offer regarding your son's care."

"And, of course, your threat of defamation," he said easily.

The man, caught off guard by the sudden switch in tone from coffee to bluntness, sat motionless for a moment. "Believe me, Senator, my client would far prefer for this to remain a beneficial experience for everyone."

"Your client has considerable control over that," he observed. "It would seem to me, after all, that there is absolutely no need for defamation of my character. Your client is surely not compelled to do that. Nor, of course, are they compelled to rewrite legislation in a way that could more than triple the number of medical bankruptcies for my constituents."

Metcalfe said nothing.

"Tell me," Tad said. "What would you do in my place, Mr. Metcalfe? When one choice would be injurious to me and the other would be injurious to my constituents? If you were the representative, what would you do?"

"I would understand that not every matter of business is a moral issue," the man said. He had been ready for this question.

He wondered if he heard it often. "You're right," he said. "Not every matter of business *is* a moral issue. This one, however, is." He stood and buttoned his suit jacket, then began to put folders in his briefcase. "I was elected for a very specific purpose, Mr. Metcalfe—to represent the interests of my constituents, many of whom have been ruined by the costs of medical care. Despite your best attempts, you haven't created a moral dilemma for me. Merely a personal one. Do you have children, Mr. Metcalfe?"

"No." The lobbyist looked worried.

"If you ever do," Tad told him, "I hope you will remember what I say next. I am raising a son, Mr. Metcalfe, and the one thing I have noticed about young men—having been one once—is that they do not pay attention to what their elders *say*. They pay attention to how they behave. If I wish to be able to look my son in the eye—and I do—I will have to reject your offer." He snapped the briefcase shut. "The choice of what to do now lies with you, Mr. Metcalfe." He made his way to the door with a smile on his face. "Enjoy the coffee."

He sighed regretfully as he made his way down the hallway and past a group of people who chanted and waved signs outside another senator's door. It was amazing how quickly he had become inured to all of it, and he was disappointed to think that he might be gone within a year, if not sooner.

But his relief was palpable. He had not realized how heavily the choice had weighed on him until he made it.

His phone rang and he muttered an expletive. He kept forgetting to silence it, half-worried that he would miss a call from Mary. Being away from California, even for a few days, troubled him.

He didn't recognize the number. "Hello?"

"Senator Williams." The voice was warm. "I wanted to talk to you about the care of your son."

Tad stopped. All the fear he had cast aside rushed back. "Yes?" His voice was clipped.

"I've heard some of the treatment your son is receiving." The woman's voice had no inflection he could pin down, but her next words surprised him deeply: "I...would like to hear more."

Mary looked up from her tea as Dr. DuBois came into the lab for the morning. Today was the first time she hadn't seen him there when she arrived, and Amber had informed her that DuBois was sleeping on Jacob's couch.

He said vague hellos to everyone in the office and placed his set of bags near the monitors he had claimed as his desk. One bag, Mary noted, was full of other bags of popcorn. A week before, she had noticed the other three keeping track of how many bags he ate, and the day before, she had added her guess to the betting for how many he could consume in a day.

Fifteen bags was high, but she believed in him.

"How are you this morning?" she asked him. "Can I get you any coffee to go with your popcorn?"

Amber narrowed her eyes from across the room and shook her head. With a guess of eight, she had been the first one knocked out of the competition and she was still bitter about some of the tactics the others had used to secure high bag counts.

"Oh, no, thank you." DuBois gave a distracted smile. "It looks like Justin is still asleep, yes? Good, good. I've noted very small—but statistically significant—changes in his brain activity after long periods of sleep."

The term "sleep" had resulted in considerable debate one night and Mary, at loose ends since Tad was in DC, had been able to witness it. Feeling very out of place in her cardigan and slacks, she had watched the debate unfold with a great deal of smartphone-searching and citations being thrown around. Before she knew it, she found she had drunk two bottles of beer and eaten her stir fry directly out of the carton.

All this pretending to be a college student would be much more fun if sleeping on couches didn't make her back ache. Age was definitely not only a state of mind.

Now she stood and walked to the desk. "Has there been any progress on Justin's birthday present?"

"It's almost ready," DuBois told her.

"You know," Mary joked, "he used to ask for a dragon to ride when he was little. I didn't think I'd ever be able to give him one."

Amber smiled from across the room. "Man, that would be amazing."

"Really?" Jacob asked. "I think I'd shit myself." He gave Mary a horrified look. "Sorry, ma'am."

"Believe it or not, I have heard swearing before." She smiled. Young people were so delightfully naïve. "With age, one simply becomes more judicious with its use. The shock value is much higher that way."

She looked at the pod, now surrounded by several of Justin's favorite toys and stuffed animals. After a month or so, the lab had a much more lived-in look than it had at the start. It was never unattended now and there were couches, blankets, and several cold mugs of coffee to attest to the fact.

A thought occurred to her. "Could...you have more than one pod? I know this was vaguely mentioned but never really discussed but could *I* be in the game with Justin?"

"Um." Jacob stared at her. Everyone in the lab had gone silent. "Uh, theoretically? It would be tricky to implement."

"Right now, the game only responds to Justin," Amber explained. "His periods of sleep are getting shorter, but we don't want the game to stay on if he falls asleep—and, for instance, have an enemy find him."

"Oh." Mary looked at her hands. It had been a foolish hope, she knew, but for a moment, she had entertained the idea that she might be able to speak to Justin in person.

"We wouldn't want to implement something that complex without outside guidance," Nick explained. He looked genuinely regretful. "It wouldn't be safe right now. And outside guidance…costs money."

"Right." She nodded and tried not to let them see the tears in her eyes. "I understand."

"We'll get funding," Jacob promised her. "As soon as there are results from Justin, we'll have funding."

"Which means we need to speed that process up," DuBois said, showing either a moment of unusual acuity or his usual logic—it was always difficult to tell which with him. She looked at him and realized that he was smiling confidently. "I thought about that this morning in the shower, and I believe I may have the answer—puzzles."

Everyone paused. Amber had her coffee cup suspended halfway to her mouth and she put it down slowly. "Interesting," she said quietly. "As he gains mental acuity—which we can see but can't necessarily prove yet—he'll have more brainpower to doubt the game. We need to distract him from that and also begin retraining his higher brain function."

"We could put a module in with a book of puzzles," the doctor suggested.

"We don't need to." Nick was excited. "Games like this have puzzles all the time. It's a kind of…tomb raider thing. You go into the old ruins and have to light the braziers in the right order or whatever. We could work puzzle elements into the game itself. It's not too far from how games work anyway but it makes it a little more obvious."

"You two get started on that," Jacob suggested. "If we can show that he's getting faster at solving puzzles, that might be the kind of evidence that could get us more funding."

Mary smiled, but her expression turned to worry when Amber frowned at her phone, picked it up, and said, "Hello, Senator." As she listened to whatever Tad said, her frown deepened. "No," she told him. "Not on our end. A woman, though? Where was the phone number from?" She pulled a piece of paper closer and began to scribble notes. "Well, I'll do what I can to find out who it is and what they want. If they know about this…" She sighed. "There's no verifiable reason why we should be worried," she said at length. "For all we know, they have a similar patient. We can only stay the course right now. Right. Of course, I'll tell her."

She hung up and looked at Mary. "Your husband is going into a vote and says he loves you. He called to say that he was contacted by someone who claimed to know what was going on with Justin's care and asked for more information."

Everyone looked worried at that—everyone except DuBois, of course, who was busy coloring something on a piece of paper that Mary hoped was a puzzle for the game.

"They're onto us," Jacob said. "We knew they would be eventually, right? DuBois says they've watched him for years."

"They have." The doctor crunched a piece of caramel corn. He didn't look up from his coloring.

"And who knows how many other people have found his research over the years," Amber said soothingly. "What I said to the senator is true—we don't know that this person has bad intentions, right?"

Jacob looked doubtful.

"Jacob." Amber raised her eyebrows. "Being doubtful and worried is kind of my thing."

"Oh. Right." He nodded. "Look, Amber, it's not like we *know* this person is trying to screw us over."

"But they could be!" she said. She folded her arms in mock worry.

"We have to stay the course," he told her. "I won't hear another thing about it."

The two of them nodded decisively at each other, sat again, and returned to work, and with a laugh of her own, Mary sat as well. She propped her feet on the pod, smiled at it, and opened her book.

Stay the course. She could try to do that.

CHAPTER TWENTY-NINE

Justin hopped on one foot as the guards approached. He had barely managed to get both boots on when the first trio arrived. With a "Ha!" he drew his sword and shook a drip of water off the tip of his nose.

The good thing about a sword fight was that it warmed the blood. His fingers hadn't had much feeling in them after his swim through the pipes, but after a few passes with his sword, he noticed sensation coming back with a prickle.

"Ow. *Ow.* Okay, never do a sword fight with pins and needles in your hand. Oh, this feels weird." He looked at Zaara. "You don't look happy."

"And you're awfully talkative for being in the middle of a fight," she responded. She slashed with one dagger and retreated awkwardly. The second trio drew closer now and she grimaced at Justin. "I wasn't able to get another dagger before we were tied in that wagon."

"Maybe one of the guards has a good one."

"Do you think they'll let me borrow it if I ask nicely?" She grinned as she ducked under one's swinging arms, but he could see that her humor was a mask for her worry.

The guards seemed to be able to sense it, too. They stayed out of range of his sword—and Lyle's furiously swinging fists—and had converged on her. Justin lunged and caught one in the heel with his sword. The guard fell, writhing, and he smirked at the wounded man and took stock of the situation. The dwarf had managed to pull one of their adversaries away and was currently turning him into a bobble-head. The one who had met the slashing sword remained out of the fight.

That left four. He waited and tried to time his opening, and as Zaara cursed and threw herself into a full-body roll, he seized his moment. The fireball that surged from his hands was perhaps more impressive than it needed to be, but it eliminated two guards with the speed of a freight train. His mana bar went down to half and he chortled.

The other two guards seemed wary of fire—maybe it was a zombie thing, he thought—and Zaara seized her moment to attack and eliminated one with a stab directly in the eye socket. He dry-heaved as the guard collapsed in a crumple of limbs.

He'd forgotten the one he'd disabled. The guard, no longer alive, was down but not out. Apparently, human-like abilities couldn't survive a stab to the brain but they could survive a tendon cut. That was good to know. Justin danced backward, steeled himself, and used the same strike Zaara had used but with a sword this time. He yanked the blade out and shuddered reflexively each time it got stuck. When it finally came free, he turned as Zaara and Lyle killed the last of their enemies in almost-perfect unison.

"There," he said. "That wasn't so hard, right?"

"Uh-*huh*." She rolled her eyes as she checked the bodies. "This isn't a great dagger but it's better than nothing."

"Ye could always use yer fists," the dwarf suggested. "If ye ask me, humans don't punch enough."

"Given your personal history, I'd say that's good for you," Justin pointed out. "Okay, let's get inside and kill this bastard. Does anyone need any bandages? Lyle, that tavern wench said you would be severely hungover."

His companion laughed. "A human would be, aye, but not a dwarf. Come along, now."

"He drank half a barrel," he mouthed at Zaara.

She gave an elaborate shrug before she followed Lyle, and Justin paused to watch them with a smile. It was strange to think that only a few hours ago, he'd wanted her to find the nearest well and fall down it—and that she'd felt very much the same.

He followed his companions into the shadowy interior of the tower and they crept up the staircase that wound along the wall of the storeroom.

"This is not OSHA compliant," he muttered at one point.

"Huh?"

"Nothing." At the first door, he leaned close to listen. "I think this is the kitchens. Let's keep going."

"Shouldn't we go straight to the top?" Zaara questioned.

"No way. The longer we take, the more XP and loot we get."

"*What?*"

"I said…the longer we take, the more…you know, never mind. There might be something useful in here. We could get you a better dagger." He paused outside the second door and listened intently. "I don't hear anythi—"

The door opened and a giant, green hand yanked him inside and slammed it shut again. Justin yelped and proceeded to go airborne as the troll in the room threw him at the far wall. He impacted hard and slid down it with a groan. He was fairly sure his companions were pounding on the door and trying to get in, but it was difficult to tell what noise was made by the troll and what was made by them.

"Okay, maybe I made a mistake."

"Just possibly," the AI told him and made a return with its usual smugness. "But I don't know what you expected. You threw fireballs at your own wrists in a wooden cart. You're not the brightest tool in the shed."

"That's a low blow for a computer." He wheezed as the troll waded into the attack. It was tall, hairy in all the wrong places, and he thought it was the ugliest creature he'd ever seen. He stood, swayed on his feet, and tried to time his duck and sideways roll and barely made it. The troll smacked into the wall at high speed and bellowed in pain.

That gave Justin an idea. "Get out of the way!" he yelled at the door and he began to run. He tried approaching a different wall first to see if his attacker would fall for the same trick twice. Unfortunately, it was marginally smarter than that and he had to edge into range again before it would swing at him.

The pounding on the door had stopped and he could only hope that the others kept their composure and didn't get found by a patrol. He made a game of getting in close, rolled around the troll's feet, and sometimes nicked it with his sword. The giant health bar over its head told him he did little real damage, but that wasn't his goal. Slowly but surely, they moved closer to the door.

FANCY FOOTWORK, LEVEL 3 flashed on the screen.

"You should try out for Riverdance," the AI told him.

"Start the bagpipes, toaster."

Now for the risky part. Justin lunged, pretended to overbalance, and pulled back sharply, only to sprawl on the floor while his sword clattered away. He crawled toward it but tried not to go too fast, and the troll bellowed and began to run toward him. Only at the last moment did he throw himself between his attacker's legs.

The massive creature pounded into the door at top speed. It was so tall that its head struck the lintel, but its fists punched completely through the wood. It stumbled back, clutching its head.

With a bloodthirsty yell, Lyle launched himself through the aperture. He delivered a flurry of punches that knocked HP off the troll in a tiny cloud of red numbers. It turned and tried to catch him, and Zaara leaped onto its back. She hung on and scrambled up with a few grunts of effort before she managed to stab it in the ear.

It toppled like a sack of bricks and she rolled free before she limped closer to yank her dagger out of the large ear.

"Why," she panted, "didn't you open the door yourself?"

"You know," Justin told her, "you'd think I would have thought of that."

"Yeah. I would. Now, where's all that useful stuff?"

"Um." He waited for the body to disappear, then triumphantly held a bracelet up. "Ha! It's good for magic—I suppose you should have this."

"Thank you." Zaara slipped it on. "You know, I do feel like I could throw more spells. Maybe it's all in my head."

He grinned and stepped onto the stairs.

"Oh, by the way, there are patrols." She caught up with him and whispered the words. "Lyle and I figured it out. Follow me." She cleared her throat and wiggled her fingers, then slouched her shoulders, let her face go slack, and marched up the stairs like a zombie.

Justin had to bite his lip to keep from laughing. A glance behind him showed Lyle doing the same thing and he almost lost it but he managed to keep it together enough to clomp along behind Zaara. They passed another patrol and the members grunted. The dwarf grunted in return.

SNEAK, LEVEL 11, the game told Justin. **FOOLISH BRAVADO, LEVEL 1.**

He couldn't argue with that.

The stairs ended soon after and a door led them deeper into the interior of the tower. Lyle looked at the others to see if they were ready and stood aside to let Zaara work her lock magic. The door swung open silently.

Kural's work lasted.

The room beyond was furnished like a living room. A large hearth held a fire that crackled merrily, a sideboard was laid with delicious food and pitchers of wine, and long couches made Justin ache to sleep. His mouth watered and he groaned.

"It's all poisoned, isn't it?"

"Yep," Lyle said gruffly.

The food looked so tasty that it took them a moment to realize that what floated above their heads wasn't some kind of airy, shimmering gauze but a spell instead. Justin looked sharply at it with a curse, but it didn't seem to come any closer. It billowed toward the ceiling and was anchored to the wall at four points. A stairway wound into the interior of the tower and vanished through the spell as it ascended.

"What do you think it is?" he asked Zaara.

Before they could stop him, Lyle picked up a little bauble from one of the side tables and threw it directly at the force field. It bounced off, returned at high velocity, and shattered on the floor when the dwarf ducked.

"What are you doing?" Zaara hissed at him.

"He'll hear us," Justin added in a furious whisper.

"Relax." The dwarf shrugged. "I think if he didn't notice the guards dying with a fireball and the troll demolishing that door, he won't notice this, right?"

"Your reasoning is somewhat flawed, but...acceptable." He looked at the shards of glass. They didn't seem to be burned. "Do you think it's only a shield?"

"It looks like it," Zaara agreed. "That's what those sigils are—they anchor it." She pointed to the four points on the wall. Each glowed a different color.

"Okay, so how do we take it down?" He approached the staircase cautiously and walked up to it until he was close enough to touch the barrier. All three of them winced when his fingers drew close to it, but it didn't shock or burn him. It merely gave slightly when he touched it like the surface of a trampoline.

Justin unsheathed his sword, tried to brace himself on the stairs as well as he could, crouched, and drove the blade up. The shield gave but immediately snapped back and jerked the weapon out of his hands. It bounced hilt-first off the stairs a few times. He threw himself against the wall to avoid it and the sword clattered to the floor below.

"My turn." Zaara marched up the stairs and motioned for him to descend. She readied herself, seemed to consider a few different options, and finally chose a jet of water.

A moment later, she turned to look at the others. Her hair and cloak were sopping wet.

"My turn," Lyle said.

"You already tried." She walked down the stairs, wiping her wet hair out of her eyes.

"Not with my fists," the dwarf argued. He approached the barrier without slowing and began to punch it furiously. His fists bounced off, but he planted his legs and gave a war cry as he continued.

"He doesn't do subtle, does he?" Zaara asked Justin in an undertone.

"He does not, no."

"Good to know." She folded her hands and watched their companion.

It took him longer to tire than Justin expected but eventually, the dwarf stumbled down the stairs with a sullen expression.

"Wizards," he said and sounded grumpy.

"It turns out you can punch a spell, though," he pointed out. "Which was one of your main objections at the start of this."

Lyle harrumphed his displeasure. "Yeah, yeah, make your jokes. But I don't see you coming up with any bright ideas."

Justin tilted his head back to look at the barrier. Its surface was a deep blood-red that rippled slightly when he looked at it, and he sincerely hoped there wasn't actual blood in it. He had to admit it was a strong possibility, however, as he turned to look at each of the sigils. They glowed the same pale gold as the lamps.

And beneath each, only faintly visible, was a dwarven door.

"It's a *puzzle*," he said and pointed to the doors. "Lyle, look. Four doors, four sigils. Behind each door must be whatever guards that anchor point."

"Ahhh," Zaara said, with satisfaction. She gave a longing look at the food. "I wish we could eat."

"We can," Justin said, "but not any of that. Everyone sit and rest for a moment. We have some fights ahead of us, I think."

"What are you doing?" she asked as he pulled the book out of his inventory.

"I'm learning another spell or two," he told her. "I think we'll need them."

CHAPTER THIRTY

Without any indication of which door to select, they chose one at random. It was sticky enough that Justin began to doubt himself, but a particularly hard headbutt from Lyle opened it with a bang.

"You could have used your foot," he told the dwarf.

"What's the fun in that?"

"What, indeed," Zaara said philosophically. "Also, I don't mean to distract you two, but there appears to be something in the dark."

When Justin looked closely, he discerned a faint blue glow in the darkness. He threw a fireball, which illuminated a giant, bear-shaped creature before it connected with the back wall and plunged the room into darkness again.

"Yes," he told her, "I think you're right."

"Oh, for—" She gave him a look and charged past him at a sprint. "For Riverbend!" She drew her dagger, only recently cleaned of troll blood, vaulted upward, and brought the point of the blade straight down. "Ow, fuck!"

With a burst of white sparks, her dagger slid off the beast, which rose to its feet with a growl. Its fur now shone the same blood red as the magical veil. It lowered its head and snarled at Justin.

"For—San Francisco!" He threw a fireball without even a moment's hesitation. It was better, he decided, to strike before it started to charge and with that in mind, he grasped Lyle and dragged him sideways out of the doorway. In their wake, the door banged closed and locked them in the room. "Typical," he muttered.

The fireball, however, also had no effect. The bear's fur took on a sickly green hue and he began to worry that it was gaining power.

"Lyle, don't!"

It was too late. The dwarf was gone and the bear thrashed and twisted to try to reach him while he kicked and punched. None of his attacks—like those of his teammates—seemed to have an effect on the animal's health bar.

Its fur began to glow blue again and Zaara readied herself.

"Zaara, wait!" Justin called. "Use a spell this time. And Lyle, punch it."

"If ye say so," the dwarf called enthusiastically. A moment later, Lyle yelled, "Ow! Still nothing."

Zaara's fireball, however, had done the trick. The bear bellowed in pain and sparks skittered across its fur. It rolled on the floor to try to put the fire out and heaved itself to its feet. The fur glowed red and Justin aligned the colors with their style of attacks.

"Lyle, I think it's you now."

"You said that last time," the dwarf complained but that didn't stop him. He took two running steps and, with more balls than Justin could imagine having in five lifetimes, punched the bear in the face. The creature reared with a shriek and its fur changed to green.

"Now, Justin!" Zaara yelled.

This time, when he attacked, he knew there was only a short window. The animal had begun to sway on its feet as he sprinted. Only a few more steps, only a few more, he told himself desperately. It began to sag and he stabbed his sword forward and up with every ounce of strength in his body.

His pixelated body, of course. Although he'd be pleasantly surprised if he woke up and found out that he'd somehow become ripped from his e-workouts.

He had no more time to think about that as the bear fell and he was thrown to the floor with a clatter of teeth. The creature pinned his legs as its fur faded to black and he couldn't squirm free. It took both Zaara and Lyle to heave the carcass to the side enough for him to get out, and when he did, his legs were covered with blood.

"Ew," he said with vehement distaste. The door clicked open and he limped to it.

"What, you've never butchered an animal before?" Zaara looked at him like he was crazy.

"I thought you were in training to be a noble lady," he told her grumpily.

"A lady can't cure ham? Skin a rabbit?"

"This world is weird." Justin shook his legs on the expensive carpet, pleased to see Sephith's riches getting ruined, and smiled at the ceiling. "Well, the good news is that one of the anchors is gone."

With a rumble and a crash, the door collapsed and was replaced by a blank wall. All members of the party stared at it for a moment, thankful that they'd stepped clear moments before.

"Huh," Lyle said finally. "I've never seen a dwarven door do that before."

"You don't say. Okay, which next?" Justin covered his eyes, spun in a circle, and pointed. "Eeny, meeny, miny…whoops, pointing at the fireplace. Moe." He strode to the door he'd selected. "Is everyone ready?"

"Ready." Zaara nodded. "Blue for magic, red for fists, green for blades."

But when he opened the next door, all they encountered was a wall of shimmering peach fire. A click and a creak behind him made him whirl as the door on the opposite wall also opened to reveal the same fire inside.

"Zaara, can I borrow your spare dagger?"

She handed it over silently and he stretched gingerly to poke the dagger into the flames. As he had expected, the tip protruded through the opposite door. He withdrew it and handed it to her. "So it's a portal."

"It's a portal to nowhere," she said. "And if two of the points are in there, how are we supposed to get there? You can't go through either door…well, maybe if you go the other way?" She went to the other door and repeated the trick, but it worked the same. "Now what?"

"Stand away from it," Justin said. He readied a fireball.

"Maybe a small one," Zaara suggested.

"Oh, good call." He knelt and pictured a tiny fireball. When it skittered from his palm, it rolled across the floor like a mini bowling ball and into the blaze, only to roll out the other side unscathed.

Zaara tried the same with water and wind, he tried his new ice spell, and for good measure, Lyle attempted to punch the spell. None of the techniques achieved anything at all. The three of them sank to the floor to think and every once in a while, turned to watch as the tiny fireball rolled past again.

"There's no way to drain magic, is there?" Justin asked.

"Not that I know of," Zaara said. "And all of ours seem to go right through."

"Wait." He scrambled up. "Go to that door, I'll go to this one."

"Okay." She hurried to stand across the room from him and raised her foot to allow the fireball to roll past again. "Now what?"

"Now, you use a water spell and I use a fire spell," he said.

"Ohhh." She nodded. "Okay, on the count of three—and we'd better go at the same time or one of us will take a spell to the face."

Lyle chortled. He'd found a safe place on the stairs and seemed to be enjoying this immensely.

"Does that mean, one, two, three, *go*, or one, two, *three*?" Justin asked.

"On the three. That's why I said, on the count of three. It's in the phrase."

"Well, you can't simply expect—"

"One, two, *three*," Zaara cut in.

With a hasty oath, he delivered a fireball. The two magic attacks met with a hiss and a puff of steam, and the peach fire seemed to weaken. He almost thought he could see her through it now.

"It's working! Go again."

It took four rounds, but the magical blaze disappeared and with a rumble, both doors vanished and the anchors winked out of existence. Only one still glowed and the veil began to look awfully weak.

"*Ha,*" Justin said. "All right, is everyone ready for one last challenge?" When both his companions nodded, he opened the door.

"You will face my wrath," a figure in a black cloak announced as it swung its arms up to cast a spell.

Justin promptly stabbed it in the chest. It fell with a scream and the door disappeared with a crash. When he turned, Zaara had her face hidden in her hands and she shook with silent laughter.

"That was amazing," she managed. "Truly amazing. Oh, gods."

He chortled as well. When he looked up, the staircase now faded into the gloom with no veil to block their path. "Let's rest again before we move on. I'd say we have a wizard to kill."

CHAPTER THIRTY-ONE

Justin sat on the floor and gnawed on a rabbit leg with little enthusiasm. It was hard to be content with the same old thing when he stared at the most delicious looking meal he had ever seen. He half-expected to reach Sephith's inner sanctum and have the wizard tell them nothing had been poisoned.

Zaara and Lyle spoke in low voices. She had tended to a scratch behind one of his ears and he had cleaned and wrapped a cut on one of her hands. The white bandage stood out vividly against her black cloak and armor. Once, Justin thought he saw them look at him, but he might have imagined it.

Finally, she came to sit beside him. She withdrew a piece of bread from her pack, broke it in half, and offered him one of the two pieces.

"Is that your last bread?" he asked.

"It won't do anyone any good if one of us dies from being weak, right?" She waited for him to take it. "Lyle gave me one of the rabbit legs. I only wish I had wine to wash it down with. Not that it would help in the fight at all—I'd simply be less worried."

He laughed.

"What about you?" she asked and fixed him with a curious look.

"What about me?"

"Are you scared?"

"Kind of," Justin told her. "Yes. I am. But it doesn't matter."

She waited, looped her arms around her knees, and looked at him as she chewed.

"I spent my whole life playing it safe," he said. "The stories I heard were supposed to inspire me to do great things and I never did."

"You're here now," Zaara pointed out. "You're saving people from a wizard. Don't you think that's a great thing to do?"

He smiled bitterly. "It isn't real, Zaara."

"What do you mean?" She crossed her legs and straightened to peer curiously at him.

Justin took a moment to wonder if it would kill him to break away from the game entirely. He was surprised to find that he was more worried to lose the friendship of Zaara and Lyle than he was to break the game. He didn't remember being in the coma before it had started. If he went back to sleep, that wouldn't hurt him.

This might.

"I come from another world," he told her. "Not another valley or a faraway city, a whole different world."

She gave a disbelieving laugh.

"Magic isn't real where I come from," he told her. "I only know about it because people tell stories about it. I was…I guess you'd call me a noble. Or a mayor's son. I wanted to make my living telling other people's stories. One day, when I was out with a woman, a cart crashed in the road and I was injured. Badly. All of this is a dream my brain is telling me while I lie asleep."

Zaara considered this. She took a bite of bread.

"I suppose you think I'm crazy," Justin said. *Who am I kidding—she's not real. She doesn't think at all.*

"I do think you're crazy," she agreed. She chewed, swallowed, and stared into the middle distance for a moment. "A little, anyway. But many people are a little crazy, aren't they? People say that all wizards are mad and that's what allows them to reach beyond the veil and bring their powers back. Maybe your soul is only wandering." She looked at him.

"But none of this is real," Justin told her desperately. "It's all in my head. You don't exist, Zaara. None of this exists." Panic welled in his throat. Why should he care about convincing a part of the AI in this game?

"If it's in your head and you're real, then it's real," she countered.

"That's—I can't…that doesn't make sense."

"It makes as much sense as what you said." She took another huge bite of bread. "And how do you know it's even in your head, anyway? You could be dead in the other world but alive here."

"Well, that's truly terrifying." He looked away and swallowed. "What…frightens me…is that, even though this isn't real, what if I die facing Sephith and that somehow kills me in my world?"

Zaara smiled at him. "So, you're worried the same as me and Lyle then. We're all afraid that death means the end. But that's why we're here, isn't it? Because Sephith is killing those villagers and now, their stories are ended before they began."

He rested his chin on his knees. She didn't understand. No matter what he said, the game wasn't made for characters to acknowledge the fact that they weren't real.

"Justin." She stretched her hand tentatively toward him before she rested it on his shoulder. "Answer me something."

"Yeah?" he asked her wearily.

"What does it change?" she asked him. "You think we aren't real. But whether we are or we aren't, you're here with us. Whether or not any of this is real, your death here could mean your death in your world. In the village, you told people it made more sense to fight Sephith than to wait for him to take them all one by one. Didn't you mean that?" She sounded almost sad.

"I…did." Justin swallowed. *I merely never thought I'd be the one with my life on the line. It didn't seem real to me then.* "It's easier to say than to do, I guess."

"It always is," Zaara agreed. "But you're still here. You've believed this whole time that you might die, but you're still here. You could easily have run away to the city. You could have spent all your coin renting a room in Riverbend."

"That's true," he said after a surprised moment.

"Instead, you came to find me," she said. "And you're still here. You didn't simply leave when you found out who I was."

"Of course not. I was tied to you."

She laughed. "You know what I mean. Think of it this way—defeating Sephith means these people will be free. They won't be afraid anymore. You coming with me and Lyle means we're less likely to fail. I know you're about to say that it doesn't matter because we aren't real. But I think it does matter…to you." She gave him a half-smile and went to speak to Lyle again, giving him time to rest his chin on his arms and stare across the room, his gaze blurred with tears.

In the PIVOT labs, Amber sat abruptly and pressed her lips together so hard she thought one might split. She was about to cry, and she hated crying.

Not only that, but she also hated people to *notice* that she was crying, and she cursed internally when Jacob spoke.

"Amber?"

She shook her head. If she spoke, it would come out all squeaky and strange and she would inevitably and unavoidably sob. She looked away and focused on her breathing for a while.

"It's stupid," she said finally. "Because it's exactly like Justin said—none of this is real. And the AI only tells him what he needs to hear."

"The point of stories isn't only to be an escape," Nick said. He patted her shoulder awkwardly—he wasn't great at emotions. "It's to make you see the world differently and do things differently, right? I feel like maybe Justin's not only getting all his puzzle-solving abilities back. Maybe he'll come out of this with a different attitude toward life."

Amber nodded and a single tear broke free of her lashes. She wiped it away and groaned. "Okay, I'm swearing all of you to secrecy. I did *not* cry over this. I didn't."

"Crying is embarrassing?" DuBois asked doubtfully.

"Yes." She wasn't sure if she wanted to hug him or roll her eyes. "Why?"

"Because if so, we should also remember not to tell anyone Justin cried," he said seriously.

She laughed. "He probably wouldn't like anyone to know. I'm glad Mary had gone grocery shopping. I feel like she'd have bawled if she heard that."

"Then we'd have more secrets to keep." The doctor shook his head. "This kind of thing gets out of hand so quickly. All right, I think he's going to sleep again. Everyone get some food and rest. I think we'll want all hands on deck when he reaches Sephith. I'll put his birthday present into the game while he's asleep."

When Justin stood, his mind was clear. For the first time he could remember, he truly felt calm.

"Are you ready?" he asked the others.

"I think so," Zaara replied. "I won't get any more ready sitting here, though, that's for sure."

"The girl has the right idea." Lyle strode to the stairs. "So let's see what monsters Sephith has cooked up for us now. Wizards have no sense of moderation."

"You drank half a barrel of ale in ten minutes," he said.

"Exactly. Moderation."

He rolled his eyes and followed with a chuckle. Zaara snatched a torch and ran ahead to hand it to the dwarf, who proceeded as if he had not the slightest worry. It seemed like a very long time until they reached the next floor, but Justin remembered how much bigger the keep was on the inside than it had seemed from the outside. It must be taller as well.

When the wooden floor appeared above them, Lyle held the torch up.

"I can't see anything," he said. "I can't hear anything, either."

"We haven't exactly been quiet," he remarked. "Whatever's up there, it's probably heard us coming. We might as well go up. Weapons ready, everyone."

The three of them clutched their weapons as they entered the next room. To his surprise, instead of rough wooden boards, the hardwood floor was ornate and brilliantly polished. On it, laid out in several concentric circles, were pieces of stone that he could see might interlock via small bumps and grooves along their sides. The three of them walked through to look at the runes carved onto the surface.

"Do we arrange them?" Zaara asked. "Or does that summon a monster?"

"There are no stairs," Justin pointed out. "And no door. So we must have to arrange them to get to the next room." This was a puzzle and he knew how puzzle games worked. "Okay, let's start trying things. Do they make a few circles or only one big one? And do they slide?" He braced his hand on one of them and pushed, pleased to see that it glided easily across the floor.

Beneath them, the wood shuddered and began to rise.

"It's a lift," Lyle told them and sighed with relief. "Dwarves have these to get from level to level in the mines. It'll take us to the next level."

"No, it won't." Justin was suddenly overwhelmed with certainty. "No, it's put a clock on us solving this."

"What do you mean?" Zaara asked him. She looked warily at the blocks.

"There's a ceiling up there somewhere, right?" He began to study the blocks hurriedly. "Well, I'd bet anything that this floor won't stop moving until we get the blocks in place. And if we don't get them in time, we'll be crushed. Everyone, take a set of blocks—quickly. Lyle, you look for ones with all the jagged lines like that one. Zaara, you look for the squares. I'll take the squigglies. We'll deal with the triangles later."

The other two, thankfully, didn't question him. They raced around in the semidarkness, muttered curses, and shifted blocks. Much of the time, he simply felt for complementary sets of grooves to fit the blocks together.

"It's two sets of two circles," Zaara called. "I see eight center pieces and ten outer pieces."

"Good," he responded. "Okay, let's find out which goes with which —once we have the sets assembled, of course. Move the pieces for each set into one corner and let's start organizing them. Move, people, move!"

"You should work in the army," she muttered.

"Less jokes, more puzzles!" He did *not* want to get smushed. Justin arranged his four pieces with far too much trial and error and hissed his annoyance each time the blocks didn't go perfectly into place. He was supposed to be hooked into this game, and if he died because his fingertips weren't sensitive enough, he would be very annoyed.

Or not, as the case might be.

"Got my set," Lyle called a moment after Justin finished his.

"Still working on mine," Zaara replied. "The grooves on the inner part of my circle have dots and squiggles. Which one of you has those that match that?"

He felt around. "Not me."

"I do." Lyle began to haul his set to her.

"Wait!" Justin stopped him. He took the torch and peered at the floor. "Lyle, you have jagged lines…put them there. See the pattern on the floor? Zaara, you bring yours to arrange around his. That means my set should go over…here. Okay."

They worked furiously, aware of the constant shudder and creak of the moving floor. He glanced constantly into the darkness and saw nothing but was always aware that the ceiling must be getting closer.

He had barely slid his inner circle into place when Lyle yelled, "I see the ceiling!"

With a hasty upward glance, he swore. He had sincerely hoped he was wrong but the spikes on the ceiling left little to the imagination.

"Go, go, go!" Zaara yelled.

Justin didn't need to be told twice. He worked as fast as he had ever worked. Pieces slotted into place in his outer circle and it wasn't long until the other two gave a triumphant shout and ran to join him. He spared a glance upward and his heart leapt into his throat. The spikes were no more than a yard above his head and the floor was still moving.

The three of them passed the blocks of stone with the triangles between one another with frantic efficiency, and as he ducked out of the way of one of the spikes, the last piece slotted into place. With a groan and a creak, the floor stopped moving.

He slid reflexively into a seated position. His legs shook and he laughed, not entirely able to control himself.

"Holy shit," he managed. "Holy shit, holy shit, holy shit."

"Holy shit," Lyle mused. "Now there's one I haven't heard before. I like that."

"There's a door over here," Zaara said. She pointed. "I think we took a little too long but the door is technically here."

"The door to…the outside of the tower?" he asked. He wondered if this was a moron test.

"There was an outer section before, remember? Maybe we can go out to it."

That was a good point. He approached the door and pushed it open. She was right. The floor had moved them beyond it enough that they had to lever themselves out somewhat awkwardly, but they were able to make their escape. With a final look at the room and shake of his head, Lyle stepped into the corridor and held the torch into the gloom. Justin couldn't hear the footsteps of any lich soldiers, for which he was grateful.

The trio climbed in the semi-darkness until they reached the next wall and door.

"I wonder what the puzzle is this time," Zaara joked. She smiled at them. "Weapons out anyway?"

"Always." He drew his sword.

"Aye." The dwarf held his fists up.

She pushed the door open and entered, Lyle at her heels. "I don't see—" Her voice cut off in a gasp and she vanished, yanked sideways.

"Zaara?" Justin pushed into the room. "Lyle!" The dwarf had been yanked away as well. Both hovered now, their arms outstretched and encased in shimmering blue light. Their mouths moved but he could not hear them speak. He looked worriedly from one to the other. They seemed to be breathing, which was something, at least.

A door on the opposite side of the room opened and a figure stepped into the light.

"What's the matter?" he asked. "You only count on two adventurers at a time?"

"No," a familiar voice said. "I wanted to face you myself." The figure walked closer and pushed his hood back to reveal a face Justin knew very well.

It was his own, after all.

CHAPTER THIRTY-TWO

Justin's jaw dropped. "Sephith?" Had he been brought all this way simply to defeat himself? Was *he* the person who had terrorized the villagers? He recalled his thoughts about having a castle full of pretty serving girls and swallowed convulsively. Had the wizard he saw in town been nothing more than a disguise?

"Sephith?" His other self laughed. "No. I'm not Sephith—I'm you, only better." Without warning, lightning erupted from his fingertips and Justin threw himself sideways. "Did you think you were the only piece of your consciousness that had come here?"

"Whoa." Amber reared away from the screen as the machines wailed to life.

"What? What is it? What's happening?" Mary had been in the kitchenette, but a mug clattered on the floor and she ran into the other room.

"His vitals are going crazy," DuBois called to Amber. He flipped the lid of the pod open to make sure Justin's chest still rose and fell.

"Everything is spiking off the charts." He looked at her. "What's going on in the game?"

"He's..." She pointed wordlessly to the screen. Warily, she looked at Mary, not wanting to say it out loud, and stepped aside as the doctor came to look.

"Ah." He cupped his jaw with one hand. "I should have anticipated that."

"You should have anticipated *what?*" Mary demanded. She shoved between them. "One of you had better tell me what's going on or I swear—"

"One of the aspects of the game," DuBois said, "is the ability to make ethical choices. The ability to choose the path of morality or immorality."

"And?" The woman looked like she would jump out of her skin.

"And Justin is at war with himself," he said quietly. "He's made some choices and he's not sure about them. As a result, he has to be sure."

"So why are his vital signs going crazy?" She sounded close to tears as she walked to the pod and stretched a trembling hand to stroke Justin's hair away from his face.

"The game has made two of him," the doctor said. "He is both of them right now and he's tearing himself apart. Unfortunately, he has to choose because only one of them can go onward."

Justin's throat closed in horror. No. This couldn't be real. He barely clung to reality as it was, immersed in the game, and he now wasn't the only version of himself?

"If you were me," his other self suggested, "you'd want to reunite the two of us. You'd want all the shards to be whole."

"Or I'd recognize that you're a useless, whining brat." His counterpart launched a hail of fireballs, one after the other, that followed him as he ran around the room. Finally, he charged directly at his other self and only barely skidded to a stop in time to avoid the point of a sword—a much better weapon than the one he carried.

His copy advanced quickly and Justin stumbled away, drawing his sword as he did so.

"You had the chance to be anything," his adversary said and shook his head. "You could have had all the power of a wizard." He attacked and swung the sword in a complex series of strikes that left him on the defensive. "But what are you instead?"

Justin narrowly avoided the last assault and spun away as he shoved his other self away with a kick. He couldn't shake the feeling that he was being toyed with.

"You're nothing," the other him said contemptuously. He gestured with a hand and slick ice appeared around Justin's feet so that he slipped and tumbled hard. His tormentor advanced and slashed viciously with the sword as he scrambled away. "You let the rest of them claim your XP and your loot. You heard there was a wizard who could level cities and you decided to kill him rather than learn what he knew? You could be *anything.* You could have any woman you wanted. You could command armies—and you're merely a nobody with a Level One sword and a dirty cloak!"

He rolled out of the way with a curse. When he cast a look at his friends, he realized to his horror that they had begun to look pale and sluggish in their movements.

"What are you doing to them?"

"The same thing we'll do to you," the other him said. "Why do you think I'm so much better than you, Justin? I have the life force of dozens inside me. Dozens like *them.* And once I take yours, I'll be even better. Do you see where the blue power leads? That's their soul— their energy—feeding the machine Sephith made. He made himself a god and he's making me one too."

"You're an idiot," Justin said. He knew that for a fact. "A guy like Sephith never shares power. He's using you to do his dirty work and then, he'll hook you up to that machine and drain all your power into himself. He'll never let you survive."

Despite his bravado, he was panicking. He had to end this and he didn't know how. Power still crackled at the end of his other self's fingertips.

How did you defeat a master swordsman with almost unlimited power?

Then, he had an idea. After all, this was apparently another shard of himself. He began to laugh.

"What?" his counterpart demanded.

"Nothing." He shrugged. "It's funny to see you throwing fireballs around. I mean, clearly, nothing's changed with all that power."

"What do you mean?" His opponent looked rightfully wary.

Justin had never tried to outwit himself before. He would have to do this carefully. "Come on. We both thought the same thing—come into this world, find a sword, start slaying monsters, and get all the tavern wenches, right? And it didn't work for either of us. So, off you went to get magical lightning and better sword skills. And…" He laughed so hard, he snorted. "And it still didn't work. You're still a loser in a coma."

"Shut up," the other Justin yelled at him. "You shut up. Once I kill you, I'll be more than you dreamed. You're the only one who's still a loser because you want to wake up. I'll stay here and rule the goddamned world, and once I kill you, I'll have the power I need to—"

His monologue cut off with a gurgle and he fell to his knees as blood spread from the wound in his chest. With his eyes wide and disbelieving, he fell sideways and lay still.

Behind Justin, two bodies thudded to the floor—and, to his great relief, two voices muttered very ornate curses about pain and magic. With a sigh of gratitude, he ran to see to his friends.

"Come see." Amber beckoned urgently to Mary, who had stayed at Justin's side the whole time and gazed at his face while tears streamed down her cheeks. She had heard the entire conversation but she hadn't seen any of the context behind it. "Come look."

Mary bent her head. "I can't hear any more of this."

"You won't." She came to take her hand and lead her to the monitors. "He knows his own worst fears and he used them to lure his other self into a trap. He was tempted with everything he wanted to be at the start of the game but he chose to be a different self instead. Justin saved his friends and he's…well, he'll go to kill the wizard now."

It occurred to her how strange it was to be emotional about someone choosing to kill a pixelated wizard. She cleared her throat and lowered her gaze.

"Well, he's not doing that yet," DuBois said. Everyone looked at him and he shrugged. "He still has to see his birthday present, after all."

"Are you okay?" Justin demanded as he helped Lyle up. He went to offer Zaara his hand. Both his companions could stand, at least. That was something.

"I feel wonderful, actually." She looked confused. "All the life was draining away from me but everything came back in a rush."

"Thought I was a goner," Lyle agreed. "Guess not. So who…" He stopped and looked from one Justin to the other.

"Yeah," he said. "Apparently, there were two of us—I hope that was all. That one said Sephith has a machine he uses to steal people's life force and give it to others."

"Wait." Zaara pointed at him. "How do we know you're the right one?"

"You tore me a new one the first time we met," he told her. "You watched me burn my hand on the ropes trying to get us both untied. Lyle, we met in the jail at Riverbend and I mortally offended you by suggesting you might have left me to drown and run off before killing Sephith. The other Justin wouldn't know that."

"I suppose that's true," Zaara said.

A roar outside shook the stone of the tower.

"What was that?" he asked wearily. His wrist lit up with a blue light and he considered it for a moment. Given everything that was happening, he should probably check his messages sooner rather than later. He pressed the button and was surprised to see Dr. DuBois's face appear.

"Your parents remembered one of your favorite aspects of games when you were younger, and they wanted to give you a birthday present. This is only a beta test so you won't be able to take it outside this zone, but if it works well, you might get it back later. And don't worry, we gave you a buff to make sure you can't plummet to your death. Have fun."

The man vanished as the roar was repeated.

"I have no idea what it is," Zaara replied to his earlier question. No time had passed for her or Lyle while the message was active. "But it's big."

He walked to the door and pushed it open as purple scales flashed past. His face broke into a smile.

"It's a dragon," he said and began to laugh. "I'm going to be a dragon rider."

<hr>

The creature soared through the night air outside the tower and swooped to hover in front of Justin.

"How much time passed while we were in there?" Zaara asked.

"*That's* what you're focused on?" Lyle asked her. "There's a dragon, girl."

"I know." She gulped audibly. "I'm trying not to think about that."

Justin stepped out onto the ledge. This high up, the wind whistled around the tower. He extended his hand as the dragon flew closer. Softly, it lowered its snout into his palm. One eye—a brilliant green with a slit pupil—closed in a long blink.

"Hello," he said.

It snorted.

"Can I...ride you?" He looked at its back.

It lowered its head and maneuvered close to the little ledge so he could slide onto its neck and down to the saddle. He made a sharp intake of breath as he stepped out onto nothing, but the creature caught him and a moment later, the air returned to his lungs. He laughed shakily.

"Already outfitted for a rider, huh?" The pommel was fine leather and he traced his fingers over it before he leaned closer to see the letter embossed there—J. "Thanks, Mom and Dad," he whispered.

"Justin!" Zaara called. When he looked at her, she pointed at the sky. He narrowed his eyes to focus and identified dark shapes in the black expanse. "You must have to do something with those! And—good luck!" With that, she turned and buried her face in her hands.

"Do you see those?" he asked the dragon. "Let's go check them out."

It must have understood because it stopped sculling in midair and flapped its wings twice before it soared into the night. Justin gave a whoop and a laugh. Air rushed past him, the beat of the dragon's wings made its body ripple with muscle, and the stars were incredibly close.

The creature spiraled as it ascended steadily. It took delight in flying, Justin could tell. It was made for this and was intelligent enough to love it. He stroked his hand along the scales and smiled.

"You're more wonderful than I ever thought," he told it, and he thought it snorted again.

The dark patches in the sky were a series of stars, each ornate and each the absence of light rather than the presence of it. They circled the very top of the tower, but he could make no sense of them. Dragon and rider were on their second circuit when a look over his shoulder revealed something strange.

"Fly close to the tower," he called to the creature, who obeyed without a flicker of doubt. They circled and descended toward where Lyle and Zaara waited, then spiraled to the top. Ornate stars were etched faintly in the stone, each like those in the sky. Justin counted eight of them. He memorized four and urged the dragon up and around until they found the first.

He bit his lip. There was only one thing he could think of to do.

"Fire," he told the dragon and pointed at the first star. It opened its mouth and roared, flames erupted into the darkness, and the void turned into pure, shining fire. Below them, there was a shout and he looked down as part of a stairway sprang into existence.

Justin had the dragon light each of the stars in turn until the stairway extended to the top of the tower. The creature swept toward the ground in a dizzying rush before it carried him up again. He clung to his saddle and his blood raced, and he honestly didn't think he had ever been this happy in his life.

When the dragon deposited him outside the wizard's inner chamber, his heart pounded. He stroked its snout a little regretfully.

"I hope we meet again," he said gruffly.

It blinked slowly at him again and banked into the night with a final roar.

"Shall we?" he asked the other two.

His companions nodded and with his heart in his throat, he thrust the door open and strode into the wizard's sanctum.

CHAPTER THIRTY-THREE

The room held nothing Justin would have expected in a wizard's tower. The only thing present was the machine—a giant computer shimmered white, its casing carved ornately of ivory with a throne atop it. Sephith sat with his head tipped back and his arms resting on the arms of the throne. One hand clutched something but otherwise, he looked as if he might be asleep.

Around him in a circle were a dozen people, each suspended as Zaara and Lyle had been. They looked as if they had been there for some time and the lines of blue power that led to the machine were very faint.

No one in the room seemed to be aware of their presence. Justin edged closer with his sword drawn and Zaara and Lyle followed. All three of them exchanged glances as they moved. Where were the guards? Where were the traps?

The answer turned out to be about a yard from the throne. Sephith's eyes flew open and the door to the stairway slammed shut. With a shout, he elevated and hovered once again on flames of black and green. He was smiling.

"So you defeated your other half." He began to laugh. "You could not even make yourself whole." He held an iron key up, the thing he had clutched with one hand. "Only together could you take this from me—and you need it to get home."

"He's bluffing," Lyle said immediately. "Humans are *terrible* at it. I know."

Sephith snarled at him. "What do you know, dwarf? You're a drunk and a brawler. I've seen dozens of your kind and drained them of their life. I'll take yours, too. All three of you will give me your talents and your thoughts—so much better, I must say, than these simpleton villagers."

"You must have learned a lot about herding cows over the years," Zaara taunted. "And breeding pigs. Who was the last person you took —the baker? Can you make a good sweet roll?"

The man's mouth twisted. "You want to play, the three of you? You have no idea what you're up against." He slipped the key into his belt. "On the count of three? One, two—*three*." With both hands, he unleashed a pure, roiling cloud of black directly at the companions.

"Oh, my." DuBois snatched his phone up and his fingers fumbled over the keys. He could barely drag his gaze away from the screens as he typed.

"What's going on?" Mary had stopped crying but she still clutched Nick's hand in a death grip.

"He's beginning…to show some progress." The doctor tore his gaze away from the monitor. "I'm ordering a portable MRI machine to be brought right now. We need to know what's going on."

"What's going on?" Tad asked from the doorway. He looked at them one by one. "I've had the worst flight you could imagine and not a single one of you has answered your phones." His look took in Mary's tear-streaked face and DuBois typing furiously. "What's going on? What happened?"

"So much," his wife said finally. "So much." She smiled. "He loved the dragon." She looked at the monitor. "But now, he's fighting the wizard."

"It looks like I got back just in time." Tad wrapped her in his arms.

<hr>

The spell surged through the air and Zaara yelled, *"Duck!"*

Lyle and Justin crowded close to her and a magical barrier suddenly activated. Her face paled as she fought to keep the shield operational. Around it, the air seemed to be at once melting and on fire, as well as being pitch black. Justin had a feeling the sight would haunt his nightmares if he ever got out of this alive.

Sephith laughed. "Oh, you little fools. This is only the smallest piece of my arsenal."

"How long can you hold the spell?" he whispered to Zaara. When he saw her strained face, his heart sank. "Hold it as long as you can. Every second counts. Let me guide you across the floor, okay?"

She responded with a jerk of her head and walked slowly forward. Her breath dragged into her lungs in shallow, rapid breaths, while Lyle and Justin crouched nearby and shuffled along with her. It wasn't, he thought, the most dignified thing he had ever done.

On the other hand, he still wasn't dead.

Sephith must have realized what was going on because he suddenly yelled. A red orb of magic soared toward them out of the black and Justin raised his blade on instinct. The sphere struck it and shattered. Another hissed toward them and he batted it away from them.

"Exactly like baseball," he said. He had sucked at baseball. For all their sakes, he had better get good, and fast.

They reached the machine and he kicked Lyle to get the dwarf's attention. "Hey. Stout."

"What?" The dwarf watched as he dispatched another ball of magic with his sword and fired ice from his hands to spear a fourth.

"Destroy the machine," Justin whispered.

"How? I'm not an engineer."

"What do you mean, how?" He spared him an impatient glance.

"What do you do with really complicated things to break them? You hit them hard."

"Oh. I can do that!" Lyle set to work with a will. He grunted continually with pain as his fists struck the ivory repeatedly, but he seemed to care less about the pain than Justin did.

The sound of flesh and bone hitting something hard like that was not a sound he ever wanted to hear again. He was grateful to have the distraction of the wizard's fireballs.

"I wish I could get in that machine for a little while!" Zaara's voice cracked. "Oh, gods. Oh, this hurts. Ow. Ow."

"Only a little longer," he told her. He felt much the same, although he knew he wasn't in as much pain as she was. Each time he managed to swing the sword to connect with the balls of magic, he counted it as a lucky coincidence. He had almost taken one directly to the face when he missed and had needed to duck hastily, unable to get a spell off quickly enough.

Still, he had been able to throw a few spells between the balls of fire. Sephith circled them at surprising speed, yelled obscenities, and taunted them, but Justin could hear the fear in his voice.

"We're winning," he called to Zaara. "Don't give up. Please don't give up. Give Lyle a little more—"

Her whimper of pain came at the same time as the dwarf's triumphant shout and a crackle of electronics. Sephith screamed, the black cloud disappeared, and twelve people thudded unceremoniously to the floor.

Zaara staggered and caught herself on what remained of the throne. Her face was an unhealthy gray but she looked practically radiant next to Sephith. The wizard seemed to age in front of their eyes. The green and black flames disappeared and his back began to hunch. His hair went white, his skin sagged, and his eyes turned milky.

"No!" he croaked. He fished the key out of his pocket but fumbled with it. He attempted to throw it but his joints gave out and he fell to his knees. "*No!*"

The people on the floor began to wake up. Men and women

rubbed their heads and looked around as if they had no idea where they were. Then, with an ominous rumble, the tower shifted and began to lean slightly.

"*No!*" Sephith's scream seemed to resonate in the very stones.

"Lyle!" Justin yelled. "Get these people out of here—and Zaara." He had to get the key but he couldn't live with himself if the rest of them died. He pointed to the side of the room where a small box was visible now that the throne had been destroyed. "Put them in that, take it to the ground floor, and get *out!*"

The dwarf began to usher the villagers toward the makeshift elevator. Zaara clung to him. Her breath wheezed into her lungs and she looked exhausted.

But Sephith uttered a last, triumphant shout. He flung his hands up and vanished in a burst of purple lightning that hung in the air for a moment and crackled before it disappeared into the machine, which hummed to life once more.

Zaara stopped. She looked at the elevator and then at Justin. Slowly, she straightened.

"I'm staying," she told Lyle.

"Zaara," Justin called.

"Go!" she shouted to Lyle. "I'll stay." She looked at Justin. "There's no way you can fight this alone. And get that key!"

He flung himself down to grasp the key, rolled sideways as the tower groaned and swayed again, and tried to keep down the rabbit he'd eaten earlier.

I'm not afraid of heights, I'm not afraid of heights, I'm not afraid of heights, I'm not afraid of heights...

A hologram of Sephith rose from the machine. The ivory crackled with power and the figure—young and glossy-haired once more —laughed.

"A true wizard is immortal," he told Justin. "You cannot kill the body and expect the mind to follow."

"I know," he said. "After all, I was trained by Kural."

"*Kural?*" Zaara whispered.

"How did you think I learned magic?" He grinned at her. "I'll tell you the story when we're done. Right now, I'd say that hologram has a bluish glow, wouldn't you?"

She grimaced with effort, but she fired a fireball from one of her palms directly at the machine. Sephith shrieked and began to cycle through the colors, which flickered in and out with a speed Justin's eyes could barely follow. The tower groaned and shook.

"Oh, it is *on*," he said. He lowered his sword, grinned, and steadied himself.

<hr>

The lift barely made it in one piece. At regular intervals, the tower seemed to sway and throw it and its inhabitants against the walls. Boards began to pop off the sides of it and people clung to one another and screamed.

When it was close to the ground, Lyle leapt free. "This way!"

Thankfully, they followed him without question. Dust sifted onto them as they ran out of the storeroom and into the yard at the main gate.

Zombie guards lay still and silent on the ground. The dwarf guessed that they had been sustained by the power of the machine. Perhaps every one of them had given their soul to it. Poor bastards. The few living servants, meanwhile, hitched horses to a cart and cast fearful looks at the tower.

"Wait!" he called. "Wait for us!"

To their credit, they did. They helped the villagers into the cart and it lurched into motion not even a second later.

"There are two more in the tower," he called.

"Then they'll need to get out on their own." A man who looked like a blacksmith extended a hand to haul Lyle into the cart by his collar. "And I've seen this tower kill too many to let you die here, too. Come along, dwarf."

<hr>

Sephith might be a wizard, but he was only one man, and Justin noticed something very interesting. Every time there was a strike, whether or not Sephith was immune, the flicker between immunities stopped for a split-second.

He waited for Zaara to notice it too and darted her meaningful looks each time it happened. When she saw it, she nodded. Her color was returning but she still looked drained and slow.

They worked in unison. One of them would attack and the other would slip in to use the correct type of secondary attack while the color was stable. Sephith's health bar ticked down slowly. He called insults to them and shouted that they were nothing and would be rubble with the rest of the tower.

Justin wished he believed Sephith would be rubble if the tower collapsed. He watched one of the wires become more and more frayed as the fight continued and began to kick at the machine each time it went past. It might have been his imagination, but it seemed as if the flickering became slower and the health bar dropped faster.

"You'll die here!" the wizard screamed. "You'll never be anything and you'll never get home!"

"It could be worse," he snapped in response. "I could be a coward." He brought his sword down with all his might and Zaara put her entire residue of strength into a stab. Sephith flickered, screamed, and vanished.

"Come on!" Justin yelled as the tower tilted.

"I don't want to get in that box!"

"The good news is that you won't have to," Justin assured her.

"What's the bad news?"

"The bad news is…well…jump!" He snaked his arms around her and lurched into midair. "Come on, DuBois, don't fail me now."

The buff did, indeed, catch them. Zaara wound her arms around his neck and let loose with a stream of promises about exactly how she would haunt him and ruin his life if she fell to her death, and he tried to hold her while laughing so hard it hurt.

The situation was rectified by the dragon, who soared around them in a quizzical circle before it situated itself so they dropped onto the saddle.

"Oh, thank the gods," Zaara muttered.

The tower groaned again.

"Uh…hold on." Justin held her in one arm and the reins in the other. "Punch it, dragon!"

The creature rocketed away as the tower collapsed into black dust and rubble and lightning began to crackle out of the air around it.

In the cart, looking back as it jostled down the road, Lyle saw the building begin to fall. The top of it was encased in purple lightning that snapped and spat fire into the air. Clouds gathered in a swirl and the ever-present drifting embers began to travel toward it as if summoned. People called out and pointed.

He swallowed. There was no way anyone inside the tower could survive what was happening now. He sat heavily in the back of the cart and buried his head in his hands.

When the shouts turned to screams and whoops, he looked up and gaped as a purple dragon soared past. It landed on the road ahead of them and Justin dismounted with Zaara. She used his sword as a walking stick and Lyle smirked as he leaned over to try to kiss her. The dwarf chortled when she jerked away and her words drifted on the wind.

"Don't push your luck." She was laughing as she said it.

"Lyle Stout," Justin called. "We found something very interesting in that tower."

He hopped down from the cart, which had stopped with the tower behind it and the dragon ahead. Everyone held their breath, seemingly afraid that they might become a post-flight snack.

"What did you find?" the dwarf asked.

Justin held the key out. "Zaara thought you might know something about this."

Lyle came to take it and his mouth dropped open. "This can't be… It's one of three keys to open the Vault of Myr."

"Yep." Zaara was smiling.

"So…are you two up for another adventure?" Justin asked.

"Always," she said.

"Always," the dwarf agreed. "But first…*beer*."

The lab erupted into cheers. Mary kissed Tad, Jacob and Nick jumped up and down, and Amber and Dr. DuBois had their arms around each other's shoulders as they watched the numbers on the screen flit past.

"That was close," she said in an undertone.

"They don't need to know that," the doctor muttered in response. "Anyway, he did it. And…oh, would you look at that." He pointed to something on one of the screens and she clapped a hand over her mouth.

"What do you see?" Mary asked. She moved closer, still holding Tad's hand.

"Dopamine," he said serenely. "Phenethylamine. Norepinephrine."

"Yes, but what does that mean?" she asked patiently. She had gotten used to DuBois by now.

The doctor smiled broadly. "Otherwise known as the chemistry of attraction, Mr. and Mrs. Williams. I wouldn't be too concerned."

"Oh, that is it." Mary looked around. "You put me in the game right now."

"I don't think we should be too hasty," Jacob suggested.

"I will not let some uppity sprite girl seduce my son," she said. "There are limits, and the hard limit is that my son's girlfriend has to exist in the real world. You put me in that game right now."

Tad laughed and shrugged. "I've learned that once she uses that tone, it's better not to argue, boys. I'd do as she says."

Amber's phone rang and she chuckled as she picked it up. "Hello?"

"Is this Ms. Garcia?" The voice was female.

"Yes," she said. All the hair on the back of her neck suddenly stood to attention.

"Wonderful." The woman sounded as if she was smiling. "A courier will be at the door within a couple of minutes. He has a check for you —for five million dollars."

"For *what?*"

"Use it well, Ms. Garcia. I'm intrigued to see what the PIVOT team has in store."

The line went dead.

PART II

CHAPTER THIRTY-FOUR

"This, above all, is our duty to our constituents." Tad Williams looked out over those gathered there and tried to make eye contact with a few senators in particular. "In this room, most of us have made campaign promises that others would be horrified by." He grinned when there was a laugh. "Maybe your constituents and mine have different opinions on some things. Maybe they have different opinions on most things. And, let's be honest, every one of us here has people who voted against us. So, in every vote, we have to ask ourselves, what is our duty to *everyone* we represent? And the answer is always the same—we do what we believe is right.

"With the greatest of respect to this bill's sponsors, it will harm their constituents and mine. I was elected to represent people, not a party, and that is why I cross the aisle on this bill and vote nay."

A storm of applause from the bill's detractors followed and stony silence from some of the members of his party. Several refused to meet his gaze as he returned to his seat. The energy in the chamber felt almost electric to him.

Of course, that electricity seemed confined to the more junior senators. The senior ones talked quietly to each other and their aides, already focused on the next vote, the next meeting, and the next initiative. One or two had begun to leave the chamber, and a few empty seats told of others who had already gone.

He shook his head as he sat. They'd all been elected to weigh in on matters that affected their constituents, and this bill would affect everyone in the country. No one had any business calling themselves a senator if they chose not to be there for issues like this.

The vote was taken, and Tad was surprised at how steady his hands were when he pressed the button. Two weeks before, his stomach had been in knots and he'd hardly been able to sleep. With his son's life in the balance, the pharmaceutical lobbyists had offered him the answer to all his prayers if he voted aye on this bill.

And blackmail if he didn't.

Several of his fellow senators, as well as news outlets and aides, had asked him what made him stand up to both the lobbyists and his party whip, and he'd answered all of them the same way—that this was what was best for his constituents.

That wasn't the whole truth, though.

The real tipping point had come as he watched Justin fighting for his life. The same companies who lobbied him had blackballed a life-saving treatment years before, one a new company was now trying to revive. The treatment—an immersive alternate reality that worked like a video game—stimulated the brain to heal itself and wake up and after Justin's car accident, that healing was something he desperately needed. It was also something that conventional treatments did not provide.

Tad had never been a fan of video games. He'd wanted to go hunting or fishing with his son. Like most fathers, he'd wanted to throw a football around, which was something Mary made him stop trying after the fifth broken window. When Justin lost himself in a make-believe world full of vampires, dragons, or spaceships, his father wanted to beat his head against a wall.

Then he'd seen Justin play this one.

Despite himself, he recognized much of his younger self in how his son played. There was the desire for acclaim...mostly from beautiful women. There was also the devil-may-care attitude toward risk and the pigheaded insistence on going directly to the most difficult target, strength and aptitude be damned. Tad had gotten more than a few black eyes and bloody noses from that in his teenage years.

What he hadn't expected was the young man's sense of justice. Lurking behind the desire to be the hero was a sense of obligation that extended even to people he knew didn't exist. He had listened to his son's fiery speeches as he exhorted his allies to fight on and villagers to stand up to a tyrant. He'd seen him throw himself into mortal danger to protect those he fought alongside.

Tad had known that when Justin woke up—and he had to wake up because his father could not even contemplate another option—he wanted him to see that he was someone who did the right thing too. He wanted to be someone his son could respect. For years, he'd tried to make his son into someone like him without realizing that Justin was lightyears beyond him in some ways.

The speaker stood and made his way toward the podium, and Tad straightened quickly in anticipation. This was it, the moment when he found out if his speech had made any dent in the balance of votes. His hands clenched as he looked at the board where the split-second ticker of votes showed before the totals populated. Was it enough?

"The nays have it," he heard dimly, and he lowered his head with a laugh that sounded more like a wheeze. Seven of his fellow senators had changed their minds, and although he had no clue if his speech was what had tipped the balance, he knew he had done what was right.

"Senator." A man came to shake his hand. There was a twinkle in his eye—he and Tad had argued opposing sides of several votes before this one, to the point that when one of them stood to talk, everyone looked automatically at the other. This was the first time they'd agreed on a vote, and the other senator clearly found it as amusing as he did. "I assume next week, we'll be back to business as usual?"

"Count on it," Tad told him with a laugh. "I can't wait to see what drivel you come up with on the infrastructure bill."

"With all due respect, Senator, you're confusing my opinions with yours." The other man left with a wide grin and his aides hurried after him with their arms full of folders.

"Senator Williams?" One of his aides tapped him on the shoulder. "Your wife called and said the car is close. Your plane is waiting and we have you on the red-eye back."

"Thanks, Kyle." He handed the man his briefcase. "Text me if anything comes up."

"I will. Also, sir, you should know there are numerous reporters outside and they'll definitely want to talk to you. Verge News had a commentator on this morning saying you'd never vote nay."

"Next time, maybe they'll listen to what I say," he responded. He followed the rush of people into the atrium and pushed toward the door. "Is there any spinach in my teeth? Wine on my tie?"

"What do you eat for breakfast?" Kyle asked rhetorically. "And no, sir, you're good."

"Excellent, thank you." Tad took a breath and exhaled quickly before he stepped out into the crush of reporters, and—exactly as Kyle had predicted—several shouted his name. "Hello. What can I do for you?"

"Senator Williams," one called, "can you discuss why you made a deal with Senator Horitz on this bill?"

"Senator Horitz and I did not make a deal," he said patiently. "Both of us happen to believe this bill is not in the interests of our constituents. Believe me, we were as surprised as everyone else to discover we'd agreed on something." A round of laughter drew a smile from him. He was tired but he genuinely enjoyed this part. He liked to imagine that his constituents saw each word he said as well as the larger meaning behind them—*I'm doing what you voted me in to do. I've got your back.*

"Senator Williams." A woman raised her hand. "Is it true that you've had your son, Justin, transferred to an unlicensed facility for a non-FDA-approved treatment?"

A sudden silence settled over the group around Tad. Nearby, reporters continued to shout to get the attention of other senators, but all of those around him were as blindsided as he was. All he could see right now was the woman's careful, reporter-esque smile.

He had no idea what he would say to that question, but rage and panic had begun to build in his chest in equal measure. A hand slid into his and he jumped, but Mary smiled calmly at him. She offered no word of explanation as she led him away, and the reporters parted silently to let him through.

"Did you hear?" Tad asked numbly.

"Yes." She was still smiling but he knew this particular smile. It was the one she'd worn at family Christmases more than once when she was furious with someone but far too polite to show it. She nodded a thank you to the agent who held the car door open for her and looked at Tad as he folded himself in beside her. Still wearing her pretend smile, she waited until the car lurched into motion before she shook her head. "They shouldn't be allowed to bring children into it."

"I'll sponsor a bill," he said but the automatic joke emerged from his mouth with far too much bitterness. "Jesus Christ."

"Tad."

"Sorry." He gave her a tired smile.

"Well, now I know where Justin got it." She rapped his knuckles affectionately.

"Justin has far outstripped me in the inventiveness of his expletives." He began to relax as the crowd grew farther away, but anger and exhaustion crept in to replace the tension. "So, this is what Metcalfe is doing. He must have decided an affair wasn't newsworthy enough so he's having the press twist what's going on with Justin...if that even was the press."

"I have no doubt." Mary shook her head. "There's always a news outlet looking to break the newest story, whether or not there's a shred of evidence behind it."

"That's what worries me." He leaned his head back. "There is evidence. It doesn't mean what they say it does, but it's there. And with this...who knows how they'll twist it?"

———

"Son of a…what psychopath arranged these cords?" Jacob crouched and peered at the underside of the desk.

"That would be you," Nick commented from above. "As I recall, your exact verbage was, 'I don't fucking care how they're fucking arranged, I just fucking want to know if it fucking works when I fucking plug it in.'"

"Oh, right," he said. "That. You know, if I could go back and smack past me on the head with a brick—"

"Within current technological frameworks, I don't think you can." His partner swore under his breath and clicked frantically with his mouse. It was a moment before he resumed the conversation. "However, you do have the opportunity to make sure your future self doesn't have the same problems by being more responsible in the present."

"Hey, now." Jacob popped his head up over the edge of the desk and gave his friend a look. "Let's not take it too far, man."

"How did I know you'd say that?" Nick wore a pained expression.

"Because you've worked with him for years." Amber came to wrap her arms around Nick's shoulders and give him a sunny smile. "And we love him despite the fact that OSHA would shut this mess down in five seconds."

"That won't be a problem…" Jacob plugged a cord in and looked around to see the lights activate on another pod. "As long as no one snitches."

She mimed zipping her lips and throwing the key away. "Oh, but I should point out that even if no one snitches to OSHA, Justin's parents will soon be here."

"What was the point of zipping your lips if you weren't going to, you know…actually zip it?"

"Fine. Next time, I'll let you get caught with your pants down." She returned to her desk. "And in five minutes, when you've moved past your stubborn insistence on resolving it yourself, Nick and I will help."

"Speak for yourself." Nick launched into another flurry of clicks. "I have a fairy egg to rescue."

"You can pause the game," Jacob called from under the desk. "It's the space bar."

"First of all, I want to have something to show Mrs. Williams when she arrives. Second of all, the AI knows when I pause it and gets all snide when I come back." He hunkered in his chair. "And it's mean, you guys. Yesterday, it leveled up my Darwin Was Wrong skill to three and told me I was in the running to be the stupidest person on the server."

"Yeah…" Amber rolled back in her chair to look at the screen. "We're gonna want to fix that before Mrs. Williams logs in. Although, knowing her, she'll find how to make it be nice to her."

"My money's on that one," Jacob agreed. "Son of a bitch. I swear to God this cord has three ends."

She checked her watch and looked at Nick. "Three minutes and twenty seconds until he taps out. Be ready."

Nick snickered. His character, who currently ran through a tunnel made of glowing blue rock, tripped and sprawled heavily. **CLUMSY, LEVEL 8**, the screen told him, and he rolled his eyes.

"It's not my fault you keep falling," the AI said in his earpiece.

"You know what, I bet if I went back and looked, I'd find out you put some polygons in my way just then," Nick retorted.

"You are such a sore loser. In fact—"

The screen froze.

"Augh…" He groaned and lowered his face into his hands. "It's an instanced level! You're smart enough to get this. Only people in Justin's level need to be held to the same timeline."

The AI made no reply.

"Did it freeze again?" Jacob asked sympathetically.

"Yes." He came to sit next to him with a sigh. "I know we're still a minute and a half ahead of schedule but let me help you with this." He began to sort through the cords. "Okay…well, the reason you think your cord has three ends is that you have one of mine. Gimme. No, not that one, *that* one—yes." He tugged at it. "Feed it through."

"The senator's plane just landed," Amber called across the room.

"Fuck—feed it through quickly." Nick looked around the room a little desperately. "We don't have much time."

"By the way, Nick, the game restarted." She leaned back in her chair to look at the screen. "Aaaaaand you're dead by pixie."

"Son of a—" He sighed. "Okay, clean-up first, then I'll respawn and I'll find a way to punt that AI into next week."

The computer dinged and she looked at it again. "You have two new skills—Inadvisable Threats and Skynet Protocol, both level one."

By the time Tad and Mary walked into the lab, it barely resembled the same place. Nick and Jacob had been busy bundling cords, which now lay tied together neatly and adhered to the floor with clearly marked pathways between them.

Still, the new arrivals looked around with wide eyes and worried expressions.

"What is all this?" Mary asked. "Is there a...problem?"

"Oh." Amber scanned the room. It looked so much neater than it had twenty minutes before that it was difficult to see the problem, and she studied it carefully with fresh eyes. After a moment, she realized that however neat the arrangement of server blocks and cords might be, the area did look more like a server room than a medical facility. Even the lighting had been dimmed to keep the temperature in the room down and only the light directly above Justin's pod was on.

It looked like something out of a dystopian sci-fi film.

She bit her lip. "Oh, dear."

"I'm sure it's all fine," Tad said comfortingly. He squeezed his wife's arm. "I've seen many places in a panic, my dear, and this doesn't seem to be one. As long as they aren't panicked—"

The unmistakable sound of a zap and an exclamation cut him off in mid-assurance, and all the lights went out except the LEDs on Justin's pod. A large generator roared to life in the distance and the lights flickered on a moment later in time to reveal DuBois, who wandered from behind a stack of servers with his hair sticking up on end.

"Sorry about that," he said vaguely. "Wrong plug. I'll fix it."

"Wait, your hair *actually* stands up on end when you get shocked?" Nick looked at Amber in disbelief.

"I don't think that's the takeaway here." She pivoted to the Williams and plastered a smile on her face. "As DuBois demonstrated for us, we now have a chain of independent backup generators as well as a battery within Justin's pod. Any disruption to the main power grid will have no effect on its function, and if everything else is shut off, we have thirty-six hours of power to the pod if we need it."

Tad's mouth twitched and she thought he was enjoying this more than his wife. "I see."

"Now, Mrs. Williams." Amber guided the woman to the table where Nick had been playing the video game. "We've perfected the controls so that you can also play the video game. Because we know your primary purpose isn't to play, though, we're working to set a number of teleport points so you can move your character to wherever Justin is in order to speak to him. You also have an invulnerability buff—ah, like armor? Yes—and are universally coded as not being a threat. Nothing will attack you."

From the look on Mary's face, she hadn't considered the idea that she would need to play the game.

"One of the issues we can't control," the engineer continued, "is Justin's sleep and wake cycles, as well as the speed with which he processes information. To make a long story short, having what he perceives as a brief conversation could take hours or days. We're working on a couple of fixes for that, although it seems like his reaction times are improving."

"Ah," Mary said. She cleared her throat. "Well, thank you very much. It seems as though all of you have been busy."

"We have." Jacob gave her a tired smile. "Thankfully, one of the express provisions given by our mystery donor was that we could spend as much on coffee as we needed to."

"Do you have any idea yet who it is?" Tad asked. His voice was a touch too casual and Amber began to see the strain in him.

"Not yet," she told him. "I've managed to find a few of the hospital's major donors as well as the causes they support, but I haven't found anyone who seems like a match."

"Of course," the senator said. "I should have known that would all be published somewhere."

She cleared her throat and hoped her cheeks weren't red. The truth was that, although the donors did need to be named, no dollar amount was required to be published. That information had been obtained via slightly—or wildly—less than legal means.

Thankfully, her two partners both knew her well enough to know that she needed them to break into the conversation at this particular moment.

"Justin's progress seems stable," Jacob reported. "The leaps ahead we saw him make a week ago have held. It wasn't an anomaly and seems, instead, to be real improvement."

Thankfully, the couple was diverted.

"So he's getting better," Mary said. She looked relieved.

"There has been no forward progress since then," DuBois said and appeared at exactly the wrong time to offer the unvarnished truth. He studied his blackened fingers before he looked up to see everyone staring at him. "Jacob is quite right, the progress is indisputable and a holding pattern is good."

"It's...good?" The woman didn't seem to believe him.

"Asking for more right now would be like..." He raised his shoulders in a surprisingly artful shrug. "Asking someone with a new hip to walk a half-marathon. They could probably do it in extremis, but it would set their healing back. Slow and steady is what you want."

"Ah." Both of Justin's parents nodded.

"And how are matters on your end?" Nick asked them politely. "Senator, we caught a piece of your speech earlier. It was quite well-articulated."

"Thank you." But Tad's smile had disappeared entirely. "Unfortunately...it looks like we may have a complication soon. The media has caught wind of some part of this. I don't know how, exactly, although I have my suspicions, and I don't know how much they know. But I can tell you how they're spinning it. The insinuation is that this procedure hasn't received FDA approval because it is dangerous and that I know it's dangerous but decided to pull him out of the hospital and have you experiment on him."

Amber covered her face with her hands.

"Oh, no," Jacob managed to croak.

The only sound in the room was DuBois crunching popcorn. When everyone looked at him, he shrugged.

"Wasn't all of this already happening?" he asked. He shrugged. "They had the project blocked last time and they threatened to black-mail the senator. The difference is that now, we have funds to keep going."

Amber stared at him.

"He's right." Mary's voice was low and clear. "Thank you, Dr. DuBois. We all knew they would try to give us bad press, but we also know this is the best course for Justin and many other patients. We need to keep working—although I realize I shouldn't include myself in that. Nick, would you mind showing me some of the fundamentals of the game?"

Amber stood aside as the group swung into action once more. DuBois was right that this wasn't anything new.

On the other hand, it reminded her exactly how uncomfortable she was about the fact that their donor was still a mystery.

CHAPTER THIRTY-FIVE

"Is everyone ready?" Lyle stroked his bushy beard and looked at Zaara and Justin.

"One moment." She rearranged her cards.

"Come on, human. How long can it take you to read those? You've had 'em all in your hand." Lyle shook his head at Justin. He added in a stage whisper, "I'm starting to think she's not too bright."

"There's no need to be rude," Zaara said mildly and for a moment, Justin thought he could see the young gold digger her father had tried to raise with perfect manners and an artful tilt to her head. "After all, this is a new game for me. Oh! What's that?" She pointed across the tavern.

"What?" Lyle turned to look, and the young man watched with weary amusement as she switched several cards between her hand and the dwarf's. A ball of multicolored light danced in the corner of the tavern to which she'd pointed.

Lyle drank his beer while he watched with a slight frown and when the bright globe faded, he looked at the table. "I dunno why that keeps happening, but it sure is pretty. Wait…hic…you can see it, too, right?"

"Yes." Zaara did not mention that she had pointed it out in the first place.

Or, as Justin could plainly see, that she had been the one who created it. She was smiling, all innocence, as she laid her cards out on the table. "Is this a good hand? I wasn't sure so I bet low."

"Never tell people why ye bet the way ye do," the dwarf said. He looked at her hand, narrowed his eyes, and looked at his. "Wait. I had that card."

"Are there two of them in the deck?" she asked and laid the innocence on with a spatula.

"No, I had it in my hand." He gave her a hard look.

"You had it in your hand in the *last* round," Zaara told him. "Remember?"

Lyle swayed in his seat and hiccupped. "Yeah. Yeah, I guess you're right."

"Unbelievable," Justin muttered. A moment later, her boot connected with his shin and he winced. "Ow!"

"Eh?" The dwarf gave him a look. "Did you get hurt killing that wizard, Justin me boy?"

"No," he said. "I'm merely marveling at Zaara's luck this evening. *Ow!*" He rubbed his shin and glared at her. "Also, I seem to keep hitting my shin on this table."

"How sad," she said sweetly. "You haven't shown your hand, by the way. Maybe you won."

"Yes." Justin took a sip of his beer. He had almost adjusted to the fact that the game's graphics didn't show the beer moving when he moved the mug—and the fact that he could only half-taste the beer. It was only a memory of what it tasted like, after all. He laid his cards down. "Ah, no. Lost again. How sad. You know, it doesn't seem to be my night. I think I'll bow out and watch you two play."

SORE LOSER, LEVEL 2 popped up on the screen and he rolled his eyes. It might be his imagination, but it seemed like the AI had been snarkier than usual.

"Eh," Lyle said. He slid a small pile of coins to Zaara. "That's the last turn for me or I won't have any for my next pint. This one's having all the beginner's luck."

"Yeah, that's what it is," he responded blandly. This time, however, he lifted his legs out of the way as she kicked and was rewarded by the sound of a boot hitting the chair leg and her muttered oath of pain. "Is there a problem, Zaara?"

"No," she said, with dignity. "I'm fine. Thank you."

"You're welcome." He grinned and put his feet down.

POKER FACE, LEVEL 1 the game announced. **REALLY BAD FLIRTING, LEVEL 1.**

"I am not flirting," he whispered under his breath. His cheeks flamed suddenly.

"What?" Zaara looked at him. From her expression, it seemed as if she genuinely hadn't heard him.

"Uh…I said… That's not…Murting."

"Who's Murting?"

"Someone I know." Justin hastened to extricate himself from the conversation. "Hey, look over there—oh. Hey. Look over there." To his utter surprise—and relief—something *was* going on. The town crier had come in with the week's new bounties, each stamped with a seal of approval from the mayor's office.

A few chairs scraped, and assorted people stood to peer at the new posters. Sephith, the wizard who once ruled this valley, had attracted a steady stream of adventurers, and over the past week, several had arrived in East Newbrook. With him now defeated, they were all looking for alternate employment.

Justin hadn't seen Zaara leave the table but a moment later, she sat and slid a piece of paper across the table. "I took the best one," she said with a wink.

Had that wink always made his stomach flip? He shook his head to clear it. She wasn't real and was merely a collection of pixels run by an AI who hated him. With his luck, she would ask him out as a joke and he'd be laughed at by an entire pixelated village.

He took a moody sip of his beer and wished it were real before he took the piece of paper to read.

"Ruins. That could be good."

"*Could* be good?" Zaara flipped her hand and uncurled her fingers to show the key they had salvaged from Sephith's castle. "There are three keys. We have one and no one's even heard tell of the other two for years. Ruins might be the only place to start tracking things like that."

"As long as there's loot, I'm in," Lyle interjected. He hiccupped. "I'll go get more beer."

"He's right. You're right." Justin blew a breath out. The group had scrounged a few minor missions but nothing that paid well, and at this point, they barely covered their stay at the inn. "We should go to the ruins. But…" He held a finger up. "We should also get a few smaller jobs with easy payouts—something to fall back on."

"Those are so boring." She tossed a piece of bread in the air and caught it in her mouth.

"Your first mission was defeating a necromancer wizard, but they won't all be like that, you know." He raised his eyebrows at her. "Mark my words, you'll find out that adventuring is equally as boring as the life you ran away from."

"Really?" She leaned forward on her crossed arms. "You think adventuring will become as boring as sitting in a backwater nowhere village, doing needlework and practicing my giggle to impress a nobleman."

"Um…" He had to admit she had a point.

With a grin, Zaara hurried to the board and pulled down another few jobs. She returned and waved them under his nose. "A missing wedding ring and a wolf going after sheep. I hope that's boring enough for you, Sir…"

"Sir…" Justin prompted.

"I can't think of anything." She sounded annoyed. "Dammit, and I wanted it to be such a good insult." She looked up as Lyle joined them. "Lyle, we're going to do tiny adventures."

The dwarf gave her a dubious look and hiccupped, but he shrugged. He was not, the young man noticed, carrying another mug of beer. The bartender must have guessed that he wouldn't see any coin for it.

"I'll go," Lyle said. "And by the way, when will we go back to Riverbend for that ten gold? I've told people about the money I'll have coming in, and it'll be good if, you know…I can pay them for things. We defeated the wizard."

Justin rolled his eyes. "Yes, but the Mayor won't pay us."

"He won't?" The dwarf looked outraged.

"The reward," he said patiently, "was for rescuing Zaara and she doesn't want to go back."

"Trust me," she said, "he wouldn't pay you anyway. He only put up the sign so someone would come to East Newbrook, find me, and drag me back. Then he'd string you along and smooth-talk you. Believe me when I say you two aren't missing out on anything."

"I still think he should pay us," Lyle grumbled.

"You haven't been in this business long, have you?" Justin asked him. He stood. "Either way, we won't get that money tonight and we need to pay for our stay at the inn. How about we go see the farmer and kill that wolf?"

The dwarf followed them as they headed out into the night. He muttered quietly, as much to himself and an imaginary audience of other dwarves as to his companions, so the other two ignored him.

"I'm sorry my father's a jerk," Zaara said after a while. "I know ten gold would help you."

"Yeah," Justin said absently. "I don't know. I guess I don't understand why you're still here, though."

"What do you mean?" She walked with her hands resting on the hilts of her daggers.

What do I mean? He had no idea, and as he tried to find the answer, he made the mistake of starting to talk. Some people could come up with a nice speech on the fly, but he was not one of them.

"It's dangerous out here, that's all."

"You don't mind," she pointed out.

"I'm stuck here, remember?"

"Oh, right." Zaara shook her head. "I keep thinking that one of these days, we'll see a poster with your picture on it and it'll say some madman escaped."

The AI snickered.

"Are you laughing at your own joke?" Justin asked under his breath. "Seriously? Come on." To her, he added, "Very funny. First of all, that's clearly Lyle."

She snorted with laughter.

"Second of all," he continued, "you don't have to believe me. I don't expect you to. It's merely...true."

"If it were true, wouldn't you sit around, drink beer, and wait to wake up?" she asked practically.

"I don't know. It seems not." He rolled his eyes. "Why don't you?"

"Oh, you are insufferable." Zaara drew her knives.

"Whoa! Hey!"

"Justin." She waved the knives at him. "Look over there."

Justin turned to look and stopped in his tracks. A massive shadow slunk around the tree line nearby and toward a pasture where he could see sheep grazing. As it moved into a gap in the shadows, the moonlight glinted off brindled fur.

"Oh, shit," he said. "Are we sure that's not a...you know...bear?"

"Wolves are big. I thought you knew that." Zaara set off briskly. "Come on, Lyle, we have a rabid wolf to kill."

"It's rabid?" He followed her and unsheathed his sword. The animal moved more quickly now and they increased their pace slightly.

"We haven't exactly been quiet," she called over her shoulder. "And it's still there, so either it's starving—which is not the case—or it's rabid."

"The lady has a point." Lyle brushed past him, his fists readied.

"I'm not a lady," she told him crossly.

"She has a point about that, too," the dwarf agreed.

"Are you going to punch a wolf?" he asked as he hurried behind them. He had a bad feeling about this wolf. Zaara was right. It should be able to hear them and it didn't seem to care at all that they were there.

The bleating of the lambs made his mind up for him. One of them trotted to its mother in the moonlight and he immediately broke into a run. There were lambs in this field and sheep that did not have a chance in hell against this monster wolf from hell. He did not intend to sit around and watch pixelated sheep die. His unease pushed aside, he held one hand out and prepared to throw a fireball—

"Are you crazy?" Zaara caught him as he moved past, held his sword arm out the way, and tripped him. "Fireballs in a pasture?"

"Ow," Justin said. "Listen, I—"

"Stoooooooooooout!"

Justin and Zaara exchanged a glance before she yanked him to his feet and they sprinted after Lyle. They hurdled the fence and pushed through the herd of sheep, all of whom seemed determined to put themselves firmly in the way.

To their teammate's credit, the wolf seemed as surprised as they were. The beast had stopped at the edge of the meadow in a larger patch of shadow than those around it, and seemed to be under the impression that no one would be stupid enough to run directly up to it and punch it in the nose.

It had not bargained on Lyle Stout, who did exactly that. After a surprised yelp, the wolf backed away and snarled suddenly. It snapped its teeth and padded forward.

With a low growl, it slunk away again as Justin tumbled over the second fence and narrowly missed impaling himself on his sword. He rolled, ended on his feet, and swiped his hand to clear the **CLUMSY, LEVEL 8** that flashed up on the screen.

The wolf now stared dubiously at him, and he didn't wait for it to recover. He went on the offensive at once with a battle cry. Over and over, he brought the sword down to slash, and thrust, and wave it like a battle-ax.

It wasn't a winning strategy, but it didn't have to be. The wolf continued its retreat and backed away step by step, so it seemed to be working.

In the next moment, Zaara barreled into it from the side. She tumbled over it and one of her knives found flesh. The animal opened its mouth in a snarl of pain, but the light was already fading from its eyes. It slumped heavily and she heaved herself free.

"Good job," she said, panting. "See? One wolf, no big deal."

"Hey!" The call came from across the field. A man hurried toward them dressed in the baggy, patched clothes of a villager. "Are you from East Newbrook? Did you kill the wolf?"

"We did," Justin said. He panted as he sheathed his sword.

"My thanks, my thanks." The farmer reached them and looked at each of the adventurers in turn. "There's a purse for you to split and another half to be given by the mayor. He knew once the wolf had finished with my flocks, he'd look for others." He held the purse out to Justin. "And there's something else for the lady."

"I'm not a lady," Zaara muttered.

The farmer smiled and withdrew something from under his shirt. It was wrapped in heavy fabric and he opened it as gently as if it were a baby. Nestled in the black cloth was a well-worn sheath and one of the most beautiful daggers Justin had ever seen.

She drew her breath sharply.

"It was my grandfather's," the farmer said. "I never had the training for it, and he was a wild soul—wouldn't like it being used for sheep shearing or a kitchen knife or naught like that. When I heard an adventurer was in town with daggers, I thought maybe I'd sell it. But you saved my flocks and because of you, my children will eat this winter. Have this knife. My grandfather would want that."

"Thank you," she whispered as she picked it up. "Oh, thank you. It's beautiful."

"If he were still alive," the man said, "he'd have gone after Sephith, himself, no matter that he was ninety and blind. Go. Free other towns."

"I will be honored to use this," Zaara told him, and for the first time, Justin saw something in her face and thought he understood why she didn't want to go home. This was the kind of story she would never hear if she were a nobleman's wife.

He was silent as they walked to town, sad without knowing why.

CHAPTER THIRTY-SIX

Birds chirped merrily the next morning when Justin awoke. He took a moment to stretch before he remembered that he wasn't stretching for any reason. This game could mimic many things, but one it didn't—hopefully by design—was the way you could toss and turn in your sleep or wake up with a crick in your neck.

"You awaken feeling well-rested," he murmured as he sat. He pushed the shutters open to see the bird that trilled so happily. It turned to look at him, chirped, and failed to notice the drifting, magical ember on the wind.

The change was rapid—the bird ignited and the flames swelled and twisted with darkness. It uttered a low cry that pierced him to the bone and collapsed into a puddle of greenish goo below the window with a muted plop.

He sat with his hand over his mouth.

"I gotta do something about that," he muttered hoarsely when he had recovered enough to talk. Although Sephith had been defeated, he had ruled the valley for years and the residue of his battle to take the tower remained—a kind of magical fallout that could sicken people, crops, and livestock. He had seen more than a few villagers with withered limbs or burns on their faces and shoulders. This was the only place where people wore their hoods down in the rain and up in the sunshine.

Downstairs, the innkeeper was serving beans, cheese, and bread to Zaara and Lyle. Justin narrowed his eyes and looked more closely. The innkeeper was serving her only, and she had decided to sit at the same table where Lyle had passed out the night before.

Justin smiled as he joined her. "How are we saving the world today?"

"First, we're eating breakfast. Do you want some?" She tipped her plate of beans at him.

They looked way too similar to the bird-goo and his stomach heaved.

Zaara raised her eyebrows. "I've never seen that look on a man before. You're not a woman, are you? Secretly with child?" She ducked under the table to peer at his stomach.

"I'm not a woman," he said in annoyance. "But…no beans. Bread."

"Right." She scooped a spoonful into her mouth and laughed at the look on his face. "Well, don't look. But do eat. We'll need our strength."

"I thought—thank you—" Justin accepted a hunk of bread from the innkeeper, along with a mug of something that was vaguely tea-like if tea were made with pond scum. "Ew. I thought we were retrieving a wedding ring?"

"Sure, but first we have to drag Lyle out to the fountain and dunk his head in until he wakes up." Zaara took a sip of her tea. "Try it. Despite appearances, it's good."

He sipped it, winced, and was surprised to find that it tasted a little like a smoothie—fruity and chalky at the same time, but warm. He could work with that, he decided.

Once they had finished, he took a piece of bread to go on Lyle's account, and he and Zaara dunked the dwarf successfully under the water a few times before the three of them set off toward the edge of town. Justin waited for Zaara to ask how he always knew where to go, but she never did. It was a shame, he thought. He'd looked forward to explaining the concept of a mini-map.

The widow lived in a surprisingly picturesque little cottage. He was sure that if he stood close enough, he'd be able to identify the pixels, but he'd taken considerable flak from his teammates about that before.

Justin knocked on the door, and it wasn't long before the widow opened it. She was bright-eyed and vibrant but frail.

"Adventurers," she said with a smile. "Are you here for potions? Could I interest you in a quest?"

"To find your wedding ring?" Zaara asked. "If so, that is why we came. We wanted to find it for you."

"Oh, bless you, children." The woman smiled and waved them to a table.

The interior of the cottage was spotless, with copper pans and ladles on the walls, a small bed with a quilted bedspread, and a merry fire in the grate. A thin workbench on the other wall was packed with bottles and herbs, a scale, and a mortar and pestle. Onions hung from the rafters in bunches and braided rag rugs covered the floor.

"I was near the sewer grates," the widow explained. "Up on the king's highway, you know. We have nothing so fine here in East Newbrook, of course." She laughed.

Justin, who had never considered a sewer to be a cause for celebration, forced a smile.

"Well, Sweetgrass grows out of the sewer grates, and as I stretched in to harvest a clump, my wedding ring fell off." She turned over a piece of paper that had lain on the table. "I marked the location very carefully. It's the grate fourteen paces west of the 485th league marker."

"Okay." He looked at his two companions and was pleased to see them both nodding. Someone, at least, seemed to know where they were going.

"I'd go find it myself, you see, except these old bones wouldn't take that very well."

She shook her head with a laugh. "And I'd wait, but the same old bones tell me there's a storm coming. Where there's a storm, there's water, and any chance of finding my ring will be gone."

"Of course." Zaara picked the piece of paper up and smiled. "We'll be back with your ring, ma'am."

"He seems to be making friendships," DuBois remarked.

"Hmm?" Amber looked up from her ledgers.

"Justin." The doctor gestured at the screens. "He's bonding with the characters in the game. He wants to keep them from getting hurt."

"It isn't surprising. Did you know a study was done with robots that looked nothing close to human, and the human test subjects still refused to destroy them? They didn't want to 'hurt' them." She smiled. "Humans will pack-bond with anything."

"Maybe." He didn't seem convinced. "Sure, he could have simply wandered around, pushed people into lakes, or swung his sword every which way, and I tend to think many people might do that—sudden freedom from social judgment, after all, and no consequences. But Zaara was right—he could also have holed up in a tavern and refused to interact."

"I was worried he would when we sent his parents' message through," she admitted, looked at her research, and sighed. She was getting nowhere fast so might as well take a proper break. "I thought if he knew there was a real chance of dying, he might simply stop trying and we'd have to back him into a corner."

"That wouldn't have been pleasant for anyone," DuBois said. He nodded at her work. "I'm sorry to have taken you from that. You did sigh almost continuously, though. I thought perhaps you could use a distraction."

"Thank you." She was always surprised when he did something human, although she had begun to think he was the type to observe carefully and interact more fully once he knew people. He now picked up everyone else's favorite snacks at the grocery store too, and if he was listening to jazz—which Nick couldn't stand—he always turned it off before the man was due to arrive for the day.

"Is there a problem?" the doctor asked.

"Well..." Amber gestured for him to approach her desk. With all the new equipment, she had moved from the center of the big room to one of the corners. She pointed at the screen. "I can find nothing that tells me who this benefactor is, and the timing is—"

"What timing?"

"When this all leaked to the press?" She raised her eyebrows and pulled her phone out of her pocket to show him. "Look—forty-eight missed calls. My old roommate's getting calls and my classmates are getting calls. I emailed the people at your lab and they told me they've had to unplug their phones."

"Ah, yes." He nodded his head seriously. "This is why I don't have a phone."

"What if someone needs to reach you?"

He shrugged. "My lab knows where I am. And the truth would come out sometime, wouldn't it? The press is always looking for something. The only thing that surprises me is that more details haven't emerged yet. They aren't very good at looking, are they?"

Amber could only laugh at that. DuBois was a man whose career had almost been ended by these same forces, and he was offended on a personal level that the people who tried to destroy them weren't better at their jobs.

"Well, why don't you see if you can resolve this puzzle." She pulled the chair out for him. "Justin's sleeping, after all, and—"

"And?" DuBois looked at her with a small frown. "What's—"

"Here's all the info." She tapped the screen. "Read it and let it sink in."

She took a careful step and sank to the floor before she slunk around the maze of desks and cords. While not exactly a ninja, she could move quietly when she needed to and the hums and beeps of the machinery covered her movement.

DuBois muttered to himself as she eased out from behind a desk, took a look at the server wall, and shook her head.

Stealth.

And speed.

And don't destroy the servers. She stood as quietly as she could, took two long, quiet steps, and put the intruder she'd seen in a headlock. The camera tumbled free and she kicked it with every ounce of strength she possessed so it skidded into the darkened interior of the room. The intruder, meanwhile, screamed.

"What's going on?" Across the room, DuBois stood with a horrified look. "Who is that?"

"A reporter, I think." Amber flipped the woman over her shoulder and onto the floor, where she yanked her hands up behind her and knelt on her back. "I'm right, aren't I? You're a reporter?"

"This is assault," the woman said shrilly.

"Oh, no." She hauled her up. "How terrible for you. You snuck into private property to try to take pictures of trade secrets, potentially disrupting experiments in progress, and with what goal, exactly?"

"The world deserves to know the truth about Justin Williams," her captive said as Amber began to force her down the hallway.

"Who?"

"You know exactly who I mean. He's in that...that pod thing, isn't he?"

"To be clear, you think there's a missing person in our lab and you've decided the best way to save him is to come in and look at our server blocks?" She shook her head, kicked the outside door open, and ushered the woman firmly into the sunlight. "Here's a fun suggestion. Why don't you...I don't know, do your research and find out who we are before you sneak onto our property. There's also a doorbell." She slammed the door, locked it from the inside, and walked away, ignoring the woman's shouts about her camera.

In the lab, DuBois stood and stared worriedly at the door. "Are you sure you should have done that?" he asked.

"Yes," she said. "Did you make any progress with the information?"

"There's hardly enough to make sense of," he said with a shrug. "We'll have to wait until—oh, look, he's waking up." He snatched a bag of popcorn and headed to the monitors, and Amber laughed ruefully before she returned to her computer.

Whether this was enough information or not, the reporter's visit had shown her one thing. They needed to identify the players in this game and they needed to do it fast. Not for the first time, she wished she could swap places with Justin.

If she had to fight mysterious strangers, she'd rather have a sword and some fireballs.

The King's Road was like an entirely different world. Justin had become familiar with the villages and dirt paths, but the big road half a league away was made of shining white stone. Weeds grew here and there, of course, but in general, it was in remarkably good repair.

"People come every year to clean it," Zaara explained. "And reset the cobbles and all that. You can see who did which parts—the stones are all engraved with who was ruling when the stone was laid. So… look, most of these are from Hieronymous, who was the first one to extend the King's Road out this way, but this stone is more recent."

"Huh." Justin shrugged. "Chipping the King's name into thousands of cobblestones seems like…maybe a waste of time?"

"The kings don't think so," she said and mirrored his shrug.

"The kings don't have to do it, I assume. Okay, there's the bridge and the mile marker, so we have to go west of that—or east?"

"West." Zaara picked out the small grey stone at the edge of the road. "I'll go count the steps." Lyle and Justin waited as she approached the marker and counted the required number of steps before she laughed in triumph. "Ha! Right where she said it would be. Now, I guess we need to find a way to get this grate up."

"Let me." Lyle marched to her, felt under the stone, and gave a satisfied grunt. He pulled his knife out and stuck it under the grate. Stone and steel scraped together jarringly before he hauled the cover up and threw it into the grass. "There it goes. It's a dwarven make and locked in so someone can't simply take a nice hunk of iron, eh? Anyhow, in we gooooo!" He sat on the edge of the opening, pushed off, and disappeared. The sound of boots hitting wet stone followed moments later.

"Did we even check to see if the ring was simply there?" Justin asked.

"Nope," Zaara said. She sighed as she leaned over. "I don't see it, though. You know, I'm not looking forward to this." She levered herself down more carefully, then called, "It's barely a drop for a human, don't worry!"

He was surprised to feel a few stabs of pain in his arms as he swung down. That had happened sometimes lately, and he wondered if it was actual pain in broken limbs—the thought made him shudder —or merely biofeedback that had been fouled up in the system.

As always, the thought of his own sleeping body made him nervous. and he decided to think about something else. The truly terrible smell in the sewer was first on the list.

"Lyle?"

"Over this way."

"How do you know you're going the right direction?"

"Put a dwarf underground and ask 'im to find gold, and he won't fail ye."

The two humans looked at one another, shrugged, and headed off, following the sound of his voice. He did, in fact, seem remarkably good at leading them through the passages of the sewer, most of which were blessedly dry.

"Lyle," he said.

"Eh?"

"You can...get us out again, right?"

The dwarf scratched his ear. "Uh...yeah. Yeah, sure."

"We'll die down here," Justin told Zaara. "Either that or we'll turn into Morlocks."

"Into what?"

"Nothing. I—oh, hey, is that—oh, no." He raced forward to yank on the back of Lyle's shirt. At the end of the tunnel, a shaft of light from another sewer grate illuminated the edge of a glittering pile. It wasn't all treasure, but there were coins mixed in with the battered knives and slivers of glass.

A scrabbling sound came from somewhere nearby, followed by sniffing.

He drew his sword, Zaara drew her knives, and Lyle edged forward with his fists ready.

"One…" he whispered.

"Two…" Zaara continued."

"Stoooooooout!" Lyle yelled as he attacked.

"Oh, for—" Justin surged into a sprint. "Leeroooooooy!" He came around the corner and slashed at the first thing he saw that wasn't Lyle.

Between the squealing, dodging dwarf and making sure he didn't trip on the metal, it took him a while to identify what he was fighting —a truly giant rat. He had never seen anything like it if the truth be told. Its eyes glinted red, its fur was thick and mangy, and its teeth looked longer than any animal's had a right to be.

"This rodent," Justin yelled as he backed out of the way of the snapping teeth, "is a truly unusual size."

"Oh, you noticed, did you?" Zaara shouted in response.

"R!" he called as he slashed. "O! U!" He stepped forward and thrust the blade into the animal's eye. "S!"

It screamed and fell to the ground, where it twitched horribly.

"ROUS?" Zaara asked blankly.

"So, it's not a human thing?" Lyle asked her.

"No. No, it's not."

"It's a long story." Justin shrugged. "Oh, hey, look." He stooped to take a gold ring off the ground. "It was hoarding things like a dragon. Off we go, I guess."

"Will you tell us about the ROUS?" Zaara asked. "We do have quite a walk ahead of us, after all."

"Fine, fine… Okay, so where do I begin? Once, there was a princess named Buttercup…"

It had begun to get dark by the time they reached the widow's hut again, and when she hobbled to the door, it was with a radiant smile.

"So you found my ring! Oh, children, let me get your reward." She hobbled away but returned quickly with a coin purse and a bag that clinked like glass. "I made you all some salves and potions."

"Thank you," Zaara said humbly. "Would you look at Justin's arm? He's tried not to let us see but it had a nasty bite."

"Of course, of course." The woman beckoned them to the table and fixed Justin with a look. "Now, let me see. Ah, good God. Child, this wound is poisoning you."

"Er…" He had seen the bleed debuff as it chipped away at his health and expected it to go away. So far, though, it hadn't. "Yes."

"And did it not occur to you to ask for help?" She clicked her teeth, hobbled to the table in the corner, and began mixing. "One of these days, that'll kill you."

"I'd say it's more important that he learn how to dodge," Zaara suggested.

"You're too clumsy," the AI told Justin. *"I keep waiting for you to figure out your role but you don't. This is excruciating."*

"Excruciating for you?" he muttered under his breath. "I'm the one with the bite on my arm."

"Look, you don't have what it takes to do all the fancy footwork. Try something else."

Justin didn't have a chance to ask what it meant as the healer had returned with a set of salves and bandages. Zaara carried a steaming bowl of water.

"Hold him," the older woman told the other two.

"What? Hold me? Why—ow, fuck!" He did his very best to levitate through the roof of the thatched-roof cottage, an effort that was thwarted by his teammates. They hung onto him as the woman cleaned the wound with brisk, efficient strokes of a brush and rubbed the whole area with salve. "God in heaven, woman, what are you doing?"

She didn't bother to answer. "Keep holding him," she told his companions. She bound the wound tightly with strips of linen and stooped to glare at him. "If I have them release you, will you leave the bandage on?"

"My arm," he said through gritted teeth, "is on fire."

"Good gracious, boy, you can see that's not true." She looked at his companions. "Give it a few more seconds."

"I'll give you all my loot," Justin said wildly to Lyle. To Zaara, he suggested, "And a new set of daggers. Maybe? An old map? Uh…a magic textbook?"

"I'd like that." She gave him that smile that made his stomach flip. "But I won't let go of you. Sit still and stop being such a baby."

Hearing her call him a baby wasn't good for his wounded pride. Justin sank into the chair and muttered under his breath, but he noticed that the wound had begun to feel better. He watched the widow darkly as she went to the corner and pulled something out from under the bed. When she turned holding a sword, he almost shoved the chair over backward as visions of demonic sacrifice ran rampant in his head. Even Lyle and Zaara surged to their feet.

Their hostess gave them a disbelieving look. "Good heavens. I'm not planning to kill you. I want to give you this sword. It's a good sight better than the one you have, and gods know, I've no use for it. Now, run along, all of you. It's getting late and you need your rest if you plan to go off adventuring. Remember to come back for potions."

It was surprisingly pleasant to have an annoying parent in the game too. Justin smiled at her and bowed awkwardly. When she handed him the sword, it felt heavy in his hands but also right. This was the kind he'd wanted when he started the game, and no amount of polishing would make his old, rusted blade into a proper weapon like this one.

"Thank you," he told the woman. "We'll be back, I promise."

CHAPTER THIRTY-SEVEN

The villagers of East Newbrook had heard of the good deeds the three adventurers had done. Justin almost thought they cared more about the lost wedding ring and the flocks of sheep than they did about Sephith's defeat.

"Of course they do," Zaara said over a lavish breakfast. The innkeeper had only reluctantly taken coin for their rooms the night before and now went out of his way to offer every amenity he could.

"I don't get it." Justin took a big bite of bread. If he didn't concentrate too hard, he really could imagine he was eating.

"Look." She considered what to say for a moment. "There are always tyrants, right? There's always some fuckhead wanting to rule the world who turns villagers into slaves. If it hadn't been Sephith, it'd probably have been the king, drafting them to fight in his wars. Sure, they hated that dude, but as far as they're concerned, another one will simply come along soon."

He put his mug of ale down and stared at her. "Are you telling me we went through all of that for nothing, in their opinion?"

"Not nothing." She shrugged. "They're always happy to see someone like that defeated. But they know that soon, there'll be another one. When it comes to things like lost wedding rings or wolf packs…well, you can deal with those. Once you fix those problems, everyone's better off for a while."

"Huh." He ate a few berries off his plate while he it though. "I never thought of it like that."

"That's plain." Zaara gave him a curious look. "Where do you come from that you don't know anyone who thinks like that?"

Justin decided against even trying to explain Silicon Valley. "It's a long story and not as cool as the one about Princess Buttercup. Let's go find Lyle and dunk him in the fountain."

"Your dwarf friend is already up," the innkeeper informed them. "He got up with the sun and he's at the blacksmith. He said he was looking for something for you."

"For me?" He exchanged a confused glance with his teammate. "I guess we'd better go see, then. We're heading to the ruins today, so we won't be back for a while."

"I'll have my boy run some provisions to the blacksmith," the land-lord told them. "And your rooms will be kept ready, don't you fear."

He would have protested but Zaara shook her head. As they walked out into the sunlight, she told him, "Tyrants are common, but heroes are rare. East Newbrook saw many adventurers come through looking for glory and almost none of them cared to help with the little things." She elbowed him. "Besides, weren't you excited to have tavern wenches falling all over you?"

"Uh…" He colored and cleared his throat awkwardly. That fantasy now seemed embarrassingly juvenile. His dreams lately had been filled not so much with curvy tavern wenches as a figure in black armor, light on her feet and with a ready smile. "Someone pointed out that was stupid."

"Eh." She shrugged. "Well, I'll be damned, the innkeeper was right." She pointed to where Lyle lounged outside the blacksmith's shop. "Lyle!"

"So ye finally decided to show up." The dwarf shook his head at them. "Lazy buggers."

"This coming from the dwarf who wakes up at noon most days,"

Justin said. "The innkeeper said you were here getting something for…me?"

"That's right." He slung his arm around the young man's shoulders. Given the difference in their heights, it didn't work very well and he settled for shoving him in the back to push him into the blacksmith's shop. "My thought was what do ye do with someone who doesn't know how to avoid his enemies?"

"Footwork lessons?" he suggested.

"Oh, should I add tap dancing to this game?" the AI asked him.

"Nah, you're too hopeless for that." Lyle delivered the insult distractedly. He looked at the blacksmith, who hammered a large sheet of metal. "Armor!"

"Oh, wow." Justin dropped his pack on the floor and hurried to look. The armor was a little rough but it was miles better than anything he'd had yet. Between this and the new sword, it would be like playing an entirely different game.

The blacksmith, a young man with his hair held back in a braid, ducked his head apologetically. "It's not as good as it should be, sir. Our master blacksmith was taken by Sephith a year past, and no one worth their salt would come to replace him. I've made it so another should be able to add to it, though."

"Don't apologize." He looked at his leather armor. "This is what it's replacing, after all. And I like it. Did you teach yourself to do this?"

"I was still learning when Geoffrey was taken." The young man flushed. "And most of what these people need is nails and plows and so on. Horseshoes too, not armor or swords."

"I'm glad to have this." He began to strip his leather armor off. "Do you want any of this for scraps? And how much do I owe you?"

"Aye, the leather would be useful. It'll be…" The blacksmith swallowed. "Fifteen copper, sir."

It was a pitifully low price for his work and barely enough to cover the cost of the metal, and after a few days of adventures, Justin had enough in his purse to spend more. He handed him two silver as well as his leather armor and his old sword. With the blacksmith's thanks ringing in their ears, the adventurers clanked away to find an alchemist.

The new armor was difficult to walk in. He noticed fatigue taking his energy every few steps and could only hope that he grew stronger as time went on. Lyle took practice swipes with his new weapons—sets of long, curved claws that he wore over his knuckles. It would turn any normal boxing match into a bloodbath—and make the dwarf's punches less ridiculous and more deadly.

Although Justin had to admit, his teammate did have a very good track record due to sheer chutzpah. Few wolves, orcs, or wizards could believe that an unarmed dwarf would run in, headlong and with no apparent concern, to punch them.

The alchemist, a man with a long beard and overly dramatic phrasing, had several things in stock. He sold "a vial of the sea's fury" to Lyle—a basic potion Justin suspected was nothing more than caffeine—and "the purest, distilled essence of the stars" to Zaara.

"What exactly is that?" he asked her once they were out of the shop.

"I'll show you." She led him to a bench, where she wet a rag with the potion and rubbed it carefully over both her daggers. When she had finished, she put the bottle away with great care and placed the rag on the cobblestones before she stated, "Ignis!" The two blades and the rag both burst into flames and she smiled, satisfied. "See?"

"So, here's how it'll work," Lyle said, as they made their way out of town, their packs heavier now with the provisions from the innkeeper. "I'll run out and surprise 'em and Justin can follow and draw their attention with that sword. Once they're all focused on him, Zaara and I will do the real damage."

"Excuse me," Justin said, with dignity. "I can be useful, you know."

"Of course you can," she said soothingly. "And this is how. You take all the hits."

"Oh." He realized now what the AI had tried to push him toward. "I'll be the tank."

"Finally." He chose to ignore the comment and the snark in it.

"What's a tank?" Lyle asked.

"Uh…nothing. It's not important. Let's head to those ruins, shall we?"

Mary took the last sip of her coffee and looked around. Normally, Tad would be whistling while he read through his briefings for the day. He probably was, she reminded herself, but he was in DC right now and she was there to be close to Justin—which meant the house was unnaturally quiet.

She cleaned her breakfast dishes with a sigh and got ready to leave. DuBois and the others were sure that, any day now, she would be able to try to go into the game world with him, and she was equal parts impatient and terrified. She had only ever seen the pods used for comatose patients and even the thought of being put under was enough to worry her.

Her desire to see her son, however, was stronger than her fear. At the insistence of the doctor, she and Tad had not sent any further messages. They weren't supposed to distract him, the man explained. He needed to focus on strengthening himself and his survival instincts and forging relationships.

Those relationships were what worried her. She had seen him form very few close friendships in his life, and she had never seen him take to someone as quickly as he had bonded with Zaara. The woman might be a figment of his imagination, but Mary was quite sure no mother would be happy with her son bringing home a black-leather-clad, dagger-wielding runaway.

Not only that, a part of her had worried since she gave Justin the dragon that he would never want to return to the real world. Why would he, after all, when he had everything he'd ever wanted? Now, he could throw fireballs, run his life without any restrictions, and ride dragons. If he fell in love too, that could be too much to come back from.

She realized she simply stood and stared into nothing with the water pouring over her hands. With a little shake of her head, she put the mug and plate into the dishwasher and was about to pick her purse up when the computer dinged.

It was probably her sister, she thought. Ever since Justin's accident, the family had tried to rally around the two of them and even offered to fly out. When he was moved to the PIVOT labs, however, Mary had tried to keep them all at arm's length—an attempt that had fallen apart spectacularly when the press broke the story of the "experiments" being done on him.

While Tad dodged reporters in DC, she had dodged them at home as well as fielded increasingly worried questions from her family. She didn't like lying but she also knew that her family wouldn't understand the range of pressures that were being brought to bear on the Williamses.

If she didn't answer this email, though, her sister might well go a little insane and fly out from Nebraska, and she shuddered to think of that. She went to the computer, brought up her email, and her face immediately snapped into a glare.

It wasn't Annette who had emailed her. It was the girl who'd almost killed Justin and who was the reason they were in this mess to start with.

Mary had refused to see Tina in the hospital. She'd ignored the calls, the texts, and the handwritten letters. She had deleted the voicemails and text messages without reading them before she blocked the girl's number and shredded the letters. When Tad's aides called her to pass messages on, she told them not to speak to the woman.

How she had gotten her email, she didn't know. On the advice of other senate spouses, she had set up a new one when Tad was elected and it wasn't linked to anything—not any of her favorite shops, not the utilities, and not even her friends.

She was about to delete the message, but the title caught her eye. *Please*, it read simply.

Only one word and nothing more.

Something about that word caught at her heart and she swallowed. *Please.* She could sense Tina's desperation, and almost of its own volition, her hand scrolled slowly. She hesitated only a moment before she clicked on the email.

Dear Mrs. Williams,

I know you must hate me for what I did to Justin. You're right to. What happened that night was my fault, and I hope you can believe that however much you hate me, it's nothing compared to how much I hate myself for what happened.

I only want you to know I'm sorry. I know I can't ever make it up to you, but I want to help in any way I can. I keep seeing news reports about Justin and every time, I think it should be me. I wish it had been. It isn't fair.

Please, if I can do ANYTHING, let me know.

I know I don't have any right to ask this, but if Justin is okay, if he's recovering, could you tell me? It's hell not to know.

I'm so sorry.

Sincerely,

Tina Castro

Mary stared at the message and fought a lump in her throat while her eyes stung with hot tears. *It isn't fair.*

She was damned right it wasn't fair. It should be Tina in a hospital bed right now, Tina who might never wake up, her parents who—

Her heart seized at that thought. If it had been, her parents would be at her bedside. They would lie awake at night, afraid to go to sleep because they knew they would see her grave in their nightmares. They would watch her cheeks grow gaunter by the week, and they would rage at the fact that she was so close to them, still breathing but unreachable.

And her parents would never have received the offer Mary and Tad had. They wouldn't have been in the news to catch PIVOT's attention, and they wouldn't even have had the offer of a bribe. They wouldn't be able to give her a dragon for her birthday.

Mary couldn't wish her pain on anyone, and it would be worse for them.

Her breathing slowed. She no longer needed to sit on her hands to keep from typing an angry tirade. She could close the email without wanting to make Tina's pain worse.

But she couldn't find kind words yet. Not yet. She couldn't face the woman who'd taken Justin's life away and exposed Tad to threats of blackmail.

Not yet.

She snatched her purse, powered the computer down, and left for the PIVOT labs.

CHAPTER THIRTY-EIGHT

The two young engineers stared at the breakfast burrito on the kitchenette table. It had been thirty minutes since Jacob had arrived with the four burritos and twenty minutes since they had finished theirs. Now, with Amber still not there, both of them began to wonder how dead they would be if they ate hers as well.

DuBois, meanwhile, wandered into the kitchenette with his hand over his sternum. "So heavy," he complained.

"You can't only eat popcorn, man." Jacob gave him a hard look. "I'm…worried about you. And I lived on ramen and vodka for a year."

"Two years," Nick corrected him and said to the other man, "And you should take him seriously. He knows what he's talking about. He got scurvy. Literal scurvy."

The doctor swung to face them, clearly interested in this development. "Really?"

"We don't need to go into this," Jacob said grumpily.

"He didn't work it out for a while," Nick said wickedly, "because when he's sick, he gets himself two cartons of orange juice and drinks them straight. You should have seen his face when he finally put two and two together."

His teammate grumbled and looked up as Amber wandered into

the room. She wore the same clothes she had the day before, and the shadows under her eyes were so dark that he had to double-check to make sure she hadn't been in a fight.

"Hi," she said distractedly and made a beeline for the coffee.

"We got you a breakfast burrito," Jacob said.

"Thanks." She drained an entire cup of coffee, wiped a drip off the edge of her mouth, and threw the mug in the trash. "Wait. That doesn't go there." She fished it out and put it in the little dishwasher. "More coffee."

"Did you sleep at all?" Jacob asked her.

"No." She came to sit, cradling a new mug in both hands. When she realized it was empty, she stared at it blankly until Nick stood and retrieved the pot. "Thanks."

"Why were you up?" Nick asked her.

"Uh…"

"She was researching the reporter who got in," DuBois said. "And who she tackled," he added darkly.

"You did what?" Jacob gave her a horrified look. "Wait—someone got in?"

"Yes." Amber gave him a weary look and gulped her coffee. "I didn't hurt her and I didn't confirm that Justin was here, but I spent the night trying to find out who she worked for and also to buy a better security system. The landlord agreed to let us put in whatever we wanted."

"Did he agree to that because you called him at an ungodly time of the morning and he simply wanted to go back to sleep?"

"Possibly." She raised an eyebrow. "Don't judge my method. I get results. I'll need you to scrounge up another ten grand for the system, though."

"Didn't we get five million from our mystery donor?" Nick interjected.

"It goes more quickly than you'd think," Jacob said. "Between the servers and everything else, we don't have much left, especially with trying to stabilize the power fluctuations."

"Oh, we resolved that last night, too." Amber finished her second cup of coffee and Nick poured her another. "I switched a few of the servers to a different block of circuits and also unplugged the most power-hungry machine we had."

"You killed Justin?"

"No, you idiot." She rolled her eyes. "There's one thing in this office that sucks a wildly variant amount of power and was made with zero thought to efficiency, and that's the giant, deluxe popcorn machine."

The two young men looked at DuBois, who regarded the ceiling with sudden, fanatical interest.

"The…the popcorn machine," Jacob said after a fairly tense silence.

"Yep."

"That's why we kept having blackouts."

"Yep."

"Well, selling it will get us some of our security money." He sighed. "It looks like it's back to store-bought popcorn for you, buddy."

The doctor muttered and headed into the lab as Mary entered the kitchenette. She looked almost as distracted as Amber and raised her eyebrows to see all of them.

"I only saw one car in the parking lot."

"Well, DuBois never leaves and Nick and I carpooled," Jacob explained. "But…Amber, where did you park?"

"I took an Uber," she said. "Do you honestly think I should be driving?"

"Good point." He smiled at Mary. "How are you?"

"I'm…not important. Did you say something about security?"

The three members of the PIVOT team looked at one another and tried to reach a silent consensus before Jacob explained. "The press seems to have found out where we are, and we'd like to make sure no one can simply walk in."

"You should call my husband," Mary suggested.

"I really wouldn't want to bother him," he said.

"No, I mean it's possible he could get you funding." She raised an eyebrow. "Senators are always meeting with donors and quite a few have had funding for their pet projects pushed through. Why shouldn't we?"

"Uh…" Unsure what to do with this sudden change in perspective on her part, he gave her a blank smile. "I'll…um, I'll give him a call. Nick, would you like to walk Mrs. Williams through the pod setup?"

"Please call me Mary," the woman said as she moved away with the other engineer. "I feel old enough as it is around you three."

Jacob smiled and followed them but returned a moment later to pull gently on Amber's arm. She shambled along in his wake, still sipping at her coffee and her eyes focused on the middle distance. He wondered idly if she'd notice if he thunked her over the head with a brick.

Not that he'd risk it, of course. In a fight between a sleep-deprived, zombified Amber and anyone up to and including a rabid bear, he'd bet on her every time.

As they had requested, Mary had come dressed in more casual clothes than she usually wore. From what Jacob could tell, she had purchased her sweatpants and long-sleeved t-shirt specifically for this experiment, and she looked—ironically—very uncomfortable when she took her coat off.

"Okay," Nick said. His tone was very soothing and he had realized she was worried. "You remember how the game started for Justin? He was alone and had to hunt rabbits, avoid wolves, and all of that. You won't have to do anything like that, okay?"

The woman nodded. Her arms were wrapped around herself now and she stared at the pod as she shivered nervously.

"When you get into the game world, you'll be in a comfortable room," he continued. "You will see windows that lead to a pleasant seaside view, and there will be sounds like waves and birds singing. You can stay there as long as you want."

Mary looked heartened at that.

"There will be different challenges around the room." He opened the pod and gestured for her to sit, smoothly beginning the preparations as he kept her mind occupied with the details. "Objects to pick up and fit together, a thin carpet on the floor for you to try to walk along, things like that. This will help you get used to the game controls."

Jacob was impressed. The woman was scared—as, he had to admit, he would be if he'd never used this technology before. The only person she had ever seen in this world was locked inside it.

Nick took her hand to help her lie inside the pod, then clipped a pulse monitor on her finger while he attached electrodes to her head. DuBois hovered at the side and watched carefully. He did not intervene, however. The group had decided together that, when it came to Mary, it would be best to have someone with a good bedside manner to introduce the world.

"We've taken your pulse every time you've been in recently," Nick told her, "so we have a good idea of your resting pulse rate. If we sense that you're stressed or uncomfortable, we'll stop the simulation— you'll see the world fade out like a sunset. You can also stop the simulation at any time by saying, 'stop the simulation.' We'll be able to hear your voice, remember, exactly like with Justin."

"Right." She looked at them. Her face was pale. "What will happen if it…doesn't work?"

"It could go wrong in a number of ways," DuBois said. He fell silent when Amber gave him a death glare of epic iciness.

"It boils down to one of two possibilities," she told Mary. The coffee must be kicking in because she looked mostly human by now. "Either you won't be able to get the input and you won't see or hear anything, in which case you can tell us that. Or the game won't take your input, in which case you won't be able to move. We'll be able to see either of those two things happen, so we'll simply stop the simulation and one of us will troubleshoot."

The woman nodded wordlessly.

"Okay," Nick said. "Now, close your eyes and when you open them, you should be in the seaside room and you'll hear my voice."

Mary closed her eyes and he pressed the button to begin the simulation. Her muscles twitched and her eyes began to move behind her closed eyelids. He watched her carefully and examined the vital sign feeds before he closed the lid of the pod.

"Mary, can you hear me?"

"I can hear you." The voice was surprised. "How am I speaking?"

"I'll have Amber show you the mechanism." Nick smiled. "What do you see?"

"I'm in a room like you said. I think it's a castle."

"Describe it in as much detail as you can."

On the screen, the team could see the room she was in—thanks to the recent upgrades the mysterious donation had purchased for them —and Amber was poised to take notes on any differences they saw between her description and reality.

"The stone is gray," Mary said. "There are rugs on the floor. One is an oriental rug, another is a very long, thin rug. They look thick—oh!" The floor rushed up as her character fell. "How do I get up?"

"Relax for a moment," Nick told her. "Breathe. Give me a long breath—in, two, three…hold…out, two, three. Now stand up."

The camera righted itself and she asked, "How did that work?"

"The game responds to your intent and what your body thinks it's doing," he explained. "You sent the nerve impulses to stand, so that's what you did in the game. But it's like juggling or knitting. If you think about it too hard, you can't do it—you have to do it subconsciously."

"Huh." She took a few unsteady steps to the window. "Oh, it's beautiful. You wanted me to describe things, right? I must be high up. I can see the water and the sunlight on it. There are no clouds. Oh, a bird! The water is so lovely, and I hear the waves, even though I don't think I should be able to. There's wind."

"Good, good. Do you smell anything?"

"No."

"That one seems to take longer," Nick said to Amber, who nodded. Justin had also taken a while to smell and taste things in the game, and the feed still wasn't perfect.

"Can you run through some of the tests?" Nick asked her. "Try picking things up and putting them down, stacking them on top of one another, et cetera."

"Okay." Mary walked slowly to the table on one side of the screen, and they watched as she began trying to pick things up. It took her a few attempts to close her fingers around something successfully, and her depth perception was a little off at first.

"Mary, do you wear glasses?"

"When I read," she said. "Oh. *Oh.* I see."

"Yeah." He considered. "I think we might have to work with things as they are for now. I wouldn't be surprised if things adjust over time, but you could have trouble with depth perception when you log in and log out."

They watched her complete the trials, mostly in silence. Amber, at Jacob's urging, left him to take notes and headed off to devour her breakfast burrito. DuBois periodically stared longingly at his now-unplugged popcorn machine. Nick fiddled with the controls.

Finally, Mary picked up one of the objects and, after a pause, threw it out the window of the room. It sailed away and she laughed before she ran to look out. The world tilted dizzily as she gazed at the city below.

"Oh, dear. Oh, I don't like heights."

"That's good to know," Nick told her. "Next time you load in, you'll be on the ground floor."

"Thank you." The view swung crazily as she looked around. "Where did the plate land? I didn't hit anyone, did I?"

"Even if you did, they're not real," DuBois said.

"I still don't want to hurt them."

"That's illogical." The doctor opened his mouth to speak again and received an elbow in the side. "Ow! What was that for?"

"She's being nice," Jacob said. "That's one of the things that'll stave off the robot apocalypse. Don't call it illogical."

DuBois shut up but he looked deeply skeptical.

"Okay, Mary," Nick said, "you can now choose what your character will look like. Three options will pop up in front of you."

In the viewfinder, three magical portals appeared. The first, with a white background, showed a woman with blonde hair caught in a high ponytail and a costume reminiscent of a certain warrior princess but with more cleavage. The second, with a blue background, showed a woman with a wide-brimmed pirate's hat and an eyepatch, her white shirt slightly translucent and thigh-length high-heeled boots over tight pants. She blew a kiss. The third wore a plunging green gown and held a ball of flame in her cupped hands. Her black hair swirled in an imaginary wind.

Mary seemed dumbstruck. No sound came from the monitor. Finally, she said faintly, "Ah…I'm not sure I'm comfortable wearing any of this."

Amber gave Nick one of her trademark Fix-It-Now looks. "I'm sorry, Mary," she said quickly. "These are some of the default characters that were here when we acquired the game. This should have been fixed. One moment." She pressed a few keys to remove the portals and leaned forward to look Nick in the eyes. "This is something I never thought I'd have to say but stop objectifying the senator's wife."

"I'm sorry!" he squeaked. He began typing furiously on another computer. "I loaded the wrong game assets. I swear. Don't kill me. Okay, this should work. One second…" He hesitated and looked genuinely frightened before he pressed a button nervously.

This set of characters, Jacob saw with relief, was much better. The first wore flowing red robes. Her face was in shadow but they could see a hint of grey hair, and black power swirled in one hand. The second wore armor much like Zaara's, although it was brown instead of black, and a deep-red cloak. She was younger but not as heavily made up as the women from the first set. The third had heavier plate armor and wore a sword strapped across her back.

"I like the first one," Mary said. She sounded quite pleased. "I see why Justin likes this so much. I'd love to be able to throw spells at people when I get older—and sweep around in fancy robes like that."

"I can't help you with the spells," Amber said, "but I'm fairly sure the robes are doable."

The woman laughed.

"Okay," Nick said. "I'll walk you through a few trials that should show us how well your buffs are working. If everything is good, I'll port you to Justin's zone, okay? Head to the door."

As they watched Mary emerge improbably into a meadow, DuBois leaned closer to murmur to Amber, "If this works, you have more than merely a recovery tool. You have a way for people to interact with their loved ones while they're in a coma."

Her mouth gaped. She'd been so caught up in tracking their mysterious benefactor that she hadn't thought about the other applications of their research.

"We could even use it for people to speak to loved ones after they die," the doctor continued.

"Shhhh," she hissed.

"Not Justin—anyone. Imagine being able to speak to a parent or a grandparent...or a spouse who'd passed away."

"Holy shit," she murmured. "Uh, Jacob? We'll want that in some marketing materials at some point."

"Wait." DuBois gestured at the screen. "Let's see if it works first."

The engineer buried his face in his hands. "Buzzkill," he said.

CHAPTER THIRTY-NINE

The ruins lay a fair distance from town—easily a day's journey, although they could see the faint shimmer of them nestled in the hollow of a mountain long before they reached them.

As they walked, Zaara and Lyle bickered good-naturedly about the various mythology of the dwarves, so Justin was able to let his mind drift. He could only think it was a shame that he wouldn't have all these hard-earned muscles in reality when he woke.

That thought led him to wonder what it would be like to wake up. Would he come out of sleep all at once, or would he go to sleep one night in the game and wake up in the real world? Would the doctors tell him what they were going to do?

Would he have a chance to say goodbye to people?

When he glanced at his companions, he felt a pang of sadness. He knew they weren't real, but the thought of vanishing out of their lives without so much as a goodbye seemed cruel. Would other people encounter them in the game and hear about Justin, the adventurer who had disappeared?

Lyle saw him looking at them and his brows snapped together.

"Yer lookin' peaky," he told him. "It's that armor. Yer not strong enough for it yet. And ye know why, don't ye?"

"Because this is the first time I've worn it?" He did feel exhausted, now that the dwarf mentioned it, and he thought that was very unfair. After all, he wasn't *really* hauling around a suit of plate armor.

"No. It's because ye don't drink enough ale." The dwarf nodded seriously. "We'll start working on that in the next town we get to."

"Uh…" Justin wondered what his parents would say if he came out of this experience otherwise recovered but suddenly a raging alcoholic.

"Hey, look." Zaara, thankfully, distracted Lyle. "There's a cart up ahead. It looks like it's broken down, though."

The three of them increased their pace and the AI made snide comments now and then as Justin panted and wished vaguely for death. Luckily, they weren't too far from the cart and soon stared at a large man who held a hammer in astonishingly well-muscled forearms.

"Greetings," he said, but his tone wasn't very friendly. Nearby, the horse tied to the cart pranced nervously, and Justin could see that the wheel beside the man's leg had cracked.

"We're on our way to the ruins in the shadow of the mountain," he said, "and I see that your cart is broken. Is there anything we can do to help you fix it?"

The man gave them a measuring glance. "Where'd you come from, then?"

"East Newbrook," Zaara explained. "We've been there for some weeks—well, I have. These two only arrived a week or so ago."

"Aye, what news of the wizard?"

"He's gone," she told him and glanced skyward. "Some of his magic lingers, but he's dead."

"That's what I'd heard." He scratched his chin, now thoughtful. "It's why I decided to come along, see. I'm looking for a job."

"As an adventurer?" Justin asked. "You could come with us. We could always use more weapons and you look like you'd be good with that hammer."

"Ha." The man chuckled. "I have no interest in adventuring. I'll leave that to you. But it seems you aren't highwaymen, so how'd you like to make a few coins?"

He bowed. "We're at your service."

Zaara gave a snort of ill-concealed amusement and his cheeks flushed.

The man, thankfully, pretended not to notice. "A wolf scared my donkey off," he explained. "A great, hulking beast came out of the woods and tried to get the donkey away from me. I had a hell of a time keeping the horse calm—that's how we struck the rock that cracked the wheel—and I managed to scare the wolf off, but the donkey ran as well. I'd appreciate you finding it before the wolf finds itself a nice meal."

"We can do that." Justin stopped himself before he bowed again. "Which direction did the donkey go?"

"Thataway." He pointed. "I hoped he'd come back, but no such luck."

"We'll take a look." He gestured to Zaara. "Ladies first."

"You know, when people say that, I don't think they mean ladies should lead the way into wolf-infested territory." She grinned as she started off. "Also, feel free to stay here. You're struggling in that armor, aren't you?"

"Shut up." He panted as he clanked after her.

The meadows sloped away from the road in a series of winding hills dotted with stands of trees. It would have been quite pretty if not for the fact that he knew he would have to climb the hills when this was over.

He considered taking the armor off, but if he did that, Zaara would laugh again.

Lyle gave a low whistle a few minutes later and stopped to point. The donkey grazed in a patch of open grass, and it looked at them warily as they approached. Zaara, thankfully, must have learned something about farm animals because she approached it from the side and let it sniff her before she slipped a hand around its halter.

"There, now," she told it. "Should we get you back home?"

"Uh…Zaara?" Justin stared at the nearby stand of trees. "Zaara, we have a new friend."

"I know, isn't he sweet?" She stroked the donkey's ears.

"Not the donkey, ye daft lass. Look," Lyle muttered. "Look at the trees."

She complied and her eyes widened when she saw the shadow lurking there. They'd found the donkey barely in time, it seemed, because the wolf that had spooked the cart had arrived.

"There's something wrong with it," Zaara said. She had stepped in front of the donkey and her other hand rested on the hilt of a knife.

"Is the something perhaps that it's twice the size any wolf should be?" he whispered in response. "Lyle, I see you're thinking of charging. Do not."

"It's part of the plan," the dwarf whisper-shouted at him.

"The tank pulls."

"What does that even mean?"

"It means I go first." Justin burst into a run without waiting for a response and immediately regretted his decision. His armor was heavy and fatigue points had him down to three-quarters health without having reached the wolf yet.

The beast didn't run and instead, charged to meet him. He didn't have the nimbleness to dodge anymore, although he tried as best he could. The only result was that he tumbled awkwardly in a heap of clattering armor pieces without changing direction at all, after which the wolf collided with him at high speed.

In the darkened lab, everyone except Nick clapped a hand over their mouth. Even DuBois, perpetually intrigued by the mechanics of the game instead of taking it seriously, looked faintly queasy.

"Oh, dear," he said.

"Ohhhhhhh." Amber shook her head in disbelief. "Oh, no."

"What's going on?" Mary asked. "What do I hear in the background?"

"I, uh—I knocked the coffee machine over," Amber told her and motioned to everyone else to be quiet. To the others, more quietly, she added, "I hope he learns about the sword soon. It won't help him if he never gets a chance to swing it."

REALLY BAD TANK, LEVEL 3

The wolf seemed as surprised to be bulldozed by Justin as he was by falling instead of dodging. As much as anything that was four hundred pounds of killing machine could trip, it did and skidded while it scrabbled to get its feet under it again.

"Stooooooooout!"

"Goddammit…" he muttered as he tried to roll over.

"You know, when I had them belabor the idea of you being a tank, I didn't think you'd be quite this bad at it."

"Oh, so you weren't trying to get me killed? That's reassuring." He glared at the sky.

"You always look up when you talk to me. I'm not God, you know. I'm an AI."

"Whatever." He managed to haul himself up and leaned heavily on his sword as he glowered at Lyle, who dodged wildly around the wolf. It wasn't quite sure what to do with a short force of nature, but once in a while, it would stretch its neck and snap its teeth to force him to dance away.

"Justin!" the dwarf panted. "The sooner you can get up, the better. My fists are doing nothing."

"Almost like punching a wolf was a flawed concept," Justin retorted as he took a step and slashed with all his might at one of the wolf's hind legs.

The effect was unexpectedly good. Fifty hit points floated away and took a chunk of the wolf's health bar with it. The creature stumbled heavily to the side. It whipped its head around with a snarl and he resisted the urge to run away. He was a tank and needed to stand his ground.

At least he'd captured its attention.

"Zaara! Hit it with everything you have."

"I'm on it!" she yelled as he planted his feet and swung his weapon. It was much harder, he discovered, to stand his ground when he was in a virtual reality. Like most people he knew, he had laughed at the videos of people in VR games who cowered and screamed while being attacked.

It turned out that your nervous system was a hell of a lot stronger than your tactical brain. He didn't curl into a ball on the ground but he hunched his shoulders, planted his feet, and held the sword out. Again, the blade sliced cleanly through fur and flesh and again, a chunk of hit points came away. Although he was thrown back several feet and ended up on his butt in the dirt, the impact didn't do as much damage as he'd expected.

Score one for the armor.

REALLY BAD TANK, LEVEL 4

"Oh, come on!" Justin yelled at the sky. "Zaara? Any minute now."

"I'm trying," she responded. "I've thrown three fireballs and they don't do anything."

"Wait, what?" Justin scrambled back as the wolf advanced. It was limping but it had murder in its eyes. The beast snapped at him once, looked at the other two, and seemed to be trying to decide what to do.

Apparently, he would have to be the one to end this. He came to a quick decision and slumped in the dirt.

"Justin!" Zaara yelled.

The wolf seized its chance and leapt.

Its weight and momentum carried it forward powerfully and into three feet of steel that pierced its belly. Justin threw his head and torso sideways as the huge body slumped onto the sword and he felt a wrenching pain in his elbow. He released the weapon with a yell and curled into a ball as he tried to push himself up on his good arm. The other wasn't dislocated, he was sure, but his nervous system sure thought it should be.

This was worse than the widow's salve. Dear God. He hobbled to the wolf's side, grasped the sword, and made to yank it out but stared as the beast shrank and faded away before his eyes. On the ground lay a bloodied, bruised man who stretched toward him.

"You have to—help them—" He gasped as he tried to speak.

"What?" Justin stared at him in horror. He hadn't felt sad to kill the zombies around Sephith's tower—they were already dead, after all— and he hadn't felt sad to kill Sephith, who manifestly deserved it. But this man was scared and now, he recalled that the wolf had only charged him once he attacked.

He hadn't behaved like a wolf because he wasn't one. Justin knelt at his side as Zaara ran closer with the bag of salves.

"Lie still," she told the man.

"No." He shook his head. "Too—late. You have to listen." His hand closed around Justin's. "There are more of us. Not werewolves. Witch…cursed us. We robbed her and she cursed us. You have to help."

"You robbed a woman and now you're preying on livestock," Zaara said, offended. "And you want us to help you?"

"Only—trying to survive," the man rasped. "A wolf still has to eat. Kill her and the spell will release them. Then…justice." He looked like he wanted to say more but before he could, he slumped in the dirt and lay still.

Justin's stomach heaved. He hadn't ever seen anyone die before, and although this wasn't the real world, it felt real. The smell of blood hung in the air and the man had talked to him moments before going still. He had felt the way his sword sliced through his flesh and with something close to horror, realized he was the reason for the body in the dirt.

To his surprise, it was Lyle who seemed to understand. The dwarf came to lay a heavy hand on his shoulder. "It shouldn't get easier t'kill men," he advised him. "When I left for a life aboveground, that's what my da told me. He said to do whatever I wished but when it got easier to kill a man, I'd know it was time to seek another life." He held a hand out and hauled him to his feet. "Let's bring this donkey back and rest, eh?"

CHAPTER FORTY

Walking the donkey to its owner was a silent affair. Zaara seemed unsure of what to say, and Lyle had spoken his piece already and didn't seem inclined to add to it.

Justin, meanwhile, did his best to not feel like he'd made a terrible mistake. Zaara's suggestion of holing up in a tavern seemed like a better and better idea with each passing moment. It was one thing to go after a megalomaniac with a horde of zombie servants, but this kind of thing made him sick to his stomach.

"Only trying to survive," the man had said.

The donkey's owner studied them critically when they arrived. "What in the seven hells happened to you?"

"We found the wolf," he said shortly.

The man gave him a long look. "Well, I think I'll camp for the night," he said at last. "You're welcome to share my fire. I don't have much coin for you as a thanks, but I'll say this. I'm a blacksmith, and a good one. When next you're in East Newbrook, I'll add touches to that armor of yours, sharpen your swords and knives, whatever you need. You, dwarf—I can sharpen those talons with what I have here."

The blacksmith gathered rocks for a fire with Lyle, who seemed to explain the fight in a low tone. Zaara took one look at Justin's face, wisely decided not to talk to him, and let him wander away from the camp.

He stripped his armor off and wrapped one of the blankets from his pack over his shirt. As the others set up camp, made dinner, and finished the wagon repairs, he prowled the outskirts. The first stars began to twinkle on the eastern horizon when he saw the woman emerge from the shadows.

She wore flowing robes and she walked confidently toward him.

The hair on his arms stood up. No one should be out there at twilight alone, and especially not without a weapon. More than that, though, she seemed familiar in a way he couldn't put his finger on.

"Are you fucking with me?" he asked the AI under his breath.

"I am not." Unfortunately, it volunteered no more information.

The woman moved closer and stared at him for a long time. When she pulled her hood back, white hair gleamed in the light of the rising moon. Her face wore an expression that he couldn't name.

"Justin?" she asked, and her voice cracked.

He took a step back. "Are you the witch?" Please, let someone at the camp see him. Why had he walked away from his sword?

To his surprise, she smiled and he saw a tear trace down one cheek. She gave a laugh that sounded a little like a sob. "I'm not a witch but you have called me that once or twice. Justin…it's me. It's Mom."

"Mom?" His voice came out louder than he wanted it to. In the camp, there was a sudden scuffle of activity and in moments, Lyle and Zaara were there. He looked at them and shook his head. "Could I, uh —could I have a moment with her? Thanks."

They retreated but he saw Lyle sink into the shadows near one of the cartwheels to keep watch on the two of them.

Justin turned to the woman. "You're…you're really Mom? No offense, but this whole virtual world scenario is playing with my head. Can you prove it?"

"Yes." She smiled again, although she still looked like she wanted to cry. "When you were seven, you broke your arm falling off the rope swing at Joey Thaler's house. I wrapped you in the green quilt

Grandma made you and we brought you to the hospital in Dad's old truck."

"Mom." He took two steps and embraced her so tightly she squeaked. "Sorry. I didn't mean to—oh, no." His heart dropped. "Oh, no. Mom. Are you okay? Why are you here?"

"I'm okay!" She clasped his hands. "I came to see you. I wanted to spend time with my boy."

Despite being twenty-four, he had the distinct urge to stomp his foot and remind her that he wasn't a little kid anymore.

"Moooooooom, I'm a dragon slayer!"

He wished hellfire and missed server connections on the AI but held his tongue rather than respond to the sniped comment. To his mother, he said quietly, "How long has it been?"

"A month and a half," she said at once with the recall of someone who had thought of almost nothing else. "They say it's only been a week and a half or so for you in here."

Justin swallowed. "Is that…good? Or bad?"

"I asked. DuBois said it simply is." His mother sounded frustrated and she shook her head. "He said these things take time and your brain needs to rest. There are good signs."

He looked at the camp. The fire crackled and the smell of food cooking drifted on the air. His stomach growled and his muscles ached. It seemed incredible that this wasn't a real place. He debated saying something about how he'd miss it but decided not to. He knew his mother wouldn't understand that.

"How's Dad?" he asked instead.

A series of expressions crossed her face too quickly to track. "He's fine," she said.

"Really?" he pressed.

She took her time to choose her words. "It doesn't take lobbyists very long to discover what motivates you. They tried money and it didn't work. Now, they're trying blackmail."

"Blackmail?"

His mother wavered, then shrugged dismissively. "They doctored photos of him to make it seem like he was having an affair. And, yes, I know they did because I remember that day—I was the one who was with him. He liked to think it wouldn't be complicated when he got to the senate and that he'd always know what to do, but he's finding out it's…not that easy."

Justin nodded.

"He's worried about you," Mary said quietly. "He flies out on the red-eye for his sessions and comes back at night. Every night, he's here and he comes to see you."

He looked away and a lump formed in his throat. "Can we…talk about something else?"

"Of course." She reached for his hand. "How are you?"

"Not that, either." He gave a watery laugh and remembered something. "Where's Tina? Why isn't she here with me?" When he saw the look on his mother's face, he had to take a moment to process it. It wasn't sadness, he realized. It was anger.

It was fury, in fact.

"Tina," his mother said, "is fine."

"Oh, thank God." He pressed a hand over his heart.

"Thank God?" His mother's voice rose. "She crashed that car at ninety miles per hour. You've been in a coma for weeks now, Justin, while she walked away with scratches. And you say thank God?"

"I don't want her dead," Justin said. He frowned at her. "It isn't like you to want someone hurt either."

"I never had someone crash a car with my son in it before," Mary said fiercely. She squeezed his fingers. "It isn't fair. She's the one who messed up and you're the one to pay the price—and, Justin, it's my fault, too. I made you go on that date. If I'd let you stay home like you wanted to that night, you'd be safe now." She pressed a hand over her mouth.

"Mom—"

"No, no. Don't you comfort me. You're the one who's hurt. I came to comfort you." She forced herself to smile.

"Mom." He took her hands. "Don't blame yourself and don't blame Tina. It was an accident. A puppy ran into the road and she didn't want to hit it. This was an accident. It isn't worth hating her over and it isn't like you to do that."

She sighed and nodded but didn't meet his gaze.

"Mom." The word came out before he knew he was speaking. "Will I be okay?"

The way her gaze snapped to his face, he knew she didn't know. On some level, that was comforting—he'd been afraid, he realized, that she was there because she knew he would never get better.

"There's progress," she told him. "Your brain function is improving. They say it's sustained, not merely a fluke."

"Okay." He nodded, dizzy with relief.

"Oh, I've missed you." His mother wrapped him in her arms. "I've missed you so much, Justin."

"I've missed you," he whispered in return. He slid his arms around her back and squeezed until his arms closed on nothing. His mother's face shimmered in the air, blurred out of focus into pixels, and vanished.

For a long moment, he stood and stared at the space where she'd been.

"That's yer mother?" Lyle said from behind him. "She's not the witch, is she?"

Justin laughed. He needed to laugh right now and he was absurdly grateful for the dwarf's presence. "She's not the witch," he said. "She's, ah…you know, it's one of those long stories that aren't as good as the Buttercup one. But if you want, I can tell you all about Luke Skywalker."

CHAPTER FORTY-ONE

Her arms closed around thin air and Justin disappeared like a ghost. Mary opened her mouth to scream as everything around her faded into deep blue studded with stars, then disappeared entirely.

"Justin! DuBois!"

Cold air rushed over her and hands touched her forehead and wrists. The first thing she saw when she opened her eyes was a flood of light. DuBois and Nick removed the patches from her head, their faces strained and pale.

"What happened?" Mary demanded. "Is he okay?"

"He's fine," the young engineer said tightly.

"Well, am I fine? My pulse wasn't rising, I wasn't panicked—"

"It wasn't that." Nick glanced over her shoulder.

"What, then?" She looked at DuBois, who now stood with his shoulders hunched. He didn't meet her gaze as she slid off the table. "Well? So help me, but if you tell me again that I can't see Justin because—"

"Mrs. Williams." Amber's voice was impressively level. Far too level, in fact. "We were instructed to pull you out of the game."

Mary turned slowly. She had the feeling she wouldn't like what she saw and she was right. Two men in suits stood near Amber and Jacob, along with four in bulletproof vests. Jacob was in handcuffs.

She used the same tone she'd used when she came into the house to find Justin setting his winter coat on fire using one of the stove burners. "What is going on here?"

"Ma'am, I'm Agent Klein from the Food and Drug Administration." One of the men stepped forward. "I regret to inform you that there is no FDA approval for this human testing, nor has approval been sought. The lab needs to be shut down."

"Shut down—no." Mary drew herself tall. "No. You can't do that." A part of her registered the oddness of the situation because it somehow felt like a few steps had been omitted from the entire process. It didn't add up, but her brain couldn't think it through.

"They can, Mrs. Williams." Amber shook slightly as she spoke. Her hands were clenched at her sides and wrinkled the sheaf of papers she held in one hand. "We have twenty-four hours to shut the lab down and Jacob is…" She looked at her teammate and swallowed.

"As the President of PIVOT Technologies, I am legally responsible for what happened here," Jacob said. He cleared his throat. "As well as ethically responsible, Mrs. Williams. I hope you won't hold Dr. DuBois, Amber, or Nick responsible for this. I led them to believe we had received FDA approval."

Mary realized what he was doing at the same time Amber did. Their jaws dropped.

"I truly am sorry, Mrs. Williams." He looked miserable and she decided he didn't need to fake that, not with jail time looming. "I had seen the research and the early results were so good, I was sure this was a good way to help Justin. But—"

"That's enough, Mr. Zachary." One of the agents stepped in front of him. "Mrs. Williams, our office will be in contact with you. Ms. Garcia, Mr. Ryan, Dr. DuBois—this lab is to be shut down within twenty-four hours. We will send an agent to oversee the process. Mrs. Williams, you will need to arrange for your son's transfer to an approved medical facility." He gave the team a cold look before he gestured to Jacob. "Mr. Zachary, come with us, please."

The officials left and the young engineers watched their friend go with horrified faces. When they were alone, Amber turned and Mary stepped forward, her chin trembling.

"You let them take him? You're letting them do this?"

Amber held the pieces of paper out. "They have the authority, it seems. The FDA has blanket authority over all drug trials except in very specific instances."

"This is the only thing that's keeping Justin alive!" Her voice was raw. She turned away, a hand over her mouth. "If they take him off this, he'll be locked in, he'll be alone—" She broke off and stared at the wall. "We knew the risks. All of us knew the risks. And they'll haul Jacob up for it and you'll let them?"

"No." The young woman's voice was firm. "Believe me, we will find a way out of this for Jacob. We have legal representation and Nick is calling them now. They'll meet him at the police station, and he knows not to say anything until a lawyer is present. Beyond that..." She faltered for a moment before her voice strengthened. "Beyond that, I'm not sure what to do, but we'll think of something. Keeping Justin on this treatment is the best way to allow him to heal. The first problem—aside from the fact that the FDA might have overstepped—is the time limit the so-called official documentation stipulates. What we need to find is...somewhere to take him where they let us keep doing this on the sly?" She shook her head. "But the agents will check when he's installed."

Mary watched her and her anger drained slowly. "You'll be arrested, too."

Amber gave her a sharp look. "Only if we get caught," she said simply.

"There are good odds of that," she insisted. She wanted so badly to agree and send Justin to another facility and make the FDA find them again—anything for a few more days. Every second they delayed was another second in which Justin might wake up. At the same time, she knew what they were risking, and the mother in her didn't want the other woman to spend her life in jail for this. She looked at Nick and

Amber. "You two may face jail time if you help us now. You know that."

"That's now how I'm making my decision," Amber said.

Mary sighed.

The friends exchanged a look.

"What?" Nick asked.

"Well," Mary said and looked around for her purse, "I can't let you all go to jail for trying to help my son. I'll call Tad. It's time to pull all the strings we can."

"No," Tad heard one of his assistants say. "The Senator is not taking interviews about his son at this time."

"—official press release from our office forty minutes ago," another man said.

A third voice cut over the other two. "—comment on that at this time—"

Tad cradled his head in his hands and groaned. He had tried to spend this morning getting some reading done. The simple truth was that he hated being away from Justin at all, which meant he needed to make every second count when he was there. With the phones ringing off the hook, however, not only was he unable to focus, his staffers couldn't get any of their work done either.

The question from the reporter had set off a furor. Reporters called at every hour of the day and night, his staff had mentioned being tailed to their homes, and deals he'd been in the process of making had begun to fall through.

Somewhere, he realized bitterly, Metcalfe was sitting back and laughing. He had dared him to do whatever he intended to do, and the man had.

His phone rang and his blood pressure spiked. He snatched the handset without looking and snapped, "For the last time, there will be no press access until otherwise stated."

"Tad, it's me." Mary's voice was tight.

"Oh, God." He squeezed his eyes shut. "I should have known. I'm so sorry. The phones are going off the hook I'm going to have to shut them off and—"

"Tad, we don't have time."

"What?" Mary was rarely this brusque. If she was, it meant something bad. "Is Justin okay?"

"For now." She tried very hard to stay calm and he could hear it in her voice. "But someone alerted the FDA to the PIVOT lab and we've been given twenty-four hours to shut everything down."

"What?" Tad lurched out of his seat. A scuffling sound outside followed immediately and one of his aides stood at the door, his earpiece still on.

"Sir?"

"I'm…it's okay." He held a hand out. "I'll, uh—it's okay."

The man backed out, his eyes wary, and Tad fought a wave of despair. Working for him was turning into political suicide for these staffers. He wasn't only ruining his career, he was ruining theirs too. He slumped into his chair and rubbed his forehead.

"It's Metcalfe," he said.

"Yes," Mary agreed. "The problem is, everything the FDA is doing is legal—apparently, although there might be a few procedural loopholes we can raise—and one of the PIVOT team has been arrested. Jacob," she added as if she'd sensed his question.

"Arrested." The bottom of his stomach dropped.

"Tad, that isn't all."

"It isn't?"

"The other three seem determined to keep the experiment going." Her voice began to tremble. "I don't want to move Justin to a hospital. I can't bear the thought of him being locked away in the dark again—" She broke off.

"Mary, listen to me. Justin knows we're here for him." His focus zeroed in on his wife. She was three thousand miles away and all he wanted to do was fold her in his arms. "And he's a fighter. No matter what, it'll be okay."

"Maybe. But what about for them?" Her voice still trembled.

"They're talking about how they want to keep this going because it's his best chance, and I want them to, Tad. I want it more than anything, but I can't let four people spend their entire lives in jail because of us. I can't ask them to do that."

Tad looked at his desk, swallowing hard.

"Is there anything you can do?" Mary whispered. "I don't know—something you can add to a bill, an exception you can get passed. We're not asking for anything bad. This project should have FDA clearance. It should have been cleared years ago. It wasn't blocked because it was dangerous. There has to be an appeal we can put through or—I don't know."

"I think there's something," he said. "I'll, uh—I'll check it out and get back to you."

"Oh, thank God." She was smiling, he could tell from her voice. "I'll let you do that. Thank you, love."

"Of course." His lips were numb. "I love you."

With a heavy sigh, he set the phone down and stared at the wall. His heart was racing now and he couldn't seem to catch his breath.

There was, of course, something he could do to make this stop. He could do one simple thing and all these problems would go away.

He could cave.

When he'd first come to Washington, his purpose had been to challenge lobbyists like Metcalfe. In his fantasies, he would stand tall and lead the way, the news would leak that they had tried to put pressure on him, and he would be hailed as a hero. Following his example, dozens of other senators would come forward. Slowly, the tide would turn away from the lobbyists, and senators would begin to represent their constituents' best interests again.

It hadn't gone that way.

Tad had spun a pencil in his fingers and now, he held it so tightly that it creaked. He put it down hastily before he broke it. Somehow, he needed to find a solution. Surely there was a way out of this.

Except there wasn't. What had Metcalfe said? Oh, right—*you're not the first senator who's come here determined to fight us.* They had won every other time, why not now?

"Sir?" Eddie had returned and held a note out. "A courier arrived with this."

"Is it laced with something?" he asked bitterly. When he saw the look on the young man's face, he regretted the joke. "Sorry, Eddie. I'm very sure it's not laced with anything. Thank you for bringing it in. Also…shut the phones down. Re-record the answering service with the message the legal team advised. You all need a rest."

"Sir." He nodded and handed him the letter before he withdrew.

Ted's name was written on the front of the letter in a scrawl that looked like a doctor's handwriting. There was no postmark. He sighed as he opened it to reveal a single sheet of paper with two lines of text. The first was a phone number and the second read, in handwritten letters, *I can help.*

He looked at the letter. This was Metcalfe. It could only be Metcalfe.

Well, hell, he needed to speak to the man anyway. He snatched the phone, dialed the number, and sat on the table while it rang.

"Diatek Industries," a female voice said. "Office of Anna Price. How can I help you?"

Startled, he made no response.

"Hello?" the woman said cautiously.

"Ah, hello." He cleared his throat. "I received a letter that asked me to call. My name is Tad Williams."

"Ah, Senator." The woman's tone brightened. "Ms. Price is expecting your call. I'll put you through, one moment."

"I—" He stopped when hold music began. Holding the phone between his shoulder and his ear, he slid into his chair and typed *Diatek Industries* into his browser's search bar. The computer was still thinking when the hold music stopped and a new voice spoke.

"Hello, Senator."

"Hello." He leaned in his chair. "You are…Anna Price, your secretary said?"

"Yes. I'd like to speak to you." This woman was brisk. "However, not over the phone. Can you meet?"

"I…yes."

"If you leave now, there will be a flight for you out of the private terminal," Anna said promptly.

"To where, exactly?"

"New York City. I'll see you soon, Senator."

She hung up and Tad stared at the handset as he put it in its cradle. His mind warred with rampant thoughts of rage, suspicion, desperation, and fear. Diatek Industries? He'd never heard of them, and the odds were beyond good that this was another player with Metcalfe's objectives. There was no way in hell he would have ever considered taking a flight like this to only God knew what waited on the other side. Then again, he'd never been quite this desperate before.

On the other hand, he had a certain grim desire not to work with Metcalfe and those he represented and he was intrigued that the CEO of Diatek—the website had loaded now—had spoken to him directly, not hired a sleazeball to conduct negotiations or turn the screws.

He pushed the negative emotions aside, stood decisively, and retrieved his briefcase and coat before he stepped into the main office.

"I'll need you to cancel all my meetings for the rest of the day," he told the aides. "I'm flying to New York. Eddie, could you call me a car? Sylvia, I'd like you to research Diatek Industries. Find me the names of any senators they've spoken to recently and any bills they've weighed in on one way or another. Forward all of that to my email. I need it before I land."

"I...yes." She nodded.

"I'll be back when I can." He spun on his heel and left before he could say anything he'd regret.

Such as the fact that they really should find other jobs before association with him turned them into pariahs.

CHAPTER FORTY-TWO

Justin slept fitfully. He woke constantly with a start, hoping he would see his mother return, but he had no such luck. While he couldn't help but be worried by the way she had disappeared, he told himself the game was still running so the issues surely couldn't be that bad.

Toward dawn, he walked a short distance away from the camp and recorded a brief message. "Mom, Dad—it was good to see Mom yesterday. I hope you're both well, and I also hope to see you both soon, in here or out there. Let me know if anything is wrong, I'm worried after Mom disappeared so quickly. I promise I'm well here. I love you." He shut the recorder off before he could start babbling.

Their breakfast with the blacksmith was a hasty meal of leftover flatbread and meat from the night before, and the three of them then watched the cart trundle away. The donkey clomped along behind, now docile.

"Well," he said finally, "I guess we should head to the ruins."

He swore that not a single word would disturb his thoughts, but Zaara and Lyle swung into a well-concerted effort to cheer him up. The banter flowed, jokes both good and bad were exchanged, and despite himself, he began to laugh at a song about a young dwarf stuck in a mine and the bargains he struck with the rock spirits to get out.

The change in the landscape around them was gradual. The rolling plains gave way to forests until the trees were packed so tightly that full sunlight reached the road only rarely. Acorns and leaves crunched underfoot. Birds chirped, squirrels skittered over the branches, and deer and foxes could sometimes be seen in clearings.

After a while, it changed again but wasn't noticeable at first. Every tree had dead branches, after all. There were always fallen leaves, and it wasn't uncommon to see the corpse of a small mammal. No matter how idyllic the surroundings, a forest had both life and death.

The death, however, began to grow stronger. Bare branches became more prevalent. The patches of shadow on the road vanished, but neither the blue sky nor the sunlight seemed particularly warm. Ahead of them, the ruins loomed large and they could now see that the dirt there was as gray as ash.

Gradually, his companions stopped joking and their heads turned at every crack of a branch. They still saw deer but the animals seemed gaunter now. At some point, the birdsong had stopped. Even the blue of the sky seemed faded.

"I don't like this," Zaara said finally. "Ruins are fine. I don't mind ruins. But this? It looks like what my father described right after Sephith defeated Kural. This isn't from a fire. It's not dark enough, and even sickness in plants doesn't kill everything."

Indeed, there was not a living thing in sight. Trees had toppled yet did not seem to be rotting. Bushes stood sparse and prickly. Leaves coated the ground, settled over time but not eaten away by animals or fungus. On the other side of the road, some areas seemed dank and swamp-like, although the expected decay usually found in moist, water-logged areas was absent.

"Nothing is rotting," Justin said slowly. "It's like the cycle stopped at death without going on to new life."

His words sounded unnaturally loud in the stillness but less so than Lyle's snort.

"What are you, a poet? Come on, lad, the place is cursed. Let's leave it at that."

He threw his hands up and caught Zaara's good-natured grin. She jerked her head at the dwarf and shrugged, and he could only nod. Besides that, it helped to have someone to keep him from getting too philosophical about all this. He continued to trudge forward and tried to emulate Lyle's wary acceptance of the place, but she stopped them both.

She didn't speak. The location seemed to discourage speaking. Instead, she gestured to where a little shack had almost fallen apart with age. It leaned precariously, the wood so weathered that its colors merged with the gray and brown forest.

Justin pointed at the shack, then at their packs. For all they knew, there might be supplies in there. In the real world, a place like this wouldn't have a mysterious sword or a helm with plus-five strength, but video games were not the real world.

The other two nodded and they inched off the road. He had many half-memories of stories where you weren't supposed to leave the road under any circumstances, but a few glances over his shoulder showed it remained where it had been. It didn't seem to be vanishing like a mirage, nor did the forest seem to close up around them.

The little house looked like it might have been a storage shed at one point, although he wasn't quite sure why one would build one in the middle of a swamp. Perhaps it was for fish, he thought. Still, there was no chimney and nothing except the four walls and the roof, all leaning on the unstable ground. The door had creaked off its hinges as the building slid and now stood ajar.

He held a hand out to indicate to his friends to wait as he pried the door open. Common sense suggested he make sure it wasn't the only thing holding the building up, so he waited a few seconds to see if there were any ominous creaks. There weren't, so he shrugged and stepped inside.

It took his eyes a moment to adjust but he made out several objects in the darkness. This would be a place to restock, he thought in excitement. There was a table, a mortar and pestle, a stool, a broom—

And a woman. She muttered a single word, rough against his ears, and blinding light burst into his eyes. He staggered back as she uttered a second word and froze the three of them where they stood.

"Justin?" Lyle called. "Zaara?"

"I'm here," Zaara responded. "Damned light. What is this?"

"There's a witch," he told her wearily.

The woman laughed. He couldn't see her, not with the light still blazing, but she could have been any age judging by those muttered words and her laugh. "A witch. A good enough assessment, I suppose. And you three are those who slew Sephith, which means I have a task for you."

"Oh?" Justin raised an eyebrow. He was able to move his face, it seemed, but none of the rest of him. Fortunately, given the fact that he'd been in the middle of a step, the spell also seemed to be holding him up. Still, every muscle strained uselessly to avoid falling.

"I'd wager you'll have heard about the wolves," the witch said. "In fact, I'd wager you've fought one or two. You have that smell."

This was the witch the werewolf had mentioned. The realization flashed through Justin's mind and it must have shown on his face.

"Ah, so you did. And you spoke to one, I assume."

"They told us to free them from the spell," he said. "They're hunting livestock because they have no choice. They don't know how to be wolves. They asked us to kill you."

"Well, I wouldn't advise that," she said simply. "You won't succeed. It would be stupid to try, as you can plainly see."

"So will you turn us into werewolves, too?" Zaara panted and it sounded as if she tried to wrench herself free of the spell.

"No. And don't strain yourself trying to undo the spell, girl. I can see what you're using, and nothing you know will free you from this." The woman muttered another harsh word and the light dimmed. To Justin's surprise, seeing her did not make her age any clearer. She wore robes that obscured her hair, and her face was not young but not old either. Her expression emotionless, she studied them for a moment. "I am glad you came to me. Tracking you was…surprisingly difficult."

Justin had some theories about that and decided to keep them to himself.

"I hope we don't have to remain enemies," the witch said pleasantly.

He snorted before he could help himself. Although he couldn't see Zaara, he could hear that she'd made a similar noise.

"You've trapped us," he pointed out.

"Indeed I have. You'll find it's wise to take precautions when three well-armed individuals stumble into your house without warning." She pulled the stool out and sat. With her fingers laced around her knees, she could be any woman sitting in the sun on a nice day.

Except, of course, that she had them all captive and was apparently responsible for wreaking havoc all across this forest.

"Besides," she pointed out, "you've already taken a job to kill me."

"We haven't taken a job," Zaara said, precisely. "We heard the plea of a dying man who was spelled as a wolf."

"A dying bandit," the witch corrected. "He and his pack would have taken everything I had and probably killed me into the bargain, so I won't trouble my conscience over their fate. Now, I would like you to do a favor for me. I would like you to kill the werewolves."

Justin's stomach twisted. He could only move his head but he made full use of that. His head shook emphatically. "No. I refuse."

"You see the forest around this place," the woman told them. "The wolves are poisoning it. Their very essence is turning the place sickly. Parts are already a swamp."

"So why'd ye make them?" Lyle asked.

She did not answer and merely looked at all three of them in turn. "Will you help?"

"I won't hunt a whole pack of them and kill them," he said. "I don't…hunt humans." He remembered the dying man on the ground. "I killed Sephith for a reason. Being a bandit isn't a good enough reason."

"Oh?" Their captor extended one hand casually and where there had been nothing, a key now glittered with a triangular handle, almost identical to the key Sephith had waved in front of the group only two weeks earlier. "Perhaps this will shift the equation. I had hoped you would aid me for the sake of the forest and that this would be an unexpected reward. But if you will not do that, perhaps seeing your true reward now will help to change your mind."

Justin's breath caught.

"Ah." She had seen the change. "Very interesting. I suspected this was what you were searching for, and it seems I was right. Do we have ourselves a deal, adventurers? You do this one thing—for me, and for the forest—and in return, you get this key, which you so clearly want." Her eyes were very bright and very watchful. "You don't want it for the coin, I can see that much. So why? Are you three secretly scholars? The girl, I could see. But you two?"

Justin said nothing. He had a hunch only, and nothing more.

"I guess I shall see if it is incentive enough." She shrugged. "I should teach you a spell. It will aid you on your quest."

"You're teaching us spells?" Justin asked incredulously. "What's to stop us from coming back to kill you?"

The witch looked at the three of them, all frozen in midair.

"Okay, good point," he said.

SLOW ON THE UPTAKE, Level 1, the game told him.

"What, I didn't get any levels from the tank business?"

"Ah, a self burn. Those are rare."

The woman paid no attention to Justin's muttered words. She moved her hand slightly and the spell relaxed enough to allow him and the others to stand upright. She placed a plain wooden bowl on the ground and she looked hard at all three of them.

"You two—you have magic. Pay attention. Look at the bowl and imagine, in your mind's eye, something being revealed. It could be anything—light falling across a room, a covering drawn away from a statue, the lid rising from a box. Imagine it and let your magic twist in with the imagining."

So she was serious about teaching them spells. Justin stared at the bowl until his eyes crossed. He thought of cutting box lids open, pulling covers off furniture, and of everything he could until he groaned in frustration. He finally gave up but, out of nowhere, an apple appeared in the bowl.

"Did I do it?"

"No." Their captor pointed. "She did."

"I did it!" Zaara sounded incredulous. "I thought of a candle in a dark room and…there it was."

"Good. Now, practice." The witch snapped her fingers and the rest of the spell relaxed. "All of you, go now. You, boy, keep thinking of different ways to visualize. I promise you, there are many things in those ruins to see if you get it right. Go now." She watched them as they approached the door warily. Her head was tilted to the side. "You know, I'm interested to see if you come back."

CHAPTER FORTY-THREE

They were barely outside the shack before Lyle announced, "We shouldn't trust 'er."

"Shhh," Justin hissed.

"What, ye think she doesn't know how ye feel?" The dwarf gave him a scornful look. "No one who strings people up can think they're well-liked. Plus, she's too clean."

"I'm clean," Zaara protested.

"Who said I trusted you?" He gave her a look but grinned after a moment. "Nah, I've forgiven you for that."

"You've forgiven me for…not smelling…" She sounded like she couldn't believe her ears. With a frown, she looked at Justin, who shrugged.

"Yeah. Yer handy with a blade." Lyle seemed oblivious to the absurdity. "Anyway, I say we don't trust her and we don't trust those wolves, neither."

"Now, hang on." He tripped over a bush and barely saved himself from an ignominious fall in the mud. His stamina was increasing, thankfully faster than it would in real life, but he still wasn't entirely used to the weight. "I thought you'd chosen a side."

"Common sense, lad." Lyle chewed meditatively on a stalk of grass. "When two sides are pointin' fingers, it's wisest not to trust either of 'em."

"I suppose that makes—wait, are you chewing on something you found in a swamp?" Justin felt slightly queasy. "That's terrifying."

"What's wrong with that?"

"What's wrong with—ohhhh, I can't." He struggled up the bank and onto the road. "Finally. I hate mud. I hate it, I hate it, I hate it. Not to mention that it looks stupid on plate armor."

"That's what looks stupid?" Zaara asked. When he gave her a sharp look, she raised an eyebrow. "You don't exactly look like a berserker."

"I'm not a berserker, I'm a…knight."

"When were you knighted?"

"Not literally."

"That makes no sense." She rolled her eyes. "But, to return to the matter at hand, I think Lyle has a good point. We need more information. Also, we need dinner."

"I'm on it." He drew his sword, turned, and slashed at a rabbit.

BUNNY SLAYER, Level 4!

"Hey, I'm getting better at that."

"You used a four hundred damage ultimate on a level-two bunny."

"I like my food dead, what can I say?" He clanked stiffly to the other side of the road where he'd seen several other rabbits take shelter in the tufts of grass.

A few deadly swipes later, the group had a set of rabbits for the next few nights' worth of dinner. Lyle began to skin them while Justin made sure to look away and Zaara made another drying rack.

Justin climbed the tumbled remains of a stone wall. He could almost forget he was in a game when he did anything like this. As things progressed and he became more attuned to the signals the game sent, he could feel the stones under his feet and the shift of the rocks when he stepped.

Either that or this was all his imagination. The thought was sobering. What if the game was only the most basic polygons and he simply built up more and more of it in his head? Worse, what if the game had truly crashed when his mother disappeared and everything since then had been a fever-dream constructed by a brain that was locked in the dark?

And how did he know his mother had been there at all? Sure, she knew about him falling and breaking his arm, but he knew about that, too.

He stopped and stared at nothing.

"Justin?" Zaara studied him carefully, a branch held in one hand and a knife in the other. "Are you sick? Do you...see something? Oh, are you practicing the spell?"

"I'm—yes. Yes, that's what I'm doing." He forced a smile. Just for kicks, he tried the spell again but nothing happened. The problem, of course, was that he didn't know if there was nothing to find or if he hadn't done the spell correctly.

With a shrug, he began to climb again.

What would he say to everyone when he got back? When he found all the keys, he assumed there would be a door—and that door would wake him up. He hoped so, anyway. Perhaps the quest for each key would teach him something new. He would wake and—would he be able to tell anyone on his YouTube channel what he'd been up to?

He had to, after all. A thing like this would be wildly popular. People would clamor to have their loved ones transferred to pods like this. His followers would definitely want to hear about it.

Those who still cared by then, of course. He hadn't put content out for weeks now so it was possible no one remembered him at all. His ad revenue would be shot to hell and he'd be behind on all the expansions.

And it wasn't like he even had friends to miss him. College had been a mess of people he didn't like and didn't fit in with. There had only been one or two people he liked reasonably well, and they hadn't kept in contact since everyone graduated. Without having anything close to the means to rent an apartment in the Bay Area, Justin had stayed at home, so he hadn't had roommates or work friends, only the few friends who came back for holidays, and that was it.

"Justin." Zaara stood in front of him, her hands on her hips. She looked at him with a disapproving expression. "You're doing it again. Be honest, are you sick? Did the witch do something to you?"

"No. No, I'm only thinking. Oh…you were joking." His brain caught up with him and his cheeks flushed. "Sorry. I'm a little out of it today."

"Yeah, I can see that. Come on, we've hung the rabbit pelts out to dry and we'll get them on the way back. Speaking of which…" She walked him to a vantage point. "Lyle's seen motion in the ruins. We should be fairly well hidden here, but there's smoke drifting up, birds circling, and everything to suggest people are there."

"So?" he asked. When he realized what she meant, his stomach dropped. "Oh, I don't want to do this. I say we go, try to find the third key, and come back another time. Plus, we might learn more about who to trust that way."

"Justin, if there's a way to get a key, we should do it." She folded her arms. "Plus, she's right. Even the one we killed said they were bandits."

"They were trying to make a living. Ugh, this is *Les Miserables* all over again. I hated that book. No, don't ask. This one's not nearly as good as Luke Skywalker's story."

"I did like that one," Zaara said wistfully. "My point is, these bandits are people who would be out on the roads, robbing and murdering otherwise. Now they're wolves and they're attacking people's herds so the farmers can't make it through the winter. Also, they are destroying the forest and the swamp, and the witch has the key."

"I agree," Lyle said.

"You said not to trust her," Justin pointed out.

"I'm not saying we should trust her. I'm saying we should kill the bandits."

Justin massaged his temples. His head was beginning to hurt.

"Or," a new voice said, "you could all come along quietly and no one will get hurt."

His head came up and his heart sank. Three bandits stepped out of the forest. No—he looked to one side and identified three more.

Two to one. He wasn't sure he liked those odds. On the other hand, whoever they were, they weren't friendly. He hopped from the wall and noted how quickly each bandit followed him with their gazes. The one on the far right was the slowest and he marked that.

"Why should we come with you?" he asked.

"I told you," the one who'd spoken before said. "So no one gets hurt."

"Ah," said Justin and promptly charged. "Stooooooout!"

"That's my line!" Lyle yelled as he joined the battle.

"Stooooooout!" Zaara yelled. A crackling noise and a yelp suggested she'd thrown a fireball.

"Both of you, stop it!" Lyle yelled. "My granda' will be spinning in his tomb!"

Justin slashed down with his sword and grimaced when the bandit he had targeted danced easily out of the way of his blade. Another ran face-first into his side, and although that seemed to hurt the attacker more than him, the heavy armor made it more difficult to recover from the impact.

He took the sword in both hands and whirled it wildly. The first bandit hadn't suffered so much as a scratch, but he stayed out of range and that was something. Others began to venture closer and he shifted the sword between hands to whip it out quickly to drive them back.

This wasn't a great stand-off for them, he had to admit. Triumphing in an outnumbered situation required the element of surprise, and they were already way past that point.

Also, the bandits seemed to have focused entirely on him, which was strange given that he could still hear his friends fighting. His head snapped around to look and, with a sinking sensation, he realized that there were no longer only six bandits.

Now, there were twelve.

"I think you can see that it would be best if you came with us," the leader said. He smiled and displayed teeth that seemed sharper than they ought to be.

"Not a chance," Zaara said tightly.

That was all Justin needed to hear. He wasn't of this world. For all he knew, it was better to go with them. If she didn't think so, however, he would go with her judgment. After all, she had kept herself safe on the road, alone and in an unfriendly town run by a crazy wizard.

He lunged and caught one of his adversaries in the leg. A fireball rocketed from his other hand and caught a second fully in the chest. The man dropped into the swamp with a scream and tried to put the flames out.

"That was a bad choice," the bandit leader snarled.

"Like we want to be taken as slaves?" Lyle retorted. Justin couldn't see his teammates from where he was, but a thud sounded a great deal like one of the dwarf's punches landing and was followed by a grunt of pain that he hoped came from a bandit.

Any chances of a peaceful resolution were gone, which made things a great deal simpler. He hacked, slashed, and fireballed his way through three more bandits. Zaara—or one of the female bandits— uttered a cry of pain before another fireball whooshed behind him.

Lyle, meanwhile, had decided that the best accompaniment to a good punching was to throw in a monologue about the parentage and proclivities of the bandit troupe, down to what they brushed their teeth with. Justin considered his particular suggestions on that last front to be improbable.

"Justin! Watch out!"

He threw himself sideways and barely avoided a battle-ax that descended with earth-shuddering force. His heart froze as he stared at it. How on earth would his brain react to thinking he'd been split in two by a battle-ax?

"Enough!" the bandit leader bellowed and to Justin's immense surprise, the next slash of his knives went to the wielder of the battle-ax. He collapsed in the mud with a gurgle and the leader pointed his bloody knives at everyone else. "All of you, enough. I said I wanted them taken alive and you three can stop trying to fight an impossible battle. Come on."

Justin was hauled unceremoniously out of the muck, his sword wrenched away, and his hands chained, and Lyle and Zaara joined him a moment later as captives.

"March," the leader said grimly, and the three of them stumbled forward, surrounded by a group of battered and manifestly unfriendly bandits.

CHAPTER FORTY-FOUR

The experience of getting to New York was disturbingly smooth. The pilot at the private terminal knew Tad's face and they were airborne within five minutes of his arrival. A car was waiting when the plane taxied to a stop and he was whisked through the ever-present New York traffic with astonishing speed.

A young woman waited for him in the lobby of Diatek Industries. Her hair was cut in a severe bob, her dress revealed a strenuously thin form, and her genuine smile was disconcerting.

"Senator," she said.

"Did we speak on the phone?" he asked her and extended his hand.

"We did." She shook it warmly. "Please, this way."

In her presence, the security gate was opened without fuss and the two of them took an express elevator to what he could only think was the top level of the building. Wherever it was, it was high enough that his ears popped on the way.

The young woman led the way down a richly carpeted hallway to a set of frosted glass doors. Immediately, both tried to hold the doors open for one another. She laughed—again, shockingly warm in contrast to her appearance—and ushered him through and into a conference room. She did not enter and simply said, "The senator is here to see you, ma'am."

"Thank you, Lauren." The woman at the window turned to give her a smile before her gaze fixed on Tad. "Senator Williams. I'm glad you came. I'm Anna Price." She came to shake his hand.

She could have been an older version of her secretary. Also strenuously slim, she wore the kind of understated suit he had come to realize meant serious money. Her hair had once been blonde but was now more than half gray, although her eyes were a clear blue and her grasp was strong.

Tad settled into a chair when she gestured to the table and cleared his throat. He had decided on the plane to let her speak first. Caution meant he didn't want to give her any ideas or anything to seize on, especially since what Sylvia had managed to dig up was incredibly sparse.

Anna Price had studied chemistry at Harvard and went on to work for a pharmaceutical company for several years before she married. Her husband and daughter had both passed away, however, the daughter apparently from a car accident, and the husband some years later, potentially from heart problems. During the years between the two deaths, Anna had founded Diatek.

If there was little on Price, there was far more on Diatek—and none of it was particularly reassuring. The company had extensive contracts with the Department of Defense and the FBI. It had flown under the radar in terms of exerting influence regarding different legislation, but Tad could only think this was because the company had direct access to the officials making the decisions.

Price sat at the table and regarded him evenly. "It will save time, I think, if I tell you what I know about your situation. I know that your son, Justin, was involved in a car crash approximately six weeks ago and that he is now under the care of Dr. Jean-Luc DuBois and the three operating members of a company called PIVOT. I can only assume he is still comatose and being treated using virtual reality.

"I know that, as of this morning, the FDA has arrested Jacob Zachary and given him twenty-four hours to shut the experiment down. I also know the leak of information to the FDA came from Dru Metcalfe, a lobbyist who works for several pharmaceutical companies, including the one that previously blacklisted Dr. DuBois's research. I know that Mr. Metcalfe has also leaked isolated details of Justin's treatment to the press. Would you say that is an accurate summation of your current situation?"

Tad clenched his teeth and gave a brief nod. This woman was businesslike and far too calm to be discussing matters of blackmail. It was almost like none of it shocked her.

He shouldn't have bothered to come.

Which was why he was surprised to hear Anna Price say, "What I believe you don't know, Senator, is that my daughter died under very similar circumstances. Like Justin, she was in a car accident. Like him, she was in stable condition. She was a fighter, Senator. Her name was Mina."

Startled, he looked at her. Her face was still and he could only now see the strain around her eyes.

"My husband and I were postgraduate students," Anna explained. "We didn't have much money and we tried everything we could. Both of us looked for different jobs. We sold our house, we sold everything we owned, and we lived out of our cars. We even tried to find research that might help Mina recover more quickly." She raised her chin fractionally. "We ran out of money. We went bankrupt, our postgraduate placements ended, and our next insurance companies would not take Mina. She died—not from her injuries but because we ran out of money to keep trying to save her."

His mouth hung open. In all analyses of what he might face, he had not expected this.

"The year after she died," Anna Price said, "I secured funding to open Diatek. My goal was very simple. I wanted to ensure that no other family would have to go through what ours had. I had worked for a pharmaceutical company and I knew the technologies that were being developed, but it wasn't an area of research that most companies were looking into, especially on the pharmaceutical side. It was always my focus. Diatek has made immense profits in other areas but all of them have been funneled into this research."

Tad swallowed. "I…see."

"Senator, I would like to fold PIVOT into Diatek Industries," Price said bluntly. "Their research and Justin's treatment would be covered indefinitely. I believe they are using an injection formula substantially similar to one we have clearance to test on human subjects. This would allow Justin's treatment to continue without interruption."

The silence dragged on as he looked at her for a long moment.

"You're wary," she said. It was not a question. "Given everything, I certainly can't blame you for that. Is there any particular area of concern I can address?"

He shrugged helplessly. "You know everything, which means you know why Dru Metcalfe is smearing me to the press."

"Yes." She raised her eyebrows.

"So you know my stance on blank checks and favors," he told her. "If you'll forgive me, your company came out of nowhere and were awarded a significant number of government contracts awfully quickly."

"Yes, that's true." She smiled bitterly. "You and I measure our morals differently, Senator. That is something you will need to come to terms with. I have made sacrifices in the name of progress and have collaborated on projects you would likely not find…ethical. I made my choice. I would not wish what happened to me—to my husband— on any other family."

"Your husband," Tad said and suddenly felt lost.

"He killed himself," Anna said crisply. He could see the precision masked an anguish that had not diminished even slightly with the years. "If I didn't have this, I might have done the same. I…was tempted."

He caught his breath and imagined the future stretching ahead. Years without Justin, where he knew that his son had not died because there was no treatment but because there was no money. The anger he already felt multiplied a hundred times and then a thousand times.

Anna's words struck a piece of him that was so raw, he wanted to press a hand over his chest.

And Mary…how would Mary take it?

Still, his reservations refused to be silenced.

"What's the catch?" Tad asked. Everything in him wanted to believe this was true, but Metcalfe had also offered the exact thing he wanted. This was even better, which he was sure meant the catch was even worse.

"There is no catch." Anna smiled now. It did not reach her eyes but given what they had discussed, he would have distrusted that even more. "I want to help, Senator. As I said, I have given a great deal to make sure other families do not face this same trial. The work done by Dr. DuBois and PIVOT is exceptional."

He considered this and nodded. "I…see." Half of him screamed to run and the other half yelled to take the deal. "Let me think about it, please."

"Of course." She did not seem surprised. Then again, he did not think she was surprised by very much. "You know how to reach me."

CHAPTER FORTY-FIVE

Justin woke in the freezing cold and his hands ached where he had curled them against his body. He couldn't determine why it was so bright or why there was so much wind. Cautiously, he opened his eyes for a moment, closed them against the glare, and opened them again as he sat far too quickly.

Dungeon cells were generally underground and deeply depressing, with a side helping of no-one-will-hear-you-if-you-scream. He had not enjoyed his brief stay in Riverbend's jail, and he hadn't looked forward to being in this one.

As things turned out, there was more than one way to keep someone in captivity. He wasn't chained, for instance, and his cell—such as it was—didn't have four walls. Whatever had happened to these ruins, the side of this building had sheared off and left it open to the wind.

Which, judging by the way it whistled and how close the fog lay, meant he was fairly high up. He estimated that it was at least ten stories, possibly more.

He struggled to remember the night before. The three of them had been brought to the ruins, at which point their weapons and armor had been taken and they'd been blindfolded. He didn't remember much after that beyond awkward stumbling over rocky ground and the sounds of muttered arguments about them. At some point, they'd been given food and water.

Of course, he hadn't noticed the bitter taste in the water until it was too late.

It was reassuring to find out he hadn't been killed, he decided morosely.

Now, if he could only find out what these bandits wanted, that would be a significant step in the right direction. He looked around. The floor wasn't particularly new but it didn't creak ominously when he moved across it either. He flattened himself onto his stomach and inched forward with what was probably excessive caution.

Still, despite the discomfort, excessive caution was better than being turned into jelly at the side of a tower.

And he definitely would be if he fell. Now that he was at the edge, he could see exactly how far up he was, and it was excessively high. He spared a thought for whoever had bothered to haul their unconscious bodies up a mountainside and so many flights of stairs before he recalled that this was a video game and they had probably simply been ported up.

Lucky bandits, he thought belligerently.

It occurred to him to wonder where the others were and if they'd been drugged.

"Zaara? Lyle?" He edged back to the wall. The floor might be stable, but he still preferred it there. "Anyone? Zaara?"

"Justin?" Her voice floated from his left. "Did you just wake up, too? Where are we?"

"Uh…are you afraid of heights?"

"Not really," she said promptly.

"Good. Because we're way the hell up in a tower." He pressed his back as far as it would go against the wall. What was the expression he'd once heard? *A fear of heights is illogical. A fear of falling from heights, on the other hand, is prudent.*

"That explains why they haven't bothered to keep us somewhere with walls." She sighed. "Not to mention that I woke up when I almost fell through the floor."

His shoulders hunched around his ears. "Oh, God." Like he wasn't already feeling the sensation of falling, he now had to worry about the next time he fell asleep. What if he rolled? What if part of the floor collapsed and he couldn't wake up in time to grab onto something?

"I'd only have fallen one floor," Zaara told him, "but still." She sounded more grumpy than anything. "Where's Lyle?"

"I don't know, I can't hear him. Maybe he's on your other side."

"One moment. Lyle? Lyle?" A creaking sound suggested she was walking. "Lyle!" More creaking followed. "He's not over here—or he hasn't woken up yet. Given how well he can sleep ale off, though, I'd say he probably woke up before we did."

"Fair point." Justin considered this but not for long. "Okay, we need to find out where he is and if he's okay, but I don't think that's priority one. What we need to do first is find out why we're here. Or...maybe escape."

"I vote escape," Zaara said. "If they only wanted to do some friendly bargaining, there wouldn't have been any need for battle-axes. That was a good dodge, by the way. I don't think even your armor would have stopped that."

He shuddered. "I think you're right. Hmmm. You said there's a hole in the floor?"

"Yeah, why?"

"Well, maybe the door in the chamber below you isn't locked," he pointed out.

"Oh. Good point. Give me a moment." Scuffling sounds followed and he imagined her hanging upside down out of a hole in the ceiling. "I think you're right," she said, her voice muffled. "Okay, so I drop down, get out, and come get you."

"No, there might be patrols. Let's have you drop down and then help me down as well." Although the thought of jumping so close to the edge was terrifying, the floor of the chamber below did extend somewhat farther.

"If you say so." She sounded dubious. "Okay, one sec—"

"Shhh!" he hissed suddenly. He could hear voices in the corridor outside and the dull thud of footsteps. A few seconds later, a key scraped in the lock and his door creaked open to admit the bandit leader. He stepped in and the door was closed and locked behind him.

"You're awfully confident," he observed and studied his captor. "I could tackle you off the edge."

His visitor only raised his eyebrows. Justin thought he saw something glimmering but the flicker of it was gone in the next moment.

"Why did you come to the ruins?" he asked.

"There was a job posting in East Newbrook," he said wearily. "Not even a job posting, really, merely someone saying there might be good loot in the ruins."

"Oh? And who was this someone?"

"I don't know. It was one of the pieces of paper the town crier put up." He threw his hands up. "Does it matter?"

"Given that this only turned into ruins two months ago and no one offered a reward? Yeah, it does." The bandit crouched to look him in the eyes.

"Wait, two months ago all of this was…fine?" He couldn't keep the incredulity out of his voice.

"Good acting," the bandit said derisively. He stood and wandered a few feet away. "Try again," he called over his shoulder. "And make it more believable this time."

He was distracted from his anger by the glimmer he saw again at the man's waist. Curious, he tried to picture a box lid opening as the witch had suggested, but nothing happened. Then, in a strange wash of inspiration, he remembered a summer day at the beach when a wave ebbed to show the stones and shells in its wake. As the water receded, the shoreline was revealed.

A chain of magic at the bandit's waist became instantly visible. Tendrils of magic extended up and down from it to burrow into his leather armor, and a trail led to the door. That was why he wasn't afraid, he realized—he knew that no matter what happened, he wouldn't go over the edge.

The man looked at his waist in surprise, then at his prisoner, and his eyes narrowed. "I knew it," he said. "The witch sent you."

"Oh?" Justin challenged. "Since you seem to be deciding everything about us, what then?"

"Then we kill you," he said bluntly.

A strained silence followed.

"If, on the other hand, you came on your own…" The man smiled and showed his teeth. "Maybe we can make a deal."

He considered his options. As far as he could tell, the best option was to play along for now, whether or not he intended to make a deal. That said, of course, was it better to admit their association with the witch or not?

His knowledge of magic was likely suspicious, he decided. He had to spill the beans.

"We set out from East Newbrook on our own," Justin said. "We planned to search the ruins for ancient artifacts. Yesterday, while trying to retrieve a donkey that had run away, we encountered a massive wolf. It and I fought and I wounded it, but it turned into a man, who told me a witch had cursed a group of bandits and that I could free them by killing her."

The bandit watched him suspiciously, his arms folded.

"We weren't sure what to do," he continued. "Shortly before we met you, we went off the road to a little shack, thinking there might be supplies we could use. It didn't look as if it had been inhabited in some time but a witch was inside. She held us captive with a spell and told us to find you and kill you—that you were killing the forest and, even before you preyed on flocks, you'd been bandits."

"She told you we were killing the forest?" Fury hardened his captor's tone. "No—that's her magic—her curse because she uses magic that isn't natural. She's the reason we became bandits. It wasn't our choice. She wanted our town and our tower, so she fought us for it. That's the reason for the ruins, and she cursed us when she couldn't drive us out. We're bandits now because it's not safe to be around humans. When the change comes over us…we can't always control ourselves. Sometimes, we attack."

Justin stared at him, genuinely torn now.

"She needs to die," the man said fiercely. "This tower was ours for the taking and it's not like she had any more right—" He broke off. "We have a potion," he stated coldly. "It will incapacitate her and make her weak enough to kill. None of us can use it as her curse alerts her to our presence. But you could do it. You could free us all. We'll give you a day to decide."

The door opened to let him through and slammed again behind him before the loud footsteps of the bandit group walked away. He peered out the tiny opening in the door but didn't see any shadows to suggest a guard had remained.

"Zaara, did you hear that?"

"Every word. How did he know you were sent by the witch?"

"I used the spell she taught us," he explained. "I finally made it work." He slumped against the wall. "I have no idea who to trust, though. Did you hear what he said? About how she had no more right to this place than they did?"

"Yes." Her voice was contemplative. "I did, now that you mention it."

"What do you think?" Justin asked her.

"I'm…not sure. If we have to side with one, I guess I'd side with her. If she were someone like Sephith, she'd have lackeys to help her fight the wolves, wouldn't she? Or she'd simply be able to kill them. And whatever they were doing before, they're hurting more people now."

"Wait." He peered at the wall. "What you just said—if we have to side with one. What if we didn't?"

"Wait, what?"

"What we need is information, right?" he asked her. "We need to get out of here, take the potion, and find out who's right before we deal with anyone." He listened and waited, but she made no response. "What do you think?"

"Let's do it," Zaara agreed.

CHAPTER FORTY-SIX

Mary looked at the clock for what felt like the twelfth time in twenty minutes.

She sighed when she realized it had only been ten minutes.

The building's owners had been able to restrict the FDA agents from entering again by citing the exact language of what appeared to be an injunction, although she didn't fully understand it. From the snippets of discussions she'd picked up, it seemed the entire process reeked of corruption and power plays. Whether this was true or not was moot on some level. Yes, they could fight it, but whoever had orchestrated it had done so with a time limitation in mind. When the twenty-four hours were up, they would have no legal grounds to keep them out.

Jacob, back from jail on bond, was cloistered with Nick and Amber as they conference-called with the lawyer. Mary had tried to sit in on some of the meetings, but between the technical terms being thrown around and her guilt, she wasn't much of a help at this point.

It didn't improve her mood that she wasn't useful at all. She couldn't help the PIVOT team, she couldn't help DuBois prep Justin for a potential move, and she couldn't help Tad with his work in the senate.

She looked at the clock for the thirteenth time. Only twelve hours and forty-two minutes were left.

A light touch on her shoulder startled her and she turned, expecting to see Tad there—hopefully with perfect news.

It was DuBois, though. She hoped her face didn't fall too obviously and cleared her throat. "Can I help with anything?" she asked him.

"No. But I can help you. I can put you back in the game."

Mary stared at him. "Are you…sure? Can you do that?"

"No," Amber called from the side of the room. "He can't. But we're all screwed anyway so I say go for it."

"Ms. Garcia, please don't say things like that while I'm on the line." The lawyer sounded pained.

"Oh. Right. Sorry. Mary, don't go into the game. Help the doctor clean up. DuBois, stop suggesting things you know are illegal." She gestured at the older woman, then the pod, and gave the man a thumbs up.

Mary smiled, but her eyes stung with unshed tears. These three kids weren't much older than Justin, and they were utterly prosaic about their chances of facing legal action. She let DuBois usher her to the pod and sat.

Tina flashed into her mind. For now, the girl was a blank, a faceless entity. She hadn't looked up her social media profiles and preferred to avoid the chance that she would send an angry message. To control the rising snarl of fury, she pressed her fists hard into the soft bottom of the pod and tried to push the thoughts aside. These people put their livelihood on the line for Justin, and where was Tina? Off Scott-free and uninjured although she claimed she was miserable.

The girl wasn't miserable enough, she decided.

"Mrs. Williams?" DuBois looked concerned. He held sterilizing wipes in his gloved hands as he frowned at her. "Are you all right?"

She thought of snapping a response that it was a ridiculous question, but she held her tongue. The doctor had his moments but he meant no harm—and he did the best he could to help her now. He had noticed her worry and it would concern him as he was putting her into the game. That was what she had to focus on. He was doing all he could to give her the time with Justin she desperately wanted.

"I'm...yes, I'm all right." She forced a smile.

He nodded, but he left an expectant silence as he swabbed her temples and wrists.

"I'm thinking about the woman who was with Justin in the car," she explained.

"Was she killed?" he guessed.

"No," Mary said bitterly. "No, she's fine."

"That's a relief." DuBois smiled at her. "Did you know her well?"

"I barely knew her and it's not—" *It is not a relief.* Mary cleared her throat. She held one wrist out for an adhesive pad. "Her parents and I set her up with Justin. She was driving the night of the accident, was going way too fast, and crashed the car. The girl is fine and Justin is like this." She gestured at the pod with her free hand.

To her surprise, DuBois still did not speak. He looked briefly at her as he put the pad on her other wrist and then began to position the neural pads around the sides of her face and at the base of her skull.

"I don't want to wish pain on her," she continued. "But it isn't fair. She reaches out to me constantly for news about Justin and I can't bear to write back. I can't—she has no idea of the pain she's put us all through. Tad and I are in hell, you and the rest of the team might wind up in jail, and none of it would have happened if she'd been careful."

The doctor nodded now. Instead of hooking her up to the machine, he took a seat nearby. "I know that feeling," he said.

"You do?" she asked, surprised.

He nodded again, his expression thoughtful. "It felt unfair when my research was shut down the first time." He held a hand up and took a very long time to choose his words. When he spoke, his voice was oddly flat and she could see how hard it was for him to try to understand the twists and turns inside someone else's mind.

"I understand that it's not the same as having a child in a coma. But I think it may be more similar than you think. I don't mean to be disrespectful, not at all. That project was my life's work. I enjoyed it because it was difficult, but I also toured hospitals and saw people in comas and their families. I did everything right so I could help them because I believed that what I needed to do was create the treatment." He shook his head and she saw that the fallout still did not make sense to him on a fundamental level. "I spent every day for years working on that research. I handpicked my team and I never took a day off. When it was shut down, it wasn't that I had done anything wrong. It was something totally meaningless, and it would cost so many people their lives."

Mary hunched her shoulders. DuBois seemed so vague that she had never considered that he might feel this way.

"You seemed so calm about it," she said hesitantly.

"It's been years since then." He smiled at her and then, as if to assure her that he was still the same person she'd known all this time, he stripped his gloves off and pulled out a bag of popcorn. "And most of this stuff…well, it took me a year before I could even go into the lab," he added as he munched on a handful of caramel corn. His low-key demeanor did not match the words but she could see that he meant it.

"What changed?"

"I realized that continuing to be angry would accomplish nothing," he said. "Other researchers didn't understand. They told me projects were called off for all kinds of reasons and I shouldn't be angry. That wasn't a good reason to me. Why would I feel less bad to know that other lifesaving projects had been shut down for bad reasons? It only made me feel worse." He looked completely baffled. "What did make me feel better was realizing that nothing I could do would change the fate of that project. I only had the skills to do research, and if I stayed in my apartment and was angry all day, I wouldn't do any research."

Mary considered this.

"I didn't like being that angry," DuBois explained. "I blamed myself for things that did not make sense at all. I would tell myself that if I had studied law, maybe I would know how to appeal things better than my university—even though if I had been a lawyer, the project would never have existed at all. I thought about what would have happened if I'd gone to one of those companies. Maybe if the treatment was beneficial to them, they wouldn't have stopped it. But I couldn't go back in time."

"You can't change the past," she agreed. How many times had she read that sentiment in celebrity interviews and self-help books?

"Exactly," he said as if she had come up with the quote on her own. "That is a good way to put it. I could not change the past and it was no use being angry at myself for not knowing different areas of study."

"I have felt useless," she admitted. "I don't understand the technology, I'm not a doctor, and I can't help Tad with any of this. I don't know what to do except feel guilty that all of you are in this mess…" She hung her head. "I've failed my child, Doctor. I can't help him."

"You can't?" DuBois fixed her with a firm look. "I don't think that's correct, Mrs. Williams. You and your husband chose together to find the best doctors you could and placed Justin in our care. You made sure the team was functioning well. You brought food in and I remember you telling Jacob to sleep. You told us things we could put in the game to make him happy." He shook his head. "I am not sure why you think you cannot help him. You have been helping him. All of us, too."

Mary shook her head. "I…don't know if I'll ever really be able to believe that," she admitted. The rest came out in a rush, an admission she hadn't even shared with Tad. "I don't go to confession anymore. I'm afraid the priest will hear how angry I am. I'm afraid God will hear how angry I am. I would never want someone else's parents to suffer for this, but I wish it was Tina in a coma and not Justin. It isn't fair and it doesn't make sense."

"I imagine she feels the same way," DuBois said neutrally.

She studied him silently for a moment. "She…does," she admitted. "She told me so in an email."

"Can you imagine writing that email?" he asked. His face was distant and contemplative. It wasn't a rhetorical question and he was not making a point. He was imagining it. "She emails you to ask how he is. She wants him to be better because she does not think it is fair that he was injured and she was not. She is…miserable." He nodded as if checking an equation and realizing that it balanced.

"She also knows that you are in pain and wishes she could take it away."

Mary said nothing. She felt the first stirrings of guilt.

"You could tell her that he is improving," he suggested. "We have seen measurable improvement. Maybe it would help her to know that."

Her lips twitched in a strange smile. DuBois was very good at putting the pieces together but he still didn't understand—not really. He could not comprehend the outward force of her anger or her desire to have Tina be miserable.

And, with his simple, easy suggestion, she felt her anger unwind somewhat. She remembered the moment when she'd stood in her kitchen and realized that to wish the coma on Tina was to wish her anguish on her parents. She didn't want that. And when she thought of the girl, she saw now that she'd wished grief on her without ever really thinking about that grief.

She remembered being young. How would she feel if it were Tad in a coma and she was at fault? She couldn't imagine that and she swallowed uncomfortably.

"Thank you," she told DuBois. She took his hand and squeezed it. "Thank you."

"Of course." He stood and motioned for her to lie back.

"Please…will you pull me out if Tad calls?" she asked.

The doctor nodded and she had the sense that he would take her directive seriously. He wouldn't let her linger in the game if it were bad news.

His assurance was comforting.

Mary closed her eyes and breathed out. Her vision began to fuzz into pure white, and in seconds, the feed from the video game took over. She did not see DuBois shut the lid of the pod but she was smiling.

Soon, she would see Justin again.

CHAPTER FORTY-SEVEN

"I want to say," Zaara called over the wall, "that if I die by falling through the floor, I'll be really angry about it."

"Only briefly, though," Justin responded. "Look on the bright side."

"Very funny." She grunted, followed by the crack of wood. "Ow. And no, I didn't fall."

"That's good to know." He sat cross-legged and drummed his fingers nervously on the floor. "Let me know when you're down."

"Uh-huh."

"Are you waiting for something?"

"I'm having an argument with my better sense," she muttered in a rough and strained tone. From the sound of it, she was halfway through the hole and held herself up on her elbows. "This is beginning to seem like a very bad idea."

"Leaving on our own seems like a much better idea than letting them send us out," Justin told her. "They'll keep something we care about to make sure we come back, and I'm kind of worried that something will be you or Lyle."

"So the 'we' is you?"

"In this case, yes. They did come to speak to me."

"For all you know…" Zaara panted and he waited. "They talked to

Lyle too. Good gods, I wonder if he sold us out. I'll stab him if he did. All right, here goes nothing." The sound of ripping cloth preceded an oath, a thud, and another muttered expletive.

"Zaara? Zaara!"

"Ow." He heard limping footsteps. "Ow, ow, ow. They couldn't put pillows down, could they? Nooooooo…"

Justin's mouth twitched. He decided to focus on that as he inched toward the edge of the floor. While he'd asked Zaara what she was waiting for, the truth was that he was none too eager to do his part. He thought of asking her to sneak up the stairs and let him out, pictured what she would say in response to that, and decided to take his chances with the several-hundred-foot drop instead.

Cautiously, he stuck his head over the edge. "Are you ready?"

The area below their cells was one large chamber and she stood under where he lay. She took a careful step to the side and gave him a thumbs-up. One sleeve was ripped down the side and a nasty bruise was already visible but otherwise, she seemed fine.

"Okay," he said. "Right. Okay. Right. Okay." He maneuvered his legs to the edge. "Right." He lay on his stomach and stared at the grain of the wood. "Okay."

"Justin?"

"Yep. I'm, uh…having an existential crisis."

"I don't know what that is." Zaara sounded exasperated. "Are you worried about falling off the tower?"

"Yes."

"Well, get over it." She didn't sound particularly sympathetic. "Now-ish would be good."

"Maybe this plan was a mistake."

"Right, I'll jump through the hole in the floor again, then." She came to peer toward the edge of the ledge. He couldn't see her, of course, but he could feel the force of her stare. "Are you kidding me, you good-for-nothing, pot-lid-wearing—I don't even know…useless, fireball-slinging donkey-wrangler?"

Justin sighed. He was fairly sure he could hear the AI laughing and that annoyed him. "Right. I'm coming down. Grab my hand, right?"

"Oh, you mean the goal is to stop you from going over the edge? Huh. I hadn't understood that." Her tone was as sweet as poison. "So help me, you will jump or I will come up there and make you wish you had."

"Right. Okay. Right. Okay."

"Stop saying that!"

"Okay." He wiggled his legs off the edge of the floor, listened to the wind whistling, and tried not to whimper pathetically. Stupidly, he told himself he should be glad she wasn't real because if she were, he'd have sunk any chances he had with her. He wiggled back farther, inch by careful inch. With his arms braced on the wood and his fingers scrabbling for purchase, he let his body hang before he grasped the edge of the floor and exhaled as he let himself down. His feet dangled a meter or so above the floor.

When Zaara began to back away, he knew the panic showed on his face because she sighed.

"Listen, you dolt, I'll grab your hand and pull you this way. Got it?"

"Oh. That's a good plan. Right."

"If you say 'okay' one more time—"

Justin pressed his lips together, prayed deeply, and released the wood. He struck the floor, threw himself forward, and sighed when he realized he wasn't still moving. Zaara had hold of both of his hands but the floor had held.

Or so he thought. With a crack and a shudder, the boards under him splintered and he felt the sickening sensation of freefall.

"Whoa—whoa!" She threw herself back, her boots braced on the floor. "Justin, throw your leg up over the edge. *Now!* I'm sliding. Justin!"

His hands slipped in hers but he managed to hook one foot onto a stable piece of a beam and wrenched both himself and Zaara sideways. She grimaced with the effort of hauling him up and tried to brace her boots on the weather-beaten wood flooring. The beam gave them enough space for them to gain better purchase and for him to scramble to safety. With one hand still clasped around his forearm, she wrenched the door open and the two of them tumbled into the hallway as the rest of the floor crumbled behind them.

A long pause followed.

"Do I want to look behind me?" his companion asked. She was close to hyperventilating.

"I don't think so." Justin looked cautiously over his shoulder and saw wind whistling and far too steep a drop. Bile rose reflexively. "Oh, God. You definitely don't want to look. I regret that."

"Okay, this way." She crawled toward the stairs. "Shut the door."

He shut it behind him, latched it, and pushed to his feet. His hands and legs were trembling and he began to laugh.

"Holy shit. Oh, God, that was such a bad idea."

Zaara laughed too. "Yeah, probably."

"Hello?" a voice called.

The teammates froze.

"Marco?"

Justin grimaced and only narrowly avoided saying, "Polo."

"Marco, is that you?"

He buried his face in his hands and tried not to laugh. The struggle continued when Zaara grabbed him by his shirt and began to drag him up the stairs.

"Now is not the time," she snapped in his ear.

Although he nodded, between the adrenaline and the name, he couldn't seem to stop. The two climbed the stairs as quickly as they could. He stumbled sometimes when he laughed too hard to lift his foot properly and she continually darted worried looks behind them.

Two floors up, she stopped to rest her ear against a door. She peered through the latch, nodded, and motioned him up the stairs.

"If you can't be useful, hide."

"I'll...I'll take care of him. By way of apology." Justin gestured for her to hide instead. He waited and bounced on the balls of his feet until the guard's footsteps drew closer. With the wind outside the tower and the creak of stone and wood, he wasn't surprised that the man wondered whether he'd heard something or not.

"Marco?" the guard called. "Marco, is that—" He stepped around the corner and stared at Justin, open-mouthed.

"Polo," he said cheerfully and punched him in the face. The man fell like a sack of bricks and he caught the front of his vest and dragged him onto the landing. When Zaara opened the door into a room that was fully enclosed, they took the opportunity to drag the unconscious body in before they began to strip him as fast as they could.

His armor, luckily, fit Justin well—or maybe that was merely the video game auto-sizing things. Given how tall the werewolves seemed to be, that was probably the case. It meant that he now had greaves, wrist guards, and a helmet, as well as a leather buckler and two knives for Zaara, although she gave him one for now.

They snuck out of the room, closed the door, and used a piece of loose wood to wedge the handle closed.

"We should go down," she mouthed and gestured to illustrate the point.

Justin gave a thumbs up and they descended. Given that he was now dressed as a guard, he went first. Two floors down from their cells, the corridor divided, straightened, and wound into utter blackness, punctuated only by flickering lanterns.

"It must be cut into the rock," Zaara said quietly. "What now?" She pointed at the stairs. "Down, or in?"

"If the tower's crumbling and they have treasure, it's probably in here," Justin said, after a moment. "Like that potion and…well, my sword, which I need if we fight werewolves. It's the only thing that hurt the last one, remember. So let's try this way."

They set off as quietly as they could. She moved purposefully, but her fingers constantly moved to where her knives should be and she looked surprisingly small without her breastplate and cloak. Funnily enough, however, with a white blouse and black leather pants, she could pass for someone in the real world. He hid his smile and didn't mention that to her.

They were halfway down the hall when they heard something that made both of them prick up their ears.

"Aaaaaand the miners heaved, and the miners hauled—"

Lyle might not have a future as a singer, but his voice was certainly distinctive. The friends exchanged a hopeful glance before they snuck closer to a door, which they found locked and heavily barred. It didn't look as if the dwarf was held in luxury.

A second later, both of them jumped when he said, "Whoever's sneaking around out there, I can hear ye."

Justin gestured to the door and motioned for Zaara to pick the lock. She folded her arms at him, sighed, and retrieved the set of keys the guard had carried.

"Oh, right. That is better."

"Yeah. Yeah, it is." She tried a few keys before one slid in and turned, then pushed the door open and motioned for him to go first.

The room inside was pitch-black. He came up short and looked around as she ran smack into him.

"Aren't ye a little short for a werewolf?" Lyle asked.

"Huh?" He stared in the direction of his voice. "Oh, the helmet." He took it off. "It's us. We're here to save you."

"Are ye now?" The prisoner hopped down from where he'd been seated—a boulder, judging by the shape. "About time. I was getting bored, you know."

"Yes, yes." Justin gestured dismissively. "Do you have any idea why they didn't have you out with us on the outside of the tower?"

"My guess? They assume I know enough about masonry to have escaped." Lyle looked around the hallway and pointed farther into the mountain. "There's gold thataway. Anyway, they put me in a room with no joins and no hinges. I have to say, it was well-done. I went over that thing three times and never found so much as a crack to work with."

Justin made a mental note to learn more about Dwarven magic and led the way down the hallway. In whispers, he and Zaara caught their teammate up on what was going on.

"I don't see why we don't kill all of 'em," Lyle said when they were done.

"Because we don't know who's to blame yet." He gave him a horrified glance.

"They've all got the look to 'em," he retorted. "Every one of 'em has dirtied their hands, let me tell you."

"So we simply kill them?"

"Why not?" Lyle sounded quite self-assured. He stopped at a door that blended into the rock. "This is the treasure." He ran his fingers around the edge, found the hidden catches, and pushed it open with a kick. As he took a torch from the wall, he said, "They'd kill you straight off. You know they wouldn't even hesitate."

"That's not the point!" he protested as he followed him into the room.

"If that's not the point what the hell is?" The dwarf gave him a confused look.

Justin had no idea how to respond to that, so he looked around the room instead.

His jaw dropped at what he saw. Not only was their armor and weaponry in a neat pile in the center of the room, but his friend had also been correct that there was gold. It wasn't Aladdin's cave levels of gold, but there were coffers that didn't close properly, more suits of armor lining one wall, and whole racks of weaponry.

The group scrambled to arm themselves. Zaara sighed with relief as she donned her armor once more and flashed him a sunny smile.

"It doesn't feel right not to have some protection."

He snickered internally and managed to not make a joke about that as he pulled his plate armor on. Lyle sifted through handfuls of jewelry and once in a while, flung a piece toward one of them with an explanation of why. One ring set with a ruby apparently increased one's ability to strike true, and a silver chain granted the wearer strength. Zaara got a bracelet that made her "light of foot," in Lyle's words, and she paused to stare at the young man's wrist.

"I wonder why they didn't take your amulet," she said and pointed to where the blue amulet was still on his wrist.

Justin looked down in a panic. He was also confused but he hadn't thought how difficult it would be if he were to lose this now when he couldn't exactly return to Riverbend easily and find another. "I don't know why they didn't take it off," he responded after a moment.

"Oh, they tried," the AI told him. "Four of them were full-on electrocuted. It was hilarious—I mean…sad."

He bit his lip to keep from laughing when something moved in the shadows and he stumbled back. His feet caught and in an effort to stay upright, he upended a suit of armor nearby and wasn't able to catch it in time. Everyone in the room covered their ears as it clanged.

"Justin?"

He knew that voice.

"Mom?" He scrambled to his feet. Again, it was jarring to see her not looking like his mother but he knew it was her. "What's going on? Why are you here?"

"I…came to see…you." She looked around. "Is something wrong?"

"Well, for one thing, I heard an alarm bell go off," Lyle said.

"Fuck," Justin said furiously.

"Justin! Language!"

"Mom?" He looked at her. "We're about to have a whole crowd of angry werewolves in here."

"Oh," Mary said. "Fuck."

CHAPTER FORTY-EIGHT

"Mom!" Justin called. "Find something to fight with."

"Oh. Right." Mary looked around, then at the ceiling. "Oh, thank you," she said to no one.

"Was that the AI?" he asked wearily.

"Yes." She smiled. "It's very helpful. It told me I'll want something made of silver and also how to throw something called a death-coil."

"You have to be kidding me."

"Try being pleasant for once."

He glared upward to the imagined location of the AI. When this was over, he would find who had created it and they would have to answer some serious questions.

The clatter and clang of feet very quickly changed into the pound of paws and the howling of wolves.

"Fuck," Zaara said under her breath. She stood in the corner of the room.

"What are you doing?" he demanded.

"Looking for something silver," she told him. "I can't find anything."

"Take this." Mary threw a silver ring at her. "Unless you want this.

Yes, you'd probably better have that." She tossed the dagger and Zaara lobbed the ring back.

He looked on, shook his head at the bizarreness of it, and looked at the door. "Are you ready to do this, Lyle?"

"Yeah. Are you? Last I heard, you didn't think people trying to kill you was a good enough reason to kill them."

"That is not what I said. You said they would kill me if they had the chance. When someone's actively trying, all bets are off."

"That doesn't make any—"

"Later, Lyle!"

The first wolf skidded through the doorway and Justin swung his sword overhand. An animal scream was quickly cut off as the beast was pushed out of the way by the momentum of the others behind it. Justin wrenched his sword free and slashed sideways.

Lyle charged into the fray, silver flashing at his knuckles, and pounded his fists into his first target. Yips mixed with battle cries and Zaara leapt into the battle from overhead.

"Justin!" Mary dragged him out of the way and launched a bolt of something black and deadly looking out of one palm. "Stay behind me."

"Are you crazy, woman? I'm the one in the plate armor."

"I'm invulnerable," she told him. "I hope."

"You hope—*Mom!*"

A wolf reared and lashed out with both claws, only to slide off her as a blue shield illuminated across her skin. The beast snarled and danced back and she threw another bolt of black magic at its face. "See?" she shouted at her son.

"I hope Dad's watching this," he muttered. He slid around her side and stabbed a wolf directly in the chest but retreated hastily when its jaws snapped dangerously close to his face. "Oooof, that was a slim margin. Fuck."

"Justin, you know how I feel about you swearing."

"Mom, you're throwing death bolts."

The last remaining wolf snarled, adjusted its shoulders, and screamed as Zaara rolled under its belly and sliced it with the silver knife. It collapsed and she waved a hand at the other three. "Come on!"

They sprinted out of the room and into the hallway.

"Will we make it?" Justin asked breathlessly as they ran. His muscles were on fire.

"I gotta be honest, I have no idea, and—oh, *shit!*" Zaara skidded to a halt when they heard the sound of boots on the stairs. "That is way too many—run! The other way."

"We don't know what's the other way," he protested.

"Is there a way out?" Mary asked.

"Mom, I don't—you're asking the AI, aren't you."

"She says it's this way." His mother caught his wrist and yanked him along.

"You know, I don't think I'll tell my YouTube subscribers about this part," he said contemplatively. Snarls and yips grew more frenzied behind them, mixed with the clangs that suggested the soldiers were bursting out of their armor as they transformed.

"Less talking and more running." Lyle chugged along at their side and reminded Justin of nothing so much as a pug. When he caught the glint in the dwarf's eye, he revised his opinion from pug to terrier.

The group pounded down the hallway and without warning, slid off the edge and down a flight of stairs into utter darkness.

"Ow!" That sounded like Zaara.

"I—oof, fuck. Are you okay?" Justin couldn't tell which way was up anymore. He constantly tried to catch hold of a handrail but didn't think there was one.

"Of course I'm not okay. You're heavy in that armor. Lyle?"

"Relax," the dwarf responded. "I've been through a ton of these. Relax, let go, and think of happy things."

"You are out of your mind." Justin gasped a breath. "Fuck, how long is this staircase?"

"The AI says not much longer," Mary replied. "Zaara, grab my hand, I think I can—"

"*Ow!*" With thuds and clanks, all four of them stopped abruptly.

The wolves shuffled around at the top of the stairs but they couldn't be sure if the beasts wanted to try coming down.

"A door," Justin said wildly. "Get it open."

"There's no door!" Zaara told him sharply.

"Are you sure? Wait, why aren't you looking? Lyle!"

"There's no door," the dwarf echoed.

"You're telling me someone carved the world's longest staircase and it goes nowhere?" He made a fireball in one hand and glared at Lyle. "There is a door here. Find it."

"Do you see a door?" His friend gestured at the blank stone wall with surprising elegance.

"No, I…oh." He stared at the wall, closed his eyes, and breathed out as he pictured waves on the beach, but his effort was disturbed.

A yip and some scuffling told him the wolves had started down the stairs and his head jerked around.

"Focus," Zaara yelled.

"What about you?" Despite his challenge to her, he forced himself to refocus. *Waves in, waves out. Don't think about the horde of angry wolves.* This was hard. *In, out. Keep the fireball going. Wolves. In, out. In…out.*

"It's there!" Lyle caught him by his armor and yanked him through the door. "You go, you go, you go…all here, okay." He slammed the door shut with his shoulder and a moment later, they were treated to the immensely satisfying sound of several wolves careening into a stone wall at high speed.

"Ah. Perfection." He blew a breath out. "Everything hurts. Does everyone else hurt everywhere?"

"I do," Zaara said.

"Not really." Mary sounded remarkably calm. "I am a little dizzy, though. Wait…no, I'm not. Thank you, AI."

"Unbelievable," Justin muttered. "Okay, all, let's find a way out of here. I think we can safely say going the other way is off the table."

CHAPTER FORTY-NINE

Justin's ball of flame guided them partway down the corridor, although his mother noticed it kept burning his hand. It wasn't far, however, before they found old, unused torches on the wall. Zaara retrieved one and lit it from the fireball before she strode away to find others. With everyone now armed with light, they set off again.

Mary looked around as they walked. The walls weren't marked and dust lay thickly on the floor. Whatever this place was, it hadn't been used in a very long time.

"What do you think this is?" Justin asked, his mind running along similar lines to hers. "The air...doesn't seem as stale as it should."

"Yer right, and that's good," Lyle said. "A closed-off mine is the worst place you can be." His voice showed the depth of his feeling. "It's part of why I left," he added gruffly after a moment.

He glanced at his friend but held his tongue, which Mary approved of. The dwarf's fear was obviously deep-seated and she had a sense that he wasn't someone who made admissions like this lightly. After all, he'd been remarkably unsentimental during the fight.

She shook her head. What was she thinking? Lyle wasn't real. He was a fake person created by the makers of the game—perhaps shaped by Justin's choices, but not real.

Unwillingly, her gaze drifted to Zaara.

While she hated to say it, she could see what her son saw in the girl. Her appearance wasn't the first thing you noticed about her. Rather, it was the way she walked—not the confidence she projected as she tried to be a dangerous outlaw but the real confidence that lay beneath. Behind the black armor and double daggers, she was watchful and protective, as well as brave. She'd been the one who ran down the corridor first, after all, even knowing they would likely face opposition.

Mary was lost in her thoughts when she heard the strange skittering sound from the darkness ahead.

Everyone froze and only the flames from the torches continued to dance and send their shadows flickering over the walls. She peered into the tunnel ahead of them and realized she was holding her breath. The battle with the wolves hadn't affected her as much as she'd expected, not with the realization that she was immune to damage.

This, though… Something about an enemy lurking and not knowing what it was made it more difficult.

She thought she saw a gleam in the pitch-black shadow and leaned forward. A pair of eyes appeared, then another pair. The two of them must be close together, and they were very far off the ground.

When she saw the other four eyes, she uttered a little sound of fear.

More than anything, she hated spiders and always had. She was a country girl and had gutted deer and fish, mucked stables out, and planted and harvested in every kind of weather imaginable. There was a time when she used to catch snakes and bring them inside.

But she couldn't stand spiders.

"What do you want to bet," Justin said slowly, "that it's poisonous?"

Mary resisted the urge to clap her hands over her face—which wouldn't be good, given the fact that she carried a torch.

"I'd say the odds are good," Lyle said.

Zaara nodded.

"So I'd propose we burn it," he said and looked at Zaara, then at Mary. "Zaara and I will throw fireballs. Do you want to join in with some of your death bolts, Mom?" He gave her a crooked smile she remembered from his childhood. "Maybe you'll feel braver around spiders if you help deal with—"

"Justin!" Zaara yelled.

The spider had come down the hallway in a rush as if sensing the team's distraction.

Mary screamed as loudly as she could and threw her hands out. The torch tumbled into the dust and black power poured out of her, flanked by bolts of flame from Zaara and Justin.

The three strikes were more than enough to kill the creature but not enough to halt its momentum. It uttered an unearthly shriek as it caught fire but still skittered forward at high speed. His mother gave another full-volume scream of her own before he tackled her sideways against the wall as the flaming body went past.

"Mom. Mom!"

She managed to stop screaming. "What?"

"You're deafening me," he told her but laughed as he held one hand up to shield his eyes and studied the spider. After a moment, he turned her away and marched her down the hall. "I wouldn't look if I were you. Suffice it to say it's taken care of. Come on, everyone. Zaara, if you'd take the front?"

"Right-o." The young woman grinned and handed Mary's torch to her before she added shyly, "And I don't suppose you could teach me that spell, could you? I've never even seen that one."

"Uh…"

"She'll think about it," Justin said firmly. He draped an arm around his mother's shoulders and steered her down the hallway behind the other two. "How about that, huh? You killed the spider to end all spiders. My mom, the spider-slayer. Did you get any levels from that?"

"Levels?" she asked. She still tried to calm the racing of her heart.

Blue letters popped up on one side of the screen, reading **FEAR SLAYER, Level 1.**

"Oh. I guess I'm a Fear Slayer."

"That's cool," he said encouragingly. "As you do more and more, you'll level up."

"As I do more?" She thought she might have a heart attack. "How do you survive this game? Good God above."

Justin laughed and hugged her. "Dad's not gonna believe this unless he's watching it right now." He looked at her and some of what she felt must have shown on her face because he said slowly, "Is everything okay? And why did you disappear like that last time?"

"Oh, I…" Mary cleared her throat and couldn't decide what to tell him. The thought of him being closed in darkness without this world around him and without friends was terrifying—and surely it would be more terrifying for him without knowing what was happening. But then again, if Tad and the others found a way to avert this, he might spend the rest of his time in this world waiting for an ax to fall, and surely that would be cruel.

She considered what to say, conscious that he was waiting.

Finally, she patted his hand. "We miss you," she said. "Putting many people in the game at once isn't something they had a good idea how to do, you see. They want to be sure everything is working. I was glad to test it, of course, but I don't want to be selfish and get in the way of your progress."

"You're not getting in the way," Justin said stoutly.

"Oh, really?" Mary raised an eyebrow. "Having your mother come along with you on your adventures isn't getting in the way?"

The light wasn't very good, but she was sure she saw him blush and Lyle cleared his throat in a way that might have been a stifled laugh.

"Mom," he said, embarrassed.

"You don't need me here," she said. As the words emerged, she realized she truly meant them—and that, in a way, she was glad. "You're doing well, Justin. I heard you speaking to—Lyle, is it? Yes— about when you should kill and when you should not. I like that you hesitate." She smiled at him. "Tell me about who we were fighting back there."

"I assume you mean the wolves," he said wryly. "I have no idea if the spider had a backstory."

"Oh, do you have to bring it up?" Mary groaned.

"Sorry, sorry." He grinned. "Ah, the wolves…long story short, there's a pack who were probably turned into werewolves by a witch. They want us to kill her so they can be set free of the curse. She wants us to kill them because she says they were robbing people and they're cursing the forest. We have no idea who's right."

She nodded. The corridor had begun to slope up slightly as they walked and it wound gently into a curve. So far, thankfully, nothing else moved in the darkness.

Justin was different here. She could hardly believe how much, in fact. No, not different. She considered the best definition.

More. She looked at briefly him, then looked away. Would he remember this when he recovered?

She hoped so and that he would be this person when he returned. He had always been smart and able to determine the best course of action. Now, though, he was decisive, willing to share his opinion and argue for it, or even take control of the situation when it was needed. Clearly, he wasn't using the video game as an excuse to go on a murdering spree and as far as she could tell, he hadn't even made a move on Zaara.

Though DuBois had been evasive when she asked about that.

With a sigh, she conceded that it was none of her business.

"Is something wrong?" Justin asked her. "Seriously, Mom."

"I have to say that when I saw you playing all those games, this isn't quite what I imagined."

He smiled. "Yeah. Me, neither." He lowered his voice slightly. "I told Zaara and Lyle the truth, kind of, but they mostly think I'm crazy. I mean…you know what I mean."

She nodded. "Lyle," she said a little more loudly. "Tell me about yourself."

The dwarf gave her a look over his shoulder. He seemed quite respectful of her, even if he wasn't particularly respectful to Justin.

"What d'ye want to know?"

"You said you left your home to come adventuring," she said lightly. "That's interesting, isn't it? And you're fighting at my son's side, so I was already interested."

"Ah, he's not so bad with a sword as we say," he said gruffly. "And me...well, there's not much to tell. I decided to find my own way rather than stay in the fortress. I haven't had as many adventures as I thought there'd be, but yer son seems to attract them."

Mary smiled at that. "Do you have any brothers or sisters?"

"One o' each. Twins. Older'n me. They were hell and never went anywhere apart. 'Course, they also couldn't stand each other. That was fun. Last I heard, they couldn't decide whether to train as blacksmiths or goldsmiths. Now, me ma was a stonemason, see, and she..."

They continued to walk as Lyle rambled about his family. To Mary's surprise, the story had the little touches she wouldn't have expected from a game. She looked at Justin and he smiled at her.

When she tilted her head curiously, he said quietly, "You wondered what I loved about games? This was part of it—all these stories."

She had never considered that. When at last Lyle began to wind down and the corridor finally showed the faint promise of sunlight, she called, "Your turn, Zaara."

"I have nothing as interesting as Lyle's story, ma'am." The girl seemed almost shy. "Or yours, I'm sure. I'm only a mayor's daughter."

Justin snorted. "Merely your average mayor's daughter. She taught herself daggers and magic and ran away to kill an evil wizard. Normal stuff."

"Justin!" Zaara flushed. "I barely know magic, especially compared to your mother."

"She's—" He looked at Mary and she saw his mouth twitch madly. "Yes, I suppose she does know magic. Mom, why don't you tell them your story?"

"Now, now," she said, "if I tell all the details, where would my aura of mystery be? I prefer to be mysterious." She smiled at Zaara and Lyle. "But it's clear I could wish for no better companions for you, Justin." She stopped him and squeezed his hands. "It was good to see you. I'll go now." She hugged him. "You're doing well. We think of you every day."

"I think of you, too," he said. "Tell Dad I said hi."

"I will."

She continued to watch him as the world dissolved around her into darkness. Moments later, she stared at the entire PIVOT team.

"Is something wrong?"

"Well, someone called the cops on us," Nick said, "because a woman screamed bloody murder. So, rest assured, Mrs. Williams, the next time we put you in the game, there will be no spiders."

Justin watched as his mother's form faded before he rejoined his friends with a sigh.

"I never learned any of her spells," Zaara said mournfully. "Justin, she's wonderful. Imagine having a sorceress for a mother. You never told us that."

"I never knew," he said philosophically. When the other two gave him a confused look, he cleared his throat. "Ah...I mean, I never knew until...oh, whatever. Maybe the next time she's here, she can teach you some spells."

"I'd like that," she said.

He stared at where the sunlight slanted into the mouth of the tunnel—werewolf-free, so far—and considered their options. "So, what on earth do we do next?"

"Well..." Lyle sounded contemplative. He held up a crystal vial of something that sparkled like stars and blood and death all at once. Looking at it too hard made the young man's head ache. "We could use this potion I stole from the werewolves and kill us a witch. What do you say?"

CHAPTER FIFTY

Jacob looked at the clock. They had eight hours and three minutes left—or, in more commonly accepted terms, it was 2:17 AM. He hadn't slept since four hours before the FDA had arrived the previous day, and he was fairly sure none of the others had either.

It wasn't that he hadn't tried. He had attempted to snatch a catnap a few times. He knew their chances of getting out of this hinged on their ability to think clearly, and that ability would go down the tubes increasingly the longer they stayed awake.

But nothing, not even pure exhaustion, could rob him of the sheer rage that circled through his brain. He was furious, he was afraid of spending the rest of his life in jail, and he was even angrier that this was what was dangled in front of him to force him to back down.

He hadn't done anything wrong.

Not that the FDA cared. The agents worked with the absolute certainty that their bosses were doing the right thing. As far as they knew, he was running uncleared experiments on a comatose patient.

With his head buried in his hands, and gave a groan that turned into a shout of frustration. "What the fuck do we do?"

When he looked up, Amber was seated in her chair and stared at the ceiling.

"We could back down," she said. "It's the first time. There's enough evidence to show we saw it would be safe and we could almost certainly get you off without jail time. I trust Jamie when he says that."

The lawyer had, to his credit, given them all their options. He was sure the man would prefer it if they backed down.

Amber, however, was a surprise—and one that made his blood pressure climb even higher.

"You want us to back down?" he asked her. "You sat through sixteen hours of brainstorming and you didn't say that. And you watched me come back from getting bail, you told Mary you'd keep fighting, and you told me you thought we were doing the right thing and now, you tell me we should back down?"

She said nothing and watched him with dark, inscrutable eyes.

"Let me tell you something." He stabbed his finger on the kitchenette table. "We did the right thing. We used technology with a good track record to give Justin a better chance to survive this. We're only in this mess because some assholes at big companies don't want their quarterly reports to take a hit, and I'll be damned if I let them get away with that. We will not back down."

"Really?" Amber said. "Because Nick and I have given you…" She looked at a sheet of paper. "Seventeen different ideas and you've shot every one of them down because the FDA might come down too hard on us. If that's what you're afraid of, you need to back down. If not…" She stood, braced her hands on the table, and met his gaze. "Then get over it. This is the last time I'm asking. Do you want to back down? You're the one facing jail time and I gave you my word fourteen hours ago that if you wanted to call this off, I'd back you. Nick said the same. Give us an answer."

Jacob stared at her. "No," he said finally. "Fuck them. I won't back down."

"Then the time for trying to stay away from downsides is over," she stated. "We have two objectives. The first is to keep Justin on this course of treatment without interruption, and the second is to make this treatment available to more people. Keeping the FDA from getting mad at us in the short term is not one of the objectives."

The two partners locked gazes until he nodded.

"Now," she said as if the prior confrontation had not occurred, "we do have an option. None of us will be particularly happy, but we do have it. We approach one of COMPANY X's competitors and give them a deal. We leak what's been going on with Justin, that the treatment got blacklisted by an FDA official who took a cushy position at COMPANY X, and we let their competitor swoop in and buy the rights to the treatment. They go to bat at the FDA and their lawyers take the heat. We'll probably be blacklisted but the treatment will survive."

Jacob and Nick—who had remained silent thus far—looked at each other. Jacob could tell the thought was as much of a gut punch to the other man as it was to him but one look showed that Amber wasn't taking it well, either.

"We said that we got into this to help people," she told them. "I don't know about you, but for me? It partly meant that I wanted to be known as someone who helped people. I don't want to have my reputation smeared, but if it's a choice between that and this treatment not getting out...I think the choice is clear."

He rubbed his face to try to move past the feeling that he couldn't think anymore, having been awake too long.

The phone rang and everyone at the table jumped. He shook his head and pushed it to Amber, who sighed before she answered.

"Hello? Hello, Senator."

The two men now straightened.

"One moment," she said. "I'll put you on speakerphone...there. It's only the three of us here. Your wife is grocery shopping and DuBois went to take a shower.'

"About time," Nick said and shuddered.

"I'm glad I caught you alone," Tad told them. "We don't have much time left, so here's the deal. Our mystery donor is Anna Price of Diatek Industries. She has offered to fund the project and smooth out any FDA wrinkles by folding PIVOT into Diatek."

The three of them fell silent.

"I assume from your silence that either the call has dropped or you feel much the same way I did," he said. "It's too good to be true, so there must be a catch, right?"

"Right." Amber's face said she knew what the catch would be.

"I've had my aides dig up every damned thing I can about Anna Price and Diatek," he said. "Much of their work is sealed, unfortunately, as it's for the Department of Defense. But with that said, she told me one story that I have fact-checked and found to be completely honest. When she and her husband were postgrads, their daughter was involved in a car accident, became comatose, and had to be taken off life support because they ran out of money. She started Diatek soon after, allegedly to make sure no other family had to go through that. A few years later, her husband killed himself. His death certificate officially says unknown causes, but we've dug up obituaries and news coverage from the time that make it very clear it was known to be a suicide and it was about Mina's death."

Jacob felt the hair stand up on his arms. All three of them stared at the phone on the table, unable to look away.

"We've found paper trails that, as far as we can tell—and we're not engineers or doctors but we'll send you what we can—suggest she's being honest about where Diatek's profits go," Tad continued. "She never took it public, so she has no shareholders to answer to, and that means many details can fly under the radar. However, she doesn't have any extra properties we can find, she doesn't have massive investment accounts, and her C-suite team doesn't seem to live the high life either. And...I don't know if I have to say this, but Department of Defense contracts are lucrative. The woman should have money."

A long pause followed before Amber blew a breath out.

"PIVOT isn't my company," the senator said finally, "so this isn't my choice."

"No, but Justin's care is." Jacob found a reserve of energy he hadn't been able to access on his own account. "What is your opinion, sir?"

Tad took his time before he answered. "I want him to stay on this program," he said finally. "I know I'm not a doctor, but I can't see how only sleeping with no brain engagement would be better for him than this. Mary tells me he's not only recovering, but he's also actually… growing up. He's making moral choices. Would I rather have him in a hospital bed, sleeping for months? No. But I don't know how to get there. Whatever other ideas you have, I'll let you think about them. Call me when you've done that."

"Yes, sir." Jacob ended the call and looked around at the other two. "So, what now?"

"Hmm?" DuBois entered the room. He smelled much better but his hair somehow looked exponentially worse.

Jacob decided to chalk that up to his sleep deprivation. He outlined Diatek's offer quickly for the doctor, who took a seat and laced his hands over his stomach. He seemed deep in thought, not yet inclined to speak.

"I'm not sure we want to do this," Nick said finally. He held a hand up to stave off argument from either of his partners. "No, listen to me. A private company that comes out of nowhere to get a ton of Department of Defense contracts?" He held his phone screen out. "Their first contract came within two years, and it was a big one. That's absurd. They've basically been bankrolled by the military and intelligence ever since, and it isn't even clear what they're paid to do. Which… well, we know what that means."

"We think we know what that means," Jacob said. "The military is also working on stuff like regrowing limbs so it's not like everything they do is bad." He sighed. "Okay, yes, it's probably bad."

"Either she's lying about the research on comatose patients or she's telling the truth, and I don't think we'll do a better job of researching that than his aides did," Amber said. "I say we start there. If we think she's lying, there's zero reason to trust her and we say no. That's only my opinion. If we think she's telling the truth, we have a judgment call to make, right? Because then, it's a greater-good kind of thing, and I'll be honest, I never liked those thought experiments."

"Neither did I." Jacob groaned again. "On the other hand, this is exactly what you were advising we do, only now, we don't have to persuade anyone. The deal is already made." He shook his head. "But I don't want to answer to someone I've never met. I need to know this won't be shut down and buried."

"If we don't work with Diatek, it will be shut down and buried," DuBois pointed out. "We can keep moving the lab but they'll keep finding us, and I don't think any of us have deep enough pockets to fight the legal battle indefinitely."

Down the hall, the door opened and the quick, light sound of Mary's footsteps followed. When she arrived in the kitchenette, she studied their expressions with laser focus. "I wondered why you were so quiet," she said. "Trouble?"

"Less than before," Amber told her. With a stab of humor, she added, "Although that's a low bar. Do you want my chair?"

"No. Sit." The woman looked at them expectantly until they explained Tad's offer.

"What do you think?" Nick asked her. "I think he wants us to choose."

"I think he does," she said slowly after a moment. "He's right that PIVOT is your company. He and I can't choose for you. But I will say that although Tad is maybe too quick to fall on his sword when it comes to his conscience, he doesn't like to force other people into bad decisions. What I've worried about for the past day is that he would sell out to the lobbyists to make this problem go away, but that's something he would never ask anyone else to do." She sighed. "I guess what I'm saying is that if he thought this was a real deal with the devil, he would either have rejected it outright or he would have made it himself rather than put it on your conscience. Him putting the ball in your court is his way to show that he thinks it's a good deal."

A surprised silence followed.

"Really?" Jacob asked finally.

"He…thinks we should team up with someone who's helping black ops?" Nick asked skeptically.

Mary raised her shoulders. "Apparently, yes. Whoever this woman is, he believes her story."

Everyone looked at Jacob. "Oh, I have to make the final call?"

"You're the CEO," Amber said, "and you're the one out on bail right now. I'd say yes."

He thought for a moment, then shook his head. "Nope. One moment." He wandered into the other room, tore up a piece of paper, and scribbled some instructions. "All of you, color in one of these bubbles. I won't look to see who does what, and I'll cast my vote in there."

They shrugged and he left them with the tiny makeshift ballots and went into the other room to think. Justin's pod hummed in the corner and the lights flickered on the side. The monitor showed that he was in a conversation with his two party members.

Jacob remembered Mary's expression when she came out of the pod the day before—oddly calm and confident. He remembered the hints that she and Tad had been disappointed in their son. They weren't anymore. The senator was right. This treatment wasn't only giving Justin a chance to return to how he had been. It was giving him a chance to try being someone new.

It was important.

He returned to his team, picked the ballots up, and scrolled through them with a smile.

"It seems we're in agreement," he said. He picked the phone up, dialed, and waited until he heard Tad's voice on the other end of the line. "Senator. Yes. We've decided that we'd like to accept Diatek's offer. How do we proceed from here?"

CHAPTER FIFTY-ONE

Lyle had stopped arguing by the time the group circled to the witch's hut, but his disapproval was clear. As far as Justin could tell, he didn't trust anyone who tried to hire killers, which gave him a wonderful mental image of the dwarf operating as the world's best and worst assassin—someone who would always get the job done, only to come back and kill his client as well.

He, however, still held out hope that one side of this argument would emerge as the reasonable one, and he'd secured promises from both his teammates not to attack the witch right off the bat.

The door to the hut still stood open as they approached, and he decided to go in first. He was the one who asked them not to attack, after all, so should take the most risk.

From the darkness, the witch surveyed them calmly. "Are the wolves dead?"

"Tell me more about what happened between you," Justin said. "It sounds like you fought over the ruins. I'm interested as to why."

She tilted her head to the side and folded her arms. "Are they dead, adventurer, or aren't they?"

"Some witch you are," Zaara said, "if you can't tell." She raised an eyebrow. The group had decided that, even if they went with his plan, it would be way too suspicious for all of them to behave nicely.

"I can tell the forest is not regenerating," the witch said, "and I can smell a potion on you that I know is meant for me. However, I also felt an extraordinarily strong bolt of death magic in the ruins, and the three of you smell of that as well. What am I to make of these facts?"

Justin had the urge to tell her the absolute truth. The death magic had come from a relatively untrained sorceress who had been imbued with her powers by an all-powerful god and let loose to kill a single larger spider.

He couldn't allow the conversation to be dragged sideways like that, but it would be worth it to see the witch's face.

"I could ask the same thing," he said. "I've heard three stories now, all different and all pointing fingers. I've heard the people in those ruins did nothing to anyone except take the ruins when you wanted them—and that they weren't even ruins two months ago. I've heard, from yet another of the wolves, that they were bandits who crossed you and stole something of yours, only to receive a disproportionate punishment. And I've heard from you that they're thieves and murderers whose very existence is causing the world to die, although you won't explain how they became werewolves in the first place. What I want to know is—"

"So you didn't kill them," she interrupted. "They're still there. Their presence still taints the forest. Their pack still hunts the villagers and their flocks. Not only that, but you also came back with the means to kill me."

She raised a hand as casually as if she might shoo them away, but what came from her fingertips was a bolt of lightning.

Justin swung his sword up in time and the bolt of magic ricocheted off the blade to punch through the ceiling with a sizzle. He stared at her and disappointment twisted in his chest.

"You couldn't answer a simple question," he said, thoroughly angry now. "You know, when you tell someone to commit mass murder, it's polite to tell them why."

That was the signal. On the word "polite," Zaara flicked the lid of the potion open and flung a few drops at their opponent. The woman gasped, curled her hand around her forearm where the liquid had splattered, and looked at Justin with venom in her eyes.

"Yeah," he said. "That's right. I ask questions. I don't come in with my weapons drawn. But I'm not stupid either. Go!"

His teammates swept into motion. Lyle charged and tackled the witch into the back wall and Zaara circled behind Justin using a nearby chair to vault into the air and descend on the witch from above. Two blades, one steel and one silver, slashed and their enemy screamed. She lashed out toward the young woman and ripped her belt pouch away.

Thankfully, Zaara didn't have the potion any longer.

Justin saw the decision form in her head, and he lunged, his blade out to catch the bolt of magic that arrowed directly toward his partner's chest. He had no idea what it was but he did know he didn't want it hitting any of them. When the witch crumpled in a daze, he realized it had been a stun spell of some kind.

Lyle flicked a few more drops of the potion on the woman before he threw the potion toward Justin and Zaara. Had the dwarf been the kind of person who hesitated before launching into battle, he might have been moved to pity by the sight of a lone woman swaying on the ground, defenseless.

Luckily, he wasn't one of those people. He delivered a strong kick and followed it up with a hammer strike on the witch's head.

"Ha!" he yelled. "You can't shoot firebolts if ye can't see straight, can ye?"

"The man has a point," Justin called to Zaara. He waited for Lyle to dodge before he sliced down with his sword.

The witch, however, had somehow managed to activate some defenses. Where blunt force had partially powered through, Justin's blade was stopped by a weakly-flickering shield half an inch above the witch's head. She looked at him with a smile.

Fire burst from her hands where they were planted on the floor.

The house was barely standing as it was and this would bring it down within minutes. He swore and dodged a line of flames on the floor before he drove the pommel of his sword down on the witch's head. It didn't strike but the shield flickered and died, which was something.

Zaara danced in and one blade inflicted a long gash down the witch's back. As she slid out of range, a death bolt like the one his mother had thrown launched to follow her. He lunged and realized too late that he didn't need to worry about whether he stepped on the witch or not. He caught the spell with the tip of his sword and batted it away.

"Take that, worst batting average in little league!" His spare hand shook the vial over the woman's head and the potion made contact with an unmistakable hissing sound.

"Oh, that is gross!" Zaara yelled.

Justin stumbled toward a fiery wall but took time to find a place to plant his feet. He looked back to see the witch's form melt into something green, tentacled, and terrifying.

"Oh, good," he said. "Medusa and Cthulhu had a baby. This is good."

"It can still be punched!" Lyle shouted triumphantly and delivered a kick as he raced past her and managed to land it squarely in her groin. When she doubled over, he punched her in the face.

"I didn't know that hurt for women." Justin slashed at a tentacle that snaked toward him and followed it up with several quick swipes as others tried to circle. "Jesus, do these things ever stop growing? Zaara, does it hurt when women get kicked in the groin or is that only a man?"

"It hurts when Lyle kicks you anywhere," she responded.

"Damned right it does," the dwarf agreed.

"Sure." He looked around. The smoke had begun to cloud the air and he could barely see the door. "Okay, last attack—all in."

"Are you sure?" she called.

"Very sure. Zaara first."

This had been part of the plan as well. The creature swayed on its feet and turned to look at her, but the woman had vanished out what was left of the doorway with Lyle at her heels.

By the time it looked for Justin, it was too late. It took the last of the potion full in the face and chest and a truly terrible scream ended in a gurgle when he ran it through with his sword. The monster's face flickered between forms as it collapsed, and he punched out a side wall without even looking for the door.

He wouldn't normally plunge his head into a swamp, but he did it this time without hesitation, bolstered by the memory that water couldn't carry magic. Then, sure that his head was not on fire, he stood with a groan.

"Okay, she—it…whatever—is dead. Very dead. Are you two…" His voice trailed off.

Zaara and Lyle stood together close by, their weapons still raised, and around them and the entire shack, a pack of werewolves had gathered. The sun was setting and the moon was rising.

A full moon, he realized in horror.

"Shit," Justin said. Thoughts tumbled through his head. Maybe the wolves had used them to kill the witch or maybe they were as bad as she'd said. Whatever the case, there was another battle to fight and unlike the last one, they didn't exactly have a potion to make this one shake out in their favor.

To his surprise, the wolf that padded toward him lowered its nose before it transformed into a human. Around the circle, fur melted away and men and women exchanged glances with one another.

"You said she's dead," the bandit leader said to Justin. "Was that true?"

"Well, she's a puddle of goo," he said. "And it wasn't moving when I left. I'd say that counts as dead." His arms ached where he held the sword. "So, let's get this over with, then."

"If you want." The man held out an amulet on a gold chain. "Take this with our thanks. You will always have a safe haven here."

He stopped and squinted at the item. "Wait, what?"

The bandit leader did not smile. "I told you we could make a deal if you freed us, and you freed us."

"We also killed several of your band," he pointed out.

Lyle uttered a sound of disgust. "Ye're not good at bargaining, are ye, lad?"

The leader did smile at that. He met the dwarf's gaze before he focused on Justin again. "Yes, you did. But you also left one of them alive in the tower when you could easily have killed him. You escaped rather than unleash your necromancer on us. And, perhaps most importantly, we would have all been dead in the end if the curse had taken hold—all of us and the forest as well. That monster was an abomination and you have freed us."

Justin took the amulet hesitantly. It looked almost like a clock and each ray out from the center was marked with a series of cross-hatches he could not interpret. "What is this?"

"Do you see the way the middle shines?" At the very center of the amulet, a piece of gold seemed to catch the light in a strange way. "That means it's charged. Anyone who wears this and dies will be returned to the last place the amulet was charged, alive and unharmed. It takes its power from old magic, the nodes between the ley lines."

He raised his eyebrows and looked at it quizzically.

"One use per charge," the bandit leader said. "Use it wisely. If you appear in the middle of our temple, we'll help you, but it won't bring your friends and not all nodes are safe places." He whistled and gestured to his team. "Goodbye, strangers. I'll be interested to see what becomes of you."

When they were gone, Justin slipped the chain over his head. He looked at the other two. "And we still don't know the story," he said.

Zaara laughed. "You'd better get used to that," she said. "I have to say, though, your principle of only killing people who are already trying to kill you got us farther than I thought it would."

"Uh-huh." He knew better than to look at Lyle, who clearly still disapproved of the tactic. "So what now?"

CHAPTER FIFTY-TWO

Mary put the last of the server cords into a large box and shook her head. Eight hours seemed to have vanished in the blink of an eye.

As soon as the PIVOT members agreed with Tad's proposal, logistics swung into motion. A fleet of trucks was being mobilized for the PIVOT equipment to bring it somewhere that was allegedly close but completely unspecified—and, she expected, classified.

While the rest of the team packed—undoing days' worth of careful setup in as little time as they could—Justin's game wound onward. There had been a battle of some kind, she gathered, but DuBois had glanced at the monitor a few times and didn't seem worried.

"I think…" Amber looked around. "I think that's it. None of the rest can be unplugged until we have the truck."

"Which was supposed to arrive an hour ago," Jacob said quietly. He shook his head. "Did we do a stupid thing?"

"No," she said stoutly. "Jamie said there was nothing too sneaky hiding in those papers…well, nothing along the lines of them hanging us out to dry. But there's a small chance Justin may now be classified as a banned weapon under the Geneva Convention."

"A small chance that what?" Mary asked.

"I didn't say anything," she said far too quickly.

"And I didn't hear anything," Nick said. Both gave her identical, pasted-on smiles.

Her quest for answers was interrupted by several men in suits. They strode into the room and stopped when they saw the smiles on everyone's faces.

"Why is this still running?" one of them asked and gestured to the pod.

"Ohhhh," Amber said. "You're not…I mean, you're from the FDA."

"Yes." He fixed her with a suspicious look. "It's been twenty-four hours. We're here to shut this down—and, apparently, take Mr. Zachary into custody again, given that shutting the experiment down was one of the conditions of his bail."

"Correction," the young woman replied calmly. She folded her arms and gave them a sweet smile. "It has been twenty-three hours and fifty-four minutes."

The agents stared at her and she returned it impassively.

"You'll make us sit here for six minutes?" the agent asked her finally.

"You could wait outside," she suggested. Her sweetness didn't waver.

The man stepped forward. "There is no way this will be taken down within the next few minutes. It wouldn't matter if it was six or thirty-six. You're done. All of you."

"And you don't have the right to shut it down until those six minutes are up," she reminded him. There was steel under the sweetness now. She gestured to the kitchenette. "So why don't you take a seat? We can make coffee if you'd like."

The older woman could only admire her resolve. Amber wasn't a Southern girl, but she could certainly slay someone with kindness as if she were.

The agents looked at one another. They looked at their young adversary, who smiled insincerely. Their attention shifted to DuBois, now perched on a desk and munching popcorn, and Mary, who had changed into a suit and pearls. The lead agent pulled his phone out and strode away as he dialed. Whoever he called, he launched into a furious, whispered tirade in the kitchenette.

The other two agents remained in position and Amber pulled a chair out and sat.

None of them broke eye contact. It started as a contest to see who would back down first but it had gone on so long that looking away would only be more awkward. Mary settled her shoulders, stared fixedly at one of the agents, and tried to think what Tad would say when he had to bail her out of jail.

But where was he? She hadn't heard so much as a word from him since the call. Papers had been sent by courier, looked over by a harried lawyer, and signed. She had given her consent as Justin's guardian, and the papers had been taken away again.

That had signaled the start of a seemingly endless wait.

The lead agent's argument ended in the kitchen and he stormed into the room to stare at them, his arms folded. He did not, however, touch a single piece of equipment. No matter how pissed he was, they were right about his jurisdiction.

Mary finally looked at the clock. Two minutes remained and as she couldn't see the seconds counting down, a minute seemed like an eternity. When they were, at last, within the final minute, she let her head slump forward—only to jerk it up when she heard footsteps in the hallway.

The lead agent didn't seem to care. He stepped forward with a smile when Tad strode into the room with a blonde woman in an expensive suit.

"Thank you for your service, Agent Hyde," the woman said smoothly. She held out a folder as the agent swung to face her in disbelief. "Your agency has been relieved of duty in this particular case. You'll find all of the details in here and your supervisor should call you—"

Hyde's pocket rang.

"Now," she finished. She handed the folder to him and moved to shake Mary's hand. "Mrs. Williams. I'm Anna Price." Quickly, she went around the room and correctly identified each of the people there—including, Mary noted, the two other FDA agents.

When Hyde returned from this particular call, he was white with fury. "Do you care to explain this?" he asked Price in a clipped tone.

She did not waste time in thought. "No," she said simply. "I must ask the three of you to vacate the premises, please. This project is now under the aegis of a different agency in partnership with Diatek Industries and is classified."

The man looked as though he couldn't believe his ears. "Classified?" He ground the word out.

"As such, given that you lack the clearance or project authorization, I must ask you to leave." Her voice held a warning now. She gestured to the door and waited.

"Who authorized this?" he snapped.

"That information is on a need to know basis," she told him. "And you do not need to know. Mr. Hyde, if you do not leave, I will be required to call law enforcement at this juncture. Should anything be lacking in the authorization paperwork—and nothing is—I encourage your supervisor to take it up with the Department of Justice."

Hyde knew when he was beaten, at least. He jerked his head at the other two agents and the three of them left. They strode rapidly down the corridor and slammed the outer door behind them.

"Excellent," Price said. She looked around the laboratory. "It looks like you've packed up almost everything. That's good. The truck will be along shortly to move Justin, and while it does have sufficient power to maintain the full operation of the pod, I would like you to keep the generator attached as a backup."

Jacob nodded.

She looked at all of them and smiled slightly. "Do you have questions?" she asked.

"Why are you helping us?" Nick asked immediately. Jacob gave him a furious look but he was intractable.

"I am not certain what Senator Williams told you about my personal life," she said. "Suffice it to say that I have first-hand experience with watching a loved one deal with traumatic brain injuries.

Our understanding of what works and what does not is woefully incomplete, and much of the operating budget of Diatek each year is devoted to various areas under the umbrella of rehabilitation, sleep cycles, and the activity of comatose brains."

"Is that what your company does for the Department of Defense?" Nick pressed.

"Nick." Jacob held his face in his hands.

"Your associate is right in the abstract," Price told him. "He would normally have a right to know who he is doing business with. Unfortunately, Mr. Ryan, I cannot give you specifics of Diatek's work with any other agencies. Those projects are classified."

Nick looked away.

"If you look carefully," the woman said, "you'll notice that your contracts specifically state that you will not be required to do any work on projects other than this one. I do not ask for your approval of my company. I have made choices you might make and ones you might not. On this much, however, we can be clear. Funding for PIVOT is secured as long as I believe you have not knowingly and recklessly strayed into territory that would be more dangerous to patients than currently-approved therapies. Are we clear?"

After a pause, Nick nodded.

"Any other questions? No?" She walked toward the pod. "Good, because I have several of my own. What did you use for the converters here?"

Mary watched the team walk away and turned to launch herself into Tad's arms. They held each other for a long time without speaking, neither needing any help to know what the other was thinking.

"I knew you would do it," she said. "I was afraid you would throw yourself under the bus sometimes, but I knew under the fear that you would do it."

"You know me far too well." He set her down. "And I take it you helped persuade them on this end?"

"I told them you wouldn't give them a deal with the devil," she explained. "Don't prove me wrong."

"I don't think I will—although I have to admit I empathize with

Nick." He shook his head. "It's always worrisome when someone has such an ironclad moral code that includes shady things."

"Yes. Then again, you never know where help will come from." Mary raised her shoulders. "You're fighting for people like her to not have to make those choices, right?"

"Right." Tad put his arm around her while she rested her head on his shoulder.

"I want to see Tina," she said finally.

She surprised him with that. He looked at her, his blue eyes quizzical. "Tina…who Justin was on a date with? That Tina?"

"That Tina." She nodded. "Don't worry, I won't yell at her. She's… emailed me and wants to know how Justin is. I couldn't bring myself to reply but I think I need to."

"It would be good if she were to come here," DuBois said. He stood nearby and he gave them an apologetic smile when they looked at him. "I didn't mean to eavesdrop but I heard the name. I'd like to meet her."

"Why?" Tad asked him. He sounded deeply dubious.

The doctor cleared his throat and looked awkward now. "Well, ah…since you ask…Justin isn't responding quite how I'd like to having Mary in the game."

"I've hurt his progress?" She was horrified.

"No. No, I don't think so. I wouldn't have let you go in if you were hurting him."

"Why did you let me go in at all?"

"Well, it was a good idea in theory, and the first time produced a significant spike of brain activity that seems to have settled into a higher cognitive level." DuBois pointed at a graph, remembered neither of them could read it, and cleared his throat again. "I realized the second time that your presence was…it's difficult to quantify. Please understand that this is a sample size of only one patient and there are many factors in play."

"Yes." Tad had his senator smile on. "I completely understand your reservations, doctor, and we won't hold you to any guarantees so give us your hunch."

"My guess is that Mary's presence forces a false dichotomy on Justin's mind," DuBois explained. "Young adults go through a phase where they have the power to begin reshaping the world. They see it differently from their parents' generation and they, in many senses, operate in a world that does not yet exist, while their parents operate in a world that no longer exists."

Mary's brain hurt. She squinted and tried to make sense of what he'd told them.

"Under normal circumstances, this would not create any kind of break with reality," the doctor continued. "Social turmoil, of course, if both generations were aligned enough with one another, but that's not at play here. My hunch, however, is that in this case, he now perceives this world as Mary's world—his parents' world—and the game as his world. Her dropping into it only serves to drive him into viewing it as a world where he can make a difference."

"Oh." She understood that, at least. "I didn't think of that."

"Again," he said carefully, "I would not have let you go in if I thought it was actively harmful. I think there's much to be said for encouraging his interactions with real minds instead of only the AI. That said, I would like to see his response to someone his age and especially, given the circumstances, I think Tina might be the right person for this."

She looked at Tad and they exchanged minuscule nods before they focused on the man.

"All right," she said.

"We'll have to clear it with Ms. Price, of course," the senator added. "But we've seen tremendous progress so far. If you tell us this is something Justin needs, we'll try to make it happen."

DuBois wandered off, probably to interrupt Price's conversation and ask immediately, and Tad looked at Mary.

"So, you went into the game again?" He sounded wistful. "I wish he hadn't said that about it being bad for Justin. I wanted to go in."

"No, you don't." She shuddered. "There are giant spiders. Like, the size of a small horse. Oh, it was terrible. It was good to see Justin, but...spiders."

He laughed. "I missed you," he said. "Also, please tell me there's video of you and the spiders. Did you scream?"

"I might have had law enforcement called," she said with great dignity.

Tad buried his face in his hands and his shoulders shook with mirth. "Oh, God. This, I have to see."

CHAPTER FIFTY-THREE

It should have been a miserable night. After all, Justin and the others had nothing to do while they waited for fire to consume the shack and reduce it to ashes. They were tired, they were injured, and a swamp wasn't a great area to try to sleep.

He wasn't sure what genius had come up with the idea of a virtual reality that included mosquitos, but he was increasingly determined that when he got out of there, he would kick some ass.

However, the mosquitos heralded a change that happened slowly over the course of the night and was more than visible by morning. The swamp and forest had begun to return to life. Green shoots of grass showed in the patches of dry, brown vegetation, buds pushed through on the various bushes, and birds building nests busily in the trees—which, he had to say, did not look quite so dead as they had the night before.

The area didn't smell quite as awful, either. There had been a stale smell before, somehow even worse than rot, and there was now a bright smell he could only describe as green.

The three of them awoke refreshed and each of them yawned and stretched. Lyle cooked sausages while Justin and Zaara wandered over to take a look at the ruins of the hut. While the remains were still surprisingly hot, the teammates were able to make some progress sifting through them with long sticks they had set to soak in water overnight.

"It smells all kinds of weird," she said.

"That's probably the goo," he told her.

"I can't wait to see that. I bet it's gross." She sounded intrigued. "I keep wondering what she was. I can't think of any myths that talk about something taking a human form that's green and covered in… what did you call them?"

"Tentacles."

"Right. I'd never even heard of tentacles before."

"Boy, would the Internet surprise you."

"Huh?"

"Nothing. I—you know what, forget I said anything." He turned the remains of a book. "It's a shame we didn't get her books out."

"I don't think so." she shook her head. "This place reeks of bad magic. You don't want to know how she did her spells."

"Didn't you want my mom to teach you death coils?" he asked her and moved a piece of what he assumed had been the table. He must be close to the witch's remains now.

"That's death magic, not bad magic."

"You'll have to explain the difference to me."

"You really don't know? Well, the clerics would say there's no difference." Zaara rolled her eyes. "But there is. Bad magic—no, let's start with death magic. Death magic simply kills things, right? It's like you made a sword but you made it out of death. You don't burn someone to death or stab them to death, you—"

"Death them to death?" he asked.

"Yeah, basically." She shrugged. "It's not bad any more than fire is bad. Death happens. It's all around us like magic. I suppose the only difference is that you couldn't use a death coil for anything else." She shrugged. "Still, it's a spell you throw like any other spell."

"Sure." Where was the damned body? Justin continued to shove pieces of wreckage out of the way.

"Bad magic isn't done with magic. If that makes sense."

"It really doesn't."

Zaara thought in silence for a moment. She dipped her hands in the water and pushed a piece of the wall off the pile. "Ha. If you move quickly enough, you don't get burned. Um...bad magic uses the life force of things to make a spell work. You can do it with anything, including a person or an animal."

"A plant?" he asked.

"I'm not sure. I guess so."

"Well..." He gestured broadly at the area around them.

"Oh." Zaara looked around. "Yes. Of course. That makes sense. You know, I wonder if she wasn't right when she said the werewolves were draining the forest. If the curse had to be maintained and the energy came from living things...yeah."

"What a charming woman." Justin scanned the mess around them. "Why do you say clerics don't see the difference between death magic and bad magic?"

"Because they both kill people." She shrugged. "To be fair, they would also say killing someone with a fireball is equally as bad. They don't think mages should be trained for wars and they don't think there should be wars at all. Or bandits. Or...you know, whatever. The problem is, that doesn't help when you're dealing with one."

"That's very true." Justin dropped his stick and sighed. "Okay, I cannot find this body. It should be here."

"If it were a puddle of goo...maybe not?" She scowled. "I guess I don't know."

"You didn't see this stuff. It was as gross as hell. It smelled—it smelled so bad. There's no way we wouldn't see a mark on some of the boards or something, or a...chunk of tentacle." He shuddered dramatically.

"What are you saying?" Zaara stared at him. "She was dead when you left, right?"

"I cut her in half and she collapsed into goo that caught fire." Justin waved his hands. "To me, that means dead."

"I...well, I can see why you'd think that." She nodded. "I probably would, too. But you're the person saying she was dead and saying her body should be here if she were, so I'm not quite sure what to do with those two pieces of information."

"Oh, this is a nightmare." He stared at the ruins. "If she's still alive, that is a very, very bad thing."

"Let's think about this logically." Zaara leaned on her stick. "The curse on the werewolves was released, so whatever happened to her, she wasn't able to maintain that."

"That's a good point."

"I know, right? Second point…I believe the key is right there near your foot." She pointed. "I don't think she'd have left that if she ran away."

He crouched, scrabbled in the ashes, and hissed when his hands tingled with the heat. After a moment, he picked the key up and juggled it between both hands. "Good. That's good. Any third point?"

"Yes. I think the sausages are ready." She set off, using her stick to balance herself as she leapt across patches of water.

Over breakfast, they relayed their findings to Lyle. The dwarf, mistrustful by nature, was inclined to believe that the witch was still alive.

"Ye can never trust a witch to be dead," he said gruffly.

Justin had also begun to suspect that most dwarves could be described as deeply pessimistic.

"What do we do, then?"

"We get the hell out of here," his friend retorted. "The ruins are crawling with wolf-bandits…or bandits that used t'be wolves, or—"

"The bandits formerly known as wolves," he said.

"Ye have an odd way of speakin', lad. I say we go to that stash of treasure we found when we were creepin' around and get it out of here before anyone else finds it. Keep the key and pretend we never saw this place."

"Hmmm." He considered the suggestion. While making their way back to the witch, the team had stumbled across a buried hoard of treasure, something he was sure they would never have found if it hadn't been for Lyle. They had covered it as well as they could and gone on, afraid the wolves might catch up if they didn't. Now, however, it might be worth returning for it. "Good enough. Shall we?"

The walk to the cache of treasure was slow. He wasn't worried that they would be killed by the bandits. At the same time, he was certain it would be fairly awkward if they were caught making off with a large number of artifacts when the last person who had opposed the bandits for these ruins was now—theoretically—dead.

Luckily, the little cart the blacksmith had made for Justin provided them with a template for makeshift sleds, and they set about excavating with enthusiasm.

"There aren't any stories about cursed artifacts in this world, are there?" he asked.

"Why, are there in yours?" Zaara raised an eyebrow. "And of course there are. Cursed rings, cursed amulets, all of that."

"You only thought to mention that after I put on the amulet from the bandit leader?" he demanded.

"Hey, you didn't think of it, either." She shrugged and struggled to secure a chest of coins closed with twigs, which didn't work well. Eventually, she gave up and ripped a few strips off the end of her cloak with a sigh. "What do you think these ruins were?"

"I don't know." He frowned. "The bandit said they weren't ruins until two months ago, but there was dust in some of the rooms and we didn't see furniture, and this doesn't look like it's been buried all that long."

"Coins, goblets, jewelry." Lyle shrugged. "Any rich person might hide this. It's odd that they took the furniture and not this, which is more valuable and more portable."

"I'm beginning to think you're right," he conceded. "This whole place has too many mysteries and not enough facts. I'm ready to be gone."

The dwarf nodded seriously.

They loaded what they could take onto the carts and sleds and returned to the road.

By the time they arrived, all three of them were in a very poor mood, not to mention sweaty and covered in mosquito bites. Justin had now achieved BUG CHOW level 3, which only vaguely helped his mood. He wondered if appreciating the AI's sense of humor was a sign of delirium and decided it probably was.

Things improved marginally on the road, but not by much. They had to travel slowly to avoid tipping any of the cargo off, and their backs soon began to ache with the strain. Once in a while, they would rotate sleds, but the way they sniped at each other about messing up the equipment had begun to take the fun out of everything.

"Mo' loot, mo' problems," Justin muttered to himself.

"Stop muttering!" Lyle snapped. "And get yer sword. I hear a cart."

"Oh, shit." He stood and panted. "Shit." He looked at the side of the road while his brain worked furiously. They should haul the treasure to the underbrush and hide it, but he couldn't see how to do that by the time the cart arrived. Besides, the thought of dragging it out afterward and setting off again was too much to bear. From the looks on the others' faces, they were thinking the same thing.

A mosquito stung him and he thought back, wistfully, to the time when the swamp was a magic wasteland full of wolves.

To their surprise, they recognized the cart's driver immediately.

"Ho, there!" the blacksmith said heartily. "I wondered if I'd find you here."

"Are you coming to trade?" Justin asked dubiously. The bandits probably needed a good blacksmith as they rebuilt, but he wasn't sure about the man's chances of being allowed to leave later.

"Nah." He drew the cart to a stop, swung down, and patted the draft horse's neck. "I got to East Newbrook and thought, 'Now, those adventurers helped me and they'll try to haul all that treasure back.' I stowed my gear and here I am."

"You're not worried they'll rob you?" Zaara asked.

"I'm the first master blacksmith to grace their town in four years," he said seriously. "The mayor would give me his house if I asked. In any case, I see I came none too early."

Justin was too tired to argue much, but he also studied the man suspiciously as they transferred the treasure. "This is an awfully big favor."

"When I was on the way here, I remembered how much I liked life on the road," their helper said contemplatively. "Nights alone by a fire with the open sky. A blacksmith can't usually stray far from his forge, and who knows the next time I'll have the time to leave East Newbrook. Plus…you could call it good business to forge a good relationship with wizard-slayers who might come through with plunder and stories. In every town I've served, I've made it a point to buy an ale for the adventurers whenever they come through and it's never steered me wrong yet." He smiled and hauled Lyle up next to him in the front seat. "You two, climb in the back and we'll set off."

"He's right," Zaara said when she and Justin were in the back and the cart started to turn. She gave a huge yawn. "My father always said the same about buying adventurers a beer. He said they were useful."

"He certainly made use of me, I guess." Justin yawned as well. Her sleepiness was contagious. "Stop yawning, dammit. Also, he never bought me a beer."

"How about…I buy you one…when we…" A snore finished her sentence. She had pillowed her head on her cloak and passed out entirely, her cheeks still flushed from the effort of lifting and loading the treasure.

His stomach did the weird sideways leap it always did where she was concerned but before he could be overly troubled by that, his eyes drifted shut and he fell asleep to the sounds of the dwarf and the blacksmith singing folk songs. His dreams were full of gold coins and foaming tankards as the cart wound its way through the now-living forests.

***

"That's it," Jacob said as he stepped into the offices again. "DuBois says it will probably take twenty minutes or so to get everything hooked up in the truck."

His partners nodded. They stood in the kitchenette of the office, and if Nick was reading Amber's expression correctly, she felt as shell-shocked as he did.

"Final walk-through?" she said finally. "We should make sure we don't forget anything important."

"Sure." He knew this was her way to cope with big changes. It had been helpful at least twice as often as it had been maddening, although the two sometimes overlapped. He, meanwhile, told too many jokes, and Jacob tried to manage everyone.

Who had ever decided to let three engineers run a company? It was madness.

It was clear that they had missed nothing in the big lab. With all the pods and servers removed and after a thorough vacuuming, the area looked oddly small. If it weren't for the glass walls that enclosed the pod area, he wouldn't have been able to remember what it looked like at all.

"I wish we'd been able to get all the tape marks off the walls," Amber said distractedly.

"The landlord said this will be turned into a restaurant." Jacob shrugged. "They'll probably gut the place." He hunched his shoulders. "No one will remember we were here, will they?"

"The people who heard Mary screaming will remember it," Nick pointed out.

The other man cracked a smile, as did Amber, but he could feel their sadness.

"Hey," he said, in a burst of inspiration. "Do you remember five years ago? We'd just had the idea for PIVOT. We were in my room—"

"We'd finished a pizza," she said. "I remember because I'd started lifting that week and I wanted to order four more and you kept telling me to order one at a time." She snickered.

"That was a lifechanging moment," Jacob said. "Not a night we had pizza. Focus on the big picture."

She laughed. "I'll tell you that the next time you're hungry. Or...I would if I wasn't afraid to die. You get hangry, man."

Nick watched them banter good-naturedly. He was glad they weren't a couple anymore. The bickering that was so easy between them as friends had acquired a bad edge to it while they were together. He'd been worried their friendship would be ruined, but they'd both gotten over the awkwardness quickly.

"Did you picture any of this that night?" he asked them when they had finished their whispered argument.

"Any of this?" Amber shook her head. "Not a single part. Hell, when we got this place, I was over the moon. I couldn't imagine having an office that wasn't in my living room. As for the rest of it…" She looked out toward the corridor and they could hear the beeps of the truck and the occasional shout. No one sounded panicked. The Diatek crew seemed to view all of this as a fascinating challenge rather than merely another boring job, which had set the PIVOT group at ease.

"I know I never pictured it," Jacob said with certainty. "I was sure we would do some good work, hit a roadblock somewhere, and all get office jobs."

"You never told us that," his friends said at the same time.

"I didn't want to be a downer."

Nick shook his head. "And now we're working for one of the main contractors with the Department of Defense."

"We also have salaries now," the other man reminded them, "and we're millionaires."

They shook their heads.

"That one still doesn't seem real," she said.

"Live in the Bay Area long enough and it won't be," Nick joked. "Plus, what's a millionaire around here? Nothing. Dime a dozen. We'd only be special if we were billionaires."

"Given that we still own forty-nine percent of the PIVOT shares, that might happen." Jacob shook his head in wonder. "What do you all think now? Do you think we'll pull it off?"

"I think if it's possible, we will," Amber said. "Before, tons of stuff could have gotten in our way. Now, the only thing we have to worry about is whether we can think hard enough to do it. Justin's results are groundbreaking in and of themselves, and we should have a much bigger suite of test subjects within a couple of years."

Nick whistled. "And then, before you know it, they'll be flying drones in some kind of Ender's-Game-for-Coma-Patients dystopia."

"Why are you always so negative?" The other man threw an elbow at him.

"I'm a realist," he said with dignity.

She snorted. "You're both pie-in-the-sky dreamers. I'm the realist here. And I'll tell you what, one of the first things we'll do is hire an accountant."

"Uh-huh," Jacob said. "And one of the next things is you firing the accountant because you can't stand giving up any of your work." His phone buzzed and he glanced at it. "They're all ready. Apparently, it was relatively simple. Wait a second, he's still typing…he wants to know if there'll be popcorn at the Diatek labs or if we should stop on the way."

Amber burst out laughing. "That man. Anna Price has no idea how much of her budget will go to popcorn, does she? And he'll weasel his way into getting that popcorn machine back, I know it."

"I'm sure he was the one who bought it from us on eBay," Nick said. "DrDPopcorn was the username, and it was created on the day we sold it."

"Jesus." Jacob rolled his eyes. "That man must give his financial advisor heart attacks."

"This may surprise you," she said as they left, "but not everyone has a financial advisor."

"What?"

"Oh, you sheltered little rich boy."

Nick waited until their voices drifted away, put his hands in his pockets, and looked around at the room. So much had happened there —their first whole prototype, the first test drive for each of them in the pods, and the marathon of late nights as they adapted the video game they had bought. There was no way to count how many boxes of takeout had been consumed there or how many pots of coffee.

He remembered that he'd always been excited to come to work, though. Even when the news coverage was snide about the cost of their product or when the initial sales numbers didn't come in as well as expected, he had come in every day excited about the work—and even more so now that they had found a use for it beyond entertainment.

"Hey, man." Jacob stuck his head into the kitchenette. "Is everything okay?"

"I'm saying goodbye." He grinned and flipped the lights off. "I don't want to be mushy, but...in case no one's said this to you yet, I think your grandmother would be proud of what you're doing right now."

His friend blinked a few times. His eyes were suspiciously bright but he didn't make any mention of it, so he also pretended he didn't see it.

"Thanks, man," Jacob said finally. His voice was a little rough. "That means a lot. I like to think you're right." He beckoned to Nick. "Come on. There's only one thing left. Once the pod is installed, we'll all go get some sleep."

CHAPTER FIFTY-FOUR

With their treasure safely stowed in the cart and Lyle chatting amiably with the blacksmith, Justin's dreams were pleasant ones of soft beds and feasts. He'd had enough turkey legs to last him a lifetime in this world. Right now, what he wanted was mashed potatoes and some of his grandma's dinner rolls.

And mac and cheese. God, he'd kill for mac and cheese.

He wasn't sure quite when his dreams began to change but slowly, the feasts began to turn darker. The beds were prickly, the food tasted like ashes, and he looked around at skeletons seated in the chairs nearby.

The air was clammy when he woke with a start. While he'd been asleep, a heavy fog had rolled in. Zaara slept with one arm thrown over her eyes. She snored softly, and he leaned against the side of the cart with a sigh. They'd certainly seen enough terrifying things to warrant a few nightmares.

He stiffened when he saw something moving in the mist.

The hair on his arms stood up and he sat bolt upright. He peered into the fog behind the cart until his eyes ached, but the shadow didn't return.

Still, his instincts prickled alarmingly.

Quietly, he clambered onto the back of the cart so he sat directly behind Lyle and the blacksmith. They had stopped singing folk songs at some point and both of them looked at him warily when they heard him approach. He couldn't tell whether he felt better or worse to know that they were both spooked as well.

"Did the silence wake ye?" Lyle's voice was unusually subdued.

He shook his head. "Nightmares." He tried not to speak too loudly and turned his head quickly when he thought he saw something out of the corner of his eye. If there had been something, it was already gone.

Or it had been nothing and he was jumping at shadows.

Lyle dashed that hope a moment later. "There's somethin' out there," he said in a tight mutter. "It came with the fog."

Justin made a snap decision. "I'll wake Zaara."

The blacksmith and Lyle both nodded, and his heart sank. He climbed down as quietly as he could before he shook Zaara's shoulder. When she turned her head and started to wake, he picked her arm up and put a finger over his lips. Her eyes opened and she frowned when she saw him.

He motioned for her to sit and peer out the back of the cart. It took long enough for them to see anything that she looked at him curiously a couple of times, but finally, something black flicked through the fog. He could almost imagine it was a tail, something impossibly fast.

She pushed herself back with wide eyes. Her face had gone pale and when she looked at him, there was genuine fear in her eyes.

That, in turn, worried him. He hadn't even seen her afraid in Sephith's tower. Angry, yes. She was easily moved to anger and contempt for those who hurt others but she was rarely afraid. Tense and fearful, she looked at him, and then at Lyle, who nodded to her and showed her his fist. Whatever was coming, the dwarf was—as ever—ready to punch it.

Zaara drew both her daggers quietly, and he went to get his sword.

They all knew they were waiting, and Justin thought not knowing what they were waiting for was the worst part. He found out very quickly that he was wrong when the first beast broke through the fog in front of them.

He honestly could not have said what it was. At first glance, he swore he saw something like the witch. Arms waved like an octopus and lashed toward him. The creature blazed closer so fast that Justin and Zaara, perched on the back of the cart, tumbled into it with a clatter of gold coins. The horse screamed and dragged the conveyance in wild jerks, and the blacksmith gave a full-throated yell.

The beast hurtled overhead. It was long, possibly scaled, and perhaps as slimy as a slug. It was gone too quickly for Justin to tell—either what it was, or how it flew. He was left with the impression of fangs and a long tail, something he decidedly would not want to meet in a dark alley.

Or anywhere, for that matter.

On the bench, Lyle yelled something. The blacksmith was hunched over his arm but still tried to calm the horses.

"He's wounded," the dwarf called to Justin. "Drive the cart."

"I don't know how to drive a cart," he responded and tried to push panic aside. "Zaara?"

"I'll do it." She clambered up the side and onto the bench. He heard her sharp intake of breath and a sudden oath to several gods. "Lyle, get him in the back—oh, *shit*."

"What?" Justin demanded. He scanned the road behind them for the giant snake-monster. "What is it?"

Lyle jumped into the cart behind him with a thud and a second, less graceful thud heralded the blacksmith joining him. Justin looked back and froze when he saw what Zaara had been looking at.

Whatever the beast was, it had claws of some kind and they had inflicted a long gash in the blacksmith's arm—he must have put a hand up to shield his head, he thought. The gash, however, was far from the worst of it. The skin at the edges of the wound had turned a deep black, a dark liquid oozed from the cut to mix with the blood, and from the hissing sound and the blacksmith's bone-white face, the pain must be horrific.

He ran to help Lyle lever the man down, who hardly seemed to notice them. His breathing was shallow and a thin film of sweat covered his face.

"Zaara!" Justin called. "Get the horse running as fast as you can. We need to get him to town."

Her reply, however, was drowned out by another scream from the horse. Above them, the beast slithered through the fog, and the clouds parted in front of the cart. What stood there, all fangs and claws and dripping blood, looked like the army of hell. The creatures were far from human and barely close enough for their appearance to be utterly horrifying.

Zaara, thankfully, did not hesitate. She whistled sharply and yanked on the reins to guide the horse into a wide arc. The cart plunged off the edge of the road into the tall grass with a jostle that made the blacksmith hiss through his teeth and circled to try to get behind the creatures.

The horse, all things considered, seemed happy to flee. She did not crack the reins—indeed, she had to pull back on them to keep the animal from running wild. The cart jostled over the ruts and her entire focus was fixed on the horse and the bumpy landscape ahead.

She spared only a moment to say, "We're still closer to the bandits' hideout and we can't get through that army."

Justin responded with a curt nod. Behind him, the blacksmith gasped with pain while Lyle yelled something. It didn't take a genius to guess what. With his heart sinking, Justin turned and unsheathed his sword.

The army pursued them with preternatural speed. Whether on two legs or four, each of the creatures seemed to be made of thick tar, melting slightly at the edges as if formed out of a void and a wish that didn't quite hold together.

He could easily bet that he knew whose wish it was.

The first to reach them looked something like a cat. Giant whiskers trailed away from its face and an all-black maw opened in a snarl as it leapt onto the open back of the cart.

Without hesitation, he swung a heavy downward slash that passed cleanly through but left a dent in its head when the tar reformed.

"That is disgusting," he muttered. He took a half-step back as it lunged and pressed forward again, slashing and thrusting.

"Justin!" Zaara yelled. A knife thudded into the cart near his foot.

"Thanks, but I'd appreciate it if you didn't try to throw knives and drive at the same time."

"No!" she yelled, exasperated. "Say the spell to light it."

"Oh." He dove to retrieve the knife, delivered an awkward, one-handed swipe with his left hand, and yanked the weapon out of the floor. "Ignis!" Before the cat-creature could react, he drove the dagger forward into the place where an eye should be.

It went up in flames so fast that his sleeve caught fire. He swore and flailed his arm, only to be entirely doused by a jet of ice-cold water in the next moment.

"I can't look right now," Zaara called. "Did I put the fire out?"

"Yes." Justin shook his head and brushed away the water that dripped down his nose. "Boy, this isn't gonna be one for the history books, I tell ya. If they're vulnerable to fire, though…"

He threw his sword to the side, kept the flaming dagger in his right hand, and began to conjure fire in his left. The army had scattered as the flaming corpse tumbled off the back of the conveyance but had now begun to reform—and they were pissed.

"Lyle!" Justin nudged him with his foot. "Go drive the cart. We need Zaara throwing fireballs."

"Someone has to keep him from bleeding out," the dwarf shouted in response. His hands were pressed against a wad of blood-soaked cloth. On the floor, the blacksmith had passed out. His face was an unhealthy gray.

"There is no time," he snapped. "Brace it with something—a chest, whatever. I don't care. We need to get to the bandit hideout and we need to keep these things at bay."

Lyle hurried to obey. He wedged the blacksmith in the corner with impressive—and, frankly, worrying—strength and climbed up to switch places with Zaara.

She dropped down with fire brimming in her palms and threw her first firebolt a second later. He thought it had gone wide until he saw the faint red glow in the fog above and a flaming bird-creature tumbled out of the sky.

He shuddered and returned to his fireballs.

By now, he was sure these creatures were not sentient. Anything that could think would know better than to pursue two humans who lobbed fireballs with wild abandon. Even chickens, he thought, were smarter than that. The beasts didn't seem to care, however. They pushed closer and closer and threw themselves into the path of the fireballs in order to give one another cover. They moved in twos and threes and some swooped down to distract the two defenders long enough for others to clamber onto the cart.

They would die there. The realization chilled him to the bone despite the heat from the fireballs that seared his face. The amulet the bandit had given him lay heavily against his chest, a reminder that he would almost certainly come back

But Zaara wouldn't and Lyle wouldn't.

With a roar of fury, Justin stepped in front of her.

"Ignis!"

He didn't have a word for the spell he tried to do. In fact, he wasn't sure if it was a spell. Still, he yelled, he drew on his magic reserves, and he pictured what he wanted. Against all odds, his vision appeared in his hand.

The sword was made of pure flame and bigger even than a claymore.

His palm seared against the hilt but he swung it anyway and whipped it viciously with a whoop of glee. The fire was so light that he might as well be swinging air despite the sheer size of the blade.

"Get—the fuck—back!" he bellowed. "Or I swear to God, I will kill you, and find you, and bring you back, and kill you again. Painfully!"

In the back of the armored truck, several Diatek employees stared, wide-eyed, at the monitors.

"Um…" one of them said faintly.

"Hmm?" DuBois, who had snored quietly in one of the seats, straightened with a jerk. He peered at the monitors and nodded vaguely. "That's normal, don't worry," he said.

Unperturbed, he rested his head again and went back to sleep.

The cart clattered into the bandit hideout with Lyle screaming hellos at the top of his lungs and Justin yelling threats at the top of his. To everyone's surprise, the army practically flattened itself against thin air as soon as they were inside. Beasts melted into goo and re-formed, howled, and clawed at a barrier Justin could not see.

"What the hell?" Zaara panted.

"Don't question it," he responded. "Just…you know…give thanks."

Bandits rushed out of the buildings around them and the leader shoved them away to reach the front. At Justin's urgent wave, he hurried to the back of the cart and his eyes snapped together when he saw the blacksmith.

"We'll take him inside."

"Wait." He removed the amulet and laid it around the blacksmith's neck. "He needs this more than I do."

"Why didn't I think of that?" Zaara asked rhetorically.

"Because we were throwing fireballs at monsters," he said. "It's the same reason I didn't."

"Right." She stood aside as the bandits lifted the blacksmith down and carried him inside.

"I'm sorry to impose," he told their leader. "We…had nowhere else to go."

"You chose well," he said bluntly. "Something is wrong out there, and it seems we're safe here. Why, I don't know—and I don't know how long it will hold. Come inside. We'll explain there."

CHAPTER FIFTY-FIVE

The man led them to what looked like a half-finished throne room. A massive stone pedestal stood in front of two tall windows. Some of the panes had shattered and the glass had, with efficiency, simply been pushed against the back wall. A fire burned in the hearth and a large table, roughly made from scrap lumber, had been placed in the center of the room. Around this, an odd assortment of chairs and stools had been placed.

Their host led the three adventurers to the hearth. "Sit and eat while I explain." He saw them look toward the door and smiled grimly. "No one will touch the goods in your cart by my order. We may not have always been friends, but without you and yours, this group would still be cursed. They know that."

Justin settled and accepted a bowl of stew. He was surprised to see both Zaara and Lyle rummage through their packs and put something in the stew pot—a piece of meat and a potato. She gave him a meaningful look and he dug out an onion and a carrot, as well as a strip of dried meat. He felt foolish. Once he had seen the custom, it seemed intuitive enough, but he had almost blundered badly.

He had never been much of a one for etiquette—all the gestures seemed meaningless and empty, merely a way to hide the truth about a situation. He had to say, however, that he had begun to appreciate social customs more since he had been in this game. When even former enemies shared food, there was something to be said for it. *We might not be friends, but we're all trying to make our way in the world. I'll give you what I have and you give me what you have.*

"So," the bandit leader said and leaned back in his chair. "The curse has been lifted. We know that to be true."

Justin paused, his spoon partway to his mouth. It didn't take a genius to see the but coming—which was good since he wasn't one. He was, however, a person who had fought a nightmare army on the way there.

"Something is…not right," the man continued. He shifted a little and stared at the flames. "What is coming back is still strong. The grass grows as it should and the sun shines. But…it is as if our nightmares grow as well. When the witch was here, her spells drained the life from the land. Now that she is gone, the land thrives but it seems some of her evil remains."

Zaara looked at Justin, and the bandit caught the look.

"What? What do you know?"

"Well, for one thing," she said delicately, "we *don't* know your name. I'm Zaara, of Riverbend. This is Lyle, of House Stout. And Justin, who comes from very far away indeed—and whose mother is a sorceress of no small power."

"And I'm Hildon," the man said. He smiled. "Apologies for the bad manners, Mistress Zaara. Events are unsettled here. Now, will you tell me what you two were looking so meaningful about?"

She nodded at Justin, who considered what—and how much—to tell him.

"I told you that the witch collapsed into a pile of goo, yes?"

"Yes," Hildon said drily. "I remember that being a particularly evocative way of phrasing it."

"The reason I said goo was that she wasn't, er…human…by the end of the fight. She was green. There were tentacles. I killed her—it—and there weren't any bones like you'd expect." He left out the part where the body had been gone when he went back to look but added, "If it wasn't human, can we expect all its power to go with it?"

"That isn't good." The man considered this but glanced at them. "Would you like more stew?"

Justin, luckily, had the good sense to know the answer to this. He patted his belly and shook his head. "My belly is full, thank you."

"That army seemed like it wasn't all…there," Zaara said thoughtfully. "I almost wonder if we saw the same creatures or if they were simply echoes of our personal nightmares."

Hildon raised his eyebrows but said nothing.

"What else do we know?" she asked. She looked at Justin.

"They were vulnerable to fire." He ticked points off on his fingers as he thought of them. "They are growing even as life comes back to the forest and marsh, and they have outpaced the original dead zone." He looked at their host. "And there was trouble here too, apparently."

"Creatures in the dark," Hildon said shortly. He nodded at Zaara. "As if from a nightmare like you said—and disappearing so quickly that no one could tell what they saw. They never came over the walls, which we realized soon enough. But we didn't notice them before some of our hunters and foragers went missing."

Justin was momentarily diverted by this. "Do you have people in your bandit crew whose job it is to simply find food?"

"Of course we do," he said. He looked at him as if he were crazy. "How else are we supposed to eat?"

For a moment, all he could do was stare. He had assumed that bandits stole food like they stole other things. He shook his head by way of apology. "So they don't come over the walls. That's right. They didn't follow us past the gate, even the big one."

"And it's not your magic," Zaara concluded, looking at the bandit. "For a spell like that, you'd have to have quite a sorcerer in your band."

"If we were that strong, we'd have killed Sephith ourselves and taken his tower," Hildon said with a snort. "No, magic is a rare enough thing—and powerful, even when the wielder is inexperienced." He gave Justin a wry look.

"Just so you know, I'm leveling up his Sick Burn skill," the AI told him.

Justin sighed but the man's words sank in and he stood so quickly his chair tipped. He picked it up, not looking at it, and walked to the block of stone.

"Justin?" Lyle called. In a stage whisper, he added to the others, "The boy's not right in the head. Ye'll have to forgive him."

"Yeah, yeah." He could see the hexagonal shape now and his fingers brushed away the dust to reveal tiny grooves—as if a frame of some kind would sit on the block of stone. "These ruins appeared out of nowhere a few weeks ago, yes? And they were perfectly preserved, as if no one had been here and no one had ever found them, yes?"

"Yes," their host said. He stood and moved to join Justin with the rest of the group. "Why?"

He pointed to the stone. "What you said about taking Sephith's tower made me think. This block of stone would fit his throne awfully well. It was a machine and sucked people's souls out of them and stored the energy to give it to him. When he sat in the chair, it gave him their power."

"This was Sephith's," Zaara whispered. She looked around. "But we only killed him two weeks ago and they said this has been here for months."

"I don't understand all of it," he said and shook his head. "It would explain some parts of it, though. The strength of the barrier spells, for instance. It seems like they protect whoever owns the ruins."

"They do," the bandit said. "When the witch said we stole something of hers, she wasn't lying—well, not exactly. She laid claim to the ruins first, but she left one day for some reason. We snuck in to check the storerooms—and when we had our people in the throne room, she couldn't get in."

Justin began to laugh.

"What?" Hildon looked confused.

"I told ye," Lyle said. "He's not all there."

"No, it's…" He wiped at his eyes. "It's…oh, God, my stomach hurts. One second. Ow. Okay. It's only the mental image of…" He broke down in tears of laughter again. "Of us trying to sneak into the ruins at night and running into an invisible wall at high speed."

Even Zaara snickered at that mental image.

"Ah, yes." Their host looked intrigued. "We did bring you here ourselves, didn't we? Otherwise, I suppose you would never have gotten in."

"Ye could have simply holed up," Lyle said.

"And lived in a stone warren for the rest of our lives?"

"It worked fer the dwarves, dinnit?"

Justin sensed the conversation going off-track and steered it back. "This is good and bad. The spells are still holding enough to protect the people inside the ruins but the ones keeping it hidden have already fallen apart. I'm not sure that staying here is something we can count on to keep us safe."

The others nodded as one of the bandits came into the room and drew Hildon away to mutter something in a low tone. The bandit leader frowned and replied, and when the man was gone, he looked at Justin.

"Your friend needs more help than we can provide. We've slowed the spread of the infection but we can't stop it."

He closed his eyes. "It's stronger magic than anyone could be expected to heal." He felt terrible guilt now. The blacksmith had returned to help them, and this was the reward he'd received for his trouble. Then, a thought occurred to him. "The widow—the one we found the wedding ring for. If anyone could cure this—"

"She could." Zaara ran to her pack and rummaged in it. "Everyone, check what you have. She gave us potions. Some might be able to keep him alive until we get him to her."

"You want us to go out there again?" Lyle demanded. "Are ye mad?"

"The boy, as you call him, is right." Hildon clapped the dwarf on the shoulder. "This is no true refuge—it's a trap. The longer we wait here, the stronger our enemy gets and the weaker we become. A bandit learns to never stay in one place for too long."

"Ye'd never make a proper dwarf," he said grumpily.

"That's as may be, Master Stout. Now, if you will all excuse me, I will tell my people to make ready."

"Your people—you're coming with us?" Justin gaped in surprise.

"You barely made it here alive and the enemy will only have grown while we sat. Not only that, but we also need to leave as well." The man paused. "And, I admit, I'm interested to meet this widow you spoke of."

"She's ninety if she's a day," he said flatly.

"That's not why." Hildon pinned him with a glare. "Any healer who might heal something like this is an ally worth having. More than that, though, curses and hidden ruins tell me we need someone with a long memory. There's no telling what she might know." He nodded at all of them. "Get some sleep. We'll be on the road within an hour or two at most, and you were near-drained when you arrived. We'll need your fire magic when we're on the road again."

"Is there anyone you can leave?" Justin called as the bandit leader strode away. "If what's out there is the witch's power, I wouldn't like the idea of it having a hideout."

Hildon paused while he considered this. Finally, he nodded and continued to walk away.

"Well, if we're abandoning this place, I'm having more stew," Zaara said. "You all should, too."

"I'd kill for a proper mug of ale," Lyle said wistfully.

"Think of it this way. If we go to East Newbrook, we can get some ale." He was only joking and so he was amused to see his friend perk up at this.

"That's true. I hadn't thought of it like that."

Lyle shook his head at Zaara, who grinned and lowered her head to hide her laughter.

"Well, then," Justin said. "For ale and honor."

"Ha." The dwarf nudged him with an elbow. "Now there's an oath. We'll make a dwarf of you yet, lad."

CHAPTER FIFTY-SIX

The bandits made ready to leave with surprising efficiency. A few came in to get bowls of stew, talked in low voices amongst themselves, and nodded at the adventurers. Some—Justin guessed it was those who had been on guard duty—came to take naps. They slept on the floor with their heads propped on their packs as if they could sleep anywhere at any time.

It was decided that a contingent would stay behind to guard the throne room and keep some of the horses.

"It's a risk," Hildon said when he asked him about it, "but so is going. A few, like your dwarven friend, had no interest in making the journey. He can stay with them if he likes."

Justin looked at Lyle, who was helping to tie packs down in the back of a cart. He was tempted to refuse on behalf of the dwarf but he knew that was unfair. However much he believed it was the safest thing to leave, he could not volunteer him for that.

To his surprise, his teammate shook his head when he asked if he wanted to stay.

"I owe ye my freedom, remember?"

"Lyle." He was smiling. "You've fought at my side since then. I think we can consider ourselves beyond keeping debts."

The dwarf gave him a considering look. "An' here I was, thinking ye were a useless city boy when we met."

"I was a useless city boy when we met." He grinned at him.

SELF BURN, Level 2

"Aye, true enough." Lyle shook his head. "But, no. I've seen enough from the two o' ye—I'll be safer at your side than anywhere else." He cleared his throat and looked away, his cheeks unusually ruddy. "Er…I mean t'say, ye'd be helpless without me. I can't leave ye, not in good conscience."

"You're a good man," Justin told him. He tried to catch Zaara's glance but she was watching the dwarf with a certain softness in her eyes. Curious, he pushed through the crush to her and helped her to load packages onto a cart. "Are you surprised by our friend's softer side?"

She didn't answer for a while. Her cheeks flushed, she swallowed. When she spoke, her voice was a little unsteady. "No one's ever wanted to…I mean…no one's ever said anything like that about me. My father never believed in me at all, not that way, and the people of East Newbrook tolerated me, but none of them would risk anything to fight with me." She cleared her throat again, a surprisingly gruff harrumph.

"Do you think you'll ever go home?" he asked curiously. "Go back, I mean. To Riverbend."

She considered this but didn't have the chance to answer. The carts had barely been loaded a moment before but they were already in motion, and Hildon trotted up to them with another of his leaders.

"Mistress Zaara," he said. "You'll ride with me. Justin, you'll ride with Mira."

He raised his eyebrows.

"Why?" Zaara asked. He was pleased to see that she didn't seem exceedingly happy about the idea of riding with the man.

"We have archers with flaming arrows in each cart," the bandit said, "but there's no knowing where we'll need reinforcement. Mira and I will keep the two of you mobile so you can help where you're needed."

She looked at him and gave a quick nod—and, before he could react properly, she crushed him close for a hug. "Be safe," she whispered fiercely in his ear before she moved away and swung up in front of Hildon.

Justin, tongue-tied and afraid he was blushing, only lowered his head. He did, however, get an unpleasant glance at Hildon's smile as the bandit leader galloped away with his head close to Zaara's.

In the next moment, however, he was glad enough that they were gone. He didn't have the faintest idea how to get into the saddle of Mira's horse, much less while she was already there, and in the end, she had to swing down and let him struggle to mount.

She, at least, said nothing about it despite her fiery red hair and forbidding expression, which might have suggested otherwise. Oddly, she seemed to have a way of moving that was disturbingly lazy for someone so well-armed. He had the impression that anyone trying to surprise her in a dark alley would have their ass handed to them, and she wouldn't even break a sweat.

"Hildon will keep your lady friend safe," she told him. She looked over her shoulder at him with a wry smile. "I mean he'll keep her alive, mind you, not keep her looking at you with those gooey eyes."

"She looks at me with gooey eyes?" He straightened a little.

Mira sighed. "Yes. But Hildon's a flirt and he's a damned good fighter. If you're trying to be impressive on this journey, you'll need all the luck you can get."

"Luck?" Justin was outraged. "I'll have you know I conjured a sword of pure fire on the way here. I—oh. You were trying to get under my skin, weren't you?"

"A little." She flashed him a smile. "I'll tell you a secret, though. The one I want to impress will be in the carts and they're not pleased to see me riding with you. So, we both have someone to impress, eh?"

He grinned. If someone had told him a day and a half ago that he'd joke and fight alongside the bandits, he would never have believed them, but this felt oddly natural. "Let's give them a show, then."

Mira laughed and spurred the horse to a gallop. "Get ready, adventurer. We have monsters to kill."

"What's going on?" One of the Diatek scientists looked up in concern as the pod was lowered to the ground.

Jacob looked at the monitor and snickered. "Ahhhh. You'll get used to seeing that."

"Yes, but what is it? It looks like…" The scientist frowned at the neural activity readouts. "Attraction."

"Mm-hmm." He grinned at him.

"But he's the only person in there." The man still looked confused.

"I tell you what." The young engineer clapped him on the shoulder. "I'll start you on a strict regimen ofvideo games. We'll get you through a few, then you can come back to me and tell me if you still don't understand."

"Video games? But—"

"Trust me." He smiled. It had been a while since he had explained this and he found himself both wryly amused and struck by how little many people understood of this world. "Games give you a chance to be who you want to be. Humans don't turn into unfeeling robots simply because a person is made of pixels and algorithms. They still care. They still throw themselves into danger and try to help." He gestured to the monitor. "That's part of why Justin's getting better. Because the game helps him to be human."

The creatures didn't attack immediately. The caravan plodded into the fog beyond the gates and for a long time, nothing stirred. The mist swirled around the carts as Justin and Mira rode up and down the line. They could not see the entire caravan at once, but the vapor was not so thick that they couldn't see the road beneath the horses' hooves. Strangely, the clopping seemed to echo somewhat.

No one sang to pass the time. The bowmen kept arrows nocked and their heads turned constantly.

Still, enough time passed without incident to wonder if they had all been mistaken and if the magical creatures had ever existed at all.

The attack, when it came, was sudden and devastating. Justin and Mira were near the head of the line when the leader of the army—the worm that had flown over the blacksmith's cart and wounded him so grievously—exploded out of the earth in front of the caravan.

Mira's horse had been trained to go through battles but it was not ready for this. It whinnied and reared as the two riders leaned forward with all their strength. He clung to the horse's neck with one arm and Mira's waist with the other, and she leaned close to croon in the horse's ear. When the animal settled onto all fours, the bandit didn't hesitate and spurred it to a gallop as she tossed a glance at him.

He gave her a nod and held his right hand out. The power warmed it and brought a sudden rush of satisfaction. The witch and her minions had thought to attack them, but the humans wouldn't back down without a fight. This fucking-worm-creature—his new name for the army leader—would get more than it bargained for.

His gaze focused on its head as it flailed and tossed. When it swung to focus on them, he locked eyes with it.

"As soon as I shoot, turn the horse," he told Mira, and he launched one of the biggest fireballs he had ever created.

The creature had opened its mouth, whether to spit poison or snap at them, he didn't know.

Either way, it ate a fireball.

Its head exploded into flames and it withdrew into the ground with startling speed. The earth closed over it again. Rubble was strewn across the road but otherwise, it might never have been there.

Mira wheeled the horse and they surveyed the line. As the fucking-worm-creature attacked, other monsters had rushed out of the mist. The bandit archers called orders to one another as they knelt on the packs of supplies and fired. They reached over their heads with precision, nocked their arrows, dipped them in fire, and sent them with deadly accuracy. Tar creatures went up in flames with shrieks and ran wild, spreading the blaze to their compatriots.

Farther down the line, the rumble and roar of the road exploding once more caught his attention. The screams of horses and humans came through eerily, but his heart unclenched when he saw the glow of fireballs arcing through the fog. Zaara was still alive and fighting.

"Perimeter sweep!" he called to Mira.

She nodded and urged her horse to a canter. Under the range of the archers, she and Justin targeted the stragglers. It wasn't long before they developed a system. He scanned ahead and behind and his fireballs eliminated the enemy that had edged close to the carts. Mira, meanwhile, drew a blade that glowed a dull red and focused on the beasts within arms' range.

It took an odd kind of courage to trust her help, but once he accepted that he could rely on her to watch his back, it released him to fight with a focus he had never had before. He felt a deep satisfaction whenever he was able to aim a fireball with particular skill and more than once, he felled an animal that had decided to attack her. She slashed and hacked with a skill that wasn't so much elegant as brutally efficient.

The caravan, aided by Hildon's bellows, kept moving throughout. The donkeys and horses had had their ears plugged and their eyes bound with cloth, and it was barely enough to keep them moving. Their flanks were shivering and coated with sweat.

The mist cleared so gradually that he didn't realize it until someone yelled from the front of the caravan. Something in the cart-driver's tone was enough to make both Mira and Hildon race to the front of the line.

Justin gaped. The witch stood in their path but she was truly monstrous. She was so tall that her head was lost in the clouds. Tentacles writhed and lashed forward, only to vanish in the space of a blink.

"Where did she go?" Justin yelled to Mira over the sound of the wind.

"Where did who go?" she called back.

"The witch—didn't you see her? The monster as tall as Sephith's tower."

She gave him a curious look and a chill ran down his spine. Whatever it meant that he was the only one who could see it, he didn't like it.

They had more pressing issues to worry about, however. At the front of the line, the first driver attempted to guide his horse out of the way as a massive worm hissed and swung its head. The archers fired as quickly as they could, but it wasn't enough.

When the worm saw Justin, it unhinged its jaw and its mouth yawned into a black void.

"Eat fireball, shithead!" he bellowed and hurled a fireball.

"What he said!" Zaara screamed and followed suit.

"Stoooooooooooout!" came the call from the back of the line.

"Thanks for the support, buddy," Justin called over his shoulder. Another fireball had already formed in his hand and he threw it. "Zaara, aim for the eyes."

And then catch it off-balance. Luckily, she seemed to understand his plan. The two of them threw fireball after fireball at the eyes while flaming arrows crackled and whizzed overhead. Finally, with a nod to one another, the two teammates gave the last of their reserves for a massive explosion that streaked forward in a white-hot inferno.

The screaming seemed to go on forever. The worm thrashed and shrieked, its skin no longer scaled or slimy but instead, burning far too fast. He had barely enough time to regret his choice before the creature expelled its last breath and black poison spewed into the air and dissipated. It fell and crumbled to ash, and the rest of the creatures vanished into the mist.

Ahead, Justin saw the widow's cottage through a swirl of fog.

"There!" he called. "Go, go! There's the cottage."

CHAPTER FIFTY-SEVEN

The door to the dwelling remained tightly closed as the caravan thundered closer. Justin tried to jump from Mira's horse and barely managed to keep his feet from getting tangled in the stirrups. He still savored the memory of Zaara's hug but he wasn't sure her admiration would last if she saw him fall face-first into a mud puddle.

Common sense said it was best not to risk it.

The bandits lifted the blacksmith down while Justin went to knock on the door. The blacksmith's chest barely rose and fell now. His skin looked so pale that he might have been carved from stone.

"Please," he whispered. "Please, please." He raised his voice. "We need help! Please, we need a healer. I'm Justin, one of those who brought you your wedding ring."

At that, there was the sound of footsteps and the door opened. The widow looked out, bright-eyed and inquisitive, and when she saw the blacksmith, she clicked her tongue.

"Come in, come in. Well, a few of you. Only so many can fit, even if I was of a mind to take a whole bandit horde into my house—and I'm not." She looked at them all and counted. "You, bandit leader."

"Yes?" Hildon said with surprising courtesy. "I am Hildon, ma'am. Well met."

"Yes, yes, well met. Tell your band to come inside the wall. There's some protection in it, at least. And you, come inside with the other three. Where's the dwarf? Ah, yes." She looked over her shoulder and continued the stream of chatter. "Yes, put him on the table. Gently, now, he's not a sack of beans."

Justin gestured to Zaara to head inside and she smiled as she passed him.

"I'm glad you're safe," she said softly.

"I'm glad you're safe," he told her. He blushed and looked back to where Hildon ushered his people into the yard. To the young man's amusement, all of them tried very hard not to step on the herb gardens.

Inside the hut, the widow waved them to the hearth. "Make yourselves tea. The leaves are in the blue jar and don't use anything else. I won't answer for the effects if you do."

Hildon began to measure tea leaves into a copper strainer and hung a heavy iron water pot over the hearth.

The widow worked quickly and sniffed at the blacksmith's wound. Her look of distaste was plain as she hurried across the room to her workbench. A complex bundle of herbs went into the mortar and pestle and she sniffed now and again to check the balance. Finally, she poured a few drops of oil in—something that made everyone else in the room sneeze and which gleamed like pure sunshine.

Back at the table, she unwrapped the bandage on the blacksmith's arm. Justin, who expected something horrifying, was not disappointed. The flesh, streaked through with black veins, looked like marble and blood began to flow again as soon as the pressure was released.

"Exactly as I thought." She spread the paste she'd mixed liberally over the wound and held her hand out to Justin. "Your sword—the one I gave you. I need it for a moment."

He handed it to her and gaped in surprise as she placed the blade flat against the wound. Something seemed to change in the air—an almost electrical charge like a thunderstorm—and the hair on his arms stood on end. The widow passed the sword to him and bound the wound tightly before she placed her hand on the injured man's brow.

Justin had thought she was checking for a fever, but he watched a flush return to the blacksmith's cheeks when her hand rested there.

Hildon lingered close to his shoulder. "This woman is no mere healer," he said quietly.

The young man shook his head. "I swear I didn't know. I thought she was only an old widow."

"Well, your instincts surely led you right," the bandit leader said, "even if your guesses did not." His smile was wry.

The widow looked at them and he had the feeling she had heard the exchange. "Now," she said briskly. "Everyone sit and tell me why there's a demon's army on my road."

A long pause followed while she waited expectantly.

"A demon?" Zaara asked finally. Her voice sounded very small.

The healer snorted. "Surely you've noticed those are no ordinary creatures—and the one who summoned them is equally unusual."

Zaara shook her head. "If there were a demon wandering around, we'd have known about it before."

"It hasn't been here long. No more than a couple of months, I would guess. I felt something pulling the magic away but I wasn't fool enough to go seek it out." The old woman poured them all earthenware cups of tea. "Drink up, it'll give you strength."

Justin drank and was not surprised to see a buff appear in the corner of the screen. "I hoped the witch was the demon instead of there being two evil things that are still hunting us."

She chortled at that. "I knew I liked you, young man. And, yes. That witch was never a human woman. I don't suppose you managed to see its true form."

"Green," Justin said. "Oozy. With tentacles."

"Really? Interesting. Very interesting. Well, that answers some questions." She sipped her tea thoughtfully. "I wonder where Sephith found one of those."

"Sephith?" Everyone else at the table spoke in unison.

"Do you know of anyone other than him strong enough to summon a demon?" she asked. "No, of course you don't."

"Wait." Justin narrowed his eyes. "So the ruins appeared about two months ago, they seem like they were Sephith's, and that's when the demon appeared as well and claimed them." It was so close to making sense but he couldn't truly say it did yet.

"Precisely." The widow went to one of the walls and waved a hand. What had been bare was suddenly full of bookshelves. She selected one with a deep red leather binding and pulled it down. When she placed it on the table, everyone drew back from the set of diagrams.

As Zaara would have said, they reeked of bad magic.

"It's a binding spell," the widow explained. "The demon's life force and magic are what power the binding—or the illusion. It's not an exceedingly useful one for most people. For one thing, it takes almost as much power to bind the demon as it does to do the rest of it, and it's riskier. For another, there's a chance that it will break free at any time—and there has to be containment when the binding is broken, even deliberately." She closed the book with a snap. "But Sephith was never exactly a cautious person. If you want my guess, it suited his purposes fine."

"How d'you mean?" Justin took another sip of tea. It really was good. He couldn't tell what it was made from but the buff helped him feel better than he had in days.

"It was flashy." Her tone dripped with derision. "And my guess is he reasoned that if someone broke it or the demon broke out...well, he'd be gone, so what did it matter if it ransacked the countryside?"

"That son of a bitch," Zaara said. Her voice sounded hot and angry.

"You're not wrong." The widow replaced the book and sat again. "The ruins—again, this is a guess—were likely a hideout, an entire city he could run to if he needed one. Whether the spell decayed and he simply didn't notice, or he pulled the power from it for some other purpose, I can't say. Either would be like him. He was sloppy. Powerful but sloppy." Her tone was deeply bitter.

He sighed. "So, I didn't kill her, did I?"

"You knew you didn't kill her?" Hildon's tone was overly sweet.

"I…might have noticed there wasn't a body or anything." He hunched his shoulders. "She'd already turned into a pile of goo, though, and the curse was gone, so that could have gone either way."

"Hmph." The man didn't look pleased but the reasoning was good enough to forestall a fight.

"No," the widow said. "You didn't kill it. To kill a demon is a tricky thing. It's not impossible but it is difficult."

"Wait," Zaara interrupted. "I don't understand something. The witch made the werewolves, right? She made that curse? But then she told us to undo it because it was draining the forest. None of that made sense to me."

"She was a lyin' bitch," Lyle interjected.

"You can hardly expect something different from a demon," the healer said wryly. "Be that as it may, however, the girl has a point. There's a reason I gave Justin a silver sword—werewolves have been known in this area for generations. I don't know how the first came to be, and when I heard mention of large wolves behaving oddly, I thought perhaps they had returned. I was both right and wrong. The demon did make them. It wanted an army of monsters to do its bidding, you see. I can't exactly blame it for wanting revenge after what Sephith did to it."

"It tried to make werewolves but realized the curse took too much power," Justin said slowly. "That makes sense. She was trapped in a weakened form—it was enough to trap us when we went into the hut but not enough to fight the entire pack of werewolves."

"And to undo a spell takes an investment of power, much like making one in the first place," the widow agreed. "It needed someone to get rid of the problem. It probably didn't see you coming up with quite that solution, of course."

"How do we kill it?" Hildon asked bluntly. He didn't seem at all interested in the lore. "You said it wasn't impossible, so how do we do it?"

The widow gave him a smile. "Very, very carefully, of course."

CHAPTER FIFTY-EIGHT

The Diatek labs were vastly more impressive than PIVOT's had been. Amber wanted to be dispirited by that. She'd been so proud to be able to rent a space of their own and now, it looked shabby by comparison.

On the other hand, she wanted to drool at how many tools were laid out within eyesight. There would be no scraping projects together and McGuyvering solutions that might go wrong at a critical moment. They would have whatever they needed, whenever they needed it.

The pods were laid out in an orderly row. Nick worked with the Diatek engineers to get each of the unused pods hooked up while another followed them and made extensive notes.

She realized that Anna Price had come to stand beside her while she watched the activity. The CEO looked quietly pleased with the scene unfolding before her, but she could not forget the tone in her voice when the woman spoke of the trade-offs she had made to bring this company to profitability. She was very, very sure she did not want to get on the wrong side of her.

"Is there anything else you can think of that you need?" Price asked her.

"Nothing you need to bother yourself with," Amber said. "I know you must be very busy. We appreciate you taking the time to do this yourself."

"It's why I started the company." The woman glanced at her. "There's nothing more important. My C-suite knows that I am prone to disappearing at times. It's why I've been so careful in choosing them. Each is authorized to make decisions regarding their initiatives."

Amber looked curiously at her. "So there are other projects like this."

"There have been." Anna's jaw clenched slightly.

She knew better than to ask any more questions, and the pit of her stomach lurched. When this started, it had seemed so simple and it had seemed to work. She had to remember that there was still a great deal that could go wrong.

"I met a neurosurgeon once," Price said. She did not look at her companion and her gaze was still fixed on Justin's pod. "He specialized in a particular type of tumor that killed one hundred percent of the people who had it. Any lives he saved were considered a victory. I tell myself that we are in a similar situation with this work." She looked at Amber now and smiled. "Do not allow fear to blind you or the complexity of the situation to overwhelm you."

She nodded in response.

"I've made sure you have my number," Price said, in a way that suggested it was somehow already in everyone's phone. "Call if you need anything—at any hour. And..." She smiled again. "You know, I would like to try one of those pods if you don't mind. Another time, of course."

"Of course," Amber murmured. She watched her stride away and shivered for a reason she didn't quite understand.

Was this someone else's life? It felt like it.

The ritual the widow described was so complicated that Justin's eyes crossed within thirty seconds of her starting the explanation. Zaara, who he was beginning to think might be a terminal nerd where magic was concerned, leaned forward to listen but wound up staring at a single diagram with a shell-shocked expression.

"All of which is to say," the woman finished sometime later, "that I'll need to come with you."

Everyone had hunched slack-jawed in their chairs but now, they sat bolt upright with wide eyes.

"Wait, wait, wait," Justin protested. "We can't ask you to—"

"To what, child?" She raised an eyebrow. "Perform the spell only I know how to perform?"

"I have a question about that," Lyle said. He drummed his fingers on the table and frowned at the widow. "D'ye care to explain exactly how a widow in a tiny cottage knows all this about magic but never thought to stop Sephith?"

"Hey." Zaara looked up. "He's right. Why did you let him terrorize everyone? You hid away here, pretending to be a harmless old woman, but you could have helped."

"I couldn't, actually," she said. "I was the one person who would never be able to defeat Sephith." She looked at their confused expressions and sighed. With a snap of her fingers, she vanished and was replaced by a man who looked vaguely familiar.

Zaara's jaw hung open.

"You're the mercenary," Justin said. "The one who sent us into Kural's hideout and had us get the book."

"Ye bastard," Lyle added, for good measure.

The man smiled at him. "That book is how your friend first learned magic. I don't think you should complain, Master Stout."

"You're a mercenary who disguised himself as an old widow?" Justin asked.

Zaara made a kind of strangled noise.

"No," the man said patiently. "I'm a defeated wizard whose magic was chained by Sephith's spells. Once I finished wandering around like a heartsick fool after my defeat, I decided to see who I could train to defeat him. The world needed it, of course."

"You *are* Kural," Justin said, awestruck and faintly smug because his suspicions had been correct.

"Just so. And you've made quite an apt second pupil, might I say."

"Second?" Justin asked.

Kural looked at Zaara. "Hello again."

She gulped and finally regained the ability to speak. Her expression one of confusion, she looked at Justin and gestured to Kural as she shook her head. "This," she said, "is my magic tutor."

CHAPTER FIFTY-NINE

"Why didn't you tell me who you were?" Zaara demanded.

"Sephith bound my power but he wanted me dead." Kural stood. "He watched closely for anyone who could defeat him—remember how he told you he knew when people spoke against him? He did because he watched the whole of the valley. I did as much as I could for you in Riverbend, which he didn't watch as closely. There was less I could do for Justin." He gave the young man a sad smile. "More details will have to wait, I'm afraid. We need to prepare for the summoning."

Justin looked at the blacksmith who lay alone on the table.

"Watch." The wizard made a gesture and his spells became visible. They covered the wounded man like a blanket. "They will keep working, even if I am not here. What he needs more than anything is rest, however. Were I here, I would simply watch and wait."

He nodded but he felt a pang of regret mixed with fear. The man had promised to make him better armor but aside from that, he should never have been mortally wounded by demons.

Kural directed Hildon and Lyle to arrange potions and salves in three groups. The first would make weapons more deadly, the second would fortify fighters' strength or health, and the third would restore health. Every bandit was to have at least one potion, perhaps more.

Zaara and Justin, meanwhile, helped Kural prepare what was needed for the summoning.

"Summoning?" the young man asked.

"Yes—an angel instead of a demon. And before you protest, know that we will not truly summon it. It is merely to draw the demon to a place of our choosing. It will do anything it can to stop the summoning of an angel, of course."

"So we kill it while it's distracted."

"Exactly." The wizard pointed to two mortars and pestles. "Justin, grind the vervain. Zaara, you grind the thyme."

"Am I making a stew?" she asked under her breath but she set to work.

The two worked until both had aching arms and he realized his magic reserves had gone almost to zero. On a hunch, he twisted his arm with the pestle and the bar decreased slightly. When he examined both the bowl and the pestle, he noticed runes carved on them. It must be set to imbue the herbs with magic as it was used.

That explained why they had been in charge of grinding herbs, then.

Kural mixed a few herbs in careful proportions and stored others separately. Each packet was wrapped in a square of cloth that was slippery and silky, held together with a dollop of hot wax that glowed with spells. When he was finished, he gave his two assistants a critical look and retrieved two potions from one of his hidden shelves.

Justin had played a number of games where his character drank mana potions but he had never felt one take hold. It was as if he had swallowed an entire packet of pop rocks and washed it down with soda. His vision went blue at the edges as his mana bar climbed to full.

"Whoa."

"It is a good feeling, yes?" The wizard smiled. "There have been more than a few who got addicted. Be careful."

He nodded. "You have what you need for the summoning now, so what's the plan?"

"I'll need your help to devise one," Kural said bluntly. "I'll set a spell within a spell. The angel summoning will draw the demon close, then I'll release the second one. What I'll need, however, is someone to watch my back and people to keep the wider demon army at bay."

"Lyle, Zaara, and I can watch your back," Justin said. "The bandits know how to fight together, so it makes sense to have them fight as a group around us, and the three of us can alternate between more than one way of fighting when necessary." He looked at Zaara, who nodded, and then at the dwarf, who had recently entered the house. Lyle nodded as well.

"I don' have more'n one way of fighting," he said gruffly. "But when I punch somethin', it stays down."

"I believe you, Master Dwarf." Kural beckoned to him. "And I have something for you. This oil here will make your knuckle weapons deadly to anything of the demon realm. It is called Angel Fire, and it is quite precious. But, if ever there was a time to use it, that time is now, I think." He used another piece of the slippery cloth to smooth the oil over the knuckle weapons Lyle used and nodded at him. To Justin, he said, "I would appreciate it if you would convey the plan to our friends. I think someone they have fought with before would be a better voice to tell them what they must do."

He nodded agreement. "I will tell Hildon first," he said. "Any reservations he has may well show us a weakness in our plan. We will call you when it is time to tell the rest."

***

"Hey." Jacob beckoned to the technician he'd spoken to earlier. "Come watch this."

Not surprisingly, the rest of them crowded around as well. The essential work was done and they were merely bringing the excess pods online and updating now.

"This may show you part of why games are important," he explained. "When Justin first came into this game, his biggest goal was to get glory and win the...er, gratitude...of tavern wenches everywhere. Whatever you're thinking, it's probably worse than that. Trust me—I'll show you the logs. But watch what he's doing now. He's speaking to multiple people, asking them if there are problems in his plan, and then he'll speak to them about why they're doing what they're doing."

"But these...aren't people," one of the technicians said blankly.

"They behave like people and they look like people," he said. "Not only that but if Justin dies in the game, he may well die in real life. It's one of the ways the game works—it forces his brain into an acceptance of life and death." He settled into his chair. "Just watch."

***

Hildon listened to Justin's explanation with a furrowed brow. At his shoulder, Mira hovered with a carefully blank expression. When he finished, the two of them looked at one another. There was clearly some communication, although he could not tell what they had agreed. He suspected that was by design.

"You know what you're asking of us," the bandit leader said at last.

"I'm asking you to be the first line of defense against the demon army," Justin said. "It is dangerous and it will be difficult."

"And you're willing to admit as much to the bandits?" Hildon asked.

"Yes."

"Then do so." He gestured with his chin. "They'll pull no punches with their questions, I warn you."

Mira gave him a smile. "Good luck."

"I have to ask." He crossed his arms. "Do you expect me to do well at this or fail miserably?"

She considered the question. "I could see it going either way." With that not very reassuring assessment, she left to take her place among her comrades and Justin beckoned the others out of the hut.

He didn't want to share the entirety of the plan at a high volume in case the demon was listening, so he abridged that part and told them only about the fact that there would be a summoning for an angel.

Then he told them which people would do what.

"Hang on." One of the bandits, a woman with hair that was almost white, leaned against the wall and pierced him with a look. He was reminded of Lyle's assessment that old mercenaries had learned how to get other people to go into danger instead of going in themselves. It seemed it was probably the same with bandits. "We'll be slaughtered if we do this."

"Not slaughtered," he said. "If I thought you'd be slaughtered, I wouldn't have suggested this. There will be many waves of demons and it is imperative that whoever stands against them be strong and accustomed to fighting as a group."

"But you're putting us on the front line," another argued. Where the first was old, he was young, although his eyes didn't look any younger. "If we wanted to fight in the wars of the powerful, we'd have stayed in our villages. We don't get caught up in those messes."

"Do you remember what Hildon said at the ruins?" Justin challenged. "To avoid confrontation with an enemy like this is to let it gain strength."

"That was when we were trapped," the woman said.

"Now we can leave," the man agreed. "Who will the army follow? They won't choose a group of bandits. They'll target the town."

"You'd let them attack the town?" he asked, horrified.

"They could be bandits too, 'cept they make themselves a target." The man shrugged. "Everyone makes their choice. If you have a house and flocks, someone will want those. If you stay in one place, you're a target."

He gaped and looked at Hildon, who seemed to be enjoying this. The man leaned against the wall of the cottage with his arms folded, and he shrugged.

"I told you they wouldn't be easy to persuade."

Justin thought about it. He did not look at Zaara or Kural and focused instead on the bandits. His father had once said that you could learn much about a person by really looking at them. At the time, of course, he had tried to convince his son to wear something other than jeans and hoodies, to which he had only rolled his eyes.

Now he thought he'd try to take the advice.

The bandits lived hard, but their gear didn't show it. Each patch was well made, and the gear was beautifully maintained. Leather armor and scabbards were oiled and worn easily. Knives were kept clean—cleaner than the bandits, in fact. These people lived and breathed defense, not comfort.

They weren't paladins, moved to protect the weak. Still, he suspected they weren't malicious, either. They merely tried to protect themselves and didn't see why other people wouldn't run as well.

In addition, they were used to being able to pick their battles.

"You came out here because you didn't want to live in their world," Justin said. The bandits had gone silent. They didn't nod but they no longer objected either. "And the odds were that you'd make it a few years before the world caught up with you. You knew there might be someone like Sephith or bored royal guards, or you knew that someday, you'd pick the wrong target or luck wouldn't go your way. That's how things go out here. Until then, you'd be free."

"Don't make a big deal out of it," a different bandit muttered at the same time that the AI popped up its input onscreen.

FLOWERY SPEECHES, Level 38

"Fine, I get it," Justin muttered under his breath. He shrugged. "You're used to being able to choose your fight. Well, this one wasn't what you thought. You chose it, way back when the demon was that one witch. You didn't even realize what you were stepping into. The thing is, now the demon is pissed and it's making an army and you have a choice—you deal with it now, or you deal with it later. You're looking at basically the only person around who can kill it, which means this is probably your best chance for a while, if not ever."

A sulky silence followed that.

"It sucks," he said. "I understand that. And if any one of you wants to switch places and guard the wizard while the demon tries to kill him, you're welcome to do that. It would probably be best if it's someone with magic if you have that. I'm doing this because the demon is attacking people I care about and I won't leave them. I think you all feel the same about those you fight with. In the end, though, it's your choice."

They began to talk and muttered among themselves. Tight knots formed. Some were arguing, he could see. Others had made their choice, and still more waited to see what others said.

They divided into two groups with two thirds on one side and one third on the other. It was clear what was happening, and he could only hope the larger group had chosen to help.

"We'll do it," Mira said, from the head of the larger group. She nodded at him. "You watched my back before, now I'll watch yours. Not to mention that I'd still be cursed if it weren't for you."

The two groups looked at Hildon now. Justin could see a certain fear in the smaller group. He didn't understand until the leader spoke.

"It's a heavy choice to make, isn't it?"

He realized then that those who didn't fight were relinquishing their right to be a part of the group. Horrified, he looked at Hildon,. "I didn't mean for this to happen."

"You didn't?" The man returned his look. "Where are you from that you'll keep someone with you even if they won't guard you through thick and thin? We don't guard townsfolk but we guard each other." He nodded at the smaller group. "I'm sad to see you go, all of you. I wouldn't have kept you in my team if you weren't worth it. May we never meet again."

"May we never meet again," the others murmured in response. They left, shouldered their packs, and vanished into the mist.

"Better to have fewer allies than uncertain ones," Kural said. "Shall we?"

"Yes." Justin swallowed and nodded. "There's a demon to kill."

"And a chance of killing it, thanks to you." Zaara squeezed his hand. "I didn't think you had a hope in hell of convincing them."

"Neither did I," Mira agreed.

"Thanks a lot, guys." He rolled his eyes.

"We weren't going to hamstring you by telling you that," Mira protested.

"Right. Let's go. And no one give me your opinions on our current odds, please." He shuddered. "I'd like to imagine a future where I survive."

CHAPTER SIXTY

Kural led the group through swirling fog. Justin couldn't see more than a foot or two ahead of himself, but the wizard seemed to know exactly where he was going.

Everyone else hung onto each other's cloaks to make sure no one got lost.

He was sure they would run into the same issue as the last time, with their enemy drawing out the suspense to breaking point and attacking en masse from the mist. Not so much as a flicker of movement caught his eye, however, and eventually, they stepped out of the fog with surprising suddenness.

Startled, he looked behind him. The mist hadn't met a wall, exactly, but it had ended within the space of a yard. It stretched up as high as he could see—which was unnerving, although he couldn't have said why.

"Come." Kural jerked his head at the group. "Down the hill. Quickly now."

They were in a piece of land that looked almost like a volcanic crater. It sloped down from sharp peaks on every side except for the small area they had walked in through, which seemed to have been worn down by the sheer number of people. The bare ground cut a path through grass of varying heights and ended at a patch of white ground—a rough panel of rock that might either be natural or somehow brought there long before.

It looked like the kind of place where druids might dance around naked, Justin thought.

Or the kind of place where someone would offer a blood sacrifice. He wondered if he should ask what exactly this ritual entailed but felt that it might be too awkward to do so now.

The wizard placed his packets of herbs on the ground next to the circle and began to work. First, he knelt and took a stick of charcoal out of a hidden pocket in his cloak. A giant diagram began to take shape on the white circle. It didn't look satanic, the young man thought. Not…exactly.

Only a little too close for comfort.

"Get ready," Kural said.

Justin, Zaara, and Lyle took their places around it and looked out. The mist had crept around the crater now.

It knew they were there. The hair on Justin's arms stood up and he gulped slightly.

The smell of herbs reached him. The wizard had cut some of the pouches open and followed the lines he had traced in charcoal as well as some he hadn't drawn at all. He didn't speak, but the sound of a muttered spell was almost audible in Justin's head.

The bandits were still fanning out when the first attack came. A set of bear-creatures lumbered out of the mist at high speed. They seemed to pull the vapor along with them as they ran.

Hildon's fighters didn't waver and flaming arrows were loosed immediately. Most struck home and all the bears met attacking bandits a moment later. Shouts erupted but so far, they seemed to be fighters calling to one another, not cries of alarm or pain.

Justin settled into a crouch. He held his sword angled and tried to breathe. Something out there in the mist was looking at him, he knew it.

It didn't come from where he expected. The ground directly ahead of him exploded and spiders poured out to skitter across grass and rock.

"Ignis!" he yelled. He shifted his sword to his left hand and swiped his right, the palm out, in an arc. Flames streaked from his palm and washed the spiders in a wave of crackling fire.

Some were obliterated but the problem with tons of spiders was that there were so many of them and they all moved in different directions.

"Spiders," he moaned. "Why did it have to be spiders?" He wasn't as afraid of them as his mother was, but that didn't mean he liked them. One of them had started to climb his cloak and he twisted and spun. "Dammit! Get off. Off!"

In the lab, Jacob looked around to see that everyone's shoulders were close to their ears. He couldn't judge, though, as his were, too.

"Hello, everyone," a cheerful voice said.

Under normal circumstances, an unexpected hello wouldn't have had much effect. However, as the technicians were watching the proliferation of demonic spiders on the screen, they were more jumpy than usual. Several uttered undignified noises that were outside their usual vocal range, two fell off their chairs, and Jacob almost took the monitors with him when he stood too quickly and promptly fell.

"Is everything okay?" Mary Williams asked. Beside her, Tad watched with an expression of deep consternation.

"It's fine," the young engineer said much too quickly. He shoved the monitor behind him. "Fine. Everything's fine here."

"How are you?" one of the technicians asked hastily.

"What's going on?" the senator asked and advanced on them. He wasn't threatening, not exactly. But it was very clear from his expression that someone had better have a good answer.

"Let's say Justin could use Mary's help right about now," Nick said. He had recovered more quickly than the others. "She pulled out one of the most powerful spells I've ever seen in-game for a single spider, and there are about eighty-five of them right now."

"Eighty-five?" Mary asked. She had taken a step back but her hands had also come up in the spell-casting pose, clearly by instinct.

Tad looked at the technicians. He looked at his wife. Still utterly silent, he repeated the looks but with a deadpan expression.

"Is there, uh…" He cleared his throat. "Is there any video of that?"

***

"Get—the fuck—off me!" Justin yelled. He launched fireballs with wild abandon at this point, which seemed like a good idea until Kural yelled in protest. "Sorry!"

"I'll deal with the spiders," Lyle told him. "You deal with the big horse thing."

"What big horse—oh fuck, what is that?" He had the impression of hooves and bright red eyes and decided there was no time like the present for an offensive strike. "Geronimoooooooo!"

The animal reared at the last minute and its hooves lashed out. He skidded to his knees and thrust the sword up with all his might. A red shield appeared at the point of impact. It glowed with demonic runes and the blade slid uselessly off it.

"Fuckballs," he said vehemently as he threw himself sideways. He barely managed to avoid rolling into the circle and the horse reared again. "How the hell do I—oh."

It was difficult to hold a visualization as he dodged around the animal, but he tried to imagine waves receding from a beach. Oddly, that focus relaxed him. He began to dodge automatically, parried the stabs of the hooves, and jerked out of the way of its snapping teeth.

Waves…wave ebbing…waves—

He saw the entire shield illuminated on the creature, along with the places that held it together. Justin ducked under another reared attack, rolled away, and whipped to stab his sword directly into one of the glowing red runes.

The spell flared and a piece of it died.

"Aha!" he yelled. "What now, you piece of horsey shit?"

"I never imagined this as the backdrop of my greatest magical work," Kural commented in a long-suffering tone.

"It's better this way." Justin was on a roll now. He could see the points of strength across the animal's body and it couldn't keep all of them away from him at once. "Alone in a tower would be boring. This way, you have an audience."

"You aren't, of course, looking at me," the wizard pointed out.

"Oh, right. I saw that throne." He recalled Kural's hideout. "Look, I promise when this is over, we'll get you a parade and a ton of beautiful women singing new songs about how awesome you are, but right now—take that, you stupid horse—I need you to focus."

"Indeed," Kural said dryly. "I'll hold you to that, you know."

"I will sing both of you a song if you please shut up for a while," Zaara shouted.

"Killjoy." Justin dodged the horse's back feet and identified his opening. "Aha. One…two…three." A long slash of his sword cut along an unarmored part of the creature's side. Without the shield, the sword bit deep and he followed it with a fireball.

His adversary dropped with a scream.

"Oh, hell yeah. Giant worms? Demonic horses? Justin can do it all." He danced back and wished he could do jazz hands and hold a sword at the same time.

IMPRESSIVE KILLS, Level 1

"Level one?" he demanded of the AI.

"Do you want me to take it away? Because I can."

"Fine, fine." Justin looked around. Lyle was punching the last spider into the dirt, Zaara was surrounded by what looked like giant dead slugs, and the rest of the bandits seemed to be reforming their lines. "Is the first wave over?"

"It seems like it," Zaara said. "Kural, how are you doing?"

"Good. But I'm not quite where I need to be yet." He spared them a grin. "So let's hope there are a few more waves."

"Uh…" Justin looked over his shoulder. "I have bad news about that."

There was the sound of a particularly thick vat of liquid bubbling, and the demon strode out of the mist.

Everyone gaped at it and panic was evident on the faces of the bandits.

"Well…" Kural said. "Shit."

CHAPTER SIXTY-ONE

The demon strode forward with earthshaking strides. Each step was slow, but Justin assumed that it was merely for dramatic effect. They had a minute or two at the most unless it decided to make an evil speech.

"Kural," he said conversationally.

The wizard was gesturing to arrange the bandits in a peculiar pattern, although it wasn't clear why. It appeared to be a kind of a cone with an arc of bandits behind the circle as well. One hand still held the lines of power in the diagram, which now glowed white. He glanced at the young man. "Yes?"

"What kind of demon is this, exactly?" he asked him.

"Theoretically, it's a water demon." Kural cleared his throat. "Salt-water, specifically."

He looked at the green and faintly slimy skin. "So…fire magic?"

"Have you ever tried throwing a lit torch into the ocean?" He was pale now. "It would have about the same effect. The demon is stronger than I thought and my spell won't be able to kill it unless it's weakened."

"Oh. Uh…any ideas, then?"

"A big enough torch would do the trick," Zaara said decisively. "And you taught me that spells can be amplified, right?"

Kural looked quickly at her. "Yes."

"I can amplify Justin's magic and you keep the spell going. Help us when you can. We'll keep moving." She looked nervously at their adversary. "Hopefully, we can hold out."

"We can tell the archers to concentrate on one place," Justin said quickly. "Kural, where is it weakest?"

"The eyes," the wizard said at once.

"All archers!" he called. "Aim for the right eye! All melee fighters, concentrate on the left ankle. Focus on slowing it and direct your damage as much as you can to one area."

A yell of acknowledgment followed.

"The sooner we kill this," he shouted, "the sooner we can go have some ale!"

For that, he got a much louder cheer.

"You're learning," Hildon said from behind him.

"Thanks. Ready, Zaara?"

"Ready."

Justin tracked the demon's path. It led directly to Kural, whose face was pale.

"Hold out," he told the man. "Whatever it costs—this being won't accept a surrender."

"And I think I've used up my luck on near escapes." He nodded. "Do some damage. I'll spring the trap as soon as I can."

He caught Zaara's hand, ducked, and began to run behind one of the lines of bandits. She muttered under her breath as she started the spell to amplify his power and after a few moments, he began to feel the same tingly feeling as when Kural had given him the potion.

"Justin," she whispered.

"Yeah?"

"Start small," she told him. "You're not used to having this much power. Trust me. The first—"

The demon took its first step into the crater and the ground shook enough to throw everyone off their feet. Only Kural stayed standing and a white shield began to rise around him like motes of dust in shining sunlight.

"Archers!" Hildon yelled.

The bandits were well trained. The demon's giant head swung to find the source of the shout and the archers scrambled to their feet, aimed, and waited for it to stop. It had barely stilled when all of them let loose. The arrows found their targets, and although they extinguished quickly, it was enough to make the being rear back. One giant hand moved to its eye and it uttered a scream that Justin didn't hear in his ears so much as his mind. A series of red numbers floated up and away

"Melee!" It was Mira's voice this time. She raced forward with the melee fighters. Their group was ragtag but with their swords alight, they looked more formidable than they might usually. The demon looked down when their group reached its foot. Swords and spears swung in a flurry of blows before the fighters scrambled when the creature stooped to sweep one giant arm. A single bandit, the younger man who had challenged Justin, catapulted away with a yell and lay still.

Justin gathered his power and waited as the demon's head swung around. It looked at Mira, at Hildon, and finally, at Kural. When it stepped forward, the young man was ready. He gathered a small fireball in his hands—only enough to divert its attention—and lobbed it gently toward the right eye that was still steaming.

His plan, unfortunately, went awry. Instead of his intended restrained assault, a fireball the size of a small sheep singed his hair as it rocketed away. He stumbled, barely held his aim, and managed to hit the demon in the neck.

"And now you see why I said to start small," Zaara said.

"Oh, mama." He grinned. "Oh, I like this. Let's do that again."

"Let's run first!" She grasped his hand and yanked.

Mira's group attacked next to switch the order and keep the demon off-balance. They didn't shout war cries as they charged and simply ran. When the being swung to face them, they were already gone, having scattered behind it to circle. They had learned from the last time, Justin thought.

He loosed his next fireball at the same time that the archers shot and this time, they did enough damage that the creature's health bar took a noticeable hit. In a somewhat amusing twist, the health bar had been made a part of it, which meant that it was also obscured by the swirling mist and the demon's sheer height.

The next few assaults followed quickly. Emboldened, the archers began to fire without pause, and the demon could not find its footing to retaliate. Several of Mira's team collaborated to target the back of its heels, and although Justin suspected it didn't have an Achilles tendon, it bellowed in pain just the same.

"You're doing well," Kural called. "Keep at it."

That was all the demon needed to remember why it was there. Its mouth opened in a silent snarl as it looked at the wizard.

"Oh, shit," Justin and Zaara said at the same time.

The creature dropped its hand from its eye and stared at Kural. It took one step, then another. As if the fighters around it had only succeeded in annoying it, it turned and swept its arms forward and back. Tentacles that hadn't been there before lashed out and bandits careened away with a chorus of screams.

"Kural!" Zaara tried to run to him, only for Justin to yank her back. "Let me go."

"Don't get in its way," he snapped in response. Years of sword-fighting and months on the road had made her strong, and she was sneaky along with it. He had trouble holding on. "Listen to me. If Kural can't hold it off, what chance do you think you have?"

That made her hesitate—and the hesitation was enough. The demon surged toward the wizard at full speed. Justin, seeing Kural as small as a mouse beside the demon, had one moment of deep regret before white magic exploded outward like a bursting bubble.

The demon skidded across the ground and lay still with its skin smoking. It was still moving, however.

He didn't want to warn it what was coming and merely raced forward and hoped the other fighters would see him and take note.

Zaara' caught up with him with enough time to pull his head down. His heart gave a sideway leap, but her words weren't quite what he had hoped for.

"I'll help Kural. Stay safe." She ducked away and left without giving him time to respond.

THIRD WHEEL, Level 1

"Now you're trolling me," he protested.

"Do you think that just started? Really?"

The demon pushed up and swatted at Justin, who skidded to a stop. It took another step toward Kural, who—he had to admit—did not look well. He was on his knees as he poured every ounce of energy into his summoning spell and his whole body shook. Around him, bandits lay prone and wounded.

And Zaara wasn't there to amplify fireballs anymore, which meant he had to get creative.

"Hey!" he called. "Hey, you. Yeah, I'm talking to you, fish-face."

The demon didn't spare him a glance.

"If I could give you negative levels for trash-talk, I would."

"Some demon you are," Justin called and ignored the AI. "You were summoned as a fucking contingency plan, you useless fucker. I bet your mom was a salmon and your father was a horny fisherman."

The demon swung to look at him. He couldn't tell if it was angry or merely bemused, but at least he had its attention now.

"You know what? You aren't even listed in the book of demons. When humans think of your kind, they think of bright red, flaming stone creatures, and now I know why. It's because you fucking suck. Where's your ingenuity? A proper demon doesn't do its own dirty work. It talks humans into doing it—but noooooo, you wanted to make an army of werewolves. How did that turn out?"

The demon began to flicker madly. One moment, it was gigantic and green, and in the next, it was the witch he and his team had encountered.

"Yeah," he said. "Yeah, you. Miss 'I need you to go fix the problem I made.' Great pitch. I guess I know why you didn't go into sales. Let me guess, Sephith found you in the discount demon bin, didn't he?"

"Discount demon bin," Nick muttered. His lips twitched crazily.

Amber, who had snorted root beer up her nose, tried to recover without coughing soda all over the monitors.

"What's a discount demon bin?" DuBois asked.

"Never mind." Jacob patted his arm. "Have some popcorn."

The demon stalked closer and its features shifted and writhed. "You are nothing, a useless human."

"Oh, yeah, sure, that's why you lost an eye and you're getting fucking owned by a horde of bandits and a level-three group of adventurers, huh? How's your eye, Cthulhu?"

Justin. It wasn't the AI, he realized, but Kural. *Lure it closer.*

"You wanna go?" He walked toward the being and spread his arms as he began to circle and drive it toward the summoning diagram. "Let's go. I'll even let you choose the weapons. You wanna—"

Someone pounded into him from the side. Justin went over with a grunt of pain and hit his head so hard the whole world turned white.

Or…wait, the whole world had turned white. It wasn't the sickly gray of the demon's fog, either. It was a pure, blinding, light-filled white that illuminated the ground in lines that sizzled and burned and finally slammed closed around the demon.

It probably would have screamed if it had time, but it didn't. Where the lines fell across its skin, they seared through like a hot knife through butter. The creature didn't even go up in flames as there wasn't time for that.

Within seconds, it was ash.

Justin looked at Zaara, who had tackled him to the ground.

"Sorry," she said. "Kural said not to shout the plan where the demon could hear."

"A broken rib is…" He winced. "Probably better than death by demon. The jury is out, though."

"Let me help you up."

"I'd rather not move, thanks." He laughed, then regretted it. "Lyle?"

The dwarf appeared overhead. His knuckle weapons dripped with black blood and he had a psychotic kind of grin. "Let's find more demons."

"Oh, God." Justin closed his eyes. "Lyle Stout, demon hunter. It has a ring to it, I guess."

Around the crater, bandits struggled to their feet. Kural limped to those who were not moving. Hildon and Mira both tried to hold each other up and consequently didn't do a spectacular job.

Everything ceased when a loud, commanding voice asked, "What in the seven hells is going on here?"

He looked up to see the blacksmith. He was still pale but stood with his hands on his hips at the edge of the crater.

"Oh, hi," he blustered. "I'm glad to see you up and about."

"I woke up in a strange cottage in the middle of the mist and with what sounded like a full war going on," the man said. "And I think I remember a giant worm. And what's that?" He pointed at the diagram. "Did someone summon a demon?"

"Sephith." Justin took Zaara's hand and stood with a wince. "Don't worry, the demon's gone. Do you want to go back to East Newbrook?"

"Only if you promise there will be no demons," the blacksmith said. "I mean it. None."

CHAPTER SIXTY-TWO

Kural sent several of the uninjured bandits to retrieve supplies from his house and had others turn the battlefield into a makeshift hospital. Those who could still walk were tended to by Zaara and Justin once Hildon had taught them a basic spell to clean wounds.

The young man had never experienced the aftermath of a battle this way. Before this, he had simply stumbled to the nearest tavern and taken advantage of game mechanics to heal his tired muscles. Now, he had an up-close and personal look at the damage done by a battle.

Every so often, his gaze drifted to the edge of the battlefield where two bodies lay still. The young man who had challenged him—and been swayed, in the end, by his speech—had died in the demon's first attack. An older man lay beside him.

"It isn't your fault," Hildon said when he caught him looking.

He was making a splint for the bandit leader's twisted knee and wrapped the bandage as neatly as he could around the hardened leather of the man's scabbard. A short silence followed as he did not reply at first.

After all, he knew it wasn't his fault. He wasn't the demon and he wasn't the bandit. But still, he'd been part of how it had all played out.

"Every choice has downsides," he said finally. "I made my choice to try to persuade all of you and two of yours died for it. I know it would be worse if we had all cut and run. There would be hundreds of dead villagers and an army of monsters. That doesn't mean those two aren't still dead."

Hildon looked curiously at him. "Everyone dies. People die young, especially bandits and warriors. If you know such things are inevitable, why let them sadden you at all?"

"He's from a very different place than this land," Zaara said. She looked up from where she was binding a long cut on a bandit's side. "You should have seen him agonizing over what to do when the witch wanted us to kill you and you wanted us to kill the witch."

"Hey," he said, a little sensitive.

She bit her lip on any further words and moved to the next bandit.

"She doesn't think less of you, lad," Hildon said in a low voice. He smiled.

Justin's cheeks were hot. He finished the splint and looked around. There weren't many left to heal, and all of those were within Kural's purview, not his. He sat on the ground and rubbed his face as he realized he was exhausted.

"It can't happen," he said finally. Zaara wasn't real, and somewhere in a lab, a doctor watched all of this. He wanted to curl into a ball and die at the thought of people watching a romance between him and a fake character.

Thankfully, he didn't have to explain this to his companion. "A mayor's daughter and an adventurer?" the bandit asked thoughtfully. "I can see why you'd have your doubts."

He responded with a tight smile.

"Still," Hildon continued. "She wouldn't be the first well-born scion to run off and be an adventurer instead of marrying up. Mayors and merchants and the like always have plans for their children. And the children don't always like to go along with those plans, do they?

It's somethin' to consider." He clapped him on the shoulder and allowed Mira to help him up. "Think about it."

Justin was saved from having to do this by Kural, who limped closer with Zaara and Lyle.

"Everyone is bandaged and healing," he said. "There aren't many serious injuries, I'm happy to say."

"Now to get back to the hideout," Hildon said. He sighed. "I'm not looking forward to a journey, I'll be honest."

"Perhaps you don't need one just yet." The wizard turned to survey the crater. He closed his eyes and bowed his head, his palms up.

The first change came with those who were gravely injured. Slowly, they elevated and thick sleeping pads appeared beneath them. An awning rose from nowhere to shelter them from the sun.

Beyond them, a creaking sound accompanied tables and chairs that sprang into being. A fire blazed into life on the white circle of rock with a whole hog on a spit. On the tables, platters of food appeared and their smell made Justin's mouth water helplessly. He could see pitchers of wine, bowls of roasted potatoes, and baskets of bread rolls. Two giant kegs of ale appeared at the edge of the crater, propped up on wooden stilts and accompanied by trays of mugs.

Kural opened his eyes and smiled. "Eat," he told those around him. "Rest. A journey should only be undertaken on a full stomach."

His suggestion was met with enthusiastic applause. Lyle appeared at the kegs with a speed that strongly suggested teleportation and began pouring ale for everyone. He appeared to have a process of drinking a mug of ale himself and pouring one for someone else, then repeated steps one and two as quickly as he could.

Justin laughed and sat. He was famished and he couldn't remember the last time anything had tasted as good as the pork and potatoes he shoveled into his mouth. He was on his third plate when he looked at Kural.

He watched the other man eating with perfect manners and asked, "Are you...I mean, is any of the three faces we've seen actually what you look like?"

The wizard glanced at him, surprised, and smiled. "You know, no one's ever thought to ask me that."

"I'll take that as a no," he said.

The man only smiled.

"So, what will you do next?" Justin asked.

Kural didn't answer immediately. He took another roll and offered him one as well, before—apparently on a whim—he conjured an opulent chocolate cake. "My biggest failure," he said finally, "wasn't in losing to Sephith. It was in leaving the people of the valley to his mercy—and mine. It was my spell, you know, that has ash floating in the air. I would like to undo as much damage as I can before anything else. There are buildings still standing at the tower and I can work from there." He looked at Justin. "What will you do?"

"I don't know," he said. "Well...I'll find the third key, I guess."

"I'll aid you if I can," the wizard offered. "I have several books that might contain some of the lore behind it. Sephith gave you my key and the demon...well, gods alone know where it found the one it gave you. I have my guesses but we'll likely never know. I'll send you a message if ever I find a hint."

"Thank you." They clinked glasses, a friendly and oddly reassuring gesture.

"And what will you do about your mayor's daughter, hmm?" Kural smiled slyly. "What will she do when she learns you're not of this world?"

Justin leaned back with a start.

"Yes, I do know." The wizard fixed him with a frank look. "It's obvious enough to anyone who has the eyes to see."

"Well, then, you make a suggestion." He met his gaze. "And she knows, anyway. She doesn't believe me, but she knows. And nothing will happen. I have to go back."

"Which is why you need the keys, eh?" Kural smiled. "We'll see."

PART III

CHAPTER SIXTY-THREE

"I feel like a new man," Nick announced as he came into the lab. This had become something of a ritual since they'd first relocated to the new premises.

Jacob studied him quickly. "You look like a new man." He refocused on his work for a moment before he looked up again. "Damn. We joke about this, but you really do look like a new man. In fact, you look good."

"Well, I think we can deduce from the exchange that I've slept enough and Jacob hasn't," he announced.

Amber snorted into her coffee. She didn't look up from her spreadsheets and a careful list she had made in a notebook.

"Amber," he said. "You also haven't slept enough. I can answer all the money questions you have in there. We have unlimited money now." He gestured broadly. "Hell, any one of us could tie up every loose end in there and still have money to spare."

She leaned back in her chair and grinned at him. "We do not have unlimited money. No one has unlimited money. For your information, I am making sure that I pass Diatek's accountants a full list of our debtors as well as a complete accounting of our current situation. I merely want to be careful."

"She's only doing that because she was making a mess drooling all over the equipment," Jacob quipped. He looked into the lab with a contented smile. "I can't blame her, of course. Will you look at that? It's gorgeous, isn't it?"

Nick put his armful of things on his desk—the last empty desk in this section of the lab—and settled into his chair to study their surroundings.

Their old lab had been a small warehouse-esque room in a facility that absolutely was not built to be a lab. While it had seemed like crazy luxury to the three founding members of PIVOT when they first rented the space, it wasn't remotely in the same league as this new premises.

The lab was divided into five unequal parts. On one side of the room, set up a few feet from the rest, was a long, thin area partitioned by panels of glass. Four desks were positioned along the wall, which allowed the PIVOT team and Dr. DuBois to work while looking out over the floor. A mirror area on the other side of the room held servers, although the glass there was misted slightly from the powerful air conditioning.

The main floor was comprised of two sections. The first was the line of pods, each with its own set of monitors to show the vital signs of the patient inside. Only Justin's pod was illuminated right now, but he could easily imagine how it would look when there were more patients there. On the other side of the room from the pods were all the tools and toys they could possibly want arranged around several black workbenches. It looked like what one would get, he thought, if you asked an engineer to draw a candy store.

DuBois was in that area now and gestured enthusiastically to a group of Diatek scientists who had been assigned as his assistants. Nick was pleased to see that they looked interested in the doctor's passion—as well as amused. Between his mannerisms and his genius, the man often reminded him of a cross between Albert Einstein and Doc Brown if either of those two had eaten inordinate amounts of popcorn. His desk was piled with bags of it, in fact.

The last area of their new offices, set behind more panels of glass emblazoned with the Diatek logo, was a comfortable seating area where the families of the patients would be able to watch the work in the lab without sitting on work stools. Mary and Tad Williams were there right now, and both also looked better rested and showered.

That was the kind of setup you got, however, when you were bought out by one of the Defense Department's top private contractors. Diatek had rocketed to the top of its industry without ever going public, instead assisting the Department of Defense and the US intelligence agencies with projects Nick frankly didn't want to think about too hard. Anna Price, the founder of Diatek, was a chemist—and Nick could come up with more than a few guesses of what kind of things she provided to the government.

Price, however, had another side as well. As a young woman, she had lost her daughter and her husband within two years. Her daughter had been left comatose after an accident similar to the one that had injured Justin Williams, but where Justin's parents had been able to turn to PIVOT for help, Anna Price and her husband had found no support. They sold everything they had, only to run out of money anyway. Price started Diatek, determined that she would find a way to make sure no other families had to go through what she and her husband had endured. Two years after their daughter was taken off life support, however, her husband had committed suicide out of grief and guilt.

He could not imagine what she had gone through, and he felt bad for judging her contracts with the Defense Department. If it weren't for her efforts and the money from those contracts, after all, she would not be able to help PIVOT with its work.

Still, the woman unsettled him. She unsettled all of them, he thought. With no family of her own left to save, she was wholly devoted to her goals in a way even the consummate workaholics of PIVOT could not be.

The young engineer shivered as he booted his computer up. They had made the final decision to allow Diatek to buy PIVOT out, and he could only hope that had been a good idea.

Mary watched as the members of the PIVOT team set up. It was enlightening to see DuBois work with a team of assistants. When he was on his own, his genius tended to manifest in unsettling ways. She recalled an instance where Justin was in mortal danger in the video game and DuBois tended to be fascinated rather than worried and simply munched on popcorn as he watched the vital signs spike.

It turned out that the man was also a good teacher. He had spent a solid hour and a half walking his students through the various monitor readouts on the pod and now waved his hands as he explained something in the area of the lab with the workbenches. Mary could not begin to imagine what they were talking about—she probably wouldn't have any clearer an idea, she thought, even if she could hear the speech—but the assistants were enthralled.

The group trooped to another of the pods and one of the assistants took their shoes off and climbed inside. The others, under the doctor's direction, began to hook their colleague up.

Beside Mary, Tad made a frustrated noise. She looked at him.

"Is there a problem?"

"Another email came in." He looked up. "I didn't read it and only saw the title. They want me to…uh, do something that current technology would make very difficult."

He forced a smile but it was impossible not to see how exhausted he was, and her heart ached for him. She'd had very little sleep as she tried to stay up with him, but he'd had even less. He had spent almost the entire night with his aides in DC going over PR strategies.

Two weeks before, a reporter had been tipped off about Justin's treatment. The resulting questions to him, shown on live television, had triggered a media storm. It was his first term as a senator and he stood up to many of the big lobbyists in Washington and sponsored bills across the aisle to limit the power of pharmaceutical companies.

His work should be the focus of the interviews he was asked for, she thought. Instead, the media painted him not as a principled new senator but as a renegade who had no principles at all and no respect for medical ethics. They either didn't understand that Justin's treatment was well-backed by research or didn't care. Mary couldn't decide which made her angrier.

The man who had stirred all this up was Dru Metcalfe, a lobbyist for several pharmaceutical companies. One of his main clients had been responsible for getting Dr. DuBois's seminal work blackballed from FDA trials. It was his research that PIVOT had stumbled across and melded with their own pod technology to enable Justin's brain to heal from the damage caused by the car accident. By engaging him inside a virtual world, PIVOT and DuBois drew him slowly back to the real world.

Meanwhile, thanks to Dru Metcalf, Tad was bombarded by inaccurate interview questions and hate mail. The other party was only too happy to jump on this as evidence of their opponent's immorality, and Tad's party, angry about his reaches across the aisle, made no effort to defend him.

Mary was seriously considering taking boxing lessons so she could kick some ass. She was not pleased by this situation.

Plus, in her opinion, no one would guess that a woman in a pink skirt suit and pearls could beat them up. She clenched one hand into a fist and made an off-season New Year's Resolution to learn some kind of martial art. She could look it up later.

Right now, he needed her. She took his hand and squeezed it.

"The team wants me to come back to DC," he said. His gaze was fixed on Justin's pod. "They have ideas for PR stuff to do. They want to drum up support."

"That sounds like a good idea," she said. "Do you want me to come with you?"

He shook his head. "I won't ask you to do that. You'd do nothing but sit in meetings."

"I could give interviews," Mary pointed out.

Tad looked at her and considered the suggestion quietly. "I suppose you could. I'll float that idea to them. For now, though, you stay here. The fewer people who have to go into that snake pit, the better." He gave her a pained smile. "At least Price is letting me use her jet to go back. I'll be able to work on the plane." He lowered his head into his hands. "And I'm sure the media will get wind of the fact that I'm using her jet and it will turn into something about how I didn't sell out to the lobbyists, I sold out to a crackpot who promised me they could cure Justin."

"That's a terrible way to talk about DuBois," she said and her lips twitched.

Her husband was startled into a bark of laughter. He looked into the pod section of the lab, where DuBois ran one cheese-stained hand through his wild hair. "Oh, that man. I have to say, he really grows on you."

"He does." She smiled. "Okay, you go. I'll stay here and…well, get DuBois to wash his hands. And his hair. Dear Lord. And you…" She stood and took his face in her hands. "You remember something—you didn't simply throw Justin's life away on a whim. You saved him from a situation where lobbyists were in charge of his life or death, and you found people who truly wanted to help him—and who had shown they could. The truth will come out, I believe that. For now, remember that you found the best care for your son."

Tad crushed her close in a hug. When he spoke, his voice was broken. "I miss him so much, Mary. He's right there, but I can't speak to him."

"You will," she promised. "We'll get him back. Now, you go to DC and fight for all the families that don't have PIVOT and Diatek helping them."

He squeezed her hand and nodded.

"And when you need to smile," she reminded him, "remember those videos of me in the game."

That drew a reflexive and genuine guffaw. He had persuaded DuBois to show him the readouts of Mary in the game, filtered through with basic graphics, and he had teased her nonstop since then about how she should be his bodyguard now. With a tender kiss, he left with his shoulders a little straighter than they had been an hour before.

Mary watched him walk away with a smile that faded as soon as he was gone. She had to keep believing that they would get Justin back. If she thought for a moment that they might lose him, she would be lost as well. She had spoken to him in the game and had seen his humor and his strength.

He was in there. She fixed her gaze firmly on his pod. He was alive and he was in there. They would get him back.

Dru had just showered when his phone rang. He put his razor in its usual place and his jaw tightened. The ringtone was familiar and he took a moment to compose himself before he moved to the bed and answered.

"Mr. White. Good morning, sir." He kept his tone hearty.

"Yes." Raymond White, CEO of IterNext, wasn't a very talkative man. He also wasn't a happy one in general, especially when one of his employees failed him.

The lobbyist had failed him for the past five months. What was supposed to be a routine operation had gone sideways when, instead of falling in line, Tad Williams had decided to go rogue. It was the longest a senator had ever held out against the man's trademark combination of bribery and blackmail, and Dru was absolutely determined to not let it be the first time he failed entirely.

"Well?" White asked. He didn't waste words.

"We're making progress, sir," he assured him. "The media is doing its job wonderfully. The exposé piece on the PIVOT offices is coming out this morning. There are four journalists waiting outside Williams' offices. He'll have to go past them when he gets back from California."

"You said you had him," the CEO reminded him. "You said he would need you to get out of legal trouble. What happened with that?"

He sat on the bed and tried not to snarl. It wasn't his fault that had gone wrong. How was he supposed to guess that the founder of PIVOT would be stupid enough to jump on the grenade to save the rest of them? You went in, you threatened legal action, and people fell in line. It was how it worked. Sometimes, they countersued and you let the lawyers go at it for a while until the other party cracked, but you always won. When you had deep pockets and enough lawyers, it always worked.

Despite the failure, he still believed he could have worked on Jacob Zachary if he'd had the time. Unauthorized human experimentation would haunt the man's career forever if he were convicted. He could have gotten him to flip in a few days if he had access.

What no one had expected was for Anna Price to swoop in. Diatek had no goddammed interest in this bill. They were in defense, for the love of Christ, not pharmaceuticals. They had all the contracts they could ever want.

Now, PIVOT belonged to Diatek, all charges against Zachary had been wiped, and interfering with anything they did was likely to land someone in a prison that didn't technically exist.

Dru had lost significant leverage.

He sketched the details for White, hopeful that the man would offer some connection to Price, preferably something they could use.

Instead, his boss said simply, "Price is a dead end. And I told you to get Williams on board, not PIVOT."

"Yes, sir." Dru fought the urge to yell down the phone line. "He's close to cracking."

"You've said that for four months and the bill is coming to the floor in two weeks," White said crisply. He was spelling it out, which was an extremely bad sign. The man hated spelling things out. "I expect to have the votes by Friday. Do I make myself clear?"

"Perfectly. Sir."

The phone went dead and he put it down slowly and took a deep breath.

He dressed mechanically. Better than anyone, he knew what happened to people who disappointed Raymond White, and it wasn't pretty. What might happen to Jacob Zachary's career was nothing compared to what might happen to him. The CEO didn't like to be concerned with details unless someone close to him screwed him over. Then, he went all out.

Dru wouldn't merely be out of a job, he would be completely

discredited. By the time White was done, his own family would believe he was a pathological liar with a drug problem. His ex-girlfriends would believe he had cheated on them, his other clients would believe he had spilled their secrets, his landlord would have evicted him, and his bank accounts would be empty.

It wasn't something he had worried about before now because he had never anticipated failure. He didn't fail—it was his entire hook as a lobbyist. Never once, before now, had he not delivered the promised results.

Which meant it was very clear what he needed to do now.

Bribery hadn't worked for Tad Williams. In retrospect, Dru thought he should have let the senator bask in his relief for a few days before he made the ask. That chance was gone now, however. Blackmail also hadn't worked. The man's wife must be a saint if the thought of doctored affair photos didn't even faze the man.

The current strategy had brought him a little closer, though. It hurt Williams deeply for people to accuse him of being a bad father who was endangering his only child. Still, he wasn't cracking.

Would it be too much to ask for to have at least one skeleton in Tad Williams's closet? Dru put his tie on with a grimace. Only one. That was all he asked for.

Since he wouldn't find one, however, he had to get creative.

CHAPTER SIXTY-FOUR

Kural drained his mug of beer and laughed heartily. "Okay, I should go now while I can still remember the way to my tower."

"Jus' keep goin' uphill," Lyle advised. He wiped foam off his beard after a long drink. "Ye can get a few more in before ye forget that."

The wizard laughed again. "I'm sure I can, master dwarf. Nevertheless, I have a great deal to do and so I shall leave the three of you to your drinks. Any of you are welcome at any time—especially my two apprentices, of course. Zaara, if I could speak to you for a moment?"

Justin watched as she followed him outside.

"Eh." Lyle clapped him on the arm. "Anyone likes a little o' the exotic, an' a sorcerer is always exotic. She'll come back, though."

He stared at his companion.

The dwarf, thinking he hadn't understood the point, elaborated. "See, sorcerers can summon all kinds o' strange things. Ye're telling me if a lovely female sorcerer appeared, ye wouldn't be even a little interested? Powers ye couldn't even dream of, eh?"

"I, uh…" He decided to take a sip rather than respond to the challenge. It was too much to try to explain to Lyle that he felt stupid being jealous of a collection of pixels over a different pile of pixels.

Thankfully, he was saved from more well-meaning advice when Zaara returned. She was unusually subdued and gazed into space for a while. The conversation ebbed and flowed around her until finally, she looked at her companions and saw the question in their eyes.

She shrugged. "He asked if I'd like to come back and be his apprentice—*really* be his apprentice."

Justin shut his mouth on several uncharitable comments about Kural's motives. He had no reason to expect that this was all an attempt to flirt, and Zaara did have a talent for magic. She could be as powerful as the wizard one day if she trained at it, he had no doubt about that.

"What did you say?" he asked as neutrally as he could.

"I told him I don't know," she admitted. "I've missed my magic studies. I want to learn to be able to do the things he can do—or your mother." She smiled.

He shook his head with a rueful smile. His mother had persuaded the scientists to let her into the world of the game, and she had proved to be a very able player. Aided in part by the invulnerability buffs they had given her, she had unleashed a truly amazing amount of power at one point.

The joke, of course, was that she had been startled into it by a spider.

Hopefully, there were videos of that somewhere. While he'd lived it, he really wanted to see it again. His mother had never been outright disdainful of his video games, but she also hadn't really understood them. He would never have guessed that she would be quite so good at playing them. Even if she weren't invulnerable, he would bet she could actually get good, given enough time.

Justin refocused on Zaara. "You know, if you want to do this—"

"And leave you two alone?" she asked tartly. "You'd be dead within a day. Lyle would run his mouth off—or if he didn't, he'd charge blindly into the fight you found. You have a remarkable talent for finding trouble, Justin Williams."

"I don't know what you're talking about," he said with great dignity. "In fact, I think you're confusing me with you. Who's the one who came to threaten me away from Sephith?"

She rolled her eyes.

"We were…" He looked over his shoulder and pointed. "Right over there, weren't we?"

"Yes." Zaara raised an eyebrow and sipped her beer. "Except, to set the scene, we really should have you ogling a bar maid."

He flushed a deep red and choked on his mouthful of beer.

"You know, she's still here," she said in a whisper. "And I hear you're the hero who defeated Sephith and a demon army. If that's not a strong opener, I don't know what is."

"I'd be willing to bet you don't know what a strong opener is," he retorted, but a smile tugged at his lips. "And there's no reason to be superior simply because your suitor is a sorcerer and mine are bar wenches."

Zaara laughed. "Wrong. My suitors are nobles who might as well wear their pants on their head for all the sense they have."

"Not Kural, then?" Lyle rumbled. He didn't seem to notice Justin kicking him under the table, but he was on his eighteenth mug of beer.

"Kural," she said, "is three hundred and ninety-seven years old."

Her companions both stared at her open-mouthed.

"And I'm given to understand he prefers the fae," she added. "He says if you live long enough, you tend to not want humans anymore."

"Uh…huh." Justin wasn't quite sure where to go with that.

"Anyway," she continued. "We should talk about our next adventure. Hildon gave us quite a few leads."

He retrieved the scroll with a nod. After their confrontation with the demon, the bandit leader and his army had withdrawn to their new headquarters to restore it and recover. Although they had spent their time together on the roads, they seemed to have had enough adventure after fighting off a force of undead demon-creatures and losing two of their fighters in the process.

When he left, the man had gifted them a list of places they had considered looting. Justin had immediately crossed the monasteries off but that still left numerous targets.

"Where do you think would have an ancient dwarven key?" he asked rhetorically. "The first two were around here, so logically—"

"Logically, the third one should be close," Zaara said with a smile.

"I intended to say, logically, my luck would be that the third one is at the bottom of the ocean," he responded.

"Nah," Lyle said. He drained his beer. "Someone'll have it." He wandered off to get more beer, returned, and drank half the mug before he looked at them. "What?"

"Were you simply being optimistic?" Justin asked. "Because that's not like you. And if you know, how do you know?"

"It's a dwarven artifact," the dwarf said as if that explained everything.

He motioned for him to keep talking.

"Do ye really not know about dwarven artifacts?"

"Let's skip ahead and assume Zaara and I know nothing." He fought the urge to scream.

"Oh. Well, when ye live in mines 'n other dark places, ye learn real quick that ye can lose jus' about anything," Lyle explained. "So anythin' of value is made to find its way back into someone's hands. 'Course, the trouble is, like as not, it'll find its way to someone who hates ye, but at least someone will know where it is."

"Huh." He considered this. "So…we should be able to find it?"

"Should," the dwarf agreed. He shrugged. "That's the legend, anyway."

"Aaaaaand there goes my hope," Justin told Zaara, who laughed.

Any reply she might have made, however, was cut off when the tavern door was thrust open and voices shouted in the doorway. He looked up with interest. Brawls in this town were rare after so many years under Sephith, and he was interested to see what could inspire one.

Wheat? Mud? Cows?

When the people came through the hallway and into the tavern, however, Zaara whispered, "Oh, no."

His heart sank. He recognized the man amongst the armed guards. It was Mayor Hausen, her father.

"Oh, hell," Lyle said and dived under the table.

"That man!" Hausen shouted and pointed at Justin. "He kidnapped my daughter!"

"What?" Justin and Zaara said at the same time.

"Sir." The man who had argued with the mayor was short with dark hair, the former cartwright of East Newbrook and newly made mayor. "There must be some mistake. You told me your daughter was abducted by Sephith, sir, and I regret to inform you that—"

"She's right there!" the other man yelled. Several of his guards moved toward her and stopped when she unsheathed her daggers and fixed them with a death glare.

"Oh." Mayor Killian, who had made a big deal of announcing that "the Saviors of East Newbrook" would sleep and eat for free from there on out, looked both relieved and confused. On the one hand, he didn't have to tell Mayor Hausen that his daughter was a mindless husk left by Sephith.

On the other hand, he didn't have the faintest idea what was going on.

"Sir," he attempted after a pause, "that woman is one of the saviors of our valley. She participated in slaying the vile wizard Sephith."

"Because she was abducted by this man," her father said dramatically.

"I was not," Zaara protested.

"She arrived some time before the gentleman," Mayor Killian interjected.

"You sent me to rescue her," Justin added.

"And did she return?" Mayor Hausen asked. "No. My only daughter, my darling child, was taken from her betrothal to Lord Howard and forced into a life of banditry."

"Lord Howard?" she demanded, outraged. "I told you I would never marry him. I told you I would rather eat cow dung than marry him. I told you I would rather—"

"Now, out of a fear of her captor, she lies," the man said dramatically.

"This is ridiculous," Justin stated to no one in particular.

"I don't want to go back," she said dangerously.

"Shh, my darling, that man can't hurt you anymore. Come over here." He beckoned.

"No," she said flatly. "I wasn't abducted and you sent several adventurers to their deaths under false pretenses. I came to free East Newbrook from Sephith—which you should have done yourself, except you—"

Something hard struck Justin on the back of the head and he fell as stars burst through his vision. By the time he came to, his wrists were bound with rope and Zaara was yelling something. The two mayors were engaged in a hissed argument while Mayor Hausen's lackeys held Justin up, his head lolling.

"Fine," Killian said eventually. He turned and cleared his throat. "Justin Williams, you stand accused of abducting Zaara Hausen and forcing her into a life of banditry. As mayor of East Newbrook, I will allow both you and Mayor Hausen to make your arguments to a jury, who will then decide the truth of the matter."

"What about my arguments?" Zaara asked dangerously.

"Both sides will be permitted to call you as a witness," he answered wearily. "Master Williams, I must ask you to accompany me to the town jail."

"My father will have his thugs kidnap me the second Justin is in there," she said. She held one of her daggers up. "Although I would warn them strongly against trying."

"You will come with us and stay in my house," Mayor Killian said. When her father began to protest, he held a hand up. "Sir, you have invoked the law of this town. That law states that I may take any and all measures to ensure a fair trial. Mistress Hausen, Master Williams, come with me if you please. Mayor Hausen, the innkeeper will see to your needs."

The two friends walked out of the inn, both struck mute. Justin didn't know when to start speaking.

Zaara did, however. As Killian handed him over to the guards, she darted between them to give him a hug.

"I'll get you out of this," she told him fiercely. "I promise."

"I…" He nodded. "Thank you." This seemed like a bad dream and he knew he didn't want to spend several years of recovery time in prison, even if it wasn't real.

"I promise," she repeated. She looked over her shoulder at him as she left with Mayor Killian.

"Sir," one of the guards said awkwardly. He clearly didn't want to clap the Savior of East Newbrook in irons but he had his orders. "This way, please."

With a sigh, he set off for the jail.

The prison hadn't been structurally well-maintained, enough so that he was fairly sure he could bludgeon his way out if he needed to. That was comforting, he thought as the guards put irons on him.

"Hey," Justin said.

They stopped and looked nervous.

"You know Zaara would have slit my throat if I tried to abduct her, right?" he asked. "I wouldn't take my chances with that one."

The men guffawed at that. It was better than the plea for mercy they'd expected, and they left with a nod to him.

He leaned back and tried to remain positive. No matter what strings Mayor Hausen could pull, he was relatively sure he could get out of there one way or another. He had begun to try to decide where to sleep when one of the piles of straw moved.

Reflexively, he yelled. The pile of straw did too. Footsteps sounded as the guards pounded back.

"Is everything all right?" one of them asked.

"Yes. I, uh…" He wanted to sink through the floor with embarrassment. "I didn't realize there was anyone else in here. I, uh—oh shit. Never mind. Nothing." While apologizing to the man in the pile of straw, he had noticed that he had only one arm.

The guards backed away, clearly trying not to laugh, and he turned to see the man looking equally amused.

"If there's a bright spot to having lost an arm," he told Justin, "it's people making that face when they notice."

He shook his head and sat quickly. He couldn't tell if he should apologize or not, all things considered. "How did you get here?" he asked finally.

"Old misdeeds," the man said poetically. "I used to be a bandit, once upon a time. I worked for a man named Hildon."

"Oh, Hildon." He smiled. "A brave man."

"Diff'rent Hildon," the man said. "Must be. No good bandit is brave and Hildon's a good bandit. He's as craven as they come."

Justin resolved to share this assessment with the leader in question at some point. "And what's your name?"

"Ah. Batholemew." The man nodded. "Anyway, I ran off to Insea for the tournament, lost my arm…came back here, and had the bad luck to be recognized while trying to get back to Hildon."

"Ah," he said. His mind caught up with him a moment later. "Insea?"

"That's the nearest city," his cellmate told him. "The king's city. Where are you from that you don't know that?"

"That's a long story."

"Well." Batholemew looked around the cell. "I think we have the time."

The AI laughed in the background.

Justin waved airily. "I'm not in the mood to tell my stories tonight. Tell me about the tournament—and the city. Let's say I'm from quite far away. Assume I know nothing."

"Anyone can assume that," the AI told him.

He rolled his eyes and decided he wouldn't miss this AI. Or maybe he would, but only a little. Still, it would be nice to not have it interrupt otherwise normal conversations.

"Insea has everything," Batholemew said, his face aglow. "It's on the River Gelatia, so there's an abundance of trade. If you want silks, you can buy 'em. Do you want spices, animals, glass, paper? Anything, you can get it in Insea. That's if you have coin, of course, but coin is like water there. It comes and goes. A man can be a noble one day, a pauper the next, and a famous poet the day after that. I never met a people more used to the way the wheel turns."

"Huh." He leaned back and considered this. "What does it look like? Paint me a picture."

"I was right-handed," Batholemew quipped. He gave a bark of laughter at Justin's look. "You're going to hear all the jokes—I don't get an audience for 'em often."

"Right." He grinned. "Well, work them all in, I guess. I should warn you, though, I've traveled with a dwarf. I might have to retaliate with bad jokes of my own."

"Ha. Well, you asked about Insea. It's a strange city built long ago by the fae. It'll never fall to ruin, no, but it's not…made for humans if you catch my meaning. Everything's a little too tall. It's carved from a block of stone."

Justin nodded, then frowned. "Wait, all of it? From one block?"

"That's the way of it. There's not a crack or a join in the whole city. Streets, houses, castle, arena, everything. Some say Insea's where the dwarves learned to work with stone—that they were the apprentices of the fae and they left to find their own mines beneath the mountains."

He gaped. His mind couldn't picture it at all.

"The stone's beautiful," Batholemew told him. "Some of its milky-pale, some's golden like the first light at dawn, and some's almost a rose color. You stop seeing it after a while, but I still dream of it, even now."

"That sounds beautiful," he murmured.

"Oh, it is."

"And the tournament?"

"Oh, the tournament." The man rested his head on the stone, a smile on his lips. "A chance at the greatest treasure in the world."

Justin sat bolt upright. "Treasure?"

"Oh, yes. The king throws his treasure stores open for the tournament and the winner of the grand prize takes home something of incredible worth. Of course, they usually sell it to one of the nobles, but ten thousand gold in your pocket is nothing small." He raised an eyebrow.

"What's the prize this time?" he asked.

"Oh, no one ever knows ahead of time. The last one I was there for, it was a rope of the most beautiful pearls you ever saw. My friend had a glimpse and he said each was the size of a strawberry and a deep purple like dusk. The time before that…ah, yes, a golden statue of one of the elven gods with diamonds for eyes. No one has ever been disappointed, I tell you."

"Ah." He leaned back and his mind rolled furiously. "I wonder what the king has in his storerooms."

"No one knows that," Batholemew said with a laugh, "least of all the king. Some say the whole tournament was devised so he could clean out the storerooms and get some goodwill in the process. It helps the city, too—people come from all over to see the tournament and fight. The inns are always busy and so are the blacksmiths. Poets come to sing songs about the contestants. There was a song about me, you know."

"Really?" He smiled.

"Yes. Well…it said there was one contestant with a nose like a turnip." His cellmate shrugged good-naturedly. "But I was in a song. Everyone knew who I was that week."

Justin tried not to laugh too hard. "You know, I used to study dwarven artifacts."

"Oh, the king has those for certain," the man said emphatically. "Remember when I said people think Insea was partly built by dwarves? Well, one of the reasons why they think that is because there are so many dwarven artifacts there. A whole academy is devoted to them, and rooms in the palace. Not that I, er…"

"Ever considered robbing them?" he asked slyly.

Batholemew cleared his throat and didn't answer.

He laughed. "Well, then. A palace full of dwarven artifacts. A tournament with the king's storerooms thrown open. Huh."

"Are you thinking of seeking your fortune?" The man looked critically at him, then into the area beyond the cell. "Is that your sword and armor?"

"Yes."

"You might have a chance, then." He sounded doubtful. "Of course, that's if you ever get out of here. What landed you in this mess?"

His irritation returned and he blew out a breath. "Did you hear about the people who defeated Sephith?"

"Ah, yes. It doesn't make much difference to me in here, of course, but everyone else seemed happy."

"Well, one of them is a woman named Zaara. She's the daughter of the mayor in Riverbend, beyond the valley. Another one of them…uh, is me."

"Oho!" Batholemew chortled. "And you got her in the family way, did you? Piece of advice, friend, get the deed done and marry her. There's a sight worse you could do than an adventurin' lass."

"I did not get her in the family way," he protested, mortified. "No, her father didn't want to admit to anyone that she ran away to kill Sephith, so he came here and accused me of kidnapping her. I didn't, everyone knows that, but he got Mayor Killian to arrange a trial."

"Then it don't matter much who knows what, do it?" the man asked.

"Wait. What?"

"A trial's a place for the rich to grandstand," his cellmate explained. "Everyone knows that. You'll spend the rest of your life in a cell like mine, you wait and see."

"No. No, I need to get to Insea. I need to get to the king's storerooms." Panic began to rise and cloud his thoughts.

"That's as may be, boyo, but if her father wants you locked up… well, you just wait, that's where you'll be."

Justin lowered his head into his hands. The future, which had looked so bright only a moment before, now seemed insurmountable.

"Cheer up," Batholemew told him.

"Oh? Why?"

"I still have a good few jokes about having only one arm. You haven't even heard the best one yet."

"This is it," he said, the words muffled. "I've survived a car crash and a coma and this is what will kill me."

CHAPTER SIXTY-FIVE

Mary was eating a very belated breakfast when DuBois found her in the seating area.

"Mrs. Williams." He smiled broadly at her.

She swallowed her mouthful of eggs. "Hello, Doctor. It's wonderful to see you in these new facilities. Your team looks very engaged and happy."

"Yes, yes, they're remarkable." He looked at the group. Some of them were chatting but they all did so as they worked. They looked as focused on their diagrams and experiments as the members of the PIVOT team did on their computers. "I wanted to ask you if you've had any word from the young woman you mentioned—Tina."

Her smile disappeared.

"She's not injured, is she?" the doctor asked. His mind seemed to spin off in another direction. "Hmm, if she initially seemed fine but now she's having symptoms, would it make sense to…no, we didn't test for that. Too much of a risk—"

"No, no." She shook her head. "I'm sure—I have no reason to think she's ill, no. I haven't…called her yet."

DuBois gaped at her. "You haven't called her yet?" he asked faintly.

"No." Mary felt a deep, squirming sense of guilt.

"Because?" He shook his head. "Mrs. Williams, Justin's recovery may require someone in his age group. I truly believe that linking Tina specifically could help him become ready to wake up."

She made no reply. Instead, she looked at her eggs, although she no longer wanted to eat them.

"Mrs. Williams." He sat down next to her. "It is clear that you do not want to contact this woman. Could I ask why?"

"Yes, why wouldn't I want to call her?" She flared in response. "The woman whose reckless driving put my son in a coma, the woman who brought all this down on us—why wouldn't I want to talk to her? Why wouldn't I want to call and explain that I couldn't help him but she could?"

The words came out before she had time to stop them and she froze. Mortified, she focused stiffly on her hands.

"Ah," DuBois said softly.

Mary pressed her hands against her eyes. She didn't trust her voice in that moment.

"So, perhaps…" he said. His words trailed off thoughtfully. "It is as if, in order to save Justin, I had to rely on those who blacklisted my treatment. I think I would be angry about that." He patted her knee absently. "And yet, I think you know what you would tell me, even if the patient were not Justin. You would tell me that my goal—to save my patient's life—was more important than my anger."

She put her hands down. This was perhaps the least cutting way he could have said this, and she was grateful. She managed to nod.

"I will," she said. "I hate that I hurt him and she could be the one to help."

"If you blame her for his condition, why shouldn't she be the one to make it right?" DuBois asked rhetorically.

"Well…that's a good point. But…" She reached for his arm as he stood. "I want to go into the game. I want to help. I can't simply watch, doctor. I *can't*."

"Mrs. Williams," he told her gently. "I told you that—"

"I wouldn't have to see him, would I?" she persisted. "Maybe there's another way I could help him. Some way that he couldn't see me and wouldn't know I was there but I would know I helped. I could be helping—smooth the way."

DuBois considered this. "You know, I think there might be a way," he said finally. "Yes. Yes, I think so. I'd have to run it past the team, of course."

"Run what past us?" Amber asked.

Mary now vaguely remembered all of them heading out for lunch—goodness, her breakfast *was* late—and they had already returned. The other woman held a bowl of noodles that smelled amazing, and Nick munched on a wrap of some kind. Jacob set a sandwich awkwardly beside her plate of eggs. He had clearly gone out of his way to get her something to eat as well. She gave him a nod of thanks.

The doctor gave them an overview of her request and his idea. To her surprise, it was quite an interesting one.

"Remember," he said, "we have the option to have each of our patients exist in the same world. Each would know of the deeds of the others, although they might not know those people were actual people."

"Are you up for this?" Amber asked her. "Because I think it sounds seriously cool. You could be a crazy legend—the death sorceress who trained Zaara the Great. Or whatever she ends up being called."

Mary smiled. "A legendary sorceress. I do like that. I'm not sure about the death part, though." She frowned. "But…how will I get her away from Justin?"

"Well," Nick said, "we may have an opening. Give us a few. Well, maybe a half an hour or…I'm not sure how long it will take. Sorry."

"That won't be a problem," DuBois said. "Mrs. Williams has a call to make." He gave her a surprisingly steely look.

"Fine," she muttered. She scooped a last mouthful of eggs into her mouth. "I'll call Tina. But I won't be happy about it."

"Okay," he responded serenely.

Tina realized she'd stared at the book in her lap for forty-five minutes without reading a single word. With a sigh, she closed it and put it beside her on the porch swing.

"Are you all right, dear?" her mother called from inside the house.

She shut her eyes and prayed for patience. Her parents had already been almost unbearable before the accident and now, they took it to an unimaginable level. Her father was absolutely furious that she'd had the accident and her mother coddled her as if she were a baby.

Frankly, she preferred her father's company at this point. However angry he was at her, it couldn't come close to how angry she was at herself—and it felt good, actually, to have someone hate her. She still hadn't heard from Mary Williams, and the thought of how angry and heartbroken Justin's parents must be tore her up inside.

All she wanted was for them to yell at her and say all the things she thought about herself.

She didn't expect her phone to ring and lurched into an ungainly sideways leap to stare nervously at the device as if it might bite her. The number was unfamiliar but it was from the area, which meant a glimmer of a chance that the impossible might have happened.

Tina's heart pounded. She picked the phone up and was shaking so hard, she had to make several attempts to answer. "Hello?"

"Hello?" It was a woman's voice. "Is this Tina?"

"Yes?"

A long pause followed. "This is Mary Williams," the woman said.

"Oh, my God," she whispered. "Oh, my God. Oh, Mrs. Williams, I am so sorry. I am so sorry, you cannot imagine—"

"I know." The woman's voice sounded strained. "Please do not apologize to me. It is Justin who deserves your apology."

Tears came to her eyes and she squeezed them shut. "I know," she managed to say in a croak. "And someday I hope I can—"

"Yes." Mary sounded brisk now. "Justin's doctors have requested to meet you. They believe you may be able to aid in his recovery."

"They do?" She stood up so fast she got a head rush. "Oh, my—"

"God, yes." The caller's tone was now impatient.

"How could I help?"

"The doctors can explain that," she said finally after another long pause.

Tina briefly considered the possibility that she was planning to murder her. Mary must have been thinking the same thing because a moment later she said, "Please understand, there are concerns around patient privacy. Justin's doctor is a man named Jean-Luc DuBois."

"Like Captain Picard?" Tina asked excitedly.

"What?"

"Jean-Luc. Never mind. Um. Yes, I can help. What hospital is Justin at?"

Another pause made her feel a little uneasy. "Ms. Castro, I need to know that you will share this address with no one," Mary said sternly.

The murder vibes had begun to increase alarmingly now. "Uh… maybe it would be best if I didn't come."

"Tina," the woman said pleasantly, "my son is in a coma because you were driving ninety miles per hour on a residential street. If I could, I would rather live the rest of my life without ever hearing from you or acknowledging you again. Trust me when I say I did not respond well to the doctor's suggestion to bring you in. However, they believe your presence might help Justin wake up, and I am determined to do whatever it takes to make that happen. Even allowing you near him again."

"See," Tina said, "that sounds a hell of a lot more honest. I'll be there."

"Really."

"Yeah. And for the record, when he comes out of that coma—"

"I think I know where you're going, Ms. Castro, and I warn you not to say anything of the sort," Mary said crisply. "I will thank you to take responsibility for your own actions before you criticize mine. When, God willing, Justin is out of his coma, I may be willing to discuss your opinions. Not before."

"Right." She swallowed. "Right. So, you need me to come somewhere."

"Yes. The medical staff would like you to stay for several days to… speak to Justin. The head of the facility will contact you and send a car. Her name is Anna Price. And Tina, you cannot imagine how much it pains me to say this—thank you."

Mary hung up and the young woman smiled ruefully at the phone. The chances that she would be murdered were slim to none, she estimated. She could tell from the woman's tone that the thank you had been hard to say and she would never have said it if she didn't have to.

Tina retrieved her phone and her book and headed inside to pack. When she passed her father on the stairs, he glowered at the sight of her smile.

"What do you have to be happy about?"

She looked at him, unperturbed by his belligerence. "I might be able to fix it," she said finally. "Mrs. Williams called me to come see Justin. I might be able to fix this."

CHAPTER SIXTY-SIX

The clang of the jail door woke Justin the next morning. He sat, winced at the pain in his neck, and spat out a piece of straw that had lodged in his mouth.

Straw from the floor that certainly wasn't anywhere near clean. He looked at it, winced again, and hoped his brain wasn't powerful enough to make him sick based on the reasonable certainty of fake microbes.

Multiple footsteps approached and his heart began to pound—all the more when the group reached his cell and he saw who it was. Mayor Killian looked deeply apologetic to see him on the floor and covered with dirt, Mayor Hausen looked triumphant, and Zaara looked furious.

Screw the crick in his neck. He scrambled to his feet and brushed himself off as quickly as he could.

"Master Williams," Killian said. He smiled at him now. "I am relieved to say that the charges against you are being dropped."

"Yeah, well—wait, what?" He broke off in confusion. "Eh?"

The man looked at Mayor Hausen. On his other side, Zaara folded her arms and glared at her father.

Hausen looked at them both and a somewhat sulky look settled on his face. He cleared his throat and sighed. "Hrm. Yes. Due to several factors, I have—"

"Ahem," his daughter interrupted meaningfully.

Justin, suddenly entertained, looked at him.

Her father was clearly not happy at this state of affairs. He sighed again and gave him a pained look that was clearly supposed to be somewhere in the realm of friendly. "After speaking to my daughter," he said reluctantly, "it seems I was, er…"

"Father." Her voice dripped with poison.

"It seems I was…wrong." The last word seemed to be dragged out of him.

"And how were you wrong?" she asked sweetly.

He darted her an annoyed glance before he cleared his throat and focused on the prisoner. "Zaara has informed me that she left Riverbend of her own free will and remained here in East Newbrook with…you…in order to help the people of this town escape another of Sephith's lackeys. As my daughter assures me that she did all of this without duress—and, importantly, as she is unharmed—I have decided to drop the charges against you." His gaze bored into him.

Against his better judgement, he felt a stirring of sympathy for the man. Sending a rescue party after Zaara under false pretenses had been wrong, but the man had come to find his daughter—a woman he was afraid for after she didn't come home. He wasn't lying when he said that the most important thing to him was her safety.

"Thank you," Justin said as courteously as he could.

"Father," she said. "The matter of the mission."

Mayor Hausen gave her a stricken look. When he looked back, his shoulders were faintly hunched. He cleared his throat. "Ahem. Yes. As a condition of your defeat of Sephith and my daughter's rescue, two things were promised. First, the freedom of Lyle Stout and second, ten gold coins were promised. I regret to inform you that the coffers of Riverbend will only support…five."

"I'll take three," Justin said promptly.

"I—wait, what?" Hausen paused, confused. Beside him, Zaara

frowned, Mayor Killian had his head tilted to the side quizzically, and the guards stared with their mouths open.

"I won't bankrupt the people of Riverbend," he said. "Three of us worked together to defeat Sephith—myself, Lyle Stout, and Zaara. Each of us will take one gold coin in recognition of this effort. I would forgo payment entirely, but please understand that my armor is my livelihood."

Hausen, now with no moral high ground to speak of, cast about for something to say. At last, he managed to speak. "That is very generous, Master Williams. There being no objection from the members of your team—"

"None," Zaara said. "I'll speak for Lyle."

"Um," the man said. "In that case, your money will be provided to you at the inn before my daughter and I leave for Riverbend."

Justin's smile slid off his face. He looked at her and saw her regret. She gave him a sad smile and a nod and he now understood that his freedom hadn't come only from facts but from a bargain.

"Now that Sephith is defeated," her father said, "Zaara has no reason to stay in East Newbrook." He looked meaningfully at her. There was no malice in his voice and instead, Justin could hear the echoes of fear.

He understood but he still hated it.

"There's still a great deal more injustice in the world," he reminded them.

"Yes," Zaara said. "My father and I have agreed that, in the future, I will inform him of my plans to fight against individuals like Sephith. He will help me assemble a team so he knows I am not fighting alone." She gave him a half-hearted smile. "I don't suppose you have a pressing injustice to fight now—"

"Zaara," Mayor Hausen said warningly.

"I'm joking," she said. "Of course. I know Mother and Yannick would be glad to see me."

"And have you home, Zaara." There was genuine softness in the mayor's voice. "All of us would be happy to have you home."

Justin swallowed and looked away.

"Yes," she said softly. She cleared her throat. "Justin, I'll…I'll be at the inn to say goodbye to you and Lyle." She left, her footsteps a touch too fast, and her father followed.

"Master Williams." Mayor Killian sounded relieved. "The guards will remove your irons. I hope there are no hard feelings."

He gave him a hard look. "What would you have done if he had insisted on the trial?"

The man had clearly considered this already. "You would have been convicted," he said.

Stunned, he gaped at him. Killian didn't sound sorry at all.

"And then," the man continued, "regrettably, due to an unfortunate clerical error, you would have been released soon after Mayor Hausen returned to Riverbend." He gave him a smile and a nod before he left.

"Huh," he said.

"Don't worry," the guard said. "If he hadn't done the right thing, we would have."

"What must it be like to have friends?" Batholemew asked rhetorically from the corner.

"Shut up," the guard said. "He saved us from Sephith. You robbed my aunt at knifepoint."

"Details." The prisoner made a show of going back to sleep but opened one eye to look at him. "Don't forget what I said about Insea."

"I haven't," he assured him. "Good luck, Batholemew."

Zaara was waiting for him in the inn. Three mugs of beer were on the table in front of her, laid out as if for her, Justin, and Lyle, but she had drunk all of them already. She wiped the back of her hand across her mouth as he sat.

"Sorry. I don't want to go back."

"So don't," Justin said. He was surprised by how urgent his tone was. He leaned forward. "We'll go right now. Grab Lyle and sneak out the back. We can disappear."

She shook her head sadly. "I thought of that. Trust me, I considered it." She hiccupped and swayed slightly.

"New plan," he said, "we hide in the basement while you sleep that beer off."

"I don't want to do that to my family." She managed a shaky laugh. "My father may be an ass, but he was really worried about me. My mother was too. My brother...well, who knows." She gave a half-smile. "I'm joking. He and I get along fine. I made Father agree to let him marry Annika when we get home."

He frowned and thought back. "The barmaid," he said as he remembered. "That's right. She said the mayor thought his son could do better than a barmaid."

Zaara raised the empty glass to him with a wry smile. "That's my dear father, all right. But he wants Yannick to be mayor after him, so there's no reason for him to marry outside the village. And he would do well as mayor, he really would. He—" She broke off. "You don't care."

"I care," he said quietly.

To his surprise, she smiled at him. "Yeah. Yeah, I know you do. The thing is, Justin..." She steadied herself. "The thing is, you need to go home."

He wasn't sure how to respond so simply said nothing. The innkeeper set three more mugs of beer down and left quickly as if to escape the awkward silence.

"That's why you need the three keys," Zaara said. "Isn't it? You never said as much, at least not straight out, but Lyle and I both knew."

"You told Lyle about where I was from?" He groaned.

"Yes, I did. And the dwarves made those keys, Justin. They're the ones who made it so the bearer could use the door. You've heard him talk. Dwarven artifacts have power woven into them, so him knowing your goal might help him remember things he wouldn't otherwise."

"Okay, I hate to admit it, but you have a point. Still. He'll make fun of me for this, you know."

"Everyone already makes fun of you," the AI said.

"Weak," Justin muttered.

"Yeah, I think I'm losing my touch. I can do better. Hang on."

Justin sighed. To Zaara, he said, "Yes. I don't...know...that it's why

I'm finding keys, but I suspect so. I think they're tests I have to pass to show that I'm ready to go back."

Zaara studied him. "When you get back, what do you think you'll do?"

He groaned, picked up a mug of beer, and drank a few gulps. "I don't know," he admitted. "My world isn't like this one. You can't simply go out and do things to help people."

"You can't?" She sounded deeply confused. "Are you sure? But…is everyone happy? Is there no injustice there?"

"Well, no—I mean, yes, there is injustice."

"And war? Poverty?"

"Well, yes."

"So why can't you help people?" She looked like she was trying to put two and two together and failed miserably. "I'm not confused because I'm drunk, am I?"

"A drunk woman, and here I am talking about life plans and injustice," Justin said philosophically.

"Huh?"

"Nothing. Uh…in my world, you can't simply pick up a sword and go kill a wizard. Things are more complicated than that. Sometimes, injustice is in the laws or stuff like that."

Zaara shrugged. "So don't kill any wizards with swords then. We were talking about injustice, not stabbing."

He opened his mouth, closed it, and nodded. She had a point. "It's not that easy," he said finally. "You don't always know that what you're doing is the right thing. No matter what you do, someone will tell you that you hurt people."

She smiled at him. "That's not only your world, you know. There are people here who will tell you that Sephith was doing important work. He was trying to learn how to resurrect people."

"Oh." He felt a stab of regret. "And we killed him."

"Yes." Zaara took a sip of the new beer. "Exactly like he killed thousands of people trying to discover how to resurrect them afterward."

"Oh. Right."

"You have to make the best decisions you can," she told him. "Here, in your world, wherever you are. And part of why I agreed to go back…" She sighed. "Well, it was so I could help you find the last key. I didn't tell you this at the time, but when Kural asked me to be his apprentice, I said what I wanted was to help you get home. He was already looking for the key, and now he knows why. And he said I can help him. He gave me this." She withdrew an orb from a pouch at her belt. It looked like clear glass but somehow, the inside was as black as night.

The pause that followed was both awkward and heavy.

"I always knew you'd have to go back," Zaara said finally and her voice broke. "And so did you."

He cleared his throat and looked away.

Lyle saved the moment when he clapped Justin so hard on the back that the young man smacked face-first into the table. He barely managed to get the mug out of the way and picked his head up, stars dancing in front of his vision, to squint at Zaara.

"Ow," he mumbled.

"Well, ye've some dwarven skills to learn yet," Lyle said philosophically. "I can't send ye home with no manners, now can I?"

"Uh-huh." Justin rubbed his forehead. "Or the same nose, apparently."

"Good point." The dwarf sat. "Hey, who drank all the beer?"

"Surprisingly, that was Zaara." He nodded at her.

"I always knew you had it in ye," Lyle said with a nod of deep respect. "But what's this I hear about you leaving?"

"I'm going back to Riverbend," she explained. "It was one of the ways I got my father to agree to Justin's release."

"Ahhhh." The dwarf nodded. "Has anyone suggested simply making a run for it?"

"Justin did." Zaara managed a smile. "I'll go home, though. My father agreed that I can go adventuring and learn magic. I only need to not run off without telling him, and—I quote—'giving your mother a heart attack.'"

"Mothers," Lyle said. "I remember the first time I fell down a mineshaft. My mother carried on about it for days. Or so I'm told. I was asleep for most of that. Knock on the head, you understand. Still, I came out of it fine."

Justin, who had choked on his beer, nodded seriously. "Ah. Yes."

"So, where are you two going?" she asked.

"I thought perhaps Insea," he told her.

"My people's first city," the dwarf said. "Grand place. I've never seen it meself, of course. Why would we go there?"

"The tournament," he explained. "I hear the king throws his coffers open for the prizes, and he has quite a few Dwarven artifacts. I thought perhaps the third key might be there."

"O' course, there's the small matter of winning the tournament first," Lyle pointed out.

He waved a hand dismissively. "Insignificant."

"Very minor," Zaara agreed. "Hardly worth mentioning. Well, when I was on your team, of course. Now, you two are screwed."

"Now, listen here," he protested. "I've gotten out of plenty of scrapes without—well, we have good combat skills—uh…hmm."

"It's all right," she said. "Other than being quite a fine hand with knives and spells, I can distill most of my use to the group into one simple piece of advice. Don't do stupid shit."

"That's it?" he asked blankly.

"The trick is getting you to follow that advice," she explained.

"Oh. Yeah, we're screwed."

"Shpf," Lyle said eloquently. "I, for one, am well-versed in careful battle plans." He saw his companions staring at him open-mouthed and bristled. "It just so happens that the element of surprise is a good tactic—and charging at someone with yer fists gives ye the element of surprise."

"You'll die," Zaara told Justin.

"Yeah," he agreed. "Yeah, I will."

"We'll find another teammate," the dwarf said. "It'd be easier if Miss Zaara would come along with us, o' course, but if she's determined to go back to Riverbend, I won't risk my life by trying to persuade her otherwise."

"A wise choice," she said serenely. "And I'll make you two a deal. If you get to the final, I'll make sure the last key is the prize."

"What if it's not in the treasury?" Justin asked.

"I didn't say if it was in the treasury, did I?" she gave him a steely-eyed smile. "You hold your end of the bargain up, and I'll hold up mine—come hell or high water."

"Come hell or high water." He clinked his glass with hers. "Lyle?"

"'Til magma swallows us all," the dwarf said seriously.

"Dude, that's intense."

Lyle gave him a grin. "It's a shame ye won't be able to see the dwarven cities before ye leave. Ye'd have a fine time. And dwarven women…ah, let me tell ye about them."

Zaara caught his eye and gestured to indicate a luxurious beard. The two of them stifled their laugher behind their beers as he waxed poetical about the charms and talents of dwarven women, insisting that the ability to make a cast iron pot or find a chunk of ore was a valuable trait in a wife.

"'Course, ye'd have to hold up yer end of the bargain," he told Justin. "But don' worry, I'll teach ye to smelt ore an' find her a vein to mine."

"Is that a double entendre?"

"No." The dwarf sounded offended. "Get yer mind out o' the gutter, adventurer. This is a serious matter. I'm not about to let ye marry a kinswoman if ye can't find her ore to mine. Are ye crazy?"

"I…sorry." He rested his chin on his palm. "Please, go on."

Beside him, Zaara smiled as she sipped her beer. "You know," she said quietly to him and hiccupped. "If I have to leave, I'm glad I could spend another hour drinking beer with you two."

Justin watched Lyle for a moment to gauge the detail with which the dwarf explained mining techniques. "I'd say you have a good four before he's finished."

She clinked her mug against his. "Even better."

CHAPTER SIXTY-SEVEN

Anna Price did very little with her life except work—something that became clearer by the day. When Tad first saw the shower and pull-out bed in the private jet, he thought it was an incredible luxury.

Then he realized it was because she combined her travel time with her showering and sleep.

On her recommendation, he showered before taking a nap. It did, indeed, ease some of the tension and allow him to relax. He was surprised at how much wearing old, rumpled clothes had affected his mood.

The thoughts were short-lived, though, and he almost fell asleep on the way to the pull-out bed. He barely made it before passing out for the remainder of the flight, only to be woken by a gentle touch on the shoulder from the attendant.

"We'll be landing soon, sir."

"Thank you." He changed from the provided pajamas into a new suit. On the one hand, the nap had made it painfully clear how much he was behind on sleep but on the other, he could now at least function.

Kevin, one of his aides, met him at the plane with a car, a breakfast sandwich, and a very large coffee. From the taste of it, the coffee had been laced with more than one espresso shot. He ate while the other man briefed him on several routine bills that were coming up for vote.

Once he had agreed with the recommendations from the aides—or, in some cases, asked for additional research—they were almost at the senate building.

"We made sure there wouldn't be word of you coming back today," Kevin said worriedly, "but some of the reporters are bound to recognize you. Alice suggests you simply say, 'I'll give an official statement tomorrow.'"

"And what will be in that official statement?" he asked.

"I'm not sure. We thought that would give us some time to decide."

Tad felt close to despair. "Does politics always work like this?"

"Mostly," Kevin said. "It's rare that there's not a crisis of some kind. But remember, this isn't a time-sensitive crisis. The accident happened a while ago. Simply because they know something about his treatment now doesn't make it imperative for you to share details immediately."

"I know, Kevin. But thank you." He sighed as the car pulled to a stop. "Ready?"

"Absolutely, sir."

He squared his shoulders and stepped out of the car when his driver opened the door. "Thank you, Bill."

"Yes, sir. Nice to see you again."

"Same." He smiled at him. "I hope your daughter is well?"

"Yes, sir." The man's gaze flicked to the stairs, where several people were already yelling in their direction. "Would you like me to walk with you, sir?"

"No, thank you, Bill. There's no need to have coffee thrown on you this early in the morning." He sighed. Most of the people there did not look like reporters but rather like protesters. "You get out of here and I'll see if I can get any of them to throw the coffee directly into my mouth."

"An admirable goal, sir." The man's mouth twitched.

The walk up the stairs, as much as he wanted to be amused by it, was hellish. People screamed Justin's name at him, along with accusations that made his blood run cold. He was in the pocket of the gun companies, was allowing military experiments to be run on Justin, and was a terrible father who didn't care at all for his son's life or happiness. By the time he reached the doors and swept inside, his heart pounded and he wanted to snarl accusations in response.

The first person he saw, by chance, was Charles Snelling. As one of the junior members of the other party, he had been one of Tad's most vocal critics—on everything except a recent bill, where the two of them had collaborated to limit the power of pharmaceutical companies. Their sparring had always been good-natured and the brief alliance had amused them both.

Still, he was wary. "Senator." He hoped Snelling wasn't in the mood for a fight because he would most assuredly get one if he was.

The man looked past him to the door, where the last of the violent shouts died away as the barrier swung closed. His mouth tightened and he paused. "Senator Williams, believe me when I say that of all the things I may think about you, I do not believe you would ever recklessly endanger the life of your son." He cleared his throat awkwardly and offered the tentative smile of someone who attempted a risky joke. "Your opinions may generally be horseshit, but you're a good man."

Tad burst out laughing. He'd needed that and without hesitation, held his hand out for Snelling to clasp. "What do you say we shake it up next time? Go out together and confuse all of the protesters?"

Snelling nodded. "Oh, and by the way, my aides will set up a meeting later. I have a bill I'd like your support on. Or, as is more likely, your pointed comments."

"I'll do my best to oblige." He smiled and headed down the corridor.

More protesters were clustered outside his door and Kevin swept him inside before he could make out what they were saying. They'd taken the time to set it to meter and rhyme, he could tell, but he definitely tried not to know what they accused him of.

"If I hear that stupid chant one more time…" the aide muttered. He guided him into the main room. "The senator's back, everyone."

"Welcome, sir." A few of his aides waved at him.

"Good morning, everyone." He checked the clock. "Afternoon. Good afternoon. So, what's on the docket, then?"

They exchanged slightly nervous looks.

"On the way in here," Tad said conversationally as he took his seat, "I was accused of turning my son into a cyborg for the military. That has set the bar rather high for ridiculous things to say. You're probably fine."

A few of them laughed.

"We're working on your public image," Alice said and took point. "We'll work with you to draft a public statement but in the meantime, we also need to garner positive publicity for you."

"Do we?" he asked wearily. "Elections aren't for two years and I clearly won't win, so…"

She gave him a stern look. "We will have you back on track soon," she said, "but what we need is for you to not get pressured into resigning between now and then."

Tad sighed. He leaned back in his chair and nodded. "Continue."

"We've compiled a list of fundraisers and events for you to appear at," she said.

"No. Absolutely not. I didn't come here to rub shoulders with the elite, I came here to—"

"To do things like tackle child cancer?" Alice suggested delicately. She pushed a dossier down the table and the other aides passed it along. "Or, perhaps, provide technological help for farmers?" Another dossier joined the first.

He looked at them, then at the group of aides. "So that was why you were all nervous. Don't you think child cancer charities is laying it on a little thick?"

"It's a bipartisan issue," Kevin pointed out as he brought him another cup of coffee.

"It has nothing to do with any of the current bills," he protested.

"Which is another reason it's good," Alice pointed out. "There isn't any especially heated rhetoric, merely an opportunity for you to speak to donors, make a donation yourself, and be seen to give your time for a worthy purpose."

Tad sighed.

"We know you don't want to spend your time this way," Kevin said, "but Alice has done good work to compile this list. We have high rollers from all walks, including several who have backed experimental medical procedures before. Senator Yaczwinski actually used one, and she'll be at the benefit for—"

"Okay, but if so many people have backed experimental medical treatments," he interrupted wearily, "why can't we set up an interview where I explain what's going on and tell the truth? That will clear things up nicely, won't it?"

After a pause, all the aides began to snicker. Within a few seconds, every one of them was doubled over, holding their sides.

"The truth!" Kevin gasped.

"It'll clear things up," Tom agreed. "Oh, man."

Alice tried to remain calm, but she looked like she might break a rib trying not to laugh. "Um, sir." She could not seem to find words to say. "While I appreciate your…um…"

"Childlike naivete?" Kevin suggested.

The woman darted him a look before she focused on the senator. "It's risky to put out a statement before we have a good idea of what people are thinking," she explained. "Ronan and Bridget are compiling the data from calls and opinion polls, and they'll help us craft the statement for tomorrow."

"I should have known," he said and sighed. "Telling the truth was too simple and too ridiculous a plan in this town."

"Mm-hmm," she agreed.

"You know who should make a speech," Tad muttered, "is Dru Metcalfe."

"He'd only lie through his teeth," Kevin pointed out. "He's notorious. Apparently, he's worked with ninety-five percent of the senators currently here."

"And how many did he run off?" he asked bitterly. A few people shuffled their papers anxiously and he sighed. "I'm sorry. It turns out it's a little stressful waiting to find out what lie will come down the pike next."

"If we could nail Metcalfe, that would be amazing," Alice said wistfully. "It would be so on-brand for you, too—expose the corruption and show how he's swayed public opinion before. We could have you on record saying how you understand why people were so horrified —" She shook herself. "It's best to have manageable goals, though."

Tad knew a lost fight when he saw one. He pulled the dossiers close and read through them. The team had done good work, he had to admit that. They'd successfully found events that would be populated by members of both major parties, and if he could make donations at some of them, he'd gain valuable credibility.

He had come to have his actions speak for him, he thought despairingly, not his donations—and not lobbyists.

"Senator?" Alice spoke again. She was smiling slightly.

"Yes?" He frowned.

"Smear campaigns are very common," she said. "Perhaps I'm out of line, but it seems like you hold yourself responsible—as if you messed up or left an opening. Remember that no matter what you did, Metcalfe would have created a smear campaign for you. We knew when we signed on that you wouldn't be popular with lobbyists. We're not surprised to have this meeting."

He smiled at her. "Thank you." He looked around the table. "You're all more sensible than I am, then. I thought this would be smoother sailing than it has been. I thought all the drama would be in the senate chambers."

"That's merely the tip of the iceberg," Kevin said. "The very smallest, tiniest tip of a gigantic iceberg. Trust me. And you've made our jobs so much easier by not going out drinking and hiring call girls and so on. You getting your son medical care? Now, that's the type of public relations situation aides dream of."

Despite the hollow pit in his stomach, he laughed. "I never knew that bar was set so low. All right, everyone. Prep me for these events, please."

Mary paced around the tiny seating area. She was bemused by her own anxiety. On a normal day, she would be happy to not leave the house at all and the downstairs wasn't really larger than the lab. However, after being stuck near Justin's pod for weeks, she was about to climb the walls.

Tina's imminent arrival didn't help to soothe her nerves. Originally, she had seen a couple of pictures of the girl—pictures she now realized had been carefully curated by her mother to give the impression of a dutiful, obedient daughter. She had found her Facebook page, and the profile picture there clearly showed both tattoos and a certain devil-may-care attitude.

When a car door slammed outside, she stood quickly. What was she feeling? Nervousness? Anger? Hope?

Tina arrived, walking in with Anna Price, and she had a small moment of amusement at how uncomfortable the younger woman looked. She wore jeans and a hoodie, and she looked overawed by her companion's suit and the general security in the lab.

The CEO pointed to a few people and items, murmured to her, and nodded to Mary and left. She was always sure to know what was going on in her facility, but she was also ready to get back to work at a moment's notice. Mary began to wonder if the woman slept at all.

The newcomer edged closer and looked a great deal more nervous now. "Mrs. Williams. Hello. It's good to—ah, thank you for—I mean—"

It would have been nice to say something and put her out of her misery, but she didn't feel incredibly nice at that moment. She waited and offered the same pleasant smile she had once given to Tad's grandmother.

That old biddy had been a piece of work, and if she could survive that, she could certainly survive this.

"I'm sorry," Tina said finally. She looked Mary in the eyes. "I've thought about what you said—about taking responsibility for my actions before talking smack about yours."

"I'm fairly sure I understand what that means from context." She nodded. "I'm glad you're here." She managed to get the word "glad" out without her voice going crazy. "Has Ms. Price briefed you on what's happening here?"

"She said someone named Dr. DuBois would explain it," the girl said.

"That's me," the doctor said from behind Mary and made her jump. "Tina, is it?" He shook her hand. "It's very nice to meet you. To be very brief, Justin is varying between an involuntary coma and a controlled one. For the past two decades, I've studied the theory that electric stimulation of certain areas of the brain might help the brain heal itself after trauma, and the team at PIVOT has developed a technology that lets a user experience an entire virtual reality. Justin is presently immersed in a game of sorts."

Her jaw dropped. "Wait, that kind of thing is real?"

"It's new," he said. "Justin is the first patient to try it. As my employer will doubtless have explained to you, there is a great deal of confidentiality to be maintained."

She swallowed. "I…we'd seen the news coverage about the allegations. You know, the experiments you were running on Justin."

"There are news stories?" DuBois asked.

"Did you think Amber tackled that journalist for fun?" Jacob asked him. He came to shake Tina's hand. "Hi. I'm Jacob Zachary, the founder of PIVOT. My two co-founders over there are Nick and Amber. We developed the pod technology that Justin is currently using, and Dr. DuBois has helped us adapt it to the needs of a trauma patient."

"And Amber…tackles people." Tina seemed more than a little nervous.

"Only when they break in and try to steal secrets," Mary said serenely. "As you've seen, there is considerable curiosity about Justin's treatment."

"How did word of it get out at all?" the girl asked, confused.

"That's not the most important thing right now," the doctor interjected. "Come, I'll show you the lab."

He led Tina to a station to wash her hands and put booties on over her shoes before they walked into the lab itself, and the rest of the team trailed after them. They went first to the pods, where DuBois opened one that was not in use to show Tina its features.

"This headset creates the input that allows your brain to perceive the game world," he explained. "Much of the game is accomplished via the power of suggestion and allows the brain to fill in details with its own memories—the smell of flowers, for instance. We've found that senses beyond sight and sound take longer to develop in-game, but we don't have a large enough sample size to tell if that's unique to trauma patients."

She touched the inside of the pod nervously. "People are shut inside?"

"Yes," Jacob said. "But don't worry, it's not frightening. Mrs. Williams can assure you of that."

Tina looked at Mary, wide-eyed. "You did this?"

"Yes." She forced a smile. "I was the first one to interact with Justin in the game world."

"Oh, I—*oh*." Tina's eyes went even wider. "Oh, you want me to do that, don't you? You want me to go into the game. In...one of the pods." She gulped.

"Precisely," DuBois said. "The game has stimulated Justin's survival and social instincts, both of which are important pieces of restoring him to a waking state. I believe that what is most necessary now is for him to engage with a more proximal piece of his situation—someone related to the accident."

Tina suddenly looked miserable.

"He knows about the accident," Mary explained. She couldn't help but feel a little sympathetic. "We made the choice to tell him why he was there so he would understand and use caution in the game." She hesitated, but her sense of responsibility induced her to add, "He asked about you as soon as he understood where he was, and he's very glad that you're all right."

"Oh." The girl put her hand at her mouth and looked even more miserable. "He's not angry?"

"He's not angry," Jacob assured her.

"I wish he were angry," she said in a small voice.

Mary felt some of her tension ease. "Remember why you came," she told her. "It was to help. Dr. DuBois has very good instincts for this kind of thing and he believes that it will help Justin to come back to a waking state if he can interact with you."

Tina simply stared, her expression worried.

The doctor broke the tension of the moment with his usual efficiency. "Come on," he said jovially. "Let's get you into a pod and start you on the tutorial."

CHAPTER SIXTY-EIGHT

Tina's heart pounded as the lid of the pod closed over her head. She wanted to do nothing more than throw all the harnesses and electronics off her and sprint out the door. Although she had never been claustrophobic before, she sure as hell felt that way now. She would hyperventilate and they wouldn't get her out in time, she thought desperately.

In a split-second, she was outside again. A weight seemed to lift from her chest and she took a deep breath as she registered blue sky. The ground beneath her feet and the walls to either side of her were made of a translucent, pinkish stone that seemed to glow faintly. It was like something out of a dream.

Unfortunately, the nice parts of outside ended there. Pink stone or no, she was undoubtedly in a back alley. The ground was textured to look like cobblestones with grime between them. There were no birds chirping except for a few bedraggled and murderous-looking pigeons nearby, and a couple of rats gnawed at something.

"Hello," a voice said, seemingly in her head.

"Fuck!" Tina jumped and looked around. "Who was that? Where are you?"

"I'm Evy," the voice said. *"I have created this world."*

"Oh." She settled and took a breath. "Um, hi."

"Hello. Would you like a tutorial?"

"Yes. That would be very nice, thank you."

"How polite." The voice sounded pleased. *"I have someone for you to meet. He could stand to learn a thing or two about manners."*

"Uh…huh."

"First things first." Several screens popped up in midair, each with a differently colored background. One showed her in flowing robes with fireballs in each hand, another showed her in chainmail and with a sword, and the third had her in leather armor and armed with two daggers. *"How would you like to engage in combat in this game?"*

"Oooh. This is hard." Tina tried to tap her chin and failed miserably. It took a few moments of flailing wildly before she was able to control her muscles enough to do so—or whatever impulses her nerves were sending. It made her head hurt if she thought about it too hard. "Did…did you see that?"

"Yes." The AI sounded like it was laughing. *"It's very common."*

"Well, at least there's that. You know, I've always liked biker jackets. I think I'll go for the leather armor and the daggers."

"Are you sure you wouldn't like to base your choice off of combat aptitude instead of aesthetics?"

"I can shiv a bitch if I need to."

"Noted." Two old, rusted daggers appeared in her hands. *"If you would, please, 'shiv' one of the rats for me."*

"Wait, I don't get nice, pretty daggers? And I'm still wearing…what is this, a burlap sack?" She looked at herself. "Okay, answer me one thing. If I follow the tutorial, will you tell me how to get the nice armor and the really sharp daggers?"

"Yes."

"Good." Tina edged closer to one of the rats, which promptly scurried away. She sighed, circled behind it, and tiptoed closer, only for it to scurry away when she was still a few steps away. She thought for a moment, then charged at high speed.

That didn't work either.

She sank into a crouch and considered her options. She had two sheaths, one on either hip, and she put her knives away before she crept closer to the rat again. With barely a moment's thought as to how stupid she would look if this failed, she threw herself at her quarry. It darted away again, but not before she managed to grab its tail.

"Ow, fuck!" She had not expected it to hurt so much when she landed flat on her face. "Damn this game and its realism. Ow, stop biting me! Fuck." She flailed to avoid the teeth and thunked the rat on the ground, then drew her knife and stabbed it.

It was far more realistic than she'd expected and she clapped a hand over her mouth. Blood had spattered on her face.

"Oh, God," she said, her voice muffled. "Oh, I don't think I'm cut out for this. Holy shit."

"You're doing quite well," the AI said. *"You've shown creativity in your approach, and you're mastering the movement controls very—"*

"I have rat blood all over me!"

"There's also that." The AI sounded bemused. *"You know this isn't a real world, right?"*

"It looks real." Tina glowered at the rat.

"Well, if it helps, rats are carriers of disease and you're helping the citizens of this city lead happy, healthy lives. Speaking of which..." A glow appeared around her hand and the bite mark went away. *"Given that this is the tutorial, I won't let you get any debuffs."*

"Can I ask a question?" She pushed up and rotated her shoulders to work out the new bruises. "What were those numbers I saw floating up when I fought with the rat?"

"Ah. Do you see the red bar at the top of the screen? That is your health. You want to keep it from reaching zero. At present, you have seventeen of twenty health—or, as they are often referred to, hit points."

"Charming."

"You lost a point from falling and two points from the bite. Those will heal over time. You will also find that you lose points when you exert energy. However, as in the real world, the more consistently you do so, the more energy you will begin to have."

"I don't know how you're hoping to sell a video game that's like going to the gym," Tina quipped. "But, okay. I level up at things."

"Yes. For instance, watch this."

RAT SLAYER, Level 1 flashed on the screen, followed by **JOKER, Level 1**.

"Huh. Okay. So, what next?"

"Next, you kill two more rats."

"Oh, no."

How she managed to make herself kill the rats, she wasn't sure. She did it, however, and even managed to talk the AI into removing the spatters of blood, which earned her **SILVER TONGUE, Level 1**.

"Now what?" she asked.

"Now, you explore the city." The AI made the end of the alley flash for a moment. Tina could see people walking up and down a main thoroughfare with carts and market stalls. *"Don't worry, they don't bite. Most of them, anyway."*

"How reassuring," she said. She raised her eyebrows at the crowds. "Everyone is better dressed than I am."

"Yes. You will want to perform small tasks from the market board, which will give you the funds to upgrade your wardrobe. Expect some snide comments in the meantime."

"Gee, thanks." She strode to the mouth of the alley. "I don't suppose you'll tell me where the market board is, will you? Of course you won't. In fact—oh, holy shit. Justin!"

The journey to Riverbend took two days, which was about how long Zaara needed to get over the truly monstrous hangover she'd brought on herself.

Her father was not particularly amused by that. He hadn't wanted to stay in East Newbrook for another day, but her carousing had lasted for several hours and she had lost track of how many beers she had consumed.

It was enough that Lyle had been proud of her, which handily explained the hangover.

She was half-afraid that her father would go back on his word when they got home, but on the second day, when they could see Riverbend in the distance, he turned to her and said, "I know you didn't have to come back. I also know I can't keep you in Riverbend if you don't want to stay."

Half-sure that the hangover was playing tricks on her ears, she stared blankly at him. "I'm...sorry, what?"

He gave her a rueful smile. "When I got to East Newbrook and saw you drinking with those men, I wanted to think they had brainwashed you somehow. You don't understand what it was like with your mother asking me when you'd be home and trying to find a way to send people after you when they might not go if they knew you'd left on your own. And then we received word that Sephith was gone, but we still didn't know if you were okay. I arrived and saw you and I was so angry that you could joke and laugh when we were sick with worry."

Zaara stared at her hands while guilt twisted in her belly. "Father—"

"Even when you were as drunk as a dwarf in that inn, you wore your daggers better than any guard I've ever had," he said ruefully. "And I remembered you running off every chance you had when you were little. You'd climb onto the roof and leap off or escape on market day. Did you think we didn't know about your magic teacher and your sword fighting lessons? We knew but we thought it might give you enough of a taste of adventure to stay home."

She cleared her throat awkwardly.

"There's nothing I could do that would keep you in Riverbend," her father said. "I'm sure you could pick locks or burn a jail cell down— and what kind of father would I be if I trapped you?"

"Then why did you make me come home?" she burst out.

"I didn't." He looked steadily at her. "You offered, Zaara, and you drove a hard bargain and made me agree to let you go adventuring again. Do you really think you'll make a noble marriage if you're known to be a highwayman?"

Zaara shrugged.

"I think you came back because you felt bad about leaving the way you did," he guessed. "You know you have an obligation to your family. Everyone does—to their family and their town. So what I'm asking you to do is find a way to fulfill that—and not only adventuring but something that will last for your children and their children."

She had thought about those words all through her tearful reunion with her mother and an ale with her brother at the inn. For some reason, she lingered around the house, helped carry pails of water, and brushed the horses. She took a long walk around the town and greeted the people she hadn't seen in months.

Finally, she went to her room and retrieved the orb Kural had given her.

The spell to activate it was simple and he appeared soon after. He looked tired as if he had not slept since she last saw him—which, she thought, he might not have.

"Zaara." His gaze took in her surroundings. "You're home, are you?"

"Yes." She explained the situation, then added, "I think I've decided what I want to do."

"Is it, 'return to East Newbrook and be a wizard's apprentice?'" he asked hopefully. "Because, let me tell you, I could use your help."

"Oh." She thought about that for a moment. "Hmm. Maybe my plan won't work, then. I wanted to stay here and be your apprentice."

"Oh, really?" He leaned back in his chair. "Explain."

"You protected the people of East Newbrook," she began. "Everyone in the valley knew you would resolve disputes and protect them from armies, everything like that. You could heal people and make sure the crops grew well. My father spoke to me about leaving a legacy for my community, and I think this could be mine. I want to build a wizard's tower here in Riverbend and protect my people."

Kural considered this with a somber expression. "Are you sure?" he asked finally. "To be a wizard is to live for nigh on a thousand years. My mentor was over eight hundred years old when he trained me, and the woman who trained him was still living at one thousand two hundred."

"So?"

"So you will not only see your parents grow old and die, but your brother as well, and his children, and their children," he explained gently. "There is a reason so many wizards settle in a different place than where they were born. There is joy to be had in a long life and much wisdom, but there is also grief, Zaara."

"I know." She swallowed. "But I want to do this. I wanted to be your apprentice when you asked before. I've wanted to learn more sorcery for years. And…I want my name to be remembered." She colored with embarrassment. "I used to get so disgusted with my father for saying that he wanted our family to be remembered, but I want the same thing. As a wizard, I could train my successor and know that I was leaving Riverbend in good hands."

He smiled. "You're forgetting how strongly the winds of fate can blow, Zaara. I'll help you, I will—but this will not make you omnipotent. People will still make their own choices, even ruinous ones. There will still be storms and droughts and wars that are out of your control. Remember that."

Zaara nodded. "Every life has powerlessness and grief and every life has loneliness. Kural, you trained me and you know me. You know I can do this."

"I do." He nodded. "And, as it happens, I have a solution to your problem that does not require me to spend as much time teaching."

"Oh?"

"Yes. A new sorceress has arrived in Insea, a woman of some renown. I heard whispers that she is seeking the sorceress who slew Sephith."

She sat bolt upright. "Wait…really? You knew this and you didn't tell me?"

"I was waiting for you to contact me—and for more confirmation. It is clear that her search is for you and it seems, from what I hear, that she is trustworthy. Or as trustworthy as a wizard can be." Kural smiled. "So, while I confirm that, I will give you a skill that will let you train with her without leaving Riverbend and will help me keep a promise to Justin."

"Oh?" She leaned forward, interested in what he had to share.

"It's called shadow-walking," he explained. "It will let you be in another place…almost entirely. You will be able to explore the king's storerooms—"

"And look for the third key," she finished.

"Precisely." He nodded. "If it is there, I believe I can convince the master of ceremonies to make it the prize for the tournament. However, I do not have the time to search for it myself and the shadow-walking would hone your skills."

"Teach me!" Zaara bounced in her seat. "Please?"

"May I say," Kural interjected, "that a little bird told me you want to be a death sorceress and I'm not entirely sure you have the proper demeanor for that."

"I know." She rolled her eyes. "Anyway, I can't be that if I take care of everyone here. It'll only be…you know, a hobby."

"Quite a hobby to pick," he said in open amusement. "Very well. Here is the spell."

CHAPTER SIXTY-NINE

The journey to Insea involved pleasant weather and deeply unpleasant terrain. The King's Road was the only thing that made the exercise bearable, providing an evenly paved path through increasingly difficult hills. More often than not, one side of the road or both plunged into marshland or cliffs, which meant that Justin and Lyle needed to walk far into the night to find a place to rest.

The dwarf was of the opinion that the road had been made this way to ward off any invading armies, while his companion argued often—and loudly—that the road was this way because the elves couldn't take a hint when they found a site for their city.

"I bet the whole place is cursed," he said on the third day. "How much clearer a sign can you get that something doesn't want you to get to this place?"

"On the contrary, I very much want you to get there," the AI said crisply.

"What, so I leave the game?" he muttered.

"No, so you stop bitching about this damned road. On the other hand, you being gone forever does have a certain appeal."

He rolled his eyes and focused on his lunch. When he looked up, Lyle had a strange smile on his face. "What? What is it?"

"So, the city is cursed?" his friend asked.

"I'm not saying it's definitely cursed. I'm only saying it's awfully coincidental that—what? Why are you smiling like that?"

The dwarf grinned like a loon. "So, there's no reason anyone would want to go to Insea?"

He folded his arms and waited for him to explain the joke. Lyle, for his part, clearly wanted to hold out but beckoned him to follow as he climbed the next rise. The road, for most of the past day, had been a series of rolling hills that made Justin's calves ache until he had cursed the doctor, the makers of the game, and everyone involved in this all too realistic simulation.

Now, he sighed and walked to the top of the hill, fully expecting to see another twenty identical hills stretched before him. Instead, the ground sloped away and the road wound through beautiful fields and gardens until it reached the city.

"Wow." Justin exhaled an awed breath.

Insea was everything he had imagined but so beautiful it made his heart ache. He had never been one for architecture but he had to admit there was something inspiring about the way the buildings gleamed in the sunlight. Distant spires and arches, solid walls of translucent stone, and everything in the city seemed almost lit from within.

"Ye sat down for lunch too soon," Lyle said, with a grin. "I noticed just now when I was stretching me legs."

He sank into a crouch, cursed his legs again, and laughed in wonder. "This is gorgeous."

"And you wondered why they moved heaven an' earth to build a city here," the dwarf said smugly. He thought for a moment. "Well… the elves were never ones to let practicalities stand in the way of being floopy, pretty bastards, 'specially when they could get someone else to do the work for them."

"They must have paid well," he said with a laugh. "Otherwise, I don't see what the dwarves got out of it."

"A blessin' an' a curse," his companion said philosophically. "We got our hands on that gorgeous hunk of rock an' all the training we'd need to make our own cities. Since then, we've chased the dream of finding a place half as beautiful as Insea—or, Elfholt. That's what we call it."

Justin began to pack his gear up with newfound energy. "Batholemew seemed to think it was only a legend that the dwarves built it. I was joking when I mentioned them but it seems like you're sure."

"I grew up hearing tales of Elfholt," Lyle said and shouldered his pack. "A city that shone like the sun, made from the most gorgeous rock you ever saw, carved by tools and magic alike, of elven design and dwarven make. No one ever told me where it was—it's a legend to us, too. But now I've seen Insea…that's it. I knew at a glance." Wistfully, he added, "This is the first time in years I've wanted to go home. I want to show me da' this."

"You can," he told him as the road led him down the long slope toward the city. "You can go home as the hero who slew a wizard and won the tournament of Elfholt and bring your family here to live in style."

Lyle responded with an unwilling laugh. "None o' them ever knew why I wanted to leave. Dwarves don't leave. For this, though…"

"So, why'd you leave?" Justin asked.

"I went…what's it you humans say? Stir-crazy, that's it. Dwarves don't even have a word for it, see. A few leave every generation. I found that out when I did. Their families cover it up. I couldn't stay— an' I had siblings, so it's not like my parents were hard up." Lyle shrugged. "Oh, they were angry, though. Still, I wasn't the eldest, so it's not like I was s'posed to carry on the family name."

Justin tried to imagine Lyle as a family man and village elder, and his brain shorted out. "Huh."

"I reckon they might forgive me if I showed 'em Elfholt, though," Lyle said contentedly. "And, after all, I promised ye a dwarven bride."

"I told you, I need to go home." That was the most diplomatic way he could find to get out of this insane marriage plan his friend was concocting.

"Don't do yourself the disservice of leaving afore ye see dwarven women," the dwarf advised. "But, first things first. We have to win that tournament."

"Uh-huh. Yes." He tried to hide the horrified look on his face. "Yep, that's a good place to focus first."

Justin expected a huge crowd of visitors trying to gain entry to Insea and was pleasantly surprised, instead, to see the gates standing open and no guards at all. When he expressed his astonishment, his companion guffawed.

"Oh, the king's craftier than ye'd think. No one's seen him in years. Everyone knows Insea has no guards an' everyone knows it's never been conquered."

"Wait, seriously?" He couldn't imagine a place as beautiful as this—with storerooms so full that the king gave away treasure to adventurers—going unconquered. "So, is the king elven?"

"Maybe?" The dwarf shrugged. "That's the guess, anyway. No one really knows. The city never has drought or famine, no riots, the nobles are merely the families that have stayed rich for generations."

"And no one ever sees the king?" He had stopped but now hurried after Lyle. "You're seriously telling me no one is curious about this? A city that runs itself? Like…an AI?"

"Good luck explaining that one to him," it snarked.

He rolled his eyes.

The dwarf, luckily, seemed to not have noticed. "Oh, people are curious, all right. There are always a few new theories floating around. Some people say Insea is the city of the gods an' they move around here unseen an' keep people safe." He shrugged. "Me, I wasn't too interested in a place where nothin' ever goes wrong, ye ken?"

Justin, who was having dreams of living in a beautiful stone city that never got dirty and never had famine or war, suddenly felt very boring. He shook his head and followed along the boulevard, keeping an eye out for shops. The blacksmith of East Newbrook had improved his armor before he and Lyle left the town, but he'd advised him to get a new sword belt, new boots, new leathers for under the armor, and a proper shield.

There was a truly astounding amount of weaponry and armor on sale for a city that never saw war, but the multiple signs advertising tournament gear explained that.

He chuckled. "Maybe the king knows there's a war coming and the tournament is a way to make sure the populace is all trained up."

"Ye've got what it takes to be a prophet," Lyle said with grudging respect.

"A prophet?"

"Ye know, one o' those on street corners, yelling about the secret cabals an' the end times."

"Oh…where I come from, we call those conspiracy theorists. Or crackpots."

"Ha, crackpots. I like that." The dwarf looked around critically. "Business don't seem to be too good. That's interestin'."

"Not for a week," one of the shopkeepers said. He was a lithe young man with boots of deep-red leather, and he sat glumly on his stool. "Not since the sixth win for the Twins."

Lyle leaned on the man's table. He raised an eyebrow for more details as he pored over the daggers on display. "Twins?" he asked.

"Sure. Ah, you're new here." The shopkeeper clearly tried to decide whether to spill the gossip or keep his mouth shut in order to drum up more business. The first instinct won out and he huddled closer and beckoned them forward. "The Twins have won the tournament for the last six weeks. They must be as rich as the king himself by now but no one knows who they are. No noble house has claimed them and no one knows where they live or where they've put the treasures. And they always wear masks."

"A kind of Battle Royale Daft Punk," Justin mused.

Lyle and the shopkeeper stared at him.

"Nothing," he said hastily. "Go on."

"Well, anyway." The shopkeeper eased onto his stool again and shrugged expressively. "With those two winning every week, no one seems to think they can win so they don't spend money anymore. No one comes to look at my wares." He gave a theatrical sigh.

"Oh, yeah?" The dwarf gave him a smile that displayed all his teeth. "I bet ye've had to lower yer prices, then."

Justin watched, his lips twitching, as Lyle and the shopkeeper launched into a round of spirited negotiations—one invoking the power of dwarven might and the possibility of defeating the Twins to bring business back and the other insisting that if his prices were any lower, it would be highway robbery and he would starve in the gutter.

"Justin!" a voice called.

He spun, not at all sure what he expected.

Of course, what he hoped was to see Zaara again.

What he did see, however, was Tina with her Valkyrie tattoo and eyeliner. Her short nails were covered in deep-blue polish and she wore Level One clothes that reminded him vividly of his first few hours in the game. They were even covered in mud.

"Tina." Before he could react properly, she barreled into his arms for a hug.

"Oh! I'm sorry. I got alley grime on your armor." She pulled away, then frowned. "Also, running full-speed into plate armor hurts. I keep forgetting this game can do that. Wait, before you say anything, I'm fine. Your mother said to make sure to say that first and I forgot. I'm okay. I only came into the game to see you."

Justin relaxed. "Okay. Okay, you're all right, that's good." He looked to where Lyle and the shopkeeper had escalated their bargaining. The dwarf now loudly beseeched the gods to look down on "this most miserable and ill-equipped of their servants," while the shopkeeper uttered pleas to "his dearest friend" to see reason. "Uh…let's go over here."

Tina waited while they trailed away, then looked at Justin. She swallowed and looked at her feet. "Justin…I'm so sorry."

"I'm not," he said and to his surprise, he realized it was true. "Tina, seriously. I've had a chance to experience a life I would never have otherwise. I'm scared sometimes that things will go wrong and I'll die, but…this place is amazing. I was already scared all the time. I let myself retreat into my room and my games and I never did anything I could be proud of. I tried but I wasn't who I wanted to be."

She stared at him, confused. "Justin, I almost got you killed."

"I know—and, I guess, maybe don't do that again."

Her laugh sounded a little strangled.

He chuckled. "That night when we went on the date, you made me ask questions about why I lived my life the way I did. I had become used to being the disappointment and I told myself that it didn't matter what I did because my parents wouldn't ever be proud of me. The thing was, that was where I focused. I never concentrated on what would make me proud of the life I lived. Here, I've the chance to change lives." He looked around at the gorgeous city and felt something shift inside him. "And I'm looking forward to bringing that back to the real world. Our world."

<hr>

"Holy shit," Amber whispered.

She realized she and DuBois were clutching each other's hands as they stared at the monitors. For the life of her, she couldn't recall how that had happened and from his embarrassed glance, neither could he. They withdrew their hands at the same time and cleared their throats.

"Ah…" He looked around and gestured at the team. "Everyone. Come see. Come see."

At Amber's urgent wave, Nick and Jacob dashed closer from their position at another pod and the assistants crowded around.

"Oh, wow," Nick said. Mary appeared, trailing wires from her headset and haptic rig. "What's going on?"

One of the assistants answered her. "He wants to wake up. He's still healing but when he's better, he'll be ready to come home."

<hr>

Justin and Tina, both with trembling chins and unsteady voices, decided to abandon meaningful talk for the time being. After much throat-clearing and pretending to look in different directions, they settled in to watch the negotiations.

The theatrics did not disappoint. After much beating of chests and bemoaning the futures of brides who had not yet been married and children who had not yet been born, the dwarf and the shop-keeper hammered out a deal and Justin ushered Tina forward to look at the daggers. Lyle and the shopkeeper chatted like old friends as she brushed her fingers over the blades—and even cut one of her fingers.

"Ah, this set." The man pulled himself away from his discussion with Lyle. "The lady will be most pleased—"

"If you talk to her directly," she finished sweetly.

He had been looking at Justin but glanced at Tina, then at Justin, then at Tina again.

"I wanted to suggest, perhaps, something not combat-oriented. My lady does not look accustomed to the use of weapons." He clearly struggled to not mention the burlap shirt.

"I've fallen on hard times," she said and fell into LARPing with ease, "but I'll have you know that in my city, my skills are well-known and I will also make my name known in…in…"

"Insea," Justin muttered.

"In Insea," she finished. "Now, your wares have surprised me with their quality. Suppose we strike a bargain." She leaned forward. "You give me the name of a good leatherworker and the daggers at cost and in return, I will mention your name to my friends and not force you to bargain with this man again." She gestured at Lyle.

"Who is this?" the dwarf asked Justin.

"I'll explain later," he muttered. He folded his arms and looked at the shopkeeper. He was enjoying himself more than he had expected to with this exchange. "You won't get a better endorsement than hers," he said loudly. "I had to beg her to come to Insea for the tournament. For weeks, she told me it wouldn't be enough of a challenge. Only when the Twins rose to prominence did she think she had found a worthy adversary."

People had begun to gather to watch, and he had to stop talking so laughter wouldn't escape him.

To his amusement, Tina took up the thread without any prompting. "I lost my family to a warlord," she told the shopkeeper and made sure her voice carried. "It took half his mercenaries to defend him from me, and with the winnings from this tournament, I will go back and avenge my loved ones."

The people nodded and murmured.

"Now," she said and smiled magnanimously. "To win the tournament, I must have the best weapons money can buy. I have looked at many stalls, but nowhere have I seen blades so sharp as this. Surely we can strike a deal, shopkeeper."

The people of Insea clearly liked good theater. They clapped and a few sighed and murmured about the new challenger's dramatic story. The proprietor, meanwhile, settled into negotiations with goodwill, apparently viewing emotional manipulation not as an inconvenience but instead, as an essential part of a good sale.

Ten minutes later, the group was on their way with Lyle's fist weapons sharpened, Tina wearing the daggers, and Justin in possession of a new boot knife. By the time they reached the leatherworker the shopkeeper had recommended, word had already reached her. She greeted them like old friends and settled into negotiations for a full set of leathers.

"Alas, I have the most perfect set of armor," she told Tina, "but it will not be completed for two more days."

"When is the next tournament match?" Justin asked.

"Tomorrow," the woman said. "Only one team is willing to try to beat the Twins. It'll be a poor showing—the Master of Ceremonies is desperate to get more entrants, but there's only so much he can do. There's talk of an ancient treasure being unveiled and still people won't sign up."

"So a team could sign up now?" he asked urgently.

"Oh, of course." She lit up. "If the Twins win unopposed tomorrow, that's the end of the tournament. But if there are more than two teams, the top two will advance." She looked at Tina. "I have to say, it would be quite a coup to have a tournament team wearing my gear. And if you are in the top two tomorrow, I'll have time to finish the better set."

"Excellent." Justin looked at Lyle, who cracked his fingers and gave a wolfish grin. "I'll let you hammer out a price with my associate."

"Since this city was built by dwarven hands," the dwarf thundered as his companions escaped with a chortle.

"Do you think I can really get good enough to—" Tina started. She stopped when he cleared his throat meaningfully.

Two people waited for them outside the shop. They were almost identical in size and tall, and lean-muscled, although he could faintly tell that one was a woman and one was a man. Both wore their blond hair pulled back in a tight braid and wore metal masks over their face.

"Well, look who it is," the man said.

"The vagrant in burlap who says she's going to challenge us," the woman finished. She scrutinized Tina and turned to Justin. "And an adventurer with no accomplishments to his name, I'll bet."

"I defeated the wizard Sephith," Justin said and made a show of studying his nails. "But I'm sure that doesn't compare with play-fighting in an arena."

A deathly cold silence followed his words, and the crowd that had gathered to watch the confrontation held its collective breath.

"You want to challenge us?" she demanded. "Fine. Do it. It's your funeral. Wear better armor tomorrow," the woman said with another derisive look at Tina. "Make it a proper fight before you die, at least."

They strode away and the murmurs in the crowd began.

"Justin," Tina said, her voice entirely too level. "What in God's name have you signed me up for?"

"Let me tell you something about this place," he said. He gave her a grin and pitched his voice for her ears alone. "I've found that the best thing to do is team up with a dwarf who gives you no chance but to charge into battle before thinking too hard about the odds."

CHAPTER SEVENTY

Tad Williams grimaced before he straightened his shoulders, plastered a smile on his face, and strode into the fundraiser. The group of people in this room was everything he had wanted to avoid when he decided to come to Washington. They were decked out in expensive clothes and talked seriously about how much they could afford to give to cancer relief efforts—as if they didn't have thousands of dollars on their fingers, necks, and wrists.

His presence wasn't noticed immediately, which gave him time to drift and listen to the conversations.

However, he had strict instructions from his aides to mingle.

It in turn necessitated small talk. He wanted to beat his head against a wall at the thought.

"Excuse me, are you Senator Williams?" A woman spoke from a nearby group.

"Ah, yes." He looked at her and made sure his fake smile was on. Hopefully, he didn't look like a psychopath. "I don't believe we've met."

"I'm Samantha Howley-Smith." She held a hand out for a hand-shake that barely deserved the name. "I must say, it's wonderful to see you here trying to help other children."

There was no malice in her voice, only deep curiosity. His aides had drilled him on exactly what to say and how, which had seemed wise at the time. Now, however, he could see the evening stretching out like one long play and he was already weary of it.

"Families who are struggling with an illness have enough to worry about," he told Samantha seriously. "They deserve our support."

The words sickened him—not the meaning behind them, but the act—and it was even worse when everyone else nodded as if he'd said something truly profound.

"Don't bring Justin up," Kevin had instructed him. "Let them bring him up. To your face, they won't repeat the bad rumors—you can take the good spin and run with it."

"I don't want to be too familiar," the woman said now as if this weren't the entire reason she'd called him over, "but I've heard your son is also…ill. I hope he's recovering well."

He pretended not to notice the way everyone in the circle and several nearby groups had fallen silent and craned to listen.

"That is so kind of you to say," he replied and met her eyes with a smile as if he didn't want to throw his glass of wine and run screaming from the room. "With so many large issues facing us here, I didn't expect anyone to remember Justin's accident. And thank you for your kind wishes. The doctors can't give us any guarantees, of course, but his condition is stable." He nodded to her as if he couldn't tell that she was practically drooling for more details. "Now, tell me. How has childhood cancer affected you?"

From their stricken looks, no one wanted to let the conversation drift to the reason for the event.

A man cleared his throat meaningfully. "Ah, Senator—I, um…I hear your son has moved facilities. I have several constituents who have asked about securing treatment for their relatives, and I would love to know your recommendations."

It was clearly a bald-faced lie, but Tad took it and ran with it. "I don't want to derail the night, but I do want to thank you for your vote the other day on the classification changes bill. I take it your constituents called in with the same comments mine did." He smiled at the man. "Between the costs and the classification changes, I am so glad we were able to get our constituents better access to care. As for Justin, I'm afraid I can't share too many details."

Anna Price had given very clear-cut constraints on what could and could not be said about the experiment, clearly wary of over-promising on such a complex issue. Accordingly, he now said simply, "We were lucky enough to find an opening in a clinical trial. It provides all the standard care for trauma patients but with a new therapy that's been in the works for several years now. The company hopes to release preliminary results as soon as possible, but on a personal note, I can't tell you how grateful we are for Justin's medical team. They are some of the most dedicated people I've ever met. As soon as I have any details I can share, I will of course pass them to your office, Senator."

It was a long, fancy way of saying not much at all, which would make it an excellent political speech, he decided.

"If you'll excuse me," he told them. "I see the director over there and there is a matter I must discuss with him. Ms. Howley-Smith, a pleasure to meet you. Senator." He extracted himself with as much grace as he could manage and headed toward the director. Since he was there, he might as well learn about any challenges the organization faced. For all he knew, there were unique issues faced by pediatric cancer patients when it came to billing, and—Lord knew—he had experience in that area.

He didn't reach the man, however, as he bumped into someone—or, rather, someone bumped into him.

Someone he knew, unfortunately, and it took every effort to school his features into urbane recognition.

"Mr. Metcalfe," Tad said. He tried to echo the pleasant tone Mary had perfected in her youth while speaking to people she despised. "Fancy seeing you here."

"And you," the man said in the same tone. "A high-profile fundraiser isn't where I expected to see a famously anti-corruption junior senator."

"And yet," he replied and managed to hold his features in a smile in case anyone was watching, "I have the sense that you did expect to see me here—and that you contrived to bump into me."

The lobbyist looked around. He held his wine glass with practiced ease. It was only half-full but he clearly hadn't drunk from it at all. This event was all business for him. "Childhood cancer touches everyone," he said musingly. "Everyone knows of a family who lost someone, don't they? And a child, too…a completely innocent victim."

Tad felt his blood pressure begin to rise. He took a sip of wine and noticed the glass shaking in his hand. The liquid burned all the way down his throat.

Metcalfe didn't go in the direction he feared, however. He chose to slip the knife in between different ribs. "I suppose that's why you're here, isn't it? Such a nice, bipartisan issue. Give a few thousand to a children's charity, offer a few sound bites, and try to boost those poll numbers. Those abysmal poll numbers." He swirled his wine although he still didn't take a sip. "There have been calls for your resignation, you know."

"I'd take those more seriously if I didn't know where they came from," he pointed out. "At some point, you'll have to face the fact that you went way out of your way to stir trouble up where there was none—and you hardly got a good return on your investment. I'm only one senator, Mr. Metcalfe."

"Has it occurred to you that your refusal to support my employer's bill might hurt your constituents, senator?" The man gave him a smile that didn't quite reach his eyes. "You never asked what the measure was, did you? Instead, you discounted it out of hand." He looked pained. "We both said some unfortunate things. You thought I was pressuring you to do something ill-advised—a worthy worry—and I was offended by your assessment of my character. I do hate apologizing…but, please, accept mine."

"You want to apologize?" he asked him. "Go out there to where all the journalists are waiting and tell them what you've done." He didn't know where these words came from. It was the wine, probably, and his aides would not approve. "I don't want an apology, Metcalfe. I want you to undo the harm you've done and it'll never be undone if people don't know what's happened in the shadows. You're one of the best people to help because you know what's been happening." He pointed at the door. "Go. Go tell them all."

Metcalfe had gone oddly pale. He swallowed at the look in Tad's eyes.

In a moment, his face cleared. It was disturbing how calm he suddenly looked. His worry had been wiped away.

"Senator," he said, and his voice was warm and comforting. He leaned in with a smile that lit up his face. He was so inviting that he leaned in as well. He could see a new path before them in which the man could be an ally. He was smiling too when the lobbyist said, "It can still get so much worse for you. Remember that."

He left and Tad stared after him.

"Senator Williams." The director of the charity clapped him on the back. "It's good to see you. Your office confirmed your attendance at the last minute but we are so happy to have you here—are you all right, sir?"

"I, ah…" Tad shook his head. "I'm afraid I haven't slept enough lately. I'm sure you've seen many junior senators with the same look."

How he stumbled through the conversation, he didn't know, but the director seemed pleased by the donations and by his questions. When he excused himself to go to the bathroom, his head was buzzing from wine and from the sheer shock of Metcalfe's words.

It can still get so much worse for you. What kind of sociopath said something like that?

The kind who doctored photos to make it look like there was an affair, he reminded himself. The kind who stirred up protesters and journalists to call him a child murderer. He shouldn't be surprised at this point. He'd seen Metcalfe show his hand enough times.

He really should go out there again and schmooze more. Thus far, he was doing well. He'd heard a few murmurs echoing the things he told the first group he spoke to, and the director had been seen accepting a check from him. Now was his moment to resume his efforts.

The problem was that he didn't want to. He simply didn't. Fighting whispers with other whispers wasn't how he wanted to do this.

On the other hand, if Mary could try to help Justin by playing a video game—he still could not believe that video—he could make small talk for another couple of hours. He dried his hands and returned to the crowd. It helped to remind himself that he had nothing to be ashamed of. He had done the best he could for Justin and hopefully, the data would help to expand the testing. All he had to do was exude that honesty.

Grimly determined, he spent the night talking, laughing, and trying not to look at the corner, where Dru Metcalfe leaned against the wall and studied him.

Zaara was excited to learn to shadow-walk, and over the moon excited that she might become a sorceress's apprentice. She even looked forward to sneaking into the king's treasure rooms. After all, how often did you get to see something like that? Life had opened up all kinds of new possibilities.

Her ebullient mood lasted until Kural informed her she would have to wear a dress to shadow-walk in the palace. He called them robes, but she wasn't fooled. It involved considerable fabric around her legs and made it difficult to get around. How were you supposed to ride a horse, for instance?

"You won't ride a horse while shadow-walking in the palace," he said and sounded deeply amused. "I promise you that if you find any horses, you will be in the wrong place."

"I don't like dresses," she retorted indignantly. She picked at the bodice of her gown—something old and musty she'd found in a chest in her room—and shifted uncomfortably. "This fits all weird."

"And it will only barely pass for ceremonial robes, so be careful," the wizard admonished her. "The king is very strict when it comes to manners. He employs some humans, but he's not happy about it."

"The king really is an Elf?" she asked, diverted by this interesting tidbit.

"Not…exactly." Kural shook his head. "I can't explain more right now. Follow the instructions I gave you, try to stay out of sight, and see if you can find that key. I'm hoping it won't be too much of a trial."

She grumbled a goodbye and slid the scrying ball into its pouch at her waist. With that secured, she stepped into the circle she'd drawn on the floor of her room, closed her eyes, and tried to drop into the trance her mentor had taught her.

It didn't work the first few times and she opened her eyes to the same white plaster walls and the fields outside her window. The carts rumbled on the main street and the villagers called to one another over the burble of the fountain in the square.

Determined, she closed her eyes tightly again and focused. All the sounds faded and she opened her eyes to darkness. She was in a cold place with stone beneath her bare feet and took a cautious step, then another and another. With one more, she would know if she'd been successful. Holding her breath, she stepped forward and thankfully, didn't collide with the wall of her room.

She had stepped beyond her body. The thought was terrifying enough to spin her back abruptly. Her gasp sounded breathless as she wobbled, tried to recover, and tipped onto her bed with a thump. She stood quickly and sighed, told herself sternly that she was absolutely fine, and returned to the circle.

This time, she walked forward with a purpose as soon as her eyes opened in the darkness. It wasn't very long before the faint, greyish light took on a tinge of gold. A lantern, perhaps? She kept walking, thinking how strange it was to not hear her footsteps on the ground even though she could feel the chill of it.

The glow wasn't from a lantern. She must be close to the outer walls of the palace, with sunlight filtering through the carved stone walls. The stone had gone from greyish-white to golden and she traced her fingers over it. Insea was said to look like any town, only with the buildings all made from one piece of stone, but this hallway didn't look normal at all. It was almost like a tunnel. The walls were eerily smooth and the floor slightly curved everywhere.

"It won't be far to the treasure rooms," Kural had told her. "You'll know them by the sigils over the doors—a scale picked out in red magic. Most cannot see it at all."

Zaara had to focus to see the glimmers of magic in the rock, and when she did, it was almost dizzying. Insea, it turned out, was not only rock but also magic. She should have expected as much. Whether it was millions of tiny pieces of rock made into one, or one piece that had been carved by spells, she could not say. All she knew was that it was shot through with both veins, as any might be, and so many spells and sigils that her eyes almost crossed.

Luckily, the red of the scales stood out from the gold-and-white of the other spells. She hurried through the first doorway she found with the scales and stepped into utter blackness.

It was quite extraordinary. There was no door and yet when she entered, the light was utterly gone. She froze but forced herself to keep walking after a moment. It helped to remind herself that she was not a coward or a thief, and she wasn't technically there. Whatever traps there were, they surely could not hurt her.

The dark was even rather comforting. It was complete but not malicious. When she stepped out of it, she was disappointed, but only for a moment. She looked around at the landscape in amazement. Her path had taken her to the top of a mountain where wind whistled around her and rough stone chilled her feet.

A few more steps took her into a field of wildflowers, their scent intoxicating, and into a forest with moss and birds singing.

It took her too long to realize that this was the treasure and not a trap. There must be thousands of worlds there—worlds she could only pass through but the owner of this room could travel to in the blink of an eye. The king could go to any place he wanted from this room, she would bet. With a small, contented sigh, she wandered through the wildflowers, the mountains, and the darkness. When she stepped into the corridor once again, she was sad to leave.

The next room held elven artifacts that took her breath away with their beauty. She examined statues and paintings, fragments of old mosaics, musical instruments that were carved from the same pale stone as the castle, and even old dresses that looked so fragile, they might fall apart if she touched them. Necklaces and rings were laid out carefully, a profusion of gold and gems and pearls.

No key was in evidence, however.

The corridor wound sideways and she followed it as she trailed her fingers on the wall but darted into the third room when she heard someone coming. Even knowing that no one could hear her, she still held her breath while the patrol walked past. The guards did not speak and they did not look into the treasure rooms. They must patrol this route so often that they were bored with what they saw inside.

Zaara could not imagine that. She turned to look at the room and gave a huge smile. This was it, she realized. This was where the Dwarven artifacts were, and the room stretched on for ages. If the key was anywhere in this world, it was surely there.

Of course, the area was massive.

She noticed a similar way of organizing artifacts, however, and was able to narrow her search quickly. Decorated saddles were intriguing, although from the size of them, they must be for something the size of a hippopotamus. Ceremonial clothes, many of them decorated with pieces of ore and rough gems caught her attention. The other side of each one was a mirror of the design but metalwork and faceted gems winked in the light.

Zaara trailed past statues, small carved balls of stone, and pieces of furniture. Numerous paintings were displayed, but she found them disturbing. All manner of clocks created a substantial collection—not surprising, she decided, if the dwarves had settled underground. Of course they would need a novel way to tell time.

Although everything was fascinating, she didn't lose focus on her purpose. Still, she had walked almost all the way down the room before she saw what she was looking for. It lay on a pillow, a three-sided key with one prong extended. She could see where it would slot in with the other two keys, although she was fascinated to see the lock it might open.

It was there. Her relief came with a sense of sadness.

She sank to her knees and studied it. Her next task was to get this to Justin and then, he would leave.

It seemed right but was still painful. When she thought of Lyle, she knew she could send a runner to promise him a pint of ale and he'd wander to Riverbend. Kural was two days' journey away, but she could see him whenever she chose to. Everyone else she had ever known lived in Riverbend and within a few hundred yards of one another.

Justin was the first friend she'd ever had who would be entirely gone to her.

But she wouldn't be selfish. She understood his desire to go home. He had a family there who were worried about him too. Finally, she stood and turned to leave but startled when she noticed a figure standing behind her.

Zaara uttered a shriek that, thankfully, could not be heard by anyone.

Theoretically.

"I didn't mean to startle you," the woman said before she folded her hood down. "You simply seemed to be deep in thought and I did not want to disturb you."

"Ah…" For a moment, she couldn't think of anything to say but the enormity of this caught up with her. "You're Justin's mother."

"Yes," Mary said.

"You're here for the key," she guessed. She stepped aside and tried to smile. "You'll be glad to have him back in your world, won't you?"

"I will." The woman had stopped with those words and she seemed deeply sad. "We miss him, Justin's father and I. And other people. But that is not why I am here, Zaara. Justin's path home is his own. I have a different purpose."

"Oh?" She looked at the key, then at Mary. "Wait, how can you hear me? I'm not here."

The woman seemed to find this deeply amusing. "Neither am I. Don't worry. No one can hear us here. Perhaps Kural mentioned me to you—a sorceress seeking an apprentice?"

"You're…" Zaara's eyes widened. She recalled the bolt of energy Mary had launched from her hands during their escape from the bandit hideout. It was power like she'd never seen. "You're the sorceress who wants to train someone?"

"Yes." She smiled. "I have been told of your desire to protect your home. It is a noble goal and one I am sure you can accomplish, given how I saw you face danger to fight at my son's side. If you will let me, I will train you. What do you say?"

"Yes," she whispered. "Wait, but—if Justin goes home and you're still here…"

"He is trapped in this world," Mary explained. Her voice broke slightly. "I can come in and out at will."

"So he might come back too, someday."

"Someday." The woman seemed intrigued by the idea. "Yes, I suppose he might. First things first, however. You have a great deal to learn."

"Fascinating," DuBois murmured. Two empty bags of popcorn lay on the desk beside him.

"What is it?" Jacob scooched his desk chair over.

"The AI is…I don't know how to put it."

The young engineer gave him a wary look. "Tell me you're not about to say the AI is becoming sentient and about to take over the world."

"Not the second part," DuBois said. "I'm actually not sure if it's aware. I don't know how we'd be sure. I only know that in order to make the connections that lead characters to one another, it fills in the gaps between actions. It doesn't write the outlines of a story, it… dreams them."

Jacob swallowed and looked at the screen. "This isn't so good. We set this game up on the bare bones of a story that was made to be fun and engaging, not the basis of an entirely new form of intelligence."

"Like I said," the doctor cautioned, "I don't know that it's awake. I'm only saying it's…dreaming."

"Don't tell Price," he said hastily, then paused to consider. "Well…will it hurt Justin?"

"No. I've seen no indications that it would harm anyone."

"Then don't tell Price. Not yet. She'd nuke it or…use it for something." He shivered. "Let's keep this to ourselves for a while, okay?"

"Okay," DuBois said, bemused, He opened another bag of popcorn and began to munch on it. "Fascinating," he murmured again.

Mary's eyes opened to a clean white ceiling and the lid of the pod open beside her. Nick waved at her and continued to remove the electrodes.

"You're smiling," he observed. "It looks like you're still enjoying the game."

"Oh, so much." She took his hand to sit. Her muscles were a little stiff after the hours inside the machine and she stretched subtly as she held her hands and feet out for him to remove the various elements of the haptic set. An assistant shadowed him and watched with rapt attention while he placed each item of the set in its designated place. Mary smiled at the assistant, who blushed bright red and made a show of taking the equipment to be cleaned.

"They're good people," he told her in an undertone. "I don't think they, ah…know all the other stuff Diatek does."

She swung her legs over the edge of the pod and watched his face as he cleared the monitors. "I appreciate you all working with Diatek. I know you have concerns about them."

Nick sighed as he worked. He handed her a bottle of water without looking up. Finally, after she had finished it and he had done all his checks, he sighed again. "I don't get it," he admitted. "She never says what Diatek does, but it's clear it's not…warm, fuzzy, Care Bear stuff. She got into this to help families, but she also does things that would give most people nightmares? I don't get it."

Mary opened her mouth but closed it again when he waved a hand.

"I know, I know, greater good. Don't worry, I won't say anything stupid. And I've heard all the arguments. But I don't see how you can be so sure you're doing the right thing when you help some people and hurt others. And don't ask if I have an answer to how doing the soft, fuzzy thing can sometimes hurt more people, because I don't." He threw his hands up.

She laughed at that. "You're very much like Tad that way."

He looked up at her in surprise. "So…"

"So?"

"So, you don't think I'm being stupid?"

"Stupid? No." She pushed herself out of the pod and winced when her feet touched the floor. "I tell you, these pods are not made for old bodies. No, don't tie yourself in knots telling me I don't look old, you'll only hurt your brain." She patted his arm. "To go back to what you mentioned, I don't think anyone has ever answered that one definitively. The only fact to remember is that for most actions, there are those who benefit, and those who are hurt. Make sure you try to help those you've hurt."

"But when you help them, you hurt someone else," he said and pressed his fingers into his temples.

"It helps if you don't think of life as a problem to be solved once," Mary said, amused. "The world is constantly in flux. There will never be one perfect solution, Nick. You do the best you can and sometimes, it's difficult. If you believe people are hurt by your alliance with Diatek, you can take steps to change the world so those people are helped." She patted his arm in a motherly gesture. "But you don't have to find all the answers tonight. If you'll forgive me being a mother for a moment, but I think you should probably have dinner and rest for a while."

Nick laughed. "It's good to have an office mom, actually." He looked stricken. "I hope you don't mind me calling you that."

"As long as I still get to play the game, I'll be fine," Mary assured him. "Now, I'd like some dinner, even if all of you won't go."

"It's a good time to get some," Jacob agreed as he approached the pod with Amber. "Okay, everyone but the evening shift, it's time to go home and get some rest. Evening shift, how are you for food?"

Several assistants were rostered but had never yet been alone with Justin and gave nervous thumbs-up while they all avoided looking at Mary. Having seen their dedication and care—not to mention having met several of the nurses and on-call doctors at this point—she had no concerns about their presence. In fact, she was comforted by their jitters as it meant they were taking this seriously.

She and the others left down the main hallway, joking about the game. She had developed quite a friendship with Zaara. "If friendship is the right word," she said with a laugh. "Since she isn't...real."

For a split-second, she thought she caught a glance between Jacob and DuBois, but it was gone quickly and the young man said smoothly, "As you noted with Justin, part of the beauty of games like this is that the emotions they provoke are real, even if the situations aren't."

Mary nodded. She had always rolled her eyes when she saw news reports of people getting addicted to games, but she thought she could understand now. In the world of the game, she was able to see the impacts of what she did. She was able to try being someone else without having to run away to join the circus, as her grandmother would have said.

They had reached the lobby when the shouting became audible.

"Oh, fuck," Amber said. She pointed outside.

Signs were being waved and people yelled insults at the building. Her heart sank. "How did they find out where we were?" She looked over her shoulder. "Did Tina tell them?"

"No," a new voice said. Anna Price strode across the lobby. She looked as elegant as she had that morning with not a hair out of place or even a slight wrinkle in her suit. "Ms. Castro was already in the pod by the time the post was made online about the location of the laboratory. Whoever did this likely trailed one of you here." She held a hand up. "Please do not apologize. I made the conscious choice to not restrict all of you to the building." Her smile was surprisingly calm.

"Now. my car is waiting and all of us can leave together. Remember, the protesters will only shout at you. Look at the car and do not look at them. Come along."

"I'm not sure I'm ready for this," Mary said quietly.

"If you stop to think about it, you won't be," the other woman advised. She placed her hand in the small of her back and ushered her forward without ceremony. "Think of something else. Distract yourself. But keep walking."

Whatever Mary had expected, the protest was worse. The doors opened into a roar of noise. A quick scan—she shouldn't look, but she couldn't help it—showed twenty or more protesters, all shouting at her. Accusations hit her from all directions, vile things she tried not to hear but that slid under her guard anyway.

She didn't remember folding into the car, only the feeling of it lurching into motion. Shocked, she laid her head against the headrest and tried not to let tears escape from the corners of her eyes.

"They don't know what's going on," Jacob said. When she raised her head, she could see him fighting for calm. "That much is clear. I don't know what they were told—"

"That Senator Williams had allowed his son to be used for a military experiment," Anna Price said simply. "It was strongly suggested that Diatek is using Justin to pilot drones without releasing him from his coma." She shook her head slightly. "The mechanics weren't explained, of course—but that's the best way to spread a rumor. Point someone in a vague direction and let them dream up horrific things to fill in the blanks. People are always more attached to the story when they dream it up themselves."

"I can't stand this," Mary whispered. "People we know must be wondering if it's true—"

"We'll need to make a statement," the CEO said absently. An assistant who had entered the car with them began to take notes furiously. "I thought we could ride this out, but not if we're playing against lobbyists. They won't let it fade away."

The passengers fell into miserable silence before Jacob said, "You know what? Screw this. If they knew the facts and it was their family, they'd do the same thing. Mary, I've never said this, but I envy you—I wish every day that I had been able to see my grandmother recover. When this is over, people will know the truth. All that's going on right now is mud-slinging."

Price nodded at him with a smile. "Exactly correct, Mr. Zachary. And Mrs. Williams, rest assured I will not let your husband's career suffer from that mud-slinging. I've built up a reserve of favors to call in for situations exactly like this. Let me use them now."

CHAPTER SEVENTY-ONE

By silent agreement, Justin and Tina didn't talk about the accident or the outside world. Thankfully, he had innumerable stories from his brief stint in the game and the conversation flowed easily. After finding accommodation for the night, they sat outside on one of the patios and watched people wander past in the streets as they chatted.

"That's a lie," she challenged and laughed. "There's no way you stabbed yourself in the chest. Your sword is too long for that."

"No, not *my* chest, my clone's chest." He grinned. "Although…I am open to any accusations of my sword being too long."

She snorted into her beer.

"Don't you laugh. You don't know. It might be."

"Uh-huh. Wouldn't you prefer a sword that's not too short, not too long, but exactly right?"

"A Goldilocks sword?" he asked and snickered.

"That's disgusting, man. She was a little girl."

"For fuck's sake—"

"Oh, did you plan to use it on the three bears?"

He dropped his head onto the table with a thud. "I give up," he said

533

over the sound of her laughter. "No swords. No bears. And definitely no porridge."

"Yeah, that's a way to get a nasty burn. But don't let me tell you how to live your life." She tapped him on the shoulder. "By the way, is that *our* lunatic dwarf running through the crowd?"

Justin raised his head to look. "Yes. Yes, it is. Good evening, Stout. Let me buy you a beer."

"Thanks." Lyle panted and dropped into the empty seat at the table. "I could use one…after that run. Oh. Three days without a fight and I'm already a goner. I had to tell ye, though."

"Tell us what?" He signaled to the bartender for a beer.

"Skirmishes," the dwarf blustered, still panting. "It's a new thing. The Master of Ceremonies… announced it… Oh, I shouldn't run like that."

"Didn't you defeat a demon army?" Tina asked him quizzically.

"Yes." He glared at her. "Which means I'd appreciate more benefit of the doubt from you, young lady. Justin tells me ye're some kind of legendary warrior but I've not seen it yet, have I?"

"Yes. He did say that." She gave Justin a hard look as she sipped her beer. "I can only endeavor to do justice to the stories he's told."

He cleared his throat and became very interested in his beer. "So," he said brightly. "Tell us about the skirmishes."

Thankfully, Lyle was diverted. "Ah. Yes. It seems the Master of Ceremonies hasn't been able to get anyone else to challenge the Twins, has he? So he decided to pause the clock before the final round. We'll have three days of open skirmishes with no standing in the final tournament. There'll be prizes for the skirmishes—not so big but nothin' t'sneeze at, it sounds like."

"Hmm." Justin frowned. "I suppose it's a good idea. People fight, they get more confident…they decide maybe they do have a shot against the Twins…"

"And the grand tournament isn't simply a sad spectacle with a foregone conclusion," Tina finished. "Smart guy. You'd think he would simply say the previous winner couldn't compete in the next tournament or something, though."

He nodded. "On the other hand, this does give us quite an interesting opportunity. The Twins are shutting the tournament down, but the ones who finally beat them...well, they'd be legends, wouldn't they?"

"You're already a legend," she pointed out.

"Not here," Lyle said. "In New Eastbrook—"

"East Newbrook," Justin corrected.

"Whatever, it's at the ass-end of nowhere." The dwarf took his mug of beer with a muttered thanks. "That's my point. No one cares. Killed a wizard? A hundred people here say they've killed wizards."

"But we actually did," he pointed out.

"They don't know that, do they?"

He gave Tina a pleading look.

"Pics or it didn't happen," she explained in an undertone. "It's the same everywhere, Williams. The thing is, they don't have cameras here so you're shit outta luck."

Justin sighed. "Okay. Well, since no one knows any of us and Tina could use some...uh...chances to adapt to our team and communication style, why don't we enter in the skirmishes?"

"Exactly my thought," Lyle agreed. "That's why I signed us up for tomorrow morning."

"You what?" she asked.

"We should get some rest," the young man said loudly. "After all, we have to get up bright and early and make our reputations, right?"

"Justin, so help me—"

He pushed smoothly to his feet and pulled her chair out so she had to stand hurriedly. "You know you'll never feel ready," he said to her with a bright grin. "So I say we dive into the deep end."

"You listen here, you shitbag," Tina whispered sharply. She clearly tried not to laugh, but she also managed a good deadpan glare. "I went out on a date with a man who didn't come out of his room all that often, and he's the one I came here to save—not a psycho who decides to enter gladiatorial contests on a whim. Too soon?"

Justin was laughing too hard to answer. He waved his hand to the inn and tried to recover his composure. "Duly noted, Madame Rogue.

Let's all go to our rooms and you can spend the night dreaming up properly pointed nicknames for me."

"Oh, I am so ready for this." She cracked her knuckles. "Hey, knuckles crack, here! I appreciate that attention to detail."

A scant few hours later, Tina bounced anxiously in place while nerves seared through her until she couldn't tell if she would levitate or fall. The waiting area for the arena was made of the same ever-present rock, now a golden color that seemed to hold the sunlight from far above. She and the others stood on a platform of stone, which had—as far as she could tell—no pulleys or levers to make it move anywhere.

"Citizens and travelers!" The voice resounded above them in the arena, magically amplified. "For the first skirmish, I bring you something truly special—two of our finest teams from Season Three of the tournament and Insea's most intriguing newcomers. First, I bring you the team that landed the most impressive strike of Season Three, the silent assassins, the sure-footed dancers themselves—*the Yanevas!*"

The stadium erupted into wild cheers and the platform beneath her feet began to move smoothly upward. Her throat lurched.

"I wonder what a Yaneva is," Justin muttered.

"Only in Insea would they think it's good," Lyle told him. "They… let's simply say they traded on certain talents."

His companions stared expectantly at him.

"O' course, Insea remembers them as a fancy, elite infantry," the dwarf continued and gestured with his hands.

"Wait, I have so many questions," Justin said, but the Master of Ceremonies' voice echoed again, almost deafening now that the group was closer to the arena.

"If you've wondered who could possibly challenge the first team, wonder no more. We have secured a repeat performance from…*Quartzfire!*"

Lyle nodded in deep approval of this name and again, his friends exchanged baffled glances.

"Yes!" the MC announced over the sound of cheering, "the most favored team of Season Three, very cruelly whisked away from Insea to avoid spoilsports such as the tax collectors"—laughter erupted in the stadium—"has returned. They assure us they have done so legally, although we have been given very questionable names, in order to give us the showdown we all wanted so many weeks ago. Please welcome our dwarven friends, *Quartzfire!*"

The laughter continued and this time, Lyle provided an explanation. "No dwarf would call themselves that. They must be humans calling themselves dwarves to dodge taxes. It's not all that uncommon for prize-fighters and it's how we get most of our non-dwarven citizens."

"Huh." Tina looked at Justin and a smile tugged at her lips. "I guess no matter where you go, people are all the same."

He grinned in response but before he could speak, the awning over their platform slid back and sunlight poured in. The group peered upward, startled.

"Who would be a fitting match for these two champions?" the Master of Ceremonies continued. "Surely the only fitting complement to two such favorites would be an entirely new team, one poised to steal the hearts of Insea's citizens. Heroes from a far-away land, these brave fighters have defeated opponents we could only dream of. I bring you...*Sephith's Bane!*"

"Good name," Justin told Lyle as the platform slid up to show the team to the stadium. The two of them waved and Tina followed suit. "Wow, it's, uh...it's quite something to see this many people looking at me."

"Ye've fought demons," the dwarf said. "An' this intimidates ye?"

"I haven't fought demons," Tina whispered.

"Sure you have," Justin told her. "The Elder Castros."

She snorted with laughter at the mention of her parents. "Truly, soul-sucking bastards."

"What do they do with the souls?" Lyle asked, intrigued.

"You wouldn't believe me if I told you," she whispered dramatically and fixed him with a somber look. She ignored Justin's unsuccessful attempt to keep from laughing. "I am the third in my line and only I have succeeded where the others failed. Two brave heroes fell before me and became their thralls."

"Oh, well done," Justin muttered. "But, uh…don't you two think we should look at the arena?"

"Right." They snapped to attention.

The battlefield looked like no landscape Tina had ever seen. She had expected there to be barriers of some kind, all on the golden rock. Instead, magic—it could only be magic—had conjured a strange, alien landscape. Tumbled boulders were piled between stands of trees with gray bark and brilliant leaves that rustled like crystals.

She scanned the area with a small frown. "What's that?" To one side of them, a few boulders away, was one that looked subtly different. "Is that one of the supply caches? It is!" Now that she studied it more closely, she could see the little door that would open and reveal the treasure inside.

"Good work!" Justin grinned at her. "Let's get some weapons." As one of the conditions of the skirmishes, contestants could bring their own armor, minus any enchantments, but all weapons would be found inside the arena. One of the trials each team would face would be to find a cache, arm themselves, and base their fighting style on what they found.

A magical border glowed around them and the whole stadium counted down together. Despite her reservations, Tina's anticipation level increased. She'd always been the one who tried to get out of presenting and had even skipped school on days she was supposed to have recitals, much to her parents' annoyance.

This, however, was something entirely different. Her blood began to pump with unexpected vigor and she grinned as she settled into a runners' crouch.

When the horn sounded to start the match, she raced forward with her two teammates. She was light on her feet and always had been, and she was able to hurdle the boulder-strewn terrain with only one slip. Lyle caught her, she did the same for him, and they both consequently reached the cache a few steps behind Justin, who grinned smugly.

He pressed the glowing rune on the side of the false boulder, and it sprang open to display a selection of daggers.

All daggers.

"Well, good for me," Tina said, her smile broad. She also took a few vials of liquid. "What are these?"

"They give yer weapon flames—or wind powers, or water." The dwarf looked suspiciously at her. "Aren't ye a legendary warrior?"

"Where I come from," she said, "we don't use hacks like this." She picked up a blue vial. "I have to say, though, I'm interested to see what the power of water will do with daggers." She opened the vial and dipped one of the blades into it.

"Well…" Justin made sample passes with his chosen weapons. "It looks like I'll have to fight at close range. I tell you, I'll be pissed if the other teams have bows and arrows."

"Nah," she pointed out cheerfully. "If they do, you simply need to wait for them to run out of arrows."

"Very true." He held a hand out, concentrated for a moment, and blew out an annoyed breath. "No magic here. Phooey."

"Less yappin', more movin'," Lyle told them shortly. He had dipped his blades into a bottle of black liquid that Tina found disturbing. "Or haven't ye noticed that we're attractin' attention?" He nodded his head to the area of the arena behind them.

She turned to look and gulped reflexively. The other team now headed directly toward them.

In fact, she realized in sudden alarm, both of them did.

"Quick," she said to Justin. "Left or right?"

He studied their two sets of opponents quickly. "Right," he said definitively. "When we get close, follow Lyle. You'll know what I mean when it happens."

Tina nodded and the three of them leapt into action. The cache had vanished into thin air as soon as the treasures were removed, and they bounded away over rocks to meet their chosen opponents.

The three were all tall and lean, unused to the terrain but clearly warriors. Two of them could only have been brothers as they had the same eyes and tousled, dark-brown hair. The third had longer hair with a tinge of red tied in a braid, and he hung back behind the other two.

Tina decided to deal with him. He had the look of someone who waited for his buddies to start the barfight, then snuck up on you with a kidney punch once you were focused on someone else.

"Sephith's Bane is heading for combat with Quartzfire!" the Master of Ceremonies boomed. "The battle is joined immediately, a good showing from our newest team here at the Insea Arena."

She tuned the voice out and made herself focus only on their opponents. They scrutinized her openly, clearly interested to see what a short, fairly scrawny woman would bring to the match.

It'll be a surprise to you and me both, she thought and shook her head. They were close, only a few seconds away from one another, and her heart pounded. "Uh, Justin—"

Her sentence remained unfinished.

"Stoooooooooout!" Lyle yelled and increased his speed dramatically. He drew both daggers, which burst into black flames, and vaulted upward in a flash of silver and purplish-black.

He took both the brothers by surprise.

Idiots. They'd had three people advancing toward them for the express purpose of combat. What did they think would happen? Tina didn't stop to think, however. She dropped back, circled behind Justin, and noticed a path that dipped down and to the side. As her friend followed Lyle with a battle cry of his own, she lingered in her position for a moment.

As she suspected, the redhead had settled into a crouch and waited to see who would slip up and create an opening first. He was armed with a sword, which gave her pause, but there was nothing she could do about it.

She could fight him now on her terms, or she could fight later on his. And, of course, they had another team incoming.

He wasn't stupid and he hadn't reached the Finals of Season three by being unobservant. When he heard her circle behind him, his gaze zeroed in on her in a flash.

"What's up, fucker?" Tina asked. She was a little surprised at the words as it wasn't what she'd have said if she'd thought first, but they were what they were.

Amusingly, he didn't seem to know how to interpret the slang and his moment of confusion gave her time to attack. She drew her blades as she moved, threw them out to the sides to counterbalance herself, and found out abruptly exactly what it meant to have a water charm on a dagger.

The blades pulled away from her and followed the momentum of a wave before it swept back.

"Ohhhh," Tina whispered. "Oh, motherfucker, you are in so much trouble."

Without giving herself time to consider the possible outcome, she threw the blades straight up.

They yanked her along with a smooth force and allowed her to pick both feet up and punch them forward. The redhead, still trying to gauge her talents, began to raise the sword but the attempted defense was too late. She had already bowled him over and tumbled away by the time he held it in front of him. Of course, by then, he was flat on his back.

She was fairly sure she bounced to a stop. "Ow, ow, ow, fuck."

With no time to think about possible injuries, she rolled to her feet, imagined the tidepools and eddies at Bolinas Beach, and allowed her thoughts to guide her movements. She'd never fought with daggers but she'd surfed storm swells. As a result, she knew the pound and momentum of water and the sheer liquid force of it.

Once or twice, she came close to a lethal blow. Redhead McGankpants—as she had nicknamed him in her head—had a longer reach with his weapon and a wave, of course, didn't fear a sword. A blade like that would pass through water without damage in the way it wouldn't with a human head, for instance.

Things improved, however, when she let her blades be the wave. She and her adversary danced across the boulders, his gaze focused entirely on her and hers on him. Justin and Lyle could be seen moving out of the corner of her eyes, but she heard no shouts of alarm or warning.

This one was hers.

He drove forward in a sudden rush, his mouth compressed into a thin line. From what she could tell, he hated it more and more every time he stumbled or one of his blows failed to land. Now, instead of slashing down or sideways, he went into a heavy lunge and stabbed directly at her.

Tina laughed. She brought her hands together and raised them so the blades crossed and caught his. The sword twisted and spun out of his hands, the two waves of her daggers collided and swirled, and she landed hard on his chest with her blades against either side of his neck.

Pure hatred burned in his eyes as he held his hands up in surrender. His form froze, encased in magic. He had surrendered and so was out.

Tina stood and took a few steps back. Her chest heaved. She didn't know quite what to do now and she was so tired she couldn't hear the stadium.

It took a few moments for her to realize the crowd had gone silent.

She looked around. Justin and Lyle were seated on boulders, kicking their legs. Around them, each of their opponents lay frozen. Some had clearly suffered wounds, although the magic seemed to protect them against death.

"The other team reached us while you were still fighting," Justin called, "so we took care of them."

"An' ye," Lyle added in appreciation, "put on quite a show, missy!"

With a long, slow breath, she looked at the waiting crowd. A grin crept across her face and she stabbed both daggers into the sky. The spectators erupted into applause.

"Sephith's Bane wins the match!" the Master of Ceremonies shouted. "With, I must say, the best one-on-one match we've seen in quite some time. Insea, give a cheer for the champions of Match One."

He hardly needed to tell them. The audience stamped and whistled as they cheered.

"There," Justin said and hurried forward to clap her on the back. "Tina Castro, legendary warrior."

Tina laughed. The adrenaline made her shaky, but she already wanted another hit. "When can we go again?"

"That's what I like to hear," Lyle said in satisfaction. "And the answer, I'll have you know, is after a beer."

"That's what I like to hear," she told him and clanged her blade against his. The three of them moved to the dais at the end of the arena. Nearby, medics rushed to attend to the various members of other teams.

"Are you okay?" Justin asked her. "You're limping."

She panted slightly. "Yeah. Yeah, I feel great. There's slight chafing, though."

"You said, I remind you, that you wanted to choose based on aesthetics," the AI told her.

"Yeah, yeah," she muttered. "I'll go find a healer. In a city full of warriors in leather, someone must have an anti-chafing balm."

Zaara lingered in the shadow of a column and watched the winning team approach the dais. She had maintained this trance for longer than she should have and could feel her energy flagging, but she had not been able to resist the desire to see her friends.

It hadn't taken long for Justin and Lyle to find someone who fit with their team, and she clearly already had an easy rapport with both of them—as well as a fighting style Zaara had never seen in her life. She'd cheered along with the spectators in the stadium, even though she knew the other would never hear her.

There was a strange poetry to the way she moved, something natural and powerful. She wondered what it was but accepted that, of course, she would never have a chance to ask.

The team walked to the platform, where the Master of Ceremonies stood in his deep-blue robes, his arms spread. Before him were two golden bowls, one piled with coins and the other with swirling blue power—an illusion, she could see. There was nothing truly there. She narrowed her eyes and leaned closer.

"A hearty hello to our first champions!" the official cried. "Sephith's Bane is the first to choose from our new prizes. Would you like to see them?"

The crowd roared. Huge images of the two bowls flashed above them.

"Should the team desire riches, they shall have them. In the first bowl, there is a hundred gold pieces for each member of the team!"

Zaara's jaw dropped. As a throwaway prize, it was ludicrously big. The grand prize, of course, was always worth thousands—but this was only a skirmish. What else could match that gift?

"In the second bowl, however…" The Master of Ceremonies beamed broadly. "Is perhaps a greater treasure—an advantage for the winners' next match. Although neither they nor their opponents shall know what that advantage will be, I assure you it is worth having."

Zaara leaned back with an intrigued quirk to one eyebrow. An advantage. That was clever. This was an intriguing set of skirmishes. She knew which Justin would have chosen once and she now waited to see what he would do.

He didn't disappoint her. A close-headed conference with his compatriots resulted in nods, and he turned to the official with a smile.

"We choose the advantage," he called and raised a fist into the air. His voice was amplified as well. "Although the best advantage would be to have this crowd cheer us on again."

"Kiss-ass," she muttered but smiled broadly. He seemed to realize how much a crowd's favor could mean. Having ten thousand people screaming your name tended to bring confidence that nothing else could match—and certain high-profile patrons might come out of the woodwork for favorites.

Her attention, however, was caught by the Master of Ceremonies. To her surprise, when he turned away from the team, she realized how false his smile was. He was sweating and rivulets trickled into the collar of his robes, and he looked pale.

To her keen study, he didn't look like someone who basked in the glow of a successful plan but like someone who was still on the edge of failure.

The stadium began to flicker in her vision, and Zaara gritted her teeth as she brought all her energy to bear on the trance. If there was danger, she had to know about it. Justin and Lyle, as well as their new friend, might be at risk somehow.

While the crowd was focused on the winning team—who now did a victory lap around the edge of the arena—she ran through the maze of staircases and corridors and tried to find the Master of Ceremonies. She almost lost him, especially with her vision flickering, but eventually she caught sight of his robes swishing out of sight. Hastily, she checked for anyone watching and raced after him.

He didn't go far, thankfully, but into a room full of couches and refreshments nearby. That kind of careless luxury still boggled her mind, even after seeing Sephith's tower and the king's treasure rooms. The couches had gilt trim, the wine that stood freely available was better than any she'd have in her lifetime, and sugared pastries were going stale.

Her mouth watered. Next time, she would have Kural teach her how to teleport and she knew exactly where she'd come first.

On the plus side, focusing on those pastries had kept her trance strong.

The Master of Ceremonies stripped his outer robe off and dropped onto one of the couches. A clerk in plain black came to pour him wine.

"It sounds like an incredible success," the attendant said with a smile.

The official did not return the smile. He drank all the wine in a few long swallows and held out his glass again. "They like it, but what if the other teams don't stay?"

"Quartzfire and the Twins will make a good final match," the clerk said soothingly.

"Numbers have fallen." He put his head in his hands. "Adventurers are leaving. A spectacle means nothing if we aren't preparing."

That must be it, Zaara realized. They needed people there who were learning to fight. But why?

Her vision began to fade. She tried to hold it but exhaustion crept in and before she could counter it, the world tilted crazily and transformed into her bedroom. While she managed to get the scrying orb out of her pocket and onto her desk, she couldn't finish the spell to contact Kural before she slid onto the floor.

"Fuck," she said succinctly. "Well…as long as I'm lying down…"

She woke sometime later to her mentor's voice emanating from the orb. "Zaara?"

"I'm here," she said from the floor with as much dignity as she could muster. "I'm lying down."

"Not on your bed."

"No." She did not feel the need to explain at this juncture.

"Uh…huh." He cleared his throat. "So, did you find it?"

"Yes." Zaara wanted to sit but was unable to. A little irritated, she settled for waving a thumbs-up in what she hoped was his line of sight. "It's there—and I found something out about the Master of Ceremonies."

"You stayed for longer than you should have, didn't you?" Kural sounded amused. "And that's why you're so exhausted."

"Oh, like you never overextended yourself as an apprentice." She knew him. Even as a traveling magician, he'd been inclined to being reckless and constantly experimented with things.

"All the time." He laughed. "It's how we weed out the dedicated. People who always stay within guidelines and never overexert themselves usually don't have enough interest to complete the training."

"Really?" It was intriguing. "That's good to know. Anyway, the Master of Ceremonies is quite scared. One team has been winning consistently and now, other teams don't want to participate. He's started skirmish events as a way to encourage more people to compete again. I heard him say something about how it didn't matter how much of a spectacle it was if they weren't preparing, but he didn't say for what."

"Presumably, the person he spoke to already knew." Kural was silent, and she was fairly sure he chewed on his lip. "That's interesting. It gives me something to work with as well. I will persuade the Master of Ceremonies to offer the key as one of the potential prizes. Meanwhile, you take care to recover. If you can find any citrus fruit, that will help. Limes are best."

"I've only had an orange once," Zaara croaked. "They don't grow here, you know."

"Hmm. I'll see what I can do. With regard to the sorceress, I haven't heard from her—"

"She came to see me," she said and waved her arm again in the direction of the scrying orb. "I met her. It's Justin's mother!"

"The death sorceress?" He sounded highly skeptical.

"Yes. I've seen her use her power before. It was at the bandit hideout."

"That was her I felt two weeks ago?" He sounded incredulous. "Very well, then. If she found you, well enough. I'll let you rest, but before you do...hang on a moment..."

Several limes dropped out of midair and onto her stomach.

"Oof!"

"Sorry, sorry. I had to guess where you were. Eat all of those before you go to sleep. They're bitter but it will be worth it. Then get some sleep. Our next lesson will be in how to grow a lime tree in your room because I sense you'll need one."

CHAPTER SEVENTY-TWO

The winners of the match, it turned out, were given seating in a special reserved area of the stadium near the Master of Ceremonies. Refreshments were served, including overly sweet pastries that reminded Justin of baklava and some of the best wine he'd ever had.

Lyle, disgusted, went off to find beer while the other two stayed behind to watch the next match.

"So, who did we beat?" she asked as she licked sugar off her fingers.

"The one you fought was a member of Quartzfire," he told her. "He's a one-on-one champion…kind of. You saw how he tried to hang back while the other two charged so he could pick people off one by one."

"If he relies entirely on the element of surprise, he can't be shocked when it backfires," she said with a shrug.

"Well, he's good," Justin replied. "I listened to some of the servants talking, see. The thing is, he's never come up against someone who fought like you did."

"That was, er…" Tina looked embarrassed. "I probably didn't do things right."

"I couldn't watch the whole time," he said thoughtfully, "but it looked like you used your advantages and learned from your mistakes. Isn't that doing things right?"

"Justin." She sounded genuinely frustrated now. "You know what I'm trying to say. We have to win the tournament—the whole tournament—to get you the key so you can wake up. And it hangs on whether or not I can fight well enough to beat the champions who have won consecutively for six seasons straight. How will we do that?"

He decided not to tell her that he hadn't realized what she'd tried to say.

Now that he understood, he had to admit it was a valid point. He had defeated Sephith with Lyle and Zaara, but both had been trained in fighting for years. His advantage had been that he'd played video games for as long as he could remember, and it had helped that Sephith clearly wasn't prepared for three people to attack him at once.

"I'm not worried," he said. "I'm serious. One of the things I liked about you when we first met was that you were brave about trying things. You apply that to your fighting and you're scrappy—you don't let a little pain hold you back."

"What if…" Tina closed her eyes. "What if we fail and—"

"Tina, it's a game. If we fail and we don't get the key I'm looking for this way, the people running the game will find another way to get it to me."

"Oh." She looked faintly embarrassed now. "Right. I…forgot. It's hard to remember you're in a game when everything around you is so realistic." Her gaze strayed over his shoulder.

"What is it?" Justin turned to look and saw a woman in the stands look away from them hastily.

"She's watched us for a while," she told him.

"We just won the first skirmish against two champion teams," he pointed out.

"Ohhhh. I'm not all on my game today mentally, am I?"

"You also drank two glasses of wine." He grinned at her. "However, the next match is about to start so I need you to—*oh*." In the air above the stadium, the three team names had come up and one of them was the Twins. He elbowed her in the side and made her snort wine up her nose. "Focus, Castro. We're about to see the Twins in action. This is where we plan our strategy against them."

"Mmf." Tina blew her nose into a handkerchief and looked at the cloth in disgust. "Don't snort wine and baklava up your nose at the same time. That is nasty. Okay, I'll try to focus."

The center of the arena faded into black fog, only to clear a moment later to reveal a desert scene of rolling dunes. Boulders and trees studded the area, and a magical glow surrounded nine caches before it vanished. The one nearest to each team was largest and the next two were smaller.

"Were there three per team?" she asked. "I guess we'll know for next time."

Justin nodded. The Master of Ceremonies announced the three teams to the sound of cheers and boos. The Twins, unsurprisingly, elicited the most emotion from the crowd. They had a large share of passionate fans and as many who—either as failed contestants or their disappointed fans—seemed to hate them.

The official saved them for last, of course, and they came up closest to the winners' viewing section. Justin and Tina leaned forward for a better look, and out of the corner of his eye, he caught the woman watching them again. She was older than he'd first thought with gray hair, and she gave him a smile this time. He smiled in response and waved, hoping he looked enough like a gracious winner.

She didn't seem overawed, he realized.

The match started, however, and he had to direct his attention to the arena. The twins had clearly chosen their battle plan before they came up because they surged in the same direction without consulting one another and bounded over the dunes. The sand was difficult to run on but it didn't slow their headlong rush much.

What was interesting, however, was that they avoided the first cache in their singlemindedness. They sprinted to the second, yanked it open, and held a brief exchange to decide who got what. A bow and arrows and two potions, together with their deliberations, were displayed on large screens above the stadium. Justin didn't recall those from his match and guessed that they weren't visible to the contestants.

The woman—Callie, he recalled, having heard their names somewhere along the way— took the bow and arrows, along with a water potion, and her teammate Dexi chose the same black-purple potion Lyle had used and spread it directly onto his hands. He seemed to be in pain, but it didn't do any immediate or visible damage.

"Bets they're not as well armed as the other teams?" Tina asked.

"Absolutely," he said in an undertone. He leaned back as the Twins began to run again. They circled toward the middle, a dangerous strategy but one that might win them the element of surprise.

"It's reckless," she pointed out with a note of confusion.

"Not entirely." He had listened to many stories from his grandfathers, both of whom had served in the armed forces. "It's better to make a decision and stay in motion early, even without all the information, than it is to be frozen while you wait for the rest of the information to come in."

"Really?" After a moment, she nodded. "Okay, yeah. I suppose that's what I did in our match, didn't I?"

"Exactly. If you'd waited, we would have fought two teams at once while Quartzfire's assassin picked us off one by one." He gave her a fist bump. "So, thanks."

She returned the gesture. "Thank you. Don't forget you guys took on the other team all on your own. Oh, look—they're getting close."

The Twins had made a plan that was as sneaky as it was quick. They had circled in a particular way and very obviously chose to approach behind another team. Now, they attacked with absolute ruthlessness. Dexi circled again while Callie fired her bow to drive the other two toward him. His strikes were brutally quick. He struck one contestant across the face with such force that the magical barrier came up at once.

The second panicked and fell prey to another arrow.

Dexi and Callie immediately pushed into motion. What they

hadn't seen, however, was that the third team had found and looted two Grade A caches by this point.

"Ohhh, I wanna see them lose," Tina said.

"Hell yeah," Justin agreed.

They were on the edge of their seat and mutual anticipation hung in the air between them.

Unfortunately, they were disappointed. Callie and Dexi separated quickly and she circled left while he moved right. They advanced in a pincer movement and began to close. When she first sighted the other team, she gave a piercing whistle like a hawk's call and began to fire.

Cannily, she altered her positions slightly between each arrow to make it look like both of the Twins were behind the dune.

The other team pushed in too deep and hadn't realized what was happening. Their strategy—a modified leapfrog—used the rush technique to push closer and closer to her. They thought that if they only got into range, the Twins would be powerless against them.

Two of the three were felled by Dexi before they even saw him. The third must have caught something out of the corner of his eye because he turned with a gasp and a snarl. Armed with a sword, he charged his attacker but fell to an arrow.

Half the stadium sank into sulky silence while the other half erupted into cheers.

"Damn." Tina shook her head and gave a golf clap. "I don't want to admit it, but they outplayed them." She raised an eyebrow at her teammate. "And yet…"

"They make snap decisions and commit entirely," Justin said and immediately caught her train of thought. "They miss caches and are aggressive. A team that lays traps for them might make them sign their own death warrants—figuratively, of course."

"That's unfortunate," she said. "They're such jerks." She saw his look and waved her hands dismissively. "Don't you look at me like that. They aren't real. It's okay to wish they would go away."

"I suppose there's that." He grinned. "Hey, should we get a meal? I, for one, don't still want to be here when the Twins come for their refreshments."

"Good call." She stood and stretched. "Let's find Lyle and see what he thinks. Okay, I know what he thinks—he'll simply charge straight in. But we might as well talk about doing something different."

He laughed and followed her. In all honesty, he hadn't expected his two friends to get along so well but he was glad they did. He still missed Zaara, though. Sometimes, he thought of the jokes she would make or the disgusted way she would have looked at the Twins.

It was different to have Tina there but in a way he couldn't describe. He shook his head and followed as he darted a glance to where the woman who had watched them had been seated. She was gone now.

Justin frowned and followed Tina into the darkness of the stadium tunnels.

<hr>

The pod cover was removed and Anna Price opened her eyes as Jacob and Dr. DuBois removed her sensor pads. They helped her sit and the young engineer waited, clearly nervous about her assessment.

"It was surprisingly immersive," she told him. "I have to say, I enjoyed myself immensely. It was rather like I imagine the colosseum of Rome—well, in some ways."

"It still annoys me that we couldn't sell them," he told her. "As a game, I mean, because it is fun, isn't it? It's super fun. And there's so much more to the world."

"Now, tell me how the procedural generation works," Price told him. She stood and slipped her shoes on. "Wherever players are present, the game prioritizes procedural generation and banks some of it for recall and so on, yes?"

"Yes." To her surprise, he now looked nervous. "There have to be priorities, you see. Otherwise, it would be too much processing power."

This was an incredibly mundane point and one he should have expected her to understand from her previous comment. That, combined with his nerves, meant he was hiding something.

Anna considered this for a split-second. She was used to people hiding things from her. The end purpose of many of her company's contracts was not always clear, which led to obtuse requests from Defense Department officials. She was accustomed to arguing for more information, which she often needed in order to create the deliverables.

What, however, would Jacob be hiding?

She had an advantage over him and decided to use it. Rather than continue, she smiled as though she had not seen the look on his face. "Well, you're doing incredible work and I have to say, DuBois's hunch about Justin's friend seems to be accurate. They're clearly bonding. Now, as much as I've enjoyed this, I do have to return to my office. Thank you all for indulging me."

The look of relief on the young engineer's face was all the confirmation she needed.

He was definitely hiding something. The question, however, was what he could be hiding when the experiment was indisputably going well.

Price intended to find out.

***

The bells in Insea's gorgeous goldstone spire tolled midnight.

Unnoticed, Kural shadow-walked through the abandoned arena. The inner corridors and contestants' chambers were locked and guarded, but the rest of it was open to the public. A few citizens slept on the long, stone benches and others sat in huddles and conversed. Dissidents, perhaps? Amateur philosophers?

The wizard felt a pang. It had been a long time since he was a young apprentice. He had been in Junor, of course, beyond the strait, but cities tended to have the same rhythms to them. The world had seemed so open to him when he was young.

He didn't worry that Zaara would fail as a wizard, not at all. She had the talent and determination in spades. He suspected, also, that it would suit her better to stay in one place and cultivate it rather than adventure the world over. She had never been suited to life as a wanderer and had simply been stifled by her parents' expectations.

But being a wizard was a bargain no one anticipated when they made it. To live in the world so long was to grow apart from it. Once you saw the same patterns play out time and again, you began to view them all differently. A human mind behaved differently at four hundred years old than it did at twenty—or even eighty, for that matter.

For one thing, he had not expected how tired he would sometimes be of himself.

Ah, well. He quickened his pace as he reached the far side of the arena from the Master of Ceremonies' post.

The door was in Insea somewhere, and the more he read, the more sure he was that it was there in the arena, itself. He couldn't explain the certainty, though. Doors between worlds tended to be remote and well-guarded. It was bizarre that one would be there in the most well-traveled venue in the city.

With his luck, it would be in the middle of one of the tiers and marked with a hidden rune. Kural rolled his eyes. He had been all around the outside of the arena and had found nothing. Then, he had checked the entire structure for the telltale signs of hidden dwarven doors and again, had found nothing. By rights, he should have given up and gone home.

However, after four hundred years, one began to learn to follow hunches—and one's hunches got stronger and better.

He darted an annoyed look at the podium and stopped, suddenly thoughtful. It extended into the arena somewhat, and the front of it was carved in a beautiful elven pattern. It was remarkable, the wizard thought as his heart rate quickened, how much that large, rectangular panel looked like an out-of-scale door.

For a brief moment, he considered hurdling the railing to sprint across the arena. No one would stop him but he would be incredibly noteworthy—as would be the fact that his footsteps didn't make little puffs of dust. He rounded the walkway at a brisk pace instead and took the time to try to recall elven symbology.

Elves were relentless when it came to organization, which could be hellish when trying to get them to do anything spontaneous but was helpful for archeologists. If the front of the podium were the door, he would see trees on either side and the rune *trulya*, which brought protection to wayfarers.

Kural moved closer and waited for the clouds above to drift and let the moon shine through.

His instincts seemed accurate. Silver light streamed down and illuminated something.

He wasn't sure what, though, and leaned forward. Those were dwarven runes, were they not? After a hasty study of the area, he hopped the fence when no one was looking and crept closer.

Yes. The runes spoke of the edge of the mountain and the edge of the forest, the gate between the sea and the land, the desert and the oasis. They were structured to evoke trees—in a very angular, dwarven way, of course. And at the center, girded by a circle around a triangular keyhole, was the dwarven prayer for the wayfarer.

The wizard exhaled slowly with a smile. The door was there.

And he now knew how he would persuade the Master of Ceremonies.

CHAPTER SEVENTY-THREE

Amber was the first one into the office the next morning. When the door opened shortly after, she looked up to call a greeting which died on her lips when she saw who it was.

"Good morning," Anna Price said pleasantly as if she hadn't committed a faux pas. "I'm glad I caught you."

"Oh?" She took a bite of toast with the distinct feeling of someone trying to enjoy a last meal and glanced at her desk. With nothing to use as an excuse to avoid the encounter, she stood and forced a smile. "What can I do for you, Ms. Price?"

"First of all, sit and finish your breakfast." The woman grasped Jacob's office chair and wheeled it to the desk. "We'll have to talk about expectations, by the way. I'm a notorious workaholic, but I keep very strict guidelines for my employees—nothing over forty-five hours per week in the office."

"I've, uh…" Amber tried to calculate in her head.

"Last week, you spent a little over seventy hours in the office," her boss told her. "I always like to work with exact numbers. I understand there's a certain energy when a project is beginning and that you all needed to bootstrap the operation when you were on your own, but I prefer my employees—especially those in creative areas— to avoid burning out."

"Uh-huh." She could sense a trap closing.

"However, right now, I wanted to go over some of the financials."

"Oh." Thankful for something practical to do, she began to bring the spreadsheets up, then stopped. "Is there a specific problem you want to address?"

Price merely raised an eyebrow.

She sighed. "Look, I'm not an accountant. I did read up on standard practices and I left a ton of notes, but I'll be honest, I wouldn't be surprised if I classified something incorrectly. Whatever your accounting team has asked about, I'd be happy to explain and buy them a pizza."

"A…pizza?" The woman looked confused for the first time since she had met her.

"Oh, sorry." Amber wanted to sink through the floor. "It's stupid. Whenever one of us on the team broke something or whatever, we'd bring in pizza as an apology. I probably don't need to do that here."

"Ah." Her boss leaned back in her chair with an amused smile. "No, but I'm sure they'll appreciate the gesture. I know our software team does the same with donuts, so I wouldn't be surprised to find out accounting has a similar practice. Why don't you take me through what you handed over? I wouldn't normally be able to digest every-thing but your company is smaller than most of the ones I acquire."

The truth was, although she still felt it was right to have Jacob make the final decision about the acquisition—he was the one facing jail time, after all—she was a little uncomfortable. She swallowed in an effort to move past that and regain a businesslike demeanor.

Thankfully, she was able to put that aside as she took Price through the financials and pointed out initial investments and Kick-starter funds, outstanding rewards and loans, and the list of equip-ment with dates of acquisition.

"Well," Price said when she had finished. "I have to say, the accoun-tants might make some tweaks but I found that to be very straight-forward."

"That's what I was afraid of," Amber said glumly. "If a non-accountant can understand, it's not good accounting."

The woman was startled into a laugh. She took a sip from a mug that had the Diatek logo emblazoned on the side. "Nick mentioned you had a good sense of humor. It's good to see it." She put the cup down and asked delicately, "Would it be accurate to say that I make you uncomfortable?"

She flushed. *Yes,* she wanted to say. *You're everything I want to be when I grow up.* Price was effortlessly elegant and clearly more invested in her work than her appearance, but still knocked both out of the park. She seemed to know exactly where she wanted her effort to go at any given point in time and never worked with competing priorities.

When she explained that, her boss responded with a rueful smile and for the first time, revealed a hint of how she had been as a younger woman.

"I would much rather," she said honestly, "wear my second-hand t-shirts and try to remember whether or not I brought my lunch. Often, the greatest accomplishments in life come from the greatest pain. I know how many families my work will save but selfishly, I would far prefer never to have undertaken it."

Amber swallowed hard.

"I can't tell you that I've picked the best path," Price told her honestly. "There are many uses I can think of for the amount of money I've made. I don't know that this is the one that will do the most good. I think that's the secret to success, Amber. You'll never know if you did the right thing, but if you aim in roughly the right direction and go with your talents, I like to think you can honestly let go of any guilt."

She nodded. "I...didn't mean to pry."

"I know," the woman said lightly. She looked at her in a quietly searching way. "Do you have any worries still?"

Amber considered the question. "Well, this feels a little frivolous, but—I was proud of what we'd accomplished even before we found this use for it. Part of me is worried that if Justin doesn't recover, you'll drop us and that either way, the senator will forget about us."

"Ah," Anna said. She sighed. "I know that feeling. Amber, I will make you a promise. If ever our interests diverge and I cut PIVOT loose, I will leave the company in better shape than when I found it."

"That's a fairly low bar," she pointed out.

Price laughed. "No one will be in legal trouble and you will be in the black."

"That's more reassuring. We weren't doing too well."

The admission met with a calm smile. "If you'll excuse me, I really should speak to Dr. DuBois. But, Amber, I appreciate your time—and your candor."

"Of course," she said automatically. She nodded and turned to her breakfast, which was why she missed the look on her boss' face.

It was one of confusion.

***

Amber had been Anna Price's first guess for a weak link. It wasn't that the woman was incompetent—in fact, it was the opposite. Her relentless focus on facts made her far more anxious than her two partners, especially where things such as funding or legalities were concerned.

After speaking to her, she was sure that whatever problem Jacob was hiding, she didn't know about it.

That, in itself, was odd. The PIVOT team seemed close-knit. At least, she thought, there wasn't a lurking legal or financial issue waiting to overwhelm the company.

Her lack of success thus far merely made her more wary when she approached DuBois.

At her insistence, he no longer ate popcorn in the laboratory. Instead, he propped the bags on his desk and looked longingly at them from time to time. When he saw her approaching, he beckoned her over excitedly.

"The data we've received from non-comatose patients is really expanding our parameters," he told her. "I've studied comatose brains for decades, of course, but this is the first time I've had the chance to test the differences between comatose and conscious brains undergoing the same stimulus."

He also, she noted, did not behave as if something was wrong. The doctor had been her other choice of a weak link, simply because he tended to be incredibly straightforward. If something was wrong, he was likely to tell her about it without realizing it.

She pored over the data for a few moments. He was correct that it was extraordinary. She could see the data from Justin's viewing of the arena trial matched hers and Tina's.

"It was good to see him in the game," she told him. "I didn't speak to him but he had a fine conversation with Tina. He seems to have made great strides. I admit, I was cautious."

"It's good to be cautious with this," DuBois agreed. "Recovery from head trauma can be so varied. It will be difficult to see the long-term patterns until we have more data. I don't think it's overstating the case to say that we lucked out with Justin. His brain was well-adapted to games already and he was therefore able to come on board very quickly."

There was no hint of evasiveness in him, goddammit. Price seriously considered, for a moment, locking Jacob in a room until he admitted what was going on.

She would rather find out about it on her own, however. Thoughtful, she tapped her fingers against her arm.

"Have you run into any limitations of the game format?" How many ways could she come up with to ask about this? Would they always say everything was fine?

"No," the doctor said promptly. "Well...Mrs. Williams going in wasn't as successful as we thought, but as you noted, Tina is doing well. Finding the general principle of when there should be external communication and when there shouldn't be will likely be quite difficult."

"Mmm." Jacob came into the lab and she glanced at him. He gave her a tight smile and went to wash his hands and put a lab coat on. *In a few minutes,* she thought, *you and I will have a chat, Mr. Zachary.*

"I didn't expect the game to be immersive enough," DuBois said. "My original concept was a few simple puzzles but I was lost on how to deliver them. I hadn't thought of it then, but the brain does not like to accept places that do not follow the rules of physics, for instance. I worried that the world would be so far from reality that it would be impossible. But the AI has…" He broke off suddenly. "Well, as you can see, the world is developing nicely."

Price had been focused on the papers in front of her when she heard the break in his voice and looked at him quickly. "Jacob mentioned that the world is procedurally generated."

"Yes," he said but looked uncertain now. "But…uh, that's not exactly my area of expertise."

The AI. There was no way he wasn't even a little curious about the AI. Whenever he spoke about anything, he either gave facts or directed his audience to someone else with the facts. Now, he was deflecting.

"It's not my area, either," she said with a smile. "I'm glad your data collection is going well. Come find me if you need anything else."

She approached Jacob with the feeling of stalking prey. "Mr. Zachary—a moment?"

"Yes?" He turned to face her. His shoulders were stiff, but she could see them creeping upward to his neck.

"I wondered if I could speak to you about naming this laboratory," Price told him. "It was never officially named, you see, and I remembered you mentioning some of your personal impetus for this project. I wondered if we could name it the Elizabeth Keegan Medical Facility in memory of your grandmother."

His jaw dropped. "Ms. Price—ma'am—I…yes, that would be appreciated. It would be an honor. My parents would be thrilled to hear it."

Whatever else he was lying about, this was not part of it. She gave him a small smile. "I'll see it done. Now, remind me—if I were to go into the game again, should I do so in close proximity to Justin or should I choose somewhere else? What would cause the least excess server load for the algorithms? I don't want to overwhelm the AI and give it too much to…dream up."

The flash of panic in his eyes was unmistakable and something clenched in the pit of her stomach that could be either opportunity or misgiving. Her mind raced ahead as he stammered a reply, and she extricated herself from the lab soon after.

In her office, she sat and stared blankly out the window. She saw none of the other buildings or the reflections on the glass.

A sentient AI. She wanted to laugh but she also wanted to cry.

If she were looking for something to cement her legacy—something that would bring untold billions to Diatek and fund as much research as she could ever need—this was it.

But she had one client, and as much as she spoke to Amber and Nick about making her peace with what she did, she wasn't ready to see how a military organization would use AI. She clenched her hands and looked at the desk. It was possible they had already made the same leap, wasn't it?

Unfortunately, she knew it wasn't. They'd sniffed around for years and offered century-long contracts for any company that could give them AI.

Price wasn't exactly superstitious. She also wasn't prone to melodrama and honestly, had no time for it. But one thing she knew for certain was that sentient programs raised all kinds of ethical questions that were, quite frankly, beyond her—together with many possibilities that didn't exactly end well for humanity.

She doubted Jacob had anything more than a hunch at this point. If he were truly worried, he would have found an excuse to take Justin out of the system. She trusted the PIVOT team implicitly when it came to their patient's safety.

Which meant she had time to think. Price nodded and proceeded to do the one thing that had become a critical priority. She had to make it absolutely impossible for any of PIVOT's servers to contact any of the others Diatek owned.

CHAPTER SEVENTY-FOUR

When Tad sent a message to Senator Snelling's office, he didn't expect the man to agree to meet with him.

He definitely didn't expect him to suggest a small, run-down diner as the venue either. When he arrived, bemused, Snelling was in the process of demolishing an improbably large plate of pancakes with gusto.

"I hope you don't mind," the senator told him. "I went running before this and..." He waved to the steaming mug of coffee on the table. "I didn't want to order you anything else but I know I've seen you drinking coffee before."

"I didn't know, uh..."

"That I go running?" the man asked with a gesture at his potbelly. He laughed at his companion's expression. "Oh, come on. It's funny. I show up at the races and I weigh more than any three of the top ten put together. I can't give up pancakes, though."

"My kind of guy," he said before he could stop himself.

"Careful. We agreed on that one bill, now it's pancakes as well—where will it stop?" The man took a bite of bacon.

Tad ordered when the waitress stopped at the table and took another sip of his coffee. "Well, it's funny you should mention that..."

"Oh?" Snelling leaned back in his seat. "I have to say, I never thought you had much of an interest in child cancer."

"What? Oh." He shook his head. "Ah…" He remembered in time that it was supposed to be a good public-relations move and decided not to proclaim loudly that he didn't care about it. After all, no parent could say the thought of child cancer didn't bring them out in a cold sweat. "My cousin's son had a scare a few years back. I saw the event was scheduled and dropped by. This isn't about that."

His companion blinked at him. "This should be good."

"Well…" He smiled at him. "You see, there's a little bill coming up to do with working research costs on different projects into treatment costs."

The man's face went stony. "And?" he asked dangerously.

"And," he continued pleasantly, "I'm almost certain it's a bill a certain CEO is trying to blackmail me into voting for."

Snelling put his fork down. "Wait…"

"Didn't you ever wonder how the news about Justin leaked?" Tad asked him.

"Oh, my God." Snelling looked thoughtful. "So, your vote on the last measure—they were angry with you about that?"

"It's a slightly longer story than that, but broadly speaking, yes. Let's simply say that Justin's accident gave them a lovely opening to exploit." He took a deep breath. "And, if we're honest…I've considered caving. More than I care to admit."

"What, you can't walk past people screaming that you're a horrible father and a child abuser without getting shaken?" The man rolled his eyes and shook his head. "Some of the things people think about us. It's difficult. It really is."

"I'm lucky Mary is as even-keeled as she is," he said and chose to omit her more bloodthirsty vows of revenge against Metcalfe. "Their first attempt was doctored photos to show me having an affair."

"They get most people," the other man said thoughtfully. "You know, I've had to bump a few lobbyist meetings in the past two months and I think I might quietly cancel those."

"It's a good idea," Tad told him, his tone acerbic. "Anyway, here's the thing. They want me to vote for this bill and I don't want to vote for it, but I'll be damned if I let them set the terms. If I lose, it'll be on a better bill than that."

Snelling's eyes lit up. "You want to write your own bill."

"I have." Tad took the sample out of his folio and passed it to the other senator.

The man took it but didn't start reading. He raised an eyebrow. "So…if you've already written it, you don't need a collaborator."

"I need votes," he said bluntly. "And I don't have them in my party."

"Ahhhh." Snelling studied him. "So you're coming across the aisle, and offering…"

"The chance to vote for a bill you believe in," he said flatly. "No more, no less."

His companion shook his head. "Nope. I want a little more from you." He put the bill down and tapped it. "I promise you that I will read this and I will either agree with it and want to vote for it, or I will tell you what I do not like and what would get my vote. In return, I want you to do the same for any bills I put forward."

Tad, who had been about to explode in fury, uttered a rueful laugh. "Man, you had me going for a second there. Okay, I'll up the ante again."

The other senator laughed. "Bring it on."

"Every year, we meet up to renew that pledge," he said, "and have a beer—my choice of beer, Snelling—and tell each other what we really think of the other's voting history."

Snelling burst out laughing and nodded. "All right. If I agree with this, do you want me to pass it on?"

"Go for it."

"And keep it quiet?"

Tad sighed. "I…don't know. You know what? No. I'm not good at all that cloak and dagger shit. I talked to my party and they wouldn't sign on. If they want to get pissed now that I'm reaching across the aisle, well…how much worse can it get? I'm already informed I've torpedoed my chances of being re-elected."

"Here's a little piece of advice. Party whips always say that when you step out of line." His companion shrugged and remained silent until the waitress had set Tad's food down and left before he added, "But if this is anything like your thoughts on the last bill, you might have more support than you think. Virtually everyone knows someone who's had trouble paying for treatment. Most senators have people calling their office about it. Don't be surprised if you really do have the votes in your party. Now." He waved his fork. "Eat those pancakes before I do."

Justin shook his limbs out and tried to focus. With the countdown dinging above them in the arena, it was hard to focus on anything at all, but he constantly ran over the team's plan in his head. It had taken several beers and an exceedingly late night to fine-tune it, but in the two days since, they hadn't found any unexpected weaknesses.

Task one was to find the closest cache and defensible position.

Task two would split them up temporarily. Justin and Tina would hightail it to the cache, get the gear and weapons, and return to their "base" to join Lyle. If they saw a second cache, Justin would hurry to retrieve whatever it contained and Tina would continue to Lyle.

Task three would be when they made a more specific plan for their defense while they waited to see what the other teams did.

Over the past day and a half, Justin and the dwarf had tested Tina with various weapons. The young man had told Lyle the lie that he merely wanted to see the technique of the world's "champion." She'd acquitted herself so well during the first match that he saw no reason to come clean about her lack of training and history.

To his surprise, she did best not with daggers or fists—which he had assumed would be her forte—but with battle-axes. The same intuitive grasp of fluid dynamics that had made her fighting style so powerful worked even better with a large, heavy weapon.

Having her in leather armor wasn't the best complement to a battle-ax, but her character still didn't have the strength to cope with both plate armor and an ax. They had paid what they had to for the leatherworker's finest armor upgrades, and he had to admit that she looked good.

He kept trying not to stare, partially so as to not be rude and partially because he was genuinely afraid that she would kill him. During their date, he had seen that she was short and fairly lean, but she had covered much of her body with layers. The armor left far less to the imagination and highlighted…well, too many things he needed to not think about right now. His only priority at that moment was to focus on the match.

The Master of Ceremonies sang their praises as the lift began to rise smoothly. Light swelled and broke over them to the sounds of applause. There weren't many boos yet that he could hear—they hadn't had the time to attract many people who hated them.

"In the last match, two of our three teams took the cash prize," the Master of Ceremonies declared. "Sephith's Bane, however, opted for the advantage in this match. Do you want to hear what it is?"

"I want to see outside this magic cage," Tina muttered. They had come above ground level and could see the vague outlines of varied terrain around them, but nothing more.

He laughed as the crowd shouted approval.

"Sephith's Bane has been given…" The man paused for effect and the stadium went quiet. "A one-minute head-start."

The crowd yelled their approbation as the magical walls came down. Justin tried to tune them out as he turned quickly to scan the area.

It was a fantasy village of some kind set on rolling terrain with small fields and gardens and two houses. He noticed one two-story house nearby and a cache surprisingly close to it.

"House," he called.

"Agreed," Lyle responded a moment later.

"Likewise," Tina said. "Two caches, one to the left of the house, the other this way."

"That one first," Justin said. "Lyle, see you there."

He and Tina leapt off the platform and sprinted down the nearby hill.

The terrain, this time, wasn't quite as treacherous under their feet. It was even, he thought in amusement, somewhat pleasant to be there. He recalled any number of idyllic, pastoral scenes in the video games of his youth. During one particularly bad year, he had liked to sit on a rock in his favorite video game forest and fish as the sky faded from day to night and back again.

The smaller cache revealed a short sword and two fist weapons, as well as a purple health-and-magic potion, and one that read *stone skin* on the side in spiky script. He grimaced. While he liked the idea in video games where he could feel the effects, he wasn't sure he wanted to feel stony skin.

There was no time to lose. A minute was a good head start but it wasn't nearly enough time to get complacent. He raced back with Tina and was pleased to see that she scanned their surroundings as they ran.

"If we find a bow, we could station someone in that tree," she called to him. "It looks like it would be possible to get into it."

Justin nodded, although he wasn't sure any of them had the skills to use a bow properly—especially without falling out of the tree in the process.

"All three teams are in the arena!" the Master of Ceremonies bellowed.

"Fuuuuuuck." He wheezed as he and his teammate increased the pace. "I never liked track."

The larger cache was a better find. There was a battle-ax in this one, although there were no water potions. He wondered if that had been deliberate. With no time to waste, he snatched the two daggers and shoved them through his belt before he bundled the remainder of the potions in his shirt. The two of them raced to the house.

Lyle emerged from the shadows under the stairs as they came into the building. They laid the items out on the floor and began a quick division. Justin chose the short sword, Lyle took one dagger as a backup for his fists, and Tina held a light-green potion up.

"Poison," she read. "Damage over time. Should I use it or—"

"If you are struck full-on with a battle-ax, a damage over time debuff is kind of overkill," he pointed out.

"Good point." She rolled it at her companions.

He opted to give it to Lyle—if the dwarf needed to fall back to blades, it would give him a way to accelerate the fight before he could be further outflanked. For himself, he took the fire buff. Ever since his fight against the demon army, he'd enjoyed flaming blades.

"There are two rooms upstairs," the dwarf said. "I say one of us stays in the shadow of the stairs, and the other two go upstairs."

"Justin stays here," Tina said. "He's best equipped to take on a range of weaponry, right? He can call to tell us what's coming. I'll wait at the top of the stairs and eliminate as many as I can with a battle-ax—"

"What, and I get no one?" Lyle sounded deeply unimpressed.

"No," she said patiently. "You man the window, tell us who's coming, and back up the two of us as needed. You have a poison blade and can move between fights very effectively."

"Hmmm." He considered this and nodded. "Fine. But next time—"

"Yes, next time we'll let you charge in yelling Stooooooout," Justin promised. "Pinkie swear."

"Eh?"

"Never mind. It's not important." He flashed a grin at Tina. "Positions, everyone."

The three of them shared a fist-bump before Tina and Lyle ran up the stairs. It wasn't long until the dwarf gave a low whistle followed by two thumps of his foot against the floor. Justin faded into the shadows and began to wish he hadn't chosen the fire potion. The blade shone slightly and he wondered if someone would see it.

Their opponents circled the house once. He could hear their footsteps and see them pass the windows, but their shapes were faint through the thick, wavy glass and he was fairly sure they had no idea he was there. Upstairs, he heard a faint creak as Tina shifted slightly on the balls of her feet.

Only one came into the house, and he wished he knew whether or not they were alone or if the other one waited outside.

With a silent prayer that Tina would understand why he chose not to engage, he decided to remain in his hiding place. The person stopped inside the door and must have scanned the room before they strode forward to ascend the stairs. Their steps were sure and light-footed.

Whether she knew what he was going for or not, he didn't know. Either way, she rose to the occasion. Their opponent—a man, judging by the voice—screamed followed by a crash.

One strike was all it had taken. He smiled.

The second team member had, in fact, waited outside the door. Now, he barreled in, yelling his team member's name. His gaze was so focused on the top of the stairs that when Justin stepped out of the shadows, he had no way to stop in time.

The man was armed with daggers. Justin drove him back with a quick attack. He wished he had his sword, which had a longer range, but he still did better than he had with the daggers, and that was what counted.

Not only that, his opponent looked genuinely unnerved by the fact that he attacked with a flaming sword. He made a half-hearted attempt to fight, circled away, and tried to strike under his adversary's range of motion, but he received a boot in his face for the trouble.

Justin hadn't trained with Lyle for nothing.

As the man reeled back, he stamped hard, directly on his hand. He had a moment of guilt and wondered how injuries were healed there, but he was certain no one would let this man die. With a swift swipe, he opened a cut in the other man's neck and wasn't surprised, after his first match, to see the blue shield come up and immobilize the contestant.

Quickly, he slid into the shadows of his hiding place.

Out of the corner of his eye and through the wavy glass, he caught sight of movement. He gave a sharp whistle and only a few moments later, all three of the other team members reached the door. There was a tense, whispered discussion before they ran to the stairs as a group.

"Lyle!" Justin yelled. Tina would need backup, and there was precious little time for her to call for it.

The last team member up the stairs spun and when Justin stepped out of the shadows, she leapt the banister and attacked without hesitation.

From upstairs, shouts and pounding feet were very audible. It still sounded like there were four people moving around. He decided his warning had to be good enough and focused on his fight. There wasn't another option because his opponent had a battle-ax, and he had the feeling that he stared into a future where Tina had more practice and was on the opposing side.

It was terrifying. The woman had swung immediately into the offensive as she came up from her crouch. Her eyes were narrowed and she fought single-mindedly. The battle-ax must have been what she trained with because she used it as if it were a piece of her own body. Muscles rippled in her arms while she parried his attacks.

Whether she simply put on a good show or she was freakishly strong, Justin didn't know, but he did remember one other piece of his grandfather's advice. The best time to end a fight was immediately—better a quick fight than a pretty one.

He launched into a counterattack of his own. Strength and stamina aside, the sheer weight of the battle-ax made its swings slower than his sword. They weren't as slow as he would have liked but he had to work with what he had. He began to slash from one side, then the other, and from directly overhead, interspersed with direct thrusts of his short sword.

She was weaker on her right but with her right hand as her dominant one, she was better able to swing the ax to cover attacks on her left side. He leaned out of the way of a swing and danced back to give her an opening.

Unfortunately, she didn't take it and instead, began to circle, panting now. Was she beginning to tire? That was interesting.

"You know, I have to say you're getting fairly good at this."

Justin was so shocked to hear words of praise from the AI that he froze and almost lost his head in an attack. "Did you do that on purpose?" he whispered.

"No, but that was hilarious."

He groaned, crouched quickly, and spun on one foot. The ax whipped overhead and his opponent, dragged off-balance by the swing, tripped over him.

Upstairs, Lyle uttered a sudden below of pain and Tina screamed—and Justin went into autopilot. He had to get there. Conscious only of his friends' predicament, he seized his opportunity and dove forward to tackle his adversary. She had tried to gain the momentum to lift the ax from the floor and he clamped one hand down over her wrist. He dragged the weapon out of her hand and hurled it against the far wall, and in the next minute, his knee pressed against her throat. Murder gleamed in her eyes, but she saw the sword within his reach and sighed. Her hands raised in surrender and she was encased in the blue magical shield.

Justin snatched both the sword and the battle-ax and sprinted up the stairs.

"Justin! Down!"

He reacted to Tina's voice on instinct and dropped to his stomach as arrows whizzed overhead. "What's going on?" he called.

"Remember that tree?" Her voice sounded choked. "The first team put their third person there. They shot Lyle in the back of the leg."

"What?" He craned his head so he could see her. The dwarf was, indeed, frozen on the floor. His hand was clamped over one leg and Justin could see how much blood had flowed out of the wound even before he was frozen. Tina, meanwhile, was pressed up against the wall under the window.

He army-crawled to where she was.

"What now?" she asked him. "We can't get near that tree and he won't come in here, not when he only has a bow."

As if in answer, huge numbers appeared in the sky—fifty-nine, fifty-eight, fifty-seven…

"A stand-off has been established," said the voice of the Master of Ceremonies. "With two members of Sephith's Bane remaining and one member of Ulgutta, Sephith's Bane will be declared the winner unless a fight is joined within the next minute."

With a shout of anger, their opponent dropped out of the tree and raced to the house. He didn't have much of a choice, although his odds weren't good.

"This one's mine," Tina said furiously. She darted a glance at Lyle, and he remembered the way she had screamed. Seeing the dwarf shot had hit her hard and she was out for blood.

In the laboratory, Mary settled onto one of the stools and watched the monitors. She still couldn't read the bulk of the output there but she could hear Justin and Tina's voices—and she knew the girl was taking this particular fight.

Along with the danger.

"She was a good choice," Amber said quietly.

She pressed her lips together and was surprised to feel a touch on her shoulder. When she looked up, she met Amber's gaze.

"I know it was hard," the young woman said so quietly that even she could barely hear her. "But you did the right thing."

Mary felt something release in her chest and she smiled. "Thank you."

Their opponent didn't have a chance. He knew it and they knew it, but he had nothing to lose and he barreled up the stairs with a berserker roar. Tina's ax thudded into the ground with splintering force directly in front of him.

He stopped so fast he tripped over it and she stepped out of the shadows with murder on her face.

"End it," Justin whispered under his breath. "Don't play with him and don't try to get revenge. End it."

She didn't hear him. Entirely focused, she advanced on their opponent, who scuttled away on his back. Justin, who melted into the shadows in the room, noticed him fumble under the back of his shirt for something—a knife?

Fuck.

"Yeah," Tina said. "Yeah, you have a knife. Do you think you're gonna shank me, fucker? Well, you won't. You'll stand up and fight me one on one like you're not a total coward. You got that?"

He stood, all six foot something of him, and Justin adjusted his hold on his sword. With one more step, he could end this. There was no way she could win a one on one fight with this man, not with daggers, and he would have to sit her down and talk to her about letting her emotions get in the way of what really mattered.

The man hadn't fully drawn his dagger out when she attacked. One fist drove into his sternum, and she slashed with one of Lyle's daggers with the other hand. Her opponent tumbled back with a scream, and she looked at her teammate.

"My grandfather taught me," she said, "to make a big, dramatic speech, have them get ready for the fight, and then take them out while they were doing that."

He burst out laughing. "I'll never doubt you again, I promise."

"Sephith's Bane has won the match!" the Master of Ceremonies shouted. Cheering came from the stands and the friends looked outside before they hurried to Lyle's side. Neither of them would leave before he was seen to.

The healers arrived soon. One had the lean, almost sinuous height that Justin could only guess came from elven blood. She readied a spell and touched a blue crystal orb to the dwarf's shield. He collapsed and she immediately began to attend to the wound. Justin thought he saw her give a look of deep distaste at the man on the ground.

"He was really scared," Tina said under her breath. "It bled so much even before the stasis field came up, Justin, and I think the guy planned it that way. Lyle might have died before they could shield him."

His blood ran cold. The two companions accompanied the healers into the open air and made a show of waving to their fans, but he could only think of the possibility of Lyle bleeding out—or Tina, or himself. He hadn't thought that was a possibility, but he began to wonder if he should have looked at the history of the tournament more carefully.

And he'd reached a point where he thought people couldn't stoop any lower.

On the dais, the Master of Ceremonies greeted them with an expansive smile. "You are fast becoming a crowd favorite," he said heartily, and the spectators cheered wildly. "Should I even ask which you prefer to take?"

He would have smiled in return but for the look on Lyle's face. He knelt next to the stretcher. "Hey," he said quietly. "You'll be okay, you know that, right?"

"I do." The dwarf's voice was faint. He was pale but Justin knew that was from nerves and not blood loss. He looked at the young man and there was a gravity in his face that Justin had never seen before. Even facing Sephith, even locked in jail, Lyle had been reckless and unimpressed by the threats before him.

This had struck him differently.

"I've been away too long," he said quietly. "I never said a proper goodbye to my family." His smile was forced. "I don' want to leave ye without a team—"

"Go," he said quietly. Something in him ached. The third key would send him home, he was sure of it now. The game was slowly taking away the people he had come to rely on and he would soon return to his own life.

Had it only been a few weeks in this world? It seemed like so much longer.

"Hey." Lyle caught his arm. "Take the advantage."

"No way," he said firmly. "If you're going home and I can't buy you an ale in person, I'll damned well send you with money so I can buy you some from a distance."

The dwarf managed a laugh as Justin stood. He caught Tina's nod as well as the suspicious glint of tears in her eyes. She looked away and pretended to study the crowd. He had the sense that she didn't like to cry in front of people.

"We take the payout," he told the Master of Ceremonies.

The man's smile fell slightly. "Don't tell me you'll bow out."

"Let him wonder," the AI said suddenly.

Justin only had a split-second to make his decision and with an internal sigh, he decided to go with the AI's suggestion. He shrugged. "We'll have to see."

He and Tina raised the bowl over their heads to the sound of cheers and left the Master of Ceremonies staring after them, stricken.

"So, why did I do that?" Justin asked the AI in an undertone.

"You'll have to wait and see, won't you?" The AI sounded as smug as usual. *"Maybe I made you do it for shits and giggles."*

He rolled his eyes.

CHAPTER SEVENTY-SIX

Tina was waiting on the back patio of the inn when Justin came downstairs. Having nothing other than burlap and armor, she had borrowed something from the innkeeper's wife—a flowing linen robe she had belted incongruously with her dagger belt. She saw him looking and threw her hands up.

"I know I look ridiculous but I couldn't stand the armor for one more minute."

"You look…really good." He cleared his throat. With her hair still wet from the bath and curling as it dried, she looked surprisingly… elegant, which wasn't a word he ever thought he'd use for her.

He cleared his throat as he gestured to the table nearby. "Food? I don't know about you but I'm starving."

"Me, too." Tina went to sit and it took a little time to make sure the robe didn't gape in any unexpected ways. "The innkeeper said he'd be out with food soon. I hope you don't mind, I…uh, splurged a little."

"Well, we have a ton of money and it's not like we'll stick around very long." Justin grinned at her. "I say we go all out. Maybe this isn't the best place to do that—"

"I won't go anywhere else in this getup," she said at once.

"You know you look good, right? Not that I'm surprised. You

always look good—I mean, you seemed surprised that…oh, I'm awful at this." He let his head thud onto the table.

She laughed. "Thank you. I know what you meant." A door opened nearby and she clapped enthusiastically. "Oh, thank you so much."

"Of course." The innkeeper approached, bearing a jug of wine and glasses as well as a loaf of freshly baked bread. "Sir, are you well?" He looked at where Justin still huddled with his head on the table.

"Yes, thank you." He raised his head, embarrassed all over again. "Could I ask you to take some refreshments to our friend in the corner room?"

"Rest assured, we were already doing so." The man nodded at Tina. "The lady requested that we give him the very finest food. Of course, he has since requested that we take it away and replace it with something heartier."

Tina hid her face with one hand and her shoulders shook in a silent laugh. "I should have expected that. Ale and…what, potatoes?"

"And sausages," the innkeeper agreed. "My wife is pleased. She takes great pride in her ale."

"Oh. Well, then." She smiled. "Thank you for this. I'm sure we'll enjoy whatever you have."

"We've taken the liberty of making a meal specially for you," he told the two of them. "And you'll have the patio to yourselves."

"There's no need for that," Justin protested.

"You're not used to being a tournament champion, are you?" The innkeeper gave him an amused look. "If I let anyone else out here, you wouldn't have a moment of peace all night."

He disappeared, but not before he waved a hand in a deft gesture. It ignited magical lanterns that hung overhead and down the walls and the friends were immediately bathed in a soft glow. She gasped and the innkeeper gave him a meaningful look before he left.

Justin cleared his throat. He suddenly felt deeply self-conscious. Between the twilight sky, the gorgeous city, the wine, and the magical lights, this was a more romantic night than he had bargained on. He took a gulp of wine to steady himself and realized too late that he might have made a mistake.

Thankfully, he and Tina were both hungry enough that he could occupy himself for a moment with the bread. He dipped hunks of it in the oil that had been provided and savored the hint of salt and the warm, fluffy texture.

She licked her fingers with a happy sigh. "Do you think they have twenty more loaves?"

He laughed. "God, I hope so. You take the last piece. I'm sure they'll have more soon and I had an ale while talking to Lyle."

Tina gave him a sober look at that. "So, he's really going home, then?"

"He is." He focused on his glass of wine. "I never thought I'd see the day, to be honest. He doesn't strike me as someone who would do well with a staid life…but then again, he wasn't fighting for much of a purpose here. He merely wandered and drank himself silly most of the time. When I first met him, he was in jail for brawling and not paying his bar tab."

"He's a good man." She ran one finger contemplatively around the rim of her goblet. "Er…dwarf?"

"I have no idea what the right term is." Justin shrugged. "And, yes, he is."

"I wouldn't be surprised if all your good deeds have made him want to go home and help his family," Tina pointed out. "You've defeated evil wizards and demons and so on, right? Maybe he wants to do more of that. The dwarves must have some enemies."

"I don't know." He looked at her in surprise. "I suppose I never knew much about the wider world. In a video game—a normal one— there's always a pressing crisis like a huge war. I never heard about anything like that. It was only things like Sephith—little villains terrorizing one village at a time."

She nodded. "Well, we can ask him. He's not leaving tonight, is he?"

"No. He said he'll take a few days and he'll go with a caravan. I think I managed to persuade him not to go as a guard." He shook his head. "I had to tell him he deserved to be carried home like a prince instead of letting him think I was coddling him."

"But you were," she guessed and took a sip of wine.

Justin nodded somberly. "The healer said it will take time before he's back to full strength. She healed the wound but apparently, only the body can do some of it. I hadn't realized someone could get injured so badly in the tournament."

Tina fixed him with a curious look. "We keep rising through the ranks. Will we continue to compete?"

"I think we have to." He shook his head. "That's how we get the key." He sank into silence.

"Justin?" Her voice was low. "You'll be able to come back, you know."

He looked quickly at her.

"You have to be here right now because you're healing," she said, "but I'm here and I'm healthy. They can put you in the game. You can see Lyle again."

"I know it's ridiculous to care." He gave her an embarrassed look.

"I read my favorite books over and over again," she responded with a shrug. "And if I could actually talk to the characters? I'd never stop reading."

Justin smiled at her. "Thank you for coming here—and for understanding."

"I'm glad your mother forgave me enough to let me try," she said.

"Wait, what?" He looked sharply at her. Now he remembered the way his mother had looked when he asked about Tina. She had been angry. "Oh, no—my mother blames you, doesn't she? You know, if our parents hadn't insisted we go on that date—"

"It was my fault." She took his hand and looked seriously at him. "And I'm glad I can come here. I wanted to help, even though I didn't know it would be this much fun." She squeezed his fingers.

He returned the smile easily until he realized how perfect this moment felt, with their fingers touching and the wine making his head buzz, and the lights the perfect muted glow.

When the door opened, they both drew back as if they'd been burned. Justin could see her blush as the innkeeper and his wife entered with heavy trays of food. They were careful not to look at the young couple, but he could sense them trying to decide if they had interrupted anything.

The amount of food they provided was truly staggering. There was a shank of something that looked like lamb but must have come from something the size of an up-armored Humvee. It was coated in spices and salt, its skin crackly, and it smelled divine. Roasted vegetables lay around it. Platters of salad were provided as well, and rice with herbs, and more bread. Dumplings sizzled in a hot dish, covered with bubbling cheese, and another bowl contained something that might be pasta.

And there was so much more wine. The innkeeper and his wife topped off the goblets and withdrew like ghosts.

"Well, I don't think we'll fight in the tournament again," Tina said. "Unless there's a way we can win by lying on the ground and crying about how full our stomachs are."

"Are you suggesting…" He felt truly sad. "That we should try to moderate ourselves?"

"Fuck no," she retorted. "This is a made-up world. They'll find another way to get you that key. Eat up." She picked a potato up with her bare hands and popped it into her mouth, only to spit it out a moment later. "Fuck! Hot. This game is too realistic."

He laughed hysterically as he served himself from the platters. While he wanted to take some of everything, it wouldn't fit on his plate. With a silent prayer that he wouldn't be full before he had tried them all, he began to eat.

Every bite was delicious but it was probably because he was literally living in a dream.

"I don't think I have words," he said after he'd swallowed one of the dumplings. "That cheese. What kind is it?"

"I don't know." Tina dipped one of the pieces of bread in it. "All I know is that it had better exist or I'm gonna kick some ass when I get out of here."

He nodded emphatically.

"You know, it's weird," she said.

"Hrm?" He looked up, his cheeks bulging with rice and meat.

"Well, I was going to say that we were finally having the romantic evening our parents had hoped for but then I saw you looking like a chipmunk." She clearly tried not to laugh.

"Nice one, Casanova. You're doing great."

"I will find the server you are stored in," he muttered to the AI, "and rip your heart out." To Tina, he raised an eyebrow. "Is the woman who came to the date in a borrowed bathrobe really getting on my case?"

"Oh, unfair!" She threw a piece of bread at him. "I don't have any other clothes."

"You could have—"

"Don't you dare finish that sentence," she warned and laughed. "Although…who knows where we'll be after all this wine?"

In the lab, Jacob looked around in a sudden moment of awkwardness. Mary was already at the door of the room. She looked at everyone, who stared at her.

"Uh…" She gave them a deer-in-the-headlights look. "Let me know when it's safe to come back."

He gave her a thumbs-up and tried not to laugh as she fairly sprinted out of the room.

The Master of Ceremonies had chambers in the Royal Palace, a fact Kural guessed correctly. This left, of course, the question of exactly where in the giant palace the chambers were. What followed his arrival was a truly boring series of excursions down similar-looking hallways until all the exquisite architecture blurred together in his head.

Thankfully, he had remembered to leave magical markers for himself so he knew which corridors he had already explored. If he hadn't done so, he would have been lost very quickly.

The palace was almost empty. The guards patrolled regularly—which wasn't a problem for the wizard, who presently floated above their heads as a dust mote—but he saw not a single noble and only a few clerks.

His curiosity grew as he searched. He had known, of course, that the king of Insea had not been seen in years. Everyone knew that. The city continued to run like clockwork, however, and there were never any invasions, so Kural had decided that whatever was going on, it wasn't a problem. He'd always had something else to occupy him, like his experiments.

Or his defeat and subsequent years spent trying not to get killed by Sephith.

Now, he wondered what was going on there. Even a sick king could be expected to be surrounded by fawning nobles and crowds of servants, but he didn't see any general direction in which the guards or servants moved.

He resolved to ask the Master of Ceremonies whenever he finally found the man. Although he would have to be careful, he might even be able to work that into the persuasion portion of their discussion.

It had been over an hour by the time he managed to find the correct set of chambers. They were palatial, although it did not appear that this was due to greed. The rooms were far from the height of luxury. A desk stood at one side of the main room and a set of low couches near the fireplace, and a full wall of windows overlooked them. Beyond, he could see a bedchamber with an eastern-style mattress laid directly on the floor.

The Master of Ceremonies worked alone at his desk with a humble meal of flatbread and yogurt next to him as well as a cup of strong tea. Kural took the opportunity to change from a dust mote into his full self and walked into the room. This took vastly more strength than shadow-walking, but he needed to be there in person if he wanted to persuade the Master of Ceremonies to part with a priceless artifact.

He rapped on the open door and waited for the man to look up. "Jaco?"

"Yes?" It had been years since they had seen each other, so it took a good few minutes for the Master of Ceremonies to realize who he was looking at. "Kural?" He stood and came around the edge of the desk, disbelief and wariness on his face. "The last I heard, you had been killed by Sephith."

"Defeated," he corrected. "And then in hiding. Sephith was killed a few weeks back, though, and so I have my powers again."

"I'd heard rumors of it, but..." The official gestured to his desk. "But I've been busy."

"Yes, I can see that." The wizard looked around the room. "I don't suppose I could trouble you with a certain detail."

"You might as well." Jaco smiled wearily at him. "I'm getting nowhere. I don't suppose you have any ideas on how to revive the tournament properly."

"You seem to be doing a fine job of it so far," he observed. He waited as the man rang a small bell and murmured something below his breath. A full tea set, complete with sweets, appeared on the table near the hearth and a fire sprang into being.

The two men sat and took refreshments for a moment.

"As it happens, however..." Kural rolled the glass of tea between his hands. "I do have a suggestion. But questions first, of course. It might inform the suggestion I make. I wasn't sure it would be you I found."

His host gave him a tired smile. Over a hundred years before, he and his visitor had been rivals, both competing for the favor of certain patrons. Kural had left to find his place as a wizard, and Jaco had taken a different route. Never a wizard himself, he possessed quite a talent for creating spectacles and entertainments. He'd always had the edge when it came to delighting rich nobles.

"I have it on good authority," the wizard said, "that this tournament is not merely an entertainment for the city." He watched the man closely and was rewarded by a flash of worry in his eyes. "Do you care to explain?" he asked silkily.

The official considered him narrowly. "And have you come steal my place?"

"Have you ever been to a party I've thrown?" he asked him archly.

"Yes, actually. You served crackers. Only crackers. There was no music."

"So you know I won't steal your job." He gestured at him. "I promise you, I have a goal that does not in any way conflict with yours."

"Ah, but you don't know what mine is." Jaco sighed. He was still wary but clearly desperate to unburden himself of his worries. "Oh, what the hell. Maybe you'll have some ideas."

The story he proceeded to tell was beyond his guest's wildest imaginings.

The King of Insea was not sick. Indeed, he had never existed in the way the people believed. He had never been elven at all but was a dragon, born millennia before even the elves walked the earth. It was his servants who had built Insea under his direction after he stumbled upon the beautiful deposit of rock that made the city. His power had allowed them to forge the finished product into one stone, which made it unbreakable.

The dragon had no interest in the wars of his people. He had escaped a battle between rival armies and had fled. Whether it was from another world or this one, Jaco did not know. He only knew that the dragon wanted to be left in peace—and that he was fascinated by the doings of lesser beasts. It was for this reason that he had convinced the elves to build Insea. The rock gave him strength and he lived within the city, endlessly intrigued by what went on, and kept it safe.

"Is he...in the palace?" Kural asked.

"I don't know." Jaco shook his head. "I've never seen him, not truly."

"So it could all be a ruse."

"It could." The man leaned back on the couch and considered the idea. "I've had time to wonder if that was the case. I can think of no other explanation, however. He has used servants, over the years, for public appearances, but now fears someone might learn the truth."

"If he's told you, and you've told me..." The wizard took a sip of his tea as he frowned in thought. "I won't spread the secret, but it won't stay hidden forever."

"I know that. So does he." Jaco swirled the tea in his glass. "That's why the tournament is in progress. Something is coming but we don't know what. It might be dragons or it might be another kind of invasion. I was called here when I reached the city and he asked me if I could put together a tournament—"

"That would create and draw a populace of talented warriors?" Kural finished for him.

"Yes," the man said softly. "And it was working until the Twins kept winning."

"Well. I have a suggestion that will help you, then." He smiled. "I happen to know that one of the teams includes a man who is searching for a very particular artifact—a dwarven key."

His host leaned forward. "I know the key you speak of, I think. And it is priceless, yes, but not to any collectors. It is valuable only to historians. Are you truly telling me a scholar has entered the tournament?"

"He's a member of the team that calls itself Sephith's Bane," he told him. "Ah, yes, now you see how I know him. I helped equip him to defeat Sephith, you see. As for why he needs the key…well, let me simply say he has the other two."

"That answers none of my questions," Jaco told him tartly. "Quite the opposite, in fact."

"Mmm. Ask your dragon where the door is that those keys open." Kural leaned forward. "I promise you—I *promise* you—if you give him the key when he wins, he will create a spectacle that will not soon be forgotten. It will revive interest in the tournament in a way you cannot imagine. And when that man travels between the worlds, he may well come back, bringing the healing that Insea needs."

His companion's jaw hung open and it was a few moments before he swallowed. "And if the Twins win?" he asked tartly.

"Then offer a different prize," the wizard said wearily. "Although I'd recommend you make sure they don't."

"I refuse to interfere," Jaco said stiffly.

"You're trying to drum up opponents," Kural pointed out.

"Strong opponents," the man told him. "It helps nothing if weaklings triumph. And if a single whisper gets out that the contest is weighted, that will undo everything I have worked so hard to create."

"Mmm." He shrugged. "Well then, I leave that up to you. Justin is resourceful and I'm confident that he can do what must be done. If he wins, however, offer him the key. Trust me."

"I'm not sure I do," his companion said wryly. "But if the king agrees, I'll do it. There's something bad coming, and if this man can bring us resources…"

The wizard nodded. "Call on me if you need me. I happen to know of two others as well—a sorceress of surpassing power and her apprentice. I shall make sure the apprentice is trained with all haste in case an invading army does come."

It wasn't long after the banter started that Justin stopped and his eyes widened.

"Everyone in the lab can…hear us, can't they?"

"Oh, my God." Tina put her hand over her mouth. She wanted to disappear. "Oh, my God, oh, my God… Yes. Yes, they can."

He tipped his head back and laughed. "We finally have a date and we have a whole army of chaperones." He looked curiously at her. "What is the lab like?"

Letters appeared on her screen: **TRY TO STEER THE CONVERSATION BACK TO THE GAME**

Huh. She shrugged and hoped she could pull this off without being too obvious. Even with no pressure, she wasn't a great liar. "It looks like a lab. You'll see it soon, right?"

"I suppose." He gave her a tight smile.

"Justin." She leaned forward. "You're close to the third key. What does that tell you?"

He stared at her.

"That you're making progress," she told him. "We you need to be careful. I know we're not supposed to let you get harmed, but I also know what people look like when they're really scared all the time and I know the doctors aren't."

The reassurance helped him to relax somewhat.

"Tell me about the game," she suggested. "Tell me all of the tiny things." She stood and held her hand out. "Come on, let's go upstairs—no, not for that. We'll people-watch out the window and have a nice glass of wine."

"Oh," Justin said. "Right." He retrieved the pitcher and glanced at the table. "All that eating, and we barely made a dent."

"Good." Tina grinned. "That means there'll be leftovers. Now, come on."

They slipped up the stairs and then, on a whim, up the next set. To their pleasure, they led to an attic with broad windows. As they ascended the final flight, Tina was fairly sure the process made the robe slip more than once, but Justin was gentlemanly enough not to mention it. He handed up the pitcher and the goblets and hauled himself after.

"It's easier when you're tall," he pointed out.

"Bah." She lay back on the roof and stared at the sky. "God, it's gorgeous here. Are all games like this?"

"Play some and you'll find out," he teased.

She looked at him with a grin. "Okay. I'll do that if you read some of my favorite books."

To her surprise, he propped himself on one elbow and nodded at her. "It's a deal."

Tina laughed. She'd spent the past few years drifting, worrying her parents with her tattoos and her attitude, but the truth was, she hadn't ever wanted to run off and go on week-long binges or anything like that. Quite simply, she had only wanted them to stop treating her like she was made of glass.

That, and she liked tattoos.

"What do you think you'll do when you get back?" she asked him.

"You mean, besides all the physical therapy I'll probably need?" Justin sounded glum.

"Yes, besides that. Everyone has health problems so don't get self-indulgent."

He smiled at her. "Well… I don't know. I guess I thought I'd talk to my dad."

"What about?"

With a sigh, he pillowed his head on his hands. "What he does for a living, I guess. He's a senator."

"Yes, I know. My parents made a huge deal of it."

"Ugh, I'm sorry. Well, before that, he was in the state senate, and before that—it doesn't matter. But I never really cared. I thought he merely argued for a living and that he wanted an excuse to tell people they were wrong about things."

"And now?"

"Well, you can't really solve problems in our world by running around with a sword. So I have to find something else to do." He shrugged. "What about you?"

"Now, mine seems stupid."

"No, tell me."

"I wanted to open a store," she said. "My grandmother would weave this amazing cloth, and you could make the patterns into rugs, curtains, whatever. I thought I'd open a store where people could buy stuff like that." She sat up enough to take a sip of wine. "It's not exactly on par with saving the world."

"I like it," he said. He hesitated and took her hand tentatively. "I do. I like it. And Tina?"

"Yeah?"

"When we get out of here, could we go out again?" The words came out a little rushed.

Reflexively, she smiled as warmth stole over her. "Yeah. Yeah, I'd like that. Of course, I'm not sure your mother will ever let us leave the house together."

"My mother got me a dragon for my birthday," he said sleepily. "She doesn't get to talk about safety."

"What?"

"Nothing." He laced his fingers with hers. "I…should go. I don't want to," he added hastily, "but I keep thinking about everyone in the lab."

Tina laughed. "You don't have to go straight from this to there. Be grateful."

"You're leaving?"

"I'll be back in the morning," she assured him. "I promise."

She waited as he climbed into the building and left and wasn't surprised when the world dissolved into black a few moments later. When she opened her eyes, the pod lid was raised and she winced when the assistants helped her to sit. Her muscles ached and she had to use the bathroom.

Desperately had to.

Tina practically sprinted through the lab and emerged a few minutes later feeling disturbingly lighter. "How long was I in there?"

"Fourteen hours," Jacob said. He produced a chair out of nowhere as she began to wobble. "Sit. Your blood sugar is very low."

"Eat this," Amber suggested. She brought over a folding table and a bowl of pho. "A little salt protein, some hydration…"

"Do you have any sriracha?"

"No. I'm not crazy. But we'll have some for you next time." She tapped next to the bowl. "Eat up. You're doing great, you know."

"He's beginning to show marked signs of being ready to wake up," DuBois said.

"Oh." She swallowed a mouthful of soup. "What happens if we don't win the tournament?"

The doctor looked offended. "I can't tell you," he said.

"Does it…" She looked at the others. "Does it break the immersion or something?"

He looked at her and almost seemed to bristle. "No. It ruins the fun."

CHAPTER SEVENTY-SEVEN

"How are we doing for time?" Nick called over his shoulder. He held a large bag of trash in one hand and a sheaf of papers in the other.

"About five minutes," Jacob said. Sweat began to prickle on his skin.

"Fifteen," Amber told Nick in an undertone.

"We want to be ready before they show up," Jacob pointed out. "If they come here and see us cleaning frantically, it won't look good for us."

"The laboratory is already spotless," Anna Price pointed out. "Not that I want to get involved." She looked genuinely amused. After the weird way she had hovered around the area a few days before, he had been worried when she appeared that morning.

However, she had no negative comments on their progress. Instead, she wanted them to allow a news team to conduct an interview. It was a rare occurrence, she'd explained. She was not in the habit of allowing media attention on anything she did, but she was pleased enough with Justin's progress that she had decided to allow this.

There had been an extensive debrief of what they were and were not allowed to say with regard to patient confidentiality, and they would pretend that Justin was in a different location. Also, they would pretend that he was not the only patient.

Jacob had been leery of agreeing to the interview, but what swayed him was her reminder that this could also help Senator Williams. The PIVOT team had shared articles amongst themselves, horrified by the vitriolic comments toward them and Justin's parents. People had clearly decided that they had hooked the young man up to untested, experimental treatment merely for the hell of it.

He shook his head and returned to scrubbing the bottom of the laboratory table.

"Do you really think they'll look under the tables?" Price asked him.

"No," he replied. "But this calms me."

"Yes. You seem very calm."

Of all the things he had expected from her, a sense of humor was not one of them. He slid out from under the table and gave her a look that drew a small smile in return. She was typing on her phone as she spoke. He had only seen her without extra work once.

Apparently, there was a rumor going around Diatek that she didn't even have a house and slept in one of her offices each night. He had to concede that it seemed likely.

They all heard the door open and everyone looked around. Mary blew out a breath and bounced slightly on the balls of her feet. She had dressed conservatively in a skirt suit and pearls, and a professional makeup artist had come in. The effort had created the very picture of an non-threatening, old-school, classy mother, the kind of person who would always have something for the PTA bake sale and never dropped her kids off for school without having her makeup done. Jacob knew she had been given extensive instructions on how to behave for the camera crew and that she did not like it.

Mary, he knew, preferred to be straightforward.

So did he. Unfortunately, they were in a battle against someone who twisted the truth every way he could.

When the camera crew arrived, he thought his heart would beat out of his chest. He went to shake the reporter's hand.

"Mr. Zachary." The man smiled at him. "David Yang, Johnsonville Chronicle. Thank you for agreeing to meet us."

"Of course." He gestured to Mary and Price. "Would you like to begin by speaking to Mary Williams or Anna Price?"

"Mrs. Williams, I think." David stepped forward to shake Mary's hand. "If that works for you, ma'am."

"Of course." She nodded. "Should I sit, should I stand..."

"Why don't you come here to the seating area?" Yang looked around. "No, one of the desks. You've been here this whole time. I think it's right to show you in the lab."

"If you think that's best." Mary slid onto one of the stools in what was clearly a practiced movement.

"Let me get set up," the man told her. He directed the camera crew into position before he launched into the interview. "Now, Mrs. Williams, can you give us your overview of the treatment Justin is receiving?"

"Of course." Mary swallowed and gestured to the pods. "A comatose patient would normally receive very limited interventions. Feeding tubes, of course, and all the monitors, as well as perhaps a medically induced coma if it was needed, but I think that's only if they seem to be coming out of it too quickly—to slow it, I guess, but I'm not a doctor. But there isn't generally a way to interact with the person. The brain is very complex and there isn't a way to predict when the patient will get better."

David nodded.

"What PIVOT did," she said, "was they gave patients a way to begin to get better while they remain unconscious. The video game that was developed by their team can be interacted with by the patient and will stimulate the brain to heal." She gave a self-conscious smile. "Dr. DuBois, how would you say I did at explaining that?"

The doctor gave a distracted nod. "Very good, yes. Yes. Now, if you'll excuse me..." He wandered away.

Amber edged closer to Jacob. "Where did you hide his popcorn?" she asked out of the corner of her mouth.

"In the ceiling tiles," he muttered. "Let's hope he doesn't think to look at the security footage anytime soon."

She snickered. They had decided it was probably best if no one saw Justin's doctor eating popcorn in the middle of the laboratory but had not been able to convince him of that. Consequently, she had lured him outside while Jacob hid the popcorn.

"So, Mrs. Williams," David Yang asked, "what do you know about the types of stimulation? You mentioned that it was a game. Is it like a logic puzzle?"

"It's a video game," Mary explained. "I've been inside it. Well, in one of the pods. As one of the early tests, I was allowed to interact with Justin."

She described her experience within the game. Although she left out the part about her killing the spider, she was incredibly animated. Her sense of wonder about what she'd experienced would translate well, Jacob thought.

Or, at least, he hoped it would. He noted the way her chin trembled with real emotion while she discussed being able to speak with Justin and send messages.

"Now, one last question, Mrs. Williams," the reporter said. "Early stories about this treatment were very negative and your husband has been pressured to resign. Do you have any comment on that?"

Mary paused and Jacob knew from having watched that this was practiced. She had gone over this several times with the lawyers and publicists as well as her husband. He had also witnessed her ranting about how disingenuous it felt to practice the speech, only to have Anna Price shake her head. "Sincerity isn't enough when it comes to the press," the CEO had said. "Not legally and not in the court of public opinion. We need to be careful."

"I know the stories were scary," Mary said and swallowed. "I guess people must think we're desperate or reckless and if they've only seen the news reports, I can't really blame them. I hope that when they learn the details, they'll think more kindly of us. We feel lucky that we were able to find this treatment for Justin and we hope more families will soon have the same opportunity."

"Thank you, Mrs. Williams. Now, Mr. Zachary…" David Yang gestured around the lab. "Would you like to provide more specifics on the treatment?"

"Of course," Jacob said. "Come with me."

He led them around the lab and allowed his genuine enthusiasm to show when he pointed out the various new pieces of equipment PIVOT had access to as part of the acquisition deal. Finally, he led the team to the pods.

"There's been considerable press coverage of these already," he told David Yang. "Obviously, we didn't originally intend these to be used for comatose patients. What first gave us the idea was my grandmother's treatment. To be frank, my family could not afford to keep her in the hospital. It put us in a terrible position and my parents and their siblings considered draining their retirement funds to help her recover."

"Your grandmother passed away, did she not?"

"Yes." He swallowed. "And I'd be lying if I said I didn't wonder, every day, if she might have recovered if she'd been able to try this treatment. She always loved stories. I remember her reading to me when she was younger. If she'd had a chance to be a hero and go on adventures, I think maybe…" He swallowed hard and kicked himself mentally because he had not wanted to cry. More than anything, he needed to be professional and present a trustworthy image. "I think maybe that would have given her strength," he finished.

"I see. And so your team is now marketing the pods exclusively as a therapy for trauma patients, correct?"

"Right now, that is the only application under development," Jacob said carefully. "However, as you can see, we're also collecting data from healthy patients to understand how their vital signs respond to the game. This gives us a good idea of how brains diverge and we're interested to see those data."

"So these are not patients?" the reporter asked.

"Yes. Obviously, we can't show you any of the treatment as the patients aren't able to sign waivers."

Yang nodded and one of his assistants checked a question off. "Do you see any other uses for these pods?"

"Many," he told him. "There are numerous potential other areas where this could be used. We'll know more when we have a good set of data regarding our patients' recovery. Depending on how recovery is affected, other conditions might benefit from the same treatment. But there are more benefits, too. People can attend college remotely. They can learn combat skills or explore landscapes. Those who have mobility issues could have the sensation of walking again. There are so many ways that this could enhance people's lives."

"Thank you so much for your time." The man shook his hand heartily. "Now, Ms. Price, if you'd be willing to answer some questions about Diatek's involvement in this process."

"Of course," she said smoothly and gave Jacob a tiny nod as she went past him.

"That went well, I thought," Nick said as the team watched her answering questions.

"I hope so," Jacob said. He swallowed. "I hope so but I'm afraid Metcalfe got too far ahead of us."

"Maybe that's the benefit to working with someone who has defense contracts," Nick suggested. "If Metcalfe tries to screw with her, I wouldn't say it would go well for him."

"That's true." He bounced on the balls of his feet. "Well, we've done what we can. Let's hope this gives the senator enough of a break to hang on for a while longer."

CHAPTER SEVENTY-EIGHT

"Are you sure about this?" Tina asked.

Justin glanced at her. The roar of the crowd reverberated through the floor and the walls, and all he could think of was home. Only three teams remained from the skirmishes, and with Quartzfire having withdrawn from the final, the Master of Ceremonies had hinted that a grand prize might be on the line for the teams that faced off that day.

The uncertainty had packed the stands. The three teams left were Tayr—the trio of women Justin, Tina, and Lyle had faced off against last time—the Twins, of course, and the remnants of Sephith's Bane. Justin and Tina were the only two to advance without one of their team members. The rules were clear. They could continue without their team member or they could drop out, but they could not sub in anyone else.

He knew she was worried about his choice to keep going. She had argued passionately against it, but he was ready and couldn't remain there any longer. He was ready to wake up and the thought of waiting another few days was torture.

The two of them would win. They had to.

"I'm sure," he told her.

She looked at the floor without speaking.

"Last time, everyone came for us," he told her. "We've had harder fights because we were the unknown. First, they thought we were weaklings and could be easily defeated. Then, they thought we were the big threat. But this time, we're in the arena with the Twins."

"And that doesn't frighten you?" Tina demanded.

Justin thought it over. It should frighten him. He had the sense that he should be worried about this because he had seen the Twins fight and he knew their record. They were clearly resourceful. So was he, though, his mind argued. He'd defeated Sephith—hell, he'd defeated a version of himself in that tower. Thereafter, he'd fought a demon army. What were two humans in comparison to that?

The truth was, though, he was itching for this fight. The others had been quick skirmishes against people who were used to arena fighting and not used to risking their lives. They were more cautious and more frivolous at the same time. The Twins were the ones he had wanted to fight all along.

He shrugged. "I think we can do it," was all he said.

Tina made no reply to that. She swallowed as the lift began to move. The Master of Ceremonies had announced the Twins first and half the stadium seemed to cheer wildly while the other half booed. Surely, with as much noise as there had been, there couldn't be many people sitting silently. Now, Tayr was being announced, and though there was less interest, he could tell that they had their fans.

"Our third team has become a fan favorite after only two matches in this arena," the Master of Ceremonies said. The covering over their platform slid back and light flooded in. Cheers began, along with a few boos.

"Aww, yeah," Justin said.

"What?" Tina looked deeply confused.

"We're being booed," he explained. "That means we've made it."

"I think you may be confused about how humans show emotion."

"No, no, think about it—you see a cool act, someone wins at a sports game, and you get into it, right? It's easy to cheer. But when you hate someone, that's when you've seen them enough to learn about them and care about them. We're not simply some extra team anymore."

"Uh…huh." She looked dubious, but as their platform reached ground level, she plastered a smile on and waved. "That's weird, the countdown hasn't started yet."

"No team has an advantage in this match," the Master of Ceremonies announced. "However, there is one difference between this match and the others…"

The whole arena seemed to hold its breath, and Justin realized he was doing the same.

"Magic is unrestricted in this round," the man shouted.

"*Yes!*" Justin yelled. He pumped his fist in the air.

"You can use magic?" Tina asked him.

"Hell yeah. I can set all kinds of things on fire—and reveal hidden things. And make a sword of fire. Oh, hell yes, I am so here for this."

"Good. That's good." She danced nervously on the balls of her feet. "One more thing, Justin."

"Yeah?" He darted her a glance but he barely paid attention. The countdown had begun in the sky and he scanned the vague outlines of the landscape.

"This doesn't change the plan," she warned him. "Remember that, Justin. It doesn't change the plan. We find a defensible location and we wait. Okay?"

"Yeah. Yes." Justin looked at her and nodded. "Of course. But we have magic once we get there." He held one palm up and made a fireball.

"Oh, shit." Tina's eyes widened. "You actually can make—" She broke off as the walls disappeared.

He had never been to Scotland, but this was how he imagined it. The landscape seemed made half of rolling hills and half of jutting outcrops of rock that were mossy on one side and chalky white on the other. The air seemed to hold mist, cold as it broke against his skin, and he noticed different parts of the landscape appear and disappear.

For a split-second, he wondered if the people in the stands saw the mist or not.

Justin exhaled a breath and did the spell to reveal hidden items. He pictured a wave ebbing away from a beach, leaving shells and sand in its wake, and he was pleased to see several caches illuminate. Three were near his platform and a second-tier one was equidistant between their platform and the one that held Tayr.

"There," Tina called and pointed at an outcrop. "That looks like a place where we will be defended from two of three sides, and it has high ground. You hold it, I'll get the weapons."

"Good. There, there, and there." He pointed to the first, second, and third-tier caches. The third-tier one was close to the first-tier.

They nodded at one another and leapt down from the platform. The ground was surprisingly slick under his boots. He grimaced, regained his footing, and raced forward. As he ran, power coiled in his palms and his magic bar in the top left of his screen, which had been rendered in gray during the past matches, now glowed a steady blue.

Magic, at last. He was excited for this. The question was, which of the other teams had magic users?

He watched from inside the tumble of rocks as the Twins pushed directly toward him. "Tina! We'll have company soon."

Tina called something in return, which he hoped was an agreement. She didn't sound panicked, anyway.

Dexi and Callie looked annoyingly sure-footed on the slick ground. He couldn't make out their faces but he knew it was them. The two figures practically oozed arrogance as they ran. If they had stopped to pick weapons up, he hadn't seen it.

Tayr circled behind the Twins—or, at least, he was fairly sure he saw flickers of people. He leaned forward and wished he had a spell for distance vision. He yelped when Tina arrived behind him with a clatter, and she dropped prone to avoid the fireball he barely refrained from throwing.

"No own goals," she admonished him.

"Right. Sorry." He gestured for her to look. "Tayr's trying to pick the Twins off."

She settled beside him. "Finally, a use for the fact that I can barely see at close range."

He gave her a horrified look. "How do you fight one-on-one?"

"I aim for the blur," she said and failed to reassure him at all. "Okay —Tayr has two of their people trying to flank. They're quick. I'm not sure where the third one is…oh, yep. She's hanging back behind the left flank. Man, if they can pick the Twins off…"

"That would be good," Justin agreed. "So, what did you find for weapons?"

"Fist weapons, a short sword, and a battle-ax with a water potion." She sounded deeply satisfied. "We may be trying a totally crazy thing, but at least I'm well-armed for it."

"It's not crazy," he muttered. "Also, what's going on out there?"

"They're…wait, where are the Twins?" She sounded panicked and scanned hastily behind their hideout. "Shit, shit, shit, where did they—"

"Oh shiiiiiit." He elbowed her. "Tina…Tina, look. Oh, shit. Oh, shit."

"What?" She looked where he gestured and her eyes widened. "Oh, no. Oh, Tayr…"

Tayr was still gaining ground, but the Twins must have known their opponents were there all along. Using the rocky ground and the constant dips and swells as a cover, they had hunkered down and hid to allow their opponents to pass them. Now, the Twins were the ones to creep up from behind, while the Tayr members slowed and began to inch through the mist. They were close enough that even Justin could see them clearly.

He readied a fireball as he watched. He had a unique opportunity in that everyone he could see was someone he wanted to strike. Tayr seemed to have realized what was happening. They spun to look around, while the Twins used every opportunity to close the distance.

When the spell came, it was strong—a gust of wind that knocked all three members of the other team from their feet.

"Well, fuck," Justin said. "I should have known the Twins would have magic. Who are these guys?"

"If it helps," Tina pointed out, "they're probably saying the same about you, what with you coming out of nowhere to get to the final of the tournament."

"That does help, thank you."

Unfortunately, any thoughts of a boost disappeared when the Twins fell on their opponents without mercy. Armed with daggers, they clearly excelled at close range. Callie's style was completely different from Tina's, her strokes shorter and sharper compared to his teammate's swells and powerful movements, but they were equally beautiful in motion. The woman made short work of her first opponent and turned to face the one Justin had fought yesterday who carried the battle ax.

Dexi had eliminated the third member of Tayr with a rush of water that tumbled her with the force of its undertow. She was now encased in shimmering blue and water dripped from her.

The woman he had fought knew she had no chance, but she clearly did not want to surrender. She feinted left and whirled to throw her battle-ax with power that didn't surprise Justin at all—not after seeing her ease with the weapon the other day.

The throw was true. Dexi had to dive sideways to avoid it, and with the magic-user taken out of commission, she hurled herself at his partner. The two grappled and the stronger woman tried to disarm Callie and get her into a chokehold. Her window of opportunity slipped away with every second as the man had begun to haul himself up.

Justin seized his chance. He scrambled onto one of the rocks and lunged forward to hurl a fireball at Dexi. In his haste, however, he had forgotten how slick the ground was. His boot slipped and the shot went wild. The man whirled and launched a gust of wind at him. It knocked him down, and Callie took advantage of her opponent's distraction to choke the other woman.

"Tayr is out of the match!" the Master of Ceremonies called to the sound of groans.

"Justin!" Tina darted her glance from him to their adversaries. "Justin, are you okay?"

"Yes." He groaned and forced himself to stand. There was no time to waste feeling sorry for himself. The Twins would be there in a moment. He shook himself out, tried to remember his grandfather's stories of marching for days through the forests, and told himself he could sleep when he was dead. "I'm ready. I—"

"Look out!" She flung herself over him as another gust of wind rattled overhead. Unnaturally strong, it swirled around them and began to pick hit points off them both.

"Back into cover!" he called. They held each other up as they limped to their shelter.

The wind couldn't reach them there. It whistled angrily around the stones before it faded. A moment later, a fireball rocketed at the opening from which they'd watched. The friends ducked before they looked cautiously out again.

The Twins now ran to their own defensible position. Justin gritted his teeth and threw a fireball with all the power he had. If he could only land one meaningful strike before the man was out of range.

It hit Dexi and took his health bar down a third, but Justin's magic now needed to tick back at an inexorably slow rate.

He sat weakly. "Fuck, fuck, fuck. What do we do?"

"What do you mean?" Tina stared at him. "We stay here and follow the plan. We have a defensible position and your magic will come back. As long as no one moves, it's you against him. We'll see if it's possible to distract him enough for me to creep out but otherwise, you two will need to chip away at each other."

Half-heartedly, he looked over his shoulder and barely ducked in time to avoid a fireball to the face. He swore. "Cowards."

"They're doing what we're doing," she pointed out. "And this is a compliment, after all. They've never gone on the defensive before. I asked around. They always go straight for the kill. They're scared of you."

"They should be," he muttered. "Because I'll fucking take them out."

"Justin, for fuck's sake. Sit and think for a minute—"

"I am thinking!" he shouted in response. "I'm thinking about the grand prize I need to win to get home. You don't get it, do you? You can go home anytime you want but I can't, Tina. I need that key and if they get it, I'll never get out of here!"

"Calm down." Her voice was fierce. "That is all the more reason to play this safe, Justin. Don't throw away the advantage you have—"

"No." He took a deep breath, remembered the sight of the cache that had nestled between the two teams, and ducked out of hiding to sprint toward it. If he and Dexi had magic, it stood to reason that the Master of Ceremonies would have a magic potion. He needed to get it first.

"*Justin!*" Tina yelled.

Totally focused on the cache, he didn't stop. He ducked incoming gusts of wind with a single-minded determination. No matter what, he would go home. He would win, and he would go home. The key was in his sights and he wouldn't make the mistake of sitting back while everything passed him by like he had so many times before.

She shouted something, but he wasn't listening. He thought he saw movement—Dexi, most likely—but he had proved he could avoid the wind and the man must be running low on magic. He skidded up to the cache, stood to open it, and was hurled sideways with brutal force.

Callie stood nearby, her hands out to throw a spell, and the last thing he saw before the world went black was his health bar flashing red and completely empty.

CHAPTER SEVENTY-NINE

Anna Price was nothing if not simple and to-the-point, but between the newsworthiness of the PIVOT pods and the potential future applications, the reporter clearly wanted to take his time. After she had finished her interview, David Yang ushered the founding members of PIVOT in for a group interview about their initial development of the technology.

Jacob watched Justin's pod out of the corner of his eye. He wished DuBois was there to oversee what was going on. There was a full medical staff, of course, but the patient's stress levels were climbing steadily beyond where they had been. There was no medical distress but the young engineer hadn't seen him like this since Justin first learned where he was.

He tuned back in time to hear the question Yang asked him. "Were there injuries during the development process?"

At last, he felt he was on solid ground. He shook his head. "We started very small. We worked up from already-used technologies and we tested them on ourselves. I have to say, having never done testing on people before and being the ones who would go into the machine, I think we probably took far longer with it than we needed to."

The others laughed. He didn't need to stretch the truth at all. Not being sure what would happen with the combination of virtual reality feeds, the team had tested each one stringently and had sometimes rerun all their calculations and diagnostics between trials of the same iteration.

"Now, you're laughing," Yang said, with his reporter-smile, "but I think everyone else is probably glad to hear you say that."

"It's good to do things like that," Jacob agreed. "I think we wonder about who we might have had a chance to help if we had gotten this technology online sooner—at least, I know I do—but it really does set my mind at ease to know that it's safe."

"Exactly," Amber added. "We had a few failures in testing but every one of those was running the current too low—never overloading the system. Besides that, all the testing really gave us a handle on the numbers we should expect to see, and that helped us when we integrated the game."

"Tell me about the game," David suggested. He smiled brilliantly at all of them.

"It's a fairly standard MMORPG," Nick explained. "We really lucked out in our collaboration there. It was a game that was already made and that we really loved. The team had run out of funds to keep the servers online, and we were able to keep the game alive and keep playing our favorite game."

"It's a fantasy world," Amber explained. "The basic premise is very similar to other games—you help people out, get stronger, take on stronger enemies. What makes it so effective as a recovery tool is two-fold. First, it engages social processes in the brain and second, there is a life-or-death component that stimulates the brain to protect itself."

"That was perhaps a poor choice of words," Jacob interjected smoothly. He saw her grimace and hoped the TV crew decided not to show that. "The game isn't dangerous. It's simply that the fantasy combat stimulates the nervous system to behave as if it is conscious and responding to threats."

"So there's no way to die in the game?" David clarified.

Amber opted to keep her mouth shut, for which Jacob was thankful. "Your character can die," he said, using finger quotes on the word, "which will provoke an emotional response due to the immersion. However, in a healthy individual, this is not—"

Alarms erupted behind him and he spun in alarm.

Justin's monitors flashed red and his heart rate flat-lined. A team of assistants had swung into action and DuBois burst through the laboratory doors in the next moment, wiping tell-tale traces of popcorn off his hands.

"What's going on?" he called.

"He flatlined," one of the assistants replied. "Death in-game and his vitals went haywire."

"*Justin!*" Mary ran from the other room, her face pale.

The TV crew looked at the pod in sudden interest, and Jacob was surprised to realize he felt nothing. He didn't care what they thought —not while Justin was fighting for his life. He ushered them to the side as he, Amber, and Nick crowded around the pod. Out of the corner of his eye, he could see Anna Price watching with remarkable equanimity.

"Tell me when we're clear," DuBois called.

"Clear!" an assistant confirmed.

DuBois pressed the button for the defibrillator. Jacob held his breath and watched the jolt on the screen.

Nothing happened and he exhaled, only to drag in another breath.

The doctor's calm demeanor did not change at all. "Tell me when we're clear," he said again.

"Clear," the assistant called. He was pale now.

DuBois pressed the button. Again, the jolt burst across the heart rate monitor.

And, again, the flatline returned.

Jacob turned away and sank onto a crouch. He wanted to pound his fist against something—anything—but there was nothing safe to punch.

"Tell me when we're clear," the doctor instructed.

"Clear," Jacob heard distantly. A moment later, there was a shower of sparks and several people yelled. Amber and Nick hauled their partner out of the way, and three assistants raced in. They called to each other, panicked, but he pushed them aside.

"You have a loose connection. It's not meant to take that charge so many times at once." He reached in, grimaced, and snapped the piece together, wincing at the jolt. He shook his burned fingers, knowing they would sting soon, and stood to see everyone staring at the heart rate monitor.

With his heart in his throat, he turned and almost collapsed in relief when he saw Justin's heart beating strongly. He met DuBois's eyes and nodded.

"Good work, Doc."

"It looks like he got reckless," the man said. "He—"

Jacob pushed the assistants forward and in the crush, managed to get close enough to DuBois to murmur, "Quietly. I'm doing damage control. They didn't know that was Justin."

"Ah," DuBois said. "In retrospect, that's rather a miscalculation, don't you think?"

"We'll talk about it later." He pivoted to the camera crew.

"Per the agreement," Anna Price said soberly, "I would like to remind you that all footage of monitors must be blurred and that written accounts cannot include any specific numbers."

"Of course," David Yang said. He looked from her to Jacob. "Would either of you like to make a statement regarding the overall safety of the device in testing?"

"*Justin!*" A red haze came over Tina's vision. Callie laughed, spread her hands, and gave Dexi a bow. His laughter echoed her amusement.

Tina screamed in absolute fury. She didn't take the time to think about what she was doing but simply wound up and let the battle-ax's momentum carry her across the field. Her momentum skidded her toward Dexi so quickly that, as he began to turn, she knew it wouldn't be in time.

She spun as she reached him. The blade of the ax whistled as it cut smoothly into a deadly arc and she felt a moment of complete peace.

Then she realized exactly how much damage the blade would do before the stasis field came down around him. Panic spiked through her. She was furious, yes, but she didn't want blood on her hands—and she couldn't stop turning.

Resisting the urge to panic, she planted her feet but was powerless to stop the skid. At last, she did the only thing she could think of. With all her strength, she wrenched the blade around as she spun. Her muscles screamed in protest, but she held on. Everything narrowed to the point of the blade as it inched slowly upward.

The flat of the blade struck Dexi with bone-crushing force. She thought she heard Callie scream as the stasis field came up around him, and a tidal wave of sound erupted from the stands to crash in on them. Deaf to it all, Tina raced to Justin. She skidded to her knees, felt his neck and his wrists, and yanked his shirt away to press her hand against his chest.

"Someone!" she screamed. "Someone—anyone, *please*!" She could hear the Master of Ceremonies yelling something, and healers ran across the arena toward her.

Her friend's face was pale. His chest wasn't moving and she couldn't think.

"Please," she babbled as the healers reached them. "Please—he's not breathing. He needs to be revived...his heart needs to be restarted. Please, please!"

They paled at her words but grasped Justin's unconscious body and magicked it onto a stretcher they conjured out of thin air. It hurtled away of its own accord toward the distant door of the arena and she sprinted after it. When hands snatched at her, she made to fight them off but it was only a healer hauling her up onto a moving platform. She held on, suddenly aware of the shouts from some of the crowd and the silence from the others.

Justin.

"Whatever you can do," she implored the AI under her breath, "*please* do it."

"I can only work within the strictures of this world," it told her solemnly. *"The rest is up to you and to Justin."*

"He's *dead*," she whispered.

"Then it is up to you."

Tina pressed her fingers against her eyes and when she opened them, she was in the shadowy interior of the arena's medical bay.

The chief healer—or so she assumed, given his ornate robes—leaned over Justin with an air of boredom.

"Dead," he pronounced. He waved a hand. "His body should be released to his next of kin."

"Wait just a moment!" She threw herself off the moving platform and landed awkwardly in front of him. Her arms folded, she glared at the man. "Bring him back."

"The rules of the arena are quite clear." He folded his hands inside his sleeves and looked down his arched nose at her. "We are permitted to stabilize the fighters should they be injured and bring them back to a certain level. Beyond that, we do not intervene. Everyone signing on for the arena knows the risks."

"Do you mean to tell me…" Her heart had begun to pound dangerously. "That you can revive him and you won't?"

He sneered and said nothing.

"Listen," Tina said. "Where I come from, you would be thrown out of your guild and strung up in front of a court for this. Where I come from, doctors swear to heal those they can and do no harm. You're no healer!"

"Take her away," he said, his expression one of irritation.

"If a single one of you touches me, you will be sorry," she all but snarled. The other healers backed away as she advanced on man—and the Master of Ceremonies, who had rushed into the room. "Listen. To me. You introduced a new mechanic into this game and you didn't know what would happen. Well, what happened was that one of your contestants unleashed a death spell on my teammate. She played around the rules of the game to kill him when she only needed to incapacitate him to win—and you let that happen."

"Madam," the Master of Ceremonies said, flustered, "rest assured that the recompense for a death in the arena—"

"I don't want recompense!" she screamed. "Do you think I want money? No. I want you to do what you should have done from the second Justin was brought in here. I want you to make him better."

"A revival potion," the chief healer said, "is incredibly valuable."

"So it's about money, huh? It's always about money." Tina grabbed a handful of his robes and pulled him close. "Listen to me, mother-fucker. I'm not from this world. I have powers you cannot dream of. If you do not bring him back right the fuck now, I will obliterate every-thing you hold dear. I will find the piece of your universe that houses you and I will destroy it with a bomb if I have to, but I'll make sure that everything you know and love is not only in hell, it is *gone forever*."

Whatever he saw in her eyes, he yanked himself back hastily. A quick look between him and the Master of Ceremonies produced a hasty nod, and he went to an ornate cabinet and withdrew a shim-mering purple potion. One of the assistants held Justin's mouth open as the chief healer poured it carefully down his throat.

She twined her fingers with her friend's while her heart pounded. He didn't move and she was terrified that something was wrong. They had waited too long.

Oh, she was not kidding. When she got out of there, she would find the server that ran this snooty healer and she would destroy it with a sledgehammer. The PIVOT team had told her how little Justin could afford to die in the game and now, she was powerless to do anything other than watch over the lifeless body of someone she cared about who should never have died.

Her eyes were squeezed shut when his fingers twitched.

"Justin!" She held him close.

"Can't—breathe—" he wheezed.

"Sorry...I'm sorry." Tina let go of him. "You're here. You're alive. Oh, my God." Tears started but she ignored them. "I was so scared for you. So scared."

"Tina." He wrapped his arms around her. "Uh—well, first of all, thank you. And what's this about you cursing the healer?"

"How did you know about that?" She raised her head.

"The AI told me. It says I owe you big time."

She sniffled and hiccupped.

"If you will rest in one of the suites provided," the Master of Ceremonies said somewhere nearby, "we will summon both teams once a ruling has been made."

"A ruling like throwing that bitch out of the ring and awarding us the prize?" Tina asked dangerously and fixed him with an icy glare.

The Master of Ceremonies flitted away as if he hadn't heard her and she sighed. She was aware of another emotion pressing close now —fury. Her first instinct was to pound on Justin's chest with her fists, but that seemed unwise at this particular moment.

Instead, she looked at him. "What the *hell* were you thinking?"

He let his head drop. "I'm sorry."

"Justin, don't apologize to me. You almost got yourself killed. All you had to do was remember what you told me—that they'd find another way to get you out of here if we didn't get the key." She whirled and put her head in her hands. "Instead, you were so caught up in wanting to leave right now that you...you could have killed yourself. Everything your parents did and all the doctors did would have been for nothing!"

His face looked stricken.

"So you aren't home," Tina continued scathingly. "So everything isn't normal. Well, guess what? You don't get everything you want, okay? I know I'm the last person who gets to lecture you about this. I'll never forgive myself for where you are right now, but you have a chance no one else in the world has ever had. If dozens of people are willing to give weeks and months and maybe even years of their lives to help you recover, goddammit, the least you could do is respect them enough to not do something stupid."

Justin stared at her for a moment before he nodded. "I'm sorry."

Tina sat in a miserable heap. All the other healers had fled, presumably scared out of their wits by the tiny woman in full leathers who yelled threats and curses.

"I'm sorry," she said. "And I'm sorry I couldn't find the words to get you to take this seriously."

"Tina." He moved closer to her and pulled her up. "You can't heal for me."

"So I can injure you but I can't make you better?" she asked bitterly.

"Yeah." He nodded. "You did what you could. In fact, when we get out of here, I'll look up what you yelled at that healer because it sounds impressive."

"Oh, please don't." Her cheeks were burning.

"From here on out," Justin said, "we work as a team. I won't run off and try to do things on my own, and you won't try to fix me. Deal?"

"Deal." Tina took his hand and squeezed. "Okay, we need to get out of here."

"Why?"

"Because I can see them bringing Dexi and Callie in and if I have to see either one of them right now, I'll kill them with my bare hands."

***

The TV crew stared at him, the recording lights overly bright, and Jacob felt the silence wrap around him like a blanket.

"I do apologize," he said finally. "We wanted to be transparent with you about how the technology worked but we did not feel it was safe to move Justin to another location. We wanted him to be close to all the medical and engineering staff." He glanced to where Mary stood with her palm on her son's pod, her eyes closed against tears.

"You were telling us that the pods were safe," David Yang said gravely.

"If I may," DuBois said. "This has been my area of study for over two decades now. What you have just seen is one of the dangers that faces any patient in a coma, particularly those who have suffered head trauma."

Everyone looked at Jacob, who nodded jerkily.

"The human body is not designed for the speeds we travel at these days," the doctor said. He walked to one of the desks and mimed bashing his head onto it. "Now, if I were to hit my head as hard as I could against this table, I would be injured but my skull could effectively insulate itself against the shock. In a car accident or other impact event, however, that is not necessarily true, and the brain is very delicate."

The young engineer could only hope that DuBois's unusual calm was helping. He and the other members of the team had gotten used to it, but what if the reporters thought it was a sign that he didn't care?

"At any time during the recovery," DuBois explained, "blood vessels can rupture. It is not uncommon for a slow or quick bleed to cause further injury or death in a comatose patient. It is also not uncommon that normal brain function cannot be restored—at least, within the time frames we've seen." He approached the pod. "What we see in this case is that brain function is being restored. Now, this might happen regardless of our treatment. The truth is, until we have a much larger sample size, we will not know every facet of this. What we can say is that different treatments work for different patients, and what we are doing here is adding another treatment to the repertoire doctors can use."

The crew took notes diligently.

"Any patient using this for recovery would have a full medical team available," Jacob added. "As you saw here and as it would be in a hospital."

"So, what…happened?" Yang asked. "Was what happened related to the treatment?"

"Yes," the doctor said bluntly. The young engineer suppressed a groan of frustration, but DuBois looked calm and completely unapologetic. "Immersion is necessary to activate the nervous system, and it means that if someone 'dies' in the game, their nervous system suffers a shock. Justin has been informed that he should be careful and not take on impossible odds, but combat can have surprises."

"If the treatment is dangerous," the reporter said, "does it make sense to add it to the repertoire?"

"That's a question for individual doctors and families to decide," DuBois said simply. "I would say it is equally dangerous to do nothing. In that case, the brain has no stimulation and no memory of the outside world. Both are a risky choice. It is a logical fallacy to assume that doing nothing is not a choice or that it is not a risk."

David looked puzzled as he wrote that down.

"We have seen multiple 'deaths' in-game from healthy players," Jacob said. "It causes a jolt to the nervous system but it is not dangerous without underlying conditions. As Dr. DuBois points out, the danger of the treatment is due to the same thing that makes it effective. Some families might decide that their family member would do better without this intervention. Other patients, like Justin—who has played video games all his life—show a natural inclination to interact with the game."

"I see." Yang now scribbled furiously.

"The game has provided him with experiences he had always wanted to have," Mary said quietly. She stood beside Jacob and smiled at him. Tears still streaked her cheeks, but she was composed. "He is able to help people in the game and his father and I have been able to send him limited communications. He knows he is not alone. It is a great comfort to us and to him that he is not locked in his own mind."

The reporter finished writing and looked at them. "This is fascinating. Thank you for your input. Ms. Price, rest assured that all drafts will be vetted by our legal team according to your specifications." He went around the room and shook the hands of the PIVOT team members, Dr. DuBois, and the assistants. He nodded and left with his crew.

A long silence followed.

"I think that went well," Mary said brightly. She squeezed Jacob's hand.

"No one cares about the upside when the downside is..." He shook his head.

"Mr. Zachary," Price said, "do you honestly believe you will do anyone any good by convincing yourself that the article will be negative?"

He gaped at her. "Well…I… No."

"Then I suggest you return to work," she suggested. "I feel confident that we can expect both supporters and detractors, whatever the outcome of this article. All that is within our power is to do the best we can. Of course, I speak metaphorically, as I am not participating in this research." She smiled. "I have every confidence in you. Keep working."

She left but paused to scan the records of Justin's fight with disturbing acuity.

When she was gone, everyone stared at one another.

"I cannot get a handle on that woman," Amber said finally.

Every person in the room nodded.

CHAPTER EIGHTY

Justin spent a tense quarter of an hour pacing around the emergency suites while the crowd in the arena muttered and shifted restlessly. Everyone wanted to know who would win and the AI constantly offered him a dispiriting account of the odds that were being given for his survival.

When a messenger appeared at the door, the two friends turned quickly. The man who entered beckoned them to follow him, his shoes clicking on the stone floor, and Justin felt a strange calm wash over him. He looked at Tina.

"It'll be okay."

"Easy for you to say," she said but she grinned. "You weren't the one who threatened the chief healer with violent death."

The messenger darted an alarmed look at them and increased his pace.

"I like you two together," the AI told Justin.

"Wait. Really?"

"Yes. She'll keep you on your toes."

"You hope she kills me, don't you?" He rolled his eyes.

"Of course not. Don't be so short-sighted. If she did, I wouldn't get to make fun of you."

He threw up his hands and mouthed "AI" to his companion, who snickered.

In the other room, the Twins waited with the Master of Ceremonies. When they appeared, Callie and Tina locked glances, and it was clear that the two women despised one another. Dexi tried to lounge as if he were bored but he didn't quite pull it off. Apparently, no number of healers could fix every bone in someone's torso in ten minutes.

Having been on the receiving end of a death spell, Justin didn't feel too charitable. Frankly, he hoped it hurt. He hoped the man felt like he'd been kicked by a horse.

"Thank you for joining me," the Master of Ceremonies said. "I am Jaco."

All four contestants looked stonily at him and he laced his hands behind his back with a tense smile. "Very well. As you have seen, there is the small matter of declaring a winner."

"We killed one of their teammates," Callie said. "We're clearly stronger."

"They exceeded any reasonable standards of sportsmanship or necessary force," Tina argued. "They should be disqualified." When she saw Justin staring at her, she shrugged. "What? I was in pre-law for a while."

"Huh." He tried to picture her as a lawyer and couldn't.

"Both teams had one member incapacitated," the official said. "Therefore, the match is declared a draw and both teams will receive a prize of their choosing." He took care to add quietly, "The prizes will be dwarven artifacts of great value from the king's private stores."

There it was—the siren call of his freedom from the game. Justin wanted to sit as a wave of dizziness swept over him. He couldn't think of anything to say beyond a strangled, "Oh."

He looked at Tina and she smiled.

"It seems like you're ready," she said. "Is it time?"

Callie and Dexi were in close-headed conversation. Both seemed upset and Justin turned and moved to the window. He looked out at the city and the bustling streets and heard the arena crowd singing above him. The thought wouldn't leave him. He could go home. Right now.

"Tina."

She appeared at his side. "Yes?"

"I may be ready," he said, "but there are a couple more things I want to do. I've tried to get out of here so much that I've...I haven't taken time to say goodbye. If I leave now, I'll never see Lyle again, or Kural, or...Zaara." He looked away so she wouldn't see the flush in his cheeks.

His friend said nothing.

"We agreed to do this as a team, though," he said. "And I know that if I stay, I'll make you spend more time here, too."

"Wait—Justin." She looked confused. "What are you talking about?"

"If we walk away now," he said with a grin, "those two won't ever get what's coming to them. Fuck a draw—I want a rematch."

Tina looked at them with wide eyes. "*Oh.*" Her jaw set. "Let's do it."

He turned to look at the Master of Ceremonies. "We've decided we're not satisfied with a draw."

The Twins both stood. Dexi leaned on Callie but he still managed to look intimidating.

"You don't want to make enemies of us," he told them.

"Oh, please," Justin said. "If you only want people to applaud everything you do, start a reality TV show or something."

"Huh?" the man asked.

He shook his head. "My point is this—they didn't win. It was a bad setup and things went sideways. Tayr lost fair and square, but neither we nor the Twins won. A draw? That's a shitty ending to all of this. Do you think that crowd will go home happy? No. They're here to see if the Twins finally get taken down a peg or two, and a draw isn't the way to do that." He stepped closer to Jaco. "We want a rematch. Us and the Twins."

The official stared at him. "I...allowing teams to appeal decisions would be a very unwise strategy."

"Uh-huh. But you're not, are you? No one won, you said so yourself. Your rules allowed deadly damage and you stopped the match before either team could win. You denied those people out there a winner. If you want to make this right, you'll give them one."

The Master of Ceremonies looked from one team to the other. "This is highly irregular."

"You don't say," Tina said dryly. "Look, you're the MC so you literally make the rules. Let's do it again and this time, you do your part right."

"What does that mean?" Callie hissed. "Do you want them to give you an advantage?"

"Last time, it seems like they gave you an advantage," she said. "No magic wielders on Tayr, one on our team, and two on yours? So be grateful we're not asking for a forfeit from you for your lack of control—or your attempted murder."

Justin stared at the Master of Ceremonies, who swayed worriedly, his frown intense.

At last, the man nodded. "I will announce it. Come with me." He looked at all of them and made a small gesture. Magical barriers sprang up around the two teams and faded to invisibility, and his magic bar went grey again. "Not that I don't trust you," the official said with a raised eyebrow.

The four contestants and Jaco appeared on the dais to the sudden sound of cheering. The man waited while people scrambled to their seats and crowded the railing.

"A unique situation has come to pass," the Master of Ceremonies said. "Each team had one player incapacitated—and, in the interests of our contestants, we paused the match to allow Justin, of Sephith's Bane, to be revived by our chief healer."

"Liar," Tina muttered.

"As the match was halted and no clear winner had been declared, we have decided to stage a rematch between these two teams," he continued. "This will be the conclusion of Season Twelve and will feature treasures from before the founding of Insea."

He raised his hands and the crowd cheered, and he was still smiling when he turned to the contestants.

"Rest," he told them. "Seek out healers of your own, if you can. I anticipate a…spirited match tomorrow, don't you?"

Justin looked at Callie and Dexi and saw death in their eyes. "Yes," he agreed. "I do."

Zaara was in her room, studying a book that had come by courier the day before, when her mother knocked on her door.

"Zaara?"

"Yes?" She took care to shut the book before she opened the door as she didn't want her to see arcane rituals and worry.

"A messenger came with a letter for you," the woman said.

"Oh?"

"Zaara…he says you're summoned to the city." She twisted her hands together in anxiety. "To Insea. Promise me you won't enter that tournament."

"Er…" Given what she knew about what was happening, she wasn't sure she could promise that. "Let's see what he wants."

"He's gone." Her mother hesitated, slid her hand into her pocket, and withdrew a scroll. It was tied with a deep blue ribbon, the kind of thing nobles had in abundance but people outside the city rarely saw. "Zaara, promise me you'll be safe."

"Of course I'll be safe," she told her. "No running off anymore. I promised you and I promised Father." She held her mother's gaze until the other woman smiled. "Now, let's see what this is." She opened the letter and scanned it. At the bottom was a complex rune she had never seen before and another slip of paper held a different rune.

She read the letter again from start to finish. While she had known this was coming, it still hurt to see it. She nodded and rolled the letter again.

"It wasn't a summons," she said, unconcerned that she lied through her teeth. "It's only an invitation, if ever I come to Insea. Someone heard about Sephith. So you see? There's no reason to worry."

Her mother looked warily at her for a moment but nodded. "Very well, then." She looked past her daughter at the candle. "It's late, my love. You should turn in."

"You're probably right." Zaara forced a smile and hugged her. "I'll sleep now. Thank you for bringing me the letter, Mother."

When the woman had left, she shut the door to her room quietly and carefully. She changed her clothes and blew the candle out. Alone in the darkness, she slipped the tiny piece of paper into one pocket, held the letter, and said the words of the spell.

Zaara barely blinked, but between one moment and the next, her room faded around her and she stood on a street of golden stone that glistened faintly in the moonlight. Nearby were the sounds of music and chatter, and she stepped out of the shadows in front of a crowded inn.

She was still trying to work up the courage to go in when a figure emerged, did a double-take, and stopped dead in his tracks.

"*Zaara?*" Lyle asked.

She smiled. "I heard…I heard Justin was leaving soon."

"Leaving?" The dwarf frowned. "I hadn't heard anything about that."

"I had a letter from him," she said. "It gave me a way to teleport here."

"Huh." He shook his head. "Well, I'm headin' to his inn. Come with me!"

"Uh, Jacob?" Nick stared at the screen, his expression one of concern.

"Yeah?" Jacob shoved off and let his chair roll to his partner's desk. "Look, if it's the voice glitch in the barmaid at Riverbend, I don't know how to fix it."

"I—wait. What have you been doing talking to barmaids?" He raised an eyebrow at his friend.

"Nothing." The man cleared his throat hastily. "So, what did you say was the problem?"

"Well, you know how we met after the TV crew had gone and went over the logs?"

"Yep."

"And how we saw that Justin didn't want to leave until he wrapped up all his unfinished business?"

"Yep."

"And then we decided I would go into the game and find a way to get Zaara to Insea?"

"Yep."

Nick looked at Jacob. He was fairly sure he could say anything right now and get the same response. He briefly considered what he could ask that would be the funniest but realized he'd missed the moment. His friend stared expectantly at him.

A raise, dammit. He should have asked for a raise.

Next time.

"Well, I went into the game," he said. "And I brought Zaara up and her asset...isn't in Riverbend anymore."

"Oh?" His friend suddenly looked cagey.

He narrowed his eyes. "Why do you look weird?"

"No reason. Nothing. It's fine. So what's wrong? Do you need me to, uh...take care of it?"

"No," he said slowly. "No, I don't. Because it's already taken care of. She used a teleportation spell she received from a messenger, which brought her to Lyle...who's taking her to see Justin."

"Oh." Jacob smiled.

"And I don't know where the messenger came from," Nick said.

"Right. Well, I'm sure Amber took care of it."

"Amber has been gone all afternoon."

"Maybe...I took care of it?" Jacob tried. "And then forgot? That's probably it. I haven't been sleeping much. Or DuBois—"

"Jacob, what's going on?" he demanded.

His friend sank his head into his hands. "Um. Okay. Look, I'll talk to you and Amber about it over dinner. We...might have a problem. Come on." He locked both their computers and ushered him toward the door. "We shouldn't talk about it here."

In the servers nearby, the AI hummed quietly to itself. It gave Justin a ton of crap but it was pleased that he would get to say goodbye to Zaara. He would be happy, of course, but there was more to it than that. After all, he could leave but it would have Zaara around forever. It didn't want her to be sad that whole time.

Cut off from the rest of Diatek's servers, it didn't know that in her office several stories above, Anna Price was seated in her chair, deep in thought as she stared at the security footage of the now-empty PIVOT desks.

CHAPTER EIGHTY-ONE

The inn where Justin was staying was crowded with people trying to catch a glimpse of him. Zaara looked around as Lyle pushed brusquely through the crowd. She noticed that he was limping but there was no opportunity to ask about it over the din.

The innkeeper and his wife were clearly having the time of their lives. They filled orders with cheerful abandon and called greetings to regulars and new visitors alike. She could only imagine how their coffers would overflow by tomorrow.

At the back of the inn, a burly guard stared belligerently at all newcomers. He recognized Lyle but gave Zaara a dubious look until her companion beckoned her through. The crowd made a disappointed noise and shouted questions after them, some of them quite intimate. She blushed a fiery red.

"How are we supposed to know which of those he'd prefer?" she asked in an undertone.

He guffawed. "I'd bet we can rule out a few right off the bat."

She grinned at him. "Are you well, my friend?"

"Ah." He grimaced. "I was injured. The teams are getting desperate an' they'll do anything they can to knock their competitors out. I took an arrow to the knee, I did. I used to be an adventurer too, but not anymore..."

The dwarf was still muttering when he led her out onto the terrace.

Zaara stopped dead. There was more food there than she thought she'd eaten in her entire life, along with a profusion of flowers, enchantments, and gifts. Fairy lights drifted overhead. Of her friend, there was no sign beyond faint noises.

"Justin?" she called.

"Back here!" he yelled. The scraping noise of a chair on the floor was immediately followed by his head popping into view. "Zaara! I thought that was you. Come sit. Help me with the food."

"I don't think any one person can help you with this much food," she said dryly. "Or any two people—Lyle's with me." She clambered over a pile of boxed gifts into an open space filled with couches and a firepit. He held his arms out to greet her.

"Justin." She hugged him and they both looked around when Lyle tumbled over the pile of presents. "I'm glad to see you again before you go."

"How did you know? Some mage trick?" He laughed self-consciously. "I intended to send a letter. I didn't know how to get in touch before I went."

"I thought you'd sent the rune," Zaara said slowly. She shook her head. "It was probably Kural and he forgot to let me know. He persuaded the Master of Ceremonies to offer you the key as your prize, you know."

"Yes, they mentioned it would be a dwarven artifact." He smiled at her. "Zaara...Lyle...I'll miss you both so much."

"Ye can visit, can't ye?" the dwarf demanded. "Yer mother can, so..."

"That's true, but I worry that...well, never mind." Justin sat on one of the couches. "Eat, please."

"Again, I don't think we'll make a substantial difference," she said. She piled her plate with meats and cheese, slices of melon and bread, and some kind of chutney made of a deep-red berry. "So, tell me about you. Tell me about the tournament."

Justin grimaced as he told her about the Twins and their stranglehold on the event. Lyle chimed in once in a while to mention the matches he'd seen and the stories he'd heard. The Twins were revered in certain parts of Insea and feared as well.

"They've trained their whole lives for something like this," the dwarf explained. "I heard their parents are merchants and wanted them to guard the caravans. It's well paying work and it'd mean their caravans would always be secure. That's why they were trained in everything—all weapons, magic, whatever."

"And then they had the chance to compete for prizes like these," Justin said thoughtfully. "And they've trained together their whole lives so they know what the other one is thinking. That explains so much."

Zaara, layering cheese and meat on a slice of bread, did not speak immediately. She took a bite and considered what she'd heard. "I wonder what really drives them," she said finally. "If one of them took a killing shot, there are two things to consider—either they like to kill, or they want to win for a larger purpose."

"A little of both," said a new voice.

Everyone turned to look, but Justin's face was a particular spectacle. He looked like he wanted to drop his plate and run away screaming.

She noticed the woman she'd watched in the Arena. Surprisingly short in person, she was dark-haired and dark-eyed and wore a simple robe. She nodded to Zaara as she came to sit on the same couch.

"I'm Tina. Are you Zaara? Lyle and Justin speak of you often."

"Yes." She tried to wipe chutney off her hands and failed utterly. "I, um..."

"Not to worry. Keep eating." Tina looked at Justin and smiled. "Do you want to hear what I learned?"

"Yes." He cleared his throat. "Yes, of course. That would be good."

"The Twins," she said and drew the word out for effect, "are convinced that a treasure of inestimable power lies at the end of this quest, which will give them the strength to become gods. Apparently, they were sought out by a…well, he calls himself a prophet. He has told them that they are prophesied to rule the entire world—if only they're willing to prove themselves worthy."

"Jesus leaping Christ." Justin put his head in his hands. "So they're deadly and crazy to boot. What now?"

The shawarma joint Jacob found nearby was dirty, noisy, and too full of an ever-shifting assortment of patrons to be bugged. Jacob waited, tapped his toes nervously as his two partners ordered, and explained what was going on in one tense sentence.

They both froze with their sandwiches partway to their mouths. Amber's eyes were wide. Nick looked like he wanted to throw up.

"Aware?" Amber rasped finally. "It's becoming…aware? Are yousure, Jacob? You're not simply messing with us, right?"

"I wish I were messing with you." He shook his head. "Because this is a wrench in the works that no one needed."

"Or is it?" she asked him. She put her sandwich down and looked seriously at him. "We talked about Justin adapting the game to his needs and seeking out what would inspire him to wake up, but what if the game was also adapting to him? There have been story twists we never encountered when we played it, and they've shown up at very convenient times."

"Okay, but that's even worse." He shook his head. "If it can choose to help, then it can choose not to help."

"Yes," Amber agreed, "but so far, it has chosen to help."

"Amber is right," Nick said.

"What makes you say that?" Jacob stared in turns at his most pessimistic friend and his most optimistic one. "Because I've never seen you two agree on something like this before."

"Exactly," the other man said. "Amber is the one who could find the reverse of a silver lining in anything." He saw her look and hastened to add, "No, no, it's one of the things that makes us a great engineering team. We're all good at engineering, and I dream up crazy things no one's done before and you find the ways things could go wrong. Remember that time I struck off on my own and my project literally exploded during finals presentation week?"

She snickered and took a sip of her coke. "That was funny. I have to admit, it was even funnier when mine didn't even turn on."

"See?" He looked at Jacob. "My point is, if Amber says things are going well so far, I believe her."

He considered this.

"I also don't know how aware it is," Amber said.

"It's doing things on its own."

"It was always doing things on its own. That's what procedural generation means." She frowned a little in thought. "You said that it seemed like it was…dreaming."

"Yeah."

"Okay, so here's the playbook. If we have the sense that it's waking up and pulling bad shit, we pull Justin out. He's ready and he's found the keys. Otherwise…we let the two of them do what they've been doing so far. Because, let's be honest, it's helping him."

Jacob hesitated, then nodded. "As long as all three of us agree."

It was the way they had approached most of the big decisions involved in their work together. He put one shawarma-covered hand on the table for a three-way handshake.

"Yeah, I'm not touching that," Nick said. "But I'm in."

"I'm in," Amber agreed.

"I'm in." Jacob grimaced. "Now that we've decided that, do you have any idea what to tell Anna Price?"

His partners looked at one another.

"You're the CEO," they said in unison.

"Cowards," he retorted.

The group ate in silence for a while as they considered the Twins' apparent belief in their divinity.

"It seems to me," Tina said finally, "that it's a moral test."

Justin looked at her in surprise. His mind hadn't been able to settle. He'd been torn between seeing Zaara again, realizing this was goodbye, worrying about the two women being in the same place, and hearing that his opponents were hellbent on his death. His thoughts had simply leapt from problem to problem without addressing any of them.

One of the things he had been surprised to realize, however, was that his feelings for Zaara weren't what he'd thought they were.

Having acknowledged that, he wasn't sure what he felt for Tina yet. He knew she turned his world on his head, infuriated him, and made him question things about himself. Despite that, he wanted to get to know her better. He merely wasn't sure where that was going.

And he was okay with that. With Zaara, things had seemed wrapped up in a nice, neat little bow. She was beautiful and smart, and she made him laugh. Plus, she looked damned good in leather armor and they'd had each other's backs in a fight. He honestly hadn't thought past the beautiful part in a long time. She had been there and she ticked all the boxes. Of course he would be attracted to her. It made sense that she was the love interest. She hadn't taken that first kiss after they defeated Sephith, but she would fall for him over time. That was the love interest arc.

But that wasn't how people worked. Sometimes, someone ticked all the boxes and there wasn't a spark. He had been so caught up in the way he expected things to go that he hadn't realized he didn't feel that way about her.

She met his eyes now and he saw the same knowledge there. Both knew they would miss each other. They had been through too much not to. But—

He jerked his train of thought to a halt. Zaara was a video game character. He was clearly reading into this. He darted a glance at her and saw her tiny smile.

It was merely a very, very realistic video game. Right?

Justin cleared his throat. Tina had been talking and he tried to remember what she'd been talking about. Oh, right.

"A moral choice?"

"The Twins," she said. "They're willing to do literally anything to defeat you because they want unlimited power. Their motives and their means are cruel and to get the key, you have to defeat them. The question is whether you'll cheat to do it."

"Cheat?" He felt a wave of revulsion. "Bribe the MC, you mean?"

"Or do things like they did," Zaara explained. "Take shots that could kill before the protective field kicks in. Try to injure them." She looked thoughtful. "You could pay someone to slip them poisoned wine—nothing that would kill them, only something that would put them off their game."

"No," he said emphatically.

"Ah," Lyle said. He nodded sagely. "So ye're goin' t'be stupid."

"That's not what this is!" he protested, stung.

"Oh?" Zaara raised an eyebrow. "You have two crazy people who are drunk on power, and the opportunity to eliminate them. Not to mention that they might be considering any of the things we mentioned. They might be trying to poison you."

Justin stood and paced. Eventually, he turned to look at the group. "This wasn't how I planned my goodbye with you two, by the way."

"You didn't plan one at all," she pointed out. "You intended to disappear into another world with only a letter." She seemed more amused than upset.

"Yeah, but I have the chance at one now and I'll take it." Justin made his mind up and sat. "I have almost two days to come up with a plan. *Tonight*, we're going to sit and talk and laugh. We're going to say a proper goodbye. Tina, you've never properly met Zaara. She helped me and Lyle take down Sephith."

"And helped take Justin down a peg or two," Tina interjected.

Justin darted her a look. "Right, because you had nothing to do with that."

"I like to think it's a group effort," she said with a grin and clinked glasses with the other two friends.

"Justin, I have a question for you," Zaara said.

He froze. Tina and Lyle looked on with open curiosity.

"Um…yes?" He cleared his throat awkwardly.

"In Sephith's tower," she said, "you told me you thought none of this was real and that you were dreaming this world." She tilted her head to the side. "Now, you're going home. D'you still think it's all fake?"

Justin felt a swell of an emotion that seemed very close to grief. Something was ending here. A door was closing. He could come back to the game but he would never have these experiences again. This night, with the food and the music from the inn, would only ever be a memory like all his battles against Sephith and the demons and the bandits.

"No," he said. "No, I don't think that anymore. I know it's real."

CHAPTER EIGHTY-TWO

Tad sat in his office and jiggled his foot with the single-minded determination of someone who both needed to not think and needed to work off the four cups of coffee he had drunk that morning. His bill was up for debate in the house at present, and he should absolutely watch the live feed from the floor.

He couldn't bring himself to do that, though. Quite simply, he had poured everything he had into this and he wasn't sure he could bear to listen to people argue against it. His aides watched in the other room. He could hear the muffled sounds of speeches and knew he should go out there and watch with them.

Instead, he stood and began to pace.

If I lose, I'll lose on my own terms—on my own turf. He wouldn't accept a yes or no vote on a fundamentally corrupt bill as his hill to die on. He intended to champion this bill and show people what was possible.

A sudden shout of celebration from the other room stopped him in his tracks. He turned his head so sharply he got a crick in his neck and had to rub it while the door opened and his aides peeked into the room.

"Sir," Kyle said.

Tad's mouth twitched. "Yes. I heard the cheer."

"Oh. Spoiler alert, I guess." The young man pushed the door open and the group came in with huge grins. "One of two down. Bipartisan support. Are you happy, sir?"

"Ask me again after the Senate vote," he said. He went to sit at his desk before he looked up and saw the awkward expressions on their faces. "What?"

His staff all looked at each other. They seemed to be drawing figurative straws.

"Should I simply choose one of you at random?" he asked finally.

"I'll say it." Kyle swallowed. "Sir, we don't have the Senate votes. We haven't from the start, and we've...well, we thought you knew that."

He frowned at him. "We didn't have the House votes to start with, either. We scraped those together."

"Sir, the Senate vote is in two days and we're so far away that it's...impossible."

"How many do we need?" He stood and leaned over his desk. "Tell me. How many? Six, right?"

"Eight, sir." The young man swallowed. "We had two calls while waiting for the House vote tally to come in."

"And you still cheered?" Tad threw a hand out in the direction of the TV. "Why? Because you were enjoying the idea of watching this get shot down in the Senate?"

"No, sir!" They all looked horrified and Kyle stepped forward. "These things take time. They take years to get pushed through. The fact that you got this through the House at all is incredible. It means there's a base of support and someday, it might actually happen. We were cheering because you clearly changed some minds. You did a good job. Simply having this debated on the floor of the Senate will make ripples."

"So, this whole time..." He struggled for calm. "This whole time I've talked about this bill and getting votes, not a single one of you thought it would be passed?"

The aides looked at one another. They didn't speak but they didn't have to. Their opinion was clear from their faces.

"I don't believe this." Tad leaned back in his chair. "Is there anything else you want to tell me? Will I be forced to resign? Am I being strung up on corruption charges?"

No answer was forthcoming.

"You know what?" He looked at them, his expression grim. "I have calls to make. I'm sure you all have things to do."

He looked at the papers on his desk until they'd trailed out miserably before he lowered his head into his hands. This couldn't be happening. He'd built his career on the impossible, running without a background or family in politics and against the prevailing party of his district. He'd been tested, but he thought his aides had been behind him.

Now he found out that they'd thought he would fail.

He shook his head once and picked the phone up, punched in a few numbers from memory, and waited. "Addie, yes, hello—it's Tad Williams, is the senator available? Thanks."

He waited for a few seconds before the other man came on the line.

"Tad. Hello."

"Eric." He leaned forward. Eric was on his second term, someone who had made his career bouncing back and forth between Tad's brand of fiery outspokenness and middle-of-the-road, bland moderation. It was always difficult to determine what he would back, but he believed there was a chance here. "I'd like to speak to you about the bill that just passed the House."

"Ah." The man's tone had become somewhat hesitant. "Senator, while I of course respect your passion, I think the bill overreaches somewhat."

"How so?" he asked bluntly.

So far, he'd had good luck with bluntness. No one seemed to know what to do with it in DC.

Indeed, the senator paused for a moment before he said, "These are some very serious blanket reforms you're proposing. Who can say what necessities might arise in the future?"

"What necessities might arise that make drug companies raise prices past agreed costs?" Tad asked.

"In my experience, forbidding something outright is a sure path to bad feeling," Eric told him.

In your experience? This is your second term. He scratched his head. "So, let me get this straight. First, the problem was that there might be a problem that would require companies who were not in financial distress to raise prices out of the range of acceptable costs. When I asked what those problems might be, you shifted to talking about bad feelings."

No response was forthcoming.

"Thank you for your time," he said as civilly as he could and hung up.

He stared at the phone for a moment. Fiery outspokenness and absolute, bland moderation. When Eric had been elected, he had been far more toward the end of fiery outspokenness, but the bland moderation had become more and more prevalent. He had not, to Tad's knowledge, authored any bills in line with his campaign promises.

Do you think you're the first senator we've dealt with? Dru Metcalfe had asked.

Frustrated, he shook his head again and went back to the drawing board. He'd tried everyone he could think of. Now it was time to call anyone who would speak to him. He wouldn't back down, not yet.

It was an hour later when he put the phone down and rubbed the bridge of his nose. One person had changed their vote. One person.

And they had changed it in the wrong direction.

Tad had learned more than he had ever wanted to know about exactly how many people the drug companies had bought off.

He sighed and dialed one more number. As it rang, he leaned back in his chair.

"Hello?" Mary said quietly.

"It's me," he said. "Do you not have my office number in your phone?"

"I do, but one day I called your aide sweetheart so I've been cautious ever since."

Despite his despondency, he laughed. He had needed to laugh. "Ah."

"So." She had a sixth sense about these kinds of things. "How did the House vote go?"

"Fine. It passed."

"That's fine? Not…good?"

"We don't have the Senate votes," he told her simply. "And, having talked to the better part of the entire Senate during the last hour, I can tell you that it won't have the votes. I don't know what it would take. I really don't, Mary."

"Someone should spill the dirt on those CEOs," she said darkly.

"I won't throw mud, especially when I don't have anything to back it up with yet," he said. "I checked. People have tried that and not a single one of them was re-elected."

"When you got into this, you said re-election wasn't important," Mary reminded him. "You said, and I quote, that compromising your morals for re-election would only give you longer in office to do the wrong thing."

"I really wish you wouldn't listen when I say things. It's very inconvenient at times like these."

She laughed. "Tad, you know you're doing the right thing. And…"

He straightened. "And?"

"Well, I wanted to wait to show you this when you came home, but I think maybe you need it now. Just a second." He heard background noise fade away. "Okay, I'm in the bathroom. Tina is in the game now, you know, and she and Justin are…getting along well."

"Mm-hmm." Tad could not, for the life of him, imagine where this was going.

"Well, the other day, they had a date. I left halfway through but when I got back, Nick showed me an excerpt of their conversation. Tina asked Justin what he would do when he woke up from his game. Do you know what he said?"

"Not a clue, but I'm intrigued." He leaned on his elbows and a smile crept in.

"He said he would spend time talking to you," she said. "Because part of why he never really left his room was that he didn't see a way to help the world like he has in the game. Now he sees that you're one of the people making a difference and bringing the villains down. He wants to know more about what you do."

For a moment, he couldn't speak. His jaw hung open. It had been years since he and Justin were on the same page. He couldn't remember the last time he'd talked about morals without his son rolling his eyes. They'd had everything from silent ice-outs to screaming matches about how to effect positive change in the world, and Justin had usually gone back to his room after those—put off, his father had thought, by a grown-up's assertions that change was more difficult than a young person thought.

And now, Justin wanted to know more.

"Tell him…" His voice was a little unsteady. "Uh. I'll forward something to you if DuBois can get another letter to him."

"Of course." Mary's voice was gentle. "Stay the course, Tad. You know you won't win them all but if I know you, I can tell you that you'll remember forever all the times you let yourself down."

"You're right. You're always right."

"I'll remind you of that," she said fondly. "I love you."

"I love you, too. I'll send that letter along in a moment."

Tad sat down to write. For a long time, nothing came at all and he made several false starts. The letter he finally sent was brief and to the point, the kind of thing his father would have sent. He wasn't very good at the emotional parts. That had always been Mary's realm.

But he remembered one of the last times he and Justin had agreed. It had been years before, and they'd had months of good-natured debates.

He addressed the letter to Aristotle and signed it Socrates.

That done he went into the main room and looked at the aides. "Do you all have a moment?"

"Yes, sir." Kyle stood nervously. "We've been talking—"

"You gave me a realistic assessment, and I had a temper tantrum," Tad said. "I am, therefore, embarrassed and hope we can stop talking about it."

The staff looked at one another as if they wondered if this might be a trap.

"I know we don't have a hope in hell," he said. "We need nine votes."

"Eight, sir."

"No, nine. It got worse." He stuck his hands in his pockets. "But I'll be damned if I simply accept the idea that I don't have enough votes. Jenny, if you'd see what we can scare up for interviews, I'd be grateful. Kyle and Teddy, you're on social media patrol. Anne, I'll send you some talking points and I'd appreciate your once-over on wording. Whatever else you think of, go for it. You all signed up for the off-the-wall junior senator and that's who you'll get."

He walked into his office and left them smiling.

CHAPTER EIGHTY-THREE

"Are you ready, Jacob?" Amber called.

"One second. I'm trying to get the proportions of this drink right." After a clattering sound in the laboratory's kitchenette, he emerged into the dining area with a full bottle of bourbon. He looked at the startled faces of those assembled. "It kept not being strong enough so I went back to basics."

"Oh, stop panicking." Nick leaned over and patted the couch. "Sit and watch. It'll be fine."

"Says the eternal optimist." He sat with a mutter. "They'll rip us to shreds. I woke three times last night from nightmares."

A few of the others nodded sadly. It had been two days since the TV crew left and yesterday, the PIVOT team had received word that the piece would air tonight—bumped forward due to the vote on Senator Williams' bill. Everyone had been on edge since then, a fact they had tried to keep hidden from Tina when she came out of the pod for food breaks.

Otherwise, they had all thought about little else.

Jacob, personally, was sure that he was about to see his life's work melt away. It was one thing to make a dud company and flame out.

That was practically a Silicon Valley rite of passage and had no place there.

Getting thrown out for medical malpractice, though? There was no coming back from that. And he'd have taken all these people down with him. He took a sip from the bottle of bourbon, decided not to half-ass things, and took a gulp. It burned.

Good.

"It's starting," one of DuBois's assistants said.

Amber turned the volume up and the room fell silent.

"Questions have been mounting for weeks about the condition of the senator's son," a news anchor said. "Leaked reports indicated that doctors were using Justin for the trial of an FDA-rejected treatment. The news sparked an international outcry and pressure on the senator to resign his post, while Jacob Zachary, the Chief Executive Officer of PIVOT, was briefly taken into custody at the end of last month. He has been released and charges were dropped, but details have been difficult to come by. David Yang reports."

"Well, if that isn't the bleakest assessment of things," Jacob muttered.

Yang's face came into view. He was outside on a cloudy day and he looked somber. "I'm here at Diatek's Elizabeth Keegan Laboratory," he said. "This lab houses one of the most noteworthy medical trials going on today—the use of an innovative new technology to help resuscitate those in comas following brain injury. While most medical trials do not attract attention, this one has faced unusual scrutiny following the revelation that a senator's son is part of it."

Justin's face and the details of his accident came up on the screen, while Yang's voice continued in voiceover. "This is Justin Williams. A car he was the passenger in crashed. He was flown to a nearby hospital in critical condition, where he was placed on life support in the ICU. While Justin's family is arguably quite affluent, they were shocked by the costs of his care."

The screen cut now to Tad making an impassioned speech before the vote on the bill he had opposed. He spoke of his constituents and his family, recalling the phone call he'd had with the claims representative at his insurance company.

"I was so relieved when he told me that Justin was covered up to five hundred thousand dollars," the senator said. "And then he told me how little that would cover. He told me that the money would be gone within a month, if not sooner. If Justin failed to recover in that time, my family would shoulder the burden alone—and there would be nothing left for his recovery."

"Although the senator did not realize it at the time, his son's accident had been noticed by two people who'd had very similar experiences. The first was Anna Price, the CEO of Diatek Industries."

The camera cut to Price in the laboratory, speaking seriously about her child's accident. "It was only a week away from Mina's fourth birthday when the accident happened. She was an incredible child. She was so inquisitive, so bright." Old footage began to play of a little girl dancing through a tiny backyard and playing with blocks in a small apartment while a male voice told her about the periodic table of elements. "She was also a fighter," Price said. A picture came up on the screen of the little girl in an ICU bed. "Her father and I never doubted that she would recover. We had no idea how much that would cost."

The reporter's voice returned. "As costs mounted, the Price family sold all their possessions and eventually took turns sleeping in their car at truck rest stops near the hospital. They had small donations from their family and a church group, but the costs were too astronomical even for the community to shoulder. Eventually, they had to take Mina off life support."

"I will never forget that decision," Price said. "Because it wasn't a decision. It was out of our hands, but we still had to give the verbal consent for it. It was incredibly cruel, and I remember that the only thing that pulled me out of those years was the determination I felt that no other family should ever have to face that. I started Diatek Industries in order to research treatments for comatose patients. I didn't simply want them to be affordable. I wanted them to be widely available and more effective. I wanted to do what I could to accelerate the research that was happening."

"Another blow came two years later, when David Price committed suicide," Yang said, "leaving a note that he could not live with the fact of his daughter's avoidable death. Still, Price never wavered."

"It was merely another reason," she said. "These costs don't only harm patients, they destroy families. If we'd had other children, how would we have cared for them while Mina was in the hospital? We didn't have to make that choice, but others do. Parents drain their savings and go into debt. People have to choose between providing a good life for their children and helping their community with medical treatment. I don't think it has to be that way."

"Price started acquiring companies quickly," the interviewer explained. "Many of the early experiments were failures, but she does not regret them. She has said in several speeches that each failed experiment has paved the way toward better treatments."

Footage of her was shown which included speeches at commencements and industry luncheons, and Amber elbowed Jacob in the side.

"The music."

"Huh?"

"The music. Do you notice how it's all epic and stirring? That has to be a good sign. Right?"

"Let's wait and see."

"But Diatek Industries was about to find a new collaborator," the reporter said. Jacob's face appeared on-screen, and he hunched in his seat.

"The other person to see the news about Justin Williams was Jacob Zachary," said the voiceover, "the co-founder and CEO of PIVOT Labs. Only months before, PIVOT faced a critical shortage of funds. Their technology, the virtual reality pod, had taken crowdfunding platforms by storm but struggled to find buyers.

"At the same time, Zachary was facing a personal battle—the hospitalization of his grandmother after a stroke. While her condition improved slowly, the family was staggered by the cost of her care.

Zachary and the PIVOT co-founders spoke about his experience to 360 News."

Nick appeared on-screen, seated in the laboratory. "I remember Jacob came into the lab one morning and we could see that something was very wrong. He told us how much his grandmother's care was costing the family and we couldn't believe it."

Yang's voice returned as a picture of Amber appeared. "Amber Garcia, the third co-founder of PIVOT, was the one who realized that the pods they had developed could be modified to provide life support."

Now Amber was on-screen. She squinted. "They air-brushed me."

"Shhhh," everyone else hissed.

"At the time," she said in the interview, "we didn't think about the fact that the virtual reality component could be used. We only thought about the cost of running the pods and we knew it was so much less than the equivalent equipment in an ICU. As we looked deeper into it, though, we found that someone else had looked at using a technology like ours specifically for comatose patients."

"That someone," David said, "was Dr. Jean-Luc DuBois of American University. In 2002, he had sought approval for the medical trial of a technology that would stimulate a comatose brain. His early research showed that if the subject regained an interest in solving problems or interacting with the outside world, recovery might proceed more quickly and reliably.

"The project was denied FDA testing, which he appealed on the grounds that no credible danger had been proved toward subjects. The FDA was unavailable for comment, but an anonymous source at Bentz & Jay Corp contacted us for this story and reported that several CEOs had lobbied jointly that his treatment not be approved."

DuBois appeared on screen and all the members of PIVOT tensed. If something went sideways, this would be one of the likeliest times.

"The research was incredibly promising," he said. "There is a temptation to be casual when approaching such delicate areas of health because the outcomes are already so bad. I was lucky to work with a team that was wholly dedicated to good outcomes for every single patient."

He explained his earlier research in plain language and with an earnest air that made Jacob realize the man would make an excellent professor.

With a small smile, he leaned over to nudge the doctor, "Hey. This is good. Even I understand the neuroscience here."

DuBois looked up from his bag of caramel corn with a smile. "I worked on that explanation all night," he said. "I practiced many times."

"You did?" Amber asked. Jacob could see she was as surprised as he was.

"Of course," the man said in surprise. "I'm not a natural public speaker and I needed to work hard to find a way that lay people could understand the research and connect with it. I wanted to show the project in a good light."

Jacob gaped. It was surprisingly touching that he had worked so hard on this aspect of things, especially when he had a laboratory with unlimited equipment at his disposal now.

"Thanks," he said.

DuBois merely smiled and offered him some caramel corn.

"PIVOT's treatment went far beyond the original concept of simple puzzles," the voiceover said. Stock footage of the video game began to play, taken from PIVOT's advertising materials. "The video game was a Massively Multiplayer Online Role Playing Game, akin to World of Warcraft or Everquest, in which a basic character could be leveled up to make it stronger."

"You know, in case you lived under a rock and didn't know what an MMORPG was," Nick said in disgust.

"Remember," Amber said idly, "half the people watching this still think D&D is about demonic summoning."

Everyone snickered.

"DuBois was excited about this development, however," Yang said. The camera panned to show him interviewing the doctor.

"It was the social aspect that interested me the most," DuBois said.

"It was something my original research had been unable to replicate. I would describe it as the Holy Grail of coma research—how to get through to patients. This game provided that, and because it waited for player input, the patient could rest and wake without having perceived the intervening passage of time. It would allow patients to interact at their own speed as they recovered."

"The next task," the reporter said, "was to convince Justin's parents that he was a good candidate for the trial. It had not been widely publicized, which meant they were unaware of it."

"I think we were cautious," Mary Williams said. She looked professional, if fragile. Her name was shown in the corner of the screen. "It was a new treatment, obviously, and that was a risk. What impressed us both, I think, was how...how much each member of that team *cared*. Often, in a hospital, it's easy to feel like you're simply another patient. There are so many who live and die that the doctors aren't surprised by anything. The PIVOT team and Dr. DuBois not only knew their technology, they really cared about Justin."

The screen cut to Jacob speaking about his grandmother. With a start, he recognized the background and phrasing. This had been after the camera crew realized Justin was in the pod. The music took on a solemn tone as he explained how much he wished his grandmother had been able to access the treatment.

"It isn't abstract for him," Nick said when he appeared on-screen. "When we first came up with the concept, we wanted the first trial patient to be his grandmother. We knew this treatment could give people a reason to live and remember the best parts of life."

"Jacob's grandmother, Elizabeth Keegan, passed away soon after," Yang reported. "Zachary has said that her death and his inability to help her have spurred his efforts to make sure other families do not go through the same thing his family experienced. The partnership between Zachary and Price could not have been more natural."

Anna Price appeared on-screen now. "As soon as I heard about the treatment PIVOT was using, I knew it might be the breakthrough we had hoped for. I was familiar with DuBois's work, and seeing him come out of retirement to team up with PIVOT meant that Diatek could truly help out."

"There's some confusion about timelines," Yang's voice said to her. "Elizabeth Keegan died on May 2nd, the day after Justin's accident. Now, at that time, there was no record of PIVOT seeking FDA approval, which was part of why Jacob Zachary was arrested in July, a few days before PIVOT's acquisition by Diatek."

Price nodded. "That was a very serious error in communication," she said somberly. "With things happening so quickly between all of us—Diatek, PIVOT, the doctor—and the transfer of the patients, there was an absolutely inexcusable lack of communication with the FDA, who very justifiably believed that there was a danger to the patients in the trial. All of us sincerely regret that Jacob was arrested as part of this confusion, and I have personally apologized. I think our greatest regret, however, has been the fallout suffered by Mary and Tad Williams."

The rest of them had not listened during this part of the initial interview, and they leaned forward with interest.

"Diatek has remained a private company in part because I knew that, as a parent of an injured child, public scrutiny would have been the last thing I could endure while Mina was fighting for her life," she said. "When the news broke of where Justin was and the speculation began about what treatment he was experiencing, his parents were on the receiving end of...truly unimaginable vitriol."

"You've said that the FDA decision was understandable," Yang said. "Do you think the public outcry was also understandable?"

Price paused. "The FDA absolutely has to act when there is a dearth of information," she said. "From their perspective, there was no indication that what was happening was safe. I am...upset, however, by the public reaction. I would have hoped that the press and the public would wait for details, especially once they learned that the FDA had withdrawn the charges."

"Can you comment on Justin's condition?" he asked.

"Details about individual patients are confidential," she responded. "What I can say is that early results are very promising. There are some patients for whom this kind of nervous system engagement would not be the best treatment, but there are also those for whom social interaction is a pathway back to consciousness. We have many rounds of testing ahead of us, of course, but I know that I am sincerely hopeful that we will be able to bring this treatment to the public."

The camera cut back to Yang standing outside the laboratory.

"Justin's parents were able to comment on his condition," he said, "and they report that he has shown considerable improvement. They believe that this would not have been possible without PIVOT's involvement."

Clips of the team in the laboratory began to play, all juxtaposed against uplifting music.

"When I asked the team if they had anything more to say about the experiment," his voice said, "it was DuBois who summed his feelings up—not with hope, but with anger."

Everyone in the room tensed as the doctor appeared on-screen again.

"It was difficult to see my work dismissed," he said honestly. "Especially knowing that there were no verifiable concerns about safety. I had to put that behind me in order to move forward with my life, and I believed that it was in the past. PIVOT's work has been life-changing, but I have also rediscovered that anger. If we had begun these trials eighteen years ago, this treatment would have been available to the public by now and I cannot imagine how many people would have been helped by it."

He paused, then looked directly at the camera. "We like to think that we leave the schoolyard behind when we grow up, but the truth is that there are still bullies in the adult world. I don't know why my treatment was blocked the first time. I only have conjecture on that and I have no interest in speculation. What does concern me is how many people—how many families—could have been helped with treatments for all kinds of conditions. Unfortunately, those treatments have been lobbied against by industry insiders."

The reporter returned to the camera for an earnest breakdown with the news anchor, and they discussed Tad Williams's measure that would go to a senate vote in two days. They mentioned the voting records of various senators and the fact that the measure had, unusually, both bipartisan backing and bipartisan opposition. This was juxtaposed against statements from lobbying groups and pharmaceutical CEOs. The piece did not connect the dots.

It did not need to. The implication was absolutely clear.

Jacob exhaled a breath. "Was it only me, or..."

"No." Amber was smiling. Her eyes were bright with relief. "They completely vindicated us. "Jacob, they...they liked us."

"Or it was profitable for them," he said grimly.

"Stop it," said a new voice and Mary Williams tapped him firmly on the shoulder. "They could be spreading scandal. Lord knows, they'd have the viewership if they did. Amber is right—they vindicated you and your research. After seeing the laboratory and speaking to all of you, they realized that you're not here to make a quick buck or sell snake oil." She squeezed his shoulder. "And Tad and I are only the first parents who will be grateful to all of you for your work."

The group broke apart into hugs and handshakes. The assistants talked excitedly to one another, DuBois moved between groups to offer caramel corn with single-minded devotion, and Nick sniffled suspiciously into a cup of coffee.

Jacob released a breath he felt like he'd been holding for weeks. "The cat's out of the bag," he said to Amber. "And it's okay."

"Yeah." She hugged him. "We did good."

"We did good," he agreed.

A beep sounded from the lab and everyone turned. They knew what that meant. For a long moment, no one spoke.

"Time to go see the fight," Jacob said. "Did someone call Ms. Price?"

"On it," an assistant said.

"I'll be there in a moment," Mary said. She looked quickly at her phone. "The Senate is going into arguments in a couple of hours. I want to see if I can get ahold of Tad before he leaves his office. He should know that at least someone in the press believes him. Hopefully, it will have changed a few minds. Whose, I don't know. But it's possible."

In his office, Dru Metcalfe switched the TV off and stared at the black screen in silence. Finally, he stood and buttoned his suit jacket, a reflex from years of business meetings.

He had one move left and it was something he had tried to avoid for years.

On the other hand, he thought with a certain grim humor, he'd made an entire career on doing things he didn't really want to do.

What was one more?

CHAPTER EIGHTY-FOUR

"*Citizens and visitors!*" The voice echoed and seemed to roll around the vast space. "Welcome to the final match of Season Twelve!" People cheered and stamped so hard that the entire cavern beneath the arena shook.

"Justin survived the car crash," Tina said in a mock-reporter voice, "only to die when a video game tunnel collapsed on him because he was...too popular. Joining him in death was Tina Castro, who had never imagined her life would end this way." She looked at him. "Too soon?"

He laughed too hard to speak for a moment so simply waved a hand. "Oh, God. You're right, though. Holy shit."

The Master of Ceremonies was clearly enjoying this match. He worked to wind the crowd up with descriptions of the two teams, some details of which were a surprise even to Justin.

"I didn't know you defeated a dragon," Tina said. "Did that slip your mind, or..."

"I rode a dragon," he said. "Damn. I forgot that the real world doesn't have dragons. This will be a serious bummer in some ways, I gotta say."

The platform began to ascend. The Twins were being introduced by name and he had a mental image of them waving to the crowd. He could see their smirks in his mind's eye and the same attitude they'd given him on the first day they met.

Now he knew what lay behind them. They believed utterly that they were meant to rule this entire world.

He had to say he wouldn't trust them as gods. They had proven that they didn't give a damn about anyone but themselves. Anyone willing to kill an unsuspecting opponent to gain godhood clearly didn't have a great grasp of ethics.

Tina caught his hand and he jumped. Her hold was so tight that his fingers hurt.

"Are you okay?" he asked her.

"I'm nervous," she said. "Last time, I wasn't fast enough to save you."

"Last time, I ran off like an idiot." He squeezed her hand. "This time…"

"This time didn't have to happen," Tina said. "You knew they would wake you up if you asked. Why are you here, Justin? Why are we still here? The truth now."

The cover slid back and dappled light covered them. He could see the tops of trees swaying above and he suddenly felt oddly calm.

"Do you remember when Zaara asked me if I thought this was real?" he asked her.

"Yeah."

"I…" Justin took a deep breath. "Look, don't think I'm crazy, okay? But I wasn't lying when I told her I think it's real. I don't know if it's only real for people like us—for players or for NPCs too, or what— but I know that you and I have the chance to stop those two from becoming gods and I think that's important for this world. I don't want to leave it with a threat I could have saved it from."

She squeezed his hand again. "You know, I'm really looking forward to seeing what you do when you're awake again." As the plat-form rose to the arena floor, she pulled suddenly on his hand, grasped his armor, and pulled him down for a kiss. "For luck," she said and her eyes sparkled. "Let's do this. And stick to the plan, Williams."

"Stick to the plan," he repeated. The wall was still around them, but they could see treetops and he pointed urgently. "Zip lines!"

"Oh, this is gonna be as fun as hell," she said as she turned to stand back to back with him. The two of them scanned the area around them for weaponry.

The countdown appeared Ten seconds, nine, eight...

"I'm ready," he said.

Five, four, three...

"I think."

Tina elbowed him with a laugh.

The shield vanished and they stared at an incredible forest, the trees as large as redwoods. Zip lines ran between them and the flat earth covered in a soft blanket of pine needles. With the ground so open, it was easy to see the cache.

Because there was only one—and it was right in the center of the arena.

The two teammates surged into a sprint. He was fast, the legacy of his father's talent in track. It was one of many things he hadn't pursued even when Tad had practically begged him to do so. He wondered if his father was watching now and hoped he was.

The thought of seeing his parents helped him push to an even greater speed. The twins pushed toward the cache with the same determination he and his friend did. He and Tina would reach the area first, but not by much.

"Stick to the plan!" he called to her.

She didn't spare any breath for a response. Her gaze was locked on a battle-ax that protruded from the ground and the tell-tale shimmer of a blue bottle toward the Twins' side of the cache.

Justin burst into the center of the cache when the Twins were still a dozen yards away. He didn't slow as he grasped a sword and went into a spin. A few passes helped him retrieve it fully and he continued to run. If he could eliminate one of them now, it would be incredible. Immensely unlikely, of course, but incredible.

That wasn't his real goal, however. Their adversaries slowed and began to circle outward as he forged forward with the sword. Neither of them was willing to risk decapitation at the start of the match—a pity, that—but they clearly thought they had a chance to defeat him two-on-one.

Idiots. He lunged at Callie and attacked with verve, dragging her partner's attention from where Tina had reached the blue bottle and now spread the water power along the edge of her blade. Out of the corner of her eye, he saw that she snatched as many potions as she could and stuffed them into a pouch at her belt but also threw swords and daggers away from the cache.

The twins realized too late what was happening. Dexi, angry, shouted and attacked him from behind. Justin pounded face-first into the ground and winced when his sword hand made impact a moment later. It stung but he tightened his grasp on it through the pain.

He maintained his hold when the entire sword shuddered. Callie had raced forward to stamp on the blade and pin it down while her partner grappled for a chokehold.

Without a doubt, Justin would have been in a bad way if he had to choose between defending himself from Dexi and retaining his sword, but he didn't have to choose. They'd made plans for a few eventualities, and their one-cache plan had been for him to take a ranged melee weapon and hold the Twins off while Tina collected as much of the cache as possible and threw the rest away. She would then distract them, and the two of them would find high ground while their opponents armed themselves.

Tina held up her end of the bargain now and barreled in with a battle cry.

She disappeared in a cloud of black smoke that stung Justin's lungs. Callie and Dexi both coughed and the weight on his back released. Whether this was what his friend had wanted, he wasn't sure. He only had one goal in mind—to push into the Twins' territory. With that purpose fixed in his head, he pushed to his feet and stumbled. Surely this cloud had to end sometime.

A hand caught his wrist and Tina hauled him along. "Come on!"

"What was that?" he asked. He coughed so violently he almost couldn't speak. "I…can't breathe—"

"We gotta keep running," she said and detoured sideways. "Not this one, not this one—okay, go!"

"Can't...*breathe!*"

"This is not the time for dying," she said succinctly. "You can die later." She hauled him around the side of a tree and up a set of stairs that wound around it. "Come on, come on, come on. One foot after the other. Keep going."

Still coughing and choking while his eyes watered, Justin stumbled up the stairs with one hand in hers and one hand wielding his sword. He held onto it as tightly as he could to keep from screaming at the pain in his lungs, and the metal ridges of the hilt dug into his palms.

When Tina let him stop, he dropped to his knees with a dull thud that shook the wooden planks beneath him. He coughed for a long time until he finally spat out something black that looked malevolently at him and crawled away with a hiss.

"So that's what gremlin-smoke is," Tina said.

"You didn't think it might kill me?" Justin looked at her in horror.

"Nope." She smiled. "And the good news is, it incapacitated both the Twins for a while too."

She pointed and he crawled to look before he gaped at his surroundings. He'd known vaguely that they were going up the side of a tree but he could see now that they were much higher than he'd realized. The forest floor spread below them and he could barely see the movement of their adversaries limping up one of the staircases.

"Whoa," he said.

"Yeah. Also, from the coughing, I learned something important." She pointed at Dexi. "His ribs aren't all better yet—like the healer warned Lyle about his leg."

"Yes, well, it's only been two days since you shattered literally every bone in his torso," he said. He shuddered dramatically. "I keep trying not to think about that."

"It was better than cutting him in half," Tina argued. "I only had the two choices."

"Yes, because you'd started a killing strike." Justin grinned at her.

"Okay, breathing doesn't hurt anymore. What's the game plan from here?"

She pointed to the zip lines. "While you and they were out of it, the Master of Ceremonies announced a change. Magic was blocked at the start of the match but it will be available in…well, probably about two minutes now. I'm not sure if either of the Twins heard, so my idea was for you to get on one of those zip lines and throw spells at them as you go. It'll be hard for them to target you in return. I'll follow and we can use the strategy we talked about."

He nodded seriously. This time, they had decided that they would stay on the move, learn about the arena, and not wait for Dexi and Callie to find a hideout. The zip lines had made that a higher-speed game than they had expected, but he was savagely glad about that.

With deft but careful motions, he spread a fire potion on his sword and buckled it to his side. Tina also had a mana potion, which he slipped into the pouch at his waist.

"So, how will the organizers prevent us from dying to magic?"

"Apparently, the arena's spells will automatically reduce the size of any spell so it can't leave you with less than one percent of your health. Each one of us was tagged before the start of the match and that portion of our life force was hidden, I guess? I'm not sure. It must be difficult to do—either that or there aren't any assassinations in this world."

"That's definitely new," he said. "Sephith would have had that if he could."

"Good point."

The two of them strapped themselves into zip lines and readied for the next phase. Tina's gaze was glued on the Twins' hideout, and she reported with a smile that they squabbled over the one potion they'd managed to get.

When Justin's magic bar turned from gray to blue, he made a running leap off the platform before his fear of heights could catch up with him. After a sickening moment when he feared the zip line wouldn't catch him, the harness bounced, the line went tight, and relief spread through him with a tingle.

Still, he had no time to dwell on that. He readied fireballs and hurled them one after another. It was immensely satisfying to see them converge on the Twins' location, and his only regret was that he couldn't take the time to enjoy the zip line. He barely recovered his focus long enough to stop himself from careening into the second tree at high speed—and to get out of the way before Tina came in hot behind him.

They'd divided their tasks at that point too. He would locate their next hideout and look for other caches, and she would report on what their opponents were doing.

"They've split up," she reported suddenly. "Callie got onto a zip line and Dexi didn't. He's going down the stairs. Justin, that zipline —*now*. We have a chance to disable him."

The Twins had run as their platform caught fire. Justin hooked himself onto another zip line and jumped before he realized fully what was happening.

This one led to the ground. He opened his mouth to scream an expletive but fortunately remembered that the element of surprise was necessary. Instead, he mouthed the word over and over until he landed with a clatter and a crash. Thankfully, the impact dislodged his harness and he tumbled free. Tina landed beside him and rolled to her feet, her battle-ax in her hand.

Dexi reached the ground before he saw them. He turned and ran up the stairs with a look of pure panic, and Justin felt a wave of satisfaction.

Surprise, motherfucker. He downed the magic potion in one gulp and lobbed a fireball at the side of the tree. It destroyed the fugitive's next stair and began to burn along the stairway in both directions.

With a curse, the man leapt free. He landed heavily and Justin saw what Tina had meant. He winced when his torso moved. Still, he was a warrior through and through. He'd trained through injury before and launched into motion without missing a beat, wielding two short swords like daggers.

It shouldn't have worked, but Dexi had clearly practiced this, along with magic and claymores and maces. He melded mid-range melee strength with quicks strikes Tina couldn't defend well against. She began to fall back almost at once before she managed to rally.

"Payback!" she called to him. When he ducked, she mouthed, "Gank him," and returned to her attack.

She wouldn't win in the long run but gave a good show of being too emotionally invested to do the smart thing. Her attack was accompanied by shouts of rage and an impressive grimace, and she insulted her opponent's lineage, his morals, and his looks. She spat insults about how little he deserved to win and how he would not even be remembered when he died.

Dexi, hamstrung by his injury, was nonetheless lured in by the slight edge he had over her. Justin remained behind him until he sensed that the man had forgotten entirely about his second opponent.

The timing was perfect when he struck. He raced forward and swung the sword in a powerful slash. Dexi's back arched as he screamed, and the blue shield came up.

"Knockout," the Master of Ceremonies reported. "Dexi has been taken out of the match by Justin."

A scream came from nearby—Callie, he guessed.

"Get ready," Justin told his partner.

"I was born ready." She adjusted her hold on the battle-ax. "Are you ready?"

"Yep." He sighed. "I hate to give her even the momentary satisfaction again, but…" He sighed, winked at Tina, and ran to one of the distant trees. While he dodged and weaved, he also made sure he was seen as if he simply wasn't very good at sneaking.

He located Callie when he was halfway to his target. She sprinted toward him and looked continually around her for Tina. Clearly, she had an idea how Dexi had been eliminated and she was wary as well as furious.

Justin wondered idly if she thought about being a god alone or if she'd let Dexi rule with her.

It didn't matter because she wouldn't win. A thrill surged in his blood. She was a formidable opponent but he'd fought Sephith and the demons. He was no longer afraid and he wasn't desperate. It meant he could choose his time.

The woman cut him off twice. She was armed with a sword identical to his and the two of them parried and clashed. They were close enough at one point for their breath to mingle. She hated him, he could see that.

"You weren't supposed to be here," she snapped. "Only Quartzfire stood between us and the crown."

"Is that what your madman told you?" Justin retorted. "You know, I could get a pet madman to tell me I'm a god too. Or even a pet dog." He braced his feet and shoved her back.

It had to be done carefully and he wasn't sure he could do it. He was tiring now. His magic was drained and his footwork grew slower each time he danced out of the way. If he could only get under her guard, he could end it.

Unfortunately, that seemed unlikely. He had used swords on the battlefield and he attacked with more strength and brutal efficiency, but Callie had trained for years. Time and again, a little trick of footwork or a tiny twist of her sword would rescue her from what he thought was a winning strike.

She had maneuvered them onto open ground too. The woman knew by now that his partner had no magic and there was no way for Tina to get out from the shadow of the trees before she saw her. It would be impossible to gang up on her.

Finally, Callie tired of the fight. Justin saw her draw on the deepest reserves she had. Her eyes went flat and cold and she launched into a flurry of strikes that he could not begin to parry. He swung his sword as fast as he could but there was no way he could hold out for much longer. Any attempt at offense was impossible and he scrambled back and jerked out of the way of the strikes. He prepared himself to make his own last stand when he tripped.

Justin sprawled full-length and the sword clattered away. A moment later, he felt the kiss of steel on his Adam's apple and looked into his adversary's flat eyes.

He smiled and a tiny flicker of confusion flared in her gaze for only a second.

A moment later, Tina bulldozed into her from the side at high speed. She had daggers now but she didn't need them. The sheer force with which she tackled her opponent catapulted the other woman into a tree. Callie struck the bark a few feet up, slid down to crumple in a motionless heap, and was immediately encased in a blue shield.

The two friends stared at one another, breathing hard.

"Sephith's Bane wins Season Twelve!" the Master of Ceremonies shouted.

The stadium crowd erupted with cheers and Justin let his head fall back with an exhausted laugh. They'd done it. Against all odds, they had finally won.

"Er-hem," the AI said.

"Oh, what now?"

"I only wanted to say one more thing."

He rolled his eyes and waited, panting slightly. When the words flashed up on his screen, he barely had the energy to laugh but he couldn't stop himself from doing so.

CLUMSY, the words read. **MAX LEVEL ACHIEVED**.

CHAPTER EIGHTY-FIVE

The reporters were gathering. Metcalfe could see them looking for Senator Williams.

He wondered if the man would actually appear. That might be amusing. He allowed himself a small smile before he stepped up to the podium.

"Thank you all for coming," he told them. "I'm Dru Metcalfe. I understand that some details of Justin Williams's care were released to the media in an expose by 360 News yesterday. However, there is a great deal of information that was left out, and I think you would all find it most illuminating."

Tad bowed his head. His hands were clenched on his desk and he took the time to relax them. He wanted nothing more than to head to the chapel but there was no time. He had worked for twenty hours at this point, and only rehearsal and caffeine kept him upright. Even when he tried to sleep, all he could dream of was giving his speech.

Mary's message had come in, telling him that the media coverage was good.

It might help. He had to hope it would soften some hearts and minds so that when he gave his speech, they were ready to listen to what he had to say. He stood, buttoned his suit jacket, and took his briefcase from the desk.

Out in the main room, his aides were clustered around a TV.

"Sir," Kyle said. "You'll want to see this."

"Will it change the speech I'm about to give?" he asked. He paused. "It's not Justin, is it?"

"No," the aide said. He swallowed. "It's not new information for you."

"Then I'll watch it later. I'll need at least one of you with me." He left and made a conscious effort not to listen to the words coming out of the TV. Whispers followed him and finally, Jared came to walk with him. Tad looked at him with a raised eyebrow.

"You said you didn't want to know, sir," the young man reminded him.

"Indeed, I did." He took a deep breath. "I tell you, I'm looking forward to sleep. Oh, I shouldn't have thought of sleep. Oh, dear."

"I'll meet you in the chambers with a large coffee, sir." Jared hurried away and Tad smiled exhaustedly after him.

He only had to get through this speech. He had thirty minutes to prepare—and thirty minutes to not think about why all his aides looked so deeply worried.

"A late-breaking news story might change or delay the vote on the pharmaceutical pricing bill up for debate in the Senate," a news anchor reported.

Eric Snelling, surrounded by his aides and several fellow senators, looked up sharply. His heart sank. After yesterday's news story, he had spent hours chipping away at his party's junior senators—the ones most likely, he had to admit, to stand up and do the right thing.

What was happening now?

He went to the TV with the others, only to find another of his colleagues giving him a smug look.

"You haven't been here long enough," she told him condescendingly, "but where there's smoke, there's almost always fire."

He gave her a look that he hoped might turn her to stone.

It didn't work and she shrugged dismissively. "This will not go well for Williams. Whatever dirt there is on him is about to come out."

"How do you know that?" Snelling asked.

"I know because that"—she pointed—"is Dru Metcalfe. Whatever skeletons are hiding in your closet, he'll find them all, polish them, and show them off for the whole world to see. You're lucky, Snelling."

"Why?" He maintained a calm expression although his heart sank even more.

"He hasn't made a demonstration of anyone like this in a couple years," the other senator told him. "In fact, I haven't ever seen him do one in person. Whatever he's preparing to drop, it has to be so big that Williams, his family, and his entire hometown will be a smoking crater by the time he's done."

In the main chamber, Tad found a surprising number of people already assembled. Several were clustered around a few at their desks, all of whom held phones. Some looked at him, did double-takes, and glanced nervously at each other.

He sighed. His intention had been to take the time to practice, but it was clear he wouldn't have the chance to practice on the floor.

Disappointed, he headed to his desk and arranged his papers before he tuned everything else out. His gaze traveled over the first few lines of his speech, and his lips moved as he read:

Nine weeks ago, at 11:15 at night, I got a call from the police about my son Justin...

Dru Metcalf wrapped his hands around the podium and looked at the assembled reporters. Now that it came down to it, he felt sick. He'd done many things over the years that he had to work to forget—the faces of the senators and their children when all the family secrets were dragged into the open were persistent ghosts.

He'd drunk some of those memories away and spent hours in the gym to banish the rest. Every morning, he reminded himself of how the world worked. He'd taken to looking at his bank account when he woke up.

It was all coming back now, though. No amount of zeroes at the end of his bank balance had made him feel better this morning. He'd looked at the latest deposit from Raymond White and wanted to throw up.

Would he actually do this?

Yes, so he might as well get on with it.

"Nine weeks ago, at 11:45 at night, I received a call from my employer," he told the reporters, "a man named Raymond White, the CEO of IterNext Solutions. I've worked for him for the past eight years. He told me that Tad Williams's son had been involved in a car crash and had been transferred to a nearby hospital by life-flight. His prognosis was not good."

The reporters wrote furiously.

"White has worked in healthcare for his entire career," he continued. "He knows intimately how costs have ballooned and how much pressure it can put on a family to face the costs of intensive care. For this reason, he asked me to pass along an offer to Senator Williams and his wife. Mr. White wanted to personally cover the costs of care for Justin Williams."

He looked at his notes and swallowed.

"I met with the senator in person several days later. Justin's condition was stable and Williams was back in DC to attend a vote. I arrived in time to hear Nicholas Ryn and Jacob Zachary pitching him on the treatment developed by PIVOT Laboratories, and I warned the senator that the treatment was untested. I passed along Mr. White's offer to him. In response, he accused me of bribery."

The reporters shifted and a new energy rose in the air. Metcalfe was getting to the good stuff now. This was what they were there for.

"I explained to him that this was an alignment of interests," he said. "There were bills coming to the floor that Williams had shown no particular interest in, and I wanted to speak to him about the negative impact they might have on companies such as IterNext. He disagreed strenuously with my characterization of the situation." He took a deep breath. "So I showed him doctored photos I had made of him with a mistress."

Total silence fell over the group.

"Williams was a junior senator," he continued, "and so I had not worked with him before. He was shocked by the photos I showed him. In response, I told him that...he was not the first senator who had been determined to not play ball with my clients. I told him that the choice was his—either he could have all Justin's medical bills paid, or not only would the bills not be paid, he would also be embroiled in scandal.

"I've checked my records. Tad Williams is the forty-second senator I have had a similar conversation with. Thirty-eight were persuaded, either by the initial offer or by similar methods of blackmail. Four, I made sure were not re-elected. I have been immensely successful in my line of work."

The reporters' jaws hung open.

"I leaked the story of Justin's treatment to the media," Metcalfe said bluntly. "I was the one who began the recall petition for Senator Williams. I told a reporter where she could find PIVOT's original laboratories and tipped the FDA off that there was unapproved human testing being conducted. At each step, I offered Senator Williams the chance to end the game. At each step, he refused.

"Yesterday, I saw the piece on 360 News regarding Diatek's creation and PIVOT's treatment technique." He looked up and focused on those present. "I have contacted federal prosecutors with the information that I can provide regarding why the FDA blacklisted the treatment pioneered by Jean-Luc DuBois, as well as information regarding the senators I have blackmailed. At this time, I cannot share specifics of any of those cases or confirmation of their names. However..."

He looked unwaveringly at one of the cameras. "I can tell you that several of them will be in the chamber today when they take their votes. I urge them to follow their conscience on this bill. The information I had on them is no longer in my possession and much of it was manufactured. They may consider themselves free of the chance of retribution. I will not be taking questions."

He walked away through the din of demands to a car waiting for him at the base of the steps.

"Mr. Metcalfe," a Federal Marshall said.

"Hello," Dru told him. "I assume we need to go to the station?"

"We do." The man held the door open and took a set of handcuffs from his belt. "You'll also need these."

Dru Metcalfe held his hands out and smiled as the words began. *Dru Metcalfe, you are charged with...*

<hr>

Tad had hardly noticed the chamber filling. When he stood to speak, low murmurs rippled through the ranks. They were probably talking about how the junior senator was about to have his ass handed to him in the votes, he thought as he made his way to the floor.

In all honesty, he no longer cared. All that mattered was the speech and looking them in the eyes and telling Justin's story. In his hands, a piece of paper crackled—the draft of the first letter he had sent to his son in the game. His wedding ring gleamed when he looked at it.

"You'll never forget it if you let yourself down," Mary had told him. She was right.

The speech passed in a blur. Tad knew he choked up at one point, a fact that would have mortified him mere weeks before. In some ways, he hardly recognized the man he'd been then. He told the stories of the constituents who had reached out to him and shared Anna Price's story. With quiet affection, he spoke about going into the lab to see Mary sleeping with her head resting on Justin's pod.

When he finished, he expected only silence. Instead, senators rose to their feet and applauded. Tad stared at the group.

"Okay, what was going on with that press conference?" he asked over his shoulder.

The Senate Majority Leader, a man who had never liked him in the slightest, shook his head. "You picked a hell of a time to tune out."

CHAPTER EIGHTY-SIX

The landscape of the arena faded away and Tina pushed to her feet and offered Justin a hand. He let her pull him up and became vaguely aware of the noise beating at his consciousness in waves. The crowd continued to cheer.

Somehow, even his eyes could see Zaara and Lyle in the crowd. She was crying openly, while the dwarf harrumphed and tried to hide the sheen in his eyes. Both clapped enthusiastically and leaned against each other.

I'll be back, He told them silently. *Someday.* He took his friend's hand. "Shall we?"

She walked with him, her shoulders set.

"Are you shy?" he asked her.

"Shy is being in front of a dozen people. I don't think it's unusual to be unnerved by this many people cheering for you. It must be twenty-thousand or more." She looked around. "I guess I only thought nothing like this would ever happen to me in real life."

"You never know," he said. "Maybe the world will start a live Battle Royale tournament."

"I'll be one of the hosts," Tina said, "not a contestant. With really high heels."

"That's good. You'll come all the way up to my sternum that way." He dodged out of the way of a kick and laughed.

The Master of Ceremonies waited in front of the dais and smiled at them. He inclined his head as he walked closer in the dust and when he spoke, his amplified voice seemed far away and they could hear him speak as one person to another.

"I promised you an artifact of unimaginable value," he said. "And now, I am pleased to present it."

He held the final key out and Justin's breath caught. He slid his hand into the pouch at his belt and retrieved the other two, placed them in his palm, and took the third. For a moment, he was afraid that he would fumble and be unable to put them together and it wouldn't work, but the keys seemed to know one another. They slotted together perfectly and the seams between them vanished. He held it out to Tina, who put her hand over his so they held it together.

"They key between the worlds," the Master of Ceremonies said. "The king has chosen his champions, citizens—champions to find us allies so that Insea will always prosper. Champions to end all threats and safeguard us against all foes." He turned to them again. "Sephith's Bane, are you prepared to be the Champions of Insea?"

In answer, the friends exchanged a glance before they lifted the key high. It gleamed in the sunlight as the official stepped back to gesture at the stone wall behind him. Now that Justin looked more closely, he could discern the pattern etched there, complete with a tiny, triangular hole for a key.

He looked at Tina. He couldn't seem to think anymore. His head buzzed and the stadium seemed to fade.

"Are you ready?" she asked.

"I'm ready." He walked to the stone and slid the key into the lock until it clicked in place. With a creak and a rumble, the stone doors opened into blinding white light. "It's a little on the nose, don't you think?" he asked.

He blinked reflexively and Tina was gone.

And a white light usually meant something else. Justin stared at it. He wanted to live. For so much of this, he hadn't cared. He'd tried to avoid danger, stepped beyond that fear, tried to escape this place, and stepped beyond that, too.

Now, more than anything, he wanted to live. It was time to find out if that would be his future. With one last breath and his heart pounding, he stepped into the light.

Tad stared at the ceiling. He had told himself that all he cared about was the speech, but he now realized that wasn't exactly true. With that stress now removed, he was desperate to know what had happened outside, and he was equally desperate to know what would happen inside.

Jared sat beside him and shifted from side to side. When he looked at the kid's face, he could see that the aide hadn't taken his eyes off the vote screen.

The Senate Majority Leader stood, and Tad leaned forward. His breath seemed to shudder in and out and he swallowed.

"The votes are," the leader said, "sixty-eight aye, and thirty-two nay. The bill has passed."

Buzzing swarmed in Tad's ears. "Sixty-eight?" he managed to say. "*Sixty-eight?*"

Jared looked like he might cry as he nodded. "The press conference, sir—it was Metcalfe. Remember when you said it would really help you out if he told the truth?"

His jaw dropped. "You have to be kidding me."

The young man shook his head. "You took the high road and now everyone knows that."

"Holy shit." Tad breathed in and out a few times. He pressed a hand over his mouth, aware that he might be under scrutiny, and startled when his phone rang. It was Mary's number and he answered the call to the sound of sobbing, barely audible over the cheers and chatter in the Senate chambers. "Mary? Mary! What's going on?"

"It's…Justin," she managed to say.

Tad sat hard. The phone slipped out of his grasp.

He'd been too late, he thought brokenly. Against all odds, he'd done all this and it was too late. None of it would matter for his son.

Regret was agonizing. He should have been there. All the times he'd left to come back here, and for what? He should have been at his son's bedside or gone into the game with Mary. At least that way, he'd have had a chance to see his son again and hug him, and he hadn't taken it.

Jared picked the phone up and listened. Tad couldn't hear him talking but gradually became aware of the young man shaking him. "Sir? Sir? Your wife needs to speak to you, sir."

He focused on his aide's face.

"Justin woke up. Sir? Did you hear me? Your son is waking up."

Tad had no recollection of moving but he suddenly realized he was taking the stairs three at a time to get out of the senate chamber. His aide was hot on his heels and called for a car to the airport. Senator Snelling jumped out of the way and pressed other colleagues back as he flashed Tad a thumbs-up.

"Thanks!" he called over his shoulder and only barely missed the door as he barreled out of the room. He blazed past a group of protesters with signs too quickly to know if they were supporting him or wishing for his violent death and skidded onto the steps outside. The car was already pulling up and he had to resist the urge to throw himself head-first down the stairs.

Remember, Tad, that won't actually be faster. He ran, wishing he was in better shape, wasn't wearing a damned suit, and that he was already back in California.

His son was waking up.

***

Justin was aware of the light first as a wash of red. He hadn't noticed any time passing since he stepped through the door. In fact, he'd forgotten about the door entirely. A little concerned, he squeezed his eyes shut and noticed that they ached.

Experimentally, he flexed his fingers.

That hurt too. His eyes opened again and he shut them again hastily when the light stabbed through him like a spear.

"Ow."

Talking also hurt. Good Lord, was anything working? His throat felt like it had been hollowed out with sandpaper.

"He's talking!" an unknown voice said. A sudden hush followed—he hadn't realized until that moment that he could hear low-voiced conversation—and the sound of footsteps grew louder.

Justin opened his eyes again slowly. At first, there was only brightness but he gradually saw shapes resolve. White…and a triangle. A dark triangle. He squinted and allowed his eyes to open a little wider. What was he looking at?

The inside of someone's nose, he realized. He sighed.

Two more faces swam into view—or, rather, two very blurry shapes that he was very sure he recognized.

"Mom? Dad?"

"We're here." His father's voice sounded choked and his mother gave a little sob. "Apparently, you're not supposed to try to sit up on your own for a while."

He immediately and completely wanted nothing more than to sit. Unfortunately, he only managed to raise one shoulder off the bed before he fell again, trembling.

"And that," said a male voice, "is why I recommended that you didn't tell him not to." A hand pressed on his shoulder. "You'll be able to sit up soon, Justin. Right now, your muscles are still waking up."

"Uh-huh." He regretted the words as soon as he said them. His throat still felt terrible.

Justin realized he must have grimaced because the doctor continued quickly. "You've just had your feeding tube removed. Your throat will feel very sore for a while. On the plus side, the time spent in your coma has allowed several bones to heal fully."

"Goody," he managed to respond. He looked at his parents. "You're…both here."

"Your mother has hardly left," his father said.

"And your father has flown here more times than most people will get on a plane in their life," his mother said fondly. Her voice trembled as she said, "It's good to see you again."

"Yes." He felt the bed shift. "What's…"

"They're sitting you up," she said. "Just–"

Exhaustion claimed him, and he laid his head back and drifted into unconsciousness for a while.

When he woke again, voices held a conversation nearby. With a start, he recognized Tina's—and, in an even bigger surprise, she was speaking to his mother. It wasn't even a fight. Justin listened, bemused, as they discussed a book they had both read. It was only a few minutes, however, before his father said,

"I believe he's awake again."

Warily, he opened one eye but was able to focus better this time. He stretched one set of fingers and his father squeezed his hand gently.

"Hi," Justin said.

"Hello." His father nodded at him. He clearly hadn't shaved in a couple of days and wore what looked like borrowed sweats.

"I've missed you."

"I've missed you too," Tad agreed. "I look forward to having you home."

"Until you move out and get a job, anyway," Mary said. She was teasing, but there was a moment of worry in her eyes.

Justin understood now, though. He had seen the way she fought for him.

He was also not above teasing her in return. "Oh, don't worry. I have it all planned. Just gimme some knives and I'll hitchhike around and do exorcisms."

Tina appeared behind his parents. She was smiling. "Can I come along?"

"Absolutely," he said. "After all, I need someone to come in on a zip line and eliminate assassins."

"I have to watch those videos," his father muttered. He looked at the edge of the room, then back. "When you're feeling better, you can meet the care team—those who made the game and the…pod. They're off sorting through applications. Tons of people want their family members to have the treatment you had."

"And you know, if you need a job," a voice called, "we could really use a spokesperson."

"Who wuzzat?" Justin asked muzzily.

"That was Nick, dear," his mother said. She patted his hand. "Don't worry, you'll meet them all soon enough. Focus on staying awake for now." She stood.

"Where are you going?" he asked.

His mother looked embarrassed for a moment before she shrugged. "I have an appointment. Didn't Zaara ever mention who her new magic tutor was?" She strolled away and he stared incredulously after her while his father laughed hysterically.

CREATOR NOTES - MICHAEL ANDERLE

JUNE 7, 2020

What happens when you get another chance to be someone you always wanted to be? That is a question I want to answer in what I personally call the *PIVOT Chronicles* (these sets of stories.)

Each book is three books in one. Eventually, we will probably break them apart.

I am fascinated with where we are going with technology, and what we can accomplish today and into the future. The challenge, I realize, is when technology engages with vested interests that want to maintain the status quo.

I too often see (here in the United States) where technology could grant opportunities to upset the status quo (and it often does) until you run up against well-funded competitors who can use the courts or public opinion to keep things as they are.

For example, with medical costs.

When I created this concept, I wanted to build a set of stories in which what is outside of the main protagonist is affecting the story as much as what is going on inside with the protagonist.

Here in book one, we see that PIVOT labs originally tried to create the ultimate game machine. Except, the team that wanted to make these immersive game machines ultimately are horrible with building a business.

Specifically, building a product their target market can afford.

If you don't follow the game console industry, trust me when I say even a $100.00 purchase price difference (paid one time) can make or break the leadership role with game machines for the home.

Imagine a game machine that costs $800.00 a day to operate?

Typically, technologies that upset the status quo are "10x" better. (10x is a term that started with the Mythical man month and mutated in time to a philosophy about making changes that result in something being 10x better.)

My thinking is that $800 in a PIVOT module to keep someone alive and working with their mind than in a hospital intensive care unit (ICU) that is between 5 and 7 times more expensive than the first PIVOT effort.

I did the research, and the daily costs for ICU could be as high as about $10,000 a day, down to $3,000 a day.

Now, someone with $150,000 worth of coverage (45 days at $5,000 a day) could have almost 200 days at $800.00 a day.

Now, what if they can actually heal someone while using PIVOT Labs' product?

In any story, you have to have a challenge (the status quo) and the "bad guys" (the medical industry that pays to keep the status quo) and the heroes to fight the system.

In this story, it's not just the one in the machine, but everyone outside as well. We don't lack heroes or villains, and frankly, most of them might mean well, but there is a life in the balance.

Who is responsible for those decisions?

If you know much about my other stories, I typically write about larger-than-life enemies or obvious challenges.

In the PIVOT books (there are three in production at the moment), we build on this technology and mix our challenges. We won't be able to overcome every challenge, but the human spirit will decide their own future in the end.

Because not every hero needs to save others. Sometimes they save themselves, and in the process, heal and bring joy to those they love.

Diary Entry Saturday, June 6, 2020 to Friday, June 12, 2020

Las Vegas is slowly opening from the Covid shutdown.

It is interesting what is going on here in Las Vegas as the city slowly opens back up (I live on the Strip, so I don't know what is going on downtown.) I have been to the Venetian / Palazzo Hotels/Casinos on Thursday night and to Gold Coast on Friday night.

Specifically, I wanted the chicken wrap with spicy sauce in the Grand Lux and Chinese food at Ping Pang Pong in Gold Coast.

It was *delicious*.

While I did gamble on Thursday night, it just wasn't the same as I remember back before the Pandemic shut all doors. Back then, every-thing was either a party, the late-night party, or the people leaving the party and more flying in to start that next night's party.

Now, I'm waiting to see if the folks from California drive here or what happens if they don't. Only a few hotels are open at the moment, and even the restaurants inside the open hotels are occasionally not open for business (or if open, they don't have the same operating hours as before.)

It's really weird.

But I'm thankful it IS happening.

I was talking w/ fellow author Craig Martelle driving to breakfast Wednesday, and I happened to be driving next to the airport and saw one jet land while another was taking off. I then looked around the runways and noticed about five jets lining up, waiting to take off.

My jaw almost dropped.

I hadn't seen jets (more than one) on the tarmac in over two months. The airport had become almost like a ghost town. I remember one night last year counting seven jets lining up, their landing lights trailing off into the sky to land, and recently I couldn't see seven jets at all unless you count a few parked somewhere.

Covid-19 has hurt the planet in so many ways. From the obvious of lives taken early to families' savings wiped out, to pesticides and machinery not able to get to locations for the swarm of billions of locusts rampaging across east Africa and India.

If I had put all of this into a story, I think more than one reader might have told me I had placed too many challenges in the mix, and they thought 'C'mon! Epidemics, swarms, floods, *and* famine? Get real, Michael!'

Real life has hit us all.

And yet, humans fight back. We fight back for all of the right reasons. Sometimes it's amongst ourselves, sometimes against the insect population and sometimes against contagions.

I know that a couple of planes crossing a lonely tarmac in Las Vegas isn't the same kind of sign as a beautiful flower amongst a destroyed landscape, but for me personally, it was a small sign that we as a world are getting back on our feet.

May you find your own flower as we rise up out of a completely horrible first half of 2020.

Ad Aeternitatem,

Michael Anderle

If you enjoyed this book, you may also enjoy Steel Dragon, from Michael Anderle and Kevin McLaughlin. The book is available now from Amazon and through Kindle Unlimited.

Dragons rule the world. Their claws are into every aspect of human life, from government to industry. But Kristen Hall is about to throw a wrench into all of that.

Because she's a dragon, too. She just doesn't know it...yet!

A dragon raised by humans, in the human world.

After graduating from the police academy, she's dropped right into the ranks of Detroit's elite SWAT team. A rookie, in SWAT? Unheard of. But what the dragons want, they get.

BOOKS BY MICHAEL ANDERLE

For a complete list of books by Michael Anderle, please visit

www.lmbpn.com/ma-books/

All LMBPN Audiobooks are Available at Audible.com and iTunes. For a complete list of audiobooks visit:

www.lmbpn.com/audible